Score One for the Dancing Girl,
and Other Selections from the
Kimun ch'onghwa

The James Scarth Gale Library of Korean Literature

General Editors: Ross King and Bruce Fulton

Score One for the Dancing Girl, and Other Selections from the *Kimun ch'onghwa*

A STORY COLLECTION
FROM NINETEENTH-CENTURY KOREA

Translated by James Scarth Gale

Edited by Ross King and Si Nae Park

Annotations by Donguk Kim

UNIVERSITY OF TORONTO PRESS
Toronto Buffalo London

© University of Toronto Press 2016
Toronto Buffalo London
www.utppublishing.com
Printed in the U.S.A.

ISBN 978-1-4426-4733-6 (cloth)

♾ Printed on acid-free paper

The James Scarth Gale Library of Korean Literature

Library and Archives Canada Cataloguing in Publication

Kimun ch'onghwa. Selections. English
Score one for the dancing girl, and other selections from the Kimun ch'onghwa : a story
collection from Nineteenth-century Korea/translated by James Scarth Gale ; edited by
Ross King and Si Nae Park; annotations by Donguk Kim.

(James Scarth Gale library of Korean literature)
Includes bibliographical references and index.
Text in Korean (Hanmun) with English translation.
ISBN 978-1-4426-4733-6 (bound)

1. Hanmun sosŏl (Korean fiction) – Translations into English.   2. Short stories,
Korean – Translations into English.   3. Korean fiction – 19th century – Translations
into English.   I. Gale, James S. (James Scarth), 1863–1937, translator   II. King,
Julian Ross Paul, 1961–, editor   III. Park, Si Nae, 1979–, editor

PL984.E8K54 2016   895.7'3010802   C2015-908256-0

Ornament image mashuk/iStockphoto.

This work was supported by the Academy of Korean Studies Grant funded
by the Korean Government (MEST) (AKS-2011-AAA-2103).

This book has been published with the help of a grant from the Federation
for the Humanities and Social Sciences, through the Awards to Scholarly
Publications Program, using funds provided by the Social Sciences
and Humanities Research Council of Canada.

University of Toronto Press acknowledges the financial assistance to its publishing
program of the Canada Council for the Arts and the Ontario Arts Council,
an agency of the Government of Ontario.

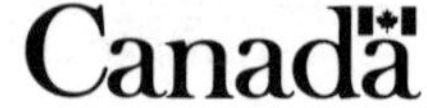

Contents

STORIES

Series Preface

The James Scarth Gale Library of Korean Literature brings together in one series the many literary translations and scholarly essays of James Scarth Gale (1863–1937), Canadian missionary to Korea, preserved in the Gale Papers at the Fisher Rare Book Library at the University of Toronto. During his forty years in the mission field, from 1888 to 1927, and with the assistance of several Korean Christian "pundits," Gale translated numerous Korean literary works into English, the vast majority of which were written in Literary Sinitic (Classical Chinese, or *hanmun*, as it is called today in Korean) rather than in vernacular Korean. Most of these translations were never published and remain in manuscript or typescript form. Thus, this series presents Gale's translations from a century and more ago of Korean literary texts dating as far back as the eleventh century, in a format congenial to the present-day reader: romanizations have been updated; Gale's prose style has been polished wherever possible without sacrificing his distinctive voice; each volume is provided with a scholarly introduction and an annotational apparatus to facilitate contextualization and understanding; and for advanced students of traditional Korea's two main literary languages, the original texts in Literary Sinitic or vernacular Korean are included in word-processed form so as to allow easy comparison with Gale's translations.

In addition to edited reproductions of Gale's literary translations and essays, the series will include an index to the Gale Papers and occasional research monographs on James Scarth Gale's multifaceted activities as a pioneer Western scholar, translator, and interpreter of Korea's literary heritage. The following is a preliminary list of volumes forthcoming in the series:

Ross King. *Courting the Cosmopolitan: James Scarth Gale's Curious Romance with Korean Literature in "Hanmun"*

Hyangsoon Yi, ed. P'alsangnok: *The Eight Marks of the Buddha*, translated by James Scarth Gale

Caleb Park, ed. 500 nyŏn kidam: *Strange Tales from Korea's Five Hundred-year Chosŏn Dynasty*, translated by James Scarth Gale and Caleb Park

Vincenza D'Urso, ed. *Footprints of the Wild Goose: A Trip to the Diamond Mountains and the East Coast by Miss Kim Kŭmwŏn (1830)*, translated by James Scarth Gale

Ross King and Caleb Park, eds. *Old Corea*, by James Scarth Gale and with illustrations by Elizabeth Keith

Ross King and Daniel Pieper, eds. *Pen Pictures of Korea*, by James Scarth Gale

Ross King and William S. Wells, eds. *Index to the James Scarth Gale Papers, University of Toronto*

Sean Bussell, ed. *Korean Poets and Poetry of the Koryŏ Dynasty, 918–1392 A.D.: Translations by James Scarth Gale*

Gregory Evon, ed. *Selected Works of Yi Kyubo (1169–1241 A.D.)*, translated by James Scarth Gale

Joohee Baik, ed. *Translation of a Korean Gentleman's Trip from Seoul to Peking, 1712–1713 A.D.*, translated by James Scarth Gale

Acknowledgments

This book has been many years in the making and the editors have incurred many debts of gratitude along the way. First to be thanked are the marvellous staff of the Thomas Fisher Rare Book Library at the University of Toronto. The late Richard Landon, Professor of English at the University of Toronto and Director of the Fisher Rare Book Library, was highly supportive of this project, as were his colleagues in the Library, Anne Dondertman and John Shoesmith. It was Professor Landon who invited Ross King to present on the Gale Papers at the annual Leon Katz Memorial Lecture in March of 2009. University of Toronto Korean Studies colleagues Andre Schmid and Janet Poole have also provided support and encouragement over the years, especially with their hosting of the symposium "The Writings of James Scarth Gale" in 2005 at the Munk International Centre at the University of Toronto. On the topic of libraries, UBC's Interlibrary Loan team has been invaluable, as has Helen Kim in the UBC Asian Library. Other super-helpful libraries and librarians on our Gale project have been Sonya Lee (Library of Congress), Minh Chung (Bodleian Library, Oxford), and the Center for Korean Classics Collection at Yonsei University.

Research funding for this project has come from several different sources. The Sunshik Min Endowment for the Advancement of Korean Literature at Harvard University's Korea Institute provided a small start-up grant in the academic year 2007–8, and we are grateful to Professor David McCann for his assistance in obtaining this support. UBC's Centre for Korean Research also provided a small grant in 2007 for field work in Toronto, and subsequent funding support has come from UBC Professor Bruce Fulton's SSHRC grant, "The Translations of

James Scarth Gale, Canadian Missionary in Korea, 1888–1927" (2008–11). Most recently this work was supported by the Academy of Korean Studies Grant funded by the Korean Government (MEST), AKS-2011-AAA-2103: an Academy of Korean Studies, Korean Studies Laboratory Grant, titled "Cosmopolitan and Vernacular in the Sinographic Cosmopolis: Comparative Aspects of the History of Language, Writing and Literary Culture in Japan and Korea" (2011–16, led by Ross King).

The editors are profoundly appreciative of the help extended by Gale's descendants. His late son George James Marley Gale (1911–2007) kindly shared valuable personal memories and insights with Ross King in 2007 before his death at the ripe age of 96, and granddaughters Wendy Earl and Rosemary Hill (daughters of Ada Alexandra Gale) in the United Kingdom have supported us with information and materials from afar, as has Margaret Farrow, granddaughter of Gale's older sister Jenny living in Kitchener, Ontario, and Marion Mosolf, his great-great-niece in Tiverton, Ontario.

Over the years, a number of Visiting Scholars from Korea at UBC have read through many of the *Kimun ch'onghwa* stories in *hanmun* with the editors and UBC graduate students: Professor Song Sŏnguk of Catholic University and Professor emeritus Yi Changu of Yeungnam University were particularly generous in this regard. Professor Sungdeuk Oak of UCLA and Brother Anthony of Taizé in Seoul have been valuable resources, as have Professors Yi Sanghyŏn (Pusan National University), Hwang Hoduk (Sungkyunkwan University), Sim Kyungho (Korea University), and Chŏng Hwan'guk of Dongguk University.

Several UBC Work Study students have put in hundreds of hours transcribing texts from the Gale Papers: Sandra Chung, Sunny Oh, Maria Kim, Joanne Lee, So Young Chang, Spencer Jentzsch, Patrick Stothers-Kwak, Jenny Kim, Chris Lovins, Scott Wells, Emily Soule, Sean Bussell, Yoonkyung Kim, Caleb Park, Elliot Cheung, Megan Chow, and Daniel Pieper.

Finally, we extend our thanks to all the UBC colleagues, graduate students, postdoctoral students, and visiting students in Korean Studies who have participated in our *Kimun ch'onghwa* reading sessions: series co-editor Bruce Fulton, Dafna Zur (now Assistant Professor at Stanford University), Ji-Eun Lee (now Associate Professor of Korean Literature at Washington University in St Louis), Hyuk-chan Kwon (now Assistant Professor at the University of Alberta), Scott Wells, Eunseon Kim, Leif Olsen, Chris Lovins, Paek Chuhŭi, Uliana Kobyakova (now Assistant Professor at Keimyung University), and Moon-sung Lee.

Translating to Inherit: An Introduction to James Scarth Gale's Translations from the *Kimun ch'onghwa*

SI NAE PARK

> The literary past of Korea, a great and wonderful past, is swallowed up as by a cataclysm, not a vestige being left to the present generation. Of course the present generation is blissfully ignorant of this and quite happy in its loss.
>
> J.S. Gale, "Korean Literature"
> *The Christian Movement in Japan, Korea, and Formosa* (1923)

James Scarth Gale (1863–1937; Korean name Kiil 奇一 [strange, wonderful one])[1] grew up to enjoy literature in rural Ontario and eventually earned a bachelor's degree in foreign languages from University College, University of Toronto. On 15 December 1888, under the auspices of the University College Young Men's Christian Association, he disembarked at Pusan from a ferry from Nagasaki, Japan, the first Canadian and the first non-ordained missionary to set foot on the Korean peninsula. Gale was based in Korea for nearly forty years, until 1927, as the country transitioned from the Chosŏn dynasty (1392–1897), through the Great Korean Empire (1897–1910), to Japanese colonial rule (1910–45). He wore many hats: pastor, traveller, educator, lexicographer, Bible translator, scholar, writer, novelist, honorary Doctor of

---

1 Rutt, *A Biography of James Scarth Gale*, 13–14. Richard Rutt (1925–2011) was an Anglican bishop who lived in Korea from the 1950s through the early 1970s, and who was himself an accomplished translator of Korean literature.

Divinity, bibliophile, translator of English literature into Korean,[2] and
– of most relevance to the present volume – translator of Korean literature into English.[3] Here I focus on Gale as a Western missionary who
chose to embody a bygone literary tradition of Korea through literary
translation from Literary Sinitic into English.

Gale's contribution to Korean literature is perhaps best reflected in
his translation of works such as *The Cloud Dream of the Nine* by Kim
Manjung,[4] and *Korean Folk Tales: Imps, Ghosts and Fairies*.[5] Those familiar with Western missionaries in early twentieth-century Korea may
also know Gale through his numerous publications in periodicals such
as *The Korea Mission Field* and *The Korea Magazine*.[6] The vast majority

---

2 Upon the urging of his first wife, Harriet E. Gibson Gale (1860–1908), and with
   her collaboration, Gale and Yi Ch'angjik co-translated into Korean Part I of John
   Bunyan's *Pilgrim's Progress*, finishing in 1895. Albeit incomplete, it was Gale's
   first literary translation as well as the first published Korean translation of a
   Western literary work. For further discussion of Gale's translations of English
   literary works into Korean, see Kim Uktong, *Pŏnyŏk kwa Han'guk ŭi kŭndae*,
   97–113.
3 For a detailed chronology of Gale's life, see Rutt, *Biography of James Scarth Gale*,
   1–88.
4 *The Cloud Dream of the Nine* is a translation of a seventeenth-century Korean fictional narrative, *Kuunmong* 九雲夢, written by Kim Manjung 金萬重 (1637–92).
   Tradition has it that Kim wrote the story to comfort his widowed mother,
   Madam Yun 尹氏, during his exile. Set in Tang China (618–907), the story relates the journey of the young and talented Buddhist monk Sŏngjin 性眞 to en-
   lightenment – his realization that Buddhist teaching is the truest teaching
   – after he is reborn as Yang Soyu 楊少遊. The figure of Christian in *Pilgrim's
   Progress* contrasts with that of Sŏngjin, in that Christian, too, achieves salvation
   at the end of his life, but only by undergoing myriad trials and tribulations.
5 *Korean Folk Tales: Imps, Ghosts and Fairies* is a compilation of excerpts from
   three story collections from Chosŏn: *Ch'ŏngp'a kŭktam* 青坡劇談 (Dramatic
   Stories by Ch'ŏngp'a [Yi Yuk]) by Yi Yuk (fl. late 1400s – early 1500s), *Ch'ŏnyerok*
   天倪錄 (Records of the Invisible Workings of Heaven) by Im Pang 任堕 (1640–
   1724), and *Ch'ŏnggu yadam* 青邱野談 (Stories from the Green Hills) by an anonymous compiler. The publisher lists Gale along with "Im Bang" (Im Pang) and
   "Yi Ryuk" (Yi Yuk) as the collection's authors.
6 For a list of works that Gale either wholly or partly wrote, see Rutt, *Biography of
   James Scarth Gale*, 373–84.

of Gale's translations, however, remain unpublished. These unpublished works were boxed up and catalogued misleadingly as "diaries" in the Thomas Fisher Rare Book Library at the University of Toronto.[7] Richard Rutt's 1972 *Biography of James Scarth Gale* notes that some of Gale's unpublished works survived, but not until Ross King of the University of British Columbia, co-editor of this volume, unearthed Gale's vast *Nachlass* in 2004 did they begin to receive serious scholarly attention.[8] The present volume, focusing on his translations from an early-ninteenth-century collection titled *Kimun ch'onghwa* 紀聞叢話 (Compendium of Records of Hearsay), represents the first scholarly endeavour to shed light on these little-known writings.[9]

In this introduction, I pay close attention to the historical context and stylistic features of Gale's *Kimun ch'onghwa* translations. In particular, I wish to show how the nostalgic pangs that Gale developed for Korea's Sinitic literary tradition led him to treat his English translations as a space to emulate the habits and conventions of late-Chosŏn transmission of *yadam* 野談 (lit. "unofficial talk"; quasi-fictional prose narratives of historical events and persons). To this end, I contextualize his *Kimun ch'onghwa* translations within the disappearance of Literary Sinitic (commonly termed *hanmun* 漢文 in Korean) at the turn of the twentieth century, the revival of interest in the 1910s and 1920s in old Korean books from the Chosŏn period, and the personal bond that Gale formed with his Korean co-translators. I then discuss Gale's source text, a four-volume manuscript edition held by Yonsei University. Then I juxtapose characteristics of late-Chosŏn *yadam* compilations with Gale's own translation methods to highlight how Gale shaped his English translation as a way of embodying the prototypical Chosŏn *yadam* compiler.

---

7 Gale's *Kimun ch'onghwa* translations are found in the ledgers labelled Diary XII and Diary XIV (Box 3), and Diary XV, Diary XVI, and Diary XIX (Box 4); Boxes 6 and 9; and a bound typescript entitled "Miscellaneous Writings II." There are no diaries. "Diary" is simply a label imposed by the University of Toronto librarians on the many ledgers containing Gale's handwritten notes, letter drafts, reports, and translations.

8 For details, see King, "James Scarth Gale, Korean Literature in *Hanmun*, and Korean Books."

9 Studies on Gale's published translations include Yi Sanghyŏn, *Han'guk kojŏn pŏnyŏkka ŭi ch'osang*; Paek, "J.S. Gale ŭi *Nogajae yŏnhaeng ilgi* yŏngyŏk pon ilgo"; and Paek, "J.S. Gale ŭi *Korean Folk Tales* yŏn'gu."

To conclude, I reflect on the significance of understanding Gale as a performative, emulative translator.

Korean Literature(s), Old and New

The first decades of the twentieth century had already brought fundamental changes to Korean language and literature. The fall of Korea from sovereign nation to protectorate of Japan in 1905 and subsequently to its formal colony in 1910 accompanied a tectonic shift in the ways Koreans perceived language, identity, and culture. The Korean language and the native script (now known as *han'gŭl*; invented and promulgated in the mid-fifteenth century) for the first time in history rose to become symbols of Korea's identity as an ethno-nation. The ascendance of the Korean script went hand in hand with condemnation of inscriptional practices grounded in Literary Sinitic, sinographs (Chinese characters), and Korea's long tradition of literature in Literary Sinitic. Privileged vehicles of philosophy, ritual, literature, and sophisticated culture for nigh on two thousand years of Korean history, Literary Sinitic and sinographs were now branded as markers of slavish dependence on a "foreign" and "Chinese" culture as well as of an elitist, time-consuming system of education.[10] Modern literary figures heralded the Korean script and spoken Korean as the basis for Korean writing and literature. For them, the literary tradition they inherited from the Chosŏn period – the "old literature" of Korea – embedded as it was in Literary Sinitic, was an awkward legacy that could only taint the modern future. Ironically, it was in the midst of this historic transition

---

10 The eventual demise of Literary Sinitic, however, should not overshadow the ponderous nature of the shift from a literary practice centred in Literary Sinitic and sinographs to one in the Korean script only. See Wells, "From Center to Periphery." That transition, despite the conventional narrative of the overnight eradication of the use of sinographs and writing in Literary Sinitic, required tremendous effort and resulted not in a *han'gŭl*-only writing system but instead a system heavily reliant on what modern scholars call "national-*cum*-Sinitic mixed-script orthography" (*kukhanmun honyong ch'e* 國漢文混用體). Im Sangsŏk, *20 segi kukhanmun ch'e ŭi hyŏngsŏng kwajŏng* offers a comprehensive overview of mixed-script orthographies in the early twentieth century.

that, Gale's admiration for the "old" Korean literature inscribed in Literary Sinitic deepened.[11]

Modern Korean writers denigrated as old and cumbersome what Gale saw as a magnificent and venerable literary tradition. An epistemological restructuring driven by modern science- and discipline-based approaches to knowledge moulded the thoughts of young Korean intellectuals and the contents and contours of their writings that began appearing at the turn of the twentieth century.[12] New epistemology, combined with nationalism and colonialism, generated competing discourses and strategies regarding how best to modernize Korean literature.[13] In the 1900s through the 1910s, with the advent of commercially successful writers such as Yi Haejo (1869–1927) and Yi Injik (1862–1916), "new fiction" (*sin sosŏl*) was serialized in newspapers and later published in book form, captivating Korean readers.[14] In Korean-language magazines such as *Hak chi Kwang* [*Lux Scientiae*] (Light of Knowledge, 1914–30), young Koreans studying in Japan wrote on vernacular Korean literature and the value of Korean as a literary language.[15] For example, visionaries like An Hwak (1881?/1886?–1946) and Yi Kwangsu (1892–1950) – the latter is considered the "father of modern (Korean) literature" (*kŭndae munhak ŭi abŏji*) – mapped out each in his own way a future trajectory for Korean literature as they agonized over whether to bring gradual and selective alterations to, or sever ties with, what they detected as the problem of the pre-existing literary tradition. For instance, in "Munhak iran hao" (What Is Literature? 1916), Yi declares a radical rupture with a past overly inflected by Chinese culture, and

---

11 For Gale's change in focus, around 1910, to Korean literature from before the twentieth century, see King, "James Scarth Gale, Korean Literature in *Hanmun*, and Korean Books," 242. In or about 1913, Gale's publications began to revolve around old Korean literature. See Yi Sanghyŏn, *Han'guk kojŏn pŏnyŏkka ŭi ch'osang*, 18.

12 For the formation of modern discipline-based knowledge in Korea at the turn of the twentieth century, see Ku, *Kŭndae ch'ogi chapchi wa punkwa hangmun ŭi hyŏngsŏng*.

13 For the intricate interrelations among colonialism, modernity, and nationalism, see Shin and Robinson, *Colonial Modernity in Korea*.

14 Pak Chinyŏng, *Ch'aek ŭi t'ansaeng kwa iyagi ŭi unmyŏng* profiles early twentieth-century Korean literature by focusing on how literary texts became objects of consumerism in the newly emerging private and public publishing industry.

15 See Yi Kyŏnghun, "*Hak chi kwang* kwa kŭ chubyŏn."

offers translations of Western literature as a solution.[16] An Hwak's *Chosŏn munhaksa* (A History of Korean Literature, 1922), the first work of its kind, advocates the more conservative approach of adopting and adapting Western literature more incrementally.[17] Some writers – many later became key figures in modern Korean literature – also experimented with writing in Japanese during this period.[18] In short, by the early 1920s Korea had witnessed explosive growth in modern literary activities, and coteries and periodicals dedicated to modern literature mushroomed.[19] Literary Sinitic as a meaningful vehicle for literature was doomed to extinction in such an environment.

Such a landscape for modern Korean literature worried Gale greatly. His concerns can be traced as far back as 1895, but not until 1917 did he begin articulating his views on the problems of Korean literature, in publications such as *The Korea Magazine, The Open Court, The Christian Movement in Japan, Korea, and Formosa,* and *The Korea Mission Field.* For example, his essay "Father and Son" notes how Korean literature in Literary Sinitic was fast becoming "a closed and sealed book," one that "up-to-date Korean men who read the papers and modern books" would not bother opening. The absence of an heir apparent is a recurrent theme in Gale's criticisms of contemporary Korean literature. In *The Open Court,* he wrote:

> This tragic death of native literature that followed the fateful edict[20] is seen in the fact that a famous father of the old school may have a famous son, yes, a graduate of Tokyo University, who still cannot any more read what his father has written than the ordinary graduate at home can read Herodotus or Livy at sight; and the father, learned though he be, can no more understand what his son reads or studies, than a hermit from the

---

16 For an English translation of this essay see Rhee, "What Is Literature?"

17 The vast majority of Korean translations of Western works from this period were adaptations and relay translations of Japanese and Chinese translations. See Kim Uktong, *Pŏnyŏk kwa Han'guk ŭi kŭndae*; and Pak Chinyŏng, *Pŏnyŏk kwa pŏnan ŭi sidae.*

18 See Kwŏn Podŭrae, "1910 nyŏndae ŭi ijungŏ sanghwang kwa munhak ŏnŏ."

19 Ch'ŏn, *Kŭndae ŭi ch'aek ilkki,* contains a timeline illustrating the kinds of reading and other cultural materials young Koreans likely found popular between 1907 and 1942.

20 "The fateful edict" refers to the 1894 abolition of the civil service examination, or *kwagŏ* 科擧.

hills of India can read a modern newspaper. So they sit, this father and this son, separated by a gulf of a thousand years pitiful to see.[21]

The blame fell squarely on the younger generation. The new literary Koreans showed little interest in the indigenous literary tradition, as Gale laments in a 1919 letter to his Anglican friend and colleague Bishop Trollope (1862–1930):

> Whereas the Korean of thirty years ago was a scholar, the young Korean of today is in many respects an ignoramus. He has a smattering of western knowledge, and some little idea of his own tongue; but his knowledge of the ancient literature of his people is practically non-existent. Therein lies a great danger. That literature contains all the idealism of his race.[22]

It is worth noting here that, as if to respond to Gale's characterizations of his generation, Yi Kwangsu, the aforementioned central figure of modern Korean literature, includes in his novel *Mujŏng* (Heartlessness, 1917) a scene where the protagonist Hyŏngsik, a Tokyo-educated young teacher in Seoul, mocks an old country scholar from his hometown of P'yŏngyang as "an absolutely incommunicative, illiterate person from another country" (chŏnhyŏ mal to t'onghaji mot hago kŭl to t'onghaji mot hanŭn ttan nara saram) and "a straggler, a man of a bygone era" (nagoja, kwagŏ ŭi saram). In fact, Yi Kwangsu's "straggler," as will be shown in later sections, is exactly the kind of conduit through which Gale explored firsthand the Korean literature of old.

In his fascination with old Korean literature and with Literary Sinitic, Gale also contrasts with his fellow missionary, scholar, and writer, the Methodist Homer Bezaleel Hulbert (1863–1949). Hulbert thought little of Korean literature in Literary Sinitic but was fascinated with spoken Korean:

> I would not belittle the enormous debt that Korea owes to China, but some of her gifts had been better ungiven … It is of course impossible to say what sort of a literature Korea would have evolved had she been left to herself, but one thing is sure; it would have been much more spontaneous and lifelike than that which now obtains. The Korean language is

---

21 Gale, "Korean Literature," *The Open Court*, 103.
22 Quoted in Rutt, *Biography of James Scarth Gale*, 67.

eminently adapted for public speaking. It is a sonorous, vocal language … Korean surpasses English as a medium of public speaking.[23]

In Hulbert's view, spoken Korean was a legitimate model for Korean literature, which was to be inscribed in the Korean script. What Gale perceived as the harmful influence of Western missionaries and Japanese education, Hulbert saw as the promise of a beneficial change for Korean literature: "It is to be hoped that the time will soon come when someone will do for Korea what Defoe and other pioneers did for English fiction, namely, write a standard work of fiction in the popular tongue."[24] As a missionary, Gale, too, was cognizant of the demotic capacity of the Korean script and readily acknowledged it as better suited for evangelism. Nevertheless, as an appreciator of literature, he was wary of the flip side of exclusive use of the Korean language and script.[25] For Gale, literature written in the medium of Literary Sinitic was just as native to Korea as anything written in the native script, if not more so.[26] In 1928, a year after the end of his long residence in Korea, he lauded Korea's contribution to world history by calling it the "Greece of the East" (Tongyang ŭi Hŭirap), precisely because of Korean literature in Literary Sinitic.

We turn now to another important backdrop for Gale's *Kimun ch'ong-hwa* translations – the revival of interest in old Korean books, a movement centred in bibliographic activities and the use of modern print technology to reissue old Korean editions.

---

23 Hulbert, *The Passing of Korea*, 304–5.

24 Ibid., 313. Hulbert also documented his views on Korean society and culture in *The Korean Review*, an English-language magazine that he founded in 1901.

25 In a 1923 report to the Christian Literature Society, Gale criticizes his fellow missionaries: "[T]he Korean language is fighting for its life as an intelligible medium of expression – can it survive against Japanese influence, western civilization, loss of classic Korea, introduction of illiterate writers? The worst enemy is the foreign missionary, putting out unidiomatic, ungrammatical, childish books. The Bible is most defective, hymns are a literary disgrace, our books bad, Sunday-school lessons ditto." Quoted in Rutt, *Biography of James Scarth Gale*, 68.

26 The two men's differences of opinion materialized into public debates on the relationship between the Literary Sinitic literary tradition and Korean literature. See Yi Sanghyŏn, *Han'guk kojŏn pŏnyŏkka ŭi ch'osang*, 208.

Old Korean Books in the 1910s and 1920s

From the 1910s to the mid-1920s, old Korean books were born again. Whether they appeared in a format old or new, these books furthered Gale's appreciation of Korean literature inscribed in Literary Sinitic.

First, numerous books from the Chosŏn period were reprinted by means of modern typography. These books had long been available in xylography (printed from woodblocks), movable type, or manuscript copies, but never before in modern print editions. The first group to launch such a revival was the Chōsen Kosho Kankōkai 朝鮮古書刊行會 (Society for the Publication of Old Korean Books, 1908–16), under the patronage of the Japanese colonial administration.[27] Barely three years later the Chosŏn Kwangmunhoe 朝鮮光文會 (Society for Promoting Korean Culture, 1911–18) was established by a group of Korean intellectuals led by Ch'oe Namsŏn (1890–1957). At the same time, some old Korean books were translated into modern Japanese as part of a series called the Kosho Chinsho Kankō 古書珍書刊行 (Publication of Old Books and Precious Books), an enterprise headed by another Japanese group, Chōsen Kenkyūkai 朝鮮研究會 (Society for Chosŏn Research, 1910–?).[28] The goal of each of these republishing projects was to represent Korea and its culture prior to the twentieth century. Gale was an avid collector of these reprints, each new title pulling him closer to Korean literature in Literary Sinitic.

Between 1912 and 1926 a few Korean-owned private publishing houses also began resuscitating stories and story collections circulating since late Chosŏn and reissuing them by means of modern typography.[29] These quasi-fictional narratives about historical events and persons, commonly known as *yadam*, which I discuss later, had previously circulated widely in anonymity. The publishers drew material from manuscript copies of Chosŏn story collections, targeting a wide readership for commercial success.[30]

---

27 King, "James Scarth Gale, Korean Literature in *Hanmun*, and Korean Books," 248.

28 For modern Japanese publications of old Korean books, see Ch'oe, "Hanmal Ilcheha chaejo Ilbonin ŭi Chosŏn kosŏ kanhaeng saŏp."

29 For bibliographical details and the contents of the story collections published during this period, see Chŏng and Yi, *Ku hwalchabon yadam ŭi pyŏni yangsang yŏn'gu*, 12–72.

30 These compilations of *yadam* appeared in mixed-script orthographical styles as well as in the Korean script only, reflecting the transition from sinographic writing in the national script.

Around the same time, a great number of Korean books from the Chosŏn period in whatever form they had existed came to be treated as collectibles. Gale soon turned himself into a bibliophile. He purchased books for himself, but most of his book-buying activity was conducted on behalf of clients in the United States and Korea such as the Library of Congress, Chōsen Christian College (the first private college in Korean history and precursor of today's Yonsei University), and other organizations.[31] Gale's research on old Korean books later materialized in the form of catalogues and indexes of Korean literature.

The resurfacing of old Korean books helped Gale discover rich repositories of the old Korean literature and had a direct impact on his *Kimun ch'onghwa* translations in the early 1920s. For example, the Chōsen Kosho Kankōkai's 1909–15 edition of the *Taedong yasŭng* 大東野承 (Unofficial Transmissions from the Great East) gave Gale "one of the greatest fillips" in his studies of Korean literature.[32] It was a comprehensive compilation of mid-Chosŏn miscellanies that had circulated in manuscript copies since the early seventeenth century. A portion of the source texts for Gale's *Korean Folk Tales* of 1913 has its roots in the *Taedong yasŭng*. The *Kimun ch'onghwa* collection resembles the contents of *Korean Folk Tales* in that both are compilations of *yadam*. In this respect, Gale's appreciation and subsequent translation of the *Kimun ch'onghwa* owes much to the 1913 publication of the *Taedong yasŭng*. And Gale's book-collecting activity led him to discover his source text, which was one of the titles he purchased on behalf of Chōsen Christian College.

Co-Translators

Gale's familiarity with old Korean texts was predicated on access to Literary Sinitic. This access would have been impossible without Korean Christians such as Yi Ch'angjik (1866–1936) and Kim Tohŭi (1866–1924). They were a dying breed of Koreans trained in classical Literary Sinitic learning, heirs apparent to the literature of old Korea (or so Gale would have perceived them). Given that Gale considered literature inscribed in Literary Sinitic as a window onto what he believed to be the psyche and culture of Korea, the influence of these "old school"

---

31 For Gale as a bibliophile and the fate of his books, see King, "James Scarth Gale, Korean Literature in *Hanmun*, and Korean Books," 247–61.

32 Rutt, *Biography of James Scarth Gale*, 49.

Korean Christian fellows must have been enormous. They taught Gale the rudiments of sinographs and of Literary Sinitic, which Gale called "the character." Their presence and guidance proved to be essential in nearly all of his translations from Literary Sinitic. Appropriating the attitude of missionary orientalists in India, Gale on several occasions called these Korean men his "pundits."[33] But more commonly he described them as colleagues, co-translators, friends, literary secretaries, and teachers.

Reconstructing his exact translation process is difficult, but a sketchy image can be achieved. Gale and his pundits generally worked early in the morning before breakfast. According to Gale's son George (Korean name Chose 助世 ["help the world"]),[34] Gale and his co-translators often engaged in heated debates as to how best to interpret the contents of a given story. George Gale's account suggests that his father's Korean co-translators made significant contributions to the preliminary drafts. It seems that some or all of the translation process involved the Koreans producing oral Korean translations of the source texts, which Gale then rendered into English based on what he heard.[35] This oral-aural process must have been conducive to discussions among Gale and his co-translators about principles of literary translation. Moreover, the co-translators' understanding of Korea's literary past and present – though Gale remains largely silent about this – must have had a lasting impact on his exaltation of Korean literature in Literary Sinitic, his lamentation over newly developing Korean speech patterns among the young generation, his disappointment in fellow missionaries influenced by modern Japanese and Western culture,[36] his choices of texts and authors to translate, and the way he approached translation. Working closely with these sinologically trained Koreans must have given Gale opportunities to develop an intimate knowledge of the stylistic features, particulars, and conventions of various literary genres

---

33 King, "James Scarth Gale, Korean Literature in *Hanmun*, and Korean Books," 245. In similar fashion, Rutt has called Gale a "revered pundit" with reference to his role in social gatherings as a repository of Korean culture, language, and history. Rutt, *A Biography of James Scarth Gale*, 75.

34 Rutt, *Biography of James Scarth Gale*, 51.

35 This oral-to-written translation process is reminiscent of Edo-period Japanese translations of Chinese vernacular fiction, and awaits further research. In highlighting this fascinating process I do not mean to suggest, however, that Gale was unable to read Literary Sinitic or sinographs.

36 See Rutt, *Biography of James Scarth Gale*, 68.

from the Chosŏn period. It is not surprising that "Student of the Orient" was one of Gale's *noms de plume*.

Source Text at Yonsei University

Gale's source text was the four-volume *Kimun ch'onghwa* currently held by the Center for Korean Classics at Yonsei University in Seoul. The Gale edition is entitled 紀聞叢話, whereas most other editions (including a one-volume edition also housed at Yonsei University) use a different character for *ki*: 記聞叢話.[37] In this four-volume edition many of Gale's own pencil marks survive, for he scribbled small circle shapes above all the entries that he translated. The Gale edition consists of some 637 stories; this is a rather large number for a story collection from the Chosŏn dynasty. Gale and his pundits read more stories than they had time to translate; at least three stories have "Read" pencilled in at the beginning of the relevant entries but no corresponding translation in Gale's *Nachlass* at the Thomas Fisher Library. Altogether 117 stories were rendered into English. Seven stories were published in the missionary journal *The Korea Magazine* and one in Gale's *History of the Korean People*. Figure 1 shows what Gale wrote as a description of his source text; the romanization and the blank spaces left for the sinographs for Korean names are Gale's own.

No less than twenty-seven manuscript editions of the *Kimun ch'onghwa* survive today. It is speculated that the progenitor-collection – that is, the non-existent original compilation – was compiled sometime between 1833 and 1869.[38] What Gale records as "Su-ke chap-nok" (= Sŏgye chamnok 西溪雜錄) and identifies as one of the source texts for the *Kimun ch'onghwa* in his "Catalogue of the Books of the Chōsen Christian College" must be a mistake for the *Kyesŏ chamnok* 溪西雜錄 (Miscellaneous Records by Sŏgye [Yi Hŭip'yŏng], which contains two prefaces dated 1828 and 1833, respectively), a *yadam* collection compiled by Yi Hŭip'yŏng 李義平 (1772–1839). According to Gale's own note, a certain Unsŭngja ("Rider of the Clouds") compiled the *Kimun ch'onghwa* in the *chŏngch'uk* 丁丑 year (1877). Although the progenitor-compiler of

---

37 The Yonsei University Library also holds a text entitled *Swaeŏ* 瑣語 (Trivial Sayings), a close examination of which confirms that it stands in either a parent-child or a sibling relationship with other manuscript editions of the *Kimun ch'onghwa*.

38 Kim Chunhyŏng, "Haeje."

No.⁴² Keui-moon Ch'ong-wha (記聞叢詁) "ABunch of Old Stoeies"

4 books.   MSS.

A book of stories collected from the following books: U-oo ｿ Ya-tam (於于野詼), P'a-soo-t'oi (破睡椎),Soo-moon-nok (隨聞錄), Su-ke chap-nok (西溪雜錄), Hai-tong I-juk (海東異跡),Han-ch'ong Ya-sa (閒叢野史),Han-po-rok (閒神補錄),Nam-sa (南史) T'ai-soo Han-wha (太守閒詁) Tong-wun-keui (東園記), The Twenty Four Capitals (二十四都記) Tong-gook Sa-keui (東國史記), Keui-yo Pyul-lam (記要便覽).

It was prepared in a certain <u>chung-ch'ook</u> (1757 or 1817 or 1877) by someone whose pen-name was Oon-sung-ja and the stories touch on the spiritual world,the official world, the world of nature etc. Tis is the most interesting collection of Korean stories dealing with Korean thought and custom that the writer has ever seen.

<u>Contents of Work</u>

Vol. ⅠI Stories of Se-jo,Sung-jong , Koo Soo-yung (具壽永)
            Yoo Haing (尹行),Hong Sum (洪暹), Sun-jo (宣祖)
            Princess Chung-sook (靖俶) Japan War of 1592 etc.
   "   II Stories of Chung Pook-chang,Mrs Yi Chung-koo (李迋龜),
            Su Kyung-tuk (徐敬德) Pak Yup (朴曄).
   "   III Stories of Yi Chi-ham (李之菡),Yi Kyung-yoo (李   )
            Yi Pyung-tai (   ), Yi T'ai-choong (   )
            Yi Pyung-jin (   ), Yi Tuk-chong (   ).
   "   IV Stories of Nim Keum-ho (林錦湖) Hong Yoon-sum (洪允成)
            Yoo Pyung (   ) Kang Hon (姜渾   ) Yoo Chung-wun (

Figure 1. Gale's description of the *Kimun ch'onghwa* in his "Catalogue of the Books of the Chōsen Christian College (Korean Department)," page 20. The same information can be found on pages 88–9 of the "Short List of Korean Books [in the Chosen Christian College Library]" appended to Bishop Trollope's "Corean Books and their Authors being an Introduction to Corean Literature" in *The Transactions of the Korea Branch of the Royal Asiatic Society* 21, 1931, pp. 1–104 (note that this "Short List" was compiled by Gale and attributed to Bishop Trollope in error).

the *Kimun ch'onghwa* remains unknown, someone identifying himself as Unsŭngja might have compiled the four-volume edition that Gale used.

The first modern Korean-language renditions of the *Kimun ch'onghwa* appeared in the 1970s. Yi Usŏng and Im Hyŏngt'aek's three-volume *Yijo hanmun tanp'yŏn chip* (Compilation of Chosŏn Short Narratives Written in Literary Sinitic) consisting of modern Korean translations of select late-Chosŏn *yadam*, includes a few entries from the *Kimun ch'onghwa*. In 1996–9, Professor Donguk Kim (Kim Tonguk) of Sangmyung University issued a five-volume modern Korean version, *Kugyŏk kimun ch'onghwa*, of the entirety of the four-volume edition used by Gale – not knowing, at the time, of Gale's personal connection with the text or the existence of Gale's translations. In 2008, a new edition of this translation was published in three volumes, newly titled *Saebyŏk kangka e haeoragi unŭn sori* (Cry of the Snowy Heron at Dawn by the River).[39]

Fluid Textuality of Late-Chosŏn *Yadam*

Let us now examine *yadam* more closely. *Yadam* is the generic category for the *Kimun ch'onghwa* entries. The word is a compound of *ya* 野 (literally, uncultivated, unofficial) and *tam* 談 (stories, chats; talk). This label, however, is a creation of modern Korean scholarship. Only a few story compilations from late Chosŏn include *yadam* in their title, though many easily fall within the embrace of this genre. In their content *yadam* deal more often than not with historical events and persons from the Chosŏn dynasty, and are imbued with an air of historical veracity. However, the plot, characterization, and details of *yadam* tend to dwell more in likelihood, probability, and tropes than in verifiable facts. To give a conclusive definition of *yadam* or the *yadam* "genre" is a difficult task, but several observations about the *Kimun ch'onghwa* as a *yadam* compilation can be made here.[40] In particular, the fluid textuality that characterizes the provenance and transmission of *yadam* throughout Chosŏn illuminates how Gale and his co-translators understood the *Kimun ch'onghwa*.

The textual fluidity of *yadam* stems from both intertextuality and manuscript culture. Writers of *yadam* drew their materials from written

---

39 Other manuscript editions are housed in various university libraries and research institutes in South Korea, Japan, and the United States. Some are in the hands of private collectors. Several have been photographically reproduced – for example, an edition held by the Karam Collection at the Seoul National University Library, reproduced in Chŏng, *Han'guk yadam charyo chipsŏng*, vol. 6; an edition held by the Tenri University Library, reproduced in Ōtani, "Yŏngin *Kimun ch'onghwa* haeje"; and an edition held by the Asami Collection at the C.V. Starr East Asian Library at the University of California, Berkeley.

40 For details of the provenance of *yadam* studies as an academic field within Korean literature studies in Korea, and discussions surrounding *yadam* as a difficult-to-define genre, see part I of Park, "A Textual Study of *Tongp'ae naksong*."

antecedents. As a result, narratives and compilations form complex ancestor-descendant and other cognate relationships.

Throughout Chosŏn, the transmission of *yadam* depended solely on human hands, and never on xylographic or typographical reproducibility. That story collections with the title *Kimun ch'onghwa* exist today in several different manuscript editions indicates that the text should be understood as a sum of reader-produced compilations by way of handmade copies, which were subsequently bound into a codex. Scholarship on medieval European manuscript culture emphasizes the fluidity of a text's form and meaning as a result of the liberties that copyists ordinarily took. Such liberties made the text "open to a wide variety of interpretations and uses" in manuscript culture.[41] The textual meaning and form could be "determined by the arrogations of a later hand,"[42] while the act of copying was interpreted as a literary practice that "mirrored [the act of] reading."[43] Chosŏn compilers of *yadam* resembled the medieval European "reader/scribe" in that their reading experience left "textual and permanent" traces that permeated the transmission of a pre-existing story or a collection.[44]

Handled by human hands and minds, transmissions of *yadam* always entailed alterations, ranging from unintended slips to exuberant decisions to excise, elaborate, and augment. The scribe might miscopy a character or inadvertently substitute an incorrect homonym for the correct character. The compiler might read another compilation and choose to reproduce a story, but leave out a large chunk of his source text while nonetheless giving his version the same title as that of his source. Or, a compiler might create an abridged version of a collection and give his collection an original title of his own, thereby obscuring

---

41 Reiter, "The Reader as Author of the User-Produced Manuscript," 163.

42 Bruns, "The Originality of Texts in a Manuscript Culture," 115.

43 Dagenais, *The Ethics of Reading in a Manuscript Culture*, xvii.

44 Reiter, "The Reader as Author of the User-Produced Manuscript," 167. This textual fluidity of *yadam* should not be taken to mean that notions of conventions and genre did not hold sway. In fact, *yadam* compilers treated their creations as literary-*like* writing, in that comments akin to literary criticism are found in framing materials such as prefaces and postscripts. See Park, "A Textual Study of *Tongp'ae naksong*," 239–311. Further research will illuminate the location of *yadam* narratives vis-à-vis the overall economy of literary genres during the Chosŏn period.

the genealogical origins of his abridged text. A compiler with creative aspirations would tamper with his source text, making author-like changes. *Yadam* collections were rarely dated and almost always circulated in anonymity.

Furthermore, the fluid textuality of *yadam* manifests certain roles that orality played in the creation and transmission of *yadam*. Earlier scholarship reflects a belief that professional storytellers – illiterate men unversed in Literary Sinitic – in the marketplaces of urbanizing Seoul were the true progenitors of *yadam* narratives. More recent scholarship has demonstrated the flimsiness of the oral storyteller hypothesis. Instead, literati networks with their casual socializing and textual circulation proved to be the predominant environment in which *yadam* originated, developed, and were transmitted. Anecdotes shared with others, or factual particulars of anecdotes heard firsthand or read in books, would count as oral aspects of *yadam* transmission. Conflicting facts surrounding pre-existing narratives spurred various new and competing versions of the same story.

All in all, *yadam* narratives were created and circulated in an environment of tremendous textual fluidity that allowed transmitters to take the liberty of leaving indelible marks of their own. The final section of this introduction will show how the *Kimun ch'onghwa* became one such malleable material in Gale's hands as he produced his English translations.

Translating and Sculpting

Much like late-Chosŏn compilers of *yadam*, Gale exerted considerable editorial freedom over his source text. He often went through multiple revisions of his translations, fixing the meaning and improving the flow of the narrative. Pressure to give translations that are both faithful and word-for-word is conspicuously absent.

The most common changes Gale made are annotations concerning reign years of kings, birth and death years of historical figures, and sobriquets of Chosŏn literati. For facts like these he consulted the *Kukcho myŏngsin nok* 國朝名臣錄 (Famous Subjects of the State; compiled by Kim Yuk 金堉 [1580–1658]). Details such as "Pak Yŏp (Graduated 1596, his wife was a sister of Kwanghae's queen)" just below the title of Story 33 suggest that Gale and his co-translators thought explanations of this nature would be useful for his Anglophone readers.

More substantial alterations include the insertion of parallels from Western history to facilitate his readers' comprehension of the context of the stories. In "The Innkeeper's Daughter" (Story 36), the protagonist Yi Kich'uk's 李起築 (1589–1645) physical strength is compared to that of the biblical strongman Samson. In "Firing the House on the Imjin River" (Story 22) about the Hideyoshi Invasions (1592–8), Gale evokes the Jewish exodus led by Moses to describe the darkness experienced by the Chosŏn protagonists of the story: "Here a great rain fell and the night was as dark as Egypt so that nothing could be seen."

Gale also furnished the stories with Western-Korean coevalness.[45] Compare, for instance, the two quotations below for how Gale elaborates on Hwang In'gŏm (Story 99) in two different pre-publication typescripts:

> Hwang In'gŏm, who graduated from the Confucian College in 1714 AD, spent much of his time as a young man in a Buddhist monastery where he studied the Chinese classics. (*Miscellaneous Writings no. 30*)
>
> Two hundred years ago there lived in Korea a well-known man by the name of Hwang In'gŏm. He graduated from the Confucian College in the year that George the First came to the throne of England – 1714 – and rose to be an officer of the first rank. While preparing for the rigid examination of that day, he spent much of his time in a Buddhist monastery. (*Old Corea*)

On at least two occasions, Gale abridged his source text, bringing a thematic transformation. In the case of "The Obstreperous Boy" (Story 51), the translation is about a prodigal boy turning over a new leaf and coming to appreciate his educator. The original, which goes on to relate one more episode, highlights the uncannily accurate prognostications of the old monk who educates the once-obstreperous protagonist.

---

45 Traces of Gale's perceptions of which are peppered throughout his *History of the Korean People* (Seoul: Christian Literature Society, 1927). Ross King (personal communication) suggests that Gale's primary historiographical principles seem to have lain in demonstrating Korea as a country with a long history and a venerable literary tradition, in the process exhibiting something like the opposite of the "denial of coevalness" that Johannes Fabian observes in anthropological writing in *Time and Other*.

At other times, Gale pens in details not so much for the quality or flow of his translation but out of personal interest and in recognition of his Korean co-translators' reactions. In "The World of the Dancing Girl" (Story 10), he writes, "This is a very extreme example of an obscene essay – seldom seen in Korea. J.S.G." In "Madness Recalls the Verse" (Story 13), he writes that the story concerns an ancestor of Kim Tohŭi, one of his Korean pundits. In the story of Yi Hangbok (Story 114), he mentions that Yi Ch'angjik, another pundit and his friend and teacher since 1889, found nothing vulgar in the story, whereas Kim Tohŭi considered it "a very dirty story." After translating "The Reward of Virtue" (Story 72) and "A Gifted Woman" (Story 88), he gives curt evaluations: "Good story" and "Not good as a story," respectively.

"The Andong Wizard" (Story 90) shows how Gale internalized the textual fluidity of *yadam* transmission within his own translations. Like many other *yadam*, "The Andong Wizard" survives in several different versions. The original opens with this phrase: "In Yu Sŏae's [= Yu Sŏngnyong 柳成龍 (1542–1607)] house in Andong lived an ignorant *suk*" (柳西崖成龍居安東家, 有一叔, 爲人蠢蠢無識). *Suk* 叔 generally refers to one's father's brothers: in other words, uncles. Therefore, in modern Korean translations, including Professor Kim Tonguk's, the protagonist is treated as the uncle of this famous scholar-official. In the translation, however, the protagonist is introduced as Yu's elder brother:

> Yu Sŏngnyong (Sŏae) (1542–1607), while he lived in Andong, had his brother with him, Yu Unnyong 柳雲龍 (Kyŏmam 謙庵). He was most simple and wholly ignorant of everything.

Why this discrepancy? The answer lies in a note provided by an anonymous reader in the top margin of Gale's source text:

> 叔, 非叔侄之叔, 是孟仲叔季之叔, 乃西崖叔兄謙庵有雲龍也.

> The *suk* [here] is not *suk* as in "*suk* and *chil*" [for "uncle and nephew"], but ["a sibling relationship"] as in *maeng* (first-born son), *chung* (second-born son), *suk* (third-born son), and *kye* (fourth-born son). Thus [*suk* in this case refers to] Sŏae Yu Sŏngnyong's elder brother [Yu] Unnyong (whose sobriquet is) Kyŏmam.

By incorporating this interpretation of the two men's relationship in shaping his English translation, Gale responds to a message the anonymous reader communicates to fellow readers of the story. In so doing, Gale participates in the tradition of Chosŏn *yadam* transmission. To reiterate, the liberties that Gale took illustrate that his translations and editorial touches share considerable resemblance with, if not conformity to, the common conventions of Chosŏn *yadam* transmission.

How conscious was Gale in his emulation of late-Chosŏn transmitters of *yadam*? Evidence elsewhere consistently suggests that Gale made conscious efforts to inscribe the stylistic characteristics of Korean traditional writing within his literary translations from English into Korean. His work on John Bunyan's *Pilgrim's Progress* with Yi Ch'angjik and his unauthorized translation of the Bible with Yi Wŏnmo are cases in point. When translating the verses in *Pilgrim's Progress*, Gale created three-to-four-syllable breath groups for the Korean translation, noting that this was a typical feature of Chosŏn vernacular lyric genres, such as *sijo* and *kasa*.[46] For prose sections, Gale ignored paragraph distinctions to make the translation flow more smoothly. He frequently dropped markers identifying interlocutors so as to follow the customary omission in the Korean language of contextually identifiable subjects. Stock phrases not originating from his source texts were at times added to make the reading experience resemble that of the traditional Korean *sosŏl* (fictional narrative) genre. Gale's Bible of 1925 was an independent project of his (hence its common byname, the "Gale Bible") and was unauthorized (read "discouraged") by the missionary community's official Bible translation committee, from which Gale had earlier resigned. The general opinion held by members of this committee was that the new Bible that they envisioned should be written in the Korean script only, be literal in its approach, and be more vernacular than classical in style and tone. Gale, however, opposed such an approach, insisting on using a type of mixed-script orthography (that is, sinographs intermixed with the Korean alphabet) and a classical style, so as not to tamper with the proper diction and dignity of the Korean literary language, which he called "Chosŏnŏ p'ung."[47]

---

46 For definitions of *sijo* and *kasa*, see the glossary in Lee, *A History of Korean Literature*, lvii, xxviii.

47 Gale's unpublished notes show his dissatisfaction with James Legge's (1815–97) translation style of the Confucian classics (published in 1879–91). Gale hoped to produce his own translations based on an understanding of the Confucian texts within the Korean tradition. See King, "James Scarth Gale, Korean Literature in *Hanmun*, and Korean Books," 247.

Once a first draft was achieved, Gale edited it to produce an improved draft in one of his manuscript ledgers. Figure 2 below shows an example of Gale's manuscript draft of story number 99, "A Question of Conscience" (Diary XIV, p. 10). A clean copy of the improved version(s) was then typed up and the manuscript original in Gale's ledger was crossed out. The typed-up draft underwent yet another round of edits before publication. When a draft was ready to go, Gale added a brief preface introducing the Korean story to his readers. A couple of unpublished stories also have prefaces. The vast majority of Gale's translations survive in clean copies, neither typed up nor edited. A few are scribbled over with Gale's editorial notes, ranging from correcting errors to revamping the text into publishable form. One significant difference between the manuscript drafts and typescript versions is that all of Gale's published stories bear an autographic preface.[48] These were clearly ready for publication.

Concluding Remarks

Score One for the Dancing Girl bears the stamp of Gale's nostalgia for the old Korean literary tradition inscribed in Literary Sinitic. In an age when new ideas and practices about language, literature, and writing were rapidly pushing out the old, Gale yearned for the riches of a bygone epoch in Korean literature before the twentieth century. Informed by an intimate knowledge of the old Korean literary tradition with the help of his Korean pundits, Gale demonstrated through his translation process that he went beyond simply rendering a text

---

48 The seven *Kimun ch'onghwa* translations published in *The Korea Magazine* and their corresponding entry numbers from the Gale source text, followed by their story number in the present volume ("Story X"), are listed here:
   1 The Innkeeper's Daughter (Jan 1919: 18–20): 196 (Story 36).
   2 The Law of Retribution (May 1918: 202–8): 205 (Story 43, therein titled "Avenged by the Gods").
   3 The Obstreperous Boy (June 1918: 255–67): 213 (Story 51).
   4 Yu Chinsa (October 1918: 444–49): 214 (Story 52, therein titled "Yu *Chinsa* and His Wives").
   5 Yi Chang-gon (September 1918: 396–400): 292 (Story 84, therein titled "Yi Changgon").
   6 High-born Prince and Worthy Girls (November 1918: 502–7): 303 (Story 93).
   7 A Second Wife under Difficulties (January 1919: 22–29): 304 (Story 94).
 The one story published in *The History of the Korean People* is
   1 Defiance to a Spirit: 198 (Story 37).

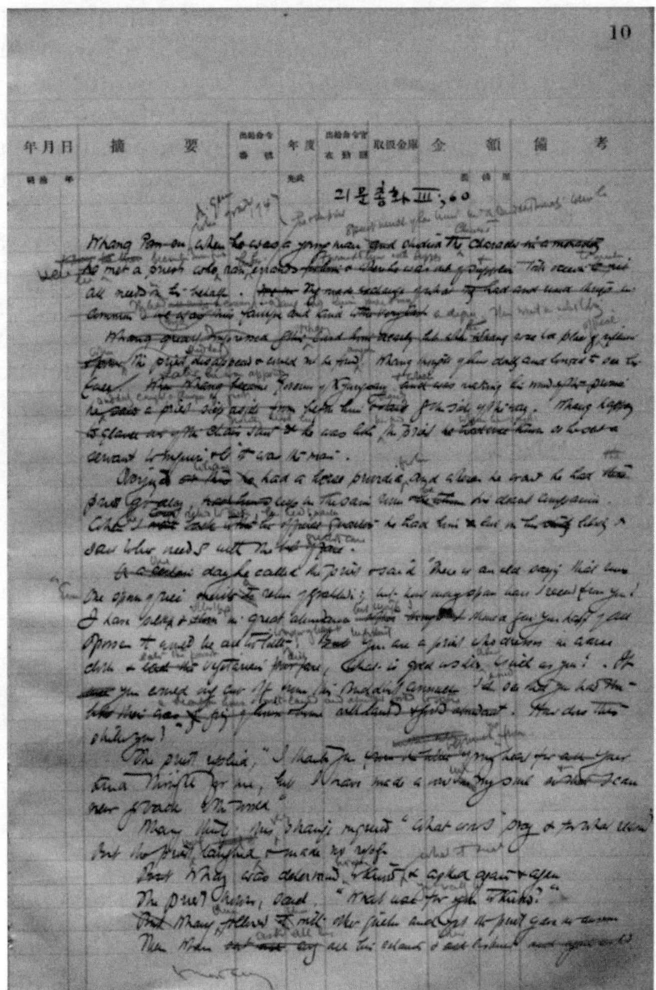

Figure 2. An example of Gale's editorial handwriting, Diary XIV, p. 10.

from one language into another (i.e., from Literary Sinitic into English). Rather, he left behind artefacts through which we discover a Western literary translator who consciously adopted and emulated a foreign literary tradition. It would be unjust to pigeonhole Gale as a de-historicizing and exoticizing orientalist of the type caricatured in Said's *Orientalism*; nor was he an uninformed armchair dilettante, oblivious to the cultural logic and practices of Korea.[49] Lauding James Legge's role as a missionary-translator who introduced the Confucian classics to the West through his English translations, Girardot calls Legge a "translator-transformer" of Chinese texts. In recognition of Gale's work on the *Kimun ch'onghwa* collection, the editors of this volume affectionately suggest that we acknowledge Gale as a legatee of the old Korean literature that he so cherished.

Though not all of Gale's manuscript translations are dated, it seems clear from other dated items in his ledgers ("diaries") that he maintained his interest in the *Kimun ch'onghwa* stories from at least early in 1918 through the end of 1921. The ledgers with *Kimun ch'onghwa* materials are: Diary XII (27 translations from the first half of 1918), Diary XIV (39 translations, mostly from the latter half of 1918), Diary XV (just three translations, likely from late 1918 and early 1919), Diary XVI (some 43 translations, mostly from May and June 1921), and Diary XIX (eight translations, completed between April and December 1921). In some cases no manuscript translation survives, and in others multiple drafts survive.

49 Yi Sanghyŏn, *Han'guk kojŏn pŏnyŏkka ŭi ch'osang*, 3.

Further Contextualizing the Translations of James Scarth Gale

ROSS KING

Introduction

This essay supplements Si Nae Park's introduction and offers additional context for understanding a) the Gale papers and the research project of which this volume is the first installment; b) the state of the art in Gale-related research; c) the quirks of Gale's translation practice and literary style, as well as d) our approach to editing Gale's drafts.

A Neglected *Nachlass*: James Scarth Gale and His Papers

Despite his enormous importance in the modern history of Korea and in the origins of "Korean Studies" as a field of research, Canadian missionary to Korea James Scarth Gale (1863–1937) remains surprisingly under-researched and under-appreciated. At least three reasons explain this neglect. The first is personal. Unlike the better-known and more fecund Underwoods of Korea, Gale had few children, and neither he nor his children remained in Korea after his retirement from the mission field in 1927. The second concerns the ways in which some of his early publications have been mistranslated, misconstrued, and misrepresented by modern-day Korean scholars of Korean literature and Korean church history, who have tended to disregard his activities and writings after 1910 and colonization by Japan, and have also inaccurately constructed an image of Gale as apolitical, anti-national, and pro-Japanese in his sympathies. The third relates again to the specialized academic field of Korean church history, and to the research biases of its practitioners. Gale left behind a substantial archive of personal papers, publications, and manuscripts, all nicely housed and organized at the Thomas Fisher Rare Book Library at the University of Toronto since 1987. However, the vast majority of these materials is literary in nature, and sheds little light on the questions of missionary policy and practice, interdenominational relations, doctrinal politics, theological debate, and church history that animate the large *kyohoesa* (Protestant church history) establishment in South Korea and its satellites in North America. Worse, the vast majority of Gale's literary *Nachlass* concerns Korean literary works written in and translated from Literary Sinitic (*hanmun*), a language that does not normally figure in the training of church historians in Korea. And of course many Korean scholars – whether working in the fields of church history, *hanmun*, or vernacular Korean literature, face a language barrier when it comes to mobilizing sources written in English.

As a result, while more than a few researchers have made the trek to the Fisher Rare Book Library to examine the Gale Papers, very few have engaged with them in a sustained fashion. The first scholar to delve into Gale's *Nachlass* was, of course, Richard Rutt (1972), at a time when the papers were still held in Montreal by Gale's son George (1911–2007). Rutt succeeded in painting a detailed and sympathetic portrait of Gale in the biographical portion of his book, and left ample bibliographic hints and clues for future researchers in the back matter of the book. Rutt's seminal book has set the tone for all future research on Gale. But it was by no means the final word on Gale, and in one particular aspect it has been somewhat misleading indeed. On page 383 of Rutt's rich "Bibliography" section at the back of the book is a small section subtitled "Unpublished Writings and Drafts" occupying barely one third of the page. In it, Rutt notes laconically, "A number of diaries and notebooks are in the possession of Dr Gale's son and daughter ..."

It would appear that Rutt never looked at them, but it is precisely these "diaries" that have become the focus of a multi-year, multi-volume project under my direction at the University of British Columbia. As described in King, "James Garth Gale, Korean Literature," these "diaries" are, in fact, bulky accounting ledgers of two hundred pages each, filled with Gale's difficult-to-decipher handwriting: draft letters and reports, the odd diary fragment, lists of books purchased and prices paid, but overwhelmingly translations from Korean literary sources in *hanmun* into English, with sources dutifully identified. There are nineteen surviving ledgers in all, which, when typed out, amount to approximately 4000 pages of text.[50]

One of the very first texts to catch my attention after my first visit to the Gale Papers in 2005 was the *Kimun ch'onghwa*. It was clear from the numerous translated excerpts from this work scattered throughout Gale's ledgers ("diaries") as well as other folders in his *Nachlass* that he had intended at some point to publish them together in one volume; the stories written out in relatively polished handwriting in Diary XVI pages 151–84, and especially the Table of Contents–like list of story titles on pages 178–9 in the same Diary, underscore this intent. So it was that the UBC team settled on the *Kimun ch'onghwa* stories in late 2005 or so. Through informal weekly reading sessions and graduate seminars, we chipped away at the texts over many years – Gale's frequently indecipherable manuscript translations and the *hanmun* originals, juxtaposed with photocopies of manuscript copies, and Professor Kim Tonguk's printed versions, *Kugyŏk Kimun ch'onghwa* (1996–9), and modern Korean translations with annotations. Professor emeritus Yi Changu of Yeungnam University, an expert on classical Korean literature in *hanmun*, guided us through many of the stories during a stint at UBC as Visiting Professor, and Professor Kim Tonguk of Sangmyung University very kindly shared the pre-publication word processor files of his *Kimun ch'onghwa* texts and translations published in 1997 in Korea. In any case, the editors often used copy-and-paste to create the present volume. In hindsight, this method was not too unlike what *yadam* compilers in manuscript culture used in their own compilation and transmission of stories (see Si Nae Park's introductory essay).

Recent Research on Gale: The Past Decade

Though Gale remains under-researched, there has been a resurgence of interest in him and the Gale Papers in recent years. For example, Kim Insu, *Cheimsŭ S. Keil moksa*, reproduces in both typed-up format and Korean translation a number of handwritten letters James S. Gale sent to the Missions Board during the period 1891–1900. KIATS, with the

---

50 As part of its ongoing Gale project, the UBC team is preparing a detailed index to the Gale papers to supersede the sketchy fourteen-page finder list prepared in 1988 and available online at http://www.library.utoronto.ca/fisher/collections/findaids/gale245.pdf.

English title *James S. Gale, the Matteo Ricci of Korea*, takes a similar approach: texts and excerpts of otherwise readily available writings by Gale are reproduced in English with Korean translation.[51] In terms of Gale's literary contributions, Kim Sŭngu, *Han'guk siga e taehan kuhanmal sŏyangin tŭl ŭi koch'al kwa insik* discusses Gale's translation of Korean verse (*siga*) in Korean, while Shin, "A Reception Aesthetic Study of *sijo*," is a useful and generally sympathetic critique of Gale's pioneering translations of *sijo*.[52] King, "Western Missionaries," examines the very substantial but overlooked role of missionaries in general and Gale in particular in Korean language reform debates at the beginning of the twentieth century, and King, in "Korean Grammar Education," analyses some of Gale's statements about Korean language grammar and pedagogy in the missionary context, while King's "James Scarth Gale, Korean Literature," is a first stab at capturing the overall contours of Gale's decades-long dedication to Korean literature and books in *hanmun* based on the archival materials in both Toronto and the Library of Congress.

In more recent research, two scholars stand out in particular: Yoo Young Sik in Toronto (Yu Yŏngsik) and Yi Sanghyŏn. Dr Yoo had the great fortune of studying for his PhD at the University of Toronto and having direct and prolonged access to both the Gale Papers and some of Gale's relatives and descendants. Himself an active member of the Presbyterian Church, both in Canada and in Korea, and a long-time Korean Canadian resident of the Toronto area, Dr Yoo has spent the bulk of his career studying James S. Gale. After an early short monograph on pioneer Canadian missionaries in Korea, *Earlier Canadian Missionaries in Korea*, and his much expanded dissertation on the same topic, "The Impact of Canadian Missionaries in Korea," Dr Yoo published an extended article on Gale's early years in Korea (2007), and a massive two-tome compendium in Korean with rich primary materials and translations in 2013. Though Dr Yoo at times indulges in antiquarian minutiae (e.g., the question of which date Gale first set foot on Korean soil), his penchant for detail yields significant dividends in

---

51 In fact, James Legge is a far more apt comparison than Matteo Ricci. See
   Girardot, *The Victorian Translation of China*, for a useful study of Legge.
52 See also in this regard Rutt's comments on Gale's *sijo* translations: "Even
   though his essentially Victorian concept of poetry made him write usually in
   iambic meter and often with rhyme, his English versions of *sijo* were landmarks
   in literary history and he unfailingly chose the best in Korean literature for presentation to the west" (*A Biography of James Scarth Gale*, 86).

his close and critical reading of the unfair treatment that Gale has suffered at the hands of church historians in Korea. Thus, in Yu, "Cheimsŭ Keil ŭi sam kwa sŏn'gyo," he shows through repeated examples how an initial misreading and mistranslation by Min Kyŏngbae, *Han'guk Kidokkyohoesa*, politically influenced by an overzealous attempt at establishing a "Koreanized Christianity" based on an anti-missionary position, has led subsequent Korean scholars like Song Kŏnho, Hong Kyŏngman, Yi Tŏkchu, Sin Pongnyong, and Chŏn Yŏngnyŏl, among others, to disparage Gale's depoliticized stance as somehow pro-Japanese and inimical to Korean independence and nationalism.[53] If anything, Yoo shows, Gale was a humanist loyal to Korean culture to the very last.[54] Dr Yoo's most recent magnum opus would require a separate essay to do it justice, but one obvious and immediate merit is its inclusion of reproductions and translations into Korean of the many personal letters sent by Gale over many years to his older sister Jenny (not available in the Gale Papers and now apparently owned privately by Dr Yoo). Given the virtual absence of any significant personal correspondence in the Gale Papers at the University of Toronto, these letters are a valuable resource and it is good to finally have them in the public domain. The second volume of Yu, *Ch'akhan mokcha*, also contains reproductions of some three hundred pages of Gale's manuscript materials, and Korean translations of many (non-literary) materials from the Gale Papers (mostly from the typescript materials).

But the Korean scholar who has delved most deeply into Gale's literary legacy and the Gale Papers is Professor Yi Sanghyŏn of Pusan National University. Trained in Korean language and literature at

---

53 See Hwang, "Han'guk kaesin'gyo ch'ogi sŏn'gyosa tŭl ŭi pi-chŏngch'ihwa sinhak" for a more recent discussion of "depoliticization theology" among early Western missionaries to Korea. Though Yu is rather harsh on Min Kyŏngbae's *Han'guk Kidokkyohoesa* and *Kyohoe wa minjok* for Min's treatment of Gale, note that Min in "Keil: Han'guk ŭl saranghago Han'guk munhwa rŭl akkin sŏn'gyosa" and "Keil: Han'gukhak yŏn'gu ŭi kŏbo" is much more sympathetic to Gale. Yu ("Cheimsŭ Keil ŭi sam kwa sŏn'gyo"), like King ("James Scarth Gale, Korean Literature in *hanmun*, and Korean Books"), is critical of Korean scholar of English literature Yi Sangnan ("Keil kwa Han'guk munhak") and her English-language essay under the name Lee Sang Ran, "Dr. James S. Gale as a Literary Translator," for her factual errors and sloppy execution, and for her knee-jerk attempt at branding Gale as an "orientalist."

54 Here it is worth recalling Rutt's comment in *A Biography of James Scarth Gale* that Gale's "loyalty was tempered with exasperation," 36. But loyalty it was.

Sungkyunkwan University in Seoul, Professor Yi was the first literary scholar in Korea to recognize the importance of the Gale Papers. A series of journal articles and book chapters based on his doctoral research beginning in 2007 culminated in his excellent 2012 book on Gale, *Han'guk kojŏn pŏnyŏkka ŭi ch'osang*. As Yi confesses in his book, he first approached the Gale Papers in Toronto expecting to find an orientalist of the type depicted in Edward Said's classic *Orientalism*, but came away with a new-found respect for Gale and his deep appreciation of and profound commitment to Korean traditional literary culture. Professor Yi's research engages primarily Gale's published translations of *yadam* fictional narratives in *hanmun* ("Ch'ŏnyerok, Chosŏn sŏrhwa," and the co-authored Sin and Yi, "Keil ŭi *Ch'ŏngp'a kŭktam* yŏngyŏk"), but also examines some of Gale's translations from vernacular fiction, including some of the unpublished works held in Toronto ("*Ch'unhyang chŏn* sosŏrŏ" and "Much'yŏjin *Sim Ch'ŏng chŏn* chŏngjŏnhwa ŭi kyebo," as well as the co-authored Kwŏn, Han, and Yi, "Keil munsŏ [Gale, James Scarth Papers] sojae *Sim Ch'ŏng chŏn, T'o saeng chŏn* yŏngyŏkpon"). His work is especially significant for its broaching of Gale's personal relationships with key Korean and Japanese intellectuals in the 1910s and 1920s and the important question of transnational currents in the formation of modern Korean literary studies in the colonial period ("Kojŏnŏ wa kŭndaeŏ ŭi pun'gi"). Another major achievement of Yi's is his co-authored book with Hwang Hodŏk (*Kaenyŏm kwa yŏksa, kŭndae Han'guk ŭi ijung'ŏ sajŏn*) on the first bilingual dictionaries of Korean produced by foreigners (mostly missionaries) and their role in Korean linguistic modernity. Needless to say, Gale and his work play a major role in that book too. Nonetheless, it must be noted that all of Yi's work to date treats the "low-hanging fruit" in the Gale Papers – those materials that are already typed up – and has left the manuscript "diaries" untouched.

Editing Gale: The Problem of Gale's Literary Style

In the case of Chosŏn-dynasty *yadam* narratives like the stories in the *Kimun ch'onghwa* here, Gale's overall "diction that echoes Shakespeare and the Authorized Version"[55] is actually quite well suited to the genre. As Rutt himself notes in his comments on Gale's style in his *History of*

---

55 Rutt, *A Biography of James Scarth Gale*, 55.

the Korean people,[56] "[h]e wrote for a middlebrow audience that enjoyed the book's anecdotal style. This style, however, was derived from the Korean historiographical tradition."

In her introductory essay to this volume, Si Nae Park discusses Gale's affinity for the *yadam* genre in greater detail, but it was Rutt who first identified the personality traits in Gale that made him an ideal person to devote many years of his life to translating various types of premodern Korean "occasional fiction" or short *p'ilgi* 筆記-type anecdotes – Gale's translations from the *Kimun ch'onghwa* are but one portion of such texts in the Gale Papers. Among these personality traits, Rutt cites Gale's "old-world feeling for women, his delight in strange tales and lyric poetry, his antiquarian pleasures, and his sense of the adventure of evangelism. He discovered in Korea a world of faery to which his Scottish blood responded"[57] and an "affinity between his own personality and traditional Korean culture, with its mixture of moralizing and fairy lore."[58]

In emending and preparing for publication Gale's manuscript translations in as sympathetic a manner as possible, the editors have had to wrestle with a number of issues related to Gale's literary style.[59] Richard Rutt has already blazed the trail to a certain extent in this regard, although he frequently evinces a rather snooty and patronizing Oxbridge attitude toward the written English of his colonial cousin from Canada.[60] One of Rutt's pet peeves we share: "Gale's habit of

---

56 Ibid., 78.

57 Ibid., 85.

58 Ibid., 87.

59 One anonymous reviewer of this volume wondered what Gale would think to find his unpolished work published. The overwhelmingly literary nature of his *Nachlass*, the several typescript book-length drafts of unpublished anthologies of Korean literature across several genres, and the almost wilful exclusion from his papers of personal correspondence and family-related quotidian and anecdotal material, suggest to us a body of material that Gale would have wanted both polished and published. Rutt in his *Biography of James Scarth Gale*, 1972, makes the interesting point that Gale's best published work was the work in which he was assisted by his first wife Hattie and that after her death his prose deteriorated (27). Our goal here is thus to edit Gale gently and generously, while preserving as best we can his voice without anachronistically modernizing his style.

60 For example, "Bishop Trollope wrote far less than Gale, and brought to the task an education of far higher quality than Ontario could provide" (*Biography of*

inverting predicates, though typical of his style when he wrote the *History*, is highly irritating when indulged too many times on one page."[61] Therefore, we have undone a great many of Gale's inverted predicates. We have also converted his Gale Romanization into McCune-Reischauer Romanization and corrected spelling and grammatical errors, but just as Rutt felt it showed "greater respect for Gale to present him without his superficial blemishes of style,"[62] we have tried to preserve most of his stylistic quirks.[63]

Four such stylistic quirks worth dwelling on here are Gale's frequently heavy-handed Westernization and Christianization of his texts, his understanding of sinographs and Literary Sinitic literary culture, his conviction that "thought translation" was preferable to slavish literal translation, and his renderings of technical terms for Chosŏn-period government offices and titles.

A Western and Christian Frame of Reference

It should come as no great surprise in the translations of a Presbyterian missionary active a century ago in Korea to find Korean terms and concepts rendered in domesticizing ways. Some trivial examples would be Gale's translation of *pok* 卜 (prognosticator) in Story 37 as "sorcerer" and his translation of *tongja* 童子 (boy; child monk) in Story 14 as "fairy" and "fairy lad." The same *tongja* 童子 is rendered as "angel" in the same Story 14, but "angel" is more often deployed for Sino-Korean terms with either *sin* 神 (spirit; deity; supernatural being) or *sŏn* 仙 (Daoist immortal). For example, Story 32 renders *sinin* 神人 as "angel." But in Story 80 *sŏn* 仙 is rendered with "fairy": "She had a son called Yang Pongnae ... The face of the <u>fairy</u>, the form of the genie was he" (産一子卽蓬萊也 … 正是<u>仙</u>風道骨).

James Scarth Gale, 78). Bishop Trollope was educated at Lancing College and New College, Oxford. Rutt himself was educated at Kelham Theological College and Pembroke College, Cambridge.

61 Rutt, *A Biography of James Scarth Gale*, ix.

62 Ibid., x.

63 Rutt was much exercised by Gale's use of "*glass* for *cup*, *pen* for *writing-brush*, *writing* for both *literary composition* and *calligraphy*; he overworked *master* for *expert* or *great man*; *soul* for *mind*; *round* for *routine* or *course*; *thought* for *meaning*; *ever* for *always*; *but* for *only* and *back of* for *behind*" (ix).We have left most of these word choices intact.

Without question the most jarring of such Gale-isms is his assimilation of various Sino-Korean terms referring to heaven, the heavens, the sky, spirits, and deities, etc., as just "God." Here too Rutt was the first to remark:

> Concern about religion shows most often in his translations of Korean writers. He translated a poem entitled "Heaven" by the sixteenth-century scholar Song Ikp'il, boldly rendering the Chinese word for "heaven" as "God," and producing what might well be a christian text. (56–7)

But there is nothing insidious or underhanded about Gale's practice in this regard, for it is easy enough to find instances where he incorporates the relevant sinograph, or its Sino-Korean reading in Korean script, directly into his translation. Thus, in Story 26 Gale glosses "God" with "(天)" (the character for "heaven") in one instance, with "(텬)" (the Sino-Korean pronunciation of 天) in another, and with "(신명)" (god, deity) in a third:

> "The boy cried and prayed to God (天)."
>
> 兒號泣禱<u>天</u>

> "Chonghŭi, your faithful spirit has moved God (텬)."
>
> 宗禧汝誠感<u>天</u>

> "His winning back his father's life from God (신명) was indeed a fitting thing."
>
> 宜其感動<u>神明</u>續父之命也

A similar example can be found in Story 29:

> "Is this not the will of God (텬)?"
>
> 此豈非<u>天</u>乎

The following two *hanmun* terms qualified for deification in Gale's book of translational equivalents, but only with a "small g":

> <u>*sin* 神 (spirit; supernatural being; deity)</u>

"She had a son called Yang Pongnae. He was a beautiful lad, born of the <u>gods.</u>"

産一子卽蓬萊也 <u>神</u>彩俊逸 (Story 80)

<u>*kwisin* 鬼神 (ghost; demon; departed spirit; disembodied soul)</u>

"Well done, done by the gods surely! The spirits must be playing some game on us by these verses."

此賦果是善作而似是<u>鬼神</u>之作 (Story 43)

Gale usually reserved "God" with a "big G" for terms that incorporate *ch'ŏn* 天 (heaven):

"surely was a filial son born of God."

出<u>天</u>之孝 (Story 26)

"Man is born into the world but names and fame are in God's giving."

人生斯世功名在<u>天</u> (Story 44)

"Such persistent praying as this God will assuredly hear."

至誠安得不感<u>天</u>乎 (Story 69)

"If we run counter to God"

若逆<u>天</u> (Story 81)

"I shall never attempt to fight against God."

吾不欲逆<u>天</u> (Story 90)

"Oh God, oh God!"

天乎天乎 (Story 97)

<u>*ch'ŏnsu* 天數 (heaven-ordained fate; pre-ordained life span)</u>

"War on us is something that is in the hands of God and cannot be blocked by man's weak hands."

我國兵禍乃是<u>天數</u>所定難容人力 (Story 90)

ch'ŏnil 天日 (the sky and the sun; the sun in the sky; the heavenly bodies)

"This is God's appointment."

天日之表 (Story 97)

ch'ŏn'gi 天機 (the workings of heaven; the secret workings of providence/nature)

"Please go back to Chŏng and ask him not to lightly make known again the secrets of God."

可歸語鄭礦使勿復泄天機也 (Story 30)

ch'ŏnŭi 天意 (heaven's will; providence)

"I've had that dream again and regard it as God's word to me."

夢又如是此必是天意也 (Story 81)

Studying "the Character"

Another somewhat idiosyncratic Gale-ism that can be jarring at first concerns Gale's understanding of traditional Sinitic literary culture and the way it hinged on a profound knowledge of what Gale called "the character" – that is, sinographs. But for Gale the character was not simply a question of knowing Chinese characters; rather, the character for Gale was a metonym for Literary Sinitic (*hanmun*) writ large: sinographs, the long and arduous training process in Classical Chinese texts, and the entire canon of Literary Sinitic literature itself.

Here again we can begin our illustration with a poem. Diary XIV (p. 74) contains a draft translation by Gale of a well-known poem by Yi Saek (李穡, 1328–96) titled "The Character." The original poem can be found in *kwŏn* 7 of Yi Saek's collected works, the *Mogŭn ko* 牧隱藁, with the title *toksŏ* 讀書, meaning literally "read books; vocalize/recite writings; study." The first two lines[64] along with Gale's translation are as follows:

---

64 The entire poem can be found in the Han'guk kojŏn chonghap DB (Database of the Korean Classics) at http://db.itkc.or.kr/.

讀書如游山　　Reading the character is like an outing in the hills,

深淺皆自得　　where hollows deep occur and places shallow;

Gale's Papers contain numerous references to the character. In an essay titled "Korea after Twenty-Five Years" and dated 5 August 1920, Gale reminisces: "Another wonder in the way of change is seen in the literary world. Twenty-five years ago Korea's reading circle was very small and very exclusive. Only those who could decipher the Chinese character ever opened a book. Literature was exalted up among the gods, and the thought of the ordinary people reading or understanding any order of script was undreamed of" (Box 9:44, p. 3). In another (undated) essay titled "The Oriental: What He Writes About" (Box 8:21), Gale begins: "By the Oriental I mean the Chinese family of nations, those who read the character and write it, and whose odd literature runs up and down the page." A typescript rendition of the traditional tale "The Turtle and the Rabbit" is prefaced with a note that reads: "Being untrained in the Chinese character, women had hitherto been shut away from the charms of the story-book" (Box 9:22B). Another essay, titled "Korea and Japan" and "written for the Japan Society in 1935" when Gale was in England in retirement, proclaims: "Here is where Korea's superiority rests, a superiority recognized by the Japanese themselves, her priceless knowledge of the Chinese character" (Box 9:43, p. 13).

Here are some examples from the *Kimun ch'onghwa* illustrating Gale's use of "the character" to translate various *hanmun* expressions connected to Sinitic literary culture:

toksŏ 讀書 (reading books; studying)

"With sword drawn, the general went in search and there he found two young men busy at the study of the character."

提督按劍而入有兩少年共讀書矣 (Story 91)

"Once when along with his associates he was studying the character,"

嘗結同儕讀書 (Story 17)

hyŏp taehak 挾大學 (carrying the *Daxue* or *Greater Learning* tucked under her arm)

"She made a trial of him by putting on a boy's dress and appeared as a student of the character, bowed low, and said,"

束條帶挾大學往拜曰 (Story 107)

hak 學 (study; learn)

"I, too, long to learn the character."

亦志學 (Story 107)

chu munhoe 做文會 (conduct a study group)

"Friends of Min who would meet to study the character, when they saw Wŏlsa go by,"

諸友做文會於路傍 月沙或過 (Story 111)

kongsi 工詩 (be adept at composing poetry [in Literary Sinitic])

"There was a dancing girl in Puan, whose name was Kyesaeng who was well-versed in the character and could play also and sing well,"

扶安妓桂生工詩善謳彈 (Story 10)

haemong 解蒙 (dispel ignorance)

"To educate him, and bring him to a place where he would do honour to his forefathers and be a master of the character would of all things be most gratifying."

大師若敎訓而解蒙則豈非萬幸耶 (Story 51)

haksŏ 學書 (study books; learn writing; engage in book learning)

"The boy, most grateful, remained and asked that he might be taught the character."

總角感謝 居數月 願學書 (Story 70)

munjang 文章 (Literary Sinitic composition)

"Knowledge and skill in the character are with Chŏng,"

文章學識固可讓於輝遠 (Story 87)

Thought Translation: Gale's Philosophy of Translation

Readers of Gale's translations from the *Kimun ch'onghwa* with one eye on the *hanmun* versions will soon notice that Gale frequently departs from the originals; a charitable way to characterize his renditions would be "loose." Si Nae Park has already discussed in her introductory essay certain excisions and exuberances that Gale typically made, and how these in fact conform with traditional practices in Chosŏn manuscript culture. But Gale was also motivated by a strong personal philosophy of translation based on more than two decades of experience translating the Bible into Korean. The essence of Gale's approach to translation was simple: translate the thought and not the word, and do so idiomatically, grammatically, and naturally. Gale abhorred literal "word translations," and branded anybody who practised them a fool: "Aquila who thought he could get an equivalent Greek word for every Hebrew word in his rendering of the Old Testament was a, what shall I call him, a fool, I expect."[65]

Although concerned primarily with English-to-Korean translation projects, Gale's "Literary Reports" to the Christian Literature Society from the 1920s contain interesting comments about his philosophy of translation in general. His March 1924 report dwells at some length on his ongoing translation of *Little Lord Fauntleroy*, and offers insights into his theory and method of translation:

> Never before have I ventured my hand at light fiction such as we find in Mrs. Burnett's *Fauntleroy*. As I go over it with Mr. Yi [Wŏnmo] I find how much there is in our world of expression that differs from that of the Korean. The main thoughts of the book are common to us both; and the heart questions that move throughout its pages are one and the same but manners of expression differ very markedly. Frequently words must be added in the Korean to make the thought clear and at times a whole paragraph of the English must be dropped else the story would become ridiculous or fall flat. It convinces me again that a literal word for word translation of fiction, or history, or Sunday School literature or anything else in fact is quite out of the question.[66]

---

65 Box 10:13 Literary Report (Bible Translation), 13 Nov. 1923.

66 Box 10:24 Literary Reports, 1924–1927, 18 Mar. 1924. See King, "James Scarth Gale and the Christian Literature Society," for a detailed discussion of Gale's work in the 1920s translating more popular literature from English into Korean with his "pundits."

Box 10 of the Gale Papers contains another collection of fragmentary items, titled "Notebook: Reports, Letters, Articles, etc.," which includes others of Gale's Literary Reports from the 1920s with valuable comments on translation. One report records a succinct summary of Gale's ultimate goal for his translation of the Bible into Korean: "All the thought, no more, no less, in the language of the common people."[67] In another report, titled "Side glimpses on Bible Revision," Gale opines: "One of the first things learned then by practical translation work is that words are not equivalents. They must each and all be tested by experiment to see if they convey the correct idea. The thought is the all-important consideration."[68] And in a discussion about education in missionary schools in his "Report of literary work etc.," dated 15 Feb. 1927, Gale complains: "The idea that translation means the carrying over of the thought into another language, grammatically, and in the idiom of that language, never seems to occur to this average Korean translator; phrase by phrase; word for word, just as the English has it. Let the result be what it will. If you offer a criticism he will reply 'But that's what the English says.' He forgets that it is not the English but the thought underlying the English we are after."[69]

We alert readers in cases where Gale has jettisoned significantly large chunks of a story, but otherwise readers of Gale's translations from the *Kimun ch'onghwa* with one eye on the originals are encouraged to enjoy the stories with this philosophical framework of Gale's in mind.

Government Offices and Titles from the Chosŏn Period

When Gale was busy working on his many translations from Korean *hanmun* sources and also on his *History of the Korean People* in the 1910s and 1920s, there was virtually nothing to guide him in the way of "best practice" regarding publishing in English about Korean history and literature. Thus, Gale had to devise his own system of Romanization to render Korean words and names and terms for his readers – a system that we have converted to McCune-Reischauer. He also had to come up

---

67 "Literary report, Station meeting, Nov. 13th, 1923 (Bible Translation)," p. 4
   (p. 39 of the larger collection of reports).
68 Ibid., pp. 46–8.
69 Page 4 of an 8-page report included in the larger collection of documents.

with his own system of equivalences for the many terms for governmental institutions and offices and government posts and ranks. Some of his choices may strike some readers as odd today: he uses "president" or "vice-president" for positions that nowadays are translated as "minister" or "deputy minister," for example. But we have decided to leave Gale's terminology intact. A survey of the small but growing number of authoritative English-language publications on pre-modern Korean history will quickly reveal that for many terms there is healthy variety, and certainly no ironclad orthodoxy, for rendering them in English. Gale's terms, if nothing else, offer a glimpse of other possibilities and of a "Korean Studies that might have been," were it not for the total lack of interest in Korea in the English-speaking world at the time Gale was working (and for decades thereafter, for that matter). For the reader of this book who cares to know, we include at the end of this essay an appendix with a list of such *hanmun* terms and their Romanizations, Gale's rendition(s), authoritative renderings by leading Korean Studies scholars today, and references to the stories where the terms appear.

The preceding sections have covered some of the main idiosyncrasies of Gale's theory and practice of translation from *hanmun*; as editors, we have felt it best to preserve them as the honest and pioneering efforts that they represent. Whatever Gale's shortcomings as a literary stylist, though, Rutt certainly got it right when he commented of Gale, "He translated with panache … Gale's work stands at the tail-end of the old Korean tradition and contains many elements from it, slightly modified by western nineteenth-century approaches and the protestant viewpoint."[70]

Editorial Conventions

The editorial conventions adopted for each story translation, original *hanmun* text, and notes are as follows:

- We have identified Gale's translations by Box number, "diary" number, date of translation (when given), sequential number in the original "Gale version" of *Kimun ch'onghwa* at Yonsei University, and

---

70 Rutt, *A Biography of James Scarth Gale*, 86, 92.

Professor Kim Tonguk's sequential numbering of the same Yonsei 4 *kwŏn* 4 *ch'aek* edition.

- The sequencing of the stories follows that in the original story collection; Gale's manuscript list of stories in "Diary" XVI indicates that such was his intention.
- "Typed-up" indicates that the story was one that Gale either intended to publish or in fact published.
- For stories that exist in both typed-up and handwritten versions, we have introduced here only the typed-up version. In the case of multiple typed-up versions of a single story, we have introduced them all.
- Notes on Korean monarchs usually include two sets of dates: reign years preceded by "r." and birth and death years. E.g., Kwanghae-gun 光海君 [r. 1608–23; 1575–1641].
- Asterisks in the annotations (e.g., Entry 93, note 32) indicate sino-graphs used to render vernacular Korean words in the documentary writing style called *idu* 吏讀.

Editorial Conventions for the Rendering
of the Original hanmun *Texts*

- In the hope that the *hanmun* originals might be of use to colleagues in Chinese, Japanese, or Vietnamese Studies, we have included annotated and punctuated versions of all the stories in Literary Sinitic.
- The punctuation of the *hanmun* texts generally follows that in the files kindly provided by Professor Kim Tonguk. Some of the spacing decisions may strike readers of Literary Sinitic who are speakers of a variety of Chinese as odd, but these usually owe to traditional Korean punctuation habits.
- Another hope of the editors is that the *hanmun* originals might serve as pedagogical materials for advanced students of Korean wishing to acquaint themselves with Literary Sinitic through Korean, to which end we have included the Sino-Korean pronunciations for each sinograph as superscript glosses in as unobtrusive a format as possible. For the sake of consistency, the Sino-Korean pronunciation glosses preserve word-initial *l-* and *n-* before *i* and *y* except in the case of names, proper nouns, style names, sobriquets, ancestral seats, and epithets.
- Character(s) in {} indicate(s) Professor Kim Tonguk's insertions.
- Character(s) in [] indicate(s) Professor Kim Tonguk's corrections.

Translation Conventions

- □ indicates that the manuscript is illegible or indecipherable.
- Office names are not italicized.
- Names of official posts are italicized.
- Province for 道; County for 郡; Prefecture for 懸; Magistracy for 府.

Editors' Notes to the Texts and Translations

- Notes to the English translations using the signs *, †, ‡, §, and ¶ are from the editors.
- Editorial notes in `Courier` font are Gale's annotations, not the editors'. All parenthetical material within his story translations consists of Gale's clarifications for either his translation or his use of expressions drawn directly from the *hanmun* original.
- Most of the notes to the *hanmun* originals are Professor Kim Tonguk's, translated by the editors from the original Korean, but the editors have created additional notes when necessary.
- Gale refers to King Yŏngjo and Chŏngjo as Yŏngjong and Chŏngjong, respectively. This is because the two kings were given the latter labels after King Kojong posthumously elevated their status in 1889 and 1897, respectively.

Works Cited

Bruns, Gerald L. "The Originality of Texts in a Manuscript Culture." *Comparative Literature* 32.2 (1980): 113–29.

Chang Kyŏngnam, and Yi Sijun. "Ilche kangjŏmgi e kanhaengdoen yadam chip e taehayŏ – *Obaengnyŏn kidam* ŭl chungsim ŭro" [*Yadam* Compilations from the Japanese Colonial Period: With a Focus on *Extraordinary Tales from the Past Five Hundred Years*]. *Uri munhak yŏn'gu* 34 (2011): 157–82.

Ch'oe Hyeju. "Hanmal Ilcheha chaejo Ilbonin ŭi Chosŏn kosŏ kanhaeng saŏp" [Old Korean Book Collecting Activities of Japanese Residents in Korea, 1890s–1940s *Taedong munhwa yŏn'gu* 66 (2009): 417–48.

Ch'ŏn Chŏnghwan. *Kŭndae ŭi ch'aek ilkki: Tokcha ŭi t'ansaeng kwa Han'guk kŭndae munhak* [Modern Reading: The Advent of Readers and Modern Korean Literature]. Seoul: P'urŭn yŏksa, 2003.

Chŏng Myŏnggi, ed. *Han'guk yadam charyo chipsŏng*. Vol. 6 [Source Book of Korean *Yadam*]. Seoul: Komunhŏn yŏn'guhoe, 1987.

Chŏng Myŏnggi, and Yi Yunsŏk. *Ku hwalchabon yadam ŭi pyŏni yangsang yŏn'gu: Ku hwalchabon kososŏl ŭi pyŏni yangsang kwa kwallyŏn hayŏ* [*Yadam* Collections Printed in Old Movable Type and Their Transformations: With a Focus on Their Relationship with the Transformations of Classical Fiction Printed in Old Movable Type]. Seoul: Pogosa, 2001.

Dagenais, John. *The Ethics of Reading in a Manuscript Culture: Glossing the "Libro de buen amor."* Princeton, NJ: Princeton University Press, 1994.

Fabian, Johannes. *Time and Other: How Anthropology Makes Its Object*. New York: Columbia University Press, 1983.

Gale, James Scarth. "Catalogue of the Books of the Chōsen Christian College (Korean Department)." 31 typescript pages. Box 11:5 of the Gale Papers. Thomas Fisher Rare Book Library. University of Toronto.

– "A Catalogue of Korean Literature: One Thousand of the Most Noted Works (6000 Volumes)." 79 typescript pages dated 31 January 1927. Washington, DC: Library of Congress.

– *History of the Korean People.* Seoul: Christian Literature Society of Korea, 1927.

– "Korea – Father and Son." *The Korea Magazine* (July 1917): 292–5.

– "The Korean Language." *The Korea Magazine* (February 1918): 53–5.

– "Korean Literature." *The Christian Movement in Japan, Korea, and Formosa* (1923): 465–71.

– "Korean Literature." *The Korea Magazine* (July 1918): 293–302.

– "Korean Literature." *The Open Court* (Fall 1918): 79–103.

– "Korean Literature I: How to Approach It?" *The Korea Magazine* (July 1917): 297–303.

– "Language Study: The Question of Translation." *The Korea Magazine* (January 1919): 20–2.

– *Miscellaneous Writings no. 30.* Box 8:15 of the Gale Papers. Thomas Fisher Rare Book Library. University of Toronto.

– *Old Corea.* With illustrations by Elizabeth Keith. Unpublished typescript. Box 8:18 of the Gale Papers. Thomas Fisher Rare Book Library. University of Toronto.

– "Why Read Korean Literature?" *The Korea Magazine* (August 1917): 354–6.

Girardot, Norman J. *The Victorian Translation of China: James Legge's Oriental Pilgrimage.* Berkeley: University of California Press, 2002.

Hulbert, Homer B. *The Passing of Korea.* New York: Doubleday, Page & Company, 1906.

Hwang Chaebŏm. "Han'guk kaesin'gyo ch'ogi sŏn'gyosa tŭl ŭi pi-chŏngch'ihwa sinhak ŭi munje: Keil sŏn'gyosa ŭi kyŏngu" [The Problem of Depoliticization Theology in Early Korean Protestant Missionary History: The Case of Missionary Gale]. *Chonggyo yŏn'gu* 59 (2010): 71–98.

Hwang Hodŏk, and Yi Sanghyŏn. *Kaenyŏm kwa yŏksa, kŭndae Han'guk ŭi ijungŏ sajŏn: Oegugin tŭl ŭi sajŏn p'yŏnch'an saŏp ŭro pon Han'gugŏ ŭi kŭndae* [Concept and History, Modern Korean Bilingual Dictionaries: Viewing Korean Linguistic Modernity through Foreigners' Dictionary Compilation Projects]. Seoul: Pangmunsa, 2012.

Im Bang, Yi Ryuk, and James Scarth Gale. *Korean Folk Tales: Imps, Ghosts and Fairies.* Translated from the Korean by James S. Gale. London: J.M. Dent & Sons, 1913. Accessible at http://archive.org.

Im Sangsŏk. *20 segi kukhanmun ch'e ŭi hyŏngsŏng kwajŏng* [The Development of Mixed-Script Writing in the Twentieth Century]. Seoul: Chisik sanŏpsa, 2008.

KIATS [Korea Institute for Advanced Theological Studies], ed. *Cheimsŭ Keil: Han'guk ŭi Mat'eo Rich'i* [James S. Gale, the Matteo Ricci of Korea]. Seoul: KIATS Press, 2012.

Kiichi [Gale]. "Ōbeijin no mitaru Chōsen no shōrai (ichi)" [The future of Korea as seen by Euro-American (I)]. *Chōsen shisō tsūshin* 787 (1928): 1.

Kim Chunhyŏng. "Haeje: *Kimun ch'onghwa* [*Kimun ch'onghwa*: Bibliographic Note]." In *Yŏnse taehakkyo chungang tosŏgwan sojang kosŏ haeje*, vol. 3, ed. Yŏnse taehakkyo kukhak yŏn'guwŏn, 113–48. Seoul: P'yŏngminsa, 2005.

Kim Donguk. *See* Kim Tonguk

Kim Insu, trans. *Cheimsŭ S. Keil moksa ŭi sŏn'gyo p'yŏnji (1891–1900)* [The Missionary Letters of James S. Gale (1891–1900)]. Seoul: K'umnan ch'ulp'ansa, 2009.

Kim Manjung. *The Cloud Dream of the Nine [Kuunmong], a Korean Novel: A Story of the Times of the Tangs of China about 840 A.D.* Translated by James Scarth Gale. Introduction by Elspet Keith Robertson Scott. Sixteen Illustrations. London: Daniel O'Connor, 1922. Accessible at http://archive.org.

– *Kuunmong: The Cloud Dream of the Nine.* Translated by James S. Gale. Introduction by Susanna Fessler. Interpretative essay by Francisca Cho. Original introduction by Elspet Keith Robertson Scott. Fukuoka, Japan: Kurodahan Press, 2003.

Kim Sŭngu. "Han'guk siga e taehan kuhanmal sŏyangin tŭl ŭi koch'al kwa insik: James Scarth Gale ŭl chungsim ŭro" [Westerners' Understanding and Investigations of Korean Verse in the Greater Korean Empire Period: Focusing on James Scarth Gale]. *Ŏmun nonjip* 64 (2011): 5–41.

Kim Tongjin. *P'aran nun ŭi han'gukhon: Hŏlbŏt'ŭ* [The Blue-Eyed Spirit of Korea: Hulbert]. [English title: Crusader for Korea: Homer B. Hulbert]. Seoul: Ch'am choŭn ch'in'gu, 2010.

Kim Tonguk, ed. and trans. *Kugyŏk Kimun ch'onghwa* [Korean Translation of the *Compendium of Records of Hearsay*]. 5 vols. Seoul: Asea munhwasa, 1996–9.

– *Saebyŏk kangka e haeoragi unŭn sori* [The Cackling of Herons by the Riverside at Dawn]. 3 vols. Seoul: Asea munhwasa, 2008.

Kim Uktong. *Pŏnyŏk kwa Han'guk ŭi kŭndae* [Translation and Korean Modernity]. Seoul: Somyŏng ch'ulp'an, 2010.

Kimun ch'onghwa. Held by the Asami Collection at the C.V. Starr East Asian Library at the University of California, Berkeley. Accessible at https://archive.org/details/kimunchonghwa00.

King, Ross. "James Scarth Gale and the Christian Literature Society (1922–1927): Salvific Translation and Korean Literary Modernity (I)." In *Una aproximacion humanista a los estudios coreanos*, ed. Won-jung Min. Ebook

distributed by Patagonia (Santiago, Chile), 2014. 40-page typescript.
Ebook available on Amazon: http://www.amazon.com/aproximaci%
C3%B3n-humanista-estudios-Coreanos-Spanish-ebook/dp/
B00PJ3AL5C/ref=sr_1_1?ie=UTF8&qid=1416445404&sr=8-1&
keywords=wonjung+min.
– "James Scarth Gale, Korean Literature in *Hanmun*, and Korean Books."
   In *Haeoe Han'gukpon komunhŏn charyo ŭi t'amsaek kwa kŏmt'o* [Research and
   Review of Old Korean Documents Preserved Abroad], ed. Sŏul Taehakkyo
   Kyujanggak Han'gukhak yŏn'guwŏn, 237–64. Seoul: Samgyŏng munhwasa,
   2012.
– "Korean Grammar Education for Anglophone Learners: Missionary
   Beginnings." In *Han'gugŏ kyoyungnon*, vol. 2, ed. IAKLE [International
   Association for Korean Language Education], 237–74. Seoul: Han'guk
   munhwasa, 2005.
– "Western Missionaries and the Origins of Korean Language
   Modernization." *Journal of International and Area Studies* 11.3 (2005): 7–38.
Ku Changnyul. *Kŭndae ch'ogi chapchi wa punkwa hangmun ŭi hyŏngsŏng* [The
   Formation of Disciplinary Scholarship and Magazines in the Modern Era].
   Seoul: K'ep'oi puksŭ, 2012.
Kwŏn Podŭrae. "1910 nyŏndae ŭi ijungŏ sanghwang kwa munhak ŏnŏ [The
   Dual-Language Situation of the 1910s and the Language of Literature]."
   Han'gugŏ munhak yŏn'gu 54 (2010): 5–43.
Kwŏn Sugŭng, Han Chaep'yo, and Yi Sanghyŏn. "Keil munsŏ [Gale, James
   Scarth Papers] sojae *Sim Ch'ŏng chŏn, T'o saeng chŏn* yŏngyŏkpon ŭi palgul
   kwa kŭ ŭiŭi" [The Discovery of the English Translations of *Sim Ch'ŏng chon*
   and *T'o saeng chon* in the James Scarth Gale Papers and Its Significance].
   Kososŏl yŏn'gu 30 (2010): 419–43.
Lee, Peter H., ed. *A History of Korean Literature*. Cambridge: Cambridge
   University Press, 2003.
[Lee, Sang Ran = Yi Sangnan]
Lee, Sang Ran. "Dr. James S. Gale as a Literary Translator." *East and West
   Studies Series* 28 (1994): 21–7.
Min Kyŏngbae. *Han'guk Kidokkyohoesa: Han'guk minjok kyohoe hyŏngsŏng
   kwajŏngsa* [History of the Korean Protestant Church: History of the Formation
   of a Korean National Church]. Seoul: Taehan Kidokkyosŏhoe, 1972.
– "Keil: Han'guk ŭl saranghago Han'guk munhwa rŭl akkin sŏn'gyosa"
   [Gale: A Missionary Who Loved Korea and Cherished Korean Culture].
   Han'guksa simin kangjwa 34 (2004): 69–80.
– "Keil: Han'gukhak yŏn'gu ŭi kŏbo" [Gale: A Giant Stride in Korean Studies
   Research]. *Han'guk changno sinmun* 1308 (11 Feb. 2012). Accessed on 16 May

2014 at http://jangro.kr/Jmissions/detail.htm?aid=1328682500&
PHPSESSID=45d9da7e73f4e762c267a7277a51a465.

– *Kyohoe wa minjok* [The Church and the Nation]. Seoul: Taehan kidokkyo
ch'ulp'ansa, 1981.

Ōtani Morishige. "Yŏngin *Kimun ch'onghwa* haeje" [Bibliographic Notes on the
Kimun ch'onghwa (Compendium of Records of Hearsay) Reproduced Here].
Chōsen gakuhō 96 (July 1980): 95–200.

Paek Chuhŭi, "J.S. Gale ŭi *Korean Folk Tales* yŏn'gu: Im Pang ŭi *Ch'ŏnyerok*
pŏnyŏk ŭl chungsim ŭro" [A Study on J.S. Gale's *Korean Folk Tales*]. MA
thesis, Sungkyungwan University, 2008.

– "J.S. Gale ŭi *Nogajae yŏnhaeng ilgi* yŏngyŏk pon ilgo" [A Study on J.S. Gale's
Translation of *Nogajae yŏnhaeng ilgi*]. *Journal of Korean Culture* 27 (2014): 283–313.

Pak Chinyŏng. *Ch'aek ŭi t'ansaeng kwa iyagi ŭi unmyŏng* [The Birth of Books
and the Fate of Stories]. Seoul: Somyŏng ch'ulp'an, 2014.

– *Pŏnyŏk kwa pŏnan ŭi sidae* [An Era of Translations and Adaptations]. Seoul:
Somyŏng ch'ulp'an, 2011.

Park, Si Nae. "A Textual Study of *Tongp'ae naksong*: Problems of Oral
Storytelling, Genre, and the Vernacular in Late-Chosŏn *Yadam*." PhD diss.,
University of British Columbia, 2012.

Reiter, Eric H. "The Reader as Author of the User-Produced Manuscript:
Reading and Rewriting Popular Latin Theology in the Late Middle Ages."
Viator 27 (1996): 151–69.

Rutt, Richard. *A Biography of James Scarth Gale and a New Edition of His "History
of the Korean People."* Seoul: Royal Asiatic Society, 1972.

Said, Edward. *Orientalism*. New York: Pantheon, 1978.

Shin, Eun-kyung. "A Reception Aesthetic Study of *sijo* in English Translation:
The Case of James S. Gale." *Seoul Journal of Korean Studies* 26.1 (2013): 175–213.

Shin, Gi-Wook, and Michael Robinson, eds. *Colonial Modernity in Korea*.
Cambridge, MA: Harvard University Asia Center, 2001.

Sin Sangp'il, and Yi Sanghyŏn. "Keil ŭi *Ch'ŏngp'a kŭktam* yŏngyŏk kwa kŭ
ŭimi" [Gale's English Translation of Ch'ŏngp'a kŭktam and Its
Significance]. *Kososŏl yŏn'gu* 35 (2013): 335–74.

Trollope, Bishop. "Corean Books and their Authors being an Introduction to
Corean Literature." *The Transactions of the Korea Branch of the Royal Asiatic
Society* 21 (1931): 1–104.

Wells, William Scott. "From Center to Periphery: The Demotion of Literary
Sinitic and the Beginnings of *Hanmunkwa* – Korea, 1876–1910." MA thesis,
University of British Columbia, 2011.

Yi Kwangsu. *Mujŏng* [Heartlessness], serialized in *Maeil sinbo* [Daily News],
1 Jan.–14 June 1917.

– "What Is Literature?" [Munhak iran hao], trans. Jooyeon Rhee. *Azalea: Journal of Korean Literature and Culture* 4 (2011): 293–313.

Yi Kyŏnghun. "*Hak chi kwang* kwa kŭ chubyŏn" [*Lux Scientiae* and Its Surroundings]. In *Kŭndaeŏ, kŭndae maech'e, kŭndae munhak* [Modern Language, Modern Media, and Modern Literature], ed. Han Kihyŏng et al., 351–97. Seoul: Taedong munhak yŏn'guwŏn at Sungkyungwan University, 2006.

Yi Sanghyŏn. "Cheguk tŭl ŭi chosŏnhak, chŏngjŏn ŭi t'onggukka-jŏk kusŏng kwa yut'ong: *Ch'ŏnyerok, Ch'ŏngp'a kŭktam* sojae iyagi ŭi chaebaech'i wa pŏnyŏk, chaehyŏndoen 'Chosŏn'" [English title: The Study of Korea by Empires, Trans-national Composition, and Circulation of Canonics: Rearrangement and Translation of *Cheonyerok, Cheongpageukdam*, Recreated "Korea"]. *Han'guk kŭndae munhak yŏn'gu* 18 (2008): 67–100.

– "Ch'ŏnyerok, Chosŏn sŏrhwa: Magwi, kwisin kŭrigo yojŏng tŭl *Korean Folk Tales: Imps, Ghosts and Fairies* sojae Oksosŏn, Ilt'ahong iyagi ŭi chaehyŏn yangsang kwa kŭ ŭimi" [Aspects of the Re-presentation of the *Ch'ŏnyerok* Stories "Oksosŏn" and "Ilt'ahong" in *Korean Folk Tales: Imps, Ghosts and Fairies* and Their Significance]. *Han'guk ŏnŏ munhwa* 33 (2007): 29–54.

– "*Ch'unhyang chŏn* sosŏrŏ ŭi chaep'yŏn kwajŏng kwa pŏnyŏk: Keil (James Scarth Gale) *Ch'unhyang chŏn* yŏngyŏkpon (1917) ch'urhyŏn kwa kŭ ŭimi" [Translation and the Reconfiguration of the Novelistic Language of *Ch'unhyang chŏn*: The Appearance of Gale's English Translation of *Ch'unhyang chŏn* and Its Significance]). *Kososŏl yŏn'gu* 30 (2010): 375–417.

– *Han'guk kojŏn pŏnyŏkka ŭi ch'osang: Keil ŭi kojŏnhak tamnon kwa kososŏl pŏnyŏk ŭi chip'yŏng* [Portrait of a Translator of the Korean Classics: Gale's Discourse on Classical Studies and the Horizons of Classic Fiction Translation]. Seoul: Somyŏng ch'ulp'an, 2012.

– "Kojŏnŏ wa kŭndaeŏ ŭi pun'gi kŭrigo pulganŭnghan taehwa ŭi chijŏm tŭl: *Chosŏn munhaksa* (1922) ch'urhyŏn ŭi kŭndae haksulsa-jŏk munmaek, Tak'ahasi, Keil ŭi han'guk(ŏ) munhangnon" [The Divergence between Classical and Modern Language and Points of Impossible Dialogue: The Modern Academic Context behind the Appearance of *Chosŏn munhaksa* (1922), and Takahashi and Gale's Theories of Korean (Language and) Literature]. *K'ogit'o* 73 (2013): 56–113.

– "Much'yŏjin *Sim Ch'ŏng chŏn* chŏngjŏnhwa ŭi kyebo: Allen (H.N. Allen), Hosoi (細井肇), Keil (J.S. Gale) *Sim Ch'ŏng chŏn* pŏnyŏkpon ŭi yŏndaegi" [A Buried Genealogy of the Canonization of *Sim Ch'ŏng chŏn*: Chronicle of the Translations of *Sim Ch'ŏng chŏn* by Allen (H.N. Allen), Hosoi, and J.S. Gale]. *Kososŏl yŏn'gu* 32 (2011): 405–56.

[Yi Sangnan = Lee, Sang Ran]

Yi Sangnan. "Keil kwa Han'guk munhak: Choyonghan ach'im ŭi nara, kŭ munhwa-jŏk ŭimi" [James S. Gale and Korean Literature: The Land of

Morning Calm, Its Cultural Implication]. *K'aenada nonch'ong* [Han'guk K'aenada Hakhoe] 1 (1993): 123–37.

Yi Usŏng, ed. *Kimun ch'onghwa* [Compendium of Records of Hearsay]. Seoul: Asea munhwasa, 1990.

Yi Usŏng, and Im Hyŏngt'aek, eds. *Yijo hanmun tanp'yŏn chip* [Compilation of Chosŏn Short Narratives Written in Literary Sinitic], 3 vols. Seoul: Ilchogak, 1973–8.

[Yoo, Young-sik = Yoo, Young Sik = Yu Yŏngsik]

Yoo, Young-sik. "The Impact of Canadian Missionaries in Korea: A Historical Survey of Early Canadian Mission Work, 1888–1898." PhD diss., University of Toronto, 1996.

Yoo, Young Sik. *Earlier Canadian Missionaries in Korea: A Study in History, 1888–1895*. Mississauga, Ontario: The Society for Korean and Related Studies, 1987.

– *The Good Pastor: In Celebration of Dr. James Scarth Gale and the First Canadian Missionary to Korea, 1888–2008*. Mississauga, Ontario: The Society for Korean and Related Studies, 2008.

Yu Yŏngsik. *Ch'akhan mokcha: Keil ŭi sam kwa sŏn'gyo* [The Good Pastor: Life and Missionary Activity of Gale]. 2 vols. Seoul: Chinhŭng, 2013.

– "Cheimsŭ Keil ŭi sam kwa sŏn'gyo [The Life and Missionary Work of James Gale]." In *Pusan ŭi ch'ŏt sŏn'gyosa tŭl* [Pusan's First Missionaries], ed. Yŏngsik Yu et al., 36–169. Seoul: Han'guk Changnogyo ch'ulp'ansa, 2007.

Yu Yŏngsik, Yi Sanggyu, Chon Pŭraun, and T'ak Chiil, eds. *Pusan ŭi ch'ŏt sŏn'gyosa tŭl* [Pusan's First Missionaries]. Seoul: Han'guk Changnogyo ch'ulp'ansa, 2007.

Appendix: Table of Translation Equivalents

❀

1. Government Offices

Hanmun	Gale's Translation	Source in *Kimun ch'onghwa*	Explanation and/or Translation
烏府 Obu	Law Office	Story 1	Office of the Inspector-General (Sahŏnbu 司憲府) (Palais)
兵曹 Pyŏngjo	War Office	Story 11	Ministry of Military Affairs; Ministry of War (Kim)
騎省 Kisŏng	Cf. "He was at this time Minister of War P'angisŏng (判騎省)."	Story 46	another name for the Ministry of Military Affairs (Pyŏngjo 兵曹)
吏曹 Ijo	Home Office	Story 16	Ministry of Personnel (Kim)
刑曹 Hyŏngjo	Office of Justice	Story 110	Ministry of Punishments (Kim)
弘文館 Hongmungwan	College of Literature	Story 18	Office of the Censor-General; Office of Special Councillors (Kim, Palais)
藥院 Yagwŏn	Royal Physician's Office	Story 31	another name for the Royal Clinic (Naeŭiwŏn 內醫院) or Palace Physicians' Court (Palais)
惠局 Hyeguk	Office of Alms	Story 53	= Hyeminguk 惠民局 = Hyeminsŏ 惠民署: Public Dispensary or Office of Benefiting the People (Palais), a relief agency for impoverished commoners
禁府 Kŭmbu	Prison Department	Story 53	= Ŭigŭmbu 義禁府 State Tribunal (Kim)
敎坊 Kyobang	"Kyobang, the music centre"	Story 104	Bureau of Music, where *kisaeng* were trained in singing and dancing

2. Official Positions and Titles

Hanmun	Gale's Translation	Source in *Kimun ch'onghwa*	Explanation and/or Translation
判書 *p'ansŏ*	*p'ansŏ*	Story 4; 7; 41	senior 2nd-rank minister of the Six Ministries (Yukcho 六曹); minister (Palais); a minister of the Six Ministries (Kim)
	"Kim *p'ansŏ* (chief of a Board)	Story 70	
	Minister	Story 67	
	Minister of Law	Story 110	
	President(s) of Boards	Story 81	
兵判 *pyŏngp'an*	Head of the War Department	Story 113	= pyŏngjo p'ansŏ 兵曹判書: senior 2nd-rank minister in the Ministry of War
相公 *sanggong*	Minister (cf. "Hong's son, minister Naksŏng" = 其伯胤相公樂性)	Story 67	Honorific term for *chaesang* 宰相 = grand councillor/councillor of state; ministers of senior 2nd-rank or higher
館伴 *kwanban*	chief host	Story 4	= *kwanbansa* 館伴使: escort of a Chinese envoy (Kim); an ad hoc government office (senior 3rd-rank) occasionally assigned to officials who welcomed foreign envoys staying in Seoul
亞 *a* = *agyŏng* 亞卿	vice-chief	Story 4	any second minister = any *ch'amp'an* 參判
亞卿 *agyŏng*	Vice-President of a Board	Story 67	

Hanmun	**Gale's Translation**	**Source in *Kimun ch'onghwa***	**Explanation and/or Translation**
座首 *chwasu*	Deputy Magistrate	Story 93	= *agwan* 亞官 = *suhyang* 首鄕: director of the Bureau of Local Yangban (Kim); Head Seat, chief of the local yangban or gentry associations (Palais)
刑房 *hyŏngbang*	Secretary of Justice	Story 93	a petty clerk (*ajŏn* 衙前) in charge of penal administration at the local yamen
及唱 *kŭpch'ang*	Public Crier	Story 93	a crier servant boy at the local yamen
使令 *saryŏng*	Constable-Runner	Story 93	a page boy at the local yamen; runner, servant (Palais)
縣監 *hyŏn'gam*	magistrate	Story 9	Magistrate to a lesser county (junior 6th-rank) (Kim)
牧 *mok*	magistrate (cf. "while magistrate of Yangju County" = *yangmok* 楊牧)	Story 93	= 牧使 *moksa*: magistrate of a *mok* = district (Palais) or county (Kim)
伯 *paek*	governor	Story 9	= *tobaek* 道伯 = *kwanch'alsa* 觀察使: provincial governor
監營道伯 *kamyŏng tobaek*	Provincial Governor	Story 26	*kamyŏng* = provincial administrative headquarters; *tobaek* = *kwanch'alsa* 觀察使
兵曹佐郎 *pyŏngjo chwarang*	attached to the War Office	Story 11; 75	*chwarang*: assistant section chief in the Six Ministries (Kim; Palais)

Hanmun	**Gale's Translation**	**Source in *Kimun ch'onghwa***	**Explanation and/or Translation**
防禦使從事官 *pangŏsa chongsagwan*	aide to the general in active service	Story 11	*pangŏsa* = junior 2nd-rank post for military officials posted to strategic locations; *chongsagwan* = chief administrative officer (Kim)
倅 *swi*	Cf.: 縣倅[守] *hyŏnswi [-su]* "magistrate"	Story 13	= *ponsu ~ ponswi* 本倅: local county or district chief; cover term for the *moksa* 牧使, *p'an'gwan* 判官 (governor's aide/magistrate's aid) or *puyun* 府尹 of a locale with a *pyŏngsa* 兵使 (army commander) or *kwanch'alsa* 觀察使
	Cf. 邑倅 *ŭpswi* "magistrate"	Story 26	
	Cf. 金山 倅 Kŭmsan *swi* "magistrate of Kŭmsan"	Story 58	
參判 *ch'amp'an*	Vice-President	Story 16	any second minister of the Six Ministries (junior 2nd-rank) (Wagner)
	vice-president of a Board	Story 66	
	Vice-Minister	Story 66	
吏曹參判 *ijo ch'amp'an*	Vice-President of the Home Office	Story 16	A second minister (junior 2nd-rank) in the Ministry of Personnel
禮判 *yep'an*	Minister of Ceremony	Story 66	= *yejo p'ansŏ* 禮曹判書 = a senior 2nd-rank minister in the Ministry of Rites

Hanmun	Gale's Translation	Source in *Kimun ch'onghwa*	Explanation and/or Translation
副學 *puhak*	Vice-President of the College of Literati	Story 16	short for *pujehak* 副提學 = first counsellor (senior 3rd-rank) in the Office of Special Councillors (Hongmungwan 弘文館) (Wagner)
	Vice-President of the College of Literature	Story 23; 41; 49; 79	
軍器直長 *kun'gi chikchang*	Guardian of the Armoury	Story 17	Superintendent (junior 7th-rank) belonging to the Government Arsenal or Weapons Bureau (Kungisi 軍器寺)
訓將 *hunjang*	Commander-in-Chief	Story 95; 96	= *hullyŏn taejang* 訓鍊大將: chief of the Military Training Administration (Hullyŏn Togam 訓鍊都監), a junior 2nd-rank military post (Kim)
	Supreme head of the troops	Story 96	
捕將 *p'ojang*	Superintendent of Police	Story 96	= *p'odo taejang* 捕盗大將: Director of the Capital Police Bureau (Kim); one of the two commanders-in-chief of the Police Department (P'odoch'ŏng 捕盗廳), a junior 2nd-rank military post
閫任 *konim*	general	Story 96	= *Konoe chi im* 閫外之任 lit. "duty beyond the doorsill/threshold" = official duties of a general taking troops off to battle beyond the borders
軍資正 *kunjajŏng*	the office in charge of the soldiers' supplies	Story 110	= *kunjagam chŏng* 軍資監正: secretary of the Military Procurement administration (senior 3rd-rank) (Kim)

Hanmun	Gale's Translation	Source in *Kimun ch'onghwa*	Explanation and/or Translation
直學 *chikhak*	An official of the College of Literature	Story 18	short for *chikchehak* 直提學: Second deputy director of the Office of Royal Decrees (Yemungwan 藝文館) (Kim); senior 3rd-rank post belonging to the Office of the Special Counselors (Hongmungwan 弘文館)
都憲 *tohŏn*	Chief Justice	Story 20	= *taesahŏn* 大司憲: Inspector-General; junior 2nd-rank official belonging to the Office of the Inspector-General (Sahŏnbu 司憲府) (Kim)
大司憲 *taesahŏn*	Chief Justice	Story 81	(see above)
道臣 *tosin*	governor	Story 25	= *kamsa* 監司 or *kwanch'alsa* 觀察使: provincial governor (junior 2nd-rank) (Wagner)
司僕正 *sabokchŏng*	Keeper of the Royal Stable	Story 25	a senior 3rd-rank post attached to the Bureau of Royal Transportation or the Royal Stable Court (Saboksi 司僕寺) (Palais)
政官 *chŏnggwan*	Government Official	Story 31	= *chŏngwan* 銓官: a generic term referring to officials belonging to the Board of Personnel (Ijo 吏曹)

Hanmun	Gale's Translation	Source in *Kimun ch'onghwa*	Explanation and/or Translation
承旨 *sŭngji*	*sŭngji* a secretary of a Board	Story 31 Story 56; 66	royal secretary (Kim): cover term referring to the Chief Royal Secretary (*tosŭngji* 都承旨), the Second Royal Secretary (*chwa sŭngji* 左承旨), the Third Royal Secretary (*u sŭngji* 右承旨), the Fourth and Fifth Royal Secretaries (*pu sŭngji* 副承旨), and the Sixth Secretary (*tongbu sŭngji* 同副承旨), all belonging to the Royal Secretariat (Sŭngjŏngwŏn 承政院)
都承旨 *tosŭngji*	Chief of Secretaries	Story 75	Chief Royal Secretary (see above)
臺諫 *taegan*	censor	Story 42	censorate (Wagner)
諫院 *kanwŏn*	censor	Story 42	= Saganwŏn 司諫院: Office of the Censor-General (Kim)
禁亂 *kŭmnan*	Officer of Order	Story 42	= *kŭmnan'gwan* 禁亂官, a sort of examination invigilator appointed to keep order during state examination sessions
吏 *ri*	Secretary; cf. 曹吏 *chori* "War Secretary"	Story 46	clerk (Kim)
	Secretary; cf. 惠局吏 *hyegungni* "a secretary of the Office of Alms"	Story 53	

Hanmun	Gale's Translation	Source in *Kimun ch'onghwa*	Explanation and/or Translation
亞銓 *ajŏn*	Vice-Minister of Home Affairs	Story 49	= Ijo *ch'amp'an* 吏曹參判: junior 2nd-rank civil official belonging to the Board of Personnel (Ijo 吏曹)
領相 *yŏngsang*	Prime Minister	Story 50	= *yŏngŭijŏng* 領議政: chief state counsellor (Kim), a senior 1st-rank official belonging to the State Tribunal (Ŭijŏngbu 議政府)
繡衣 *suŭi*	secret commissioner	Story 63; 77	lit. "silken clothing" = *amhaeng ŏsa* 暗行御史: royal secret inspector (Kim) or Secret Censor (Palais)
應敎 *ŭnggyo*	Royal Preceptor	Story 67	drafter, a senior 4th-rank post (Wagner); expectant candidates "awaiting instruction" (Palais)
參奉 *ch'ambong*	Cf. "Keeper of the Tomb of Queen Cho of Injong" (for Hwirŭng *ch'ambong* 徽陵參奉)	Story 69	tomb guardian (Palais); junior 9th-rank posts that belong to local yamen
陵別檢 *nŭng pyŏlgŏm*	superintendent of the tomb (*nŭng* 陵)	Story 69	*pyŏlgŏm* 別檢: special monitor (Palais); junior 8th-rank post belonging to the Bureau of Ceremonial Tents (Chŏnsŏlsa 典設司)

Hanmun	**Gale's Translation**	**Source in *Kimun ch'onghwa***	**Explanation and/or Translation**
齋郎 *chaerang*	keeper of a tomb	Story 69	junior 9th-rank post such as *ch'ambong* 參奉, caretakers of ancestral halls (*sadang* 祠堂) or royal tombs and gardens (*nŭngwŏn* 陵園)
校理 *kyori*	Keeper of the Records	Story 84	Second drafter of the Office of the Diplomatic Correspondence (junior 5th-rank) or fifth Counselor of the Office of the Special Councillors = Hongmungwan 弘文館) (senior 5th-rank)
宰列 *chaeyŏl*	chiefs of Departments	Story 110	Lit.: "ranks of the counselor"
知事 *chisa*	royal secretary	Story 110	Third minister of the Office of Ministers-without-Portfolio or director of the Royal Academy or second deputy director of the Royal House Administration (all senior 2nd-rank)
重試試官 *chungsisigwan*	public examiner	Story 116	examination official(s) for the special *chungsi* 重試 state exam held once every ten years
摠管 *ch'onggwan*	Chief Examiner	Story 116	cover term for Commander (*toch'onggwan* 都摠管) and Deputy Commander (*puch'onggwan* 副摠管) of the Five Military Commands Headquarters (Owi toch'ongbu 五衛都摠府)

Score One for the Dancing Girl,
and Other Selections from the
Kimun ch'onghwa

— 1 —

King Sŏngjong's Love for His Son

Vol. I: 1; translated 24 May 1921; Diary XVI, pp. 151–2; 2.

King Sŏngjong (1457–94 AD)* had a youngest son that he greatly loved. Many things in his treatment of him broke the recognized forms and laws. The officials of the Law Office consulted over it. Hearing of this, the King called them and they came. "Come near to me," said the King. He wrote a line and gave it to them, which read, "People love the chrysanthemum of the ninth moon and ninth day because it is the last flower of the season." The officials hearing this dropped tears and left, understanding thereby that the King would soon die. Shortly after this the King took his departure to the Distant Home.†

* These dates, provided by Gale, are inaccurate. See note 1 for the correct dates.
† ms. is barely legible.

成廟 1) 鍾愛 2) 一王子　多有過制之事 3)　烏府 4) 論之

上命召入掌令 5) 某　入謁上使之前　遂書一句而賜曰：

世人最愛重陽菊 6)　此花開後更無花　其人拭淚而出

未幾上登遐 7) 「五山說林」 8)

1 成廟: the years from 1469 to 1494, the reign of Sŏngjong 成宗.
2 鍾愛: dote on someone.
3 過制之事: incidents that transgress the law or regulations.
4 烏府: another name for the Office of the Inspector-General (Sahŏnbu 司憲府).
5 掌令: a senior fourth-grade government post attached to the Office of the Inspector-General (Sahŏnbu 司憲府).

6 重陽菊: chrysanthemums that bloom during the season of the Double-Nine
  Festival (ninth day of the ninth month by the lunar calendar).
7 登遐 = *sŭngha* 昇遐 ~ *yesŏp* 禮陟: the passing away of a ruler.
8 「五山說林」: a literary miscellany by Ch'a Ch'ŏllo 車天輅 [1556–1615; sobriquet Osan 五山].

———— 2 ————

Queen Han of Injo (1623 AD)

Vol. I: 4; translated 25 May 1921; Diary XVI, p. 152; 14.

When Kwanghae was driven from the throne, it was a question of taking the life of his son Chil. Queen Inyŏl (Han) said to King Injo (her
husband), "I do not know whether Chil's offence is one that merits
death or not. I am a woman and so do not know, but I do know that a
state's hope rests on virtue. As it is safeguarded so the state flourishes.
If we restrain our passions, all goes well. I can soon decide that matter
in my heart as we all know where virtue lies. There is an old saying,
"Emperor in the morning and a beggar at night." If Your Majesty does
not safeguard your heart today, where will there be another to do better
than you? Those who follow after take the pattern of those who have
gone before. I pray you not to kill Chil and leave a precedent open for
our own posterity to live later."

  King Injo hearing this wept and while he wished to spare Chil's life
the officials were opposed to it and Chil had to die.

光海 1) 廢世子桎 [祗]2) 之將死也　仁烈王后 3) 告仁

朝 [祖]4) 曰: 桎 [祗] 之罪　可生可死　非婦人所知

而國之興亡　在於德之修否　係於心之操舍 5)

결어아경　고고유어왈　조위천자　모구위필부이
決於俄頃　故古有語曰：朝爲天子　暮求爲匹夫而

불가득자　전하지조심불여금일　즉안지무부유현
不可得者　殿下之操心不如今日　則安知無復有賢

어전하자호　전인소위　후인소효　원물살질　지
於殿下者乎　前人所爲　後人所效　願勿殺桎 [祇]

이위타일보아자손지계　인조　조　수옥루　경청
以爲他日保我子孫之計　仁朝 [祖] 垂玉淚 6) 傾聽

이훈신　대신　계청안법　경사사
而勳臣 7) 臺臣 8) 啓請案法 9) 竟賜死

1 光海: Kwanghaegun 光海君 [r. 1608–23; 1575–1641].
2 仁烈王后: Queen Inyŏl [1594–1635] was the queen of King Injo. Her
   surname was Han 韓, ancestral seat 淸州 Ch'ŏngju. Her father was Han
   Chun'gyŏm 韓浚謙.
3 仁祖: the sixteenth Chosŏn king. His name was Chong 倧 [r. 1623–49;
   1595–1649; styled Hwabaek 和伯; sobriquet Songch'ang 松窓]. His grandfather was King Sŏnjo 宣祖 [r. 1567–1608; 1552–1608], his father Prince
   Chŏngwŏn 定遠君 (posthumously enthroned as Wŏnjong 元宗 [1580–1619]).
   King Injo's mother was Queen Inwŏn 仁元王后, the daughter of Ku Samaeng
   具思孟 [1531–1604]. King Injo's second wife, whom he married after Queen
   Inyŏl died, was Queen Changnyŏl 莊烈王后 [1624–88], the daughter of
   Cho Ch'angwŏn 趙昌遠 [1583–1646].
4 操舍: holding or discarding; here the expression specifically refers to killing
   the dethroned prince or letting him live.
5 勳臣: a meritorious subject.
6 玉淚: teardrops of the king.
7 勳臣: merit subject.
8 臺臣: *taegwan* 臺官, a cover term for officials in the Office of the Inspector-
   General (Sahŏnbu 司憲府) ranging from Minor Inspector (*chip'yŏng* 持平)
   all the way up to the Inspector-General (*taesahŏn* 大司憲).
9 啓請案法: briefing the king on the implementation of legislation.

——— **3** ———

Kyŏngju and Bob-Tailed Dogs

Vol. I: 7; translated 25 May 1921; Diary XVI, p. 152; 30.

Kyŏngju has no mountains at its back (to the north) and because of this dogs bred there have no tails. For this reason tailless dogs are called "Tonggyŏng" (TŌKYŌ)* dogs. Dogs seen even in the capital are so called.

* Gale seems to have been struck by the fact that Tonggyŏng 東京 "Eastern Capital" (capital of Silla; present-day Kyŏngju) and Tokyo, the capital of imperial Japan, share the same sinographs.

경 주 풍 수 무 후 여　　고 토 구 개 단 미　　속 칭 이 동 경 구
慶州風水無後餘　故土狗皆短尾　俗稱以東京狗

지 금 경 중 역 목 단 미 구 왈　　동 경 구　　회 은 잡 기　　지
至今京中亦目短尾狗曰：東京狗「晦隱雜記 [識]」1)

1 「晦隱雜識」: a miscellany compiled by Nam Hangmyŏng 南鶴鳴 [1654–1722; sobriquet Hoeŭn 晦隱].

——— **4** ———

The Envoy from Loochoo*

Vol. I: 7; translated 25 1921; Diary XVI, p. 152; 33.

There came an envoy from Loochoo who was feasted at the Nam Pyŏlgung (South Special Palace). Yi Sejwa (*p'ansŏ*)† was chief host and Ch'ae Su was vice chief. When the feast was over the envoy said to the interpreter, "The physiognomy of the chief is very bad, but Ch'ae's is very good."

The interpreter answered, "The chief is not only a successful man but his three sons have all passed the examinations and fill important offices. He is a man who has been greatly blessed, far above the average. How can you say that his face bespeaks evil?"

The envoy was silent for a time and then answered, "I can't tell you as to that."

Yi Sejwa was a handsome man of great stature. One sight of him would have had one to mark him a man of blessing. All laughed and said the envoy was a fool.

But a little later Yi's whole house died (in some national scramble) while Ch'ae lived and flourished.

He was a wise envoy after all.

* Loochoo is another name for Ryūkyū, present-day Okinawa. See note 1.
† *p'ansŏ*: senior second-grade minister of the Six Ministries (六曹), which are the Ministries of Personnel (Ijo 吏曹), Tax (Hojo 戶曹), Rites (Yejo 禮曹), War (Pyŏngjo 兵曹), Justice (Hyŏngjo 刑曹), and Public Works (Kongjo 工曹).

琉璃 [球] 國 1) 遣使來　宴于南別宮　李判書世佐 2)

爲館伴 3)　蔡仁川壽 4) 亞 5) 焉　宴已　其使謂舌官

6) 曰：判書於相法凶惡　亞則善　舌官曰：判書不

獨身顯　三子皆捷科 7) 到要津 8)　其福罕世　何以爲凶

使默然曰：非吾知也　蓋慶 [廣] 陽 9) 長大豊碩

望其貌　知其爲福人　聞者皆笑其妄也　未幾　慶 [廣]

陽闔門遭禍　仁川能獲終吉　方知其善相也「龍川

[泉] 談寂記」 10)

1 琉球國: the Ryūkyū Kingdom, an independent island kingdom [1429–1879],
  south of Kyūshū. It was composed of fifty-some islands including the
  present-day Okinawa.
2 李世佐 [1445–1504; styled Maengŏn 孟彦; ancestral seat Kwangju 廣州]:
  scholar-official under Yŏnsangun 燕山君 [r. 1494–1506; 1476–1506].
  Yi Sejwa was honoured as Prince Kwangyang 廣陽君 in 1477. His father
  was Yi Kŭkkam 李克堪 [1427–65].
3 館伴: an ad hoc government office (junior third-grade) occasionally
  assigned to officials who welcomed foreign envoys staying in Seoul.
4 蔡壽 [1449–1515; styled Kiji 耆之; sobriquet Naejae 懶齋; ancestral seat
  Inch'ŏn 仁川]: scholar-official under King Chungjong 中宗 [r. 1506–44;
  1488–1544]. He was honoured as Prince Inch'ŏn 仁川君 in 1506 and given
  the posthumous epithet (*siho* 諡號) Yangjŏng 襄靖. His father was Ch'ae
  Sinbo 蔡申保 [1420–89].
5 亞 = *agyŏng* 亞卿: any second minister = any *ch'amp'an* 參判.
6 舌官: lit. "tongue officials" = *yŏkkwan* 譯官: official interpreters during
  the Chosŏn dynasty.
7 捷科: passing of the civil service examination.
8 要津 = *yoro* 要路: important government posts.
9 廣陽: Yi Sejwa.
10 「龍泉談寂記」: collection of stories compiled by Kim Allo 金安老
  [1481–1537; sobriquet Yongch'ŏn 龍泉] under King Chungjong 中宗
  [r. 1488–1544; 1506–44].

———— 5 ————

Story by Sŏng Hyŏn

Vol. I: 9; translated 26 1921; Diary XVI, p. 153; 43.

When Sŏng Hyŏn (1439–1504 AD) was a young man he went travelling
about the country, and once when he rested his horse on the road he sat
down by the side of a stream. While there a stranger who was riding on
a mule came up and joined him. He also dismounted to rest. It was now
time for breakfast.

The stranger had a servant along with him who unwrapped a bundle, in which were two dishes. One dish was filled with red frogs and
the other had in it a boiled baby.

Seeing this, Sŏng gave a great start but the stranger divided the portions and said to Sŏng Hyŏn, "Eat, won't you?"

Sŏng looked on with disgust and declined, saying, "I don't know how to eat this kind of food."

He wondered over the matter and inquired of the servant lad, "Who is this master whom you serve?"

The boy answered, "I really don't know."

"Since when have you followed him?" was Sŏng Hyŏn's next question.

"Since the fourteenth year of Ch'ŏnbo [755 AD], but as to how many years there are I do not know."

Sŏng then inquired as to the two bowls of food. He replied, "The one is filled with red *chich'o* (that elixir of life) and the other with ginseng."

Hearing this, Sŏng was greatly astonished.

The guest then mounted his mule to ride on his way when he said to his servant, "We must cross the Choryŏng Pass today," and he laid on the whip and departed. Where they went Hyŏn could not tell.

Sŏng returned home with a lonely lost feeling in his heart. He then realized that he must have met Lü Dongbin. It was indeed the year 755 that Lü became an immortal.

成傭齋倪 1) 少時出遊郊園　途中歇馬　臨溪而坐

俄有一客騎驢隨之至　亦憩溪邊　而各進朝餉　客之

僕開袱進兩器　一器盈赤蝌蚪 2) 溢　一器烹小兒爛熟

倪甚驚　客勸倪喫其半　倪甚惡之辭曰：食不曾慣

倪異之問其童曰：客何許人　僮曰：不知　曰：何時

從遊　曰：自天寶十四年 3) 至今不知幾何歲月

이 소 식 량 기 하 물 야　왈　기 일 기 자 지　야　기 일 기 인
而所食兩器何物也　曰：其一器紫芝 4) 也　其一器人

삼 야　현 대 경　객 내 기 려 이 거　위 동 왈　금 일 당 유
蔘也　倪大驚　客乃騎驢而去　謂僮曰：今日當踰

조 령　휘 편 이 매　수 불 지 수 향　현 귀 가 황 약 유 실　잉
鳥嶺 5)　揮鞭而邁　遂不知逾向　倪歸家怳若有失　仍

식 기 소 우 자　내 려 진 인　야　개 천 보 십 사 년　려 진 인
識其所遇者　乃呂眞人 6) 也　盖天寶十四年　呂眞人

태 화 지 추　야　어 우 야 담
胎化之秋 7) 也　「於于野談」 8)

1 成倪 [1439–54; styled Kyŏngsuk 磬叔; sobriquet Yongjae 慵齋 or
　Hŏbaektang 虛白堂; ancestral seat Ch'angnyŏng 昌寧; posthumous epi-
　thet Munjae文戴]: scholar-official under King Sŏngjong 成宗 [r. 1469–94;
　1457–94] and the brother of Sŏng Kan 成侃 [1427–56].
2 蝌蚪: tadpole.
3 天寶十四年: the year 755, the 14th year of the reign of King Kyŏngdŏk
　景德王 [r. 742–65] of the Silla dynasty [57 BC–AD 935].
4 紫芝: a type of red-coloured fungus; considered auspicious.
5 鳥嶺 = K. *saejae* "bird pass": a mountain pass in present-day Mungyŏng
　聞慶, North Kyŏngsang Province.
6 呂眞人 = Lü Zhenren [name Yan 嵒; styled 洞賓 Dongbin or Lü Zu 呂祖;
　sobriquet Chunyangzi 純陽子 or Sidaoren 四道人]: a famous Daoist master
　from the Tang dynasty 唐 [618–907].
7 胎化之秋: just when he was about to turn into a Daoist immortal.
8 「於于野談」: collection of stories compiled by Yu Mongin 柳夢寅
　[1559–1623], scholar-official at the court of Kwanghaegun 光海君
　[r. 1608–23; 1575–1641].

—— 6 ——

Cho Pan's Love

Vol. I: 11; translated 26 May 1921; Diary XVI, pp. 153–4; 61.

Cho Pan had an aunt who was married to the Mongol Tuotuo. He went in his early years and lived in the home of Tuotuo in China. Tuotuo fell on evil days and his house was ruined. Cho took with him a young woman whom he greatly loved and a young servant and started off for his native country.

On the way the servant proposed thus: "We three have made our escape by flight and have come thus far. If anyone should inquire of us the reason, we shall be like sliced fish – done for all time. If we go along thus with this pretty girl we shall be the question and the wonder of all passers. Let's drop her by this way and make □ of our lives."

Thus they consulted together.

This girl was a very gifted and wise woman and said, "It is difficult indeed to have both fish and bears' paws to dine off at one and the same time. It is not meet that you should die through taking me along."

She wept as she said this. And then they dined sparingly and said their farewells.

The two then rode for their lives laying on the whip for some one hundred *ri* or more.

Thinking constantly of this pretty girl, Cho was in great distress and finally said, "I cannot go any further."

He decided to go back, find her, and join fortunes together.

The servant said, "Don't go yourself. I'll go, give your message, and return."

Cho gave his consent.

The servant went, and when he met the girl, she had thrown herself from a high pavilion and was dying. She gave her finger-ring, saying,* "You can place no confidence in women. I found her with two officials drinking and teasing and not a beast did match her countenance. What a low, depraved creature she is."

When Cho heard this he spat and went on. When, however, they reached the Amnok River, the servant told all: how she had died, how she had given the ring, how she had instructed him to □.† On hearing this, Cho had a fit and nearly died.

He came home, married, and had five children all of whom held high office. Cho became a minister; however, he never forgot his Chinese wife and he kept her dying day by sacrifice and tears.

* Gale's translation is in error here. The original reads: "the servant removed her finger-ring, returned, and gave it to his master, saying."
† Gale's translation contains both errors and exuberances. The original reads: "the servant told all of her fall from the pavilion. He produced her ring and gave it to him."

조 복 흥 반　　유 기 고 위 탈 탈　　승 상 부 인　　고 유 종 고
趙復興胖 1) 有其姑爲脫脫 2) 丞相夫人　故幼從姑

양 어 탈 탈 씨　　탈 탈 패　　공 여 소 행 미 인 급 일 소 관
養於脫脫氏　脫脫敗　公與所幸美人及一小官

피 화 본 국　　중 로 소 관 모 어 공 왈　　오 삼 인 도 화 지 차
避禍本國　中路小官謀於公曰：吾三人逃禍至此

약 유 의 이 문 지 자　　시 궤 상 륙　　우 미 인 동 행　　우 해 인 견
若有疑而問之者　是机上肉 3) 又美人同行　又駭人見

불 여 할 애 이 도 존 야　　상 여 언 의　　이 미 인 역 영 민
不如割愛以圖存也　相與言議　而美人亦英敏

내 언 어 여 웅 장 불 가 겸 득　　불 가 이 첩 지 고 병 수 취 륙　　야
乃言魚與熊掌不可兼得　不可以妾之故駢首就戮 4) 也

현 연 읍 하　　설 소 작　　상 여 결 별 어 가 로　　이 인 책 마 겸 정
泫然泣下　設小酌　相與訣別於街路　二人策馬兼程 5)

행 백 륙 칠 리 허　　공 비 념 미 인 불 이　　촌 보 불 능 진　　기 의
行百六七里許　公悲念美人不已　寸步不能進　其意

욕 환 도 미 인　　갱 서 정 야　　소 관 왈　　불 수 공 왕　　노 당 치
欲還導美人　更敍情也　小官曰：不須公往　奴當致

공 의 이 환 야　　공 왈　　락　　소 관 왕 견　　미 인 타 루 이 절
公意而還也　公曰：諾　小官往見　美人墮樓而絶

해 기 지 환 이 귀 급 공 왈　　귀 왈　　아 녀 지 불 가 신 여 차
解其指環而歸給公曰 [歸曰]：兒女之不可信如此

方與二官員　設酒唱歌　畧無愧色　可鄙之甚也　公

亦唾之之　旣到鴨綠江　俱道墮樓之事　出指環與之

公痛哭幾絶　到本國　娶妻生子五人　俱顯位至勳相

猶終身悼念　每遇忌日　流涕而祭之　「靑樓別談」6)

1 趙胖 [1341–1401; ancestral seat Paekch'ŏn 白川; posthumous epithet Sugwi 肅魏]: scholar-official of the late Koryŏ [918–1392] and early Chosŏn period. He was honoured as Prince Pokhŭng 復興君 for his meritorious contributions to the founding of the Chosŏn dynasty. His father was Cho Segyŏng 趙世卿 [dates unknown].
2 脫脫 Tuotuo [1314–55]: minister and official of the Yuan dynasty 元 [1271–1368], also known as the "Great Historian Tuotuo."
3 机上肉: lit. "a piece of meat on a cutting board" = dire straits.
4 骿首就戮: lit. "tidy up one's hair in preparation for decapitation."
5 兼程: make a two-day journey in one day; rush to one's destination.
6 「靑樓別談」: Chosŏn story collection of unknown date.

——— 7 ———

Yun-ssi, Mother of Yŏnsan

Vol. I: 12; translated 27 May 1921; Diary XVI, p. 154; 62.

Yi (*p'ansŏ*)* Sejwa had a wise and far-seeing wife. When King Sŏngjong dismissed his Queen Yun for the evil of her ways Yi Sejwa was a secretary and he brought the hemlock brew for her to drink and die.

In the evening he returned home, and his wife said, "What about the Queen whom they dismissed—have they not yet settled the matter?"

Yi replied, "I just took her her dose of poison today so that she is dead."

On hearing this, the minister's wife gave a great start, arose and said, "My children, you are all dead. No posterity will remain to us. As the mother has died in her innocence, will not her son see that all those concerned in it are punished?"

When Yŏnsan was King in the year *kapcha* (1504), Yi Sejwa's son Sujŏng was killed and Yi Sejwa himself was beheaded. The wife's foresight was very great for she saw with unerring eye.

* *p'ansŏ*: senior second-grade minister of the Six Ministries (Yukcho 六曹), comprising Personnel (Ijo 吏曹), Tax (Hojo 戶曹), Rites (Yejo 禮曹), War (Pyŏngjo 兵曹), Justice (Hyŏngjo 刑曹), and Public Works (Kongjo 工曹).

李判書世佐 1) 之夫人某氏　成廟罪廢尹氏之時

公以承旨持藥而去　其夕還家　夫人問曰：

朝廷論廢妣 [妃] 不已　畢竟何如　公曰：今日已賜

死矣　夫人愕然起坐　傷哉　吾子孫其無遺類乎

母旣無罪而被殺子　豈無報復他日乎　至燕山甲子

2) 而公之子守貞 3) 被殺　公亦爲東市之斬　夫人先見

實非常人所及也 「松窩雜說 4) 」

1 李世佐 [1445–1504; styled Maengŏn 孟彦; ancestral seat Kwangju 廣州]: scholar-official under Yŏnsangun 燕山君 [r. 1494–1506; 1476–1506]. Yi Sejwa was honoured as Prince Kwangyang 廣陽君 in 1477. His father was Yi Kŭkkam 李克堪 [1427–65].

2 甲子: indicates the year 1504 (Yŏnsan 10), the year of the Literati Purges of the Kapcha Year 甲子士禍.

3 李守貞 [1477–1504; styled Kanjung 幹仲; sobriquet Kŏnch'on 乾村 and
 Chŏngjae 貞齋; ancestral seat Kyŏngju 慶州]: scholar-official under
 Yŏnsangun 燕山君 [r. 1494–1506; 1476–1506] and a son of Yi Sejwa.
4 「松窩雜說」: miscellany by Yi Ki 李墍 [1522–1604; sobriquet Songwa 松窩].

———— 8 ————

The Loyal Dancing Girl

Vol. I: 12; translated 27 May 1921; Diary XVI, pp. 154–5; 64.

Non'gae was the name of a famous dancing girl of Chinju. She was attached to the Government Bureau. In the year 1592, when the city fell before the Japanese, Non'gae, dressed in her best with rouge and powder, prepared as for her wedding day. She stood on the high cliff just beneath Choksŏngnu Pavilion. Here the drop is very great – many hundred feet.

A Japanese, seeing her, was greatly delighted but feared to go near her as she stood in a place of danger. One Japanese, however, of special bravery, came forth and she smiled to meet him. He was a high officer and came forward to put his arms about her. At once she sprang forward and threw her arms about him and with a bound was over the cliff with him.

Many, yes – very many of these dancing girls died rather than be spoiled by the Japanese soldiers. Their names, however, are lost. They were only dancing girls and women given over to a licentious life, not people from whom one could expect loyalty and devotion. They died as though it were as easy as going sweetly home. Thus they escaped dishonour and made a name for themselves.

론 개 자 진 주 관 기 야　계 사　당 성 함 지 일　개 응 장
論介者晉州官妓也　癸巳 1) 當城陷之日　介凝粧

성 복　립 우 촉 석 루　하 초 암 지 령 기 하 만　장 직 입 파 심
盛服　立于矗石樓 2) 下峭巖之巓其下萬　丈直入波心

왜 견 이 열 지　개 막 지 근　독 일 왜 정 연　직 진　론 개 소
倭見而悅之　皆莫之近　獨一倭挺然 3) 直進　論介笑

이 영 지　　왜 장 유 이 인 지　　론 개 포 지 기 장　　직 투 우
而迎之　　倭將誘以引之　　論介抱持其將　　直投于

담 구 사　　임 진 지 란　　관 기 지 우 왜 불 견 욕 이 사 자
潭俱死　　壬辰之亂　　官妓之遇倭不見辱而死者

불 가 승 기　　비 지 일 론 개　　이 다 실 기 명　　피 관 기 야 음
不可勝記　　非止一論介　　而多失其名　　彼官妓也淫

창 야　　불 가 이 정 렬 칭　　이 시 사 여 귀　　불 욕 어 적
娼也　　不可以貞烈稱　　而視死如歸 4)　　不辱於賊

가 가 야　　어 우 야 담
可嘉也　「於于野談」5)

1 癸巳: 1593 (Sŏnjo 26); the year following the outbreak of the Imjin Invasion
  (1592).
2 矗石樓: a pavilion in Chinju 晉州, North Kyŏngsang Province.
3 挺然: conspicuously.
4 視死如歸: lit."view death like going home" = be unafraid of death.
5 「於于野談」: miscellany compiled by Yu Mongin 柳夢寅 [1559–1623;
  sobriquet Ŏu 於于] during the reign of Kwanghaegun 光海君 [r. 1608–23;
  1575–1641].

—————— 9 ——————

The Dancing Girl

Vol. I: 13; translated 27 May 1921; Diary XVI, p. 155; 65.

Yu Hŭich'un, called Miam, was made magistrate of Namp'yŏng
(Chŏlla). At the same time, Paek In'gŏl was made magistrate of
Mujang. Song Insu was governor of Chŏlla at the same time. The three
were special friends and had much in common; they were very happy
in each other's company.

Song was very fond of a dancing girl of Puan, but he never had any
sexual relations with her. It was purely platonic love. He always had her
in his company. Whenever he went to Namp'yŏng or to Mujang he always had her along. They used to picnic and have specially good times

together. The people of the district called them the Three Attendants of the governor (Yu, Paek, and the girl).

Song filled his term of office and on departure, his two friends and the girl came to see him off. Song said on this occasion, "I always liked this dancing girl because of her training and her special charm. I have had a whole year with her but I never entered into any unlawful acts with her. My reason was that I feared I might die as a result of it."

The dancing girl pointed with her finger at the graves on the hillside: "You are right for all those moundy graves bury my husbands under their sod."

This she said with a sense of complaint against his hard treatment. All laughed over this joke.

류 희 춘　　자 호 미 암　암　　위 남 평　　현 감　　백 휴 암 인 걸
柳希春 1) 自號眉菴 [巖] 爲南平 2) 縣監　白休菴仁傑 3)

재 무 장　　지 시　　송 규 암 린　린　수　　위 방 백　　삼 인 상
宰茂長 4) 之時　宋圭菴獜 [麟] 壽 5) 爲方伯　三人相

득 환 심　　규 암 심 권 부 안 기　　불 여 지 통　　견 권 지 재 이
得歡甚　圭菴心眷扶安妓　不與之通　繾綣只載而

수 행　　매 교 격　　소 무 장 남 평　　항 동 유　　처 일 도 인 위 지
隨行　每撽 [檄] 召茂長南平　恒同遊　處一道人謂之

삼 차 비 운　　송 공 과 만　　장 전 우 려 산　　이 인 급 기 수 지
三差備云　宋公瓜滿　將餞于礪山 6)　二人及妓隨之

송 공 왈　　정 애 차 인 지 공 혜　　일 년 동 석　　불 급 란 자
宋公曰：政愛此人之巧慧　一年同席　不及亂者

실 공 기 사 야　　기 개　즉　지 전 산 중 총 왈　　과 연 야
實恐其死也　妓皆 [卽] 指前山衆塚曰：果然也

피 루 루 자 개 아 부 야　　개 원 사 야　　일 좌 대 갹
彼累累者皆我夫也　盖怨辭也　一座大噱 7)

파 인 지 소 록
「巴人識小錄 8)

1 柳希春 [1513–77; styled Injung 仁仲; sobriquet Miam 眉巖; ancestral seat
   Sŏnsan 善山; posthumous epithet Munjŏl 文節]: scholar-official under
   Kin Sŏnjo 宣祖 [r. 1567–1608; 1552–1608]. His father was Yu Kyerin 柳桂麟
   [1478–1528].
2 南平: a town in Naju 羅州, South Chŏlla Province.
3 白仁傑 [1497–1579; styled Sawi 士偉; sobriquet Hyuam 休庵; ancestral seat
   Suwŏn 水原; posthumous epithet Mungyŏng 文敬]: scholar under King
   Sŏnjo. His father was Paek Ikkyŏn 白益堅 [dates unknown].
4 茂長: a town in Koch'ang 高敞, North Chŏlla Province.
5 宋麟壽 [1487–1547; styled Misu 眉叟; sobriquet Kyuam 圭庵; ancestral seat
   Ŭnjin 恩津; posthumous epithet Munch'ung 文忠]: scholar-official under
   King Myŏngjong 明宗 [r. 1545–67; 1534–67]. His father was Song Seryang
   宋世良 [1473–1539].
6 礪山: a town in Iksan 益山, North Chŏlla Province.
7 一座大噱: lit. "everyone at the scene burst out laughing."
8 「巴人識小錄」: *Sŏngong chisorok*「惺翁識小錄」: compilation by Hŏ Kyun
   許筠 [1569–1618], scholar-official under Kwanghaegun 光海君 [r. 1608–23;
   1575–1641].

———— **10** ————

The World of the Dancing Girl*

Vol. I: 14; translated 28 May 1921; Diary XVI, pp. 156–8; 70.

```
This is a very extreme example of an obscene essay
        — seldom seen in Korea. — J.S.G
```

There was a dancing girl in Puan, whose name was Kyesaeng who
was well-versed in the character and could play also and sing well. Her
special name was Maehwa Ch'ang (Plum Flower Window). She was
selected as one of the most beautiful and gifted in the south and was
sent to Seoul.

Those of Seoul who loved the dancing girl came to see her. They
strove for first place in her attention. On a certain day a Yu (Samun) To
paid her a visit. Here he found two disreputable characters Kim and
Ch'oe already with her seated in the same room.

Kyesaeng was pouring out drink for them and they were already half drunk. Each one of the three tried his best to win over the attention of the girl.

She laughed and said, "I have a command that I wish to give you and that is this – that you sing me a song that will delight me and help us pass the time and yet I do not [care for] one like this:

> The white jade arm that serves a thousand men for pillow,
> The red lips that lend a fragrance to a hundred guests;
> Your body is neither sword nor blade,
> Why so soon cut off my love that binds me,
> The legs that beat time with the midnight moon,
> One motion underneath the quilt,
> The delights of such a time as this are for those two alone.

"This kind of song is for the low-class man alone or for a soldier who runs away. I do not wish to hear any such thing as this. But if you have something that I have never heard before that will delight my heart, I will yield my favour to you."

The three said, "Very good."

Kim then sang a song written by Kim Myŏngwŏn, seven characters in each and four verses:

> Midnight without the softly falling rain
>> Keeps step with two whose hearts beat close as one.
> Before they have enough the breaking dawn
>> Drives them apart. "When shall we meet?" says she.

Ch'oe then sang a song of Sim Hŭisu:

> We sport together by the silken screen
>> So pretty she so sweetly half-ashamed.
> Whisper soft to know she thinks of me
>> She pats her locks and bows a blushing smile.

The dancing girl Kyesaeng said, "The first song lacks charm. The last is pretty, but there is no special skill demonstrated in either. There is nothing special here to delight me. A *yulsŏng* is one that is sweet and pure of seven characters such as are seen today. The thought, the expression,

the meaning all combine to make it very difficult. This is what I want
– something truly gifted."
   Kim then sang one of Chŏng Chadang:

> So pretty she a sweet sixteen or so
>   By far the rarest of her gentle kind.
> Her love and favours are a deep deep sea
>   Her dignity and form are stern as law.
> Late of the night and early with the dawn
>   The pine trees □□ on rapid shoes we head
> Farewells are frequent but the meetings rare.
>   On clouds and rain our fairies come to earth.

   Ch'oe said, "This is a very beautiful song but there are better than
this."
   He then sang one from Ko Kyŏngmyŏng, "*The horse waits by the sandy
flats how long* [sic]."
   Kyesaeng said, "This is a song of the old Kingdoms of Lu and Wei.
They show purity and form and yet they would never move one's heart.
She then turned to Yu and said, "Have you alone no song to sing me?"
   Yu said in reply, "I am an ignorant man and know only the use of
the washer made by Lao Ai" (the paramour of the mother of Qin
Shi Huang).
   The dancing girl laughed on hearing this while Ch'oe flew into a rage
and said, "You may be gifted as you say but today's trial hangs on sing-
ing a verse."
   Kim congratulated himself, feeling that his verse was the best. He
looked to each side and said, "One verse of mine will put all others out.
It is by Chŏng Chisŭng:

> The autumn nights are all too short for me.
>   Before the lamp's off with your silken robe
> Let me look in these half-closed eyes so deep.
>   Our forms meet close and fragrant perfumes rise,
> Our legs beat time a □ water mill
>   We rise and fall as dips the dragonfly.
> How strong and stiff I □* not in my soul
>   But ask how deep her love runs now for me.

   Kyesaeng said, "This is well done."

Yu then said, "Your various poems are old though well done. They are not such as will win the day. I will give a sample of a new song that will win me victory."

He then asked Kyesaeng for a rhyme character and wrote in response:

> The valiant lord meets fresh the balmy spring.
>> Beneath the silken folds he finds his mate.
> The jade white rod between the lifted legs,
>> Drives straight into the rosy gate that opens.
> The pretty eye looks out from mists that wake,
>> The blue expanse is but a penny wide.
> How great delight – what words can ever speak?
>> A thousand gilders for one night is cheap.

Kyesaeng read this and sighed, "So great a master of the pen I never would have dreamed to see in such an unsavoury place as this. Heretofore I have known your writings and have been crazy over them; for example, 'I ride my white horse out into the night.' I had long desired to see thee. Now we have met, drink this glass, I pray, that I have prepared. I could give many things to you for the misty eyes you speak of and the penny-wide heaven. The other poems are not worth a glass of water."

Hearing this, Kim and Ch'oe hurried away.

* The same story appears in Yi Hŭip'yŏng's 李羲平 [1772–1839] *Miscellaneous Writings by Kyesŏ* (*Kyesŏ chamnok* 溪西雜錄), volume 1, entry 64.

부 안 기 계 생　　공 시 선 구 탄　　호 매 창　　이 선 상 경
扶 安 妓 桂 生 ₁) 工 詩 善 謳 彈 ₂) 號 梅 窓　以 選 上 京

귀 유 자 제 막 불 요 치　　쟁 선 여 지 수 창　　일 일 류 사 문 도
貴 遊 子 弟 莫 不 邀 致　爭 先 與 之 酬 唱　一 日 柳 斯 文 塗 ₃)

왕 방 지　　김 최 량 성 이 광 협 자 부 자 이 선 재 좌　　계 생 설 작
往 訪 之　金 崔 兩 姓 以 狂 俠 自 負 者 已 先 在 座　桂 生 設 酌

이 대 반 훈　　삼 인 개 주 목　　욕 도 지　　계 생 소 이 거 령 왈
以 待 半 醺　三 人 皆 注 目　欲 挑 之　桂 生 笑 而 舉 令 曰：

제 군 각 송 풍 류 장 시　　이 조 일 환　　지 여 옥 비 천 인 침　　단
諸 君 各 誦 風 流 場 詩　以 助 一 歡　至 如 玉 臂 千 人 枕　丹

唇[脣]萬口香　爾身非刀劍　何遽斷剛腸　且足舞三

更月　衾生一陣風　此時無限味　惟有兩人同等詩

乃是賤隷走卒之誦　不足傾耳　若有傳誦前所未聞

當於我心者　當與一歡　三人曰：諾　金生誦金命元 4)

七言絶句曰：

　　窓外三更細雨時　　　　兩人心事兩人知

　　歡情未洽天將曉　　　　更把羅衫問後期

崔繼鳴沈喜壽 5) 七言絶句曰：

　　抱向紗窓弄未休　　　　半含嬌態半含羞

　　低聲暗聞[問]相思否　　手整金釵乍點頭

桂生曰：前詩太拙　後詩差妙而手段俱低　皆未足聽

凡律詩　詩之精者　而七言近體響韻意趣俱難　吾當

取其難而（精）金遂唱鄭子堂 6) 七言律曰：

　　年纔十五窈窕娘　　　　名滿長安第一坊

蕩子恩情深似海　　花長威令嚴如霜

蘭窓日晏朝粧急　　松峴風高夕履忙

相別每多相見少　　襄陽（陽臺）雲雨惱襄王

崔曰：此詩雖佳　又有佳於此者　仍謂高霽峯 7)

立馬沙頭別故遲之句　桂生曰：此詩眞是魯［鄭］衛 8)

以下　詩雖有淸光風韻 9)　亦不足動人　因顧謂柳曰：

此間子獨無吟乎　柳曰：我本無文　但嫪毒貫輪

之才 10) 耳　桂生微哂哂崔咈［怫］然 11) 曰：子雖有

長才　今日之事　當行詩令　金頰有自矜之色　顧謂

左右曰：一律可以壓倒諸詩壓　卽朗吟鄭之升 12)

七言律曰：

秋色［宵］已曙莫言長　　促向燈前解繡裳

獨眼微開晴土［吐］氣　　兩胸纏合汗生香

脚如螻蛞 13) 翻波急　　腰似蜻蜓 14) 點水忙

강건향래심자부
强健向來心自負

애랑심천문랑랑
愛娘深淺問娘娘

계생음영칭의　류왈　제군소송　개시이진　추
桂生吟咏稱意　柳曰：諸君所誦　皆是已陳　蒭

추　구　하족괄목　아당점신시일률립치어금일
[蒭]狗 15) 何足刮目　我當占新詩一律立幟於今日

석상　수령계랑호운　응성이대
席上　遂令桂娘呼韻　應聲而對：

탐춘호사기앙연
探春豪士氣昂然

비취금중결호연
翡翠衾中結好緣

탱거옥경쌍각흘
撑去玉莖雙脚屹

관래단혈량현원
貫來丹穴兩弦圓

초간교안혼여무
初看嬌眼渾如霧

갱각장천소사전
更覺長天小似錢

저리약론자미별
這裡若論滋味別

일소고가직금천
一宵高價直金千

계생영탄왈　불료존공림차루지야　습문공광심
桂生咏歎曰：不料尊公臨此陋地也　習聞公狂心

유미이　백마우황혼지시행　앙　모자구의　금행
猶未已　白馬又黃昏之詩幸 [仰] 慕者久矣　今幸

우지　내작진일배주　왈　약사안여무천사전　즉
遇之　乃酌進一杯酒（曰）：若使眼如霧天似錢　則

기가기독천금이지재　향자제공허다소음　불직일
其價豈獨千金而止哉　向者諸公許多小吟　不直一

작랭수　김최개무연퇴거　속고금소총　홍봉사
勺冷水　金崔皆憮然退去　「續古今笑叢」16) 洪奉事

금종　저
金宗 17) 著

 1 桂生 [1513–50; Yi Hyanggŭm 李香今; styled Maech'ang 梅窓, Kyesaeng
   癸生, or Kyerang 桂娘 / 癸娘]: renowned *kisaeng* from Puan who flourished during the reign of King Myŏngjong 明宗 [r. 1545–67; 1534–67]. A
   kisaeng is a professional entertainer trained in song, dancing, and poetry
   composition.
 2 謳彈: singing with musical accompaniment.
 3 柳塗 [dates unknown; styled Yujŏng 由正; sobriquet Kwiban 歸盤; ancestral seat Munhwa 文化]: His father was Yu Kwisu 柳龜壽 [dates unknown].
 4 金命元 [1534–1602; styled Ŭngsun 應順; sobriquet Chuŭn 酒隱; ancestral
   seat Kyŏngju 慶州; posthumous epithet Ch'ungik 忠翼]: scholar-official
   under King Sŏnjo 宣祖 [r. 1567–1608; 1552–1608]. His father was Kim
   Man'gyun 金萬鈞 [?–1549].
 5 沈喜壽 [dates unknown; styled Paekku 伯懼; sobriquet Ilsong 一松;
   ancestral seat Ch'ŏngsong 青松; posthumous epithet Munjŏng 文貞]:
   scholar-official during the reign of King Sŏnjo 宣祖 [r. 1567–1608;
   1552–1608]. His father was Sim Kŏn 沈鍵 [1519–50].
 6 鄭子堂 [dates unknown; styled Sŭnggo 升高; sobriquet Ch'ŏngsong 青松;
   ancestral seat Tongnae 東萊]: poet during the reign of Yŏnsangun 燕山君
   [r. 1494–1506; 1476–1506]. His father was Chŏng Ki 鄭期 [dates unknown].
 7 霽峰 = sobriquet of Ko Kyŏngmyŏng 高敬命 [1533–92; styled Isun 而順;
   ancestral seat Changhŭng 長興; posthumous epithet Ch'ungnyŏl 忠烈]:
   famous leader of the "righteous army" (*ŭibyŏng* 義兵) during the Imjin
   Invasion (1592). His father was Ko Maengyŏng 高孟英 [1502–?].
 8 鄭衛: short for "(the sounds of the states of) Zheng and Wei 鄭衛之音"
   (Spring and Autumn period = 722–481 BC) = decadent and lascivious music.
 9 清光風韻: the elegant charm of a clear moonlit night.
10 嫪毒貫輪之才: lit. "Lao Ai's skills in sexual intercourse." Lao Ai [?–238 BC]
   was the fabled and well-endowed paramour of Zhao Ji 趙姬 [dates
   unknown], the Queen Dowager of Emperor Qin Shi Huang 秦始皇帝
   [r. 246–221 BC as the king of the state of Qin; r. 221–210 BC as the First
   Emperor of China; 259–210 BC].
11 怫然: in sudden anger.
12 鄭之升 [1550–?; styled Chasin 子愼; sobriquet Ch'onggyedang 叢桂堂 and
   Ch'ŏnyuja 天遊子; ancestral seat Onyang 溫陽]: poet during the reign of
   King Sŏnjo 宣祖 [r. 1567–1608; 1552–1608]. His father was Chŏng Hyŏn
   鄭礥 [1526–?].
13 螻蟈: long-legged frog.
14 蜻蜓: dragonfly.
15 芻狗: dog made of straw used at ancestral worship ceremonies and
   discarded soon afterwards; an object that has outlived its usefulness.

16 「續古今笑叢」: collection of stories of unknown dates; possibly compiled
by Hong Kŭmjong [dates unknown]. See note 17 below.
17 洪金宗 [dates unknown]: no information. *Pongsa* 奉事 is a junior eighth-
rank post within the Chosŏn bureaucracy. See note 16 just above. This is
presumably a mistake on the part of the Chosŏn compiler(s) for Hong
Manjong 洪萬宗 [1643–1725; styled Uhae 宇海; sobriquet Hyŏnmukcha
玄默子, Monghŏn 夢軒, or Changju 長洲; ancestral seat P'ungsan; 豊山].

——— **11** ———

Spirit of the Dead

Vol. I: 15; translated 27 May 1921; Diary XVI, pp. 155–6; 71.

In the Imjin War (1592) a certain Yi Kyŏngnyu attached to the War
Office was made an aide to the general in active service. He was in an
engagement at Sangju, where they were defeated and where he was
killed. His brother, whose name was Kyŏngjun, was a general of great
renown. He was in command of soldiers in Suan (Hwanghae).

On a certain sacrificial day he had made special preparations by fasting and bathing. Here as he sat alone, he suddenly heard the sound of
a crying outside his screen and a voice spoke, saying, "Brother, I have
come."

Kyŏngjun looked out to see and there was the ghost of his brother.

Weeping, Kyŏngjun inquired of him, "Whence came you?"

"When I was killed," answered the spirit, "I longed to come and see
you but so many guns and spears blocked my way that I could not. I
came but could not get close enough, but now that you are alone and all
is quiet I have taken advantage of this opportunity."

"Where were you killed?" asked his brother, "and where now is your
body buried?"

The spirit said, "On the day when defeat overtook us, I made my
escape from the mêlée and hid among the grass and reeds. The next
day as I was making my way to a monastery among the hills I met a
Japanese on the way and he killed me."

The brother said, "Even though you go thus and appear to us brothers, I trust you will not go near father and mother. Their grief would be
increased, I fear, by such a visit."

He answered, "I'll do so. I have no desire to appear thus to them."

He came and went thus among the brothers for a space of three years. He talked of all that had taken place in the family just as though he were alive.

壬辰之亂　兵曹佐郎李慶流 1)　爲防禦使從事官　戰敗

死於尙州　其兄慶濬 2) 武將也　領大軍防守順安　適値

忌辰　淸齋獨坐　忽聞帷壁間有哭聲曰：兄氏吾來

審之則慶流魂也　慶濬哭而問曰：爾自何來　曰：

吾死後欲訪吾兄所居　兵衛甚盛　迫不敢近　今兄

靜處乘閒而來　曰：爾死何地　骸體亦在何處

曰：兵敗之日　董抽身亂兵中　埋伏草苞　翌日

步上山寺　路遇倭而見殺　兄曰：爾可以往來

吾兄弟之間　勿往父母之傍　恐益疚其懷也　曰：

然　吾亦不忍使父母知之　自此往來于兄弟之家

家中事無不言之　諄諄 3)　如平日者三年不止

「於于野談」4)

1 李慶流 [1564–92; styled Changwŏn 長源; sobriquet Pan'gŭm 伴琴; ancestral
   seat Hansan 韓山]: scholar-official under King Sŏnjo 宣祖 [r. 1567–1608;
   1552–1608]. He died in Sangju during the Imjin War. His father was Yi
   Chŭng 李增 [1525–1600].
2 李慶濬 [dates unknown; ancestral seat Hansan 韓山]: son of Yi Chŭng 李增
   and brother of Yi Kyŏngnyu 李慶流.
3 諄諄: offering whole-hearted help.
4 「於于野談」: miscellany compiled by Yu Mongin 柳夢寅 [1559–1623],
   scholar-official under Kwanghaegun 光海君 [r. 1608–23; 1575–1641].

———— **12** ————

Ghosts

Vol. I: 15; translated 30 May 1921; Diary XVI, pp. 158–9; 72.

Ha Ŭngnim (a *such'an*) when some ten years of age was a wonderful
lad. He passed his examinations very early. His name and great ability
were known abroad. Once when sending off a friend he wrote a verse:

Sadly we reach the sandy flats
   A drink and fare we part asunder.
Lost to my sight among the hills,
   I trace my steps just as the sun goes under.

At that time critics compared what he had written with an ancient
line which runs:

The day is late and closed the thorn gate stands.

Those who understood such things said, "He will not live long, we
fear; an early death appears in his time."
Shortly after, Ha died.
A friend of his was at that time in distant Chŏlla. Once just as evening
was falling he was returning home. He reached Ch'ŏngp'a just outside
the South Gate. There in a sudden he met Ha Ŭngnim. They greeted
and asked how all was with them. He gave several commissions regarding his home, saying that he was to be absent.

He came home and made inquiry as regards Ha but was told that he was dead already for some time and his funeral was over and past.

There was also a man called Im Kwang (*pin'gaek* – teacher of the Crown Prince) who was in the train of Prince Sohyŏn (son of Injo) and went with him to Peking. There he fell ill and died.

Im Yunsŏk, his son, was magistrate in Kaeryŏng (Kyŏnggi) when suddenly on a certain day he saw his father, dressed in ceremonial robes, step up into the official office. All the people in the place saw it and were frightened to death. His words and manner were exactly as they used to be when in the flesh.

As he left he said to his son, "In the world of the dead I am appointed decider of the judgments of the dead. On my way by here, my love for you as my son made me think of you, for death makes no difference to our love. That is why I have come."

He called all the servants and said to them, "Be faithful to your master and avoid laziness or carelessness. Make haste with the evening meal."

He ate some and then ordered it away.

"A spirit," said he, "desires only the spirit and not the material."

He sat and talked for a time and then arose to go. A step and two and he disappeared from view.

河修撰 1) 應臨 2) 甫　十歲以奇童稱　少年登第　名聲

正溢　嘗送客西郊 3) 有詩曰：

草草西郊別　　　　春風酒一杯

青山人不見　　　　斜日獨歸來

當時以

山中相送罷　　　　日暮掩柴扉

竝稱 而識者知其延命不久 未幾沒 其友人遠

遊湖外 日暮歸到靑坡 4) 忽於橋邊遇應臨

問寒暄 因托家事而去 歸問 應臨死已葬矣 任賓

客紲 5) 從昭顯世子 6) 入燕京病逝 其子允錫 7)

爲開寧 8) 縣監 忽一日 公儼然來坐衙軒 一家驚倒

其言語動止宛如常日 去時謂其子曰：冥府界

我以按察之任 今適過此 父子之情生死何間

欲見汝而來 仍招僮僕謂之曰：汝等盡心主家之事

毋或怠慢 急其夕飯以進 半餉使之撤去曰：神

（食）氣而飽非如生人也 坐語移時起去 數步之外

不見其形云 「菊堂俳［排］語」9)

1 修撰: counsellor (sixth grade) of the Office of the Special Counselors
   (Hongmungwan 弘文館)
2 河應臨 [1536–67; styled Taei 大而; sobriquet Ch'ŏngch'ŏn 菁川; ancestral
   seat Chinju 晉州]: scholar-official under King Myŏngjong 明宗 [r. 1545–67;
   1534–67]. His father was Ha Yŏngsu 河永水 [dates unknown].
3 西郊: the area outside the West Gate in Seoul.
4 靑坡: a station outside the South Gate in Seoul.

5 任紘 [1579–1644; styled Chajŏng 子瀞; sobriquet Samhyudang 三休堂;
  ancestral seat P'ungch'ŏn 豊川; posthumous epithet Ch'unggan 忠簡]:
  scholar-official under King Injo 仁祖 [r. 1623–49; 1595–1649]. His father
  was Im Iksin 任翊臣 [dates unknown].
6 昭顯世子 [1612–45]: the firstborn son of King Injo 仁祖 [r. 1623–49; 1595–
  1649]. His mother was Lady Han, Queen Inyŏl 仁烈王后 韓氏 [1594–1635].
7 任允錫 [dates unknown; ancestral seat P'ungch'ŏn]: son of Im Kwang 任絖
  [dates unknown].
8 開寧: a town, Kŭmnŭng 金陵, in North Kyŏngsang Province.
9 「菊堂排語」: miscellany compiled by Chŏng T'aeje 鄭泰齊 [1612–?].

—— **13** ——

Madness Recalls the Verse

Vol. 1: 15; translated [30 May] 1921; Diary XVI, pp. 159–60; 73.

There was a certain Kim Chidae (forefather of Kim Tohŭi),* whose
posthumous name was Prince Yŏnghŭng. A poem of his had been posted up in the Ŭisŏng Guest House, which read:

The garden of the Guest House wood
    Holds in its shade a towering hall.
The perfumed wind makes dance the □
    And tinkling sounds greet late the moon.

The silken smoke enwraps the trees,
    The rains recede, the hills step forth.
A distant scholar takes first place
    And rules his province from this hall.

These verses were repeated from lip to lip but later the hall was
burned in the war and the post-board was lost. Many years passed and
it was forgotten. A certain governor came to the county to find the old
verse that was so famous. The people of the county, however, did not
know and had no idea of how it went.

At that time the magistrate O had a daughter who was engaged to
be married to a son of a Minister Chang. O brought his daughter with

him. His daughter went crazy and began to recite the poem. The people of the county recorded it gladly and there it is today.

* Kim Tohŭi [1866–1925] was a close friend of Gale and one of his *hanmun* "pundits." After Kim's death, Gale arranged for his private library to be purchased by the Library of Congress.

金英（憲）公之垈 [岱]1) 題義城館詩曰 :

聞韶 2) 公館後園深　　中有危樓百尺餘 [餘尺]

香風十里捲珠簾　　明月一聲飛玉笛

烟輕柳腰 [影 7)] 細相連　雨霽山光濃欲滴

龍荒（折臂）3) 甲枝郎 4)　仍按憑軒 [闌] 尤可惜

當時膾炙人口　後十年樓火於兵板隨而亡

後又數十年　有一按廉到縣　索金詩甚急　邑人

無如 [知] 之何　時縣倅 [守] 吳某有一女　曾與約婚

於張宰相之子　而吳携與之任　女發狂亂語忽詠

出金詩　邑人大喜錄呈按廉　詩至今懸在壁上

「東人詩話」5)

1 金之岱 [1190–1266; born Chungnyong 仲龍; posthumous epithet Yŏnghŏn 英憲]: military official under Wŏnjong 元宗 [r. 1259–74; 1219–74] of the Koryŏ dynasty [918–1392]. Founder of the Ch'ŏngdo Kim-ssi 清道 金氏 clan.
2 聞韶: old name used during the Silla dynasty 新羅 [57 BC–AD 935] for Ŭisŏng 義城 in North Kyŏngsang Province.
3 龍荒折臂: battle-scarred from long experience on the barbarian wilderness frontier.
4 甲枝郎 = *changwŏllang* 壯元郎: a candidate who wins first place in the state examination.
5 「東人詩話」: collection of remarks on poetry (*sihwa*) compiled by Sŏ Kŏjŏng 徐居正 [1420–88], scholar-official under King Sŏngjong 成宗 [r. 1469–94; 1457–94].

——— **14** ———

Sin Sukchu's Angel

Vol. I: 16; translated 31 May 1921; Diary XVI, p. 160; 75.

When Sin Sukchu was a young man he came to Seoul to try the *alsŏng* examination.* He was on his way with a friend to the Confucian temple when they came upon an object in the way that attracted their attention that stood with its mouth open. Its upper lip touched heaven, its lower the earth. The friend, afraid of it, sidled away while Sin went straight into the mouth between the lips.

There he met a green-coated fairy lad (*tongja*) who bowed and said, "I desire to attend Your Excellency and whatever you may order or desire, I shall serve you."

Sin said, "Good."

From that time on the fairy attended his every [need] and never left his side. Sin won first place in the examination. Whatever was to happen the fairy always gave him word.

On the day of his death, the fairy wept and took his departure. Sin died momentarily afterwards.

* *alsŏng* examination: lit. "royal visitation examination"; a special civil service examination given in celebration of the royal visitation to the National Shrine to Confucius (Munmyo 文廟) at the Confucian Academy (Sŏnggyun'gwan 成均館). See note 2 below.

신 문 충 숙 주
申文忠叔舟 1)　少時赴謁聖試 2)　與友人同往成均館

견 로 중 일 물 장 구　상 순 순 착 어 천　하 순 순 접
見路中一物張口　上唇[屑]着於天　下唇[屑]接

어 지　동 행 황 포 각 보　취 타 로 이 행　숙 주 직 입 량 순
於地　同行惶怖却步　就他路而行　叔舟直入兩唇

순 중　유 청 의 동 자 배 이 언 왈　원 종 조 대　유
[屑]中　有靑衣童子拜而言曰：願從措大 3) 遊

유 소 지 사　숙 주 암 지　자 차 동 자 수 숙 주 불 소 리
惟所持使　叔舟頷之　自此童子隨叔舟不少離

수 첩 괴 과　범 유 길 흉　막 불 선 사 이 언 급　기 사 야
遂捷魁科　凡有吉凶　莫不先事而言及　其死也

동 자 읍 이 사 거　미 기 이 졸　어 우 야 담
童子泣而辭去　未幾而卒　「於于野談」 4)

---

1 申叔舟 [1417–75; styled Pŏmong 泛翁; sobriquet Pohanjae 保閑齋; ancestral seat Koryŏng 高靈; posthumous epithet Munch'ung 文忠]: scholar-official under King Sŏngjong 成宗 [r. 1469–94; 1457–94]. His father was Sin Chang 申檣 [1382–1433].

2 謁聖科: an ad hoc civil service examination held before the king. The occasion began with a royal procession to the Confucian Academy (Sŏnggyun'gwan 成均館), at which the king paid homage to Confucius's tablet.

3 措大: a student of Confucian learning; a scholar living content in honest poverty.

4 「於于野談」: miscellany compiled by Yu Mongin 柳夢寅 [1559–1623], scholar-official under Kwanghaegun 光海君 [r. 1608–23; 1575–1641].

——— 15 ———

Brotherly Love

Vol. I: 16; translated 30 May 1921; Diary, XVI, p. 160; 76.

Sŏng Misu was a religious man of the hermit order who had a brother Tamnyŏn. They were the sons of Sŏng Hŭi and great-grandsons of Sŏng Yong. They were both great scholars. Together with their family they made some fifteen persons.

Three years after their father and mother had passed away, Misu called his brothers and relations in order to divide the inheritance.

When anything was specially precious, he said, "Give it to so-and-so." When one of the slaves was particularly capable, he said, "Give him thus-and-such." If anything was old or broken, he would say, "This was used by my father and mother; very precious, I'll take it."

His sister was wife of Yi Chŏnggyŏng who had no house. When Misu desired to give them the house he was in, his brothers urged him not to do it.

Said they, "The home goes to the eldest son."

But Misu said, "We are all born of the same father and mother. Shall I take all this for myself alone?"

He gathered together all the cloth goods that he had in hand and gave it to Chŏnggyŏng so that he could buy a house. All was peace and gladness in the home.

성 처 사 담 수　　자 미 수　　성 정 재 담 년　　자 이 수
成 處 士 聃 壽 1) 字 眉 叟　成 靜 齋 聃 年 2) 字 耳 壽

인 수 이 수　　개 인 재 희　희　　지 자　　문 숙 공　석　용
[仁 叟 耳 壽] 皆 仁 齋 禧 [熹] 3) 之 子　文 肅 公 (石) 瑢 4)

지 증 손 야　　구 이 문 아 저 명　　형 제 남 매 십 여 인　　부 모 망
之 曾 孫 也　俱 以 文 雅 著 名　兄 弟 娚 妹 十 餘 人　父 母 亡

삼 년 지 상 필　　회 형 제 분 재　　견 물 지 유 색 자　　즉 왈
三 年 之 喪 畢　會 兄 弟 分 財　見 物 之 有 色 者　則 曰：

여모　노지유실자　즉왈　여모　기파쇄파렬　즉왈
與某　奴之有實者　則曰：與某　其破碎罷劣　則曰：

차부모지의야　아기위지　이매리정［정］견
此父母之意也　我其爲之　以妹李廷［庭］堅 5)

지처무가　우욕이본택여지　제제고간（왈：）（부모）
之妻無家　又欲以本宅與之　諸弟固諫（曰：）（父母）

가사（당）전지장자　미수왈　균시부모지자
家舍（當）傳之長子　眉叟曰：均是父母之子

아불（가）독유가야　즉출소유면포　위정［정］견
我不（可）獨有家也　卽出所有綿布　爲廷［庭］堅

매가지자　일문지내인무간언　청파극담
買家之資　一門之內人無間言　「靑坡劇談」6)

1 成聃壽 [?–1456; styled Misu 眉叟; sobriquet Injae 仁齋 and Mundu 文斗;
  ancestral seat Ch'angnyŏng 昌寧; posthumous epithet Chŏngsuk 靖肅]:
  one of the "six surviving subjects" (*saengyuksin* 生六臣). In narratives about
  early Chosŏn history, King Sejo 世祖 [1455–68; 1417–68] is generally remembered as a usurper of the throne from his nephew King Tanjong 端宗
  [r. 1452–5; 1441–57]. In 1456, four months after King Sejo's enthronement, a
  group of civilian and military officials attempted to reinstate King Tanjong,
  to no avail. This failure cost the lives of six members of the Hall of Worthies
  (Chiphyŏnjŏn 集賢殿), a research institute refurbished by King Sejong
  [r. 1418–50; 1397–1450] for recruiting the best scholars in the country. These
  six scholars are commonly referred to as the "six martyred subjects" (*sayuksin*
  死六臣). The term "six surviving subjects" refers to six other scholars who
  withdrew from their official posts due to their disillusionment with King
  Sejo's usurpation (and were spared execution).
2 成聃年 [styled Insu 仁叟 or 仁壽; sobriquet Chŏngjae 靜齋; ancestral seat
  Ch'angnyŏng 昌寧]: scholar-official under King Sŏngjong 成宗 [r. 1469–94;
  1447–94] and brother of Sŏng Tamsu 成聃壽. His father was Sŏng Hŭi 成熺.
3 成熺 [dates unknown; styled Yonghoe 用晦; sobriquet Injae 仁齋; ancestral
  seat Ch'angnyŏng 昌寧]: scholar-official under King Munjong 文宗
  [r. 1450–2; 1414–52]. His father was Sŏng Kae 成槪 [?–1440].
4 成石璘 [1352–403; styled Paegok 伯玉; sobriquet Hoe'gok 檜谷; ancestral
  seat Ch'angnyŏng 昌寧; posthumous epithet Munsuk 文肅]: scholar-official

under King T'aejong 太宗 [r. 1400–18; 1367–1422]. His father was Sŏng
  Yŏwan 成汝完 [1309–97], great-grandfather of Sŏng Tamsu [?-1456].
5 李庭堅: Sŏng Tamsu's brother-in-law.
6「青坡劇談」: miscellany compiled by Yi Yuk 李陸 [1438–98]. Gale's translations of several entries from this collection are found in *Korean Folk Tales:
  Imps, Ghosts and Fairies* (London and New York: J.M. Dent & Sons, E.P.
  Dutton & Co., 1913).

——— **16** ———

Bringing Up a Son

Vol. I: 17; translated 30 May 1921; Diary XVI, pp. 160–1; 79.

Yi Hugi was a man of Chŏnŭi and a grandson of Yi Chesin. His son was
Yi Haengjin, Vice-President of the Home Office and Vice-President of
the College of Literati. The two sons were recipients of high office and
yet the father treated them as though they were his slaves. He forbade
their ever touching drink of any kind.

On a certain day a minister brought wine and drank along with the
Vice-President of the College of Literati (THE SECOND SON).

Yi Hugi heard of this and sent a servant to summon his son. He called
out, "Have him arrested."

He prepared to have him beaten across his buttocks, but the minister
who had brought the wine, anxious for his forgiveness and pardon,
came and made special request.

The gateman came in and said such-and-such minister has come.

Yi Hugi shouted out, "My boy has gone counter to my commands
and so I beat him. Has the minister never had a father that he so acts?"

The minister, in great fear, did not dare to enter but turned and went
home.

The ancestors thus brought up their sons.

李正 1) 厚基 2) 全義人　清江濟臣 3) 之孫　而吏曹參判

行進 4) 及副學 5) 行遇 6) 之父也　兩子俱顯於朝　而管

속 지 무 이 노 예　　상 시 금 주 엄　　일 일　　모 재 패 주 래
束之無異奴隷　常時禁酒嚴　一日　某宰佩酒來

부 학 여 지 음　　정 문 지　　사 노 초 부 학　　지 즉 졸 입
副學與之飲　正聞之　使奴招副學　至則捽入

장 장 비　　모 재 걸 침　　종 부 학 이 지　　혼 자 입 고
將杖臂　某宰乞寢　踵副學而至　閽者入告

모 재 승 초 지 입 문 의　　정 대 성 왈　　오 자 위 오 언
某宰乘軺至入門矣　正大聲曰：吾子違吾言

고 오 장 지　　모 재 독 무 부 호　　기 재 대 해 불 감 입
故吾杖之　某宰獨無父乎　其宰大駭不敢入

종 외 환 거　　선 배 엄 속 자 제 여 차
從外還去　先輩嚴束子弟如此

1 正: senior third-grade post in the Office of the Royal Clan (Tonnyŏngbu 敦寧府) or the Office of the Royal Genealogy (Chongch'inbu 宗親府). *Chŏng* indicates a *tanghagwan* 堂下官 (lit. "officials of the lower end of the hall" = high-ranking officials whose rank did not reach higher than senior third grade).

2 李厚基 [dates unknown; styled Sŭpchŏng 習靜; ancestral seat Chŏnŭi 全義]: scholar-official under King Injo 仁祖 [r. 1623–49; 1595–1649]. His grandfather was Yi Chesin 李濟臣 [see the following note].

3 李濟臣 [1536–84; styled Mongŭng 夢應; sobriquet Ch'ŏnggang 清江; ancestral seat Chŏnŭi 全義; posthumous epithet P'yŏnggan 平簡]: scholar-official under King Sŏnjo 宣祖 [r. 1567–1608; 1552–1608]. His father was Yi Munsŏng 李文誠 [1503–75].

4 李行進 [1597–1665; styled Sagyŏm 士謙; sobriquet Chiam 止菴; ancestral seat Chŏnŭi 全義]: scholar-official under King Hyŏnjong 顯宗 [r. 1659–74; 1641–74]. His father was Yi Hugi 李厚基 (see note 2).

5 副學: short for *pujehak* 副提學, senior third-grade post in the Office of the Special Counselors (Hongmungwan 弘文館); *pujehak* is a *tangsanggwan* 堂上官 (lit. "officials of the upper end of the hall" = high-ranking officials whose rank reached higher than senior third grade) position.

6 李行遇 [1606–51; styled Sahoe 士會; sobriquet Su'nam 水南; ancestral seat Chŏnŭi 全義]: scholar-official under King Injo 仁祖 [r. 1623–49; 1595–1649]. His father was Yi Hugi (see note 2) and his brother was Yi Haengjin 李行進 (see note 4).

——— **17** ———

Great Courage

Vol. I: 18; translated 31 May 1921; Diary XVI, p. 161; 83.

Hŏ Chong (Sangudang) Prince Ch'ungjŏng was a man of Yangch'ŏn. He was from earliest years of a very steady and strong nature. When on the way he would look neither to the right nor left. He always seemed to be deeply engrossed in thought. Sometimes, too, he would go the wrong way thus.

Once when along with his associates he was studying the character, a thief came into the room and carried away his clothes and his shoes as well. All his companions were deeply incensed about it but Hŏ Chong paid no noticeable attention to it. He dipped his pen in the ink and wrote:

> If you've decided to steal my clothes,
>   Leave my shoes, I pray;
> But here you've taken clothes and shoes as well –
>   You've broken the laws of the stealing world.

His companions learned by this something of his inner strength. He passed his examinations and became Guardian of the Armoury.

At that time an eclipse of the sun occurred. And then too he sent a memorial concerning the state. In his petition he crossed the king's wishes very greatly so that he was commanded to his presence. He took from the petition several sentences and pretending to be very angry, said, "I have made no hundred day excursions for sport or pleasure. I never have made a dough ox to serve instead of the real one in sacrifices. How dare you compare me with Xia Kang or Liang Wudi?"

He ordered a strong man to bring him forth and to beat him with the heavy bastinado. Those who looked on trembled in their legs.

The king then drew his sword and laid it with its sheath across his knees and said, "When I draw thus my sword from its sheath, strike off his head."

He drew and drew and drew. The blade shone and glinted in their eyes. Little by little it all came forth but the merest point. The headman with his axe raised looked to see when all was out.

Still Hŏ's face changed not but was as □□ hadn't been shaken in the least by the gesture.

The king then suddenly put back his sword into its sheath and said, "A brave man, a brave man, indeed. I shall have use for you."

尚友堂許忠貞公琮 [1] 字宗卿　陽川人　梅叟憕 [2]

之曾孫　野堂錦 [3] 之四代孫也　自少沈毅　嘗於行路

未嘗見左右　凝然若沈思者　或至迷道　嘗結同

儕讀書　偸兒入其室　盡將衣屨去　諸伴莫不懊恨

公怡然不以爲意　取筆書壁上曰：

既奪吾衣兮

宜吾鞋之莫偸

既奪衣又偸鞋兮

竊爲盜先生不取也

識者始服其量　及釋褐 [4] 爲軍器直長 [5]　有日食

上疏論時事　凡六語多批鱗 [6]　上趣召內閣

摘疏中語　佯加威怒以試之曰：予无十旬不返 [7]

이 면 대 희 지 실
以麵代犧之失 8)　　爾何以予比於夏康梁武 9)
이 하 이 여 비 어 하 강 량 무

명 력 사 졸 하
命力士捽下　以圓杖杖之　傍侍股栗　上又取匣
이 원 장 장 지　방 시 고 률　상 우 취 갑

검 횡 슬 상 령 왈
劍橫膝上令曰：　見吾劍拔盡匣　卽令行斬　徐徐拔出
견 오 검 발 진 갑　즉 령 행 참　서 서 발 출

상 인 조 인 섬 섬
霜刃照人閃閃　（拔）垂盡　力士方挾斧
발 수 진　력 사 방 협 부

질 목 기 검 이 대 지
鑕目其劍以待之　公猶不變色　對隨問無錯
공 유 불 변 색　대 수 문 무 착

상 환 납 갑 검 왈
上還納匣劍曰：　眞壯士也　自是大奇之　終至大用
진 장 사 야　자 시 대 기 지　종 지 대 용

룡 천 담 적 기
「龍泉（談）寂記」10)

1 許琮 [1434–94; styled Chonggyŏng 宗卿 or Chongji 宗之; sobriquet
   Sangudang 尙友堂; ancestral seat Yangch'ŏn 陽川; posthumous epithet
   Ch'ungjŏng 忠貞]: scholar-official under King Sŏngjong 成宗 [r. 1469–94;
   1457–94]. He is a descendant of Hŏ Kong 許珙 [1233–91] and son of Hŏ Son
   許蓀 [dates unknown].
2 許惼 [dates unknown; styled Wŏndŏk 元德; sobriquet Maesu 梅叟]: his
   father was Hŏ Kŭm 許錦 [see note 3], the grandfather of Hŏ Chong 許琮
   [1434–94].
3 許錦 [1340–88; styled Chaejung 在中; sobriquet Yadang 野堂; ancestral seat
   Yangch'ŏn 陽川; posthumous epithet Munjŏng 文正]: scholar-official from
   the late Koryŏ period. His father was Hŏ Kyŏng 許絅 [dates unknown].
4 釋褐: pass the highest-level civil service examination (*munkwa* 文科) and
   enter the bureaucracy for the first time.
5 軍器直長: a junior seventh-grade post in the Government Arsenal
   (*kun'gisi* 軍器寺).
6 批鱗 = *yŏngnim* 逆鱗: lit. "go against the *kirin*" = offend the king.
7 十旬不返: lit. "not return after ten *sun*" (*sun* is a unit of measure for counting days in a month; three *sun* constitute a month) = engrossed in hunting
   and not attending to affairs of state. The expression comes from the story

of Taikang 太康, a descendant of King Wu 禹王 [dates unknown] of the
State of Xia 夏 [2070–1600 BC], who went hunting and did not return for
some hundred days.

8 麵代犧之失: lit. "the transgression of using dough instead of meat for
sacrificial ceremonies." This expression comes from the episode in which
Emperor Wu 武帝 [464–549] of the Liang dynasty 梁 [r. 502–49] upheld
Buddhism and used flour-based comestibles instead of meat in sacrifices.

9 夏康梁武: Kang, descendant of King Wu of Xia, and Emperor Wu of Liang.

10 「龍泉談寂記」: collection of stories written by Kim Allo 金安老 [1481–
1537], scholar-official under King Chungjong 中宗 [r. 1506–44; 1488–1544].

———— 18 ————

A Great Man

Vol. I: 18; translated 31 May 1921; Diary XVI, p. 162; 84.

Chŏng Okhyŏng was a man of Naju and son of Chŏng Sugang. He passed
his examination and became an official of the College of Literature.

Once on the road he met a man who was overloaded with drink and
he turned toward Chŏng's servant and said, "You are the rascal that
beat me."

He caught him by the topknot and beat him over the face.

Though beaten and pummelled thus, the servant made no reply but
simply put down his head and held fast to the bridle.

Chŏng was pulled here and there and nearly upset □□ and □, but
never once did he show the slightest sign of anger.

The drunken creature when he had exhausted his strength let go and
went off.

When he had gone a half dozen steps, he came back and bowed before his horse and said, "Your Excellency will become Prime Minister
surely." Chŏng just nodded but asked nothing □□ and □□.

정 공 안 공 옥 향　　형　　　자 가 중　　라 주 인　　월 헌 수 강

丁恭安公玉享 [享]1) 字嘉仲　羅州人　月軒壽崗 2)

지 자 야　　위 직 학　　시　　어 도 중 봉 일 사 주 자

之子也　爲直學 3) 時　於道中逢一使酒者 4)

謂執鞚者 5)　曾搏己　曳其髮批頰無數　其執鞚者

雖見曳而猶不釋鞚　丁公隨其鞚者見曳而或東或西

良久而終不怒　使酒者力疲乃解　去五六步　復來拜

於馬前曰：夫 [大] 人當作政丞云　公竟唯唯而不問

1　Chŏng Okhyŏng 丁玉亨 [1486–1549; styled Kajung 嘉仲; sobriquet Wŏlbong 月峰; ancestral seat Naju 羅州; posthumous epithet Kongan 恭安]: scholar-official under King Myŏngjong 明宗 [r. 1545–67; 1534–67]. His father was Chŏng Sugang 丁壽崗 [see note 2].
2　丁壽崗 [1454–1527; styled Pulbung 不崩; sobriquet Wŏrhŏn 月軒; ancestral seat Naju 羅州]: scholar-official during the reign of King Chungjong 中宗 [r. 1506–44; 1488–1544]. His father was Chŏng Kŭp 丁伋 [dates unknown].
3　直學 = 直提學: senior third-grade post in the Office of the Special Counselors (Hongmungwan 弘文館).
4　使酒者: drunkard.
5　執鞚者: lit. "one who controls the reins" = a groom.

———— **19** ————

Holidays

Vol. I: 27; translated 1 June 1921; Diary XVI, pp. 162–3, 123.

The various holidays of the year are as follows. On the evening of the last day of the year, there are fire works (*p'okchuk*) and the beating of gongs (*myŏngbal*). These are called drivers of devils (*pang maegwi*).*

On the morning of the first of the first moon, pictures are pasted on the doors and walls of the entrance, such as horned demons and hobgoblins. These are called scarers away of evil spirits (*pyŏksa*).†

Also on the last day of the year friends are visited as a farewell to the old year (*kwase*). Visits on the first of the first moon are called New Year Greetings (*sebae*). The first day of the New Year is a holiday and no work is done even in public office. All meet for a good time. The first *cha, o, chin,* and *hae* days are also holidays (the rat, horse, dragon, and pig days). The fire on the Pig Day is to scorch the snout of the wild hogs that injure the fields, and the fires on the Rat Day are to scorch the snouts of the rats that □ fields as well.

For three days in the New Year no work is done all □. The fifteenth day of the first moon is called the Great Night (*wŏnsŏk*) and *yakpap* or sweet cake is eaten.

The first day of the second moon is called the Flower Morning (*hwa-jo*); pine leaves or needles are scattered about the court. Thus is done to rid the place of evil smelling insects – the pine needles so do.

The third day of the third moon is called the Upper Snake Day (*sangsa-il*). It is called the Festival of Trampling the Green (*tapch'ŏngjŏl*). People go out for picnics and there make Flower Bread (*hwajŏn*) and drink spirits.

The eighth day of the fourth moon is commonly called the Birthday of Sŏkkamoni and so at each house a lantern is hung up – JUST AS LANTERNS ARE HUNG UP BY CHRISTIANS. The rich use silken lanterns of many colours.

The fifth day of the fifth moon is Tano when they hang an artemisia tiger at the door and brew the sweet calamum. The people of Seoul specially hang up swings.

The fifteeth day of the sixth moon is called Yudu (Washing the Head). In olden days the eunuchs of Koryŏ would go to the east side streams to escape the heat, pull down their hair and let it soak in the water. They would drink and call the day Yudu. This was also called a holiday. They ate a kind of bread called *sudan* and also the leaves of the *hoehwa* tree.

The fifteenth day of the seventh moon is called the Day of One Hundred Seeds. In the honour of the Buddhists they plant a hundred different kinds of flowers. Women and girls bring grains to offer sacrifice for the soul.

On the fifteenth of the eighth month is the day for beholding the moon.

The ninth day of the ninth moon is the day for going to high places.

The Winter Solstice is the day for eating bean (*p'at*) porridge.

The *kyŏngsin* day is one on which no one sleeps – an old-fashioned custom.

* See note 2 below.
† See note 5 below.

歲時名日所擧之事（非一）　除夜 1) 前日爆竹鳴鈸

而逐出曰：　放枚鬼 2)　淸晨付畵物於門戶窓扉

如角鬼 3) 鍾馗 4) 之狀者曰：辟邪 5)　除日相謁曰：

過歲　元日相謁曰：歲拜　元日人皆不仕［事］

爭聚遊　新歲子午辰亥日如之　且兒輩聚蒿草 6) 燒

苑園　亥日燻貛啄［喙］7) 子日燻鼠啄［燻鼠］8)

諸司限三日　不仕是月十五日爲元夕 9)　故設藥飯

二月初一日爲花朝　乘曉散松葉於門庭　俗曰：

惡其臭虫 10)　作針辟也　三月三日（曰：）

上巳 11)　俗云踏靑 12) 之節　人皆出遊郊野　煮花設

酌　作鐥而食　四月初八日　俗言釋迦如來生辰也

是日　家家樹竿燃燈　豪富大張彩繃［棚］13) 以爲樂

五月五日曰：端午　懸艾虎 14) 於門　泛菖蒲 15) 於

酒　都人樹繃［棚］於街市　設鞦韆之會［戲］16)

六月十五日曰：流頭　昔高麗宦侍輩　避熱於東川

散髮于水　浮沈飲酒曰：流頭　世俗因以是日爲名日

作水團餅 17) 而食之　盖槐葉冷淘 [淘] 18) 之（遺）意也

七月十五日俗稱百種　僧家聚百種花果　設盂蘭盆 19)

婦女坌集　納美 [米] 穀　唱亡親之靈而祭　中秋 20)

玩月　（九月）九日 21) 登高　冬至豆粥 22)　庚申不眠

亦皆古之遺意也　「傭 [慵] 齋叢話」 23)

1　除夜 = *chesŏk* 除夕: the last day of the year.
2　枚鬼 = *maegwi* 埋鬼: a type of agricultural folk festival from the second to the fifteenth day of the first month by the lunar calendar; a musical group visits each and every house in the village while playing music for the purpose of dispelling evil spirits and praying for good luck.
3　角鬼: *tokkaebi* = a horned goblin.
4　鍾馗: a spirit that dispels pestilences or other evil spirits.
5　辟邪: dispel evil spirits.
6　蒿草: mugwort; artemisia.
7　燻豭喙: lit. "scorch the snout of a hog."
8　燻鼠: lit. "scorch mice"; cf. modern *chwibul nori* – the custom of setting fire to the rice paddies and fields to scare away rodents on the eve of the first Rat Day (*sangja-il* 上子日) of the month.
9　元夕: the night of the fifteenth of the first month by the lunar calendar.
10　臭蟲: foul-smelling insects; the common form of 蟲 is 虫.
11　上巳: third day of the third month by the lunar calendar.
12　踏靑: a spring custom of taking a walk on new grass.
13　彩棚: a temporary pavilion decorated with coloured fabrics.
14　艾虎: grass tiger made of mugwort, used to chase away misfortune.
15　菖蒲: *Acorus calamus* (a type of plant that grows by ponds and lakes); sweet flag.

16 鞦韆之戲: playing on a swing.
17 水團餅: a small cake made of rice or wheat and served in honeyed water, sprinkled with pine nuts.
18 槐葉冷淘: rinsing locust leaves in ice-cold water.
19 盂蘭盆: a Buddhist ritual invoking and honouring the spirits of deceased ancestors; seventh month by the lunar calendar.
20 中秋 = *chungch'u* 仲秋 ~ the Harvest Festival, *ch'usŏk* 秋夕: fifteenth day of the eighth month by the lunar calendar.
21 九月九日: also known as *chungnyangjŏl* 重陽節; the Double-Nine Festival.
22 豆粥: red bean soup.
23 「慵齋叢話」: miscellany compiled by Sŏng Hyŏn 成俔 [1439–1504].

———— **20** ————

Nam Iung (1575–1648 AD)

Vol. I: 36; translated 2 June 1921; Diary XVI, p. 163; 164.

Nam Iung was a man of most determined disposition. When he was Chief Justice a certain *mudang** carried on much deception among the people.

He had her arrested and was about to punish her when she brought her miraculous power into play and caused the chair where he was seated to be beaten. The people standing about were greatly alarmed and turned pale.

Disturbed by this, Nam was more determined than ever to carry out his will so he pushed the chair away and sat on the mat. The mat also was shaken, and then he changed his place to a seat on the floor where he leaned against the wall. There he was solid and ordered her killed.

* A female practitioner of ceremonies in the service of departed souls or for the purpose of telling fortunes.

南春城以雄 1) 性剛果 其爲都憲 2) 也 有巫挾妖

術惑衆者 拿致憲府 3) 將刑之 巫能施其術

뇨 공 소 좌 교 의　　　사 불 득 안 신　　　좌 우 막 불 경 황 실 색
撓公所坐交椅　　使不得安身　　左右莫不驚惶失色

공 의 연 불 동　　　각 교 의 이 좌 석　　　무 우 뇨 지　　　공 내 철
公毅然不動　　却交椅而坐席　　巫又撓之　　公乃掇

석 급 지 의　　　의 헌 벽 이 좌　　　무 불 능 뇨　　　수 장 살 지
席及地衣 4)　　倚軒壁而坐　　巫不能撓　　遂杖殺之

1 南以雄 [1575–1648; styled Chŏngman 敵萬; sobriquet Sibuk 市北; ancestral seat Ŭiryŏng 宜寧; posthumous epithet Munjŏng 文貞]: scholar-official under King Injo 仁祖 [r. 1623–49; 1595–1649]. His grandfather was Nam Ŭngun 南應雲 [1509–87].
2 都憲 = *taesahŏn* 大司憲: Inspector-General.
3 憲府 = Sahŏnbu 司憲府: Office of the Inspector-General.
4 地衣: a straw mat decorated with cloth edges used for ancestral worship.

——— **21** ———

Kim Chip's Virtue

Vol. I: 37; translated 3 June 1921; Diary XVI, p. 163; 167.

Kim Chip (Sindokchae), when a young man, saw the little girl servant of a friend who brought a letter. A great rain came on at the time and she had no opportunity to return. He had her sleep in the little side room next to his. She was young and quite pretty. He thought of her in the night and found it very hard to keep his mind in control. He therefore locked the door and came back and lay down. Still his mind went out toward the little maid. He then threw the key up onto the roof and so saved himself and his good name.

김 신 독 재　　소 시　　유 친 우 가 비 자 지 소 찰　　적 치 대 우
金愼(獨)齋 1)少時　有親友家婢子持小札　適值大雨

종 일 불 득 환　　공 불 득 이 지 숙 기 비 어 별 방　　기 비 년
終日不得還　　公不得已止宿其婢於別房　　其婢年

소 색 미　　공 야 와 심 동 난 제　　내 기 이 약　　쇄 기 문
少色美　公夜臥心動難制　乃起以鑰 2) 鎖其門

환 와 이 심 유 동　　우 투 기 쇄 시　　어 옥 상　　공 가 위 불
還臥而心猶動　又投其鎖匙 3) 於屋上　公可謂不

부 기 호 의
負其號矣

1 愼獨齋: sobriquet of Kim Chip 金集 [1574–1656; styled Sagang 士剛; ancestral seat Kwangsan 光山; posthumous epithet Mungyŏng 文敬]: scholar-official under King Hyojong 孝宗 [r. 1649–59; 1619–59]. His father was Kim Changsaeng 金長生 [1548–1631].
2 鑰: a lock.
3 鎖匙: a key.

—————— 22 ——————

Firing the House on the Imjin River

Vol. I: 38; translated 3 June 1921; Diary XVI, p. 163; 171.

Yi Haego had a slave called Aenam. When the Japan War of 1592 came on and the king had to fly north for his life, Yi Haego was in office in the palace. He therefore started out on foot with the king.

Hearing of this sudden departure, Aenam hurriedly prepared a saddle and horse and hurried after, overtaking his master at Hongjewŏn. There he mounted and rode. By night they came wading the streams as far as the Imjin River.

Here a great rain fell and the night was as dark as Egypt so that nothing could be seen. All the village people had fled for their lives and no one could see where the boats were. The whole government was in a state of indescribable distress. What to do they knew not. Aenam then set fire to the houses on the bank of the river so that the night shone as the day. Here boats were seen fastened by the bank of the river and so the king got across.

King Sŏnjo asked who had set fire to the houses and so provided the light, and was told it was Aenam. The king was greatly astonished at this and from this time on sent food from his table to Aenam.

Aenam liked to gather all kinds of dried things in his pocket. They arrived in Paekch'ŏn and found how all the armoury was impoverished and Aenam gave forth all the things he had gathered together. The king was once again greatly astonished.

When the war was over they returned to Seoul. Here he called Aenam and with his own hand gave him a pair of buttons (gold). Aenam took them and put them in his pocket. He never wore them on his headdress.

리 해 고　　노 자 명 애 남 자　　임 진 왜 구 졸 지 대 가 서 행 시
李海皐 1) 奴子名愛男者　壬辰倭寇猝至大駕西幸時

공 이 설 서　　직 궐 중 도 보 호 종　　애 남 문 변　　급 구 안 마
公以說書 2)　直闕中徒步扈從 3)　愛男聞變　急具鞍馬

조 공 어 홍 제 원　　이 승 공 성 야 발 섭　　행 도 림 진
遭公於弘濟院 4)　以乘公星夜跋涉 5)　行到臨津 6)

대 우 하 주　　야 흑 여 칠　　지 지 척 불 변　　촌 민 진 도
大雨下注　夜黑如漆　只［咫］尺不辨　村民盡逃

불 지 선 박 하 처　　거 조 초 황 황　　계 무 소 출　　애 남
不知船泊何處　擧朝焦惶［遑］7)　計無所出　愛男

내 이 화 설　　강 변 촌 사　　통 명 여 주　　어 시　　견 선 수 척
乃以火爇 8) 江邊村舍　通明如晝　於是　見船數尺

계 재 강 변　　득 이 리 섭　　선 조　　문 소 려 멱 주 수 지 계 야
係在江邊　得以利涉　宣祖 9) 問燒廬覓舟誰之計也

시 신 대 이 애 남　　상 심 기 지　　자 시 어 선　　필 사 애 남
侍臣對以愛男　上甚奇之　自是御膳 10) 必賜愛男

애 남 매 이 건 물 성 제 포 대　　지 백 천　　이 어 선 궐 공
愛男每以乾物盛諸布岱　至白川 11) 而御膳闕供

애 남 출 대 중 진 지　　상 우 기 지　　란 정 환 도　　소 견 우 차 비
愛男出岱中進之　上尤奇之　亂定還都　召見于差備

문　　친 사 금 권　　애 남 납 제 낭 중　　종 신 불 착 운
門 12)　親賜金圈 13) 愛男納諸囊中　終身不着云

 1 海皐: sobriquet of Yi Kwangjŏng 李光庭 [1552–1627; styled Tŏkhwi 德輝; ancestral seat Yŏnan 延安]: scholar-official under King Injo 仁祖 [r. 1623–49; 1595–1649]. His father was Yi Chu 李澍 [1534–84].
 2 說書: a senior seventh-grade post in the Crown Prince Tutorial Office (Seja sigangwŏn 世子侍講院).
 3 扈從 = hoga 扈駕: escorting the king's procession.
 4 弘濟院: a post station outside the West Gate in Seoul.
 5 星夜跋涉: climbing a hill and crossing a river at night.
 6 臨津: a quay by the Imjin River.
 7 焦遑: anxious and flustered.
 8 火爇: set fire to.
 9 宣祖: King Sŏnjo [r. 1567–1608; 1552–1608].
10 御膳: dishes served at the royal table.
11 白川: a village in Hwanghae Province.
12 差備門: the front gate to an informal royal council hall at the palace (p'yŏnjŏn 便殿).
13 金圈 = kŭmgwanja 金貫子: gold buttons on a headdress.

—— **23** ——

Chang Hyŏn'gwang (1554–1637)

Vol. I: 37; translated 3 June 1921; Diary XVI, pp. 164–5; 173.

Chang Hyŏn'gwang, whose pen-name was Yŏhŏn, lived at Indong (Kyŏngsang). Once he was engaged in threshing out his barley on the court when a heavy rain came on. He had it gathered up and piled in the open hall. He was then an old man and his face was very dark. His clothes and headgear were old and soiled and gave him the appearance of an ordinary old man of the town.

At this time, the son of the governor, overtaken by the rain, came in and sat down in the open hall. He offered no greeting of any kind but bluntly asked, "You have a heap of barley here and will have something to chew at through the winter."

Chang replied, "We have been busy at labour and shall have enough to get through on."

Seeing the gold buttons behind his ears, the young man asked again, "Did you change some of your grain for those gold buttons?"

Chang replied, "There are lots of gold buttons about these days, so that even we dwellers in the country come in for a share."

The young man again asked, "Have you a son?"

"I have," said the old man.

"Is he at home?" inquired the governor's son.

"He has work just now in Seoul and is not here."

"What work has he in Seoul, pray?"

"He is Vice-President of the College of Literature at present."

At that time Chang's son Ŭngil was indeed Vice-President of the College.

"I have heard that Master Yŏhŏn lives somewhere near here. Do you happen to know him?"

Chang replied, "The young people of the neighbourhood who know nothing call me Yŏhŏn."

Startled at this, the son of the governor stepped down onto the court and said, "Your servant is ignorant and unenlightened. And I have committed a great fault. I ask to be punished."

Chang told him to come up to sit down but chided him, saying, "The son of the gentry must always be careful in his speech. Don't commit such an error again."

The governor brought his son and told that he had failed to teach his son and ha[ving] him [w]as such a disgraceful thing. He wanted to beat him but Chang compelled him to forget.

張旅軒 1) 居仁同 2)　嘗打麥 3) 于庭　大雨暴至

收置于軒上　公年老貌鬖 4)　衣冠甚巍 5)　頗似村老

時本道方伯之子　爲避雨入坐軒中而不禮焉

卒然問曰：打麥不少　君似食粟矣　答曰：能力穡僅

免飢餒矣　見鬖着金圈 6)　更問曰：無乃納粟 7)

호　답왈　근래가자　심다　고향인역득지의
乎　答曰：近來加資 8) 甚多　故鄉人亦得之矣

우문　군유자호　답왈　유계자　문　재가부
又問：君有子乎　答曰：有繼子 9)　問：在家否

유역방상경이　문　하역　답왈　방위부학역의
有役方上京耳　問：何役　答曰：方爲副學役矣

시공지자응일　위부학고야　우문왈　문려헌장
時公之子應一 10) 爲副學故也　又問曰：聞旅軒張

선생재차읍　혹지지부　왈　근처소년무지
先生在此邑　或知之否　曰：近處少年無知

칭아려헌의　도백자문지　불승경오 [황]
稱我旅軒矣　道伯子聞之　不勝驚悟 [惶]

하정이립왈　소자우미　획죄어선생　청수기벌
下庭而立曰：小子愚迷　獲罪於先生　請受其罰

공권사승헌이책지왈　사자언어불가불신　시후
公勸使升軒而責之曰：士子言語不可不愼　是後

수물부연　우후도백솔자이래　사기불능교자지죄
須勿復然　于後道伯率子而來　謝其不能敎子之罪

욕태기자　공력지지　내지
欲答其子　公力止之　乃止

1 旅軒: sobriquet of Chang Hyŏn'gwang 張顯光 [1554–1637; styled Tŏkhoe 德晦; ancestral seat Indong 仁同; posthumous epithet Mun'gang 文康]: scholar-official of King Injo 仁宗 [r. 1544–5; 1515–45] and a descendant of Chang Anse 張安世 [dates unknown].
2 仁同: a town in Kumi 龜尾 in North Kyŏngsang Province.
3 打麥: thresh barley.
4 貌黧: dark-skinned, swarthy.
5 彘: lit. "pig" = dirty.
6 金圈 = *kŭmgwanja* 金貫子: gold buttons on a headdress.
7 納粟: bribe the local government in order to gain an official post.
8 加資: (the king) promote somebody to a higher government post; a third-grade post or higher.

9 繼子: adopted son.

10 張應一 [1599–1676; styled Kyŏngsuk 經叔; sobriquet Ch'ŏngch'ŏndang 聽天堂; ancestral seat Indong 仁同; posthumous epithet Munmok 文穆]: scholar-official under King Sukchong 肅宗 [r. 1674–1720; 1661–1720]. He was adopted by Chang Hyŏn'gwang. His father was Chang Hyŏndo 張顯道 [dates unknown].

———— **24** ————

Who Was Ch'ŏnhwang-ssi's Father?

Vol. I: 40; translated 4 June 1921; Diary XVI, p. 165; 179.

There lived an official *tosa** who had to do with the examination of those who desired literary promotion. There was among these a white-haired old man who came in with the first volume of the *Saryak*† and asked that he might read the portion that dealt with Ch'ŏnhwang-ssi. The *tosa* looked with contempt on the old fellow with the child's book in his hand. He desired to shut him off and so asked a difficult question: "Do you know the name of the father of Ch'ŏnhwang-ssi?"

The man replied, "Does the *tosa* know the name of the father of the deputy governor of this county?"

The *tosa* in anger said, "Have could I know such a question as that?"

The old student then said, "If you don't know the name of a man living here and now, how could you expect me to know the name of the father of Ch'ŏnhwang-ssi who lived thousands of years ago?"

* Inspector. See note 1.
† *Outlined History.* See note 1.

석 유 일 도 사　　고 교 생 강　　유 백 발 교 생 협 사 략
昔 有 一 都 事 1) 考 校 生 講　有 白 髮 校 生 挾 史 略 2)

초 권 이 입　　청 천 황 씨　　대 문　　도 사 심 모 지　　욕 사 락 강
初 卷 而 入　請 天 皇 氏 3) 大 文　都 事 心 侮 之　欲 使 落 講

문 왈　이 지 천 황 씨 지 부 명 호　대 왈　아 사　지 차 읍 곽
問曰：爾知天皇氏之父名乎　對曰：亞使 4) 知此邑郭

좌 수 지 부 명 호　도 사 대 질 왈　오 하 지 지 호　교 생 왈
座首之父名乎　都事大叱曰：吾何知之乎　校生曰：

금 세 생 존 지 인 명　아 사 상 불 능 지　소 생 안 지 루 만 년 전
今世生存之人名　亞使尙不能知　小生安知累萬年前

천 황 씨 부 명 호　도 사 대 소
天皇氏父名乎　都事大笑

1 都事: a junior fifth-grade post, just below that of governer (*kamsa* 監司
  or *kwanch'alsa* 觀察使) at each provincial administrative headquarters
  (*kamyŏng* 監營).
2 史略 *Shilüe*: lit. "summaries of histories"; also known as the *Summaries
  of Eighteen Histories* (*Shiba shilüe* 十八史略) = a textbook of summaries of
  the eighteen dynastic histories compiled by Zeng Xianzhi 曾先之 [dates
  unknown] of the Yuan dynasty [1271–1368].
3 天皇氏: lit. "the august one in heaven" = one of the "Three August Ones"
  (*Sanhuang* 三皇) in ancient Chinese mythology.
4 亞使: lit. "the second in order" = another name for *tosa*.

——— **25** ———

The Faithful Spirit

Vol. I: 41; translated 4 June 1921; Diary XVI, pp. 165–7; 181.

In the days of Sŏngjong (1470–1495 AD) there lived in the village of
Hwaryong (Transforming Dragon) in the county of Hŭngdŏk, of Chŏlla,
O Chun who was a descendant of the gentry. He served his parents
with a most loyal and faithful spirit.

When they died he buried them on the Yŏngch'wi (Spiritual Hawk)
Hills. He built himself a house at the side of the grave and there he
ate only a bowl of thin gruel daily. His cries were so pitiful that he
was heard throughout the neighbourhood and all hearing wept tears
of sympathy.

Each night and morning before he offered sacrifice he would pour out a libation of "black" wine (water). The place of the spring was among the hills. The water was clear and sweet and the road to it ran some five *ri* or thereabouts. He went each time for a fresh supply with his bottle. He cared not for rain or wind, heat or cold.

One night he heard a great rumbling like thunder and it seemed as though the hills were falling. When he arose in the morning here was a spring of water that had burst forth from the side of the hut where he was. It was clear and sweet and a little sharp □ just like the spring that he had visited in the hills. He went into the hills to see how the first spring did □ and lo it was dried away. He used the spring water just before his door and no longer needed to take the journey. The people of the place called the spring *Hyo-gam ch'ŏn* (Spring of the Filial Son).

The grave was situated deep among the hills and there were tigers and leopards about, thieves as well. The members of his family were all anxious for him.

When he had passed the first anniversary of his father's death* he suddenly saw a great tiger come to the door of his hut and wait.

O reprimanded him, saying, "Do you mean my injury? If so, I cannot escape, do your will. But I am free from wrong."

The tiger wagged his tail and bowed his head as doing reverence.

O said further, "If you do not wish to do me wrong, why do you not go away?"

The tiger then went just beyond the enclosure and lay down and there he was day after day. He used to rub him and pet him just like an animal of the house.

On the first day of the month and the fifteenth the tiger would bring him a pig or a deer and so he would prepare his sacrificial meal. For two years from the first sacrifice days till the end no fierce beast or thief dared come anywhere near. When O had finished the whole course and returned home the tiger took his departure.

There are many evidences of this faithfulness of spirit moving the □ but few that equal this spring of water and the wonder of the friendly tiger.

At that time the governor of Chŏlla, hearing of this, made this matter known to King Sŏngjong and the king gave special orders that a gate of honour be erected to his memory, also that rice and silk be given him.

O lived to be sixty-five when he passed away. He was given the posthumous rank of Keeper of the Royal Stable. Sacrifices were offered at his shrine.

The present king (*? Yŏnsan or Chungjong*)[†] when ascending the throne was anxious about the multiplicity of shrine halls throughout the country and ordered that all erected since the year of *kabo* be destroyed.

On this, the scholars of Hŭngdŏk sent a petition relating all of the special acts of O Chun [whereupon] the king gave orders that that shrine be not touched. He declared this as a very special case.

Since that time the shrine had fallen into decay when O T'aeun came and made representations to the Sŏnggyun'gwan and had them send an order to the county *hyanggyo*[‡] that the shrine be restored and that the scholars of the county join in its repair.

I have heard that there was a man of the Han Kingdom called Jiang Shi who served his mother with a most faithful heart. His mother liked greatly to drink of river water and also liked the fresh sliced fish of the river. His wife used to go five or six *ri* daily to get the water. She would prepare this sliced salad with great care.

One day at the side of the house a spring of fresh water burst forth like the river water in flavour. Every morning there sprang forth from the spring two carp that could be used ☐ for the mother. The great Chimei rebels (적미)[§] said, "Such faithful service as this moves the spirit."

The Emperor Guangwu later appointed Jiang Shi a *langzhong*.

I have also read in the *Chouhai zhiyi* of a Cao Zeng, a man of Lu, who faithfully served his parents. In a great drought when all the wells dried up his mother desired fresh pure water to drink. Cao took a bottle and went to the side of the well where he knelt down, and lo a spring of water burst forth at his feet – a like case with O Chun.

It is said, "A devoted spirit moves heaven." A note to this reads, "Devoted loyalty can move anything." It is a faithful saying indeed. There we see the *Hyo-gam* Spring so clear and sweet. All the people of the place value it as gold and have surrounded it with stones. This is the first case of such devotion in the Kingdom of Chosŏn. Wonderful indeed.

---

* Mistranslation. Gale translates as "had passed his first examination."

† The king is most certainly King Yŏngjo, despite Gale's notes.

‡ *hyanggyo*: local school.

§ Gale gives the Korean reading of Chimei, 적미 Chyŏngmi.

성묘조시　호남흥덕현　화룡리유오준　자사족야
成廟朝時　湖南興德縣 1)　化龍里有吳浚 2)　者士族也

사친지효　친몰　장령취산　결려　묘측　일철
事親至孝　親沒　葬靈鷲山 3)　結廬 4)　墓側　日啜 5)

백죽일구　곡읍지애　청자운체　제전상설
白粥一甌　哭泣之哀　聽者隕涕 6)　祭奠常設

현주　이유천재산곡중　극청감　가거 거가　오리
玄酒 7)　而有泉在山谷中　極淸甘　可距 [距可] 五里

오군필친자제호급지　불이풍우한서소해　일석유
吳君必親自提壺汲之　不以風雨寒暑小懈　一夕有

성자산중여뢰　전일산진감　조기시지　즉유천용
聲自山中如雷　轉一山盡撼　朝起視之　則有泉湧

출려측　청결감렬　일여곡천　왕시곡천이갈의
出廬側　淸潔甘冽 8)　一如谷泉　往視谷泉已渴矣

수취용정천　득면원급지로　읍인명지효감천
遂取用庭泉　得免遠汲之勞　邑人名之孝感泉

려재심산지중　호표지소택　도적지소췌　가인
廬在深山之中　虎豹之所宅　盜賊之所萃 9)　家人

심우지　기과소상　일일홀견일대호준좌
甚憂之　旣過小祥 10)　一日忽見一大虎蹲坐 11)

우려전　오군계지왈　여욕해아야　기불가피임여이
于廬前　吳君戒之曰：汝欲害我耶　旣不可避任汝耳

단아무죄　호편도미　저두부복이궤　약치경
但我無罪　虎便掉尾 12)　低頭俯伏而跪　若致敬

자　오군왈　기불상해　하가불거　호즉출문외
者　吳君曰：旣不相害　何可不去　虎卽出門外

복이불거　일이위상　지어무롱　약가견시
伏而不去　日以爲常　至於撫弄 13)　若家犬豕 14)

이 매 당 삭 망 　 호 필 치 일 대 록 　 혹 산 저 어 려 전
而每當朔望 15)　虎必致一大鹿　或山猪於盧前

이 구 제 수 　 주 년 불 일 궐 　 맹 수 도 적 　 잉 이 병 적
以具祭需　周年不一闕　猛獸盜賊　仍以屛跡 16)

급 오 군 결 복 　 환 가 이 호 시 거 　 기 타 효 감 이 적 심 중
及吳君闋服 17)　還家而虎始去　其他孝感異跡甚衆

이 천 호 사 특 기 최 저 자 야 　 기 시 　 도 신 　 상 문 어 조
而泉虎事特其最著者也　其時　道臣 18)　上聞於朝

성 묘 특 명 정 려 사 미 백 　 오 년 륙 십 오 졸 　 증 사 복 정
成廟特命旌閭賜米帛　吳年六十五卒　贈司僕正 19)

읍 인 향 지 향 현 사 　 금 상 즉 조 　 심 환 근 래 원 우 지 폐
邑人享之鄉賢祠　今上卽祚 20)　深患近來院宇之弊 21)

명 철 갑 　 무 　 오 이 후 사 　 흥 덕 유 생 열 군 효 행 이 문
命撤甲 [戊] 午以後祠 22)　興德儒生列君孝行以聞

상 명 독 불 훼 　 역 광 전 　 야 　 기 사 근 파 상 폐 　 오 군 지
上命獨不毀　亦曠典 23)　也　其祠近頗傷弊　吳君之

후 태 운 　 구 사 래 고 우 태 학 　 청 자 태 학 행 간 통
後泰運 24)　具事來告于太學 25)　請自太學行簡通

우 본 읍 향 교 　 령 기 장 보 　 동 력 수 즙 　 오 이 득 문
于本邑鄉校　令其章甫 26)　同力修葺 27)　吾以得聞

동 한 　 시 촉 인 강 시 　 사 모 지 효 　 모 호 음 강 수 　 우 기
東漢 28)　時蜀人姜詩 29)　事母至孝　母好飮江水　又嗜

어 회 　 시 처 방 씨 　 거 사 륙 칠 리 급 수 이 계 　 시 력 작 공 회
魚膾　詩妻龐氏　去舍六七里汲水以繼　詩力作供膾

일 일 　 사 측 홀 용 감 천 　 미 여 강 수 　 매 조 약 출 량 리 이
一日　舍側忽湧甘泉　味如江水　每朝躍出兩鯉以

공 기 용 　 적 미 　 치 병 이 과 왈 　 경 대 효 　 필 촉 귀 신
供其用　赤眉 30)　馳兵而過曰：驚大孝　必觸鬼神

光武 31) 拜詩郎中 32) 又見稠海拾遺 33) 云 曺曾 34)

魯人 事親盡禮 亢旱 35) 井地皆渴 母思清甘之水

曾跪而操瓶 則甘泉自湧 吳君之事與此若符合契

蓋曰：至誠感神 傳曰：誠未有不動者 信哉 孝

感泉至今尚在觱沸澄澈 36) 邑人愛護 以石築云

此誠自有東國所未有之事也 奇哉奇哉

1 興德縣: a village in present-day Koch'ang County 高敞郡 in North Chŏlla Province.

2 吳浚 [1444–94; styled Hŏsu 虛受; sobriquet Kamch'ŏn 感泉; ancestral seat Tongbok 同福]: famous filial son of Hŭngdŏk in Chŏlla Province during the reign of King Sŏngjong 成宗 [r. 1469–94; 1457–94]. His father was O Ch'iin 吳致仁 [dates unknown].

3 靈鷲山: a mountain in present-day Yŏnggwang County 靈光郡 in South Chŏlla Province.

4 廬 = yŏmak 廬幕: a thatched ad hoc dwelling for a mourner to live in for the duration of the mourning period.

5 啜: drink gruel or broth.

6 隕涕: shed tears.

7 玄酒: sacred water offered in place of spirits for ancestral rites.

8 清潔甘冽: clear, pure, sweet, and icy-cold.

9 萃: gather.

10 小祥 = sogi 小朞 ~ kinyŏnje 朞年祭: ancestral rite honouring the first anniversary of the deceased.

11 蹲坐: crouch down.

12 掉尾: wag one's tail.

13 撫弄: caress and fondle.

14 家犬豕: domestic dogs and pigs.

15 朔望: first and fifteenth days of the month by the lunar calendar.

16 屏跡: disappear without a trace.

17 闋服: lit. "doff [mourning attire]" = complete the three-year mourning period for one's parents.

18 道臣 = *kamsa* 監司 or *kwanch'alsa* 觀察使: provincial governor.

19 司僕正: a senior third-grade post attached to the Bureau of Royal Transportation (Saboksi 司僕寺), in charge of palanquins and horses.

20 即祚 = *chŭgwi* 即位: assume the throne.

21 院宇之弊: evil practices at private academies (*sŏwŏn* 書院).

22 戊午以後祠: shrines built after the year 1738 (Yŏngjo 14), when King Yŏngjo ordered the abolition of shrines.

23 曠典: rarest privilege.

24 吳泰運 [1700–?; styled Hwabo 和甫; ancestral seat Tongbok 同福]: scholar-official under King Yŏngjo 英祖 [r. 1724–76; 1694–1776]. His father was O Sangt'aek 吳尙澤 [dates unknown].

25 太學 = Sŏnggyun'gwan 成均館: the Confucian Academy.

26 章甫 = *yusaeng* 儒生: a student of Confucianism.

27 同力修葺: join forces to repair a building.

28 東漢 = 後漢: Eastern Han = Later Han (25–220).

29 姜詩 *Jiang Shi*: famous filial son from the early Eastern Han period.

30 赤眉: lit. "red eyebrows" = peasant rebels who dyed their eyebrows red during the Xin Dynasty 新 (8? –25).

31 光武 = Liu Xiu 劉秀 [r. 25–57; 6 BC–57 AD]: Emperor Guangwu, the founder of the Later Han Dynasty.

32 郎中 *langzhong*: palace security post attached to ministers (*shangshu* 尙書), installed during the Qin dynasty 秦 (221–206 BC).

33 「稠海拾遺」: *Chouhai shiyi*, an undated text by an unknown compiler.

34 曹曾: Cao Zeng [dates unknown], a famous filial son of the state of Lu 魯.

35 亢旱: long-lasting drought.

36 觱沸澄澈: pristine water gushing forth.

——— **26** ———

A Most Faithful Son

Vol. I: 42; translated 6 June 1921; Diary XVI, pp. 167–8; 182.

There was a man called Yi Pal whose boyhood name was Chonghŭi. His home was in Chŏnŭi County in Ch'ungch'ŏng Province. When he was nine years of age, his whole house fell ill of an epidemic. His father, mother, and servant were all down together. Chonghŭi alone escaped and remained well.

His father Kwangguk was ill for a long time and the fever refused to leave him. His strength failed and for two days he lay unconscious and all his body began to grow cold from the feet up. No one came to see him.

Chonghŭi alone was left in his distress to see to his father. He got the servant on his feet and had him make some *miŭm*.* He then took a knife and cut his fourth finger off and let the blood drop into the bowl so that it coloured the *miŭm* red. He opened his mouth with a spoon and fed his father and gave him half a bowl in all.

On this, new life seemed to return and the boy, greatly delighted, gave him the whole. His father thus lived so that he spoke again and lived.

But the following day he returned to the same state of complete unconsciousness.

The boy cried and prayed to God (天). He then cut off other fingers and much blood flowed further.

Seeing this, the servant gave a great cry and tried to prevent him so doing, but the boy motioned him away and had no one else know it.

This blood was put in the *miŭm* and thus a bowl was prepared. When he was giving this to his father there was a sound heard in the room calling, "Chonghŭi, your faithful spirit has moved God (텬) and orders have gone forth from the court of the Hades (Myŏngbu) that your father live. Therefore be no longer troubled. No need to cry or rend your soul."

All in the house heard these words without any exception. All said it was the voice of the master of Changdan, his maternal grandfather, Yun Kyŏm, who had long been dead.

His father lived, his fever left him and day by day he grew in strength. His mother, too, survived. And all praised Chonghŭi as the author of this good fortune.

The rumour went abroad. The people assembled and wrote a petition to the magistrate of Chŏnŭi. He was greatly moved by this and made a report of the same to the Provincial Governor.

The governor at this time was Yi Sŏngnyong. He gave freedom of the county to the family and made a report of it to the king so that they erected a shrine of honour to his memory.

His age now as I write is thirty-two (23 years afterwards). He now lives in Aogae, Seoul. I paid a visit to see him and found him neat and well ordered, a man of great dignity – certainly an honour to the scholar class.

There are many faithful sons who have severed a finger for the sake of parents but these acts of a boy of nine, who thought not of the pain he suffered and never dreamed of name or fame, nor of pain nor suffering, surely was a filial son born of God. His winning back his father's life from God (신명) was indeed a fitting thing.

* rice gruel.

리발　　소자종희　　가본호서전의　　현야　　구세치합
李潑 1) 小字宗禧　家本湖西全義 2) 縣也　九歲値闔

실구병　　기부모노복일시병와　　독종희미통
室遘病 3)　其父母奴僕一時病臥　獨宗禧未痛

기부광국　통이구이미퇴열　　기질자이일
其父光國 4) 痛已久而未退熱　氣窒者二日

전신궐랭　이무성시자　　종희독자황황축기
全身蹶冷 5) 而無省視者　宗禧獨自惶惶蹙起

병비급자미음흘　　장도작파사지　　혈주완중
病婢急煮米飲訖　將刀斫破四指　血注椀中

만완은적　　용저계부지치　　람화　련관
滿椀殷赤 6)　用箸啓父之齒　攬和 7) 連灌

용반완이유기식미미출비구　　아경희수진용일완
用半椀已有氣息微微出鼻口　兒驚喜遂盡用一椀

부내소발어성　행득생　익일향포　　기우질여전
父乃甦發語聲　幸得生　翌日向哺 8)　氣又窒如前

아호읍도천　우작중지어궤상　혈대출　일병비견지
兒號泣禱天　又斫衆指於几上　血大出　一病婢見之

경호부옹　아극휘지　사거비무경동가중　화혈어
驚呼扶擁　兒亟揮之　使去俾無驚動家衆　和血於

粥 又進一椀 方進粥時 室中忽聞有呼云：宗禧

汝誠感天 冥府 9) 已許汝父之生 汝其放心勿悲痛

家中內外臥者莫不聞之 皆曰：長湍 10) 生員聲

也 長湍生員卽宗禧之外祖尹謙 11) 其死已久矣

其父得生卽退熱 日向 12) 蘇完 而其母亦繼瘳 13)

宗禧事無不稱道藉藉 14) 里人遂狀報於邑倅

倅大奇之 轉報監營 道伯 15) 李聖龍 16) 給 17) 復聞

于朝旌 18) 其閭 宗禧今年三十二 來居京師阿峴 19)

余嘗見之 貌端潔壯雅士也 夫親病斷指者多矣

今以九歲兒行之 不計身命 不求聲聞 20) 不知痛苦

粹然 21) 出天之孝 22) 宜其感動 神明續父之命也

1 李潑 [dates unknown]: cannot be identified.
2 全義: a village in South Ch'ungch'ŏng Province.
3 闔室遘病: the entire household comes down with an illness or the plague.
4 李光國: Yi Pal's father [dates unknown].
5 蹶冷: get a sudden chill.
6 殷赤: become red all over.
7 攪和: amalgamate.
8 向晡: around 4 PM.
9 冥府: the underworld.

10 長湍: a village in Kyŏnggi Province.

11 尹謙 [1601–65; styled Yŏok 汝玉; ancestral seat P'ap'yŏng 坡平; sobriquet
   Oong 梧翁]: scholar-official under King Injo 仁祖 [r. 1623–49; 1595–1649].

12 日向: dusk.

13 繼瘳: one person after another recovers from an illness.

14 稱道藉藉: spread words of admiration far and wide.

15 道伯: provincial governors (*kamsa* 監司 or *kwanch'alsa* 觀察使).

16 李聖龍 [1672–1748; styled Chau 子雨; sobriquet Kihŏn 杞軒; ancestral
   seat Kyŏngju 慶州]: scholar-official under King Yŏngjo 英祖 [r. 1724–66;
   1694–1776]. His father was Yi Yŏju 李汝柱 [1649–?].

17 給: report swiftly.

18 旌: erecting a gate at the entrance to a village to recognize its filial children,
   loyal subjects, and faithful wives.

19 阿峴: a neighbourhood in present-day Map'o-gu, Seoul.

20 聲聞 = *myŏngsŏng* 名聲: fame, renown.

21 粹然: naively.

22 出天之孝: heaven-endowed filial piety.

—— 27 ——

Fate

Vol. II: 2; n.d.; Box 9:21, pp. 115–16; 184.

King Sŏngjong (1470–94 AD) used to go about incognito and one night
as he was making his rounds with two or three servants, he passed before Namsan. It was then about the third watch of the night and all was
quiet about him, except a little thatched hut where he saw a dim light
and heard the sound of reading.

With his hat and his outer robe on, the King went in. The master gave
a start, arose, and after being seated inquired, "What guest do I have
the honour of meeting at this hour of the night?"

The King replied, "I heard the sound of reading as I went by and so
came in. What book is this please?"

"I am reading the *Book of Changes*," was the reply.

The King asked all sorts of questions concerning it and found him
ready with an answer in each case – a great scholar evidently.

"How old are you?" asked the King.

He replied, "I am over fifty."

"Do you not attend the Examination?"

His reply was, "Luck is against me and so I have never passed."

The King then asked to see some of his compositions and he showed them. They were all most excellent.

Thinking it very strange indeed, the King asked, "Such a scholar as you not passing is due to some wrong on part of the examiners."

The scholar replied, "No, not that; it is Fate – Luck is against me, not the examiners."

The King then looked over the compositions once again and examined one specially as he asked, "Did you hear of an examination the day after tomorrow?"

He replied, "I did not hear of it; when did such an order come forth?"

"The King has just issued such an order. Be on hand, won't you, and do your part."

He then said his farewell and came away, but not without first having his servant see to leaving two bags of rice and a few pounds of meat.

After returning to the Palace he gave orders for this special examination.

When the time came the subject posted was the same as the midnight visitor had seen among the old man's papers.

The King waited for that composition to come in and sure enough it finally came – the same as he had seen that night. He praised it beyond measure and marked it first.

When the announcement was made the King called the successful candidates but a young man came instead and not the old scholar he had seen.

In doubt, he inquired, "Did you write this?"

He replied, "No, it is my teacher's. I took it from his compositions."

The King inquired, "Why did your teacher not come himself?"

His reply was, "My teacher has had a serious attack of indigestion from having dined too freely on rice and meat; that's why I came instead."

The King was silent for a little and then told him to go.

The truth was the meat and rice was too much for the old man. It was indeed the old man's fate not to succeed. He died a few days later.

成廟 1) 時或微行 2)　一夜雪月照耀　上與數三宦侍

微服而行　行到南山下　時政三更後　萬籟俱寂

而山下數間斗屋 3)　燈火明滅　有讀書聲　上以幅巾 4)

道服　開戶而入　主人驚起　延坐而問曰：

何許客子 5)　深夜到此　上曰：偶然過去　聞讀書

聲而來　仍問所讀何書　曰：易經 6) 也　上與之問難

應對如流　眞大儒也　問年紀 7) 幾何　曰：五十餘矣

(曰：) 不廢科工 8) 乎　曰：數奇之故　屢屈科場 9)

矣　請見其私草 10)　乃出示之　箇箇名作　上怪而

問之曰：如許實才　尙未登科　此則有司 11) 之責也

對曰：奇窮 12) 之致　何可怨有司之不公乎　上熟視

其中一篇題與所作　仍問曰：再明 13) 有別科 14)

其或聞之否　對曰：不得聞知矣　何時出令乎

上曰：俄者自上有命　第爲努力見之　仍辭出

사 액 예　이 이 곡　미 십 근 륙　자 외 투 지 이 거　환 궁 후
使掖隸 15) 以二斛 16) 米十斤肉　自外投之而去　還宮後

잉 명 설 별 과　급 기 어 제 이 향 야　유 생 사 초 중 제 출 게
仍命設別科　及期御題以向夜 17) 儒生私草中題出揭

이 지 대 기 문 지 입 래　미 기 시 권　입 정　과 시 향 야
而只待其文之入來　未幾試券 18) 入呈　果是向夜

소 람 지 부　자 상 대 가 칭 상　다 하 어 비　이 탁 제 일 의
所覽之賦　自上大加稱賞　多下御批　而擢第一矣

급 기 탁 방 지 시　호 입 신 은　즉 비 향 야 소 견 지 유
及其坼榜之時 19) 呼入新恩 20) 則非向夜所見之儒

즉 일 소 년 유 야　상 아 연 이 교 왈　차 시 여 지 소 주 호
卽一少年儒也　上訝然而教曰：此是汝之所做乎

대 왈　비 야　과 봉 어 소 신 로 사 사 초 중 서 정 의　상
對曰：非也　果逢於小臣老師私草中書呈矣　上

우 교 왈　여 사 하 불 부 거　대 왈　신 지 사 우 포 미 륙
又教曰：汝師何不赴擧　對曰：臣之師偶飽米肉

졸 환 관 격　불 득 입 래　고 소 신 회 기 사 초 이 래 의
卒患關格 21) 不得入來　故小臣懷其私草而來矣

상 묵 연 량 구　사 지 퇴　개 소 사 미 륙　과 포 어 기 장 이 생
上黙然良久　使之退　盖所賜米肉　過飽於飢腸而生

병 야　유 시 관 지　기 비 명 야　차 유 인 차 병 불 기 운
病也　由是觀之　豈非命耶　此儒因此病不起云

1 成廟: refers to the years from 1469 to 1494, the reign of Sŏngjong 成宗.
2 微行: (a high-ranking official) travel incognito.
3 斗屋: small house.
4 幅巾 = *pokkŏn* 幞巾: a bandana-like headgear, part of Daoists' attire (*tobok* 道服).
5 客子: guest; traveller.
6 易經 = *Zhouyi* 周易: *The Book of Changes*.
7 年紀: age.

 8 科工: studying for the civil service examination.

 9 科場: venue for the civil service examination.

10 私草 = *sago* 私稿 ~ *wŏngo* 原稿: a manuscript in one's own hand.

11 有司: person in charge; here, an invigilator of the civil service examination.

12 奇窮: indigent.

13 再明: the day after tomorrow.

14 別科: a special state examination (*pyŏlsi* 別試) held on auspicious occasions
   or held every ten years in a *pyŏng* year (*pyŏngnyŏn* 丙年).

15 掖隷: palace servant.

16 斛: one *sŏm* = 10 *mal* (about 18 litres); a unit of volume for measuring grain.

17 向夜: the other night; the previous night.

18 試劵 = *siji* 試紙: examination answer sheet.

19 坼榜之時: "when the names of successful exam candidates are posted."

20 新恩: a new exam passer.

21 關格 = *kŭpch'e* 急滯: acute stomach upset.

—— **28** ——

Playing Magpie

Vol. III: 1; n.d.; Diary XII, pp. 83–4, with the title
"Man and Woman Magpies" (crossed out);
Diary XIV, p. 48; Box 9:21, p. 120; 185.

King Sŏngjong (1468—94 AD)* used to go about at night a great deal incognito. Once when passing a blind alley in the southern part of the city, he saw indistinctly among the shadows a front gate. Suddenly it opened and out came a woman. From a tree just in front of the gate there came the clack of a magpie.

When the woman came out she looked first to one side and then to the other to see if anyone was nearby and finding no one she went stealthily over toward the tree. Then the sound of a magpie was heard from the foot answering the one heard from the tree itself. The woman then picked up a small branch and placing it in her mouth, proceeded to climb the tree while the magpie in the tree received the branch with a clack of response.

Seeing this, the King was mystified beyond measure and gave a cough to announce his presence. Hearing this, the woman gave a start, jumped down from the tree and fled into the house.

The King then saw a man descend from the tree and go into the house as well; he followed him and asked what this all meant.

The man replied, "I have since my earliest days been a candidate at examinations and now I am fifty years of age but have never had any luck. I have heard that if a magpie builds its nest to the south of your house, your success will be insured. I have had a tree planted here for ten years and more and yet not once has a magpie ever come to build. Tonight my old wife and I thought we would act the magpie's part, chatter and carry sticks up in our mouths and build a nest and see what luck would come. In the quiet hours of the night we two were intent on this bit of foolishness when suddenly you have broken in upon us. I would like to ask who Your Excellency is and why you go about at this time of the night?"

The King laughed, though he really felt sorry for the disappointed couple. His reply was, "I am a stranger who happened to be going by."

He then left and returned to the Palace.

The day following there was a sudden announcement that there would be a special examination and when the subject was posted, it was *injak* (human-magpies). The candidates looked at the subject, mystified, unable to guess what it could mean. This scholar, however, knew and wrote accordingly; he passed his composition in and won the day.

There is a truth about the magpie's nest to the south of the home giving success at examinations, but this case was due to the happy meeting with the King.

* There is a discrepancy between the reign years given by current Korean historians and those given by Gale here. Current scholarship gives 1469 as the beginning of King Sŏngjong's reign, while Gale writes 1468 here. In Story 27 Gale gives 1470.

成廟₁₎ 夜又微行過一洞　洞是幽僻處　遠見柴門₂₎

開處　見一女子出來　而門前之樹有鵲聲　其女子

四顧而無人　仍往樹下　又作鵲聲　而以口含木而上

上有鵲聲而受之　上心竊訝之　仍咳嗽 [3]　則其女子

驚避于門內　又有一人　從樹上跳下而入柴門

上追到而問故　其人答曰：自少業科工

年近五十而尙未得科　曾聞家有南鵲巢則登科云

故此樹種于門前者　已過十餘年　而鵲不來巢

吾今夜與老妻　作雌雄鵲相和之聲　而含木枝作巢

以爲閒中劇戲 [4]　而不幸爲客所見　請問客子何

許人而深夜到此　上笑而憐之　以過客爲答還宮

翌日出科令　以人鵲爲題　一場士子皆不知解

此士獨知之　呈券而登科　南鵲之靈有如是

此亦會時而然矣

1 成廟: the years 1469–94, the reign of Sŏngjong 成宗.
2 柴門: twig gate.
3 咳嗽: cough.
4 閒中劇戲: comic theatre enjoyed in one's leisure time.

————— **29** —————

The Strange Story of Yi Sŏk

Vol. II: 2; translated 6 June 1921; Diary XVI, pp. 168–9; 186.

In the days of Sŏngjong, His Majesty the King had a dream in which he saw a dragon coming in at the South Gate that had on its brow written "Yi Sŏk."

The King gave a start and awoke. He asked of his eunuchs what time of the night it was. They replied that it was *p'aru** time on the Water Clock (4 AM). He summoned a *pyŏlgam*† to go at once to the gate, open the gate, and take the first person coming in, good or bad, take him to his house and await orders.

Thus ordered, the *pyŏlgam* went forth and a little later opened the gates. Just then there came in a boy with his hair down his back who carried a limestone on his back.

The *pyŏlgam* stopped him, saying, "Wait!" The boy was frightened and did not know what it meant. He trembled as he waited. Then he took him to his house and told the King.

It was just the time of the *alsŏng* Examination. It was just two or three days away.‡ The King ordered the *pyŏlgam* to keep this lad at his house, to give him food, and when the exam came off to put up his hair, put a cap on his head, and a scholar's dress, but not to give him paper, ink, or pens.

"You are to come in with him and take special note of what happens regarding him in the examination enclosure."

The *pyŏlgam* received these orders, retired and asked the boy, "Do you wish to go into the Exam Enclosure?"

He answered, "I am an ignorant person, a seller of lime. How could I ever get into the Exam Enclosure?"

The *pyŏlgam* then, in accord with the orders from the king, had him dressed in cap and coat, forced him into the Enclosure, and made him sit down in the Changwŏn Peak where he could see. By and by the day grew late, and soon the announcement would be made and the many candidates met beneath the Changwŏn Peak.

Among them was a white-haired old scholar who looked at Yi Sŏk again and again till finally he came close up to him and asked, "Are you Tor-i?"§

He answered, "Yes, I am."

The old scholar took him by the hand and with tears in his eyes said, "And so you live after all. I was a special friend of your father's and studied for many years along with your father. Once an epidemic came about and all your house was taken down and died. At that time your wet nurse took you and made her escape. You were then only about two years old. How could I ever recognize you now that you are grown up? When I saw you, an impression came into my mind that said it was you. And so it is. Is this not the will of God (텬)? I have a composition of your father with me and this subject today is just what we two have written together. I have written my own composition but I have your father's still with me. Have you ever written an exam?"

Yi Sŏk said, "What could I ever do with an exam? I was forced in here by this man and am merely here as a sightseer."

The old scholar said, "I have these writings of your father unsigned. Let this be yours." Then he wrote the name Yi Sŏk and handed it in.

In a little the announcement was made of the successful candidates and the first of all was Yi Sŏk's name, and when he was called the King asked to see him.

The King asked, "Did you write this?"

Yi Sŏk answered truly, "No, Your Majesty, I did not."

The King then called the old scholar to himself, and gave orders: "I appoint you as guardian of such-and-such a tomb. Go then and teach Yi Sŏk his lessons."

Thus he taught him.

Finally Yi Sŏk became a *ch'amp'an* and a special minister of Sŏngjong.

* See note 4 below.

† See note 5 below.

‡ Error: Gale translates as "It was to last two or three days."

§ The "I" signals that Gale read the original phrase "石伊 (Sino-Korean *sŏk* + *i*)" according to *hundok* (reading Chinese characters in accordance with their vernacular glosses). *Sŏk* thus reads as *tol* (native Korean for "stone") plus –*i*, the diminutive suffix that attaches to names ending in a consonant.

성 묘　　몽 견 황 룡 유 숭 례 문　　이 입　　액 상 서 이 리 석
成廟 1) 夢見黃龍由崇禮門 2) 而入　額上書以李石 3)

상 경 이 각 지　　문 내 시 야 여 하　　기 대 왈　　기 지 파 루
上驚而覺之　問內侍夜如何　其對曰：幾至罷漏 4)

時矣　仍命一別監 [5] 卽往于（南）門　內門鎖開後

如有初入之人　毋論某人　率置于汝家後回奏

別監承命而出　少竢于門內　少焉開門　而有一總

角負灰石 [6] 而入　別監仍執留　其人驚遑戰慄　仍携

至渠家而來奏　時謁聖科 [7] 只隔數日矣　上命別監

姑留汝家而饋朝夕　及科期　加冠而備給儒巾靑袍 [8]

如試紙 [9] 筆墨勿給　而汝與偕入場內　第觀其動靜之

如何　別監承命而出　問其兒曰：汝欲入科場乎　曰：

小人無識之人　以賣灰爲業　何由而入場內乎云云

則別監依下敎備給巾服　而强使入場而同坐壯元峰

只觀光矣　日稍晚榜幾出時　多士會于壯元峯下

傍有白髮老儒　頻頻熟視　仍近前問曰：汝乃石伊乎

對曰：然矣　老儒執手垂淚曰：汝果生存於此世乎

吾與乃翁 [10] 卽切友也　與乃翁同硏不知幾年矣

某年疾疫　汝家闔門 11) 病死　伊時汝之乳媼 12) 抱

汝而逃走云矣　時汝年不過數三歲　今於長成之後

吾何以記得汝乎　今於此相逢　吾心忽爾有感認

汝也　丁寧如是　此豈非天乎　汝翁私草 13) 在於吾

而今日之題　吾與汝翁舊時宿搆也　吾則以吾之

所搆用之　今餘汝翁之作　汝已觀科乎　對曰：

何敢觀科　爲此人所勸　以欲瞻闕內威儀而入來矣

其儒曰：吾有空正草 14)　汝可觀科　仍書秘封以

李石書之而 15) 呈券矣　未幾榜出　李石居魁 16) 矣

呼新恩 17) 後　上命入侍而問曰：此是汝作乎

李石對以實　上命尋其老儒入侍　下敎曰：

令除汝 18) 齋郎可敎李石以文字也　仍除一齋郎而使

李石受業矣　李石位至參判 19)　爲成廟朝名臣云爾

1 成廟: the years 1469–94, the reign of Sŏngjong 成宗.

2 崇禮門: South Gate (Namdaemun 南大門) in Seoul.

3 李石: dates unknown.

4 罷漏: Korean custom of banging a metal drum thirty-three times around 4 AM (*ogyŏng samjŏm* 五更三點) in the capital in order to mark the end of the nightly curfew.

5 別監: assistant belonging to offices like the Bureau of the Palace Court (*Aekchŏngsŏ* 掖庭署), in charge of delivering miscellaneous paraphernalia within the royal palace, such as brushes, ink stones, and keys.

6 灰石 = *sŏkhoe* 石灰: plaster.

7 謁聖科: a special civil service examination held before the king. The occasion began with a royal procession to the Confucian Academy (Sŏnggyun'gwan 成均館), at which the king paid homage to Confucius's tablet.

8 儒巾青袍: gentleman's hat and blue robe; Confucianists' attire.

9 試紙 = *sigwŏn* 試券 ~ *chŏngch'o* 正草 ~ *siji* 試紙: examination paper to be submitted at the civil service examination.

10 乃翁 = *naebu* 乃父: your father.

11 闔門 = *kŏga* 舉家: the entire household.

12 乳媼 = *yumo* 乳母: wet nurse.

13 私草 = *sago* 私稿 ~ *wŏn'go* 原稿: a manuscript in one's own hand.

14 正草: See note 9.

15 呈券: hand in one's examination paper at the civil service examination.

16 居魁 = *changwŏn* 壯元: take first place in the civil service examination.

17 新恩: a new examination passer.

18 齋郎: a junior ninth-grade post such as *ch'ambong* 參奉, caretakers of ancestral halls (*sadang* 祠堂) or royal tombs and gardens (*nŭngwŏn* 陵園).

19 參判 = *adang* 亞堂: a major second-grade post in the Six Ministries (*yukcho* 六曹).

—— **30** ——

Chŏng Pukch'ang

Vol. II: 2; n.d.; Diary XII, pp. 53–5 (crossed out); 187.

Chŏng had a friend who was very very ill and physicians' efforts proved of no avail. His father, believing that Chŏng had spiritual powers, came and inquired of him.

Chŏng replied, "He has finished his appointed course and there is nothing can be done for him."

His father then broke down and cried and still begged that something be done.

Chŏng felt sorry for him and said, "Very well then – I apportion him ten years of my own appointed life and let him live on that. Tomorrow night at the third watch you must go up Mount Namsan and when you arrive at the top you will meet two priests, one with a red coat on and one with a black, who will be seated there. Go before them and ask that your son be given life. These priests will reprimand and threaten you and order you off, but do not go. Though they take a rod and beat you, still do not go. If you will continue on with all your heart to entreat, you will know and understand in the end."

The father, just as Chŏng had instructed, went up Namsan in the moonlight, and sure enough, there were the priests. He went up to them and in tears made his request.

The priests gave a start and said, "We are two priests who are merely going by and have come here for a little to rest. Why do you ask such an outrageous thing of us? As to your son's appointed span of life, what are a pair of poor priests such as we to know about it? Get away with you."

The man paid no attention to this whatever but kept on with his requests.

The priests grew very angry and said, "You crazy idiot! We shall have to beat you."

So with their staffs they beat him.

Though sore and in pain, he still kept up pleading for his son.

Then the priest with the red coat on laughed and said, "This is evidently a matter that Chŏng Pukch'ang has put up. He has done a useless and foolish thing and yet if he wishes to give ten years of his life to the boy of yours, all is well and good."

The black-coated one then nodded his head and said, "That's so."

The two then took hold of the man and lifting him up, said, "Let's do so."

The priest with the black coat took a book out of his sleeve and gave it to the red-coated one. The red-coated one received it and in the moonlight took a pen and writing in it said, "Your son will live ten years more. Please go back to Chŏng and ask him not to lightly make known again the secrets of God."

Suddenly the two were gone. The red-coated one was the South Polar star and the black one the North star.

On going home, he found his son recovering and ten years later he died. And Chŏng only passed fifty and died.

北窓 1) 之友一人病重　醫藥無效　其老父知北窓

之神異　來問則答曰：年數已盡　無可救之道矣

其父泣而哀乞　願知其可救之方　北窓憐其情理曰：

然則不得不減吾十年之壽　以添公之子年限矣

仍曰：公於來夜三更後　獨自步上南山絶頂

則必有紅衣黑衣二僧相對而坐矣　伏乞於其前

哀乞公子之命　其僧雖怒而逐之勿退去　雖以杖毆

之亦勿去　務積誠意 2)　則自有可知之道矣　其人如

其言　至其夜獨自乘月而上南山　果有二僧如其言

仍於前泣乞　二僧驚曰：過去山僧　暫憩于此矣

公是何許人　來作此駭擧也　公子之命壽脩短 3)

貧僧何以知之　斯速退去　其人聽若不聞而一樣哀乞

기 승 로 왈　차 시 광 인 야　가 구 축 의　거 장 타 지　통 불
其僧怒曰：此是狂人也　可毆逐矣　舉杖打之　痛不

인 이 여 전 복 이 읍 걸　량 구 주 의 승 소 왈　차 사 필 시 정 렴
忍而如前伏而泣乞　良久朱衣僧笑曰：此事必是鄭磏

지 소 지 도 야　차 아 소 위 가 한　당 이 거 지 수 감 십 년
之所指導也　此兒所爲可恨　當以渠之壽減十年

이 첨 차 인 지 수 무 방 의　흑 의 승 점 두 왈　연 의　이 승
而添此人之壽無妨矣　黑衣僧點頭曰：然矣　二僧

시 부 이 기 지 왈　료 시 지 의　흑 의 승 자 수 중 출 일 책
始扶而起之曰：聊試之矣　黑衣僧自袖中出一冊

이 급 주 의 승　주 의 승 수 지　대 월 광 거 필 약 유 서 자
以給朱衣僧　朱衣僧受之　對月光舉筆 若有書字

양 이 언 왈　공 지 자 종 금 연 십 년 수 의　가 귀 어 정 렴
樣而言曰：公之子從今延十年壽矣　可歸語鄭磏

사 물 부 설 천 기 야　잉 홀 불 현　개 주 의 승 남 두 야
使勿復泄天機 4) 也　仍忽不見　盖朱衣僧南斗 5) 也

흑 의 승 북 두 야　기 인 귀 가 의　기 자 지 병 점 추
黑衣僧北斗 6) 也　其人歸家矣　其子之病漸瘳 7)

십 년 후 내 사　북 창 년 과 오 십 이 졸 여 기 언
十年後乃死　北窓年過五十而卒如其言

1 北窓 = Chŏng Nyŏm 鄭磏 [1506–49; styled Sagyŏl 士潔; ancestral seat
   Onyang 溫陽; posthumous epithet Changhye 章惠]: scholar-official and
   physician under King Chungjong [r. 1506–44; 1488–1544]. His father was
   Chŏng Sunbung 鄭順朋 [1484–1548].
2 務積誠意: lit. "make efforts to accumulate sincerity."
3 天機: (secret) workings of heaven; the will of heaven; the cosmic mechanism.
4 脩短: short life span.
5 南斗: Six Stars of the Southern Dipper.
6 北斗: Seven Stars of the Northern Dipper = the Big Dipper.
7 瘳: illness gets better.

——— 31 ———

The Wife of Wŏlsa

Vol. II: 3*; n.d.; Diary XIX, p. 38; 188.

The wife of Yi (Wŏlsa) was the daughter of Kwŏn Kŭkchi, a very worthy woman; she had two sons, one named Paekchu and one Hyŏnju. They both attained to high office and were great and noted scholars. She was most careful in her management of the home, dressed plainly and kept down expenses.

At this time there was a wedding in the home of one of the Royal Princesses, a son to be married. The King ordered that all the wives of the ministers attend this wedding.

All the ladies dressed in their very very best, each vying with the other. It was a great occasion for silks and gems the like was never seen.

Later a two-man chair came in and an old woman leaning on a staff came out. She was dressed in sackcloth and coarse cotton. She made as though she would come into the gorgeous assembly.

In haste, the Princess quickly pushed on her shoes and hurried down to meet her. The younger women looked in wonder and yet, with questions as to who it could possibly be. The Princess led her up and had her seated in the highest place of all and there treated her to the most exacting forms of politeness. The guests were more mystified than ever.

When the feast tables were brought the old lady arose and said that she would go. The Princess, however, remarked that the day was early and that she should not think of going.

The old lady said, "My husband is just now engaged in the Royal Physician's Office, my oldest son is one of the Government Officials, and my second son is in waiting on His Majesty as a *sŭngji*. I must get home and see to their meals and have them ready when they return."

Then all the guests recognized that it was Lady Yi, wife of Wŏlsa.

* Instead of a title, this entry in Gale's ms. ledger carried a heading that reads "긔문총화 (Yi's edition) II;3." Thus, it would appear that Gale's *hanmun* pundit, Yi Ch'angjik, also owned a manuscript edition of this text.

月沙 1) 夫人 權判書克智 2) 女也 有德行 二子白洲 3)

玄洲 4) 皆顯達 而治家儉素 華麗之衣未嘗近於

身 時某公主家迎婦 5) 自上命滿朝命婦 6) 皆赴宴

諸家婦女競以華侈相尙 伊日之宴 珠翠綺羅奪

人眼目 追後有轎子入來 而一老婦人扶杖而來

葛衣布裳麤劣極矣 將升堂 主人公主倒屣下迎 7)

年少諸婦莫不指笑 而驚訝不知爲誰家夫人

主人迎之上座 執禮甚恭 人尤訝之 進饌 8) 後

其老婦人先起告歸 主人以日勢之尙早挽之

則老婦人曰: 鄙家大監以藥院 9) 都提調 10) 曉已赴闕

伯兒以政官 11) 赴政席 12) 小兒以承旨 13) 坐直 14) 老身

歸家 可備送夕飯 座中大驚 始知爲月沙之夫人

1 月沙: sobriquet of Yi Chŏnggu/Yi Chŏnggwi 李廷龜 [1564–1635; styled Sŏngjing 聖徵; ancestral seat Yŏnan 延安; posthumous epithet Munch'ung 文忠]: scholar-official under King Injo 仁祖 [r. 1623–49; 1595–1649]. He was a great-great-grandson of Yi Sŏkhyŏng 李石亨 [1415–77].

2 權克智 [1538–92; styled T'aekchung 擇仲; ancestral seat Andong 安東; posthumous epithet Ch'ungsuk 忠肅]: scholar-official under King Sŏnjo

宣祖 [r. 1567–1608; 1552–1608]. His father was Kwŏn Tŏgyu 權德裕 [dates
unknown].

3 白洲: sobriquet of Yi Myŏnghan 李明漢 [1595–1645; styled Ch'ŏnjang 天章;
ancestral seat Yŏnan 延安; posthumous epithet Munjŏng 文靖]: scholar-
official under King Injo 仁祖 [r. 1623–49; 1595–1649]. His father was
Yi Chŏnggu.

4 玄洲: sobriquet of Yi Sohan 李昭漢 [1598–1645; styled Tojang 道章; ancestral seat Yŏnan 延安]: brother of Yi Myŏnghan and son of Yi Chŏnggu.

5 迎婦: welcome a new daughter-in-law.

6 命婦: court ladies; members of the royal family and its relatives; the
primary wives of the royal family and its relatives, and of the civil and
military officials of the first grade; a woman's designation as *myŏngbu* was
determined by the status of her husband.

7 倒屣下迎: lit. "come out to greet someone not noticing that one's shoes are
on backwards" = greet someone ecstatically.

8 進饌: royal feasts, less formal and less elaborate in comparison with royal
banquets (*chinyŏn* 進宴).

9 藥院: another name for the Royal Clinic (Naeŭiwŏn 內醫院), the bureau in
charge of medical and pharmaceutical supplies for the palace.

10 都提調: a junior first-grade post attached to the Border Defence Council
(Pibyŏnsa 備邊司).

11 政官 = *chŏn'gwan* 銓官: a generic term for officials in the Board of Personnel
(Ijo 吏曹).

12 政席: a venue where matters of state are conducted.

13 承旨: a cover term referring to the Chief Royal Secretary (*tosŭngji* 都承旨),
the Second Royal Secretary (*chwasŭngji* 左承旨), the Third Royal Secretary
(*usŭngji* 右承旨), the Fourth and Fifth Royal Secretaries (*pu sŭngji* 副承旨),
and the Sixth Secretary (*tongbu sŭngji* 同副承旨), all belonging to the Royal
Secretariat (Sŭngjŏngwŏn 承政院).

14 坐直: remain in one's place.

―――― **32** ――――

Sŏ Kyŏngdŏk's Power

Vol. II: 3; translated 7 June 1921; Diary XVI, pp. 169–70; 189.

Sŏ (Hwadam) Kyŏngdŏk was a great scholar of wide experience. He
knew all about astronomy, geomancy, and various magic subjects.

He built his home at a place called Hwadam in Changdan and thus his pen-name became Hwadam.

One day he had his students before him and was giving them a lecture on the Classics. Suddenly an old Buddhist priest came, made his salutations and was off. Hwadam wished him well on his way and when he had gone a great sorrow seemed to overcome him. The students asked what this meant.

Hwadam asked, "Do you know that priest?"

They said, "No, we know him not."

Hwadam then said, "He is the spirit of a tiger that walks about as a man. There is a young woman who will be married shortly and will die at the hands of this creature. I feel so sorry for her."

One of his students asked, "Master, you already know of it. Have you no means of saving her?"

Hwadam made answer, "There is a way, true enough, but there is no man whom I could send."

The student said, "I'll go – send me."

Hwadam said, "Very well, if you will go, it will be well."

Hwadam gave him a book and said, "Here is a Buddhist Book. Take this to such-and-such a house but say nothing of the tiger or of danger, but have all the materials made ready for the wedding and let the bride stay fast in her room and lock the doors. Get five or six strong women to lay hold on her and keep her from coming out and you yourself stay in the open hall and read aloud the book. Be careful that you pronounce all the endings and connectives correctly.* If you but pass the time of cockcrow all will be well."

He repeated his orders and told him to be most careful.

Thus directed, he hurried off to the place where he found everything in a state of commotion.

They said, "Tomorrow is the wedding day and so today we receive the gifts."

He then went in and saw the master and after introduction said, "Tonight there is a great disaster likely to overtake your house. I have come on this account and want to shield you from it. Will you please do what I ask of you?"

The master did not believe this but said, "A crazy passer comes to me with such a story as this."

The young man said, "Never mind about my being a crazy lunatic; you will know tonight whether it be so or not. If my words do not turn out true then you may drive me off or do to me as you please. Only do what I ask of you."

The master then began to have doubts and, thinking it over, said, "Let's try what you say."

He then had the bride stay in the room as had been ordered, while he himself took his place under the lights and read the Buddhist Book. As the third watch of the night drew on there was a crack of thunder so that all the people in the house trembled from fear and then ran for dear life.

Just then a great tiger came bounding into the court and there sat down. But the man did not change his countenance in the least and kept on reading as though nothing was wrong.

During this time the bride, on plea of going to the closet, tried to press her way out, but the women in charge held onto her and forbade her going.

The bride raised a terrific uproar on this and jumped and pulled. The tiger then sprang up into the hall and took the bar of the door in his teeth. This he did three or four times, then he turned and was gone. The bride had a fainting fit.

The people of the house then gathered their senses about them and gave her warm water and gruel to eat. And after a little while she came to.

The student then ceased from his reading and went out beyond the court. All the house now came to make their bows and speak their thanks, calling him an angel (신인 神人).[†] They desired to give him much gold to reward him for his services. But he said, "I came not for money."

So he shook his clothes and started off, came back to Hwadam, made his bows and said, "I have done as you ordered me."

Hwadam laughed as he said, "How comes it that you made three mistakes in your reading?"

He said, "I made no mistakes in my reading."

But Hwadam said, "That priest passed here again and thanked me for saving a life and added, 'Because he made three mistakes in the reading, I bit the bar of the door three times'."

Then he remembered that he must have read it badly.

---

[*] We speculate that Gale and his pundits understood (*kudok~kudu* 句讀) in the original to mean inserting *kugyŏl*-style *t'o* – grammatical particles and inflections for vocalization. After all, the tiger was Korean.

[†] "神人" means a man with supernatural powers. In Gale's Christian worldview, he has taken this term to be an equivalent of "angel."

서 화 담　　　경 덕　　　박 학 다 문　　　천 문 지 리 술 수 지 학
徐花潭 1)敬德　博學多聞　天文地理術數之學

무 불 통 효　　　복 거 우 장 단　　　화 담 지 상　　　잉 이 위 호　　　일 일
無不通曉　卜居于長湍 2)花潭之上　仍以爲號　一日

회 학 도 강 론　　　홀 유 일 로 승 래 배 이 거　　　화 담 송 승 지 후
會學徒講論　忽有一老僧來拜而去　花潭送僧之後

홀 이 차 탄 불 이　　　학 도 문 기 고　　　화 담 왈　　　여 지 기 승 호
忽爾嗟嘆不已　學徒問其故　花潭曰：汝知其僧乎

왈　　　불 지 의　　　화 담 왈　　　차 시 모 산 지 신 호 야　　　모 처 인
曰：不知矣　花潭曰：此是某山之神虎也　某處人

지 녀 방 영 서　　　이 장 위 기 해 의　　　가 련 의　　　일 학 도 문 왈
之女方迎婿　而將爲其害矣　可憐矣　一學徒問曰：

선 생 기 지 지　　　즉 유 하 가 구 지 도 호　　　화 담 왈　　　유 지 이
先生旣知之　則有何可救之道乎　花潭曰：有之而

단 무 가 송 지 인 의　　　학 도 왈　　　제 자 원 왕 의　　　화 담 왈
但無可送之人矣　學徒曰：弟子願往矣　花潭曰：

약 연 즉 호 의　　　잉 수 일 서 왈　　　차 시 불 경　　　왕 기 가　　　물 선
若然則好矣　仍授一書曰：此是佛經　往其家　勿先

설 이 단 사 지 구 상 탁 촉 화 어 청 상　　　사 기 처 녀 처 지 방 중
泄而但使之具床卓燭火於廳上　使其處女處之房中

이 쇄 사 면 문　　　우 사 건 비 오 륙 인 견 집 물 방　　　여 어 청 상
而鎖四面門　又使健婢五六人堅執勿放　汝於廳上

독 차 서 이 물 오 구 독　　　즉 애 과　　　계 명 지 시　　　자 가 무 사 의
讀此書而勿誤句讀　則挨過 3)鷄鳴之時　自可無事矣

계 지 신 지　　　기 인 승 교 이 치 왕 기 가　　　즉 상 하 분 운
戒之愼之　其人承敎而馳往其家　則上下紛紜 4)

문 지 즉 이 위 명 장 영 서　　　금 방 수 채　　　기 인 입 견 주 인
問之則以爲明將迎婿　今方受綵　其人入見主人

寒暄 5) 罷後　仍言曰：今夜主家有大厄　吾以此而來

欲使免焉　可如斯如斯　主人不信曰：何處過客

作此病風 6) 之言也　其人曰：無論吾之病風與否

今夜則自有可知之道矣　過後吾言如無靈　則伊

時毆逐　無所不可　第須依吾言爲之可也　主人心

甚訝然 7)　依其言鋪設而俟之　其女亦如其人之

言處之房內　其人端坐廳上燭影之下　而讀經矣

三更時候　忽有霹靂聲　家人皆戰慄走避

見一大虎蹲坐 8) 於庭下而咆哮 9)　其人顏色不變

讀經不撤　此時其處女稱以放矢 10)　限死欲出

諸婢左右執挽　則處女跳踉 11) 不可堪　其虎忽爾

大吼 12)　而噬 13) 破窓前木　如是者三矣　仍忽不見

而處女昏絶矣　家人始收拾精神　以溫水灌之口

須臾得甦　其人讀罷出外　則擧家揖謝　皆以爲神人

以數百金欲酬其恩　其人曰：吾非貪財而來者

仍拂衣 14) 告辭　還拜花潭而復命　則花潭笑曰：汝

何爲誤讀三處　其人曰：無誤讀處矣　花潭曰：俄者

其僧又過去而謝我活人之功　又曰：經書誤讀三處

故噬破廳木而識 15) 之云　其人思之果是誤讀也

1 徐敬德 [1489–1546; styled Kagu 可久; sobriquet Hwadam 花潭; ancestral seat Tangsŏng 唐城; posthumous epithet Mun'gang 文康]: a scholar-official during the reign of King Chungjong 中宗 [r. 1506–44; 1488–1544]. His father was Sŏ Hobŏn 徐好蕃 [dates unknown].

2 長湍: a town to the southeast of Kaesŏng 開城 in Kyŏnggi Province.

3 挨過: insist on having one's way.

4 紛紜: boisterous and unruly.

5 寒暄: lit. "coldness and warmth" = *munan* 問安 = inquire after someone's well-being; exchange pleasantries.

6 病風: short for *pyŏngp'ung sangsŏng* 病風喪性; become mentally unhealthy after suffering from a physical illness.

7 心甚訝然: find something extremely strange.

8 蹲坐: sit in a crouching position.

9 咆哮: the roaring of a beast.

10 放矢 = *pangbun* 放糞: defecate.

11 跳踉: thrash about in order to break free.

12 大吼: give out a loud cry; roar.

13 噬: take a bite out of.

14 拂衣: dust off one's clothes.

15 識 = *p'yoji* 標識: leave one's mark.

——— 33 ———

Pak Yŏp (Tiger Transformation)

Vol. II: 5; n.d.; Diary XII, p. 71 (crossed out);
typed up as "Tiger Transformations" in 9:21 "A Trip to Japan,"
but apparently never published; 192.

Tiger Transformations

Pak Yŏp (Graduated 1596, his wife was a sister of
Kwanghae's Queen).

When Pak Yŏp was Governor of P'yŏngan Province, a Minister in Seoul sent his son with this message: "I find from a mathematical calculation of a fortune-teller that this boy, not yet married, is destined this year to some great misfortune, but that if I leave him in the care of Your Excellency he will be kept safe from harm. For this reason I send him. Kindly see that he is protected and guarded."

Pak gave his consent and had him safely lodged.

Once when the lad was asleep during the day Pak waked him and said, "Tonight trouble awaits you and unless you do as I tell, you will find no escape."

The boy replied, "I shall certainly do as Your Excellency commands."

Pak then said, "Wait here."

Toward evening, as dusk came on, Pak had the mule brought that he was accustomed to ride, saddled it and had the boy mount, saying,

"Now ride just as fast as you can in whatever direction the mule desires to go. When it reaches a place some miles from here it will stop. Then you will dismount and go some distance afoot till you come to a temple of an old vacated monastery. As you enter the main hall you will see a tiger skin. Take it and wrap it round you and lie down. A little later, an old priest will come and try to take the skin away from you, but you must not give it up. If it looks as though he would take it by force, draw your knife and threaten him and he will cease. If you can, keep this up till cockcrow; then you are all right – let him have it then if he wishes. Do you understand?"

He replied, "I shall do just as you tell me."

So he rode forth and the beast fairly flew as with wings till the wind whistled by his ears. Over the mountains he went, though he knew not where he was, and down into a valley where he alighted. There he unsaddled the mule and tied it to a tree and in the light of the moon went on some distance further till he came to a deserted temple.

He approached and found the door unlocked. Entering, he saw how the dust had gathered in heaps upon the floor, while just over the fireplace was flung a great tiger skin. He wrapped this about him and lay down for an hour or so.

Later a rattle at the door called his attention and in came an old priest with a very twisted face and fierce expression.

Said he, with a start, "What's this?"

He came close up and inquired sternly, "What are you doing with my skin on? Give it to me at once."

The boy made no reply but simply lay low and watched. Then it was that the old priest came close up and attempted to take it by force. But the lad drew his knife as though he would run him through and he withdrew. This was repeated five or six times.

While they were thus facing each other the distant village cock crew. The old priest smiled and said, "This is one of Pak Yŏp's tricks; I am helpless."

He then called the boy and said, "Nothing will happen to you now even though you give it – let it go."

Mindful of what Pak had said, the boy gave it and then sat up and watched.

The old priest continued, "Give me your clothes, inner as well as outer, but remain here behind the screen and don't look."

The boy gave his clothes and the old priest took them and the tiger skin and went out. The boy watched him, however, through the chink and when the priest had put on the skin he changed into a great tiger. With a roar of thunder he came bounding in and, taking the boy's clothes, tore them all to pieces.

A moment later he took off the skin and again resumed the form of an old priest in which he came into the hall and, opening a chest, took out special clothes and had the lad put them on.

Then he took a roll of names he had and with red ink marked off from the list the lad's name, saying, "Go now and tell Pak Yŏp not to let out God's plans any more. From this time on you are free to go among tigers without any fear of harm."

He gave him also a piece of oiled paper, saying, "Take this and go forth and if anyone attempts to block your way, just show it."

The boy then set out and on his way home he met a tiger at each corner, but on showing the paper, it bowed and went away. Just as he was about to leave the hills a great beast rose up against him and while he showed the paper, the creature paid no heed but rushed forward as though it would devour him.

The boy said, "If you are so inclined to do me harm, let us both go and lay our case before the old priest."

The tiger assented and away they went to find the old man sitting where he had left him. When the case was laid before him the priest berated the tiger and said, "How is it you have disobeyed my orders?"

The tiger replied, "I was not unaware of your orders but for three days I have had nothing to eat; how can I restrain myself at the sight of flesh? Though it breaks your orders I cannot let this youngster go."

The priest replied, "Then suppose I give you something instead – how will that do?"

The tiger replied, "Good, very good."

Then said the priest, "You go there along the road to the east for half a *ri* or so and you will meet a man with a felt hat on his head; let him suffice you for your meal."

Hearing this, the tiger went forth, and after some time the sound of a gun was heard in the distance. The priest smiled and said, "He's dead, that rascal, dead."

"Why do you say he is dead?" inquired the boy.

The priest replied, "That tiger was my servant and yet he failed to obey me. My sending him off by the east way was to bring him into the hands of the hunter."

The boy left the temple and when the day had lighted up he found his mule once more feeding off the grass. So he rode it home and told all that had happened to him to Pak Yŏp.

Pak Yŏp nodded his head and said, "Yes, yes, I see."

He then sent him home and he grew up a highly successful man.

朴燁 1) 之按關西　有親知之宰相　送其子而托之曰：

此兒姑未冠 2) 而使卜者 3) 推數 4) 則今年有大厄　而若

置將軍之側無事云　故茲送之　乞賜留置　俾得度厄

爔許使留之 一日 此兒晝寢 爔使之攬睡5) 而言曰:

今夜汝有大厄 若依吾言則可免矣 不然則不可免矣

其兒曰:敢不如命 爔曰:第姑俟之 日暮黃昏後

牽出自家所騎之騾 鞴鞍而使其兒騎之戒之曰:

汝騎此而任其所之 此騾行幾里 到一處當立 汝

始可下鞍 尋逕而行 行幾里 必有一巨刹 而年久

廢寺也 入其上房 則有一大虎皮 汝試可蒙其皮

而臥 有一老僧來索其皮矣 切勿給 如至見

奪之境 則以刀欲割之 彼不敢奪 如是而相持

至鷄鳴後則無事矣 鷄鳴後 許給其皮可也

汝能行此乎 對曰:謹受教矣 仍騎騾而出門 則其

行如飛 兩耳但聞風聲 不知向何處 而度山踰嶺

至一山谷之口而乃下 仍卸鞍6) 而帶微月之光 尋草

路而行 行幾里 果有一廢寺 入其寺而開上房之戶

즉 진 애 퇴　　적　　이 방 지 하 돌　　　유 일 대 호 피 일 장 의
則塵埃堆 7) 積　而房之下埃 8)　有一大虎皮一張矣

잉 의 기 언　　몽 피 이 와 의　　수 식 경 후　　홀 유 박 탁 지 성
仍依其言　蒙皮而臥矣　數食頃後　忽有剝啄之聲 9)

일 로 승 상 모 흉 녕　자　　입 문 이 언 왈　　차 아 래 의
一老僧狀貌兇獰 10) 者　入門而言曰：此兒來矣

잉 근 전 왈　　차 피 하 위 몽 이 와 호　　속 환 아　　기 아 불
仍近前曰：此皮何爲蒙而臥乎　速還我　其兒不

답 이 와 자 여 의　　기 승 욕 탈 지　　즉 거 도 작　　욕 할 지 상
答而臥自如矣　其僧欲奪之　則擧刀作　欲割之狀

기 승 퇴 좌　　여 시 자 오 륙 차　　이 여 시 상 지 지 제　　원 촌 계
其僧退坐　如是者五六次　而如是相持之際　遠村鷄

성 악 악　　기 승 미 소 왈　　차 시 박 엽 지 소 위　　역 부 내 하
聲喔喔 11)　其僧微笑曰：此是朴燁之所爲　亦復奈何

잉 호 기 기 아 왈　　금 즉 환 피 어 아　　고 무 방 가 기 좌
仍呼起其兒曰：今則還皮於我　固無妨可起坐

기 아 기 문 박 엽 지 언　　고 잉 급 기 피 이 기 좌　　기 승 우 왈
其兒旣聞朴燁之言　故仍給其皮而起坐　其僧又曰：

여 가 탈 상 하 의 급 아　　이 절 물 개 호 견 지 야　　기 아 의 기 언
汝可脫上下衣給我　而切勿開戶見之也　其兒依其言

해 의 급 지　　기 승 지 기 의 여 피 이 출 외　　기 아 종 창 극 규 견
解衣給之　其僧持其衣與皮而出外　其兒從窓隙窺見

즉 기 승 거 피 몽 지 변 위 일 대 호　　대 성 포 효　　잉 향 전 함 의
則其僧擧皮蒙之變爲一大虎　大聲咆哮　仍向前啣衣

폭 폭 렬 지　　잉 환 탈 피　　우 위 로 승　　입 호 이 개 일 폐 상
幅幅裂之 12)　仍還脫皮　又爲老僧　入戶而開一弊箱

출 승 지 상 하 의　　사 복 지　　우 출 일 주 지 축　　피 이 견 지
出僧之上下衣　使服之　又出一周紙軸　披而見之

이 주 필 점 기 아 지 명 자 상　잉 왈　여 가 출 거　어 박 엽 운
以朱筆點其兒之名字上　仍曰：汝可出去　語朴燁云

불 가 설 천 기 야　여 종 금 입 호 군 중　결 무 상 해 지 려 의
不可泄天機也　汝從今入虎羣中　決無傷害之慮矣

우 급 일 편 유 지 왈　지 차 이 출　여 유 란　우 로 자
又給一片油紙曰：持此而出　如有攔 13) 于路者

출 시 차 지　기 아 의 기 언　출 문　곡 곡 유 호 이 차 로
出示此紙　其兒依其言　出門　曲曲有虎而遮路

매 시 차 지　즉 저 두 이 거　미 급 동 구　우 유 일 호 차 전
每示此紙　則低頭而去　未及洞口　又有一虎遮前

고 출 시 차 지　즉 불 고 이 장 서　기 아 왈　여 약 여 차
故出示此紙　則不顧而將噬　其兒曰：汝若如此

즉 여 아 해 지 사 중　결 송　우 로 승 지 전 가 야　호 내 점 두
則與我偕至寺中　決訟 14) 于老僧之前可也　虎乃點頭

여 지 해 지 사 중　즉 로 승 상 재　도 기 상　승 질 왈
與之偕至寺中　則老僧尚在　道其狀　僧叱曰：

여 하 위 령　호 왈　비 불 지 명 이 아 이 삼 일　견 륙 이
汝何違令　虎曰：非不知命而餓已三日　見肉而

하 가 방 송 호　수 위 령 이 차 즉 불 가 방 송　로 승 왈
何可放送乎　雖違令而此則不可放送　老僧曰：

연 즉 급 대 가 호　왈　연 즉 행 의　승 왈　종 동 행 반 리 허
然則給代可乎　曰：然則幸矣　僧曰：從東行半里許

즉 유 일 인 착 전 립　이 래 의　가 작 여 료 기 지 자 야
則有一人着氈笠 15) 而來矣　可作汝療飢之資也

기 호 의 기 언 출 문　수 식 경 후　홀 유 포 성 지 원 출　승 소
其虎依其言出門　數食頃後　忽有砲聲之遠出　僧笑

왈　궐 한 사 의　기 아 문 기 고　승 왈　거 시 아 지 졸 야
曰：厥漢死矣　其兒問其故　僧曰：渠是我之卒也

불 종 령 고 아 사 왕 동 급 포 수 의   개 착 전 립 인 운 자
不從令故俄使往東給砲手矣 盖着氈笠人云者

즉 포 수 고 야   기 아 사 이 출 동   즉 천 효 이 라 흘 초   의
卽砲手故也 其兒辭而出洞 則天曉而騾齕草 16) 矣

잉 기 이 환   견 박 엽 이 언 기 상   엽 점 두 이 치 송 기 가
仍騎而還 見朴燁而言其狀 燁點頭而治送其家

기 아 과 대 달 운 이
其兒果大達云耳

1 朴燁 [1570–1623; styled Sugya 叔夜; sobriquet Kukch'ang 菊窓; ancestral
   seat Pannam 潘南]: scholar-official during the reign of Kwanghaegun 光
   海君 [r. 1608–23; 1575–1641]. His father was Pak Tongho 朴東豪 [dates
   unknown].
2 未冠: not yet capped, not yet come-of-age (*kwallye* 冠禮).
3 卜者: fortune-teller.
4 推數: prognosticate.
5 攪睡: wake someone up.
6 卸鞍: unsaddle.
7 塵埃堆積: accumulation of dust and dirt.
8 下埃: warmer part of a heated floor.
9 剝啄之聲: the sound of knocking at the door.
10 兇獰: a wild and vicious personality.
11 喔喔: the sound of a cock crowing.
12 幅幅裂之: tear something asunder.
13 攔: obstruct, block.
14 決訟: receive a verdict or final judgment.
15 氈笠: cylindrical felt hat that was part of the formal attire of the warden
   of a military prison.
16 齕草: graze.

34

Pak Yŏp

Vol. II: 5; n.d.; Diary XIV, p. 30; 194.

In the third month of the year *kyehae* (1623), Pak Yŏp sat alone with the light burning by him handling a sword and sighing whereupon he heard the sound of a footstep outside the window.

He called, "Who are you?"

The reply was, "I am so-and-so of this camp."

Pak asked, "Why have you come?"

His reply was, "What will Your Excellency do under the circumstances?"

Pak answered, "It's not for you to ask me, but rather for me to ask you. What had I better do?"

The answer was, "I have three plans: first, second, third. I would ask that Your Excellency choose from among them."

Pak said, "What is your first plan?"

The answer was, "Take soldiers and oppose the government. If you make friends with the Kŭm (Jin 金)* you can become king all the way to the Imjin."

Pak again replied, "And now your second plan – what is it?"

"Make haste to raise thirty-thousand troops, put me in charge, make a rush to the capital and take your chances."

"Now your last plan? What is that?"

"You have for generations stood by the state. Take what comes gently and count that best."

Pak said nothing for a time and then gave a long breath and said, "The third plan is best."

Then said the officer, "I shall leave then," and left. Though it was not known who that was, as his name was not known, some say it was Yonggoldae (Longguda).†

* The Jurchen state of Jin (K. Kŭm; 1115–1234).

† See note 11 below.

계 해　삼 월 반 정 후　박 엽　독 좌 촉 하　무 검 발 탄
癸亥[1] 三月反正後　朴燁[2] 獨坐燭下　撫劍發歎

창 외 유 해 수 성　문 수 야　대 왈　막 객　모 야　왈
窓外有咳嗽聲[3]　問誰也　對曰：幕客[4]某也　曰：

하 위 이 래　대 왈　사 도 장 하 이 위 지　왈　시 문 어 여 장
何爲而來　對曰：使道將何以爲之　曰：試問於汝將

하 이 위 지　대 왈　소 인 유 상 중 하 삼 책　사 도 택 어
何以爲之　對曰：小人有上中下三策　使道擇於

삼 책 가 야　하 위 상 책　왈　사 도 거 병 이 반　북 통 금 인
三策可也　何謂上策　曰：使道擧兵而叛[5]　北通金人

즉 림 진　이 북　비 조 가　지 유 야　하 불 실
則臨津[6]以北　非朝家[7]之有也　下不失

위 타 지 계　야　왈　하 위 중 책　왈　급 발 병 삼 만 인
尉佗之計[8]也　曰：何謂中策　曰：急發兵三萬人

사 소 인 장 지　고 행 이 향 경　즉 승 패 미 가 지 야　왈
使小人將之　鼓行而向京　則勝敗未可知也　曰：

하 위 하 책　왈　사 도 세 록 지 신　야　순 수 국 명 가 야
何謂下策　曰：使道世祿之臣[9]也　順受國命可也

박 엽 묵 연 량 구　위 연 장 탄 왈　오 종 하 책　왈　소 인 자
朴燁默然良久　喟然長嘆曰[10]：吾從下策　曰：小人自

차 고 사　잉 불 지 거 처　미 지 차 인 위 수　이 성 명 역 불
此告辭　仍不知去處　未知此人爲誰　而姓名亦不

로 어 세　혹 운　차 시 룡 골 대　운
露於世　或云　此是龍骨大[11]云

---

1 癸亥: 1623, the year of the Restoration of King Injo (Injo *panjŏng* 仁祖反正), involving the dethronement of Kwanghaegun 光海君 [r: 1608–23; 1575–1641] and the enthronement of King Injo 仁祖 [r. 1623–49; 1595–1649].

2 朴燁 [1570–1623; styled Sugya 叔夜; sobriquet Kukch'ang 菊窓; ancestral seat Pannam 潘南]: scholar-official during the reign of Kwanghaegun 光海君 [r. 1608–23; 1575–1641]. His father was Pak Tongho 朴東豪 [dates unknown].

3 咳嗽聲: sound of coughing.

4 幕客 = *pijang* 裨將: unranked military attendant attached to regional government offices or envoys.

5 擧兵而叛: raise an army of rebels.

6 臨津: the Imjin River, originating in Tŏgwŏn County 德源郡 in Hamgyŏng Province and entering the Yellow Sea.

7 朝家 = 朝廷: the court.

8 尉佗之計: lit. "the ruse of Zhao Tuo [ca. 240–137 BC]." Zhao Tuo 趙佗 is also called Wei Tuo 尉佗 because he was a military defender (*wei* 尉) in Nanhai 南海 during the Qin dynasty 秦 [221–206 BC]. After the fall of the Qin, Zhao Tuo enthroned himself as King Wu of Nanyue 南越武王. When Liu Bang 劉邦 [r. 202–195 BC; 256/247–195 BC] established the Han dynasty 漢 [206 BC–AD 220], Zhao Tuo pleaded the Han court for an investiture with the title of King of Nanyue. Whenever the constellation of forces around him grew weak, he would proclaim himself hegemon, and whenever those same forces grew strong, he would petition for investiture.

9 世祿之臣: a retainer whose clansmen have held government office over several generations.

10 喟然長嘆: let out a long sigh of lament.

11 龍骨大 = Ingguldai 英俄爾岱 / 英固爾岱 [1596–1648]: a Manchu general whose talents in organizational skills earned him a promotion to be president of the Board of Revenue of the Qing 淸 [1644–1912].

—— 35 ——

The End of Pak Yŏp

Vol. II: 6; n.d.; Diary XIV, pp. 29–30; 193.

In the year *kyehae* (1623) Yi Kwi (Yŏnp'yŏng) and his followers laid a plot to rid the throne of Kwanghae and set Injo. Ku Inhu (later Prince Nŭngsŏng) was also privy to the plan. He was there in the camp of Pak Yŏp, being one of his aides.

One day on speaking his farewell, Pak Yŏp gave him thirty horse loads of red cloth but Inhu declined to take them, saying they were of no use to him.

Yŏp said, laughing, "You'll have use for them by and by; take them with you."

He then took Inhu by the hand and said to him, "Later on please spare my body and save it from the rabble."

But Inhu replied, "I don't know what you mean by such a speech as this?"

Yŏp said, "Never mind. Do not forget it, is all I ask."

And so Inhu left and made his way to Seoul.

Later when Pak Yŏp was commanded to die, all the court were alarmed over it and no one wished to take the responsibility. Inhu then asked that he go.

Pak was hanged according to royal order and his many enemies about flocked into P'yŏngyang with their knives to have each a piece of his body but Inhu forbade it and safely guarded him. He placed it in a coffin and set out for Seoul, reaching Chŏnghwa. Inhu was suddenly made a general of the guards and so he had to go forward, ahead of the procession.

On this, the enemies following after broke open the coffin and carved up the body and cut it into minute pieces. This was as a reward for the thousand people whom Pak Yŏp had killed.

When Pak Yŏp was young he had his fortune told: "If you don't kill a thousand men, a thousand men will kill you." The "Thousand men" was Inhu's boy name. He was called Ku Thousand-men.

Pak Yŏp mistook this to mean literally one thousand men and so killed one thousand, many of them perfectly innocent, and now he had on his head the guilt of all these unfortunate ones.

When the uprising took place there was no ready way of marking King Injo's troops, so they made red caps of Pak's red cloth and had them wear them. Red caps for soldiers take their rise from that time. Pak knew this in advance and so gave it.

癸亥 1) 李延平 2) 諸人 將謀擧義 3) 具綾城仁垕 4)

亦預 而時在朴燁幕下 一日告辭 朴燁贐 5)

以紅氈 6) 三十馱 7) 仁垕辭以無用 燁笑曰：

將有日後之用 第爲持去 仍執手而托曰：

일 후 군 행 수 오 시　인 후 경 왈　차 하 교 야　엽 왈
日後君幸收吾屍　仁垕驚曰：此何敎也　燁曰：

군 제 명 우 심　인 후 사 퇴 의　후 박 엽 수 후 명 8) 시
君第銘于心　仁垕辭退矣　後朴燁受後命 8) 時

거 조 개 공　무 인 감 하 거 자　인 후 자 청 하 거 이 처 교 9)
擧朝皆恐　無人敢下去者　仁垕自請下去而處絞 9)

즉 엽 다 수 가 10)　제 인 일 시 지 도 이 입　인 후 일 병 금 지
則燁多讐家 10)　諸人一時持刀而入　仁垕一併禁之

입 관 송 상 행　행 도 중 화　인 후 제 어 장 11)　잉 선 환 의
入棺送喪行　行到中和　仁垕除御將 11)　仍先還矣

수 가 추 지　파 관 이 촌 단 이 거　차 시 살 천 인 지 해
讐家追至　破棺而寸斷以去　此是殺千人之害

야　박 엽 소 시 추 수 즉 왈　불 살 천 인　천 인 살 여
也　朴燁少時推數則曰：不殺千人　千人殺汝

천 인 내 구 인 후 소 자 12)　이 엽 오 지 이 다 살 불 고 13)
千人乃具仁垕少字 12)　而燁誤知而多殺不辜 13)

이 충 천 인 지 수　량 가 탄 야　반 정 시　인 묘 지 군
以充千人之數　良可嘆也　反正時　仁廟之軍

무 이 구 별　이 기 홍 전　작 전 립 이 착 지　금 지 홍 전 립
無以區別　以其紅氈　作氈笠而着之　今之紅氈笠

즉 기 제 야　박 엽 지 지 이 유 차 증 지
卽其制也　朴燁知之而有此贈之

1　癸亥: 1623, the year of the Restoration of King Injo (Injo *panjŏng* 仁祖反正), the dethronement of Kwanghaegun 光海君 [r: 1608–23; 1575–1641] and the enthronement of King Injo 仁祖 [r. 1623–49; 1595–1649].

2　李延平 = Yŏnp'yŏng puwŏn'gun Yi Kwi 延平府院君 李貴 [1557–1633; styled Ogyŏ 玉汝; sobriquet Mukchae 黙齋; ancestral seat Yŏnan 延安; posthumous epithet Ch'ungjŏng 忠定]: scholar-official during the reign of King Injo [r. 1623–49; 1595–1649]. His father was Yi Chŏnghwa 李廷華 [1520–58].

3　擧義: raise a "righteous army" (*ŭibyŏng* 義兵).

4 具仁垕 [1578–1658; styled Chungjae 仲載; sobriquet Yup'o 柳浦; ancestral seat Nŭngsŏng 綾城; posthumous epithet Ch'ungmu 忠武]: military official during the reign of King Injo [r. 1623–49; 1595–1649]. His father was Ku Sŏng 具宬 [1558–1618].

5 贐: give to one setting out on a journey a token of remembrance.

6 紅氈: a piece of red woolen cloth.

7 三十駄: thirty bales.

8 後命 = *sayak* 賜藥: (the king) send an exiled criminal a bowl of arsenic-based medicine as a form of capital punishment.

9 處絞: execute by means of strangulation.

10 讐家: the household of one's enemy.

11 除御將: (the king) appoint a person to an official position as the commander of one of the capital guard units (*ŏyŏng taejang* 御營大將; a junior second-grade post) at the Capital Guard (Ŏyŏngch'ŏng 御營廳) without going through the ordinary appointment procedure of a recommendation (*ch'ŏn'gŏ* 薦擧) by the Board of Personnel [Ijo 吏曹].

12 少字: one's childhood name.

13 不辜 = *mugo chi in* 無辜之人: a person without guilt; innocent person.

———— 36 ————

The Innkeeper's Daughter

Vol. II: 7; n.d.; Diary XIV, pp. 31–2 (crossed out);
typed-up in Miscellaneous Writings II 30, pp. 18–19;
published in The Korea Magazine (January 1919), pp. 18–20.

Is such a matter as this a leading of Providence or is
it a case of pure chance? Koreans have an idea that the
minor events of life are a definite part of the great
warp and woof that make up the world and its doings.
Doubtless many such stories as this have been written
after the events happened but many again seem true to fact
and have the mark of the prophetic imprint upon them.

Yi Kich'uk was a slave in a wine-seller's shop. He was a very stupid fellow who did not know east from west, but thought only of what he ate. Strong, however, he was a giant as to the power of his arm. The innkeeper made him his general servant.

This innkeeper had a daughter about fifteen years of age who had been educated somewhat, very highly gifted and bright for her years. Her parents loved her dearly and sought high and low for a young man to whom she might be wedded, but all such proposals the daughter refused to listen to. Said she, "I have found my good man. Yi Kich'uk is my choice."

Her parents were greatly scandalized and furiously angry over this proposal. They scolded her, saying, "For what earthly reason can you wish to wed with a slave? We forbid your ever mentioning such a thing again."

She replied, however, "I shall die rather than allow anyone else to be given me."

The parents advised and coaxed, but all in vain, and having no other recourse, at last gave consent.

The daughter said, "Now that I am married to Kich'uk I do not wish to remain here. I shall go up to Seoul, where we can get a little house and live together."

Realizing that her presence at home was a cause of mortification, the parents gave their approval and, providing them with so much by way of a start, let them go. Thus they went to the capital and settled in Ch'ang-dong where they sold drink.

The spirit they vended became noted for its excellent flavour and was praised by all the neighbourhood.

One day the wife brought out the first volume of the *Shilüe* (史略) and, having marked the page that tells how Yi Yin (伊尹) drove out Taijia (太甲) and locked him up in the Wutong Palace (1753 BC), gave it to her husband and said, "Take this book to the pine grove by the north gate of the palace where you will find a group of men gathered together. Open it and place it before them and say, 'I'd like to learn this part of the book, please teach me.'"

Kich'uk went as his wife directed him, and there he found seven or eight men seated and talking together. Hearing what Kich'uk said, they looked at each other with a start and asked, "Who sent you here on this errand?"

He replied, "My wife sent me."

The group inquired, "Where is your house?" and thither they went together.

The wife brought out mats on which they could be seated and added wine and refreshments. She then said, "I am aware of what you gentlemen are about. My husband is a fool as regards most things but he is a veritable Samson as regards strength. If you have any occasion to use him he is at your service, and may his name be finally recorded among the faithful servants of the King. We have plenty of wine here, well flavoured. If you have occasion to meet and consult, meet in my house. It is quiet, too, and unknown to anybody."

The group was greatly surprised at this but agreed to her proposal. Among them were Kim Yu (金瑬) and Yi Kwi (李貴).*

Later when the soldiers arose to put out the wicked King Kwanghae and put Injo on the throne, they entered by the West Gate of the palace. Kich'uk led the way by breaking with his own hands the bar that held the doors.

When they had accomplished their purpose and the names of those specially praiseworthy were recorded, Yi Kich'uk was found among the highest officials of the 2nd class.

* Kim and Yi were leading figures of the Restoration of King Injo.

리 기 축　　점 사　　고 노　　야　　위 인 심 로 둔　　불 지 동 서
李起築 1) 店舍 2) 雇奴 3) 也　爲人甚魯鈍　不知東西

이 지 이 포 반 위 호　　유 절 륜 지 력　　점 주 이 노 예 사 지
而只以飽飯爲好　有絶倫之力　店主以奴隷使之

주 가 유 녀 년 급 계　　이 초 해 문 자　　성 우 민 민
主家有女年及笄 4)　而稍解文字　性又穎敏 5)

부 모 종 애　　욕 택 가 서 이 가 지　　기 녀 불 원 왈
父母鍾愛 6)　欲擇佳婿而嫁之　其女不願曰:

오 지 량 인　　오 자 택 지　　원 가 우 리 기 축 의　　기 축
吾之良人 7)　吾自擇之　願嫁于李己丑矣　己丑

자 기 축 생　　고 잉 이 명 호 지 기 축 운 자　　후 개 지 고 야
者己丑生　故仍以名呼之起築云者　後改之故也

기 부 모 대 경 이 질 책 왈　　여 하 소 연 이 욕 가 우 고
其父母大驚而叱責曰: 汝何所緣而欲嫁于雇

노 야　　사 물 갱 언　　즉 기 녀 이 사 자 기　　불 원 타 적
奴也　使勿更言　則其女以死自期　不願他適 8)

부 모 책 지 유 지　종 불 청　계 무 내 하　수 허 지
父母責之諭之　終不聽　計無奈何　遂許之

녀 왈　기 이 기 축 작 배　불 원 재 차　여 지 욕 상 경
女曰：旣以己丑作配　不願在此　與之欲上京

매 두 옥 이 자 생 운 운　기 부 모 역 이 위 재 차 야 인
買斗屋而資生云云　其父母亦以爲在此惹人

치 소　불 여 각 거 지 위 호　잉 급 가 산 지 자 이 송 지
耻笑　不如各居之爲好　仍給家産之資而送之

기 녀 여 기 축 상 경　매 사 어 장 동　이 고 주 9) 위 업
其女與己丑上京　買舍於壯洞　而沽酒 9) 爲業

주 심 청 렬 10)　인 개 칭 지　일 일　이 사 략 11)　초 권 수 지
酒甚淸冽 10)　人皆稱之　一日　以史略 11) 初卷授之

이 표 어 이 윤 12)　폐 태 갑 13)　방 동 궁 14)　편 이 시 왈
而標於伊尹 12)　廢太甲 13) 放桐宮 14) 篇而示曰：

지 차 책 왕 신 무 문 15)　후 송 음 하　유 제 인 지 취 회 16)　자
持此冊往神武門 15) 後松陰下　有諸人之聚會 16) 者

이 책 치 우 전 이 원 수 학 언　기 축 의 기 언 이 왕　즉 과 유 칠
以冊置于前而願受學焉　己丑依其言而往　則果有七

팔 인 단 회 17) 이 수 작　문 기 언 이 상 고 대 경 왈　수 소 사 야
八人團會 17) 而酬酌　聞其言而相顧大驚曰：誰所使也

대 왈　소 인 지 처 여 시 운 의　제 인 문 기 가 이 해 왕
對曰：小人之妻如是云矣　諸人問其家而偕往

즉 기 녀 영 지　좌 이 설 주 효 대 지　잉 타 왈　렬 위 18) 지 사
則其女迎之　座而設酒肴待之　仍打曰：列位 18) 之事

첩 이 지 지　가 부 우 치 19)　이 유 려 력 20)　일 후 자 유 용 처
妾已知之　家夫愚痴 19) 而有膂力 20)　日後自有用處

사 성 지 후　득 참 훈 록 21)　행 의　오 가 유 주 이 지 차 다
事成之後　得參勳錄 21) 幸矣　吾家有酒而旨且多 22)

의 사 시 필 회 우 첩 가 무 방　　첩 가 정 벽　　무 유 인 지
議事時必會于妾家無妨　妾家靜僻　無有人知

중 개 경 이 이 허 지　　개 시 승 평　　급 연 평　　제 인 야
衆皆驚異而許之　盖是昇平 23) 及延平 24) 諸人也

기 후 거 의 이 입 창 의 문　　시　　기 축 거 전　　절 장 군 목
其後擧義而入彰義門 25) 時　己丑居前　折將軍木 26)

이 입　　사 정 책 훈 참 이 등 공 신
而入　事定策勳參二等功臣

1 李起築 [1589–1645; styled Hŭiyŏl 希說; ancestral seat Chŏnju 全州; posthumous epithet Yangŭi 襄毅]: eighth-generation descendant of Prince
  Hyoryŏng 孝寧大君 [1396–1486] and a military official under King Injo
  仁祖 [r. 1623–49; 1595–1649].
2 店舍 = chŏmmak 店幕: tavern; a place where travelers buy food and/or stay
  the night.
3 雇奴: servant; employee.
4 笄 = kyerye 笄禮: lit. "hairpin ceremony" = rite-of-passage for girls;
  equivalent to boys' capping (kwallye 冠禮).
5 穎敏: smart and quick-witted.
6 鍾愛: dote on someone.
7 良人: husband.
8 他適: marry into another family.
9 沽酒: sell alcoholic beverages.
10 清冽: clear and ice-cold.
11 史略 Shilüe: lit. "summaries of histories," also known as the Outline
  (or Summaries) of Eighteen Histories (Shiba shilüe 十八史略); a textbook of
  summaries of the eighteen dynastic histories compiled by Zeng Xianzhi
  曾先之 [dates unknown] of the Yuan dynasty [1271–1368].
12 伊尹 Yi Yin: a legendary Chinese who helped King Tang 湯王 of the Shang
  dynasty dethrone King Jie 桀王 of the Xia dynasty 夏. Yi Yin and King Tang
  established the Yin dynasty 殷 (1600–1046 BC; Late Shang dynasty) and
  governed with virtue.
13 太甲 Taijia: name of Taizhong 太宗, the second king of the Yin dynasty 殷
  (1600–1046 BC). After suffering under Taizhong's tyranny, Yi Yin plotted
  to dethrone him.
14 放桐宮: banish to Paulownia Palace.
15 神武門: the north gate of Kyŏngbok Palace 景福宮.

16 聚會: gathering.

17 團會: gather around in a circle.

18 列位: honourable superiors.

19 愚痴: foolish and ignorant.

20 膂力 = *yongnyŏk* 用力: lit. "backbone strength" = exert one's strength.

21 勳錄: roster of meritorious deeds rendered to the state.

22 旨且多: tasty and plentiful.

23 昇平 = Sŭngp'yŏng puwŏn'gun Kim Yu 昇平府院君 金瑬 [1571–1648; styled Kwanok 冠玉; sobriquet Pukchŏ 北渚; ancestral seat Sunch'ŏn 順天; posthumous epithet Munch'ung 文忠]: King Injo 仁祖 [r. 1623–49; 1595–1649]. His father was Kim Yŏmul 金汝岉 [1548–92].

24 李延平 = Yŏnp'yŏng puwŏn'gun Yi Kwi 延平府院君 李貴 [1557–1633; styled Ogyŏ 玉汝; sobriquet Mukchae 黙齋; ancestral seat Yŏnan 延安; posthumous epithet Ch'ungjŏng 忠定]: scholar-official during the reign of King Injo 仁祖 [r. 1623–49; 1595–1649]. His father was Yi Chŏnghwa 李廷華 [1520-1558].

25 彰義門: Chahamun 紫霞門: a gate in Seoul.

26 將軍木: crossbeam used to lock a gate.

———— **37** ————

Defiance to a Spirit

Vol. II: 8; n.d.; "A Trip to Japan" 9:21, pp. 116–17; Diary XII, pp. 75–8 (crossed out); also in *Miscellaneous Writings II*: 30, pp. 105–6; 198.

Yi Hangbok (1556–1618 AD) was for a time Prime Minister
and is known today as Paeksa Sŏnsaeng (White Sand
Teacher). He is said to have had occult powers that
gave his name a special fear among all
classes of the people.

In learning, ability, religion, and uprightness of character, Yi Hangbok was first of all. When he was young he had special friends among the ministers' sons whom he saw frequently. Among them was a special friend who had been invalided for a long time with no hope of recovery. The father on account of this only son of his was in constant distress. He had called the best physicians of his day, fortune-tellers, too, but all in vain.

One day, hearing of a certain blind sorcerer who could cast lots and tell the future, he sent a horse and had him brought. Said he, "Cast your lots now and tell me about my son."

He shook the box and repeating his prayer for a time, cast the die, saying, "Bad luck! He will die this year, in such a moon, on such a day, and at such an hour."

With tears streaming down his face, the father asked, "Can you do nothing for him? Save him, I pray you."

The sorcerer replied, "There is only one way to save him. But I cannot speak of it."

The father wanted to hear it.

But the sorcerer continued,* "If I mention it I shall die myself, and so I dare not and cannot. Why should I die to let someone else live?"

Weeping, the father called on him to speak and tell him.

With changed countenance, the sorcerer said, "You have no consideration for another. Every man likes to live and hates to die. You love your son better above everything in the world; why should I not love my life, too? Please don't ask me any further."

Reduced to hopelessness, the master shed bitter tears.

Hearing this, the invalid's young wife picked up a short knife and, bounding out of the kitchen, took the sorcerer by the collar and said, "I am the sick man's wife. If my husband dies I have decided to die with him. If you did not know how to cast the lot in his favour, you need not have said anything at all, but now you have thrown and you admit that there is a way to save him, and yet you will not tell us. This I have heard with my own ears. In a case like this, I care nothing as to my being a woman, and demand that you tell. If not, I'll drive this knife into you and then into my own neck. You shall die anyway; why not tell what will save the man and spare his life?"

The sorcerer remained in thought for a little and then said, "What the ancients said as to guarding the tongue is true; swifter does the wrong word fly forth than a galloping horse. I will tell you then, so please let me go. There is a man near here called Yi Hangbok."

The master said, "Yes, I know him well – he is my son's friend."

The sorcerer said, "Have him come here and see that he stays till such-and-such a day and all will be well." Again he said, "I shall die on that day and so I ask that you will please look after my wife and children and treat them as your own."

Having said this, he took his departure.

Immediately the Master called Yi Hangbok, told him all and urged him to stay. He gave consent and from this time on remained with the invalid and slept in his room.

On the night mentioned by the sorcerer, he was sleeping on the same pillow as the sick man, when with the third watch there came an eerie cry at the door and a wind that threatened to blow out the light. The sick man lay in a semi-conscious condition. Hangbok, who was awake, suddenly saw a spirit standing back of the light with a drawn sword in his hand. He called, "Yi Hangbok-*a*!† Bring me out this sick man."

Hangbok inquired, "Why such a request?"

The spirit answered, "This man and I were enemies in a former existence and now the time has come for me to square accounts with him and take vengeance. If I miss this moment, no opportunity, as far as I can see, will ever come again."

Hangbok said, "The master of this house has put his son in my care; I shall never give him to you."

The spirit shouted, "Beware! Unless you give him up I'll destroy you, as well."

Hangbok answered back, "My death is no concern to me, but give him up? Never!"

Then the spirit, in fierce anger, rushed at him with uplifted knife, but three times bounced back. Then he threw away his sword and, bowing down humbly, said, "May Your Excellency please take pity on my case and hand over to me this man."

Hangbok replied, "Why do you not kill me?"

The spirit said, "You are a great pillar of state; your name will be recorded in history – an upright man, a superior man. How can I harm you; give me that man only."

Hangbok replied again, "The only way you can get him is to kill me." He then lay down with his arms around the sick boy.

Just then the cock of the distant village crew. The spirit then gave a great cry, "I shall never have a chance again to take vengeance; is this not something to feel resentful over? This is due to your having been warned by a certain sorcerer who lives in such-and-such a village. I'll take it out of him."

He then picked up his sword, passed out of the main gate and was gone.

Just then the sick man passed into a swoon. They gave him warm water to drink and in a little he came to.

On the day following, word came that the blind man was dead and the master took his wife and family under his care.

* Gale seems to have skipped a line; we have reconstructed the text here.
† "-a": vocative particle used to summon or address close friends and intimates.

오 성　　　문 학 재 서　　덕 행 명 절 지 겸 비　　당 추 위 제 일
鰲城 1) 文學才諝 2) 德行名節之兼備　當推爲第一

소 시　　여 린 거 재 상 지 자 친 숙　　상 여 왕 래　　기 인 적
少時　與隣居宰相之子親熟　相與往來　其人積

년 침 아　　장 지 무 가 내 하 지 경　　기 부 이 기 독 자 지 병
年沈痾 3)　將至無可奈何之境　其父以其獨子之病

주 소 초 심　　요 의 문 복　　무 소 불 지　　일 일　　문 유 일
晝宵焦心 4)　邀醫問卜　無所不至　一日　聞有一

맹 명 복 지 인 지 사 생　　송 기 영 래　　사 지 복 지
盲名卜知人之死生　送騎迎來　使之卜之

즉 복 자 작 괘　　심 음 요 두 왈　　필 불 행 의　　장 어 금 년 모
則卜者作卦　沈吟搖頭曰：必不幸矣　將於今年某

월 일 시 사 의　　기 부 체 읍 왈　　기 혹 유 가 구 지 방 호
月日時死矣　其父涕泣曰：其或有可救之方乎

복 자 왈　　제 유 일 사 지 가 구　　이 차 즉 불 가 발 설 의
卜者曰：第有一事之可救　而此則不可發說矣

기 부 원 문 지　　복 자 왈　　약 언 즉 오 필 사 의
其父願聞之　卜者曰：若言則吾必死矣

하 가 위 타 인 이 대 사 호　　기 부 우 읍 이 힐 지
何可爲他人而代死乎　其父又泣而詰之

복 자 작 색　　언 왈　　주 인 지 언　　가 위 비 인 정 지 언 야
卜者作色 5) 言曰：主人之言　可謂非人情之言也

호 생 악 사　　인 지 상 정 야　　주 인 욕 위 기 자 이 오 독 불 위
好生惡死 6)　人之常情也　主人欲爲其子而吾獨不爲

오신호 차즉불필갱문야 주인무내하이체읍이이
吾身乎 此則不必更問也 主人無奈何而涕泣而已

기병인지처 자내지소도이출래 수파복자지항이
其病人之妻 自內持小刀而出來 手把卜者之項而

언왈 오시병인지처야 부사즉오역종사결우심
言曰: 吾是病人之妻也 夫死則吾亦從死決于心

여약불지점리 즉불언용혹무괴 이기해지의
汝若不知占理 則不言容或無怪 7) 而旣解之矣

차유가구지방운 이이사위언종불언지 오기문지
且有可救之方云 而以死爲言終不言之 吾旣聞之

도차지두 하가고남녀지별호 오장이차도자여
到此地頭 8) 何可顧男女之別乎 吾將以此刀刺汝

이오역자자 의 여지사즉일야 기지일사즉하
而吾亦自刺 9) 矣 汝之死則一也 旣知一死則何

불명언이구인지명호 복자묵연량구 내왈 사불
不明言而救人之命乎 卜者默然良久 乃曰: 駟不

급설 정위차야 오장언지방지가호 잉언왈
及舌 10) 政謂此也 吾將言之放之可乎 仍言曰:

유리항복자호 주인왈 과유이즉오아지붕우야
有李恒福者乎 主人曰: 果有而卽吾兒之朋友也

복자왈 자금일요차인 여지동처 사지불잠리
卜者曰: 自今日邀此人 與之同處 使之不暫離

과모일즉자가무사의 차왈 오어이일 당사
過某日則自可無事矣 且曰: 吾於伊日 11) 當死

오지처자가선고휼 시동가인 운 이잉사
吾之妻子可善顧恤 12) 視同家人 13) 云 而仍辭

거 주인요오성 도기사이강청동처 오성허지
去 主人邀鰲城 道其事而强請同處 鰲城許之

自其日鰲城來留其家　與病人同坐臥　至伊日之夜

鰲城與病人同枕而臥矣　三更時陰風入戶 14)　燭光

明滅 15)　而病人昏昏不省 16)　鰲城臥見燭影之後

有一鬼卒　狀貌獰悍 17)　杖劍而立　呼鰲城之名曰：

李某　汝可出給我此病人　曰：何謂也　鬼曰：

此人與我　有宿世之仇 18) 怨　而某時欲報讐之期 19)

也　若失此期　則又不知何時可報　鰲城曰：人既托

我以子　則吾何給汝而使之殺之乎　鬼曰：汝不給

我　則我將併與汝　而殺之　鰲城曰：吾死則已矣

不死之前　決不給汝矣　鬼乃大怒　舉刀而向之

忽爾悚然而退　如是者三　仍擲劍俯伏請曰：願大監

憐我之情事 20)　而出給此人　鰲城曰：汝何不殺我乎

鬼曰：大監國之棟樑 21)　名垂竹帛 22)　之正人君子 23)

吾何敢害之　只願出給　鰲城曰：殺我之外無

他策矣　仍抱病人而臥　如是之際　遠村鷄鳴矣

鬼乃大哭曰：不知何年可報此讐　豈不寃恨哉

此必是某處某盲之所指也　吾可洩［雪］憤於此人矣

乃杖劒而出門　不知去處　此時病人昏絶 24) 矣

以溫水灌之口得甦　而翌朝向日之卜者訃書 25) 來矣

其主家厚遺其初終葬需 26)　優恤其妻子

1 李鰲城 = Osŏng Puwŏn'gun Yi Hangbok 鰲城府院君 李恒福 [1556–1618; styled Chasang 子常; sobriquet Paeksa 白沙; ancestral seat Kyŏngju 慶州; posthumous epithet Munch'ung 文忠]: scholar-official during the reign of King Sŏnjo 宣祖 [r. 1567–1608; 1552–1608]. His father was Yi Mongnyang 李夢亮 [1499–1564].
2 才諝: talents and wisdom.
3 積年沈痼: suffer from a chronic illness.
4 晝宵焦心: fret day and night.
5 作色: make a facial expression displaying discomfort.
6 好生惡死: love life and hate death.
7 容或無怪: within the realm of possibility, and therefore not strange.
8 地頭 = chibo 地步: circumstances; plight.
9 自刺 = chagyŏl 自決: slit one's own throat.
10 駟不及舌: lit. "even a four-horse chariot cannot match an eloquent tongue" = rumours travel fast.
11 伊日: that day.
12 善顧恤: take good care of someone.
13 視同家人: treat someone like family.
14 陰風入戶: a gloomy wind enters the room.
15 燭光明滅: a candle flickers.
16 昏昏不省: remain unconscious, remain in a swoon.
17 狀貌獰悍: one's appearance is vile and ferocious.
18 宿世之仇: an age-old enemy.

19 報讐之期: an opportunity for vengeance.
20 情事 = *sajŏng* 事情: circumstances.
21 棟樑: lit. "ridge pole and crossbeam" = a pillar (of state).
22 名垂竹帛: lit. "have one's name recorded on the bamboo and silk" = have one's influence documented in history ("bamboo and silk").
23 正人君子: gentleman of upright character, virtuous conduct, and great erudition.
24 昏絶: faint.
25 訃書 = *pugo* 訃告: news of someone's death.
26 初終葬需: all the necessary funeral paraphernalia.

——— **38** ———

Wŏlsa in Peking

Vol. II: 10; n.d.; Diary XII, pp. 86–7 (untitled and crossed out); listed in Diary XVI, p. 171, as "Wŏlsa in Peking"; 199.

When Wŏlsa arrived as envoy in Peking, he had a special friend in Wang (Yanzhou) Shizen and, both being scholars, they found great delight in each other.

On a certain day, Wŏlsa arose early in the morning and went to seek Wang, when Wang, who was dressing to go into the palace, said, "I am going in to audience, but shall not be long. Please wait here in my library till I return and choose anything you like to read."

He told his servants to prepare a specially good meal and give it to Wŏlsa. When Wang had gone, food was brought in: bread, vermicelli soup, wine, meat, fish, and fruits came in great quantity. Wŏlsa sat and while he glanced through books, he ate and so the day passed.

Finally Wang Yanzhou returned. Wang inquired, "Have you had breakfast?"

Wŏlsa replied, "I have not yet had breakfast."

Wang gave a great start and called to the steward, "How is it that you have not yet brought breakfast as I ordered?"

The servant replied, "We did, sir, bring it. And His Excellency has breakfasted."

Then Wang gave a laugh and said, "Oh, I forgot. Koreans have to have a dish of rice and a dish of soup before they call it breakfast or dinner. I made a mistake. Have it prepared at once."

Wŏlsa came back and told a friend how ashamed he was about this little affair.

Again Wŏlsa went to Wang's house, when the prince of Shu came and asked Wŏlsa to write a biography of his father for a memorial stone. He had brought a cart-load of silk, and a set of *ssangnyuk* pieces, fifteen on each side, made like dancing girls, one side dressed in red and one in blue, and finished in gold.

This was how they estimated a piece of composition such as Wŏlsa's.

月沙 1) 赴燕京 2) 與王弇州世貞 3) 親熟　結以文章之交

一日早朝往見　則弇州具公服而起曰：適有入闕之事

少間當還　君須吾書樓上披覽諸書而待吾來也

仍囑其家丁　使備朝饌而進之　弇州出門後

餅麵酒肉魚果之屬　相續而進　月沙且啖且看書

日晚弇州出來　問月沙朝膳已罷否　對曰：朝飯曾不

喫矣　弇州驚訝而責家丁　對曰：俄者已進矣　弇州

大笑曰：吾忘之矣　朝鮮人　以一椀白飯一器藿湯 4)

爲朝夕飯矣　豈如吾儕之所啗 5) 耶　斯速備飯而來

吾忘之矣云　月沙還歸後　嘗對人而言　吾於此羞

愧欲死云矣　一日　月沙往見弇州　則蜀郡 6) 太守

爲其父（求）碑文　而禮單 7) 以蜀錦一車　人雙陸

8) 一隊分美人　青紅裳各十五而以黃金爲飾而送之

大國餽遺 9) 之風如是矣

1 月沙: sobriquet of Yi Chŏnggu 李廷龜 [1564–1635; styled Sŏngjing 聖徵; ancestral seat Yŏnan 延安; posthumous epithet Munch'ung 文忠]: scholar-official during the reign of King Injo 仁祖 [r. 1623–49; 1595–49]. His great-great-grandfather was Yi Sŏkhyŏng 李石亨 [1415–77].
2 燕京 = Beijing 北京: Yanjing was the capital during the Qing Dynasty 淸 [1644–1912].
3 王世貞 Wang Shizhen [1526–90; styled Yuanmei 元美; sobriquet Yanzhou shanren 弇州山人]: scholar and poet of the Ming 明 [1368–1644].
4 藿湯: a soup of wild herbs.
5 啗 = *tam* 啖: eat, nibble on.
6 蜀郡: Shu County in Sichuan Province 四川省.
7 禮單: list of wedding gifts.
8 雙陸 = *ssangnyuk* 雙六 ~ *sangnyuk* 象六: lit. "double sixes" = backgammon.
9 餽遺: send as a gift.

—— 39 ——

Chŏng Ka

Vol. II; 10; n.d.; Diary XII, pp. 185–90; 201.

When Chŏng Yangp'a was a young man he went with two of his friends to a temple to study. They talked over one day all that they hoped to do but one man of the three was silent wholly as to what his ambitions were.

The two asked him, "How comes it that you have not a word to say?"

His reply was "My ambitions are wholly different from yours. There is no reason to ask."

But they demanded of him an explanation.

His reply was, "I have the misfortune to be born in this little country – here at one side off from sovereignty. I see no place in the world where I can have freedom of action and so my ambition is to become the chief of a band of villains in some of the deep hills with ten thousand followers who will do my bidding, rob those who have won ill-gotten gains and so provide for their troops, travel from these hills to those, have dancing girls galore and those who sing, eat the choicest harts of the hills and the best fish of the sea. This is my ambition."

The two laughed and reprimanded him for his evil desires.

Later Chǒng rose rapidly in rank till he became Prime Minister. One of their number made nothing of himself and died unknown, while one of them had wholly disappeared.

After Chǒng Yangp'a had graduated, he became governor of Hamgyǒng and the other former associate who had made nothing of himself, feeling the pangs of hunger, went on his journey to Hamgyǒng begging on the way. He reached Hoeyang.*

Here a certain man with a saddled horse came and bowed to him, saying, "Your humble servant comes by order of the general and has been waiting a long time. Please mount and ride."

The scholar, in doubts as to what this meant, asked, "Who is your general? And where does he live?"

He replied, "If you come along, you will see."

So he mounted and rode along the way for a distance. There was another horse awaiting him, and there was wine and food prepared as well.

Wondering what this could mean, he again asked what it meant, when the answer was the same as before, "When you go you will find out."

Again he went on a number of *ri* till he found himself in the hills. Night overtook him but that made no difference. With a torch ahead, a man ran before him leading the way. All night he rode without in the least knowing where he was going or what it meant. He merely followed the *mapoo*.

On the day following he came to a settlement among the hills with three red gates before it. He dismounted and walked through them and came to a flight of steps where a gentleman dressed in green silk and with a shining hat met him. He had a red girdle around his waist and black shoes on his feet. He was tall, eight feet or so in height, and a face fair and handsome, "eyes like a river and a mouth like the sea." He was a most commanding personage.

He laughed as he took the poor scholar by the hand and took him up,† saying "What a long time since we saw each other last."

At first the scholar could not make him out, but looking more closely he saw he was his comrade who studied in the temple and said his ambitions were an outlaw chief.

The scholar gave a great start and said, "When we separated at the temple, I lost all trace of you till now. Today I find you here."

The Outlaw laughed and said, "Didn't I tell you so? I have come to the height of my ambition and have nothing more to wish for. Every man wishes to make a name for himself but seeing that he is in the power of other people he has to bow his head and wag his tail like a dog, or a fly; once a fault and off goes his head and his posterity are made slaves for all time. I have said good-bye to all such works as that and with my thousands here in the hills have heaped up wealth in abundant store. I have nothing whatsoever to do with rat-thieving or dog-stealing or any such petty acts as carrying off another's pocket or his basket. My agents are found in all the provinces to watch for goods from China or from Japan and all such come my way. The goods too of evil-minded magistrates or prefect secretaries – all are gathered in. My power and my riches are second to none, not even the king. How short this life is! My wish is to have my desires fulfilled."

Here he shouted out, "Bring us drinks!"

A pretty pair of girls came in with others following with food and drinks such as the poor man had never seen or known. They ate together and had a happy time. They ate at the same table and slept in the same room.

The next day he said, "Let's have a walk out among our troops and see what my kingdom and its treasures mean."

When they walked and saw this and that together, the Outlaw said, "Your journey now is to see Chŏng the governor of Hamgyŏng because you wish to ask him for a little help, isn't it?"

He replied, "Why, yes it is."

"But I fear you do not know Chŏng's mind and what an exacting man he is. Though he gives you something, can you imagine him giving you anything like what you want? Give it up and stay a few days with me and then return to your home."

But the scholar replied, "But it is not so. There is old friendship that has □ these years. He likes me too. I must go to see him."

The Outlaw replied, "You will no doubt give him something but how little in value it will be. I'll give you something. Don't you go."

But he would not listen to this and still remained determined to go.

"If you wish to go, I'll not prevent you. Go and □ in peace."

He remained several days longer and then prepared to go when the Outlaw called the servant, had him saddle the horse and show the scholar safely out.

When he departed he said, "Now don't tell Chŏng that I am here. For though Chŏng tries to take me, he cannot do it. I shall hear it before he can move. If that rumour gets out, your own head will be in danger. Be careful then and say not a word."

He agreed to this and made an oath that not a word would he utter.

The Outlaw laughed and sent him off. He mounted outside the gate and the servant saw him safely as far as the big road. There the *mapoo* bowed his good-bye and was gone. From this point on he took up his weary walk to Hamhŭng.

This place he finally reached and after greeting they talked over their experiences together as boys.

The poor scholar said quietly to the governor, "Do you know where the student has gone who used to study with us together in the temple?"

"I have no idea whatever. Since we said good-bye, I have heard nothing of him."

Then the scholar said, "That man is a great outlaw and lives within the district that you govern. He says he has thousands of agents out through all the provinces but the soldiers he has with him are only a very few, all thieves that □□ and then again disappeared. If you will entrust me with thirty or forty good men, I'll go and take him and bring him to you."

The governor laughed and said, "He may be an outlaw, but no one here is robbed. The different towns too are not disturbed. You too are not his equal in wile or plan or artifice. You will get yourself into trouble and meet disaster. Don't you try it."

But he replied with a □ colour, "If you leave an outlaw in your district unmolested and there is trouble later on, who will be to blame for it? If you will not hear me, I shall go up to Seoul and report the matter."

The governor could not persuade him otherwise and so consented. A few days later, he sent him off. He gave him most sparingly of money, just as the Outlaw had said. He gave him policemen as he had asked.

He led them to the same place where he had entered the hills and finally reached the place and had the police hide in the bushes. He said, "Wait here till I go in and come out again."

He then went in alone only several *ri*, when lo he met the same servant who came without a horse and said "Let's go in."

They passed in through the narrow opening of the hills when suddenly a great shout resounded, "Arrest him."

A crowd appeared at once and with ropes they tied him fast as a rabbit is taken by a lot of falcons.

Then, all fearful and catching for his breath, he was taken into the court.

He looked up at the Outlaw, who shouted, "With what face dare you appear before me?"

He replied, "What sin have I committed that you treat me thus?"

The Outlaw said, "Didn't I tell you that you would get just what you got. You also did not keep the oath that you swore, but went and told the governor everything."

The poor scholar said in reply, "What report did you hear that you have such unjust suspicion of me?"

The Outlaw shouted, "Have those police arrested and brought here. And in a little all were brought under arrest into the court. When he pointed to them and asked, "Whose are these fellows?" he replied with a look of shame, "I am indeed worthy of death."

The Outlaw said, "I shall not dirty my sword on a rotten rat like you. Bring those paddles and have him beaten."

They beat him but he set free the police and said, "Why did you follow a crazy idiot such as this?"

He gave them each twenty *yang* and sent them off, saying, "Tell your master not to listen again to such a crazy fool as this."

He had servants bring out all their goods and treasures and load them on ponies and on the backs of carriers. Then he had their houses set on fire, saying, "People know we are here. There's nothing for it but to go."

He had one of the soldiers hustle the old scholar out of the place to where he could find the main road. Having thus made his escape by the skin of his teeth, he hurried home but he found that his people had all moved away. He set out to find where they were and was surprised to see a much better house than before.

He asked, "How comes it that you have got yourselves into this fine house?"

His people replied, "But you sent us letters and things from Hamhŭng, didn't you?"

He gave a sudden start, saying, "Where is the letter?"

He looked it over and while it was like his writing, it was not his letter. Money, linen, silk in great quantities accompanied it.

It was without doubt the Outlaw who had □ his writing and sent him all these things. Some say that the governor then was not Yangp'a at all.*

* Hoeyang is in that part of Kangwŏn Province lying in present-day North Korea.
† Gale erroneously translates as "Calling him by his name."

鄭陽坡 1) 少時 與親友二人讀書于山寺 一日論懷 2)

而各言平生所欲 陽（坡則 願早科 致君堯舜 3)

名垂竹帛 4) 一人曰：吾）則不願仕宦 擇居于山明

水麗之地 以山水娛平生 一人獨無言 兩人問曰：

君何無一言乎 其人曰：吾之所欲大異於二君

不須問矣 二人强之 乃曰：吾不幸 而生於偏邦

自顧此世 無可容身之所 不如自橫 5) 吾志爲大

賊之愧 而處於深山窮谷中 率數萬之衆

奪不義之財 以供軍粮 橫行山間 而歌童舞女

羅列于前 山珍海味 6) 厭飫 7) 於口 如斯度了 8)

則幸矣 二人大笑而責之以不義矣 其後陽坡

果登第 位至上[宰]相 一人以布衣 9) 終老

一人不知下落 10) 矣 陽坡之按北關 11) 也 其布衣之人

窮不能自存 恃同研之誼 12) 徒步作乞馱之行 13) 向

北關而行 到淮陽 14) 之地 忽有一健奴 鞴一駿驄 15)

而迎於前曰： 小人奉使道將令來到於此 亦已久矣

快乘此馬而行可也 其人怪而問之曰： 汝使道誰也

而在於何處 奴對曰：去則自可知之矣 其人仍上馬

則其疾如飛 行幾里 又有一馬之待者 且有盃

盤之供 16) 怪而又問 則其答如前 行幾里又如是

漸入深峽之中 而夜又不息 炬火㪺[導]前而行

其人不知緣何向何處 只從其奴之言而行矣 翌午

入一洞口 深山之中 人居櫛比 中有一大朱門

入三重門 而下馬而入 則階下一人 頭戴驄笠

身被藍色雲紋緞 17) 天翼 18)   腰繫帶　足穿黑靴

而身長八尺　面如塗粉 19)   河目海口 20)   儀表堂堂

威風凜凜　軒然而笑 21)   執手而共升階曰：某也

別來無恙乎　其人初不知何許人矣　坐定熟視

則乃是山寺同苦之時　願爲賊將之人也　其人

大驚曰：吾輩山門各散之後　不知君之踪跡矣

今乃至於斯耶　賊將笑曰：吾豈不云乎　吾今得吾志

不羨世上富貴矣　人生此世　豈不有志於功名進取乎

然以其命懸於他人之手　而畏首畏尾 22) 平生　作蠅

營狗苟之態 23)　一有所失　則身棄東市 24)　妻子爲奴

此豈所可願耶　吾今擺脫塵臼 [垢] 25)　入深山之谷

有衆數萬　財積阜陵 26)　吾非如鼠窮狗偸 27) 之爲

而探囊袪 [褛] 28) 筐之爲也　吾之卒徒　遍於八道

燕市 29) 倭館 30) 之物　無不致來　貪官汚吏之財

필야양탈 권여부불양왕공 인생기하야 이자적오
必也攘奪 權與富不讓王公 人生幾何耶 以自適吾

의이 잉명진배반 유미녀수쌍경반이진 수륙필진
意耳 仍命進盃盤 有美女數雙擎盤而進 水陸畢陳

이주지이효풍 여지진환 동탁이식 동상이침
而酒旨而肴豊 31) 與之盡歡 同卓而食 同床而寢

명일 여지동람군중재환급산수승개 잉언왈
明日 與之同覽軍中財貨及山水勝槩 32) 仍言曰：

군지차행 욕견정모 이거자장유소구야 왈
君之此行 欲見鄭某 而去者將有所求耶 曰：

연 적장왈 차인규모 군기불지야 수지유증
然 賊將曰：此人規模 君豈不知耶 雖之有贈

미흡어군지소망의 불여갱류기일자차직귀야
未洽於君之所望矣 不如更留幾日自此直歸也

기인왈 필불연의 구일동연지정 피역념지의
其人曰：必不然矣 舊日同研之情 彼亦念之矣

적장왈 량기신 물 불과기량의 하가위차이작원
賊將曰：量其贐 33) 物 不過幾兩矣 何可爲此而作遠

행호 오당유신의 물왕가의 기인불청이결의욕행
行乎 吾當有贐矣 勿往可矣 其人不聽而決意欲行

적장왈 기여시 오불갱만 유군의행지 우류수일
賊將曰：旣如是 吾不更挽 惟君意行之 又留數日

기인욕행 적장사노마호송여래시 이림행계지왈
其人欲行 賊將使奴馬護送如來時 而臨行戒之曰：

군견정모 절물언오지재차야 정모수욕포아 불
君見鄭某 切勿言吾之在此也 鄭某雖欲捕我 不

가득의 언출지일 오당문지의 약연즉 군지두불
可得矣 言出之日 吾當聞之矣 若然則 君之頭不

可保矣　愼之勉之　勿出口可也　其人發矢言 34) 曰：

寧有是理　賊將笑而送之出門　其人依前乘其馬

出外山大路　牽夫辭而去　其人徒步作行　到北

營 35) 而見監司　寒暄禮罷後　其人低聲密告曰：

令公知吾輩少時山寺讀書時　作伴之某人去處乎

監司曰：一自相別之後　不知下落矣　其人曰：今在

令公之道內而卽大賊也　渠言則　有衆數萬餘云

而皆散在各處　渠之部下無多　俱是烏合 36) 之賊徒也

令公若借我伶俐之健卒三四十人　則吾當縛致營

下矣　監司笑曰：渠雖賊魁而姑無作弊於郡邑者

且量君之智勇才力　恐不及此人矣　空然惹起禍機乎

君且休矣　其人作色曰：令公知大賊之在境　而掩

置不捕後　若滋蔓 37) 則責歸於誰也　若不從吾言

吾於還洛 38) 之後　當告變 39) 矣　監司不得已許之

留數日而送之　所贐之物數　符賊將之言　擇校

卒 40)　如數而給之　其人率校卒更向此路　埋伏

於山左右叢樾之間 41)　而戒之曰：吾將先入去矣

汝等姑竢之　行至幾里　來時牽騎來邀之人又來

而傳其賊將之言　與之偕來　而不送騎矣　心窃

怪之　行到洞口　一聲號令　使之拿入　無數健卒

以繩縛之　前擁後遮 42)　如快鶻搏兎樣 43)　而入門

其人喘息未定　拿至庭下仰見　賊將盛備威儀而坐

怒叱曰：汝以何顏來見我乎　其人曰：吾有何罪

而待我至此之辱也　賊將叱曰：吾豈不云乎　汝往

北營所得　豈不符我言乎　且汝以吾事泄于北伯 44)

不念臨別之托而何撓舌 45)　其人曰：天日在上

吾無是事　君從何聞知而疑我乎　賊將號令卒徒曰：

可拿入北營校卒　言未已數十個北營校卒　一時

被縛而伏於階下　賊將指示曰：此是何許人也

其人面如土色 46)　無語可答　只請死罪死罪　賊將冷

笑曰：如渠腐鼠狐雛 47)　何足汚我刃也　棍之可也

仍下十餘杖而依前縛之　使之解諸校卒曰：汝等良苦

何爲隨此人而至　命各賜二十兩銀子而送之曰：

歸於爾主將　更勿聽此等人之語也云云　仍使卒

徒　出各庫財帛銀錢器用等物　而或馱或擔 48)

一時擧火燒其屋宇曰：既被人知　不可以處矣

更使一卒驅逐其人出之門外大道　仍不知去處

其人艱辛得脫而前進歸家　則已移他洞矣　尋其家

而入　則門戶之大比之前家大不同矣　問於家人

則以爲在北營時豈不作書而送物種乎　其人驚訝

出而示之　則恰如自家之筆　實非自家之爲也

其錢與布帛之數甚夥　然黙而思之　此是賊將之

<ruby>所</ruby><ruby>送</ruby> 而做自家之筆跡而送之也 後乃悔之云爾

或云北伯非陽坡云 未可知也

1 陽坡: sobriquet of Chŏng T'aehwa 鄭太和 [1602–73; styled Yuch'un 圄春; ancestral seat Tongnae 東萊; posthumous epithet Ch'ungik 忠翼]: scholar-official under King Hyŏnjong 顯宗 [r. 1659–74; 1641–74]. His father was Chŏng Kwangsŏng 鄭廣成 [1576–1654].
2 論懷: discuss one's thoughts.
3 堯舜: Yao [r. 2357–2257 BC] and Shun [r. 2255–2205 BC], the two legendary kings who ruled over ancient China.
4 竹帛: lit. "bamboo and silk" = history.
5 自橫: rampant, unbridled behaviour.
6 山珍海味 = *sanhae chinmi* 山海珍味: surf and turf.
7 厭飫: be fed up with something.
8 度了: plot; scheme.
9 布衣 = *paegŭi* 白衣: a Confucian scholar without an official rank.
10 下落 = *nakch'ak* 落着: come to a conclusion or settlement.
11 北關: Hamgyŏng Province.
12 同研之誼 = *tongyŏn chi ŭi* 同研之義: social bond formed through the experience of studying together.
13 乞駄之行: be on one's way to borrow provisions or food supplies.
14 淮陽: a town near the Diamond Mountains (Kŭmgang-san 金剛山).
15 駿驄 = *chunma*: swift steed.
16 盃盤之供: set a table with food and drink for a guest.
17 雲紋緞: cloud-patterned silk.
18 天翼 *ch'ŏllik*: (native Korean word rendered in sinographs as phonograms) a kind of formal attire worn by military officers.
19 面如塗粉: lit. "face looking as if it were powdered" = fair skin.
20 河目海口: big-eyed and wide-mouthed.
21 軒然而笑: laugh self-assuredly and imposingly.
22 畏首畏尾: lit. "afraid of the heads and tails"; be apprehensive of having one's acts or thoughts known to someone else.
23 蠅營狗苟之態: lit. "flies buzzing around and dogs hanging about" = pathetic appearance of ingratiating oneself for minute gains.
24 東市: the Eastern Market in Luoyang where executions were carried out.
25 擺脫塵垢: free oneself from the yoke of the mundane world.
26 財積阜陵: pile up mounds of treasure.

27 鼠竊狗偷: lit. "mouse steals, dogs purloin"; act the petty thief.

28 探囊楛筐: rummage through someone else's pockets or bags.

29 燕市: Yanjing Market, site of trade between Korea and China.

30 倭館: Japan House in Pusan, site of trade between Korea and Japan during the Chosŏn period.

31 酒旨而肴豊: lit. "the wine was fine and the dishes abundant."

32 山水勝槩: places of natural beauty.

33 賻: give a farewell gift.

34 矢言: pledge, words of promise.

35 北營 = kamyŏng 監營: headquarters of the Hamgyŏng provincial governor.

36 烏合: short for ohap chi chung 烏合之衆; lit. "gaggle of crows" = undisciplined rabble or mob.

37 滋蔓: spread out gradually.

38 還洛: return to the capital.

39 告變: inform the authorities of crimes of treason.

40 校卒: military officers and their underlings attached to a local yamen.

41 叢樾之間: street shaded by trees on both sides.

42 前擁後遮: block in front and cut off in back.

43 快鶻搏兔樣: lit. "like an agile falcon seizing a rabbit."

44 北伯: governor of Hamgyŏng Province.

45 撓舌: lit. "wag the tongue" = run off at the mouth.

46 面如土色: lit. "face becomes clay-coloured" = turn pale.

47 腐鼠狐雛: lit. "rotten mouse and fox cub" = insult directed at a person of low station.

48 或馱或擔: load items on a horse or on one's shoulder.

——— 40 ———

King Hyojong (1650–59 AD) Overhears

Vol. II: 13; n.d.; Diary XIV, pp. 32–3; 202.

Kim Hyojong used frequently to go out incognito at night and once he thus passed through the gate on foot when there was snow on the ground and it was very very cold. He had to walk and on return as he passed the guards that kept the gate, one of them said, "Such weather is this! How can we outlive the night?"

Another said, "Do you call this cold? Plenty worse than this."

The other replied, "What do you mean?"

The first said, "When we go to Liaodong and sleep out in the open, we will think a night like this warm."

The friend said, "What reason have we to go to Liaodong and sleep out in the open?"

The other said, "His Majesty has plans now on foot to strike a blow at the north in which case we'll have to go."

The other said, "He'll never do anything of the sort."

The other said, "When General Song Siyŏl came the other day and had a conversation alone with the king, it was so decided."

The first said, "I don't believe a word of it."

The other said, "How do you know?"

The first said, "His Majesty has no fiber in his soul to make any such decision. A great undertaking of this sort he is not hand at."

The other said, "How do you know all this, pray?"

The first said, "If the king had had any such □ in his spirit when he was prince and had hold of Kanghwa, he would have smashed the head of Kim Kyŏngjing. If he couldn't deal with a creature like Kyŏngjing what could he do to China? I know from this."

When Hyojong heard this he was □ with rage and went into the palace.

효 묘　　역 간 간 미 행　　　일 일 야　　보 과 궁 장 후
孝 廟 1) 亦 間 間 微 行 2)　一 日 夜　步 過 宮 墻 後

시 설 야 엄 혹　　군 포　　포　　수 직 일 인 자 외 입 왈
時 雪 夜 嚴 酷　軍 舖 [鋪]3) 守 直 一 人 自 外 入 曰：

한 위 여 차　　하 이 경 야　　일 인 왈　　금 야 하 위 이 한 호 운 재
寒 威 如 此　何 以 經 夜　一 人 曰：今 夜 何 爲 而 寒 乎 云 哉

일 인 왈　　하 위 야　　왈　　오 배 료 동　　야 로 숙 시
一 人 曰：何 謂 也　曰：吾 輩 遼 東 4) 野 露 宿 時

기 가 왈 한 호　　기 인 왈　　오 배 하 위 이 로 숙 료 동 야　　왈
豈 可 曰 寒 乎　其 人 曰：吾 輩 何 爲 而 露 宿 遼 東 耶　曰：

주 상 금 방 의 북 벌　　여 차 지 시　　오 배 기 불 종 정 호　　왈
主 上 今 方 議 北 伐　如 此 之 時　吾 輩 豈 不 從 征 乎　曰：

무 시 리 의　왈　회 덕 회 상　대 감　일 전 입 래 독 대
無是理矣　曰：懷德宋相 5) 大監　日前入來獨對 6)

이 위 정 계 운 의　기 인 왈　필 불 연 의　왈　여 하 이 지 지
已爲定計云矣　其人曰：必不然矣　曰：汝何以知之

왈　주 상 무 위 단　차 등 대 사　하 이 판 지 호　왈
曰：主上無威斷 7)　此等大事　何以辦之乎　曰：

여 우 하 이 지 지　기 인 왈　주 상 약 유 강 단　즉 년 전
汝又何以知之　其人曰：主上若有剛斷　則年前

이 왕 자 수 강 화 시　김 경 징　기 불 참 두　일 경 징 상 불
以王子守江華時　金慶徵 8) 豈不斬頭　一慶徵尚不

득 정 기 죄　하 황 상 국 호　오 시 이 지 지　효 묘 문 차 언
得正其罪　何況上國乎　吾是以知之　孝廟聞此言

불 승 분 한 이 환 궁
不勝忿恨而還宮

1 孝廟: reign name of King Hyojong 孝宗 [r. 1649–59; 1619–59].
2 微行: go out incognito.
3 軍鋪: hut for watchmen (*sulla'gun* 巡邏軍) outside the palace.
4 遼東: lit. "East Liao" = Liaodong; the peninsula south of Manchuria and to the east of the River Liao 遼河.
5 懷德宋相: lit. "Minister Song, Hoedŏk"; refers to Song Chun'gil 宋浚吉 [1606–72; styled Myŏngbo 明甫; sobriquet Tongch'undang 同春堂; ancestral seat Ŭnjin 恩津; posthumous epithet Munjŏng 文正], a scholar-official during the reign of King Hyojong 孝宗 [r. 1649–59; 1619–59]. His father was Song Ich'ang 宋爾昌 [1561–1627]. In 1659 (Hyojong 10), Song Chun'gil served as Minister of War (Pyŏngjo *p'ansŏ* 兵曹判書). He and Song Siyŏl 宋時烈 [1607–89] promoted the anti-Manchu military campaign under the name "Northern Expedition (*pukpŏl*)." Song was honoured (*chehyang* 祭享) at the Sunghyŏn Confucian Academy (Sunghyŏn *sŏwŏn* 崇顯書院) in Hoedŏk 懷德 in Ch'ungch'ŏng Province.
6 獨對: a tête-à-tête between an official and the king.
7 威斷: a decision rendered with majestic authority.
8 金慶徵 [1589–1637; styled Sŏnŭng 善應; ancestral seat Sunch'ŏn 順天]: During the Manchu Invasion in the year *pyŏngja* (1636 Pyŏngja horan 丙子胡亂:

lit. "barbarian disturbances in the year *pyŏngja*"), Kim Kyŏngjing was serving as the inspector of Kanghwa Island (Kangdo *kwanch'alsa* 江都檢察使). Later he was impeached by a censor (*taegan* 臺諫) for the crime of failing to defend Kanghwa Island successfully and was eventually sentenced to death by poison (*sasa* 賜死). His father was Kim Yu 金瑬 [1571–1648].

———— **41** ————

King Sukchong's Joke

Vol. II: 13; translated 8 June 1921; Diary XVI, p. 171; 203.

King Sukchong was about to build a pavilion of three *kan** beside the pond in front of the Ch'undang Pavilions that he intended calling Kwanp'ung Tower.

At that time a certain Yun *p'ansŏ*,† who was Vice-President of the College of Literature, wrote a memorial in protest that said, "When wood and earth are disturbed out of season, it becomes evidence that the state is in danger."

The king replied with kingly and gracious words and rewarded him with a tiger skin. He asked that he come into the palace and receive it from his hand. Yun, thus ordered, came into the palace and one of the eunuchs led him to the Ch'undang Pavilions.

In a little an order was repeated by the soldiers: "Arrest him."

At once they arrested Yun and put him face down in the king's court.

The king then in plain clothes sat on a slightly raised platform and said, "Look now and see the house that I am building. It is not more than three *kan*; how can you say that such is out of season or that this little pavilion can be a danger to the state? You and your like build where you please in the hills and on the water and yet you tell me that I must not build even a little house like this. You have thought to make a name for yourself by such a memorial as this. It makes me wild, such nonsense as this. I shall have to have you beaten."

Yun replied, "I have done a wrong for which I ought to die, but my office compels me as a member of the College to such and to expose me to this insult of being beaten would surely be a great wrong."

The king said, "Is an official not to be punished when he does wrong?"

He then ordered him to be beaten with five blows, and said, "You are an official who has been beaten and this is a disgrace that covers me with confusion. If you go out and complain that for a brave act you have been beaten, it will be my disgrace not yours."

He then ordered a tiger skin to be furnished and sent him off.

* *kan*: a counter for the space (length or breadth) between supporting members of a structure, such as walls or pillars. *Samgan* (lit. three *gan*) = small, humble.

† See p. 14 n *.

肅廟 1) 朝　於春塘坮 2) 池邊　建三間樓　名曰：

觀豊樓　時尹判書某以副學 3) 上疏諫曰：非時土

木之役　亡國之兆　上優批 4) 而豹皮 5) 一領賞之

以命使之親受　尹承命而入闕　則一宦侍㜕 [導

] 前　至春塘坮　已而軍卒高聲　而有捉入之命

尹被拿伏於庭矣　上以便服坐於一小樓上　敎曰：

汝試見之　此樓不過三間也　有何土木之非時

而亡國之可言乎　汝輩所居有山亭水閣 6) 而

吾獨不得建此小閣耶　汝輩欲釣名 7) 而有此疏

心常痛恨　可以決棍矣　尹乃對曰：小臣罪雖萬死

顧其職則玉署 8) 之長也　殿下不可以辱儒臣也

上曰：儒臣獨不可治罪乎　命決棍五度 9) 後　敎曰：

汝以儒臣受此棍治　已是汝之羞辱也　汝可出而言之

在予爲過擧　而汝獨不謬辱身名乎　命給豹皮而出送

1 肅廟: the years from 1674 to 1720, the reign years of King Sukchong 肅宗.
2 春塘坮: a pavilion inside Ch'anggyŏng Palace 昌慶宮.
3 副學: short for *pujehak* 副提學, a senior third-grade post in the Office of the
  Special Counselors (Hongmungwan 弘文館); *pujehak* is a *tangsanggwan*
  堂上官 (lit. "officials of the upper end of the hall" = officials higher than
  senior third rank) position.
4 優批: excellent criticism.
5 豹皮: leopard skin. Gale's "tiger" is a mistranslation.
6 山亭水閣: pavilion on the mountain and tower by the water.
7 釣名: fabricate things to make a name for oneself.
8 玉署 = Hongmungwan 弘文館: Office of the Special Counselors.
9 五度: five blows.

—— 42 ——

King Sukchong's Second Joke

Vol. II: 14; translated 8 June 1921; Diary XVI, pp. 171–2; 204.

Once when King Sukchong was feeling unwell he called for a band of
music and dancing girls. At that time one of the censors, Yun, went
alone and said to the king by way of protest, "These dirty girls and
unsavoury music are a proof of destruction to those who love them.
Please pack them all off and out of the palace."

On getting this, the king was very angry and issued an order to
have a personal investigation. All the palace was put into a state of

consternation. He ordered the censor and his secretary arrested with a loud voice, and the various officers of the law were all called into requisition and made ready. He then hurried to the music and dancing without a further word of any kind regarding the sinners.

After a day had passed and evening was drawing on, he issued an order: "As I think it over, the censor's words were greatly to the point and very good. Let that order to arrest and try and all the rest of it be rescinded."

He let go of the secretary and servants, as well, but said something would have to be done to reward the faithful censor and so sent him two tables of food and two bottles of wine. He gave him also a tiger skin.

At that time the censor and his secretary were beside themselves with fear and now they ate to repletion and drank till drunk. When they were ordered to withdraw, the servant who saw them out wrapped himself in a tiger skin and roared as a beast so that people along the way asked what it meant.

His answer was, "The king has had a round with the dancing girl, has drunk deep, and has been arrested by his Officer of Order – I have just come forth with the price of the offence."

All hearing this laughed themselves stiff. The censor still has the tiger skin.

肅廟 1) 朝有患候 2)　一日命入梨園 3) 樂及妓女

自內張樂　時臺諫 4) 尹某獨詣臺廳 5)　啓以不正之色

不雅之樂　此是前代帝王所以亡國也　亟賜撤去云云

上大怒卽有親鞫 6) 之命　擧朝遑遑　爲先自禁 7)

臺官書吏喝漿 [導]8)　並蒙頭 9) 捉待　禁堂 10) 捕堂 11)

皆命招諸事預備　而無動靜　管絃之聲不絶　申後 12)

下敎曰：更思之　臺言好矣　俄者設鞫之命還收

臺臣及下隷　一併放送　而不可無褒　異之 13)

典內　下茶啖 14) 二床　御酒二瓶　一則餽臺隷

乃賜虎皮 15) 一領 16)　臺諫及下隷驚魂　纔定盡

意醉飽　上下俱沉醉　及其退歸之時

前導 [導] 下隷蒙虎皮 17) 而呼唱 18) 於大路

路傍觀者問其故　則答曰：主上殿下　挾倡會飮 19)

見捉 20) 於禁亂 21)　吾方收贖 22) 而歸云云　聞者絶倒

諫院 23) 至今有虎皮之藏焉

1 肅廟: the years from 1674 to 1720, the reign years of King Sukchong 肅宗.
2 患候: (honorific) illness.
3 梨園: lit. "pear garden" = the place where court music was taught under Xuanzhong 玄宗 [r. 712–55] of the Tang 唐 dynasty [618–907]; another name for the Bureau of Music (Kyobang 敎坊), where music and theatre were taught during the Chosŏn dynasty.
4 臺諫: a blanket term for officials in the Office of the Inspector-General (Sahŏnbu 司憲府) ranging from minor inspector (chip'yŏng 持平) all the way up to the Inspector-General (taesahŏn 大司憲).
5 臺廳: a venue where officials remonstrated to the king.
6 親鞫: king's personal interrogation of felons on trial.
7 禁 = Ŭigŭmbu 義禁府: State Tribunal, the office in charge of arresting and prosecuting criminals according to the king's orders.

8 喝導 = *kaldo* 喝道: slaves in charge of clearing the way for scholar-officials of the Office of the Censor-General (Saganwŏn 司諫院) and the Office of the Special Counselors (Hongmungwan 弘文館) on their way to and from work.

9 蒙頭: a head covering that prevents criminals from looking up at the sun.

10 禁堂 = Ŭijŏngbu *tangsanggwan* 義禁府 堂上官: a *tangsanggwan* 堂上官 (lit. "official of the upper end of the hall" = officials higher than senior third rank).

11 捕堂 = P'odoch'ŏng *tangsanggwan* 捕盜廳 堂上官: a *tangsanggwan* in the Capital Police (P'odoch'ŏng 捕盜廳).

12 申後: lit. "after the *sin* hour (*sinsi* 申時 = 3–5 PM)" = after sunset.

13 異之: share it with someone.

14 茶啖: tea and snacks for entertaining guests.

15 虎皮: tiger pelt.

16 一領: a set of clothes.

17 蒙虎皮: put on a tiger pelt.

18 呼唱: shout out.

19 挾倡會飲: gather to drink in the accompaniment of entertainers.

20 見捉: be/get arrested (passive).

21 禁亂: prohibit the violation of laws and public order.

22 收贖: collect money or other property from a criminal as a penalty.

23 諫院 = Saganwŏn 司諫院: Office of the Censor-General.

—— **43** ——

Avenged by the Gods

8 typescript pages titled "Avenged by the Gods" in Box 6:4;
typed up from Vol. XII, pp. 176–81 (crossed out);
"The Law of Retribution" in 9:21 "Trip to Japan," pp. 123–5; 205.

The Law of Retribution

It seems to the writer that Koreans could teach Sir Oliver Lodge and his company many things in regard to the spirit world that are beyond what they have discovered in interest, in dignity and in definite purpose. In the following story such would appear to be the case. Korean spirit appearances have thought back of them that put mere table-rappings and liftings and such useless antics to shame.
Please read the following.

There was once upon a time a certain literary man who threw down his pen in disgust and decided to take to the bow and become an archer. So daily outside the city at Mohwagwan he practised and trained his hand.

Once in the evening, on his return home, he saw a woman's closed chair passing along with a very pretty maidservant following it. With his bow over his shoulder and his arrows under his belt he sauntered along, sometimes ahead of, sometimes behind the palanquin.

As the wind blew and swung aside the curtains, he saw inside the chair the very pretty face of a woman dressed in mourner's white garb. Seeing her most comely features, the scholar wondered who she was, where she had come from, and where she was going. So he followed on til eventually the palanquin passed in through the West Gate and turned in the direction of South Mountain where it entered a well-to-do home.

The literatus walked back and forth before the door, thinking over the woman he had seen, till the shades of evening began to fall, and then he turned into a nearby inn and had his meal.

Later in the night with his bow still over his shoulder, and his arrows through his belt, he walked round the house to make a closer inspection, but found no possible way of entrance. However, there was a little hill against which the rear wall abutted. This he climbed, and looking in, beheld a flower garden and fruit trees. There were bamboos as well, and places here and there where one might easily hide.

In the light of the moon he scaled this wall and went softly on till he came to the rear of the house. In two rooms, one to the east, and one to the west, there were lights burning. He went quietly up to the window of the east room and peeked in, and there he saw an old dame leaning on an arm-rest, while the young woman whom he had seen in the chair was reading to her from a story-book. Her voice was sweet and low.

The scholar kept perfectly still and watched, till a little later the old woman said, "You've been on a journey today, my dear, you'll be tired; go to your room now and sleep."

The young woman bade her good-night and retired to the room on the west side. Following her along the outside the scholar slipped over to this room and watched through the chink.

She on the inside called her servant and said, "You'll be tired after your journey to-day; go home now to your mother, have a good rest and come tomorrow morning early."

The servant left while she herself arose and closed the upper windows, the scholar watching meanwhile.

He said to himself, "She seems to sleep alone. I must endeavor to make my way in," and he held his breath with his eyes close up to the chink.

She opened the wardrobe box, took out quilts and made her bed. Then she had a smoke under the lamplight and sat as though she was waiting for someone to come. The archer wondered what this could mean, when suddenly he heard, as it were, the sound of footsteps from the bamboo grove. Startled, he stepped within the shadows and hid himself, when he saw a close-shaven priest come out of the darkness, go straight to the window and rap.

At once the shutter opened, and in he went while the scholar again resumed his place watching by the chink. He saw the priest take the young woman in his arms and indulge in all kinds of familiarity.

She then poured a drink from a bottle and offered it. He drank and as he did so asked her, "When you went to the grave today did you feel sorry?"

She laughed as she replied, "I have you, what cause have I for sorrow? Why should I feel tearful over a grave with nothing in it?"

While the archer watched this proceeding, his former mind departed from him like a morning cloud and instead a fierce anger burned in his soul. He strung his bow, drew full the arrow and let fly through the paper window. It struck the priest square on the head and drove through to his chin.

The woman in a terrible fright gazed speechless, and then wildly rolled the body in a quilt and then dragged it by main force up the stairway to a room above.

After he had taken careful note of all that she had done, the archer scaled the wall and quietly took his departure. Already it was past midnight.

He returned home and in his sleep had a dream in which a young gentleman of the scholar class of eighteen years or so dressed in a green robe came in and bowed before him, saying, "I have come to thank you for taking vengeance on my enemy."

The scholar answered, "Who are you, pray? What enemy have you, and how have I taken vengeance? Why do you thank me?"

He bowed again and made reply, "I was the son of such-and-such a Minister and in my studies went to one of the neighbouring monasteries where I read the Classics. When there I used to send a priest to my home on errands, and so he often went and came. It seems that my unfaithful wife looked with favour upon him, so that they met at times clandestinely together.

"Once on the way to see my parents, he being with me, we were crossing the hills. All of a sudden, he stopped, kicked and killed me and left my body in a crevice of the rocks where it still lies. I died unjustly and yet no one has come to be my avenger, till last night your shaft drove through his head and killed the criminal who did me wrong. The woman is my wife. Thank you beyond words for this vengeance you have taken, but I have still one favour to ask. Go to my father, please, and tell him where my body lies, and have him give it burial. If you do this I shall be forever most grateful." Thus having spoken he disappeared.

The scholar awoke and it was a dream. He wondered over what had taken place and so went next day to this gentleman's home and sent in his card. The old Minister arose to invite him in.

The scholar inquired, "How many sons have you, Sir?"

The Master, tears flowing from his eyes, answered, "A most unfortunate old man am I. I had no children till after fifty years of age when a son was born to me; a jewel in my hand he was. I had him married and sent to a monastery in the mountains to study, but on his way home one day he was killed by a tiger and devoured and we are just now completing the time of mourning."

The scholar said, "I have a question on my mind about this matter. Won't you come with me please till I show you where his body lies?"

The Master gave a great start of terror and inquired, "How do you know?"

The reply was, "Let's go and see."

A horse was made ready and the old man went along till they reached the monastery, where he dismounted. Together they went some distance up the hill to the rear where there were rocks. Here was a cave with the mouth closed by stones and earth. They had the servant remove these and peering inside they found the dead body of the son, his face fair, unmarred by death, looking just as when he lived.

The old man, on seeing it, fainted away and only after some time did he revive. He then looked at the scholar and said, "How did you know this? You must have killed him."

The scholar laughed and made reply, "Had I done such an evil deed, is it likely that I would have informed you? Let's take the body, get it ready for burial, and then when you have returned home ask your daughter-in-law about it. There is something in the upper storey of your house that bears on this matter. Let us make haste."

The old Minister had the body taken to the temple and after the preparation for burial he returned. At once he went to the daughter-in-law's room and said, "My palace robe is upstairs in the box; I want to get it out. Unlock the door for me."

In a state of unspeakable fear, the daughter-in-law replied, "I'll get it, I'll get it. You needn't go up, I'll get it."

A look of death was on her face.

At this the minister's suspicions were suddenly aroused. He unlocked the door and went in to where a fearful odour met him. Behind a box was something wrapped in a quilt. He dragged it out and here was the body of a fat young priest with an arrow shaft through his head.

He shouted, "What is this?"

A face of ashy gray colour was her only reply. He then called the girl's father and brother, told them all that had happened, and finally drove her off the place. A moment later her own father struck her through with a knife and killed her.

The body of the son was taken and buried on the hill with his ancestors.

Again the scholar had a dream where once more the young scholar lad came and said, "I shall never be able to repay the kindness you have done me. There is one matter, however, in which I may be able to render you assistance and show my gratitude. The time for examinations is near at hand. The subject to be given is something I have already written on, and so I shall repeat it to you. Listen now and catch every word, for if you attend carefully and write it down you will indeed win first place."

He then repeated a poem of twenty verses, the subject of which was "Ch'up'ung hoesimmaeng" (Amid the Autumn Winds My Repentant Heart Awakes).

The scholar repeated it over and over in his dream and after awaking wrote it down. A few days later he entered the lists of the *kwagŏ* (examination) when, sure enough, this very subject was given. Inspired by the thought, he wrote the poem as revealed in the dream and passed it in.

In this poem was the verse,

(Ch'up'ung saphye sukki)
    A rustling wind at eventide,

(Og'u hwagi chaengyŏng)
    A marble hall both high and wide.

Now instead of writing *ch'u* for "autumn" he had written *kŭm* "metal" as that is used sometimes as a synonym.

The examiner at that time was Kim Chukch'ŏn (Kyujin), and when he saw the poem he said, "Well done, done by the gods surely! The spirits must be playing some game on us by these verses."

But when he came to the line where *kŭm* was written instead of *ch'u** he laughed and said, "Not the gods after all but some man's superior gift." He marked the writer as the winner of the day.

Someone standing by asked the examiner how he drew a distinction between what was by the gods and what by man.

He replied, "The spirits hate *kŭm* or metal. No spirit would ever use the metaphor 'metal wind' for 'autumn wind.'"*

When the results were announced the archer scholar was first, crowned with the honours of the day. If you look up the *Kukcho pangmok*† you will find the winner's name marked there, though I have not yet made search for it myself.

* Gale is in error. The original reads that the scholar's use of *kŭm* (金) was an "unintentional replacing" (誤換). The reference to *kŭm* as a common substitute for *ch'u* (秋) seems to have been information he obtained from his pundits.

† Registers of the Successful Candidates of the Higher Civil Service Examination during the Chosŏn Dynasty.

일 유 생 투 필 이 업 무 예　　습 사 우 모 화 관　　　석 양 시 파 귀
一儒生投筆而業武藝　習射于慕華館 1)　夕陽時罷歸

유 일 내 행 가 교 이 래　　후 무 배 행　　지 유 일 동 비 수 후
有一內行駕轎而來　後無陪行　只有一童婢隨後

이 파 연 미　　유 생 견 이 욕 지　　요 시 견 궁　　이 수
而頗妍美　儒生見而欲之　腰矢肩弓 2) 而隨

혹 전 혹 후　　풍 취 렴 권　　별 견 교 내　　녀 인 소 복 이 좌
或前或後 3)　風吹簾捲　瞥見轎內　女人素服而坐

진 국 색 야　　유 생 신 정 황 홀　　심 내 암 촌
眞國色也　儒生神精怳惚　心內暗忖

此是誰家女子也　第隨往而探知其家　仍隨後而行

遵大路入新門 4)　轉向南村某洞　一大第而入

儒生彷徨門外　日勢已暮　仍轉向店舍買食

而帶弓矢周察其家前後　無可闖入 5)

處　其家後墻依一小阜而不高　登阜而俯視

則其墻內有花園　叢竹菀密 6)　可以隱身　乃帶月色

踰後墻田園而下　則其下卽其家後面　而東西兩房

燈火熒然 7)　照後雙窓　仍往其窓下　潛窺東房

則有一老嫗依於枕上　而俄者所見之女子　讀諺冊 8)

於燈下　聲音琅琅如碎玉　儒生暗伏於窓下

而以窓隙窺見而已　老嫗謂其女子曰：今日似必困憊

可歸汝房休息　其女子承命而退歸西房　儒生自外

又往西邊窓外窺見　則女子喚童婢謂曰：行役之餘

汝亦困憊矣　可出宿於汝母家　明朝早來　童婢出門

女子起而閉上窓戶　儒生暗喜曰：此女旣已獨宿

吾當乘間突入可也云　而屛氣 9) 窺見　則其女子開

籠而出鋪錦衾　吸烟茶而坐燈下　若有所思想者然

儒生心窃訝之　少焉　後園竹枝有聲　若有人跡

儒生驚怯而隱身以避而見之　則一禿頭和尙 10)

披竹林而來叩後窓　自內開窓而迎之　儒生隨其後

而從窓窺見　則其和尙摟抱 11) 其女子　淫戲無所

不至　已而其女因起　向于卓上　拿下酒壺饌盒

滿酌而勸之　和尙一吸而盡　問曰：今日墓行

果有悲懷否　女子含笑曰：惟汝在吾何悲懷

且是虛葬 12) 之地　亦有何悲懷之可言乎　又與

僧一場淫戲　而裸體同入衾中　相抱而臥　此時

儒生初來欲奸之心　雲消霧散 13)　而憤慨之心倍激矣

仍彎弓注矢 14)　從窓戶滿的射 15) 去　正中和尙之禿

두정문　　　상삽거　　　녀자경기전률　　　급이금과승지시
頭頂門 16) 上挿去　女子驚起戰慄　急以衾裹僧之尸

치지루상　　유생세찰기동정　　갱유후장이출래　　시
置之樓上　儒生細察其動靜　更踰後墻而出來　時

이파루　의　　잉위환가　　기야사몽비몽간　　유일청
已罷漏 17) 矣　仍爲還家　其夜似夢非夢間　有一靑

포유생　　년가십팔구　　래배어전왈　　감군지보수
袍儒生　年可十八九　來拜於前曰: 感君之報讐 18)

시이래사　　유생경이문왈　　군시하허인　　이소구하인
是以來謝　儒生驚而問曰: 君是何許人　而所仇何人

오무위군보구　　지사　　하위래사　　기인엄억
吾無爲君報仇 19) 之事　何爲來謝　其人掩抑 20)

이대왈　　모내모동모재지자야　　독서우산사시
而對曰: 某乃某洞某宰之子也　讀書于山寺時

사주인승　　지량찬왕래우가중의　　음부견이욕지
使主人僧 21) 持粮饌往來于家中矣　淫婦見而欲之

수여통간의　　모어귀근　　지로　　차승동행　　도무
遂與通奸矣　某於歸覲 22) 之路　此僧同行　到無

인지지　　축오살지　　이시체치지어산하암혈자
人之地　蹴吾殺之　以尸體置之於山下巖穴者

우금삼년의　　모기원사　　이무이보구설한　　의
于今三年矣　某旣寃死 23) 而無以報仇雪恨 24) 矣

작야군지소사살자　　즉기승야　　기녀자즉오지내야
昨夜君之所射殺者　卽其僧也　其女子卽吾之內也

차구이설　　감사무지　　우유일사봉탁자　　군수왕견오
此仇已雪　感謝無地　又有一事奉托者　君須往見吾

부친　　고오지시체소재처　　사지이폄　　즉은우대의
父親　告吾之尸體所在處　使之移窆 25) 則恩尤大矣

言訖而忽不知去向　儒生驚覺則一夢也　心甚異之

翌日　更往其家　通刺 26) 而入　則有一老宰起迎

坐定儒生問曰：子弟有幾人　主人揮淚而言曰：

老夫命途奇窮 27)　無他子女　五十後得一兒子

愛如掌玉 28)　成婚往山寺課工　爲虎所噬去

終祥 29)　未過矣　儒生曰：小生有一疑訝事　第隨

我而訪屍身所在處可乎　主人大驚痛（哭）曰：

君何由知之　對曰：第往見之可也　主人卽具鞍馬

與之同行　至其寺　下馬登山由寺後　行幾步有

巖石而有穴　以土石塞其口　使下隸去其土石

而以手探之　則有一屍體出　而見之　果是其子

而顏色依舊　其老宰抱尸而哭　幾絶而甦 30)　仍向

其儒生而問曰：汝何由知之　此必是汝之所爲也

其儒生笑曰：吾若行兇　則何可見公而道之乎

第爲治喪　而歸問其由於令子婦　其房樓上

有一物之可證者　公須速行之　其老宰一邊運屍

安于僧舍之內　使辦喪需　而歸家直入子婦房

問曰：吾有朝服之置於汝樓上矣　吾可出而見之

須開樓門　其子婦慌忙而對曰：此則兒當出來

何須尊舅之親搜也云　而氣色頗殊常　老宰仍向樓

開鎖而入　則有穢惡之臭　搜至籠後　有以衾裹者

出而置之於房內　則卽一少年胖大 31) 和尙之屍

而揷箭於頂門之上矣　老宰問曰：此何爲也

其子婦面如土色　戰慄不敢對　仍出請其父與

兄　道此事而黜之　其父以刀剮而殺 32) 之云矣

仍改葬其子之屍於先山之下矣　一夜　其儒生

又於似夢非夢之間　其少年又來　百拜致謝曰：

君之恩無以酬之　今科期不遠　而場內所出之題

卽吾之平日所做之文　吾可誦傳之　君須書之

入場後呈劵　則必做第 33) 矣　仍誦傳一首賦

題是秋風悔心萌也　其儒生受而書之　數日後　科期

已迫入場　則果出此題矣　仍書其賦而呈劵　至秋

風颯 34) 兮夕起　玉宇 35) 廊而崢嶸 36) 之句　秋字

誤換書以金字矣　時竹泉金公鎭圭 37) 主試　見此

劵曰 : 此賦果是善作　而似是鬼神之作　無乃欲試

吾輩試鑑 38) 之故耶云矣　讀至金風 39) 颯兮夕起之句

笑曰 : 此非鬼作　乃擢第一　人問其故　竹泉答曰 :

鬼神忌金　若鬼作則必不書金字也　故知非鬼作云矣

榜出其儒生登魁　其姓名考之科榜則可知爲誰某

而未及考見

1　慕華館: lit. "hall of revering [Chinese] Civilization": an official reception hall for greeting Chinese envoys during the Chosŏn Dynasty; located just to the northwest of Tonŭi Gate 敦義門.
2　腰矢肩弓: fasten one's arrows around one's waist and sling one's bow over one's shoulder.

3 或前或後: now in front, now behind.

4 新門: lit. "new gate"; Tonŭimun 敦義門 = Sŏdaemun 西大門: so called because it was the last of the three large gates in Seoul to be built; the two others were Sungnyemun 崇禮門 (Namdaemun 南大門 = South Gate) and Hŭnginmun 興仁門 (Tongdaemun 東大門 = East Gate).

5 闖入: espy an opportunity to steal in.

6 叢竹菀密: luxuriant bamboo thicket.

7 燈火熒然: brightly lit with lamplight.

8 諺冊: books written in the Korean vernacular script.

9 屏氣: hold one's breath.

10 禿頭和尚: tonsured/bald monk.

11 摟抱: draw someone into one's embrace.

12 虛葬: perform a fake funeral for a missing person.

13 雲消霧散: lit. "clouds scatter, fog disperses" = disappear without a trace.

14 彎弓注矢: pull a loaded bow to full draw.

15 滿的射去: release an arrow on target.

16 頂門: crown of the head.

17 罷漏: a Chosŏn dynasty custom of banging a metal drum thirty-three times at around 4 AM (*ogyŏng samjŏm* 五更三點) in the capital in order to mark the end of the nightly curfew.

18 報讐: take vengeance.

19 報仇 = *posu* 報讐: take vengeance.

20 掩抑: hide one's resentment.

21 主人僧 = *chujisŭng* 住持僧: head abbot.

22 歸覲: return home to see one's parents.

23 冤死: die a resentful death.

24 雪恨: resolve one's spite.

25 移窆 = *ijang* 移葬 ~ *myŏllye* 緬禮: change a burial site.

26 通刺: send in one's calling card; seek an audience by presenting a card.

27 命途奇窮: be born under an unlucky star.

28 愛如掌玉: lit. "love like a gem in the palm of one's hand."

29 終祥 = *taesang* 大祥: ceremony commemorating the second anniversary of someone's death.

30 幾絕而甦: repeatedly lose and regain consciousness.

31 胖大: fatty and fleshy.

32 以刀刲而殺: use a knife to stab and kill.

33 做第: achieve first place in the civil service examination.

34 颯: cool breeze.

35 玉宇: lit. "jade house" = dwelling of the Celestial Emperor (*ch'ŏnje*; *tiandi* 天帝).

36 峥嶸: steep and towering.
37 金鎮圭 [1658–1716; styled Talbo 達甫; sobriquet Chukch'ŏn 竹泉; ancestral seat Kwangsan 光山; posthumous epithet Munch'ŏng 文清]: scholar-official under King Sukchong 肅宗 [r. 1674–1720; 1661–1720]. His father was Kim Man'gi 金萬基 [1633–87].
38 試鑑: (a civil service examination invigilator) have a discerning eye for excellent composition.
39 金風: autumn wind.

—— 44 ——

The Robber Chief

Vol. II: 16; n.d.; Diary XIV, pp. 33–7; 206.

A certain Kim *chinsa** was a wise and courageous man; very poor, however, and lacking in any hope of office. He was distressed at his bad luck and one day as he was thinking over his failures, a son of a minister, a friend of his, proposed that they go outside the East Gate and pay their condolences to a returning funeral party. To this Kim agreed.

On the appointed day before it was light a man came to Kim's house and called from outside the door. "So-and-so sends a horse and his word is, 'I hear the funeral party returns before daylight; we shall have to start at once to meet them, so I am sending this man and this horse. Come as quickly as you can.'"

Doubting nothing, Kim mounted and rode out of the city. It was as though he flew, so fast he went. He reached the Bell Rock beyond the East Gate and yet there was no sign of day.

Kim asked of the servant, "Where is your master waiting for me?"

He replied, "Just ahead here some little distance."

So he applied the whip and they pushed on faster than ever. Passing Taragwŏn, they went along the main road till they came to a resting place where a tall servant and a freshly saddled horse awaited them. At the side was another servant who had a meal prepared and wine to drink.

Kim was more mystified than ever over this and asked, "Who are you, I pray, and what does all this mean?"

The servant made reply, "Please have some refreshments; never mind anything else. We change horses here and then move on as quickly as possible. You will know a little later as to what it means."

Not understanding in the least but being helpless in their hands, Kim did as was suggested. Passing on some fifty or sixty *ri* more he again found a fresh horse newly saddled and food and drink again prepared.

He again partook without any question and so pushed on day and night without cessation, a fresh horse and food awaiting him every fifty or sixty *ri*.

He passed the great Iron Pass and then turned into the hills and, keeping along the ridge among the hills, went several days till they came to a place entirely surrounded by hills. In it was a settlement with an official yamen. There were a great many houses crowded together and one great building like a governor's headquarters with three red-arrow gates before it.

He dismounted and passed in through the middle gate when he found a great imposing personage lying under a quilt and girls about on each side. They were waiting attendance on him.

The sick man seemed at last gasp and looking at Kim said, "I too am from Seoul originally but have been here for several years; and now I am sick and dying with no one to take my place. I heard you are wise and have courage. I have had you brought here. I trust you will have no doubts or fears. If you attempt to get out of it, there will be great danger for you. Be careful, I pray you, and most guarded. I have here under my command about one thousand soldiers and storehouses full of goods and grain.

"I trust you will take up my command, for though I am a robber chief, I have never descended to low stealing or anything of that sort. What I have taken has been the stolen goods of avaricious officials or lying secretaries, the pay and alms that the rich owe the poor, goods that have come from Peking in the envoys' train in the hands of the rich, leaving the poor man to keep his own. These things I have used for my soldiers and my people. This is what you are expected to do.

"Man is born into the world but names and fame are in God's giving; he cannot claim it of himself. But what is fame and name to my place here with my soldiers about me, my singing maidens, all the treasures of the hills and the riches of the sea, with no care or anxiety over anything that lacks. I would not change with any minister or president of a board that lives. Bend your □ to make your post a success."

He finished speaking and, turning his face, never spoke again.

Kim then realized that he had been talking to a great robber chief and gave a great start in his soul but saw no way of escape and so took his seat at the place of command and a dozen or so officers came and bowed in the open court. The soldiers all came as well and made their bow and brought a special fine hat for him to don and a green coat for him to wear.

Helpless in their hands, Kim put them on. The food and clothes were specially fine and most abundant. He took up his abode just opposite to the dying chief and that night he died. A great mourning took place with sackcloth and ashes. They dressed the dead chief in the finest robe and buried him on a mountain at the rear.

Kim thought over this and that but saw no way of making his escape and so spent a week or so. Among the soldiers he saw groups gathered here and there talking.

Said they, "Our former chief is dead and our new chief sits in his place. Still ten days have passed and he has no plan or scheme. It looks as though he were merely a bag for meals; what shall we do about him? Let's wait a few days and see. If he continues thus, we'll have to kill him and bring somebody else."

Hearing this, Kim was scared out of his life. On the next morning as he sat to receive the morning greetings, he called the underchiefs and said, "When the funeral ceremonies for the late dead chief were under way I could not consult you. How about the supplies at present – are there plenty in hand?"

They replied, "We had supplies put away but they have nearly all been used up by the funeral service and so what is left is but very little. We are a bit anxious over this."

Kim said, "Let the soldiers whose turn comes tomorrow bring me their list of names."

This order the chiefs took and withdrew and in a little came in with the prescribed list. Here all the names of the rich and those worth plundering were marked.

Kim marked off the name of Chu *chinsa* of Yŏnghŭng, when the chief bowed before him and said, "This man is a great millionaire but there is no way of getting at his goods. In his town are four or five hundred houses, all servants and relatives of this lord. At every gate and minor door there is a great bell hung, tied by a string to every other bell, all bound together and then made fast to the master's. If there is any alarm whatever a bell is struck and every other bell in the place responds.

Once you get into that place I know of no possible way to get out. How about that?"

Kim scolded him, saying, "Your commander has given you this order; yours is to carry it out through fire and water. How dare you talk in a way that takes the heart out of your soldiers? Have him arrested."

After they had given him six or seven blows with the paddle, Kim ordered, saying, "I shall go myself in this case."

Kim dressed in the uniform of an officer of the provincial government with a green coat, a scepter stick, large clothes boxes and hampers, twenty horseloads and more that followed after him. His soldiers were all dressed as post station guards and when the day was drawing to a close they reached Chu *chinsa*'s place.

Kim said, "I am the military officer of the governor and now am on my way to Seoul to present the provincial tribute supply."

As he went into the gate, Chu *chinsa* came out respectfully to meet him. They passed their greeting and he said to the master, "My visit is on a mission of special tribute to the government; these goods I have are very valuable and cannot be left out in the open. Kindly let me have the use of your storehouse."

The master opened the storehouse and then prepared the evening meal and entertained them royally. At night he slept on the same pillow with the master.

The master in the night had a dream in which he seemed to be bound about the breast and stifled. In his fear he awoke and looked and there was the supposed officer of the government with his foot on him and a long knife raised.

"If you make the slightest sound," said he, "I'll have your head off in a trice. You have no cause for fear or alarm, and make no noise. I am not an officer of the government, but the chief of a band of outlaws. I have come to get from you supplies for my men. If you will tell me where your money, your goods, and your grain is, that's all I ask. If not, your life will end this night. Is your life of value, or your money and goods?"

With a face of clay in a case of cold sweat, the master pled pitifully, saying, "I'll tell you where each and everything is – don't harm me, I pray you."

The Chief promised and then he called his followers and had the storehouses opened till they saw everything in his possession.

When this was going on the people of the house were all in a state of alarm, but when any of them attempted to approach, Chu called out,

"Don't go near them, but let them have free access to everything in the stores."

So the crowd of thieves went here and there as they pleased. They carried off goods and money, everything they could lay hands on, and put it on their horses; finding their animals insufficient, they loaded the owner's horses and cows as well.

When they had all been sent off, Kim took the master by the hand and holding a knife in his own right hand had him go with him outside the gates and outside the town. There he pushed him aside and said, "Go now."

Then he mounted and was off like the wind or the rushing rain.

This one haul meant thousands of dollars. Kim then became a great chief of the outlaws.

Four or five days later he again ordered the prescribed list to be brought and upon it he marked off Sŏgwangsa. The officer, however, said, "There is only one way into this temple. If we once get in and the official soldiers shut the entrance, you are caught bag and baggage. What about this?"

Kim again reprimanded him, saying, "I shall have to go this time as well."

This time he dressed as a police captain with the Hamhŭng Crest and with an army of constables, and in the midst of them he had a number bound with red cords as bandits whom he had captured. He went into the monastery and seated himself in the tower. There he had the thieves put down and questioned them under torture. And they gave the names of this priest and that as having engaged in thievery.

Kim had these priests arrested one by one as they were called. Little by little the whole monastery, three or four hundred, were all bound and helpless. Then he had his followers gather up all the temple dishes to be found, money, goods of every kind, and loaded them all on horses and sent them off one after the other.

At that time several of the priests who had gone to the hills for wood found this state of things on their return and at once ran to Anbyŏn and gave the word.

The magistrate gave a great start, summoned all his soldiers and guards, and went in by the entrance, closing the exit.

The outlaws, hearing this, told Kim and Kim at once had four or five of his men cut their heads and dress as priests and, with blood marks on them and battered visages, say to the magistrate that "robbers have gone by the rear road over yonder hill. There is no use of coming in this way."

Hearing this, the magistrate went by the rear road in hot haste on their track, while Kim made his escape out of the east entrance and got away. Again his haul was very great and sufficed for his soldiers for a long time.

Then he planned and schemed not twice only but many, many times, passing two or three years as the outlaw chief.

Once he called his followers all to him and said, "You were once on a time all common folk of the land, but have been driven by cold and hunger to work such as this. This is not a calling that one should continue on further. Divide what you have here and you will all have something and to spare, and give up this life of the outlaw. I, too, have no intention of being long here. Divide now what we have and let each return to his home where he lived before and be a decent man of society once again. What is your mind in this matter?"

They all said, "We'll do whatever our Chief orders."

Then Kim had out all their goods and divided them piece by piece and gave each his part and sent them home. Then he set fire to every thing, house, and hall that they had built and on a pony rode back to his house in Seoul.

* *chinsa*: literary licentiate.

김 진 사 모 자 유 지 략　　이 가 빈 락 척　　　울 울 불 득 지
金進士某者有智畧　　而家貧落拓 1)　　菀菀不得志

시 유 친 지 재 상 지 자　　약 여 명 일 동 왕 동 교　　영 조
時有親知宰相之子　　約與明日同往東郊　　迎弔 2)

친 우 지 반 우　　기 일 미 명　　창 외 유 인 래 언 왈　　모 가 모
親友之返虞 3)　　其日未明　　窓外有人來言曰：某家某

송 기 운　　문 모 우 반 우 미 명 입 래　　오 배 예 어 평 명 출 성
送騎云　　聞某友返虞未明入來　　吾輩預於平明出城

인 마 자 송 지　　급 급 기 래　　김 생 신 지 불 의　　기 마 출 문
人馬玆送之　　急急騎來　　金生信之不疑　　騎馬出門

其行如飛　由東城外鍾巖　而日尙未出　金生問

于牽夫曰：汝家上典在於何處　對曰：在於前面

仍加鞭而行　度樓院遵大路而行　行到一處　則又

有一健夫　具鞍馬而待　傍有一人　具酒飯而進之

金生心益疑怪而問曰：汝輩是何人　而此何爲也

其人答曰：第可飮喫　換騎而行　則自可知之

金生不得已依其言　換騎而行　行到五六十里

又有備酒食鞍馬如俄者樣　金生第又如前飮而換騎

晝夜不止　每於五六十里　必有人之留待　而由

鐵嶺 4)　轉而入山路　踰嶺度山　行幾日至一處

則四山環圍之中　有一洞府　洞中人家櫛比　有一

大舍如公廨 5) 樣　朱門而有三　下馬而歷重門而入

則有一丈夫擁衾而臥　左右有侍娥數人　扶將而

坐　氣息奄奄 6)　向金生而言曰：吾亦京洛之人 7)

誤入於此　積有年矣　今則病且死矣　無人可代

聞君有智畧　故奉邀到此地頭　不必苦辭　若欲圖

免 8)　則必有大禍　愼之愼之　麾下軍卒有千餘名

倉庫亦實　可代吾而善處置　吾雖賊魁　而未嘗行

不忍之事　如貪官汚吏之物　富民之吝而不給人者

燕市倭館之物貨財寶之出者　量其可取而取之

以充軍需之用　君亦依此爲之可也　人生斯世

功名在天　非人可爲者　曷若坐此而號令軍中

歌姬舞女　山珍海錯 9)　不患不足　可謂公卿不換

者也　勉之勉之　言訖而臥　更無所言　金生始知

其爲賊將　而滿心驚訝　無計脫身　第坐於廳上

則如軍校者十餘人　來拜於庭下　軍卒一時來謁

以絲笠藍袍加之於身　金生不得已受而着之　其供

饋等節　極其豊潔　金生處於越房　是夜賊將殞命

軍中擧哀 掛孝 10) 治喪 極其侈麗 成服 11) 後禮瘞

12) 之于山後之麓 金生左右思想 無計可脫

留七八日後 軍中往往有偶語曰：舊帥已歿

新帥代坐 而于今近十日 別無出謀發慮之事 13)

似是一箇飯囊 14) 將焉用之 更竢幾日 若一

向如是 則不可不殺之 而更求他人爲好云云

金生微聞 15) 此言 大生恐怯 翌日之朝 坐廳上

招軍校之爲首者分付曰：間緣舊帥之喪禮未畢

無暇問之 見今軍中 需用能無匱乏 16) 者耶

對曰：如干所儲 幾盡於喪需見今餘者無多

方以此爲悶矣 金生曰：自明當分送軍卒 軍令

板 17) 斯速入來 其校承命而退 未幾入軍令板

而背後列書可偸之人家 金生乃以永興 18) 朱

進士家劃出 則首校俯伏請曰：此家果是巨富

이 실 무 가 투 지 망　기 동 중 사 오 백 호　구 시 노 속
而實無可偸之望　其洞中四五百戶　俱是奴屬

이 매 호 문 미　현 일 대 령　이 기 삭 두　도 취 우 일 삭
而每戶門楣 19) 懸一大鈴　以其索頭　都聚于一索

괘 어 주 가　여 유 경 즉 일 요 령 삭　허 다 지 령　일 시 응 지
掛於主家　如有驚則一搖鈴索　許多之鈴　一時應之

일 입 지 후　만 무 출 래 지 망　차 장 내 하　김 생 내 질 왈
一入之後　萬無出來之望　此將奈何　金生乃叱曰：

장 기 출 령　즉 수 수 화 고 불 가 사 언　감 란 언 이 요 군 심 호
將旣出令　則雖水火固不可辭焉　敢亂言以撓軍心乎

즉 위 나 입　엄 곤 륙 칠 도 후　분 부 왈　차 즉 오 당 친 왕
卽爲拿入　嚴棍六七度後　分付曰：此則吾當親往

명 일　김 생 장 출　영 비　양　이 청 천 익　패 장 비
明日　金生妝出 20) 營裨 21) 樣　以靑天翼 22) 佩將牌 23)

여 대 상 자 대 롱 등 속　수 십 태 재 지 어 마　수 후 인 개
如大箱子大籠等屬　數十駄載之於馬　隨後人皆

이 역 졸 양 장 출　이 일 모 시　치 입 주 진 사 가　이 위
以驛卒樣妝出　而日暮時　馳入朱進士家　以爲

함 영　진 상 령 거 비 장 운　입 문 즉 주 진 사 황 망 연 접
咸營 24) 進上領去裨將云　入門則朱進士遑忙延接

서 한 훤 후　향 주 인 이 언 왈　차 시 영 문 별 진 상 물 종 야
敍寒暄後　向主人而言曰：此是營門別進上物種也

유 소 중 불 가 치 지 외　가 치 지 우 대 청 상　주 인 의 기 언
有所重不可置之外　可置之于大廳上　主人依其言

치 지 청 상　비 석 반 궤 지　도 야 여 주 인 련 침 의　주 인 수
置之廳上　備夕飯饋之　到夜與主人聯枕矣　主人睡

몽 지 중　흉 격 색 울　경 각 이 개 안　즉 아 자 영 비 자
夢之中　胸膈塞菀 25) 驚覺而開眼　則俄者營裨者

거 흉 이 좌　수 집 장 검 이 언 왈　여 약 출 성　즉 당 이 검 참
據胸而坐　手執長劍而言曰：汝若出聲　則當以劍斬

지 의　수 물 경 겁　역 물 발 성　오 비 영 비　내 시 적 괴 야
之矣　須勿驚怯　亦勿發聲　吾非營裨　乃是賊魁也

욕 차 군 량 어 여　여 지 시 전 포 소 재 처　즉 여 가 활 의
欲借軍粮於汝　汝指示錢布所在處　則汝可活矣

불 자 여 명 지 어 금 야　명 위 중 호　전 포 위 중 호　주
不者汝命止於今夜　命爲重乎　錢布爲重乎　主

인 면 여 토 색　황 한 협 배 이 애 걸 왈　근 당 일 일 봉 행
人面如土色　惶汗浹背而哀乞曰：謹當一一奉行

행 물 상 아　적 장 허 락　잉 초 졸 도 지 수 래 자　개 고 이
幸勿傷我　賊將許諾　仍招卒徒之隨來者　開庫而

일 일 수 출　여 사 지 시　가 인 개 경 동　혹 유 근 지 자
一一搜出　如斯之時　家人皆驚動　或有近之者

즉 주 자 련 성 왈　수 물 근 아　이 고 중 지 물 임 기 수 거
則朱者連聲曰：須勿近我　而庫中之物任其搜去

어 시 적 도 란　란　입 고 중　포 목 지 속　은 전 지 물
於是賊徒攔［欄］26)入庫中　布木之屬　銀錢之物

출 이 태 지 병 기 주 인 가 우 마 이 태 지　사 지 운 출 동 구 후
出而駄之并其主人家牛馬而駄之　使之運出洞口後

내 좌 수 집 주 인 지 수　우 수 집 장 검　동 행 출 문 지 어 동
乃左手執主人之手　右手執長劍　同行出門至於洞

구 외　이 포 각　주 인　내 상 마 이 거　여 풍 우 지 취　일
口外　而抛却7)主人　乃上馬而去　如風雨之驟28)　一

행 소 득　태 과 수 만 여 금　군 중 막 불 칭 신　과 사 오 일 후
行所得　殆過數萬餘金　軍中莫不稱神　過四五日後

우 사 입 군 령 판　획 출 석 왕 사　수 교 자 우 품 왈　차 사
又使入軍令板　劃出釋王寺29)　首校者又稟曰：此寺

동부　지유일로　약심입이관군색동구　즉무이출래
洞府　只有一路　若深入而官軍塞洞口　則無以出來

차장내하　김생우질퇴이분부왈　금번오우당작행
此將奈何　金生又叱退而分付曰：今番吾又當作行

잉장함흥　중군　복색　이다솔교졸　적도중수인
仍妝咸興 30) 中軍 31) 服色　而多率校卒　賊徒中數人

이홍사결박수후　이입사좌우루상　이착입적한
以紅絲結縛隨後　而入寺坐于樓上　而捉入賊漢

구문악형　비지적초출승도　수출수박　사중사
鉤問惡刑 32) 備至賊招出僧徒　隨出隨縛　寺中四

오백여승　무불박지　잉사수출불기급전포등속
五百餘僧　無不縛之　仍使搜出佛器及錢布等屬

일병태지어마　이린차　출송　시유수승채초어
一倂馱之於馬　而鱗次 33) 出送　時有數僧採樵於

산견기상　급고우안변　관　본쉬대경급발노
山見其狀　急告于安邊 34) 官　本倅大驚急發奴

령급군교배　엄입동구　적도문차보　급보어김생
令及軍校輩　掩入洞口　賊徒聞此報　急報於金生

내이적도중사오인　삭발위승도양　이대혈흔
乃以賊徒中四五人　削髮爲僧徒樣　而帶血痕

작통성이출　향관군왈　적도유후산이거　관군속
作痛聲而出　向官軍曰：賊徒踰後山而去　官軍速

유후산지로　불필입차동구　관군문지　일병유산후
踰後山之路　不必入此洞口　官軍聞之　一倂由山後

이거　김생내종동구　탈신이도　우득전포백여태
而去　金生乃從洞口　脫身而走　又得錢布百餘馱

군수지용유족의　여차설계이수납자　불지어차
軍需之用裕足矣　如此設計而收納者　不止於此

이 불 득 진 록　　과 수 삼 년 후　　김 생 집 졸 도 이 언 왈
而不得盡錄　過數三年後　金生集卒徒而言曰：

여 배 개 평 민 야　　이 박 어 기 한　　내 유 차 거　　연 비 장 구
汝輩皆平民也　而迫於飢寒　乃有此擧　然非長久

계 야　　여 배 각 분 금 백　　이 의 식 불 간　　즉 하 필 여 시 야
計也　汝輩各分金帛　而衣食不艱　則何必如是也

오 역 비 구 거 차 지 인 야　　고 중 소 재 지 물　　각 자 균 분
吾亦非久居此之人也　庫中所在之物　各自均分

환 귀 고 리　　이 작 평 민 호 야　　미 지 여 배 지 심 하 여
還歸故里　以作平民好也　未知汝輩之心何如

제 인 개 왈　　유 장 군 명　　김 생 내 출 소 적 지 재　　일 일 균
諸人皆曰：惟將軍命　金生乃出所積之財　一一均

분 이 급 각 인　　사 각 귀 향 리　　이 화 소 기 옥 우　　기 마 출 산
分以給各人　使各歸鄉里　以火燒其屋宇　騎馬出山

환 귀 본 제 운 이
還歸本第云爾

1 落拓: fall into unfortunate circumstances.
2 迎弔: meet and convey one's condolences.
3 返虞 = *panhon* 返魂: bring the ancestral tablet of the deceased home after the funeral.
4 鐵嶺: a large mountain pass located between Hoeyang County 淮陽郡 in Kangwŏn Province and Anbyŏn Prefecture 安邊郡 in South Hamgyŏng Province.
5 公廨 = *kwanch'ŏng* 官廳 ~ *kwana* 官衙: local administrative office.
6 氣息奄奄: one's breathing loses its vitality and energy.
7 京洛之人: resident of the capital.
8 圖免 = *momyŏn* 謀免: escape, evade.
9 山珍海錯 = *sanhae chinmi* 山海珍味: surf and turf.
10 掛孝: lit. "don filial piety" = put on mourner's garb.
11 成服: lit. "attain clothing" = begin wearing mourner's garb three or five days after a funeral.
12 瘞: inter, bury.
13 發慮之事: anxiety-inducing matter.

14 飯囊: lit. "rice pouch" = good-for-nothing.

15 微聞: eavesdrop.

16 匱乏 = *kyŏlp'ip* 缺乏: lack, be insufficient.

17 軍令板: wooden token of command.

18 永興: a town in South Hamgyŏng Province.

19 門楣: door jamb.

20 妝 = *punjang* 扮裝: decorate; dress up as.

21 營裨: unranked military attendant (*pijang* 裨將) attached to the headquarters of the provincial governor's office.

22 天翼: *ch'ŏllik* (native Korean word rendered in sinographs as phonograms),
a kind of formal attire worn by military officers.

23 將牌: wooden badge worn at the waist by a military officer or a clerk.

24 咸營: headquarters of the Hamgyŏng governor's office.

25 胸膈塞菀: lit. "lower chest contracts and feels constricted" = feel frustrated.

26 欄入: enter without permission, trespass.

27 抛却: throw away.

28 風雨之驟: sudden thunderstorm.

29 釋王寺: temple at Sŏlbong Mountain 雪峯山 in Anbyŏn Prefecture 安邊縣
in South Hamgyŏng Province.

30 咸興: a town in South Hamgyŏng Province.

31 中軍: commander of a garrison (*kunyŏng* 軍營).

32 鉤問惡刑: lit. "ask deceptive questions and give harsh punishment" =
interrogate and punish (a criminal).

33 鱗次: arrayed one after the other like fish scales.

34 安邊: a town in South Hamgyŏng Province.

—— **45** ——

Mrs. Kim, the Prophetess

Vol. II: 18; Diary XII, pp. 84–6 (crossed out); *Miscellaneous Writings* No. 30,
pp. 100–1; Box 9:21, pp. 120–1; 207.

The wife of the Prime Minister (1672) Kim Suhang was of the Na clan,
a sister of Na Yangjwa. She was a woman of the keenest powers of per-
ception. In an effort to find a son-in-law she sent her third son Kim
Ch'anghŭp (Samyŏn) to one of the Min's to see if there was a suitable
mate for her daughter in his household.

Ch'anghŭp returned, saying, "The boys in Min's home look weak and homely – not at all suitable."

The mother said, "But that cannot be so. A family so widely known must have gifted lads."

Later on Ch'anghŭp made choice of his own from the home of a certain Yi and came to his mother to say, "I have indeed found a suitable son-in-law, mother."

The mother asked, "Who is he and what does he look like?"

Ch'anghŭp replied, "He is very handsome and highly gifted with a great future before him."

The mother said, "Very good."

On the day of the wedding the mother looked at him but sighed, saying, "My third son has eyes and yet he really cannot see."

In wonder at this, Ch'anghŭp, said, "Why do you say that, mother?"

Her reply was, "He is a nice young man, but he is destined for a short life and will assuredly never pass thirty. Why did you recommend him?"

A moment later she said, "My daughter will die first, however, so I suppose it makes no difference. Alas, why did you ever do such a thing as this?"

Ch'anghŭp opposed this, however, and maintained that it would never be so.

On a certain day Min Chinhu (Chijae) and Min Chinwŏn (Tanam), two cousins with their bridegrooms' hats on their heads, came on a visit to Kim's home. Ch'anghŭp then went in and called his mother, saying, "Mother, you have mourned over the fact that we did not arrange a marriage with the Min's; the two young men you thought of have now come – please take a look through the window chink and see if what I told you is not true."

The mother looked and again reprimanded Ch'anghŭp, saying, "You have eyes but certainly you cannot see. These are very rare and gifted lads with a great future before them. I am so sorry that we did not decide in their favour."

Later on it came to pass as she had foreseen. The Mins grew to greatness and renown, while Yi simply became a *ch'ambong** and died before thirty. The daughter died one year earlier.

This same mother had woven with her own hands three rolls of silk. Of one she made a ceremonial robe for her husband, while two rolls she put away for special use. When her third son Ch'anghŭp graduated it was suggested that she make a dress for him from one of them, but she refused. Later her son Ch'angjip (Mongwa) who had held office without graduation now graduated and she at once took out one of the rolls and made him a ceremonial robe.

The third roll she still kept by her till her granddaughter's husband Cho Munmyŏng graduated, whereupon she took it out and made him a dress from it. These three all became Ministers of State but not the others. Her thought was to give of her woven goods only to him who would rise to highest office.

When Ch'anghyŏp (Nongam) graduated he went in to see his mother, but she merely twisted her face and said, "You look like some hermit from the hills."

But when Ch'angjip came in she smiled and said, "A great Minister of State has come to see me."

* *ch'ambong*: caretaker of royal tombs and gardens (*nŭngwŏn* 陵園); junior ninth-grade post.

文谷金公諱壽恒 1)　夫人羅氏也　明村羅良佐 2)

之娣也　有識鑑 3)　爲女擇婿　使第三胤 4) 三淵 5)

往見閔氏諸少而定婚　三淵往見而告曰：閔家兒

皆氣短 6)　且貌不揚　無可合者　夫人曰：此是名家也

後進必不然矣　其後　三淵擇定於李氏兒　而來言曰：

今日果得佳郎 7) 矣　夫人問爲誰　而風範 8) 何如

對曰：風儀動盪 [蕩] 9)　才華發越 10) 眞大器之人也

부인왈　약연즉호의　급영혼합근지일　부인견
夫人曰：若然則好矣　及迎婚合卺之日 11)　夫人見

이 탄왈　삼아유목무주　의　삼연괴이문지
而嘆曰：三兒有目無珠 12)矣　三淵怪而問之

즉부인왈　신랑가즉가의　수한　대불족원
則夫人曰：新郎佳則佳矣　壽限 13)大不足遠

불과삼순　여하소취이정혼야　이이숙시
不過三旬 14)　汝何所取而定婚也　已而熟視

이우탄왈　오녀선사의　역부내하운운
而又嘆曰：吾女先死矣　亦復奈何云云

이책삼연불이　삼연종불이위연　일일　민지재진후
而責三淵不已　三淵終不以爲然　一日　閔趾齋鎭厚

단암진원　제종형제　구이약관　적유사이래의
15)丹巖鎭遠 16)諸從兄弟　俱以弱冠　適有事而來矣

삼연입고왈　모씨매이민가지불득련혼　위한의
三淵入告曰：母氏每以閔家之不得連婚 17)爲恨矣

금민가소년래의　모씨가종창극규견　필하량소자
今閔家少年來矣　母氏可從窓隙窺見　必下諒小子

언지불무야　부인종이규견　우책삼연왈：여안과
言之不誣也　夫人從而窺見　又責三淵曰：汝眼果

무주의　차소년구시귀인　명수후세지대기야　석호
無珠矣　此少年俱是貴人　名垂後世之大器也　惜乎

불득련혼의　기후과부기언　민공구대달　이리씨년
不得連婚矣　其後果符其言　閔公俱大達　而李氏年

재과삼십이참봉　요　이부인지녀　선일년이몰
纔過三十以參奉 18)夭 19)　而夫人之女　先一年而歿

부인상직금　포삼단　이이일단조문곡지관복
夫人嘗織錦 20)布三端　而以一端造文谷之官服

이단심장　而第二胤農巖 21) 登第　而不許造朝衣
二端深藏

後夢窩 22) 以蔭官 23) 登第　仍使造朝衣　一端又藏之

孫婿趙文命 24) 登第　又使造朝衣　三人俱位至三公 25)

夫人之意以爲未至三公之人不可許故也　農巖登

第而入謁　夫人顰眉曰：何爲而如山林處士樣也

其後夢窩登第而入謁　則笑曰：大臣出矣

1 金壽恒 [1629–89; styled Kuji 久之; sobriquet Mungok 文谷; ancestral seat
   Andong 安東; posthumous epithet Munch'ung 文忠]: scholar-official under
   King Sukchong 肅宗 [r. 1674–1720; 1661–1720]. His grandfather was Kim
   Sanghŏn 金尙憲 [1570–1652].
2 羅良佐 [1638–1710; styled Hyŏndo 顯道; sobriquet Myŏngch'on 明村;
   ancestral seat Anjŏng 安定]: scholar-official who served as assistant section chief of the Board of Works (Kongjo *chwarang* 工曹佐郎) under King
   Sukchong 肅宗 [r. 1674–1720; 1661–1720]. His father was Na Sŏngdu
   羅星斗 [1614–63].
3 識鑑: discerning judgment of human nature.
4 三胤: third son.
5 三淵: sobriquet of Kim Ch'anghŭp 金昌翕 [1653–1722; styled Chaik 子益;
   ancestral seat Andong 安東; posthumous epithet Mun'gang 文康]: son of
   Kim Suhang. See note 1 above.
6 氣短: have a weak disposition.
7 佳郎: handsome bridegroom.
8 風範 = *p'ungmo* 風貌: appearance.
9 風儀動蕩: have a dignified disposition and ample features.
10 才華發越: lit. "talent and efflorescence are transcendent" = be exceedingly
   talented.
11 迎婚合巹之日: lit. "day of greeting the in-laws and exchanging nuptial
   cups" = wedding day.

12 有目無珠: lit. "has eyes but no pupils" = lack a discerning eye.

13 壽限 = *sumyŏng* 壽命: life span.

14 三旬: thirty (years of age).

15 閔鎮厚 [1659–1720; styled Chŏngsun 靜純; sobriquet Chijae 趾齋; ancestral seat Yŏhŭng 驪興; posthumous epithet Ch'ungmun 忠文]: scholar-official under King Kyŏngjong 景宗 [r. 1720–4; 1688–1724]. His father was Min Yujung 閔維重 [1630–87].

16 閔鎮遠 [1664–1736; styled Sŏngyu 聖猷; sobriquet Tanam 丹岩; ancestral seat Yŏhŭng 驪興; posthumous epithet Ch'ungmun 忠文]: scholar-official under King Yŏngjo 英祖 [r. 1724–76; 1694–1776]. Leader of the Northerner Faction (*pugin* 北人). His father was Min Yujung 閔維重 [1630–87].

17 連婚: create a relationship through marriage.

18 參奉: caretaker of royal tombs and gardens (*nŭngwŏn* 陵園); junior ninth-grade post.

19 夭: die before one's time.

20 織錦: weave silk.

21 農巖: sobriquet of Kim Ch'anghyŏp 金昌協 [1651–1708; styled Chunghwa 仲和; posthumous epithet Mun'gan 文簡]: second son of Kim Suhang. See note 1 above.

22 夢窩: sobriquet of Kim Ch'angjip 金昌集 [1648–1722; styled Yŏsŏng 汝成; posthumous epithet Ch'unghŏn 忠獻]. Kim Ch'angjip was one of the four leaders of the Northerner Faction (Pugin 北人) and first son of Kim Suhang.

23 蔭官: an official who has been conferred a position due to his ancestors' merit.

24 趙文命 [1680–1732; styled Sukchang 叔章; sobriquet Hagam 鶴巖; ancestral seat P'ungyang 豐壤: posthumous epithet Munch'ung 文忠]: scholar-official under King Yŏngjo 英祖 [r. 1724–76; 1694–1776]. His father was Cho Insu 趙仁壽 [dates unknown].

25 三公: three ministers = Prime Minister (*yŏngŭijŏng* 領議政), Minister of the Left (*chwaŭijŏng* 左議政), and Minister of the Right (*uŭijŏng* 右議政).

——— **46** ———

Deceit of the First Order

Vol. II: 19; translated 8 June 1921; Diary XVI, pp. 172–3; 208.

Cho T'aech'ae (Ch'ungik *kong*) Iudang lost his wife and never could overcome his grief. He was at this time Minister of War. On one occasion when a quick call came to the palace he arose early and went in and there waited for the War Secretary to come before going to audience, but no word came. It was long after daylight before he turned up. The minister was very angry and went into his office alone. He had the secretary arrested and had him beaten on the hips.

The secretary wept while he said, "I am a man in a very pitiful case; let me say a word before I die."

"What have you to say?" asked the minister.

The *ajŏn** replied, "I have lost my wife and I have three little children. The oldest being five, the second three, and the youngest, a girl, is only one. I have had to be mother as well as father to them. I desired to get out early this morning but my little girl cried so that I had to call a woman from another house to feed her. A little later the others complained that they were hungry. I sent out for gruel that I bought for them. It was thus that my morning passed before I knew it. I knew that there was work and I also knew that Your Excellency was to be feared. I would not dare do such a thing."

Hearing this, the minister was moved to tears and said, "Your circumstances are like mine."

So he let him go, and gave him rice and grass cloth to feed his children.

The secretary had no such home but knowing the minister could be moved, played this trick in order to get safely out of his fist.

* *ajŏn*: clerks and petty officials.

二憂堂 1) 趙忠翼公喪配後　悲不自勝 2)　時判騎省 3)

而適有公故 4)　曉起而俟曺吏之來請坐 5)　因無消息

幾至日出而不來矣　公大怒　趣駕 6) 而赴　公該吏使

之捉待　拿入而將棍　吏乃泣而對　小人有切

悲之情事 7)　願白 8) 一言而死　公問何事　吏曰:

소인상처　이가유삼유치　일자년재오세
小人喪妻　而家有三幼穉　一子年纔五歲

이자재삼세　일녀생재일기　소인신겸자모이양육지
二子纔三歲　一女生纔一朞　小人身兼慈母而養育之

금효욕기　즉치녀제호　고청린가녀유지소언
今曉欲起　則穉女啼呼　故請隣家女乳之少焉

량자우기호　소인이전매죽이궤지　여사지제
兩子又飢呼　小人以錢買粥而饋之　如斯之際

자이만시　소인기지유공고　차지대감위령언
自爾晚時 9)　小人旣知有公故　且知大監威令焉

감고위범과　호　공문이비지　휘루왈　여지사정
敢故為犯科 10) 乎　公聞而悲之　揮淚曰：汝之事情

흡사여의　잉방석우급미포　이위양아지자
恰似余矣　仍放釋優給米布　以為養兒之資

개리무차등사　이지공지정사　고이차식사
蓋吏無此等事　而知公之情事　故以此飾詐 11)

이도면　야
而圖免 12) 也

1 二憂堂: sobriquet of Cho T'aech'ae 趙泰采 [1660–1722; styled Yuryang 幼亮; ancestral seat Yangju 楊州; posthumous epithet Ch'ungik 忠翼]: scholar-official under King Sukchong 肅宗 [r. 1674–1720; 1661–1720]. His father was Cho Hŭisŏk 趙禧錫 (1622–?). He was one of the leaders of the Northerner Faction (Pugin 北人).

2 悲不自勝: unable to overcome one's sorrow.

3 騎省: another name for the Ministry of War (Pyŏngjo 兵曹).

4 公故: participate in palace affairs.

5 請坐: dispatch a clerk (*ajŏn* 衙前) to request a high-ranking official to report to his post.

6 趣駕: hastily prepare a means of transportation.

7 切悲之情事: extremely pitiable circumstances.

8 白: report to someone socially superior.

9 自爾晚時: be inadvertently delayed.

10 故爲犯科: make a deliberate mistake.
11 飾詐: concoct fabrications = lie.
12 圖免 = *momyŏn* 謀免: escape, evade.

——— **47** ———

Yu Ch'ŏkki

Vol. II: 20; n.d.; Diary XIV, p. 38; 209.

When Yu Ch'ŏkki went as governor of Kyŏngsang he made a tour of the state and on his way reached Kyŏngju, at which time the magistrate was Cho Munmyŏng, whom the governor knew to be a man of great parts.

He was anxious to try him and find just what quality of man he really was. He took occasion of an offence committed by official servants to have them arrested and beaten. Not one did he let off. After this he said to the magistrate, "I came to your county and have beaten many of your servants; are you not disappointed at my behaviour?"

Cho smiled and said in reply, "Your Excellency is governor of the whole province and so they are all your servants; they too have their own sins to answer for – what concern is it of the official in charge?"

He did not change colour but held his temper perfectly even.

Yu laughed, saying, "I have on this tour of mine seen really a great man."

Later Yu, from being a chief minister, fell to the humble office of magistrate of Yangju, while Cho was a general who had jurisdiction over Yangju.

On a certain day Yu sent his card in to Cho and when he had entered they passed their greeting. As he was coming out Cho laughed and said, "The time was when I did obeisance to Your Excellency and now Your Excellency does obeisance to me. The world operates in strange ways!"

Yu thought for a moment and said, "Alas! He will never be Prime Minister."

Cho became Minister of the Left but never Prime Minister. And so the ancients foretold a man's future by a single word from his lips.

兪文翼公拓基 1) 按嶺南時　巡到慶州　尹 2) 卽趙相

文命 3) 也　知其爲人之大可用　故欲試其量

因一微事　推治 4) 邑隷　無人免者　旣罷　顧謂府尹曰：

吾到令監邑　推治下隷若是之多　於令監之心得

無如何底意 5) 乎　趙相笑而對曰：使道旣按一道

則此是使道下隷也　且下隷輩渠自得罪

而被刑杖於下官 6) 何關焉　氣色自如 7) 公笑曰：

吾今行得一大臣矣　其後　公以正卿 8) 出補楊牧 9) 而

趙相時帶摠戎使 10)　楊是摠廳之管下　兪公以牧使

一日　投刺 11) 於摠使 12)　禮畢而將出門　趙相笑曰：

年前吾於大監之前　作此禮矣　今大監又作此禮

於吾之前　世事未可知矣　公熟視而笑曰：惜乎

未得爲首相 13) 矣　趙相果位至左相 14)　未躋領相 15)

古人之以一言定其位限者　定如此也

1 俞拓基 [1691–1767; styled Chŏnbo 展甫; sobriquet Chisujae 知守齋; ancestral
   seat Kigye 杞溪; posthumous epithet Munik 文翼]: scholar-official under
   King Yŏngjo 英祖 [r. 1724–76; 1694–1776]. His father was Yu Myŏngak
   俞命岳 [dates unknown].
2 尹 = Kyŏngju *puyun* 慶州府尹: magistrate of Kyŏngju.
3 趙文命 [1680–1732; styled Sukchang 叔章; sobriquet Hagam 鶴巖; ancestral
   seat P'ungyang 豐壤; posthumous epithet Munch'ung 文忠]: scholar-official
   under King Yŏngjo 英祖 [r. 1724–76; 1694–1776]. His father was Cho Insu
   趙仁壽 [dates unknown].
4 推治: interrogate and punish a criminal.
5 底意 = *ponŭi* 本意: one's innermost feelings/thoughts.
6 下官: your humble servant (used by an official to refer to himself humbly).
7 氣色自如: lit. "facial expression same as before" = with no change in facial
   expression.
8 正卿: an umbrella term for chief ministers ranking senior second and above
   vis-à-vis vice-ministerial positions (*agyŏng* 亞卿); includes second minister
   (*ch'amch'an* 參贊) of the State Tribunal (Ŭijŏngbu 議政府), minister (*p'ansŏ*
   判書) of the Six Boards (Yukcho 六曹), mayor (*p'anyun* 判尹) of the Bureau
   of the Capital (Hansŏngbu 漢城府), and director (*taejehak* 大提學) of the
   Office of the Special Counselors (Hongmungwan 弘文館).
9 楊牧 = 楊州牧使: magistrate of Yangju.
10 摠戎使: military official (senior second-rank) belonging to the Command
   of the Northern Approaches (Ch'ongyungch'ŏng 摠戎廳).
11 投刺: lit. "throw in a name card" = send in one's credentials to request
   a first audience.
12 摠使 = *ch'ongyungsa* 摠戎使: see note 10 above.
13 首相 = *yŏngsang* 領相 ~ *yŏngŭijŏng* 領議政: Prime Minister.
14 左相 = *chwaŭijŏng* 左議政: Minister of the Left.
15 未躋領相: unable to attain the position of Prime Minister.

—— **48** ——

The Skilful Swordsman

Vol. II: 20; n.d.; Diary XIV, pp. 38–9; 210.

Kim Ch'anghŭp (1653–1689; died with his father and Song
Siyŏl),* when he was up in years went to live in Sŏrak Temple in
Kangwŏn Province. He took a priest's name to indicate that he had left

172   The Skilful Swordsman

the world and lived with the priests. One night a priest who occupied the same room was caught and devoured by a tiger and Kim wrote a poem in his memory; a most sad and pitiful case it was.

A few days later his son-in-law Yi Tŏkchae came to visit him, a lad of some seventeen years of age. Kim told him of the dangers in the hills and warned him not to go outside the enclosure, but after the evening meal Yi disappeared somewhere and was not to be found. Kim called him again and again but there was no reply. Great alarm overtook him and he gathered the priests together and had them go out with torches everywhere to search under the moonlight which was as bright as day. They found him at last sitting alone on the topmost peak of a great mountain to the rear.

Finding him, Kim gave him a sound rating: "Didn't I tell you?" said he, "that a priest of the same room as myself was devoured by this beast. How could a mere child like you venture off here alone among the hills? If you had come on a tiger, what chance would you have had? Is this the way you pay heed to what your seniors say to you?"

Yi merely laughed but made no reply.

When they had come to the temple and were seated Kim gave him another dressing down.

Yi smiled and replied, "My good father-in-law, because of the priest from his room who was killed by the tiger and the tragedy that went with it, has tiger on his brain. I did meet a tiger on the hill but I did him in and so have paid the debt owed to the dead priest."

Kim did not understand what he was driving at and replied, "What □-ings are these you are now talking?"

But the next day he went with the priests and there beneath the hill where he sat was a great tiger prodded full of sword thrusts. Everyone was astonished above measure.

Yi was a wonderful athlete and a practised hand at the sword.*

* Gale's note is confused. Kim Ch'anghŭp died in 1722, as did his brother Kim Ch'angjip; his *father*, Kim Suhang, was put to death in 1689 along with Song Siyŏl.

삼 연 김 선 생 창 흡   만 거 우 설 악 암 이 영 시 위 명
三淵金先生昌翕 1)   晚居于雪嶽庵以永矢爲名

여 승 동 처   일 일 야   동 방 승   위 호 람 사   연 옹 위 문 조
與僧同處 一日夜 同房僧 2) 爲虎噬死 3) 淵翁爲文弔

之不勝慘惻　數日後　女壻李公德 4) 載來拜

時年不過十六七矣　淵翁言前狀　戒勿出外　夕飯後

李公不知去處　淵翁連呼而無應聲　始大驚

聚會僧徒　火炬而推尋 5) 　而月色如晝 6)

李公獨坐後山絶頂之上　明月之下　淵翁見而

大責曰：吾不云乎　日前同房僧爲虎所噉汝以幼穉

之兒　獨自登陟於昏夜無人之中　倘 7) 有虎豹之患

其將奈何　汝之不聽長者之訓有如是矣　李公含笑

隨後而下來　到庵坐定　淵翁又責之戒之　李公笑而

對曰：岳翁 8) 以同房僧之爲虎所噉　久愈 9) 疚懷 10)

故小子俄於山上刺殺 11) 大虎　爲僧報仇 12) 耳

淵翁不信曰：寧有是理云矣　翌朝　與諸僧往見

則山下之壑　有一大虎亂刺而倒　人皆大駭異

蓋李公有絶人之力 13) 又善劍術故也

1 金昌翕 [1653–1722; styled Chaik 子益; sobriquet Samyŏn 三淵; ancestral
   seat Andong 安東; posthumous epithet Mun'gang 文康]: son of Kim Suhang
   金壽恒 [1629–89].
2 同房僧: a monk with whom one shares the same room.
3 囓死: be mauled to death.
4 李德載 [1683–1739; styled Hugyŏng 厚卿; ancestral seat Chŏnŭi 全義]:
   scholar-official under King Yŏngjo 英祖 [r. 1724–76; 1694–1776]; son of
   Yi Chingha 李徵夏 [1655–1727] and son-in-law of Kim Ch'anghŭp 金昌翕
   [1653–1722].
5 火炬而推尋: lit. "light a torch and look for a person."
6 月色如畫: lit. "moonlight as bright as daylight."
7 倘: perhaps; maybe; suddenly.
8 岳翁 = *akchang* 岳丈 = *changin* 丈人: father-in-law.
9 久愈: more and more as time goes by; increasingly.
10 疚懷: mourn the death of a relative or a close friend.
11 刺殺: stab and kill.
12 報仇: take revenge.
13 絶人之力: extraordinary strength.

—— 49 ——

Overdrunk

Vol. II: 20; translated 8 June 1921; Diary XVI, p. 173; 211.

Min Chŏngjung (Nobong) had a brother who was Prince Yŏyang, Min
Yujung. They loved each other very dearly and were very fond of drink.
Their father was Governor of Kangwŏn and he was very much opposed
to drink and tried to keep his sons from it.

When their father was in Kangwŏn, the two brothers went to visit him
and inquired for his health. While on their way there, Min Chŏngjung
was appointed Vice-Minister of Home Affairs and was summoned by
the king, while Prince Yujung was made Vice-President of the College
of Literature.

Greatly delighted at this, the governor gave permission for wine to
be drunk. The two drank to repletion and were very drunk. They returned to the Governor's house and there sat down and more wine
was brought. The servants said, however, that the governor had given
orders that no more wine should be brought.

Very drunk, the two said, "You, Governor, don't you know how to treat distinguished guests?"

They then fell asleep and after waking they learned what fools they had made of themselves and were frightened. They put a mat on the ground and begged pardon.

The old Governor, however, only laughed and did nothing.

로 봉 민 공 정 중　　여 제 려 양 민 공 유 중　　우 우　　애
老峰閔公鼎重 1) 與弟驪陽閔公維重 2)　友于 [愛]

독 지　　상 기 주　　이 감 사 공　　금 지 사 불 득 방 음 의
篤至 3)　常嗜酒 4) 而監司公 5) 禁之使不得放飲矣

감 사 공 안 절 원 영　　형 제 구 작 근 행　　백　　즉 이 아 전
監司公按節原營 6)　兄弟俱作覲行 7)　伯 8) 則以亞銓 9)

승 소　　계　　즉 이 부 학　　승 소　　일 시 병 도　　민 공 어 차
承召 10)　季 11)　則以副學 12)　承召　一時並到　閔公於此

일 사 지 허 음　　형 제 대 작 황　　니　　취 후　　잉 출 왕 객
日使之許飲　兄弟對酌況 [泥] 13)　醉後　仍出往客

사 좌 청 상　　이 련 사 진 주　　하 예 이 순 사　　분 부
舍坐廳上　而連使進酒　下隷以巡使 14) 分付

불 감 계 진 위 언　　이 공 취 중 대 언 왈　　여 지 순 사
不敢繼進爲言　二公醉中大言曰：汝之巡使

접 대 별 성　　고 불 당 여 시 운 운 이 혼 수 의　　성 후
接待別星 15)　固不當如是云云而昏睡矣　醒後

문 기 주 중 실 언　　형 제 대 경　　석 고　　어 문 외
聞其酒中失言　兄弟大驚　席藁 16) 於門外

감 사 공 소 이 불 책
監司公笑而不責

<hr>

1 閔鼎重 [1628–92; styled Taesu 大受; sobriquet Nobong 老峰; ancestral seat Yŏhŭng 驪興; posthumous epithet Munch'ung 文忠]: scholar-official under King Hyojong 孝宗 [r. 1649–59; 1619–59]. His father was Min Kwanghun 閔光勳 [1595–1659].

2 閔維重 [1630–87; styled Chisuk 持叔; sobriquet Tunch'on 屯村; ancestral seat Yŏhŭng 驪興; posthumous epithet Munjŏng 文貞]: scholar-official under King Hyojong 孝宗 and the royal in-law of King Sukchong 肅宗 [r. 1674–1720; 1661–1720]. His brother was Min Chŏngjung 閔鼎重.

3 篤至: sincerity is extreme.

4 嗜酒: enjoy drinking.

5 監司公 = Min Kwanghun 閔光勳 [1595–1659; styled Chungjip 仲集; ancestral seat Yŏhŭng 驪興]: father of Min Chŏngjung and Min Yujung; son of Min Ki 閔機 [1568–1641].

6 按節原營: serve as governor of Kangwŏn Province. "Wŏnyŏng" refers to the headquarters of Kangwŏn Province in Wŏnju 原州.

7 覲行: pay a visit to one's parents.

8 伯: the eldest (= Min Chŏngjung). See note 1.

9 亞銓 = Ijo ch'amp'an 吏曹參判: junior second-rank civil official belonging to the Board of Personnel (Ijo 吏曹).

10 承召: receive a royal summons.

11 季: the youngest (= Min Yujung). See note 2.

12 副學 = pujehak 副提學: senior third-rank post belonging to the Office of the Special Counselors (Hongmungwan 弘文館).

13 泥醉: overdrunk, "smashed."

14 巡使 = kamsa 監司 ~ kwanch'alsa 觀察使: provincial governor.

15 別星 = pongmyŏng sasin 奉命使臣: subject who upholds a royal order.

16 席藁 = sŏkko taejoe 席藁待罪: spread out a straw mat, prostrate oneself on it, and await punishment.

—— **50** ——

History of Yu Ch'ŏkki

Vol. II: 21; translation 9 June 1921; Diary XVI, pp. 173–6; 212.

President Sin (Hanjuktang), who had a special knowledge of people, had but one son and that son died. However, after he died the son's wife gave birth to a daughter. When she had come to the time of doing up her hair, the mother asked the father-in-law to please select for her a husband, someone that he specially knew.

Sin replied, "What kind of son-in-law do you desire?"

She replied, "One who will live till eighty, with whom his wife can grow old, one who becomes a chief minister, someone rich, one destined to many sons."

Sin replied, "How could you ever expect to find any such man on earth? It would be very difficult all of a sudden to get any such person as you suggest."

Whenever Sin made a journey and returned, his daughter-in-law asked him if he had found a suitable person. Thus she continued to do.

One day Sin mounted his official chair and passed Ch'angdong, where he saw a lot of children playing together. Among them was one about thirteen years of age, who had a curly head and high cheek bones. He was riding a bamboo horse, jumping from side to side.

Sin stopped his chair and gazed at him for a long time. His clothes were ragged and did not cover his body. His almond eyes were pulled longwise upward. He had a "sea" mouth of great extent. His whole appearance marked him as one differing greatly from all others. He then ordered one of his servants to call the lad.

He, however, shook his head and refused. He then sent others and said to pick him up and bring him. The boy, however, cried out, "What official is this that seeks to arrest me without cause? What fault have I ever committed to be thus treated?"

The servants, however, finally brought him, whereupon Sin asked him, "What status are you of?"

He replied, "Status? What have I to do with status? I am a *yangban*."

Sin again asked, "How old are you and where is your house? Where are you going just now?"

His answer was, "Have you arrested me to make me a soldier? Why do you ask my name, my age, and my home? My name is Yu; my age is thirteen, my home is in the village just over the way. Why do you ask? Let me go at once – I want to get away."

Sin let the boy go and went to find his home. It was a little hut, with little or no protections against wind and rain. The widowed mother of the boy was there alone.

Sin called for a servant and gave an order, saying, "I am Sin So-and-so from such-and-such a place and have a grand-daughter who has come to the marriageable age. I am looking for a husband for her. I have come to ask if you will consent to have your son become my grand-daughter's husband."

He ordered his servants to say nothing whatever about the matter. He then took his departure for another place and when evening had fallen returned home.

His daughter-in-law again met him and asked, "Have you found me a son-in-law?"

Sin laughed and asked, "What sort of son-in-law do you wish?"

She made the same reply as before.

Sin laughed and said, "I have found the one you desire."

She was delighted at this and asked, "Whose son is he? And where does he live?"

Sin said, "Never mind about his house. You'll know by and by."

He said no more about it.

When the day of the wedding came he told more particularly whom he had chosen. At once his daughter-in-law sent an experienced old woman servant with orders to see if his home was rich or poor, as to whether he was handsome or not.

The servant returned to say, "His house is a little hut not bigger than a rice measure, with little or no protection against wind or rain. I looked in the kitchen and moss has grown over it. There are cobwebs in the rice kettle. As for the lad, he has eyes big as baskets, and his hair is tousled like roots of the Artemisia. He is most undesirable and altogether unattractive. When our young bride goes there she will have to do the kitchen work with her own hands. Our little girl who has grown up like a flower or a precious piece of jade, and has grown up with silks covering her body. How can you ever send her to such a place as this?"

When the daughter-in-law heard these things her spirit failed her and seemed to die within her and yet this was the day to pass the presents. There was nothing for her to do, however, but to submit. She wept as she thought of it. All was made ready for receiving the bridegroom. The day following, the bridegroom came in and they passed through the ceremony. When the daughter-in-law looked carefully at him, he was indeed just what the servant had said. A hateful sight he was to see. Her inner soul failed her but there was no help for it and so the three days were passed and he was to return to his home.

That night, however, he returned, whereupon Sin asked, "Why have you returned?"

The boy said, "I went home but found nothing on hand for an evening meal and seeing the chair about to return empty I just stayed in and have come back."

Sin laughed and said, "Very good."

Thus he remained and made Sin's his home and every night he went into the inner room where his bride slept.

Little by little Sin saw how his delicate granddaughter was worn down by this rough and ready husband. He was anxious about it and said to his grandson-in-law, "Why do you sleep every night in the inner room? Tonight you must stay outside and sleep with me."

The bridegroom said, "I'll do as Your Excellency suggests."

When it was night and time to go to sleep, he had the bridegroom's bed arranged beside his own. Just as he was falling asleep, the bridegroom let go his arm and struck his grandfather in the chest.

Sin awoke with a start and said, "What do you mean by this?"

He replied, "I cannot sleep quietly as do others but beat about, for in my dreams I have this experience."

Sin said, "Don't do so again."

"I'll do so," he replied.

A little later, however, he kicked his grandfather with his foot. Sin again awoke and scolded him, but it was no use for arms and legs were flung about in hopeless disorder. Unable to endure this longer, Sin said, "Go inside and sleep there. I can't stand you here."

At once he gathered up his bed clothes and went inside to his wife's room. At that time a number of relative women of his had come and were now having a great time together in the bride's room. It was then about the third watch. In a state of consternation, they got up and made their escape to another room.

The husband called out, "All you ladies may go but see you leave Yu's wife behind you."

Because of this all the people in the place got to dislike him.

Sometime later, Sin went as governor of Hwanghae and his household made ready to go with him. Yu was ordered to bring the members of the family and the ladies and follow. The daughter-in-law said, however, "Do not take Yu but leave him here in Seoul and so give my daughter a rest from him."

Sin refused to listen to this.

The time came round for presenting the king with Haeju ink. The governor called Yu and said, "Have you any use for ink?"

He replied, "Thanks very much, I have."

"The ink is there. Take what you want," answered the governor, pointing to it.

Yu then went and selected what he wanted, one thousand pieces of the largest blocks. The guard in charge of the ink came to the governor and said, "If he takes as much as this, there will not be left the requisite amount for the king."

Sin said, "Never mind. If it is short, make some more."

Yu brought this back to his study rooms and there he divided it all among the servants. As to who this Yu was, he turned out to be Yu Ch'ŏkki. He lived to be eighty, he and his wife together. He became Prime Minister. He had four sons. Rich he was and prosperous. All came to pass as Sin had foreseen.

Later Yu Ch'ŏkki became governor of Hwanghae. He took with him his son-in-law, Hong Ik, and at that time the gift of ink was almost to be given. He called Hong and told him to take what he desired. Hong took two wraps of the large kind (twenty), three of the smaller (thirty), and five of the smallest (fifty). These he set aside.

Yu asked, "Why have you not taken more?"

Hong said, "The things of earth have their definite limit and we should not take more than we can use. If I take all, how about the presents to the king? What will Your Excellency do in the way of gifts to your friends? If I have ten wraps, I'll have enough."

Yu looked at him for a time and said, "Very good. He'll make a petty magistrate but not more."

申判書鉦 1) 號寒竹堂　有知人之鑑 2)　喪獨子而

有遺腹女　年及笄矣　其孀婦 3) 每請于其舅曰：

此女之郞材 4)　尊舅必親自相之而擇之　申公曰：

汝求何許郞材　對曰：壽至八十而偕老　位至大官

家富而多男則幸矣　公笑曰：世豈有如許兼備之人乎

若副汝願　猝難得矣　伊後　出門而歸　則必問郞材

之可合者　每每如是矣　一日　申公乘軒 5) 而過壯洞 6)

群兒嬉戲 7) 叢中　有一兒年可十餘歲　而蓬頭突鬢 8)

騎竹 9) 而左右跳踉 10)　公停軺熟視　則衣不掩身

而河目海口 11)　骨格異凡 12)　仍命一隸使之招來

則掉頭不肯 13)　公使諸隸扶持而來　其兒號哭

曰：何許官員　空然捉我　我有何罪而如是也

諸隸擁至軺前　公曰：汝之門閥何如人也　對曰：

門閥知之何爲也　吾是兩班也　公又問　汝年幾何而

家何在　汝往 [姓] 云何　對曰：欲捧疤 14) 軍丁 15) 乎

何爲而問姓名年歲居住也　吾姓兪氏也　吾年十三也

吾家在於越洞 16) 矣　何爲問之　速放我去　公放送而

尋其家　則不蔽風雨之斗屋也　只有寡居之母夫人

公招出婢子傳喝 17) 曰：我是某洞居申某也　吾有

一箇孫女　方求婚矣　今日定婚於宅都令而去云云

而仍飭下隷歸家愼勿言　仍適他暮歸　則孀婦又問

郎材　公笑曰：汝求何許郎材　孀婦對如初　公笑曰：

今日得之矣　孀婦欣然而問　誰家之子家在何處

公曰：不必知其家矣　後當知之　仍不言矣　及到

迎綵 18) 之時　始乃言之　則自內急送解事一老婢

往見其家計 19) 之貧富　郎材之姸醜　婢子回告曰：

家是數間斗屋 20)　而不蔽風雨　廚下生苔 21)

鼎中有蛛絲 22)　而郎材則目大如筐 23)　髮亂如蓬

無一可取　無一可見　吾小姐 24) 入門之後 25)　則杵

臼 26) 必當親執 27) 矣　以吾小姐如花如玉　生長綺

紈 28) 之弱質　何可送于如此之家乎　孀婦聞此言

膽落魂飛 29)　而受 30) 綵之日也　事到無奈何之境

仍飮泣而治迎郎之具矣　翌日　新郎入來行禮　孀婦

審視　則果如婢言而卽一可憎之郎也　心焉如碎 31)

而無奈何矣　過三日後　送郎而夕時新郎又來矣

申公問　汝何爲更來　新郎曰：歸家則夕飯無期 32)

且有順歸 33) 人馬　故還來矣　公笑而留之　自

此每每留在　而連日內寢 34)　新婦以質弱之女子

見惱 35) 於丈夫　幾至生病之境矣　公憂之諭之曰：

汝何爲連日內寢也　今日可出外與吾同寢可也

新郎曰：敬受敎矣　及夜　公就寢　而新郎寢具

鋪之於前矣　公闔眼 36) 則新郎以手槌 37) 公之胸

公驚曰：此何爲也　新郎對曰：小壻果不安寢

昏夢 38) 之中每有此等事　公曰：後勿如是　對曰：

諾　未幾又以足　擲 [躑] 之公　公又驚覺而責之

已而又以手足或打或擲 [躑] 39)　公不堪其苦　乃曰：

汝可入內而宿　吾則不可與同寢矣　新郎仍捲其寢具

荷而入內　則時其家族黨婦女來者　適留於新房中

夜三更驚起而避　新郎高聲而言曰：諸家婦女

皆急避　而獨留兪書房宅可也云云　如是之故

妻家上下皆厭苦 40) 之　申公按海藩 41) 也　內行將率去

而使兪郎陪來　孀婦曰：兪郎不可率去　姑留之

使吾女暫時休息可也　公不許而率去矣　及墨進

上 42) 時　公呼兪郎而問曰：汝欲墨乎　對曰：好矣

公指示而言曰：任自擇去　兪郎躬自擇之　大折 43)

墨百同 44) 別置　該監裨將 45) 前奏曰：若如此則恐有

闕封 46) 之慮矣　公曰：使之急急更造　兪郎還至書室

幷給下隷無一餘者云　兪郎卽兪相國拓基 47) 也

享年八十而偕老　位至領相 48)　子有四人家又富

果符申公之言　其後兪公爲海伯 49)　率女婿洪南原益

50) 而去矣　又當墨進上之時　呼洪郎而使之任自擇去

則洪郎擇大折二同中折三同小折五同而別置　公曰：

하 불 가 택　홍 왈　범 물 개 유 한 용 처　소 서 약 진 수 택 지
何不加擇　洪曰：凡物皆有限用處　小壻若盡數擇之

즉 진 상 하 이 위 지　락 중 지 구　하 이 문 지　소 서 즉
則進上何以爲之　洛中知舊 51) 何以問之　小壻則

십 동 우 가 용 의　공 예 시　이 소 왈　긴 막 긴　의
十同優可用矣　公睨視 52) 而笑曰：繁莫繁 53) 矣

가 작 음 관　지 재 운 의　과 여 기 언
可作蔭官 54) 之材云矣　果如其言

1　申銋 [1642–1725; styled Hwajung 華仲; sobriquet Hanjuktang 寒竹堂; ancestral seat Pʼyŏngsan 平山; posthumous epithet Chʼunggyŏng 忠景]: scholar-official under King Sukchong 肅宗 [r. 1674–1720; 1661–1720]. His father was Sin Myŏnggyu 申命圭 [1618–88].

2　知人之鑑: ability to appreciate a person's character and capability.

3　孀婦: widowed daughter-in-law.

4　郎材: suitable bridegroom.

5　軒 = chʼohŏn 軺軒: carriage conveying a high official.

6　壯洞: old neighhourhood in Seoul that used to be located between Hyoja-dong 孝子洞 and Chʼangsŏng-dong 昌城洞 in Chongno-gu 鍾路區.

7　嬉戲: playing and horsing around.

8　蓬頭突鬂: unkempt hair and protruding sideburns.

9　騎竹: ride on a bamboo horse.

10　跳踉: leap; jump up and down.

11　河目海口: lit. "eyes as big as a river and mouth as big as the ocean" = handsome.

12　異凡 = pibŏm 非凡: extraordinary.

13　掉頭不肯: lit. "shake head and not comply" = shake one's head no.

14　捧疤: create a sketch of a person's facial features and clothing.

15　軍丁: able-bodied man eligible for corvée or military service.

16　越洞: neighhourhood over yonder.

17　傳喝: deliver a message.

18　迎綵: wedding gifts sent from the groom's family to welcome the bride.

19　家計: household management.

20　斗屋: tiny house.

21　廚下生苔: lit. "kitchen grows moss" = a kitchen that has not been used for a long time because of poverty.

22 蛛絲: cobweb.

23 筐: round wicker basket.

24 小姐: young lady; mademoiselle.

25 入門之後: lit. "after entering the gate" = after marriage.

26 杵臼: pounding a mortar.

27 親執: take personal command of.

28 綺紈: silk gauze.

29 膽落魂飛: lit. "gallbladder drops and spirit flies away" = be overwhelmed, devastated.

30 受綵 = *yŏngch'ae* 迎綵: ritually welcome the wedding gifts.

31 心焉如碎: lit. "heart feels like it is being ground up" = heart-rending.

32 無期: no promise.

33 順歸: return.

34 內寢: sleep in the inner quarters.

35 見惱: suffer from mental anguish.

36 闔眼: shut one's eyes.

37 槌: hit, beat. (This character can be read as either *ch'u* or *t'oe*.)

38 昏夢: feel dizzy or woozy.

39 或打或躑: beat and kick.

40 厭苦: loathe and feel vexed by.

41 海藩 = 黃海道: Hwanghae Province.

42 進上: present local products as tribute to the king or high-ranking officials.

43 大折: a large piece cut out of a whole.

44 同: a bundle; ten ink-sticks make one *tong*.

45 該監裨將: [unranked] official supervisor.

46 闕封: unable to procure tribute.

47 俞拓基 [1691–1767; styled Chŏnbo 展甫; sobriquet Chisujae 知守齋; ancestral seat Kigye 杞溪; posthumous epithet Munik 文翼]: scholar-official under King Yŏngjo 英祖 [r. 1724–76; 1694–1776]. His father was Yu Myŏngak 俞命岳 [dates unknown].

48 領相 = *yŏnŭijŏng* 領議政: senior first-grade official belonging to the State Tribunal (Ŭijŏngbu 議政府).

49 海伯: Hwanghae'do *kwanch'alsa* 黃海道觀察使: Governor of Hwanghae Province.

50 洪益: unidentified. In the Tenri University edition of *Ch'ŏnggu ch'onghwa* 靑邱叢話 [Compendium of Tales of the Green Hills], the same character is referred to as Hong Iksu 洪益壽 (unidentified) while the Tenri University edition of *Tongp'ae naksong* 東稗洛誦 [Repeatedly Recited Tales of the East] reads as Hong Iksam 洪益三 [?–1756].

51 洛中知舊: old friend in Seoul.

52 睨視: look askance; give a fierce sidelong scowl.

53 繁莫繁: lit. "as far as tightness is concerned, there is nothing tighter" =
incredibly tight.

54 蔭官: an official who has been conferred a position due to his ancestors'
merit.

———— **51** ————

The Obstreperous Boy

Vol. II: 22; n.d.; Diary XII, p. 193–7 (crossed out); Box 9:12, two typed pages;
typed version in *Miscellaneous Writings* No. 30, pp. 29–30;
published as "The Obstreperous Boy" in *Korea Magazine* (June 1918),
pp. 255–67; included as "The Spoiled Boy" in the unpublished typescript
book *Old Corea* pp. 89–91; 213.

From *Korea Magazine*

This is an interesting story that shows the workings
of an unruly boy's mind and also how to handle
him. It shows also how a kindly bearing can sweep away
the long enmity of years. It is taken from the Kimun
ch'onghwa Vol. II: 22.

The magistrate of Hapch'ŏn had a son born to him when he was about
sixty years of age. In his foolish love for the child, he spoiled him completely, and failed altogether in his teaching so that at thirteen years of
age the lad knew nothing and was quite unable to read.

There was a famous priest living then in Haein Monastery with
whom the magistrate had been on friendly terms for a long time. This
priest came one day and seeing the boy, said, "Your son is growing up,
and you have never sent him to school. What do you mean by it?"

The magistrate replied, "I have tried to teach him myself but he is
obstinate and will listen to nothing that I say. I cannot bear to beat him,
so there you have it – a very distressful case."

The priest replied, "If a gentleman's son is not educated, he is of all
men the most useless. To merely lavish love on him and plan nothing
for his improvement will surely never do. He is handsome and bright,
and it seems a pity that he should be so neglected. Will you give me
permission to take him in hand and teach him?"

"I would be delighted," said the magistrate, "but it seems over much to ask of anyone. To educate him, and bring him to a place where he would do honour to his forefathers and be a master of the character would of all things be most gratifying."

The priest then said, "If this is to be decided upon, there is one matter that must be settled. Live or die, I must have the power to command him rigorously and for this I would ask a written contract, properly signed and sealed. Also, after sending him to the monastery, there must be no coming or going of servants, and you must give up your love here and now if I am to undertake the task. I shall see to his food and clothing myself, and if you have any occasion to send messages, let them be sent by priests who come and go, and addressed to me personally. Will Your Excellency consent to this?"

The magistrate replied, "I shall consent to anything you suggest."

Thus an agreement was made out, signed and sealed, and that day the boy was sent to the hills and all communication with him cut off.

He began by doing just what he liked, all license dispensed with. He answered his preceptor back, called him names, struck him in the face; in fact, there was nothing he did not venture to do.

The priest pretended not to see, paid no attention, said nothing, and left him to do just as he pleased.

After four or five days of this, the master arose early one morning, put on his official hat and robes, took his seat in the place of command, and had thirty or forty of his priests gather before him with their books. The strictest order was maintained with the most exacting ceremonial form. He then sent a young priest with orders to bring the magistrate's son before him.

On being arrested, the boy screamed and cried and took on in the most defiant way, saying, "You dogs of priests, how dare you put your dirty hands on a gentleman? I'll go back and tell my father, and he will assuredly have you slaughtered, everyone of you."

Again he shouted, "Thieves and robbers, a thousand deaths to you! Though I die I'll not do your bidding."

The master then shouted out to have him pinioned and brought in by force.

A crowd was on to him at once, and, fastened like a criminal, he was brought to the master's presence.

The priest then unfolded the contract that had been written, spread it out and said, "Your father wrote this, signed it, and gave it to me, and from now on your fate is in my hands – life or death. Here you are, the son of a gentleman, and yet you do not know a single letter. Evil deeds only and ungoverned ways are your accomplishments. What use for the like of you to live? Without a definite reform, you will be the ruin of your family and a disgrace forever. I shall have to punish you, and severely at that."

He then heated an iron barb red-hot, had it turned against the boy and speared his leg with it. The lad had a fit, and for a time lay unconscious. A little later he revived and the priest again ordered him to be speared, when all of a sudden the boy dropped on his knees, prayed for his life, and confessed that he had done very badly:

"I shall hereafter do whatever Your Excellency commands. Please do not spear me."

While the master had him view in terror the threatened iron, he gave him a short but very impressive lecture. He then had him unbound, and told him to sit down beside him and begin his work on the *Thousand Character Classic*. He gave him his appointed task each day so that he had no time to idle, and from this start, little by little, his knowledge grew and his general character developed. On hearing one thing he learned ten, and through ten he learned a hundred.

In four or five months he had mastered The *Thousand Character Classic*. Day and night he was constantly at it. So diligent and faithful a boy did he become, that in less than a year he had made marked progress. In three years of this training at the temple he became a young man of liberal culture.

However, as he studied he had but one thought in mind: "I was insulted by these priests because I was ignorant. I shall study now with all my might, and when I pass my examination, I'll kill this master tyrant, and wipe out the disgrace that I have suffered at his hands."

With this purpose in mind he worked harder than ever.

The priest had him taught how to write Chinese compositions, so that he soon acquired a practised hand. One day he called him and said, "Your attainments now are sufficient for you to enter the examination lists as a candidate. Come with me tomorrow and see."

The next day he took him to his father and said, "The young man's progress is such that if he keeps on he will be able to pass the examination and hold office without shame. I herewith resign my responsibility and give him back to you."

The father then planned for his wedding, and they as a family returned to the capital.

For several years he was a candidate at examination contests, till finally he graduated with honours and some years later became Governor of Kyŏngsang Province. He thought with keen zest, "I shall now square up my account with that priest of Haein-sa and wipe out the disgrace he did me."

He reached his official place, and from there prepared to make a tour of the province, but before starting out he gave orders to his Officer of Justice: "Get ready special paddles and find me three or four skilled beaters. There is a priest in these hills," said he, "whom I intend to have arrested and beaten to death."

He started then on his tour and finally reached Hongyu-dong, where the old priest of Haein-sa came out with his disciples and stood by the side of the way to meet him.

On seeing him, the Governor alighted from his chair, took him by the hand and spoke kindly.

The priest, now an old man, smiled and said, "I still live to see Your Excellency seated in the place of honour, and surrounded by all the dignity and power of office. How glad my heart is."

He then led him to the temple and said, "The room I use now is where Your Excellency used to live and study, and tonight you shall sleep there. I wonder if you would mind my occupying the same room with you?"

The Governor said, "No, not in the least, I should be very glad."

When the night had grown late and all was quiet, the priest said, "When you were here and studied, you would like to have killed me, wouldn't you?"

The governor said, "Yes, I would."

The priest continued, "Till after you passed your examination you had the same mind still, did you not?"

"Quite right," said the Governor.

"Also the other day just before you started on your tour, you gave orders to prepare paddles and find skilful hands to beat me?"

"Yes I did," said the Governor.

"Then why did Your Excellency not have me killed at once, instead of dismounting from your chair and meeting me so kindly?"

The governor replied, "I did have that thought in mind all along till I met you. Seeing your kindly face, however, all my resentment melted away like snow and only delight and gladness remained."

The priest replied, "I followed you all along your course and noted your progress and attainment every foot of the way."*

---

* Gale ends his translation here but the original story goes on to relate one more episode regarding the old monk's good deed for the erstwhile obstreperous boy. By finishing

here abruptly, Gale turns the story into a tale about a prodigal boy turning over a new leaf and coming to appreciate his educator. This theme contrasts with that of the original, which concerns the old monk's uncannily accurate prognostications. In the original, the old monk's final remark of "follow[ing] you all along your course" is revealed as his prognostication as to what will befall the Governor of Kyŏngsang in the near future – that he will become Governor of P'yŏngyang, whereupon the old monk will dispatch a monk from Haein Temple to pay him a visit, and that on the night of the monk's arrival, he and the governor must sleep in the same room. Several years later, the Governor of Kyŏngsang does indeed become Governor of P'yŏngyang and one day his gatekeeper informs him of a visit by a monk from Haein Temple. After the two exchange pleasantries and enjoy a good meal, they sleep in the same room. Late at night the governor and the monk trade places because the governor finds his side of the heated floor unbearably hot. In the middle of the night, a foul odour awakens the governor, who discovers that his guest has been murdered and his blood and guts are scattered all over the room. The next morning, an investigation into the murder reveals that a jealous servant, in love with a *kisaeng* doted on by the governor, mistook the monk for the governor and killed him instead. The old monk's prognostication about the obstreperous boy's life thus proves true once again.

합 천 수　모 년 륙 십 지 유 일 자　　이 닉 애　　이 교 훈 실
陝川守 1) 某年六十只有一子　而溺愛 2) 而敎訓失

방 년 지 십 삼 세　이 목 불 식 자　　해 인 사　유 일 대 사 승
方年至十三歲　而目不識字 3)　海印寺 4) 有一大師僧

자 전 친 숙 왕 래 아 중 의　일 일　래 견 이 언 왈
自前親熟往來衙中矣　一日　來見而言曰：

아 지　년 기 성 동　이 상 불 입 학　장 하 이 위 지　쉬 왈
阿只 5) 年旣成童　而尙不入學　將何以爲之　倅曰：

수 욕 교 문 자　이 만 불 종 명　불 인 초 달 이 지 어 차
雖欲敎文字　而慢不從命　不忍楚撻以至於此

심 이 위 민　대 사 왈　사 부 자 제 소 이 실 학
深以爲憫　大師曰：士夫子弟少而失學

즉 장 위 세 기 인　전 사 자 애 이 불 사 과 공 가 호
則將爲世棄人　全事慈愛而不事課工可乎

기 인 물 범 백 가 이 유 위　이 여 시 포 기 심 가 석 야
其人物凡百可以有爲　而如是抛棄甚可惜也

小僧將訓學矣 官家 6) 其可許之乎 倅曰:

誠好矣 固所願不敢請也 大師若敎訓而解蒙 7)

則豈非萬幸耶 大師曰：若然則有一事之可質者 8)

以生死惟意爲之只可嚴立課程之意

作文記踏印而給小僧 且一送山門之後

限等乃 9) 官隸之屬 一不相通 割斷恩愛 然後

可矣 至於衣食之供 小僧自可辦之 如有所送者

僧徒往來便 直送于小僧 許爲宜官家其將行之乎

倅曰：惟命是從矣 仍如其言 書文記給之 自伊日

送兒于山門而絶不相通 其兒上山之後 左右跳踉 10)

慢侮老僧 辱之頰之 無所不爲 大師視若不見

任其所爲 過四五日後平明 大師整其弁袍

對案跪坐 弟子三四十人橫經 11) 侍坐 禮儀整肅 12)

大師仍命一闍梨僧 13) 挐致厥童 厥童號哭詬辱 14)

曰：汝以僧徒　何敢侮兩班至此也　吾可歸告大人

將打殺汝矣　仍罵曰：千可殺萬可殺　賊禿云云

限死不來　大師大聲叱之責諸僧　使之縛來

諸僧齊來　縛致之前　大師出示手記曰：汝之大人

書此給我　從今以往　汝之生死在於吾手　汝以兩

班家子弟目不識字　全事悖惡之行 15)　生而何爲

此習不袪 [袪] 16) 將亡汝之門戶矣　第受吾罰

仍以錐末　灸火待赤 17)　而刺于股　厥童昏塞

半晌而甦　大師又欲刺之　乃哀乞曰：自此以後

惟大師之命是從更勿刺之　大師執錐而責之誘之

食頃後始放　使之近前　以千字文 18) 先授　而排 19)

日課程　不許少休　此童年旣長成　智慮 20) 亦長

聞一知十　聞十知百　四五朔之間　千字通史 [鑑]

21) 皆通曉 22)　而晝夜不輟 [撤] 23)　孜孜不懈 24)

一年之餘　文理 25) 大就　留山寺三年　工夫已成

每於讀書之詩　獨語于心曰：吾以工夫受辱於山僧者

皆不學之致也　吾將勤工得科後　必欲打殺此僧

以雪此今日之恨云　而一念不懈　尤用功力　大師

又使習科工　一日　大師使近前而言曰：汝之工夫

優可作科儒　明日可與我下山　翌日　乃率來衙中而

言曰：今則文辭將就 26) 登科後文任 27) 亦不讓於他

小僧從此辭歸　仍留置而去　其童子始議親成婚

上京後　出入科場　數年之後決 [登] 科　數十年

之間　得爲嶺伯 28) 始乃大喜心語曰：吾今而後

可殺海印寺僧　以雪向日之憤云矣　及按到而出巡也

申飭刑吏 29) 作別杖　而擇執杖之善者三四人以從

將到山門而欲撲殺此僧之計也　行到紅流洞 30)

此老僧率諸僧　祗迎 31) 于路左 32) 巡使見之　仍下

轎執手而致款 33)　老僧欣然而笑曰：老僧幸而不死

及見巡使威儀　幸莫大焉　仍與之入寺　老僧請曰：

小僧之居房　卽使道向年工夫之處也　今野移下處

與小僧聯枕無妨矣　巡使許之　與之同寢　更深後

僧曰：使道兒時受學時　有必殺小僧之心乎　曰：

然矣　僧曰：自登科至建節 34) 而皆有此心乎　曰：

然矣　僧曰：發巡時　矢于心而欲打殺小僧　至有別

刑杖擇執杖之擧乎　曰：然矣　僧曰：若然則使道何

不打殺而下轎致款乎　巡使曰：向來之恨心乎不忘

及對君顏　此心氷消雲散 35)　油然 36) 有欣悅之心故也

僧曰：小僧亦已揣 37) 知 [之] 矣　使道位可至大官

而某年月日按節箕城 38) 也　當是時　小僧當送上佐矣

使道必須加禮　而如見小僧樣　與之同寢可也　愼

勿忘置　必須如是　巡使許諾　老僧乃出示一紙曰：

此是小僧爲使道推數平生而編年者也　享年幾許

位至幾品昭然可知　而俄所言箕營 39) 事　愼勿

忘却　巡使唯唯　翌日　多給米布錢木之屬而去

其後過幾年　果爲箕伯 40)　一日闇者 41) 告曰：

慶尙道陜川郡海印寺僧欲入謁矣　巡使怳惚覺悟 42)

卽使入來　使之升堂　把袖促膝 [膝] 43)　問其師之

安否　夕餐與之聯床　至夜又與之同寢　至更深後

房堗 44) 過溫　巡使乃易寢席而臥矣　昏夢之中 45)

忽有腥穢之臭 46)　以手撫僧之背　則臥處有水漬手 47)

仍呼知印 48)　擧火而見之　則刃刺於僧腹　五臟突出

血流遍地　巡使大驚　急使運置於外　翌日朝窮查

則巡使所嬖之妓　卽官奴之所眄　而彼此大惑也

以是含憾爲刺巡使而入來　意謂下堗 49) 之臥者卽

巡使也　而刺之矣　仍拿致嚴覈 50)　則一一直招

遂置之法　治僧之喪　送于本寺　盖大師預知有

차 액　이 고 사 상 좌 대 수 고 야　기 후　공 명 수 한
此厄　而故使上佐代受故也　其後　功名壽限 51)

개 부 대 사 지 추 수 의
皆符大師之推數矣

1 陜川守: magistrate of what today is the Hapch'ŏn region in South Kyŏngsang Province.

2 溺愛: lit. "drown in love" = dote on, love excessively.

3 目不識字: lit. "eyes do not recognize characters" = completely illiterate (in sinographs).

4 海印寺: a temple in Hapch'ŏn County in South Kyŏngsang Province, famous for owning a complete set of the woodblocks for the Buddhist Tripitaka.

5 阿只: native Korean word *agi* (baby). In traditional Korean "borrowed graph orthography" *chi* 只 is typically read *"ki."*

6 官家: county magistrate (as referred to by local residents).

7 解蒙: make someone aware of; enlighten.

8 可質者: collateral; proviso.

9 等內: an *idu* expression meaning "within the period of"; while (an official is serving in his official capacity).

10 跳踉: leap; jump up and down.

11 橫經: lit. "lay out Buddhist sutras horizontally" = open up a sutra.

12 禮儀整肅: courteous, solemn, and decorous.

13 闍梨僧: a form of address used for a monk who is originally the son of a noble family.

14 詬辱: scold and heap abuse upon.

15 悖惡之行: depraved offence.

16 袪: abandon, shake off.

17 炙火待赤: heat something until it becomes red-hot.

18 千字文: The *Thousand Character Classic* by Zhou Xingsi 周興嗣 [? – 521] of the Liang dynasty 梁 [502–57], consisting of two hundred and fifty-four character phrases, comprising a total of one thousand unique characters.

19 排: sort; arrange in groups.

20 智慮: a wise and quick-witted thought.

21 通鑑 = *Zizhi tongjian gangmu* 資治通鑑綱目 (Outlines and Details of the Comprehensive Mirror): Zhu Xi's 朱熹 [1130–1200] historical critique based on his critical restructuring of the *Comprehensive Mirror to Aid in Government* (*Zizhi tongjian* 資治通鑑) by Sima Guang 司馬光 [1019–86] according to "outer guidelines" (*gang* 綱) and "details" (*mu* 目).

22 通曉: have penetrating knowledge of; be well-versed in.

23 晝夜不撤: lit. "day and night no stopping" = work around the clock.

24 孜孜不懈: work assiduously without a moment of indolence.

25 文理: logical sequence of a written composition.

26 將就 = *ilch'wi wŏlchang* 日就月將: lit. "with steady progress every day and every month" = make steady and continual progress.

27 文任: counsellor positions (*chehak* 提學) attached to the Office of the Special Counselors (Hongmungwan 弘文館) and the Office of Royal Decrees (Yemungwan 藝文館).

28 嶺伯 = Kyŏngsang-do *kwanch'alsa* 慶尙道 觀察使: governor of Kyŏngsang Province.

29 刑吏 = *ajŏn* 衙前: clerks and petty officials belonging to the Chamber of Punishment (*hyŏngbang* 刑房) in a local administration.

30 紅流洞: a ravine near Haein Temple 海印寺 in Hapch'ŏn County in South Kyŏngsang Province.

31 祗迎: greet the procession of someone socially superior.

32 路左: roadside.

33 致款: wait on someone with utmost devotion.

34 建節: be appointed governor of a province.

35 氷消雲散: lit. "ice melts and clouds scatter" = disappear without a trace.

36 油然: (clouds, etc., gather) thick and fast.

37 揣: comprehend, realize.

38 箕城: P'yŏngyang 平壤.

39 箕營: headquarters of the governor of P'yŏngan Province in P'yŏngyang.

40 箕伯 = P'yŏngan-do *kwanch'alsa* 觀察使 平安道: governor of P'yŏngan Province.

41 闍者: gatekeeper.

42 怳惚覺悟: lit. "be enraptured and then regain one's wits."

43 促膝: lit. "touch knees" = sit face-to-face (implying intimacy).

44 房堗: under-floor heating flues.

45 昏夢之中: "in darkness and dream" = dizzy; not fully conscious.

46 腥穢之臭: lit. "fishy/bloody and disgusting smell."

47 漬手: something gets smeared on one's hands.

48 知印 = *t'ongin* 通引: a factotum belonging to a local administration.

49 下堗: warmer part of a heated floor.

50 嚴覈: interrogate rigorously.

51 壽限 = *sumyŏng* 壽命: life span.

───── **52** ─────

Yu *Chinsa* and His Wives

Vol. II: 24; Diary XII, pp. 172–6 (crossed out, but listed as "No. 42 C. C. C.," referring to the Chosen Christian College collection of books); fragments of a typed version in Box 9:12 ("36"); published in *Korea Magazine*, October 1918, pp. 445–9, as "One View of the Korean Woman"; 214.

Note: This remarkable story taken from the Kimun Ch'onghwa (記聞叢話) is evidently true for the characters are historical and lived in the lime-light. Though the story might shock readers in the home land seeing it has to do with polygamy, it will be understood by those who live in the East.

The interesting fact of the story is the faithfulness of these women to one another and their spirit of self-abnegation.

Yu *chinsa** was a man of Kyŏnggi. As a lad he was especially clever at his studies and at twenty years of age passed his first examination; but he was poor in this world's goods and avoided the capital and lived quietly near Suwŏn.

His wife was a highly gifted woman – far above her peers. Among other things, by her skill at the needle she obtained their daily bread.

Now it happened on a certain day that a report came to them that there was a girl in the neighbourhood who was giving exhibitions as a sword-dancer. Hearing this, Yu *chinsa* asked that she be invited to their house so that they could all see.

She entered, but suddenly stopped short, startled apparently as she looked at Yu *chinsa*'s wife. Then she stepped hurriedly up onto the verandah, where the two clasped each other and began to cry.

Astonished at this behaviour, Yu *chinsa* asked what it meant.

His wife replied, "She is a friend whom I used to know very well, indeed; that's why." Though the stranger remained a day or two, no further word was said about the sword dance. Then she quietly took her departure.

Five or six days later as Yu was standing before his home, he saw three palanquins borne by horses making their way in his direction. A pair of mounted lackeys rode just in front of each, but there was no one following. They were evidently coming his way.

In doubt, Yu sent a messenger to inquire where they were from, and to suggest that they had evidently made a mistake in coming to his house.

The servants, however, came straight in without any reply and the chair went through the door into the inner quarters. The horses were then unhitched and taken away.

More perplexed than ever and not being able to enter the women's quarters, Yu *chinsa*, seeing as women guests were there, sent a note into his wife asking what it meant. Her reply was, "Never mind, you'll know later on."

Thus the mystery deepened. From that time on his meals were of the very best: fish and fowl with no end of other choice fare.

This, too, added to his uncertainty, so he again sent a note to inquire, whereupon the answer was, "Don't ask, please; only dine well and be happy. You will know by and by. I ask you as a favour not to come into the inner quarters for several days."

The day following it was again a mystery as to how his meals were so well ordered.

Some days later he received a note from his wife saying, "Let's go in to Seoul."

Yu *chinsa* had grown impatient over this procedure and had sent a servant to ask rather sharply that his wife come out to the middle door.

When she came, he asked, "Who are these people who are here; and how comes the change in our fare? What do you mean by asking that we go to Seoul? Some purpose must lie back of it. I have no means sufficient to pay for so extravagant a journey."

His wife merely laughed in reply and said, "Please don't ask any questions; you'll know the meaning by and by. Really you need have no anxiety about going to Seoul; all you have to do is simply go."

Although more mystified than ever, there seemed nothing for Yu but simply to yield.

So the next day the three palanquins were all put in order with horse and saddle for Yu to ride. Thus, in the wake of the chairs he finally reached the capital and passed through the South Gate. A little further on, in Hoedong, they came to a large house where the chairs entered the main gateway.

Yu was here shown into the main hall. It was a large and splendid mansion with everything in perfect order: mats, screens, tables, pens, pipe-pan, etc. A man dressed as a steward stood at the side, and several servants waiting at the head of the stairway bowed low to greet him.

Yu *chinsa* inquired, "Who are you?"

They replied, "We are Your Excellency's servants."

Again he asked, "Whose house is this, tell me, I pray?"

Their answer was, "This is Your Excellency's home."

Yu *chinsa* again asked, "To whom does all this furniture belong, and whose are these goods?"

"They are yours, sir," was the reply.

Bewildered beyond words to express, Yu thought he must have lost his wits or be in a dream. After his evening meal was over and he had sat some time with the lights trimmed, he received a letter from his wife, saying, "I am sending a very lovely person to be with you and to delight your heart."

He wrote back, "What do you mean by a lovely person; who is it and what's it all about?"

Her reply was, "By and by you will know."

As the night wore on and all the servants had gone, a maid-servant entered his room with a very beautiful woman who took her seat just below the light while the servant arranged his sleeping apartment and then withdrew.

Yu *chinsa* asked, "Who are you?" but she only smiled and answered not a word.

Thus the night passed.

The next morning a letter came from his wife, saying, "I hope you enjoyed the friend I sent you. I am sending you another this evening."

More than ever at a loss to know what it meant, Yu let matters take their course. On this next night another person accompanied by a servant came in; not the same person but quite another, as he readily saw by her face. Again this night passed.

The wife wrote once more asking, "Do you like her? I hope so."

About noon that day the sound of an approaching company was heard from beyond the gate, coming with calls and clamour. A servant rushed in to say that His Excellency Minister Kwŏn would call.

Yu *chinsa* went out to meet him, and a moment later a white-haired man riding on a wheeled palanquin came in at the gate. Yu took him by the hand and led him up into the main hall, where he bowed low and asked, "Who may Your Excellency be; and why have you come, I pray?"

When they were seated the old man laughed and said, "You have not yet realized the dream you are passing through, have you? Listen to what I have to say. You are a man born to most peculiar fortune; surely there was never such a case known as yours. Years ago your wife's home, my home, and Hyŏn *chisa*'s,[†] all stood side by side.

"In these three homes of ours on the same day of the same year a daughter was born to each. As this was a most extraordinary and unusual thing it brought our homes into close relationship, and these girls as they grew played together morning, noon and night. They made an oath, it seems, though we knew it not, that they would marry one and the same husband and so never be parted. We parents had no idea of this.

"When you were married your wife stepped out of our circle and was suddenly gone we knew not where. My daughter, as you know, is a child of my secondary wife. When it became time for her to marry I endeavoured to form plans thereto, but she refused absolutely and said that even though she died she would not consent: 'I have sworn an oath', said she, 'that I will marry the same man as so-and-so.'

"It transpired that Hyŏn's daughter had the same mind, so that though he rated, coaxed and tried to wheedle her into doing his way, not an atom would she bend to his will, and thus matters went on till they were twenty-five years of age.

"I then learned that Hyŏn's daughter had gone in search of your wife and that she had found her at Suwŏn. You will understand then that the stranger who came to your room the night before last was my daughter and the one last night was Hyŏn's. This house with the servants, the furniture, the books, the fields and rice-lands are set aside for you by Hyŏn and myself. Your fortune has won for you two very worthy women besides your first wife, a bountiful home and sufficient supply. Not less is your good luck than that of Yang Soyu. Such gifts as these come only from the gods."

"Call Hyŏn *chisa*," he shouted.

In a little, an old man with white hair came stepping in. He had gold buttons behind his ears and wore a red girdle.

He bowed to Kwŏn and then Kwŏn said to Yu, "This gentleman is Hyŏn *chisa*."

The three, having thus met, sat and passed the glass together and only when night came on did they separate. This Kwŏn was the famous Kwŏn Taeun 權大運 (1612–1699 AD).

Yu passed many happy years of life with his three wives.

Some years later his first wife said to him, "Just now the political situation in Seoul gives me cause for alarm. The Namin,[‡] it is true, have all power and Kwŏn Taeun is their chief, but danger lurks on every side and a little later he will assuredly be defeated and death will be the portion of them all. It may easily include us within its circles. Let us get away while there is yet time."

Yu took the advice, sold out, and moved to the country never to return.

In the year 1694 the Queen regained her place and power, and onslaught was made upon the Namin, who were beheaded and driven into exile, Kwŏn Taeun among them. But Yu *chinsa* was far away and safe. Assuredly, Yu *chinsa*'s wife was a wise and far-seeing woman.

* *chinsa*: literary licentiate.

† *chisa*: any of various civil posts ranging from junior third-grade to senior second-grade and belonging to various government organs.

‡ Namin = Southerner faction: one of the four political factions of the later Chosŏn. See note 42 below.

柳生 1) 某者　洛下 2) 人也　早有文名　年二十登司馬 3)

家甚貧窶　居於水原地　其妻某氏 4) 才質俱美

以針線 5) 資生 6) 矣　一日門外傳言　有一女子

善劍舞戲云　柳生招入內庭而使之試藝　其女子入來

熟視柳妻　直上廳而相抱放聲痛哭　莫知其故

問于其妻　則答以曾所面熟之人 7) 故也

仍不試劍技　而留數日而送之矣　越五六日後

望見前路　三箇新轎駕駿馬　而前有婢子數

雙亦騎馬　後無陪行而直向其家　柳生訝之

使人問何來內行誤入吾家　下隷不答而入門

下轎於內門之內　人馬皆息於店幕　柳生倍生疑訝

書問其內　則以爲從當 8) 知之　不必强問云云　　而

自伊日夕飯　饌品豊潔 9)　水陸備陳　柳生心尤疑惑

又書問則以爲只可飽喫 10)　不必問之　從當知之數日

則不必入內云矣　其明日朝夕飯又如是　過數日

其內書請以爲作京行云云　柳生怪之　請於中門內

暫面而問曰：內行從何而來也　朝夕之供　何爲而比

前豊厚也　洛行云云　何爲而言也　洛行有何委折 11)

而何以治行 12) 而發程耶　其妻笑曰：不必更問

從當知之　至如京行之人馬卽不必掛念　自當備待

只可治行而已　柳生怪訝　而任其所爲矣　翌日

三轎依前駕馬　而自家所騎之馬　亦已具鞍以待矣

第騎馬而隨後矣 到京城南門而入會洞 13) 一大第 14)

三轎入於門內 自家下馬於中大門之外而入 則卽一

空舍也 而鋪筵設席 書冊筆硯之屬 唾壺 15) 溺器 16)

之物 左右羅置 有冠者數人 如傔從樣者待令而使

喚 已而奴輩四五人入庭現謁 柳生問曰：汝輩誰也

對曰：皆是宅奴子也 柳生曰：此宅誰人之宅也

對曰：進士主 17) 宅也 又問曰：左右鋪設之物

何處得來者也 對曰：進士主需用什物也 柳生驚訝

如坐雲霧中 夕飯後 擧燭而坐 其妻作書曰：

今夜當出送一美人 庶慰苦[孤]寂之懷 18) 也云

柳生答以爲美人誰也 此何事也 妻曰：從當知之云

而至三更深後 傔從輩皆出外 自內門一雙丫鬟

19) 擁出一個絶代美人 凝粧盛飾 20) 而坐於燭下

侍婢又鋪寢具而入 生問以何許人 則笑而不答

仍與之就寢　明朝　其妻以書賀得新人而又曰：

今夜當換送他美人云云　柳生莫知其故　任之而已

其夜侍婢如前擁一美人而出來　察其形容　乃是

別人　柳生又與之同寢矣　明朝　其妻又以書賀

午時門外忽有喝㗧[導]聲　一隷入來而告曰：

權判書大監行次入來矣　生驚而下堂拱立 21)

俄而一白髮老宰相乘軒而來　見柳生欣然把手

上堂坐定　柳生拜而問　大監不知何許尊貴人

而小生一未承顏 22)　何爲降臨也　其宰相笑曰：

君未覺繁華夢 23)耶　吾第言之　如君之好八字

古今罕倫 24)者也　年前　君之聘家 25)與吾家譯官

26)玄知事者家俱隔墻　而同年同日　三家俱産女

事甚稀異　故三家常常互相送兒而見　及稍長之時

三女朝夕相送而遊嬉 27)　渠輩私自矢心 28)　同事

一人 29) 相約　而吾亦不知　彼家亦不知　其後君

之聘家移去　而不聞聲息 30)　矣　吾女卽側生 31) 也

年及笄 32) 欲議婚 33)　則抵死不願 34) 曰：旣有前約

當從君妻而事一人　其外雖老死父母家　決無入

他門之念云云　玄家女子又如是云　責之諭之

終不回心　至於過卄五歲 35)　而尙未適人 36) 矣　向聞

玄女學劍技　粧男服出遊八方　將尋君聘家去處云矣

日前逢着於水原地云矣　再昨之夜出來佳人卽吾

庶女也　昨夜之出來佳人卽玄家女也　家舍 37) 及

奴婢什物 38)　書冊田土等屬　吾與玄君排置 39) 者也

君一擧而得兩美人及家産　古之楊少遊 40)　無以加

此　君可謂好八字也　仍使人呼玄知事以來　須臾

一老者　金圈 41) 紅帶　來拜於前　權判書指而言曰：

此是玄知事也云　三人盛設酒肴　終日盡歡而罷

權卽權大運 42) 也　柳生與一妻二妾　同室和樂者數年

一日　柳妻謂其夫曰：見今朝廷　南人 43) 得時

權判書南魁 44) 而當局 45) 也　近日事　無非滅倫 46) 之

事　不久必敗　敗則恐有禍及之慮　不如早自下鄉

以爲免禍之計　柳生然其言　盡賣家産　携妻妾還鄉

更不入京矣　甲戌 47) 坤殿 48) 復位之後　南人皆誅竄 49)

權大運亦參其中　而柳生獨不被收坐之律 50)

柳妻可謂女中知識者也　豈凡人耶

1　柳生: identified in *Anthology of Yadam from the East* (*Tongya hwijip* 東野彙輯) as Yu Chagyŏn 柳綽然 [dates unknown]. *Saeng* 生 is a title for students who have yet to pass the civil service examination.
2　洛下: capital.
3　司馬 = *samasi* 司馬試 = *saengwŏn chinsasi* 生員進士試: civil service examination for both classics licentiates (*saengwŏn* 生員) and literary licentiates (*chinsa* 進士).
4　其妻某氏: identified as Madam Yi in the *Tongya hwijip*.
5　針線: needlework.
6　資生: manage a household.
7　面熟之人: familiar face.
8　從當: will eventually.
9　饌品豊潔: (of food) fresh and abundant.
10　飽喫: eat to one's heart's content.
11　委折 = *kokchŏl* 曲折: reason; whys and wherefores.
12　治行: prepare oneself for a journey.
13　會洞: a neighbourhood in the capital = present-day Hoehyŏn-dong 會賢洞.

14 大第: mansion, manor.

15 唾壺: spittoon.

16 溺器: chamber pot.

17 進士主: *chu* 主 here is meant to be read as *-nim*, the vernacular honorific suffix. Cf. Korean *nim* (= lord, master).

18 孤寂之懷: lonely and forlorn thoughts.

19 丫鬟: unmarried female slave.

20 凝粧盛飾: heavily made up and decked out.

21 拱立: put one's hands together in deference.

22 一未承顏: lit. "has yet to encounter your honourable face" = "pleased to make your acquaintance."

23 繁華夢: sweet and sumptuous dream.

24 罕倫: rare in this world.

25 聘家: (for a man) parents-in-law's household.

26 譯官: official translator-interpreters of the Bureau of Translators (Sayǒgwǒn 司譯院) who are the "middle people," or members of the hereditary class of technical specialists (*chungin* 中人).

27 遊嬉: playing and horsing around.

28 矢心: firm pledge.

29 同事一人: serve the same man together.

30 聲息 = *sosik* 消息: news, tidings.

31 側生: offspring of the union between a man and his secondary wife.

32 年及笄: lit. "age reaches the hairpin ceremony" = (for a girl) reach marriageable age.

33 議婚: discuss marriage.

34 抵死不願: decline obstinately, refuse upon pain of death.

35 廿五歲: twenty-five years old.

36 適人: (for a girl) marry.

37 家舍: home.

38 什物: household paraphernalia.

39 排置: arrange.

40 楊少遊: protagonist of the fictional narrative *Kuunmong* 九雲夢 (lit. "nine cloud dream") by Kim Manjung 金萬重 [1637–92].

41 金圈 = *kǔmgwanja* 金貫子: gold buttons for a headdress.

42 權大運 [1612–99; styled Sihoe 時會; sobriquet Sǒktam 石潭; ancestral seat Andong 安東]: scholar-official under King Sukchong 肅宗 [r. 1674–1720; 1661–1720] and a leader of the Southerner faction (Namin 南人). His father was Kwǒn Kǔnjung 權謹中 [1586–1650].

43 南人: the Southerner faction (Namin 南人) – one of the four factions, also known as the Four Colours (*sasaek* 四色), of the Chosǒn dynasty. The other

three were the Northerners (Pugin 北人), the Old Doctrine (Noron 老論), and the Young Doctrine (Soron 少論).

44 南魁: leader of the Southerner faction.

45 當局: be charged with important matters of state.

46 滅倫: contravene, go against human morals.

47 甲戌: the year 1694 (Sukchong 20). In 1694, Queen Min, who had been dethroned, was reinstated as Queen Inhyŏn 仁顯王后 (1667–1701), as a result of which the Southerners lost their political dominance at court.

48 坤殿 = *wangbi* 王妃: Queen Inhyŏn.

49 誅竄: be executed or exiled.

50 收坐之律: law of guilt-by-association.

——— **53** ———

The Act of Hong Tongsŏk

Vol. II: 26; n.d.; Diary XIV, p. 44; 215.

Hong Tongsŏk was a secretary of the Office of Alms, and steward of Cho T'aech'ae. In the troubles of the years 1721–2 when the officials of the Soron* party made request to the King, they pretended not to know that he was Cho's steward and asked that he outline the petition that would do Cho to death. Tongsŏk threw down his pen and said, "A son never writes out the sins of his father; neither should a steward turn traitor by his master. I shall not do it."

Angry at this, the officer arrested him and put him to torture a month of time, but he was firm to the end and refused.

When Cho was sent into exile to Quelpart,† Hong gave up his office as secretary to the Alms department and followed him.

When his hemlock came from the King for Cho to drink, his son Hoehŏn, learning of it, started at once on a swift horse but before he had gone thirty *ri* the messenger with the poison passed ahead of him. This he hurriedly carried and ordered Cho to drink.

Hong was at his side when this was given and said, "The offender's son is on the way here and will soon arrive. Can't you wait a few hours till he comes so that he may see his father?"

But the messenger said, "No, I cannot."

Hong then gave the glass a kick that sent its contents flying and all the spectators turned pale. But it was done and there was nothing to do for it.

The messenger returned home and said the glass had been lost in the sea.

In the meantime, Hoehŏn arrived and while the deadly dose was being sent for from the Prison Department, one month went by so that when it came a second time, Cho said to his son, "Reckon Hong to be your brother."

Hong followed the coffin back and again became secretary of the Office of Alms and had a long line of posterity that was reflected in the sons and daughters of Cho.

* Soron: the Young Doctrine faction, one of the four political factions of later Chosŏn.
† Quelpart: Cheju Island.

洪東錫 1) 者惠局 2) 吏而二憂堂 3) 僚人也　辛壬之間 4)

少論 5) 臺官發啓　而故使東錫寫之　東錫投筆曰：

子不可以手寫其父之罪名　僚從之於官員　有父子

之義　小人不可寫　諸臺怒使囚之　至於受刑數三次

而終不書之　及二憂堂之謫濟州也　東錫自退而隨往

至下後命之 6) 時　悔［晦］軒 7) 聞此報　走馬發行

未及三十里　而都事 8) 先入去矣　藥椀 9) 促使飲之

則東錫在傍請曰：罪人之子不久入來云　少延

晷刻 10)　以爲父子相面之地云云　則都事不許

東錫乃蹴其藥椀而覆之　諸人皆失色　而無奈何矣

都事不得已以藥椀爲海水漂沒 11) 修啓 12)　而悔 [晦

] 軒入來矣　自禁府更送藥水之際　拖至月餘 13) 矣

及受後命之時　二憂堂顧謂悔 [晦] 軒曰 : 東錫汝

可視以同氣　東錫隨喪上來　復爲惠吏　世世永襲 14)

而其子孫出入趙公門下而通內外 15)

1 洪東錫: unidentified.

2 惠局 = Hyeminguk 惠民局 = Hyeminsŏ 惠民署: Public Dispensary, a bureau supplying pharmaceuticals to improverished commoners.

3 二憂堂: sobriquet of Cho T'aech'ae 趙泰采 [1660–1722; styled Yuryang 幼亮; ancestral seat Yangju 楊州; posthumous epithet Ch'ungik 忠翼]: scholar-official under King Sukchong 肅宗 [r. 1674–1720; 1661–1720]. He was one of the four leaders of the Northerner faction. His father was Cho Hŭisŏk 趙禧錫 [1622–?].

4 辛壬之間: lit. "at the time of the *sinim* incident." The *sinim* incident refers to the literary purges (*sahwa* 士禍) of 1721 (*sinch'uk* 辛丑; Kyŏngjong 1) and 1722 (*imin* 壬寅; Kyŏngjong 2), which arose from attempts by the four leaders of the Old Doctrine faction (Noron 老論) to invest Prince Yŏning 延礽君 (later King Yŏngjo) as the heir apparent to the throne soon after the enthronement of King Kyŏngjong 景宗 [r. 1720–4; 1688–1724]. The four leaders were Kim Ch'angjip 金昌集 [1648–1722], Yi Imyŏng 李頤命 [1658–1722], Yi Kŏnmyŏng 李健命 [1663–1722], and Cho T'aech'ae 趙泰采 [1660–1722]. All were put to death on the same day.

5 少論: Young Doctrine faction, one of the factions during the Chosŏn dynasty.

6 後命 = *sayak* 賜藥: (the king) send an exiled criminal a bowl of arsenic as a form of capital punishment.

7 晦軒: sobriquet of Cho Kwanbin 趙觀彬 [1691–1757; styled Kukpo 國甫; ancestral seat Yangju 陽州; posthumous epithet Mun'gan 文簡]: scholar-official under King Yŏngjo 英祖 [r. 1724–76; 1694–1776]. His father was Cho T'aech'ae 趙泰采 [1660–1722].

8 都事: inspector belonging to the State Tribunal (Ŭigŭmbu 義禁府); ranks between junior sixth and junior eighth.

9 藥椀: a bowl of medicine.

10 少延晷刻: postpone; extend the limit.

11 漂沒: drown and sink to the bottom.

12 修啓: write a report to be offered up to the king.

13 拖至月餘: take a little more than one month.

14 世世永襲: inherit something from generation to generation.

15 通內外: (among distant relatives and friends) disregard the rule of keeping one's distance from the opposite sex (*naeoe* 內外).

——— 54 ———

Kim Su, the Face Reader

Vol. II: 26; translated 10 June 1921; Diary XVI, pp. 176–7; 216.

There was a man of Yŏnsan called Kim Su who could read people's faces. He used to visit in the homes of the Four Statesmen (Kim Ch'an gjip, Yi Imyŏng, Yi Kwanmyŏng, Cho T'aech'ae). Before the fateful years of 1721–2 (*sinim*), he once saw the king out on procession and all the ministers and others that surrounded him. He sighed to himself and said, "Alas, alas." Finally, after all had passed he saw one straggler bringing up the rear whose face was bright and who rode a poor, neglected horse.

Kim Su asked who he was and someone answered that he was Sim *ch'ŏmji.**

He again asked, "Where is his house?"

After knowing this, he went the next day to pay him a call. Sim was greatly surprised at this and rose to meet him, saying, "I have heard of you for long but have never had an opportunity to meet you before. What wind blows you here?"

Kim Su replied, "I am a reader of faces and I have come to ask permission to read your face. You are indeed a man of great destiny. In a few years you will be elevated to the rank of minister."

Sim replied, "How is that possible?"

Kim answered him, "If there be no law that reads faces, I cannot say. But if there is, then my words will come true."

Kim also said, "I have a wish to express. Please keep it specially in mind and make a note of it."

Sim replied, "Tell me what it is."

Kim asked for a pen and paper and wrote: "Today, on such a year, month and day a certain Kim of Ch'ungch'ŏng will return to his native place, close his door and never go out again."

He wrote this and posted it on the wall, saying, "Hereafter great things will happen. I will leave for home and shall not come again to Seoul. Keep these things in mind and save my life, I pray you."

Sim was greatly startled at this and said, "What wandering words are these?"

Kim said, "We had better not discuss as to whether these words of mine are foolish words or not. Keep this proof up, I pray you, as a witness." He bade farewell and was gone. Sim was in doubts as to what all this meant. Sim Tan was his name.

In the years 1721–2 (*sinim*) in the investigations, Sim became the master judge and in the investigation when servants were asked as to who frequented this place they said it was Kim and that he still was seen here and there.

Sim suddenly awakened to the sense of fraud. Kim Su was indeed a man of clairvoyant gifts, a very spirit. He said, "Kim is not in Seoul at all. I know definitely of this."

Thus he saved his life.

* *ch'ŏmji*: short for *Ch'ŏmji chungch'u pusa* 僉知中樞府事, a sinecure position of senior third grade.

련 산　　 김 수　　 자 선 상 인　　 출 입 사 대 신　　 문 하　　 신 임 전
連山 1) 金銖 2) 者善相人　出入四大臣 3) 門下　辛壬前 4)

견 교 외 동 가　　 편 관 반 행 제 인　　 이 독 자 돌 탄
見郊外動駕　遍觀班行諸人　而獨自咄歎 5)

지 최 후 산 반　　 유 일 조 사　　 모 형　　 이 기 기 마　　 참 반
至最後散班 6) 有一朝士 7) 貌瑩 8) 而騎駑馬 9) 參班 10)

이 과 자　문 기 수 즉 혹 왈　심 첨 지 운　우 문 기 가 재 하 동
而過者　問其誰則或曰：沈僉知云　又問其家在何洞

이 탐 지 지　익 일　왕 방　즉 심 첨 지 경 기 이 영 왈
而探知之　翌日　往訪　則沈僉知驚起而迎曰：

문 명 구 의　무 유 요 래　금 언 심 풍　취 도　김 모 왈
聞名久矣　無由邀來 11)　今焉甚風 12) 吹到　金某曰：

모 유 상 인 지 술　청 상 령 감 지 상 이 래 의　잉 언 왈
某有相人之術　請相令監之相而來矣　仍言曰：

령 감 대 귀 인 야　수 년 지 간　위 필 지 일 품 의　심 왈
令監大貴人也　數年之間　位必至一品矣　沈曰：

령 유 시 리　왈　무 상 법 즉 이 의　약 유 즉 언 불 무 의
寧有是理　曰：無相法則已矣　若有則言不誣矣

우 왈　생 유 소 탁 어 령 감 자　령 감 능 기 유 이 불 망 부
又曰：生有所托於令監者　令監能記有而不忘否

심 왈　제 언 지　김 청 지 필 서 왈　모 년 월 일　호 서
沈曰：第言之　金請紙筆書曰：某年月日　湖西

김 모 환 귀 고 토　이 갱 불 출 문 운　이 부 지 벽 상 왈
金某還歸故土　而更不出門云　而付之壁上曰：

일 후 필 유 사 단 의　생 금 일 자 차 직 환 향　이 갱 불 입 락 의
日後必有事端矣　生今日自此直還鄉　而更不入洛矣

령 감 수 명 념 이 활 아　심 경 아 왈　하 기 언 지 망 야
令監須銘念而活我　沈驚訝曰：何其言之妄也

김 왈　무 론 언 지 망 여 불 망　제 이 차 위 증 운 이 사 출
金曰：毋論言之妄與不妄　第以此爲證云而辭出

심 심 절 아 지　심 즉 단　야　신 임 년 이 판 금 오　당
沈心窃訝之　沈卽檀 13) 也　辛壬年以判金吾 14) 當

대 옥　국 정 지 초　호 서 김 모　잡 출 어 노 겸 지 초
大獄　鞫庭之招 15) 湖西金某　雜出於奴傔之招 16)

이 상 금 출 입 운　심 시 내 대 각 왈　김 생 가 위 신 인 야
而尙今出入云　沈始乃大覺曰：金生可謂神人也

수 언 김 생 년 래　불 재 경　오 소 임 지　야　수 극 력 구 지
遂言金生年來 17) 不在京　吾所稔知 18) 也　遂極力救之

1 連山: a town in Nonsan County 論山郡 in South Ch'ungch'ŏng Province.
2 金銖: unidentified.
3 四大臣: the four leaders of the Old Doctrine faction (Noron 老論) =
   Kim Ch'angjip 金昌集 [1648–1722], Yi Imyŏng 李頤命 [1658–1722], Yi
   Kŏnmyŏng 李健命 [1663–1722], and Cho T'aech'ae 趙泰采 [1660–1722]).
4 辛壬前: lit. "prior to the *sinim* incident." "*Sinim* incident" refers to the literary purges (*sahwa* 士禍) of 1721 (*sinch'uk* 辛丑; Kyŏngjong 1) and 1722 (*imin*
   壬寅; Kyŏngjong 2), which arose from attempts by the four leaders of the
   Old Doctrine faction (see note 3) to invest Prince Yŏning 延礽君 (later King
   Yŏngjo) as the heir apparent to the throne immediately after the enthronement of King Kyŏngjong 景宗 [r. 1721–4; 1688–1724]. The four leaders
   were put to death on the same day.
5 獨自咄歎: lit. "click one's tongue and lament alone."
6 散班 = *sangwan* 散官: a ranked official without portfolio.
7 朝士 = *chosin* 朝臣 ~ *chogwan* 朝官: official serving in the royal court.
8 貌瑩: lit. "appearance is radiant": beautiful appearance.
9 駑馬: old and sluggish horse.
10 參班: keep company with *yangban*.
11 無由邀來: lit. "no reason to come and greet."
12 甚風: lit. "what wind?"
13 沈檀 [1645–1730; styled Tŏgyŏ 德興; sobriquets Yakhyŏn 藥峴 and
    Ch'uudang 追尤堂; ancestral seat Ch'ŏngsong 靑松]: scholar-official
    under King Yŏngjo 英祖 [r. 1724–76; 1694-1776] and member of the Young
    Doctrine Faction (Soron 少論). His father was Sim Kwangmyŏn 沈光沔
    [dates unknown].
14 判金吾 = *p'an Ŭigŭmbu sa* 判義禁府事: junior first-grade post attached
    to the State Tribunal (Ŭigŭmbu 義禁府).
15 鞫庭之招: lit. "summons for state interrogation [by an *ad hoc* tribunal]."
16 奴僕之招: lit. "summoning of the slaves and servants."
17 年來: for many years.
18 稔知: be well aware.

——— **55** ———

Celebrations on Graduating

Vol. II: 29; translated 10 June 1921; Diary XVI, pp. 177–8; 217.

Chang Pungik (Prince Musuk) was born of a poor family and his parents were old. He cast aside the pen and went in for archery. He rose in rank to be minister of an office.

In the troubles of 1728 and 1729 he put on his helmet and his coat of mail and with a knife stood outside the palace gate as guard. Seeing this, Yŏngjong* was able for the first time to sleep comfortably. He took all the dangers of the state upon himself.

He later became general of the Hullyŏn† and P'odo‡ and rode on a *ch'ohŏn*§ chair. On a certain day, he went outside the walls and passing a certain district, he heard announcements of someone who had passed the examination; a great celebration was going on in honour of the winner. Songs were sung and harps struck; dancers and tight-rope walkers were called for.

At a well by the side of the road was a woman servant, drawing water, when someone asked her, "How does your house's winner expect to celebrate his victory?"

She replied, "Celebrations can be held when nothing else remains to do, but just now he is in straits as to his breakfast and dinner. The old master of our house starves with the rest of us, worn down thin. What celebration could be thought of under these circumstances?"

When Chang Pungik heard this, he stopped his chair and called the servant to him, saying, "Where is your master's house? And will your master share in the celebration?"

The servant replied, "Our house is in such-and-such a place," and pointed it out with her hand.

Chang saw that it was not far but really close at hand – a little house scarcely fit to shield them from the wind and rain.

Chang went at once and when he had reached the door, shouted, "*Sillae-wi!*"¶

Not at all pleased with this, Yu refused to come out. "What military man can think thus to call me? I shall not move a foot."

Chang said, "I, too, am a literary graduate; what is wrong about me, a graduate, calling another? Come out at once."

Hearing this, there was nothing for it but to come out. He put him through his paces a time or two, as the custom is, and they both entered the house.

Chang asked, "How do you propose to celebrate?"

His reply was, "I cannot even provide breakfast and supper for my parents. What celebration could I think of?"

Chang said, "I'll see that you have one." Also he said, "You have your parents with you and you must have something to make them glad."

"Even though I have my parents, I have no means of any celebration. How could I ever engage an acrobat?"

Chang said, "Not so at all. Those who have their parents alive must have a good time."

He then called the police office to choose one singer, one rope-walker, etc., four in all and send them at once with all their dresses, etc. complete and have them stay the night before beginning the display.

"I shall sleep here tonight and join in the celebration. Let all the food necessary for the night be prepared and sent here. Let all the ropes and equipment necessary be sent from the police office."

Thus he gave his orders. That night they erected a great awning and placed mats on the ground. The music kept up the night through and when morning came it ceased. He gave two hundred *yang* for the old parents. Thus it was in old days.

---

* Here and below Gale renders King Yŏngjo as Yŏngjong.

† Hullyŏn = Hullyŏn Togam: General Directorate for Military Training. See note 7 below.

‡ P'odo: Police Department. See note 8 below.

§ *ch'ohŏn* 軺軒: hand-held palanquin sometimes with a single wheel.

¶ *Sillae-wi* = "call *sillae*": *Sillae* refers to new civil service examination passers or the occasion itself. "Call *sillae*" refers to a kind of hazing ritual conducted by seniors to congratulate new civil service examination passers. The ceremony involved seniors drawing designs on the *sillae*'s face in ink and ordering him around.

張武肅鵬翼 1) 以家貧親老投筆 2) 而位至（秋）判 3)

當戊申及乙亥變逆 4) 躬環甲冑 杖劍立（寢）殿門外

英廟 5) 始乃就寢 其佩 6) 國家安危如此 以（秋）

判兼訓將 7) 及捕將 8)　常乘軒車　一日出城過一洞

則時當生進 9) 放榜　曲曲歌絃 10)　家家選優 11)

路傍井邊　有一婢子汲水　而傍人問之曰：汝家新恩

何以應榜 12)　對曰：應榜猶屬餘事　朝夕難繼 13)

吾家老上典　方在頷顧 14) 中　應榜何以念及乎云

時武肅公聞其言　停輅而使厥婢近前問曰：

汝家何在　而汝主方應榜乎　答［對］曰：家在某處

手指而示之　不遠之地　而不蔽風雨之數間斗屋也

公仍呼新來　則儒生不肯曰：武將何可呼我

我不可以出　公乃曰：吾亦生進　以生進呼生進

無所不可　斯速出來　儒生不得已出來　數次進退 15)

偕入其門　問曰：應榜何以爲之　對曰：朝夕難供

可論應榜也　公曰：此吾當備給矣　又曰：

既是侍下 16)　則當率倡 17) 矣　對曰：雖是侍下

응 방 역 무 이 위 지　　하 감 의 도 어 솔 창 호
應榜亦無以爲之　　何敢議到於率倡乎

공 왈　　불 연 의　　시 하 이 하 가 불 솔 창 호　　잉 분 부 포 청
公曰：不然矣　侍下而何可不率倡乎　仍分付捕廳 18)

창 우　　사 인 극 택　　이 복 식 무 령 선 명　　창 방 전 대 령　이
倡優 19) 四人極擇　而服飾務令鮮明　唱榜前待令　而

오 당 류 숙 어 차 이 일 유 의　　자 도 감　신 영　　성 설 야 찬
吾當留宿於此而一遊矣　自都監 20) 新營 21) 盛設夜饌

비 대 우 차 처 좌 우　산 붕　　사 포 청 대 령 사 분 부　일 모
備待于此處左右　山棚 22) 使捕廳待令事分付　日暮

후　포 진 어 기 가 전 통 가 지 상　　종 야 장 락　급 효 이 파
後　鋪陳於其家前通街之上　終夜張樂　及曉而罷

우 이 전 삼 백　헌 수 어 기 로 친　　이 선 배 지 풍 류 유 여 차
又以錢三百　獻壽於其老親　而先輩之風流有如此

1 張鵬翼 [1674–1735; styled Un'gŏ 雲擧; ancestral seat Indong 仁同; posthumous epithet Musuk 武肅]: military official under King Yŏngjo 英祖 [r. 1724–76; 1694–1776]. His grandfather was Chang Ch'aju 張次周 [1606–51].

2 投筆: lit. "cast aside the brush" = give up intellectual pursuits for a military career.

3 秋判 = Hyŏngjo p'ansŏ 刑曹判書: minister of punishments.

4 戊申及乙亥變逆: lit. "the treasons of the *musin* and *ŭrhae* years" (1728 and 1755, respectively). The treason of *musin* 戊申 concerns an attempt by Yi Injwa 李麟佐 (?–1728) and others to install Prince Milp'ung Yi T'an 密豊君 李坦 (1698–1729) as king in place of King Yŏngjo 英祖 [r. 1724–76; 1694–1776]. The treason of *ŭrhae* 乙亥 seems to refer to the incident of "slanderous writing on the wall" (*pyŏksŏ* 壁書) in which a critique of the state was discovered in Naju 羅州 in the second month of 1755 (Yŏngjo 31); however, this incident happened long after the death of Chang Pungik.

5 英廟: temple name (*myoho* 廟號) of King Yŏngjo 英祖 [r. 1724–76; 1694–1776; name Kŭm 昑; styled Kwangsuk 光叔; sobriquet Yangsŏnghŏn 養性軒]. King Yŏngjo was the fourth son of King Sukchong 肅宗 [r. 1674–1720; 1661–1720], brother of King Kyŏngjong 景宗 [r. 1720–4; 1688–1724]. His mother was Sukpin Ch'oe-ssi 淑嬪 崔氏 [1670–1718] and his wife was

Queen Chŏngsŏng 貞聖王后 [1692–1757], the daughter of Sŏ Chongje 徐宗悌 [1656–1719]. After Queen Chŏngsŏng's death, he married Queen Chŏngsun 貞純王后 [1745–1805], the daughter of Kim Han'gu 金漢耉 [1723–69].

6 佩: have a mind to, fix one's mind on, be determined to.

7 訓將 = Hullyŏn *taejang* 訓鍊大將: Chief Commander of the General Directorate of Military Training (Hullyŏn Togam 訓鍊都監; see note 20), a junior second-grade military post.

8 捕將 = P'odo *taejang* 捕盜大將: one of the two chief commanders of the Police Department (P'odoch'ŏng 捕盜廳), a junior second-grade military post.

9 生進 = *saengwŏn chinsasi* 生員進士試 = *samasi* 司馬試: lower state examination. *Saengwŏn* is a classics licentiate and *chinsa* is a literary licentiate.

10 曲曲歌絃: songs and strings at every turn.

11 家家選優: lit. "each and every house summons acrobats/entertainers."

12 應榜: (for a passer of the civil service examination) throw a banquet for relatives and neighbours.

13 朝夕難繼: lit. "morning and evening, difficult to carry on" = lead a life of half-starvation.

14 頷顑: starvation.

15 數次進退: lit. "many times advance and retreat"; push and pull several times.

16 侍下: support one's parents.

17 率倡: lit. "command/be escorted by acrobats/entertainers"; (for a passer of the civil service examination) command acrobats/entertainers to play flutes (in celebration of his success).

18 捕廳 = P'odoch'ŏng 捕盜廳: Police Department.

19 倡優: acrobats/entertainers.

20 都監 = Hullyŏn Togam 訓鍊都監: military garrison established after the Japanese Invasions (1592–8) due to the collapse of the five military commands.

21 新營: lit. "new garrison"; a branch office of the General Directorate for Military Training (Hullyŏn Togam 訓鍊都監), located by the main entrance of Kyŏnghŭi Palace 慶熙宮.

22 山棚 = *sandae* 山臺: mask dance.

—— **56** ——

Score One for the Dancing Girl

Vol. II: 28; n.d.; manuscript translation crossed out in Diary XII, pp. 87–9;
Box 9:21 "A Trip to Japan," pp. 121–2, typed up as "Jealous Wife,"
but crossed out to read "Score One for the Dancing Girl";
also in Box 6:18, typed up as "Score One for the Dancing Girl,"
but crossed out to read "Clever Dancing Girl," which appears
to be the most recent version; 219.

```
Korea, like the rest of the Far East, has a liking for the
dancing girl. She is a national institution and her name,
her place and her part are definitely recognized. Many good
stories are told of her, showing that frequently within
her soul there is something worth the while, in spite of
her degraded and loathsome calling. Often, too, though
a dancing girl, it is by no will or choice of her own.
```

Cho T'aeŏk, a Minister of State, had for wife a member of the Sim clan, a most jealous woman, who forbade her husband's casting even a glance in the direction of any other member of womankind.

His older brother was Governor of P'yŏngan Province while T'aeŏk himself was a secretary of a Board.

While in charge of this office he received orders from the Government to proceed at once to P'yŏngyang (`capital of P'yŏngan Province`). He made the journey safely and while spending some days at the Government Headquarters fell in with a dancing girl for the first time in his life.

A rumour of this got abroad, and coming to his wife, she at once ordered her travelling kit made ready and prepared for an immediate departure for P'yŏngyang. She took her brother along, grimly determined that she would make an end of this unspeakable dancing girl.

Hearing of it, Cho turned pale, while his brother the governor was equally alarmed. Said he, "What shall we do about it?"

In haste, he gave orders that the dancing girl escape for her life.

This dancing girl, however, calmly said in reply, "There is no reason to run away that I know of. Even though I stay here, what special danger is there, pray? I am so wretchedly poor that I have not the necessary means to carry out what I'd like to do. If you will give me a little money, I'll see that all is managed successfully."

The governor inquired, "What do you propose to do with money?"

Her reply was, "I want some clothes. That's what I mean."

The governor said, "If you really have some plans to see this thing through, then you may safely ask what you please and I'll give it."

He ordered the steward to give her whatever she required.

He then sent messengers as well to Chunghwa and Hwangju to meet the lady on the way to express his special compliments and see to her food and fare.

When Madame Sim reached Hwangju and met people from P'yŏng-yang with abundant supplies of food and dainties, she looked at them with a sniff of contempt and inquired, "Am I a Minister of State that you come out thus to meet me? I have means enough, and am quite capable of looking after my own affairs," and so she sent them all about their business.

When she reached Chunghwa a like scene followed, for a group met her which she again contemptuously drove off. She passed Chaesong-wŏn and reached Changnim (Long Wood).

It was then toward the close of the spring season that this happened and so along the three miles of trees the early glory of summer was all about her; the river too at every turn was most delightful to see.

Sim-ssi, or Madame Sim, as we would call her, lifted the curtain of her chair and peeked out as she went by. After passing the avenue of trees she came to the white sands of the shore where the river like a great mirror lay before her. Walls skirted the bank along which the trading boats lay thickly crowded together. The East Gate, too, Yŏn'gwang Pavilion, and Ŭlmil Outlook stood high up in front. The decorations of the upper towers flashed in the light and dazzled her eyes. Seeing it, she said, "Assuredly this P'yŏngyang is a noted place worthy of its name."

While she was passing over the sands she saw in the distance something that looked like a bouquet of flowers but which, on nearer approach, turned out to be a dancing girl, dressed in green and red, riding a prancing palfrey specially saddled and decorated. She was surprised at this and asked the bearers to wait a moment till she could see.

When the rider came near she dismounted and said, "I am such-and-such a dancing girl and have come to greet Your Ladyship."

Hearing her name, Madame Sim recognized her as the guilty party, and immediately her soul revolted at the thought of her and rose three thousand feet into mid-air in fiery indignation. She roared out, "What business have you, bold-faced huzzy, to come out and greet me? Come here till I look you over."

The *kisaeng* (dancing girl) came with a kindly face and submissive manner, and Sim-ssi, seeing her fresh as the bloom of the peach, her lithe waist like the willow, and her rich and comely dress, realized that she was indeed the rarest of beauties. She looked at her for a few minutes and then asked, "How old are you?"

"I am eighteen," replied the girl.

Sim-ssi went on, "You are a rare beauty, no question about that. I don't wonder men seeing you are unable to resist your charms. I came to kill you but now that I meet you, I am persuaded otherwise. Go back and stay with my husband. Know, however, that he is a fool and has no sense whatever. Be careful of his health. If he contracts a disease while under your care, you shall die."

When she had said this she ordered her caravan turn right about and started back to Seoul.

When the governor heard of her having turned back, he sent a messenger in hot haste, saying, "Wait, Madame, please. Seeing you have come all this way, come into the city and rest a day or two before you return."

Madame Sim replied, "Not a bit of it. I am not a beggar asking alms; what reason could I have for staying?" and with that she was off.

The governor then called this *kisaeng* and asked her how she had dared face the tigress and get off scot-free.

The dancing girl replied, "The woman's nature is vehement, beyond all word, and thus has she come these many miles. But even a kicking horse, when it has kicked its fill, gives up at last. So a woman, likewise, when she has had time to expend her fury, gives way. I thought, 'If I die I die,' and so put on my best dress and went out to meet her humbly, made my bow, and that won the day."

趙相國泰億 1) 夫人沈氏　性本猜妒　故未嘗有

房外之犯 2) 也　其伯氏爲箕伯 3) 以承旨適作奉命

之行 4) 於關西 5) 留營中幾日　始有所眄之妓 6)

沈氏聞其由　乃卽地治行　使其娚陪行　而直向

箕營 7) 將欲打殺其妓　趙相聞其狀　失色無語

伯氏亦大驚曰：此將奈何　欲使其妓避之　其妓曰：

小人不必避身也　自有可生之道　而貧不能辦矣

問其由　對曰：小人欲飾珠翠於身　而無錢故恨歎也

答曰：汝若有可生之道　則雖千金吾自當之矣

唯汝所欲可也　仍使幕客 8) 隨所入得給云　而中和 9)

黃州 10) 出送裨將而問候　且備送廚傳 11) 而支供 12) 矣

沈氏之一行到黃州　則有箕營裨將之來待　且有支供

之待者　乃冷笑曰：吾豈大臣別星 13) 行次有裨將乎

且吾之路需 14) 優足　何用支供爲哉　並使退出

到中和又如是斥退　發行過栽松院 15)　入長林之中

時當暮春　十里長林　春意方濃　曲曲淸江　景物

頗佳　沈氏褰 16) 轎簾而賞玩過長林　林盡而望見

則白沙如練　澄江似鏡　粉堞 17) 周繚 18) 於江岸

商舶紛集於水上　練光亭19)大同門20)乙密垈21)

超然垈之　樓閣丹靑照耀　屋宇縹緲22)　奪人眼目

沈氏嗟嘆曰：果爾絶勝之區23)　名不虛得24)矣

且行且玩之際　遠遠沙場之上　忽有一點花　渺渺25)

而來　漸近則一箇名妓　綠衣紅裳　騎一匹繡鞍駿驄

橫馳而來　心甚怪之　駐馬而見之　及近其女子下馬

以鶯聲唱喏26)曰：某妓請謁　沈氏問其名　則曰：某

業火衝起27)三千丈矣　仍聲叱責曰：某妓渠何爲來謁

第使立之于馬前　其妓歛[斂]容28)而敬立馬前

沈氏見之　則顔如含露之桃花　腰似依風之細柳

羅綺珠翠飾其上下　眞是傾國之色　沈氏熟視曰：

汝年幾何　曰：十八歲矣　沈氏曰：汝果名物也

丈夫視此等名妓而不近　則可謂拙夫　吾之此行

初欲殺汝而來矣　旣見汝卽名物也　吾何必下手乎

여 가 왕 시 오 가 령 감　이 령 감 탄 객　야　약 사 심 혹 이
汝可往侍吾家令監　而令監炭客 29) 也　若使沈惑而

생 병　즉 여 죄 당 사　신 지 신 지　언 파　잉 회 마 향 경 락
生病　則汝罪當死　愼之愼之　言罷　仍回馬向京洛

영 문 문 지　급 주 팽 전 창 왈　수 씨 행 차 기 래 도 성
營門聞之　急走伻傳唱曰：嫂氏行次旣來到城

외　이 잉 불 입 성 하 야　원 잠 도 성 내　류 영 중 기 일
外　而仍不入城何也　願暫到城內　留營中幾日

이 환 행 가 야　심 씨 랭 소 왈　오 비 걸 태 객　야
而還行可也　沈氏冷笑曰：吾非乞駄客 30) 也

입 성 하 위　불 고 이 치 환 경　제 기 후 영 문 초 치 기 기 이
入城何爲　不顧而馳還京　第其後營門招致其妓而

문 왈　여 이 하 대 담 담　직 향 호 구　이 반 획 면 언
問曰：汝以何大胆 [膽] 直向虎口　而反獲免焉

기 기 대 왈　부 인 지 성 수 한 투　이 작 차 행 어 천 리 지 지 자
其妓對曰：夫人之性雖悍妬　而作此行於千里之地者

기 구 구 아 녀　소 가 판 호　마 지 제 교 설　자
豈區區兒女 31) 所可辦乎　馬之蹄嚙 [齧] 32) 者

필 유 기 보　인 역 여 시　소 인 사 즉 사 이　수 피 지 기
必有其步 33) 人亦如是　小人死則死耳　雖避之其

가 면 호　고 자 응 장 이 왕 배　약 피 타 살　즉 무 내 하 의
可免乎　故茲凝妝而往拜　若被打殺　則無奈何矣

불 연 즉 혹 기 유 견 련 련 지 심 고 야 운 이
不然則或冀有見憐憐之心故也云爾

1　趙泰億 [1675–1728; styled Taenyŏn 大年; sobriquet Kyŏmjae 謙齋; ancestral seat Yangju 楊州; posthumous epithet Munch'ung 文忠]: scholar-official under King Yŏngjo 英祖 [r. 1724–76; 1694–1776]. His father was Cho Kasŏk 趙嘉錫 [1634–81].

2 房外之犯: lit. "offence of (going) outside the (bed)room": have an extra-marital affair.

3 箕伯: governor of P'yŏngan Province.

4 奉命之行: lit. "be on one's way to carry out a royal order."

5 關西: P'yŏngan Province.

6 所眄之妓: a *kisaeng* with whom one has an especially intimate relationship.

7 箕營: headquarters of the governor of P'yŏngan.

8 幕客 = *pijang* 裨將: unranked military attendant or envoy attached to a regional government office.

9 中和: a town in Hwanghae Province.

10 黃州: a town in Hwanghae Province.

11 廚傳: inn.

12 支供: feed.

13 別星: envoy dispatched by the king.

14 路需: travel gear.

15 栽松院: a station (*yŏgwŏn* 驛院) near P'yŏngyang.

16 褰: roll up (sleeves or pants).

17 粉堞: additional fortification made of plaster around the walls of a castle.

18 周繚: surround; encircle.

19 練光亭: a pavilion by the Taedong River in P'yŏngyang.

20 大同門: a gate by the Taedong River in P'yŏngyang.

21 乙密坮: a pavilion by the Taedong River in P'yŏngyang.

22 縹緲: boundlessly wide and vast.

23 絕勝之區: place of outstanding scenic beauty.

24 名不虛得: lit. "fame that does not come for nothing" = live up to its fame.

25 渺渺: faraway and difficult to discern.

26 唱喏: call out to in a long, drawn-out fashion.

27 業火衝起: the hellfire of bad *karma* shoots up.

28 斂容: make oneself (one's face) presentable.

29 炭客: a naive, clueless person.

30 乞駄客: mooch, freeloader.

31 區區兒女: unattractive, ungainly woman.

32 踶囓: be kicked or bitten.

33 步 = 運數: fortune.

—— **57** ——

A Pair of Spectacles

Vol. II; 30; n.d.; Diary XIV, pp. 44–5; 223.

While on a trip about his province when Minister Yi Sŏngwŏn was governor of Kangwŏn, he went to visit the Diamond Mountains and reached the Nine Dragon Pool; there he desired to have his name carved in the rocks but all the stonecutters among the priests were absent.

At this time the magistrate of Kosŏng was in his train and he said, "There is a man in the lower village who has great skill in cutting stone; he could do it."

A messenger was sent to call him and he came, and was ordered to cut the name. He wore a pair of spectacles, a very fine pair, the very best.

Minister Yi liked fine spectacles very much and asked to see them. He had them in his hand and was turning them over and over in his delight when they slipped from his fingers, fell on the stone and were broken.

Minister Yi gave a start and in his distress offered to pay the price but the stone-cutter, refused, saying, "Things have their appointed course to run and life to live." And then he said, "Don't bother about it, please."

Minister Yi said, "You are a man of the hills, living in sparse surroundings. You have lost your spectacles – how can you afford to buy another pair? Take this please." And he forced him to take it.

The man then opened the spectacle case and said, "If you look at this you will know my reason for not accepting."

Minister Yi looked and there he saw written: "On such-and-such a year, month and day you will meet the governor at the Nine Dragon Pool and be broken."

The minister gave a great start and asked, "Who wrote this?"

The stonecutter said, "I found this written here when I bought them but who did it I know not. I have never heard."*

A very strange story.

---

* Gale's translation is in error. The original reads: "I found this written here when I bought them. In the end, he never said who wrote it."

李相性源 1) 按原營 2) 也　巡路入楓嶽 3)　到九龍淵 4)

欲題名 5)　而刻手僧 6) 皆出他矣　高城倅 7) 以爲

此下村民有一人之來留者　頗有手才 8) 可刻云矣

使之呼來而刻之　則其人着眼鏡　而鏡是絕品 9)

李相素有此癖　使之持來　愛玩不已　偶爾失手

落于巖石之上而破碎　李相錯愕 10) 而使給本價

則其人辭之曰：物之成敗亦有數焉　不必關念也

李相謂曰：汝以山峽貧民失此鏡　而又何可買得乎

此價不必辭也　強與之　其人解示鏡匣 11) 曰：覽此

可知矣　李相受而視之　書以某年月日遇巡使 12) 破

之于九龍淵　李相大驚問曰：此是汝之所書乎　曰：

當初買之時有此書云　而終不言誰某所書　亦可異矣

1 李性源 [1725–90; styled Sŏnji 善之; sobriquet Hoŭn 湖隱; ancestral seat
　Yŏnan 延安; posthumous epithet Munsuk 文肅]: scholar-official under
　King Chŏngjo 正祖 [r. 1776–1800; 1725–1800]; descendant of Yi Chŏnggwi
　李廷龜 [1693–1766] and son of Yi Tŭkpo 李得輔 [dates unknown].
2 原營: headquarters of Kangwŏn Province in Wŏnju 原州.

 3 楓嶽: autumn appellation of the Diamond Mountains (Kŭmgangsan
   金剛山).
 4 九龍淵: a pool in the Diamond Mountains.
 5 題名: engrave one's name on a stone at a scenic spot.
 6 刻手僧: stone-carver monk.
 7 高城倅: magistrate of Kosŏng County in Kangwŏn Province
 8 手才: lit. "hand skills" = dexterity, manual adroitness.
 9 絶品: top-quality product.
10 錯愕: be surprised.
11 鏡匣: eyeglasses case.
12 巡使 = *kwanch'alsa* 觀察使 ~ *kamsa* 監司: provincial governor.

———— **58** ————

A Wonderful Physician

Vol. II: 31; n.d.; Diary XIV, pp. 45–6; 224.

Kim Ŭngnip, who lived in North Kyŏngsang, was a low caste man. He really did not know ten from a bull's foot but he was a physician whose fame filled all the south country. In his diagnosing of a case he did not trouble to feel the pulse or make inquiries as to causes or symptoms; he only looked at the face and took note of the expression to know the cause.

There was a man named Yi Myŏng, magistrate of Kŭmsan, whose daughter-in-law since her marriage had been troubled with tuberculosis. Yi also was a man who understood something of medicine and had tried many remedies, but with no success.

His daughter-in-law, however, grew worse and worse till at last she was unable to rise. He then called Ŭngnip and asked of him. He said, "I must see her face once before I can prescribe, and thus you will not be able to call me."

Yi Myŏng said, "She is at the point of death. What matter about seeing her face!"

And so he had her seated in the main hall and then called him and asked that he see her.

Ŭngnip came into the gate and after looking at her for a time, said, "This is not a difficult case – not at all. There is something raw that has found its way into her stomach."

He bought two or three pieces of candy, dissolved them in water, and gave it to her, saying, "You will now vomit it up."

She drank it and a little later vomited up a lump of mucus in which, when they had cut and opened it, they found a small eggplant that was perfectly whole.

He asked, "When did you swallow this?"

She replied, "When I was about ten years old I pulled off a small eggplant and as I was about to chew it, it slipped down my throat. That's what it is."

From this time on she grew well and strong.

Yi Myŏng's nephew had a son-in-law who had been an invalid for years. He had him come in □ and called Ŭngnip to see him. He looked him over and laughed, saying, "No need to use anything else. It is now autumn and the leaves are falling. Take any leaves – that is, those that are whole and unchanged. Put them in a large kettle and steep them till the water is evaporated down to a small bowl. Drink this as you find opportunity."

He did as told and was cured.

There was also another man who was crippled with rheumatism so that he could not straighten himself out. Ŭngnip saw him and said, "Make a small spear of crushed paper."

And then he stuck it in his nose till he sneezed and sneezed all day long and the man was cured. His healing was such and his name was sounded far abroad.

金應立 1) 者嶺右 2) 常賤人 3) 也　目不識丁 4)　而以神醫

名于嶺外　其術不診脈不論症　但觀形察色而知

其病祟 5)　李銘 6) 之爲金山 7) 倅　其子婦自入門之初

咳嗽苦劇 8)　李亦曉醫理 9)　雜試藥餌 10)　終無動靜

至於委臥垂盡之境 11)　乃邀應立而問之　對曰：

일 첨 안 색 이 후 가 의 약　차 즉 불 감 청 지 사　리 명 왈
一瞻顔色而後可議藥　此則不敢請之事　李銘曰：

금 지 사 경　일 견 하 상　사 좌 우 청　초 사 견 지　응 립 입
今至死境　一見何傷　使坐于廳　招使見之　應立入

문 이 숙 시 왈　차 시 지 이 지 병　장 위 유 생 물 지 체
門而熟視曰：　此是至易之病 12)　腸胃有生物之滯

이 연 야　사 매 이 수 개　화 수 용 화　이 복 지 왈　필 토
而然也　使買飴數箇　和水容化 13) 而服之曰：必吐

출 운 의　복 지 미 기　토 출 일 담 괴　부 이 시 지　즉 유
出云矣　服之未幾　吐出一痰塊 14)　剖而視之　則有

일 소 가 자　일 매　이 소 불 상 패　문 우 병 인　즉 이 위 십
一小茄子 15)　一枚　而少不傷敗　問于病人　則以爲十

여 세 시　적 식 가 자　일 개 오 탄 하　필 시 차 물 야 운
餘歲時　摘食茄子　一箇誤呑下　必是此物也云

자 후 병 근 수 차　리 명 질 서　적 년 침 고 태 병　이 래
自後病根遂差　李銘姪壻 16)　積年沈痼駄病 17) 而來

우 사 응 립 진 시　즉 견 이 소 왈　불 필 복 타 약　금 당 추 절
又使應立診視　則見而笑曰：不必服他藥　今當秋節

락 엽 무 론 모 엽　택 기 불 상 불　자 수 태　이 대 부 사 오
落葉毋論某葉　擇其不傷朽 18) 者數駄　以大釜四五

개 전 지　차 차 전 지 일 완 후　무 시 복 가 야　여 기 언 내
箇煎之　次次煎至一椀後　無時服可也　如其言乃

득 효　우 유 일 인　병 여 각 궁 반 장　응 립 견 이 사 작
得效　又有一人　病如角弓反張 19)　應立見而使作

지 침　자 비 공 작 해 역　여 시 종 일 이 병 유
紙針 20)　刺鼻孔作咳逆 21)　如是終日而病愈

기 소 명 약　류 개 여 시　역 가 이 의
其所名藥　類皆如是　亦可異矣

 1 金應立: unidentified.
 2 嶺右: western part of Kyŏngsang Province.
 3 常賤人: lit. "person of either commoner or low-born status."
 4 目不識丁: lit. "unable to recognize even the character 丁" (a very easy character) = completely illiterate.
 5 病祟: cause of illness.
 6 李銘: unidentified.
 7 金山: a town in present-day Kimch'ŏn 金泉 in North Kyŏngsang Province.
 8 咳嗽苦劇: severe/chronic cough.
 9 曉醫理: be well-versed in medical knowledge.
10 藥餌: medicinal food.
11 委臥垂盡之境: lit. "be in a bedridden, enervated state."
12 至易之病: lit. "illness extremely easy to cure."
13 和水容化: lit. "dissolve in water and mix."
14 痰塊: lump of phlegm.
15 茄子: eggplant (source of Korean *kaji*).
16 姪婿: nephew-in-law.
17 痼駄病 = *kojilpyŏng* 痼疾病: inveterate disease.
18 傷朽: spoil/rot.
19 角弓反張: a febrile or neurogenic disease causing the vertebrae to bend
   toward the chest in the shape of a bow.
20 紙針: needle made of thinly rolled-up paper.
21 咳逆: sneeze.

—————— **59** ——————

A Spook for a Husband

Vol. II: 31; n.d.; Diary XIV, pp. 46–7; 225.

There was a seller of ginseng who lived in Wŏnju with name Ch'oe who
was a millionaire of untold wealth. I heard from the people of Wŏnju
that Ch'oe's mother had a son when she was some twenty years of age.
Her husband died and she lived alone with her little son and kept in
memory her late husband with untarnished name.

On a certain day a great rough fellow with dishevelled garments and
a golden* pouch hanging from his waist came into the open verandah.

Alarmed and in doubt as to what he meant, Mrs. Ch'oe said, "How dare you enter this loyal wife's home?"

The man laughed and said, "I am the master of this home. Why are you alarmed and what reason to feel strange about it?"

He came into her room and forced her to □.

She was helpless in his hands and bore the pain of it with submission. From this time on he came every night. But he brought with him silver, money, silk and cotton goods, till he filled her storehouse full. Mrs. Ch'oe recognized him as a hobgoblin yet she felt a certain care for him.

On a certain day she asked, "Is there anything you are afraid of?"

He said, "There is really nothing I fear especially but yellow things – I can't stand yellow colour and when I see it, I fly."

Knowing this, Mrs. Ch'oe the next day prepared a lot of yellow paint, coloured the walls of her house, her face and body as well, and her clothes, too, all yellow.

The same night her hobgoblin husband came but gave a fearful start and asked, "What does this mean?"

He sighed and said, "Our destiny has been fulfilled and now I must go. Rest in peace. The things I brought you I have no desire to take back. Make them your means of livelihood."

And he disappeared suddenly and did not come again. From then on, the house of Ch'oe became great and rich in goods. She lived until eighty and was a rich and honoured woman.

* Gale's translation is erroneous. See note 2 below.

原州蔘商有崔哥者　累萬金巨富也　聞原之人所

傳言　則崔哥之母　才［纔］過廿歲而生子　喪其夫

與穉兒守節孤居　一日　忽有一健夫　衣服草草 1)

腰紅鬙金 2)　而來坐于廳　崔之母驚訝之　言曰：

守寡3)之室 何許男子唐突入來 其人笑曰：吾是家

長也 何須驚怪之 仍入房逼奸4) 崔母無奈何而

任之 但交合之時 氣逼骨痛5) 不可堪 自此以後

每夜必來 而銀錢布帛 每每輸來 充溢6) 庫中

崔母知其鬼物 而自爾情熟矣 一日問曰：君亦有

畏怯者耶 其人曰：別無所畏怯 而但惡見黃色

見黃色不敢近焉 崔母乃於翌日 多求染黃之水

塗於屋壁 且染其顏面身體 又染衣而衣之 其夜

其人入來驚而退出曰：此何爲也 咄嘆不已 仍曰：

此亦緣分盡而然也 吾從此辭去 汝須好在

吾之所給之物 吾不還推去 俾作汝之產業云

而仍忽不見 自其後 仍無蹤跡 崔之家因此致富

甲於一道 崔之母年近八十 而家産依前饒富

1 草草: extremely plain and unadorned.
2 紅鬖金: a red pouch worn at the waist in the shape of a goldfish.
3 守寡 = *sujŏl kwabu* 守節寡婦: a widow who declines to remarry to honour
   her deceased husband.
4 逼奸: maltreat and ravage; violate.
5 氣逼骨痛: lit. "breathing is obstructed, joints ache."
6 充溢: fill and overflow.

——— 60 ———

The Death Potion

Vol. II: 32; n.d.; Diary XIV, pp. 47–8; 226.

There was a certain head of a department called Cho Un'gyu who was
governor of Chŏlla Province. On a certain night his favourite dancing
girl had occasion to be away and he was above in his official hall. Late
at night he heard the rattle of metal from the room at the side, at which
he gave a great start.

Suddenly a voice was heard to ask, "Is anyone in the official hall?"

The governor replied, "Who are you?"

The answer was, "Your humble servant is a prisoner now under lock
and key."

The governor was more startled than ever, saying, "If you are a prisoner, how comes it that you are here at large?"

He answered, "Tomorrow morning avoid eating the broth that is prepared for you. But get the under-steward to eat it for you. Now that I
have saved Your Excellency's life, may Your Excellency think kindly of
me and save me, too."

He then left.

Alarmed at this, he did not sleep a wink but sat up waiting for the
day.

At the appointed time there came a steaming dish of broth from the
kitchen quarters. But he said he was not feeling well and pushed it
away and asked to call the under-steward.

When the fellow had come he took the dish with trembling hands but
the governor shouted out, "Eat it at once."

He then took a spoonful and at once fell to the ground.

The governor had his body taken out and when the investigation followed he had the prisoner who informed him reported formally to the king for pardon.

The governor then called him and inquired, "How did you know?"

He answered, "There is a restaurant just below the prison rear wall. One day I overheard people talking below the wall and I looked through to see and there was an under-steward so-and-so talking to the woman cook.

"He gave her twenty *yang* and a package of drugs, saying, 'Put these drugs into the broth for the master □□. If this thing works, I'll give you another twenty later.'"

"The cook asked, 'Why do you want to do this?'"

"He said, 'Such-and-such a dancing girl has won my heart so that I cannot give her up. You know about it. Since this governor came, I have never once seen her face; my longings make one day like three seasons. I must get him out of the way.'"

"The woman agreed and so I came out in the night to tell you."

趙判書雲逵 1) 爲完伯 2) 時　一日夜　守廳妓 3)

適有故出外　獨寢宣堂 4) 矣　夜深後　自夾室

有錚然聲 5)　心甚訝然　忽有一人問曰：上房有人乎

巡使 6) 驚曰：汝是誰也　對曰：小人乃是殺獄罪人 7)

也　巡使尤驚訝曰：汝是殺獄重囚　則何爲來此

對曰：明朝粥進支 8) 必勿喫　而使吸 [及] 唱 9)

某喫之也　小人旣活使道　使道亦須活小人也云

이 직 출 거　심 심 경 황　미 접 일 면　대 효 정 좌
而直出去　心甚驚惶　未接一眠 10)　待曉靜坐

미 기　조 죽 자 보 선 고　비 진 의　잉 칭 기 불 평 이 퇴 지
未幾　朝粥自補膳庫 11)　備進矣　仍稱氣不平而退之

호 흡　급　창 모 야　급 죽 기 사 지 끽 지　즉 궐 한 봉
呼吸 [及] 唱某也　給粥器使之喫之　則厥漢奉

기 전 률　순 사 내 대 질 최 끽　즉 수 일 흡 이 도 우 지
器戰慄　巡使乃大叱催喫 12)　則遂一吸而倒于地

사 지 예 시 이 출　기 후 심 리 시　차 수 치 지 생 도 이 등 계
使之曳屍而出　其後審理時　此囚置之生道而登啓 13)

문 기 위 절　즉 옥 장 지 후 즉 식 모 가 야　일 일　우 이 방
問其委折 14)　則獄墻之後卽食母家也　一日　偶爾放

뇨 어 장 하　유 인 어 성　종 장 극 규 견　즉 흡　급　창
溺於墻下　有人語聲　從墻隙窺見　則吸 [及] 唱

모 야　초 식 모 도 장 하　급 이 십 량 전　차 급 일 괴 약 왈
某也　招食母到墻下　給二十兩錢　且給一塊藥曰:

이 차 약 화 어 조 죽 이 진　사 약 성 즉 갱 이 차 수 상 지 의
以此藥和於朝粥而進　事若成則更以此數償之矣

식 모 비 문　하 위 이 여 시 야　왈　모 기 즉 오 지 미 망 야
食母婢問　何爲而如是也　曰:某妓卽吾之未忘也

여 역 당 지 지　일 자 시 사 도 지 후　불 득 견 면 목　사 상
汝亦當知之　一自侍使道之後　不得見面目　思想

지 심　일 일 여 삼 추　불 득 불 행 차 계 야　식 모 왈
之心 15)　一日如三秋 16)　不得不行此計也　食母曰:

락 운　고 모 야 참 출 이 고 지 운 운
諾云　故暮夜潛出而告之云云

---

1 趙雲逵 [1714–74; styled Sahyŏng 士亨; ancestral seat Yangju 楊州; post-humous epithet Ch'unggan 忠簡]: scholar-official under King Yŏngjo 英祖

[r. 1724–76; 1694–1776]. He became the governor of Chŏlla Province in 1755. His father was Cho Yŏngguk 趙榮國 [1698–1760].

2 完伯: governor of Chŏlla Province.

3 守廳妓: *kisaeng* who attends to a local magistrate in his private chamber.

4 宣堂 = Sŏnhwadang 宣化堂: general term for a provincial governor's office.

5 鐺然聲: sound of metal ringing; metallic sound.

6 巡使 = *kwanch'alsa* 觀察使: provincial governor.

7 殺獄罪人: murderer.

8 粥進支: (honorific) a bowl of porridge. *Chinji* (honorific) = "meal."

9 及唱: a boy servant at a local yamen.

10 未接一眠: lit. "unable to sleep a wink" = pass a sleepless night.

11 補膳庫: local bureau in charge of food supplies at a local yamen.

12 催喫: urge someone to eat.

13 登啓: offer up an official report to the king.

14 委折 = *kokchŏl* 曲折: circumstances, the whys and hows.

15 思想之心: lit. "heart that misses someone."

16 一日如三秋: lit. "one day [feels] as long as three autumns."

—— **61** ——

The Faithful Magpie

Vol. II: 33; n.d.; Diary XIV, p. 48; 229.

Pak Uwŏn was a man who lived in the country.* He went to the south as a provincial magistrate. His wife found a young magpie that had fallen from some nest. She fed it night and morning till little by little it grew and its feathers came out. It did not go away but remained in and about her room. Sometimes it would fly off to the woods but would come again and sit upon her shoulder.

When the husband was removed to Changsŏng as magistrate, on the day on which he was to remove, the magpie disappeared. When Mrs. Pak arrived at the magistrate's office, the magpie was seen sitting on the roof calling to her and dancing with delight. The lady fed him as before. It built a nest in the tree of the courtyard and there it had its young and went and came as of old.

When they left for Nŭngju it followed again as it had done before. Also when they came to Seoul, it followed them again.

When the lady died it went and came, fleeted about and cried, and remained by the body awaiting burial. When the funeral started out it sat on the coffin till it reached the place of burial and there it sat on the coffin and kept up its crying.

As the coffin was lowered into the earth, it flew down with the coffin and cried and showed its sorrow. Then it flew away and was gone. This was only a poor dumb beast, but it had a grateful heart and did not forget a kindness. People at that time wrote poems on the Spiritual Magpie.

* Gale is in error. A more accurate translation would be "Pak Uwŏn belonged to a
    different academic lineage from [the compiler of this text]."

朴綾州右源 1) 門外人也　在南邑時　其夫人見樹

上鵲雛之落下者　朝夕飼之以飯而馴之　漸至羽

毛之成　而在於房闥之間 2) 而不去　或飛向樹林

而時時來翔于夫人之肩上　及移長城 3) 將發行之日

忽不知去處　內行到長城衙門　則其鵲自上

噪而飛下　翺翔 4) 于夫人之前　夫人如前飼之

巢于庭樹而卵育 5) 之　去來如常　其後又移綾州 6)

又復如初隨來　及其遞歸京第 7) 又亦隨來

其後夫人之喪　上下啼號　不離殯所　及葬而行喪

좌 우 구 상　　도 산 하　　우 좌 묘 가 상　　이 조 지 불 이
坐 于 柩 上　　到 山 下　　又 坐 墓 閣 上　　而 噪 之 不 已

급 하 관 시　　비 향 구 상　　제 호 불 이　　잉 비 거　　불 지 거 처
及 下 棺 時　　飛 向 柩 上　　啼 號 不 已　　仍 飛 去　　不 知 去 處

수 시 미 물　　개 역 지 은 의　　시 인 유 작 령 작 시
雖 是 微 物　　盖 亦 知 恩 矣　　時 人 有 作 靈 鵲 詩

1 朴右源: unidentified.
2 房闥之間: indoors.
3 長城: a town in the north of South Chŏlla Province.
4 翶翔: (birds) fly around in a circle.
5 卵育: lit. "raise/take care of eggs" = tend to like a mother bird to its eggs.
6 綾州: a town in Hwasun Prefecture 和順郡 in South Chŏlla Province.
7 京第: a residence in the capital.

——— **62** ———

Plum-Blossom, the Dancing Girl

Vol. II: 34; n.d.; Diary XIV, pp. 49–51; 230.

Plum-Blossom was a dancing girl of Koksan, who was very beautiful. An old minister went down to Haeju as governor of Hwanghae Province and later on his round of the province he called at Koksan. Finding this attractive girl he kept her with him and had her stay at the official headquarters. He was fascinated with her and thought of no one else.

At this time also a young officer of note came down as a magistrate of Koksan. He came □ to Haeju and there saw for a moment this very beautiful girl. His desires arose and his longings for her, so that on his return to Koksan he called the mother and treated her in the most lavish way. From this time on this woman had free entrée to the yamen and received freely of rice, money, meat, and dress goods. For several months, this treatment went on.

The woman wondered over this and thought it very strange. One day she asked, "How is it that you treat an insignificant creature like me so kindly? I wonder if Your Excellency has some favour to ask of me or if there's something that I could do in return?"

The magistrate replied, "You are now up in years but your name is known as a once-famous dancing girl. I wanted therefore to □ and know you. That explains it. I have no special purpose otherwise."

On a certain day, the old mother again asked, "Has Your Excellency any suggestion as to what I may make return for all your kindness? Why do you not command me? I have been so greatly favoured. If you should ask me to enter fire or boiling water I would gladly do it for you."

The magistrate replied, "When I was at the governor's I saw your daughter and I have never forgotten her, so dear she was. I am like a sick man with longing to see her. If you could have her brought so that I might meet her even once, death itself would have no regrets for me."

The old mother laughed and said, "That is not difficult – why did you not tell me before? I'll have her come."

She went home and wrote a letter to her daughter, saying, "I have been attacked by an unknown sickness and am like to die. I must see you for if I die without it my eyes will never close. Get permission at once and come down to me so that we may say a long farewell."

She sent the letter at once.

Plum-Blossom read the letter and cried and told the governor of the news and that she would like a leave of absence to go and be with her mother.

The governor granted it and gave her rich presents as he sent her away. She came to her mother and her mother told her all the reasons for this summons. She took her to see the magistrate.

The magistrate was a young man of thirty about, a most handsome fellow, while the governor was old and ugly. As compared with the governor this magistrate was like an angel of light. Peach-Blossom fell in love at first sight and from that time on was his closest companion. They were wholly devoted to each other and so a month passed and the time of her leave had all expired so that she had to think of returning. The magistrate more and more felt it impossible to give her up and said, "When you leave me today, it is uncertain as to whether we shall ever meet again. What shall we do?"

Plum-Blossom shed tears as she replied, "I have given myself to Your Excellency. I shall see that there is a way of return and shall be yours forever."

She then left and arrived in Haeju and called on the governor. The governor asked her about her mother and she replied, "She was very dangerously ill but was healed by a skilful physician and now is somewhat better."

She was then assigned to a little room where she remained some ten days or so. Suddenly, however, she fell ill, so that she could neither sleep nor eat and seemed downcast and weary.

The governor was greatly disturbed and tried this remedy and that but with no effect. Ten days or so passed when she seemed quite unconscious till all of a sudden she jumped up and tore her dishevelled hair. With dirt on her face she ranted and kicked and beat her hands, while all kinds of ravings came from her lips. Sometimes she laughed, sometimes she cried. She came out into the main hall and danced through the governor's office calling the governor by his personal name. When they attempted to stop her, she would kick and butt with her head so that no one dared approach her. They decided that she was crazy.

In fear and consternation, the governor had the servants drag her out and the day following he had her bound, placed in a chair and sent home.

This pretended illness she soon recovered from, so that on the day of arrival she visited the magistrate and told him all about it. She remained there in one of his inner rooms. They loved each other more than ever so that a rumour of it got abroad. The governor heard of it so that when the magistrate of Koksan came to Haeju, the governor asked, "How about the dancing girl from your place, who was here and went back home ill. Is she any better? Have you had word with her or not?"

He replied, "They say she is somewhat better, but how could I have to do with a dancing girl who was already at the service of Your Excellency?"

The governor gave a cold leer and said, "Please keep her safe for me, I pray you."

Seeing that the cat was out of the bag, the magistrate at once asked leave to return to Seoul for a little.

On return he saw one of the ministers and made representations so that the governor was relieved of his office. From this time on he made Plum-Blossom his secondary wife and when he returned to the capital for good, he brought her along. In the troubles of the year *pyŏngsin* (1776), the former magistrate of Koksan fell under suspicion. In tears, his wife said to Plum-Blossom, "You see where my husband is – I am decided to die with him. But you are a young girl. Don't stay here any longer, I pray you, but hasten home."

In tears, Plum-Blossom, made reply, "I, a low-class woman, have been greatly loved and favoured by His Excellency. Yes – for years. When he was in prosperity I was happy with him and now in this day of his adversity how could I think of casting him aside and going home? If he dies, I die, too."

A few days later the husband was beaten to death, and the wife hanged herself. With her own hands, Plum-Blossom had her body laid in the coffin and prepared for burial and when finally the body of the husband came forth from the prison, she had it wrapped in grave clothes and placed in the coffin. She had the two buried together on their ancestral hill and there at the side of the grave she struck her neck through with a knife and was buried in the same grave. So faithful was her love. She was not afraid to face the contempt of the governor and finally, for her husband she died this better death. She was like Yu Rang who died for his second master.

梅花者　谷山妓也　有姿色　一老宰爲海伯 1)

巡到時嬖之　率置營下　寵幸無比　時有一名士之爲

谷山倅者延命 2) 時　霎見 3) 其姸美　心欲之　還衙後

招其母　賜顔 4) 而厚遺之　自此以後　使之無間出入

而米錢肉帛　每每給之　如是者幾月　其母心窃怪之

一日　問曰：如小人微賤之物　如是眷愛　惶悚無地

未知使道有何所見而若是也　倅曰：汝雖年老

自是名妓　故與之破寂　自爾親熟而然也　別無他事

一日　老妓又問曰：使道必有用小人處　而如是

款曲　何不明言敎之　小人受恩罔極　雖赴湯火

自當不辭矣　本倅乃言曰：吾往營門時　見汝女

愛戀不能忘　殆乎生病　汝若率來　更接一面

則死無恨矣　老妓笑曰：此至易之事　何不早敎也

從當率來矣　歸家作書于其女曰：吾以無名之疾

方在死境　而以不見汝　死將不瞑目矣　速速得

由5) 下來　以爲面訣之地云　而專人急報　梅花

見書　泣告于巡使　請得往省之暇6) 巡使許之

資送甚厚　來見其母　道其由　與之偕入衙中

時本倅年才三十餘　風儀動盪7) 巡使則容儀老

醜　殆若仙凡之別異8) 梅花一見而亦有戀慕之

心　自伊日薦枕9) 兩情歡洽　過一朔　由限已滿

梅花將還向營中　本倅戀戀不忍捨曰：從此一別

後會難期　將若之何　梅花揮淚曰：妾既許身矣

今自有脫歸之計 10)　非久更當還侍矣　仍發行

到海州　入見巡使　則問其母病之如何　對曰：

病勢委篤　幸得良醫　今則向差矣　依前在洞房 11)

過十餘日後　梅花忽有病　寢食俱廢　呻吟度日 12)

巡使憂之　雜試藥物而無效　委臥近一旬　一日

忽爾突起　蓬頭垢面 13)　拍手頓足 14)　狂叫亂嚷 15)

或哭或笑　跳躍於澄淸閣 16) 之上　斥呼 17)　巡使之名

人或挽止　則蹙之囓之 18)　使不近前　卽一狂病也

巡使驚駭之　使之出外　而翌日縛置轎中　送于渠家

蓋是佯狂　安得不差 19)　還家之日　卽入衙　見本倅

語其狀　留在挾室　情愛愈篤　如是之際　所聞傳

播　巡使亦聞之　其後谷倅往營下　則巡使問曰：

府妓之爲廳妓者　以病還家矣　近則其病如何

^{이 시 혹 추 견 부} ^{대 왈} ^{병 즉 소 차 운} ^{이 순 영 청 기}
而時或招見否 對曰：病則少差云 而巡營廳妓

^{하 관 하 가 초 견 호} ^{순 사 랭 소 왈} ^{원 공 위 오 선 수 직 언}
下官何可招見乎 巡使冷笑曰：願公爲吾善守直焉

^{곡 쉬 지 기 상} ^{청 유 이 상 경} ^{주 일 대} ^{박 순 사 이 파 지}
谷倅知其狀 請由而上京 嗾一臺 駁巡使而罷之

^{잉 솔 축 매 화} ^{체 귀 시} ^{여 지 해 래 경 제 의} ^{급 부 병}
仍率畜梅花 遞歸時 與之偕來京第矣 及夫丙

^{신 지 옥} ^{전 곡 쉬} ^{사 련 체 옥} ^{기 처 읍 청 매 화 왈}
申之獄 20) 前谷倅 使連逮獄 其妻泣請梅花曰：

^{주 공 금 지 차 경} ^{오 즉 이 유 소 결 어 심 자} ^{여 즉 년 소}
主公今至此境 吾則已有所決於心者 汝則年少

^{지 기 야} ^{하 필 재 차} ^{환 귀 여 가 가 야} ^{매 화 역 읍 왈}
之妓也 何必在此 還歸汝家可也 梅花亦泣曰：

^{천 첩 승 령 감 지 은 애 이 구 의} ^{번 화 지 시 즉 여 지 안 향}
賤妾承令監之恩愛已久矣 繁華之時則與之安享

^{이 금 당 여 차 지 시} ^{안 인 배 이 귀 가} ^{유 사 이 이} ^{수 일}
而今當如此之時 安忍背而歸家 有死而已 數日

^후 ^{죄 인 장 폐} ^{기 처 자 액 이 사} ^{매 화 궁 자 빈 렴 입 관}
後 罪人杖斃 其妻自縊而死 梅花躬自殯殮入棺

^{이 급 죄 인 시 지 출 급 야} ^{우 부 치 상} ^{부 부 지 관} ^{합 부}
而及罪人屍之出給也 又復治喪 夫婦之棺 合祔

^{우 선 영 지 하} ^{잉 자 재} ^{어 묘 방 하} ^{종 기 절 개 렬 렬 의}
于先塋之下 仍自裁 21) 於墓傍下 從其節檗烈烈矣

^{초 어 순 사} ^{즉 용 계 도 면} ^{후 어 본 쉬} ^{즉 립 절 사 의}
初於巡使 則用計圖免 後於本倅 則立節死義

^{기 역 녀 중 지 예 양} ^의
其亦女中之豫讓 22) 矣

1 海伯: governor of Hwanghae Province.
2 延命: ceremony whereby a newly appointed local magistrate visits the governor of the province.
3 覘見: catch a glimpse of.
4 賜顏: grant an audience to a visitor.
5 得由: take a furlough; go on leave.
6 往省之暇: lit. "furlough to visit one's parents."
7 風儀動盪: handsome and dashing.
8 仙凡之別異: lit. "difference between Daoist immortal and common mortal."
9 薦寢: sleep with (one's master).
10 脫歸之計: lit. "stratagem for making one's escape."
11 洞房: bed-chamber.
12 呻吟度日: spend the days groaning in pain.
13 蓬頭垢面: lit. "unkempt hair and soiled face."
14 拍手頓足: lit. "clap one's hands and stomp one's feet."
15 狂叫亂嚷: lit. "scream as if crazy and make a commotion."
16 澄淸閣: name of a pavilion in present-day Taegu 大邱.
17 斥呼: call out a senior's name disrespectfully.
18 魘之噛之: lit. "glare at and bite."
19 差: convalesce.
20 丙申之獄: lit. "a major criminal case regarding murder or treason in the *pyŏngsin* year" = (details unknown).
21 自裁 = *chagyŏl* 自決: commit suicide.
22 豫讓 Yu Rang: assassin from the Warring States period 戰國時代 [403–221 BC]. When Zhao Xiangzi 趙襄子 [?–425 BC] killed his master Zhibo 智伯, Yu Rang made multiple attempts to avenge the death of his master. When all his plans failed, he committed suicide.

———— **63** ————

The Propitiated Spirit

Vol. II: 35; n.d.; Diary XIV, pp. 51–2; 232.

Minister Ryu Ŭi (graduated 1769) once went as a secret commissioner to the south of Korea and reached the county of Chinju. Here was a deputy who had held office through the terms of four different magistrates and had done many lawless deeds so that the Commissioner decided after hearing his case to have the man beaten to death.

He was on his way to the official quarters but still had some miles to go, when night came on. Being very weary, he decided to go into the first house he encountered to pass the night. He reached a place that looked neat and orderly and sat himself down on the verandah.

Here a young lad of about thirteen came out to greet him and had him seated in the place of honour. He was an extraordinarily bright and interesting lad who looked after horse and servants well and had the servants ready the evening meal. His entertainment of the guest was most exceptional.

The Commissioner asked his age and who he was.

"Thirteen years old," he said, and he was the son of the deputy magistrate.

He again asked, "The son of the deputy is you?"

The boy's reply was, "I am."

"Then, where is your father?" inquired the stranger.

The answer was, "He is over in the magistracy on official business." The lad's replies and his behaviour were most exceptional – so gentle and respectful.

Ryu Ŭi looked at him in wonder and said to himself, "A rascal of a deputy to have such a lovable lad as this for son surely beats all."

In the night as he was asleep he felt someone's hand touch him to awaken him. Opening his eyes he found the lights burning. There was a large table spread with special dishes and dainties.

He inquired in a startled way, "What does all this mean?"

The lad replied, "This year my father's fortunes are fraught with real danger and many evils are □ ; I called a medium and asked of her and that explains the spread of food. Will you please not accept and have something to eat?"

The Commissioner laughed to himself and partook greatly so that his long fasting of many days was more than made amends for.

The morning following he left and entered the official □ where he announced himself as Royal Commissioner, had the deputy arrested and also questioned concerning all his past deeds. He then said, "I had decided to beat to death all evil doers such as you, but last night I slept at your house where I met your son, superior a thousand times to his father. I slept there and ate of your hospitality. I cannot kill you – such return would be unthinkable."

He had him beaten and sent into exile. When he returned home he said to his people, "The prayers of a medium are not such vain things as many think. I was the devil after the deputy's house and I was propitiated with good food and drink so that he escaped death. A very laughable story indeed!"*

* The original reads: "All realized and collapsed in laughter—so the story goes/it is said."

柳叅判誼 1) 以繡衣 2) 行嶺南　到晉州　聞首鄉 3)

連四等仍任　而多行不法之事　期於出道 4) 日打殺

方向邑底未及十餘里地　日勢已晚　又有路憊 5)

偶入一家　家頗精潔　升堂有一十三四歲童子

迎之上座　其作人聰慧　區處人馬 6)　使之喂 7) 之

呼奴備夕飯　接待凡百　儼若成人　問其年而且

問是誰之家　答曰：年是十三歲　卽是座首 8)

之家也　問汝是座首之家也　問汝是座首之兒乎　曰：

然矣　汝翁何去　曰：方在邑內任所矣　其應接極

詳而謹敬　柳奇愛之　獨于心曰：奸鄉 9) 有寧馨兒 10)

云　而至夜就寢　忽有攪之者　驚起則燈火熒然

前有一大卓　魚骨饌餌酒果之屬　皆高排 11) 矣

起而訝問　此何飲食　其兒曰：今年家翁之身數

不吉　必官灾 12) 云　故招巫而禳之　此其所設也

玆用接待客子　願少下箸　柳忍笑而啗之　久飢之餘

腹果氣蘇 13)　其翌日辭去　入邑底出道　拿入其

座首　數 14) 其前後罪惡　而仍言曰：吾之此行

欲打殺如汝者矣　昨宿汝家　見汝兒　大勝於汝矣

既宿汝家　飽汝之酒食　而殺之有非人情　仍嚴刑

遠配　而歸來語於家中曰：巫女禱神　亦不虛矣

殺座首之神即我也　而以酒肉禱之　而免其禍

儘覺絶倒云爾

1 柳誼 [1734–?; styled Ŭiji 誼之; ancestral seat Chŏnju 全州]: scholar-official under King Chŏngjo 正祖 [r. 1765–1800; 1752–1800]. He was a secret royal inspector (amhaeng ŏsa 暗行御史) in Kangwŏn and P'yŏngan provinces. His father was Yu Sŏnyang 柳善養 [1710–?].

2 繡衣 = amhaeng ŏsa 暗行御史: secret royal inspector.

3 首鄉 = chwasu 座首: head of a local yamen.

4 出道 = short for ŏsa ch'ultu 御史出頭: official announcement of the identity of an amhaeng ŏsa.

5 路憊: travel fatigue.

6 區處人馬: lit. "be adept at handling both people and horses."

7 喂: feed animals.

 8 座首 = *suhyang* 首鄉: see note 3 above.
 9 奸鄉: wicked local yamen overseer.
10 馨兒: exceptional child.
11 高排: (food or food receptacles) piled high.
12 官災: calamity induced by a government office.
13 腹果氣蘇: lit. "stomach is filled, spirit is revived."
14 數: interrogate a criminal.

------ **64** ------

The Faithful Widow

Vol. II: 36; n.d.; *Miscellaneous Writings II*, no. 30, pp. 106–8.
Typed. Box 9:21, pp. 117–19; Diary XII, pp. 78–82 (crossed out); 234.

In the county of Yŏngch'ŏn there was a scholar named No who had a son that died shortly after his marriage. His widow Pak-ssi dressed in sackcloth and spent three years faithfully as a mourner. She also served her husband's parents with all faithfulness so that the people of the neighbourhood praised her.

When she first came as a bride she brought with her a slave whose name was Mansŏk.

As No's home was very poor, Pak did weaving to help out while Mansŏk gathered wood and prepared meals, and thus she saw to the comfort of the home.

In the same town there lived a man called Kim Chosul who was of the aristocracy and very rich. He had taken note of Pak-ssi through the paling and saw how beautiful she was and his spirit was inflamed with a desire to possess her as his own.

On a certain day No, who had to make a somewhat distant journey, went to Kim's house and asked to borrow a head-cover. This he obtained and left.

Chosul, knowing definitely that the master was away from home, sent a servant to find in which room Pak-ssi slept. Then in the moonlight he put on his scholar's cap and went to the house, Pak-ssi being alone in her room. It was next to the room of her mother-in-law, however, with only a thin partition between.

Pak-ssi had been asleep, but was awakened by the sound of a foot-fall just outside her window. She saw also the shadow of a man against the light. Alarmed at this, she immediately went into her mother-in-law's room.

The mother-in-law inquired the reason, and she told her, so that they both sat down and watched the night through.

At this time Mansŏk was sleeping at Kim's house for he had been married to a slave attached there, and so there was no man about.

Suddenly a voice sang out in the night: "The widow Pak and I have been keeping company for a long time – hand her over to me."

The mother-in-law then screamed out her rejoinder, "A thief! A thief!"

The town people came hurrying with lights to see while Chosul made his escape to his home.

The mother and daughter talked it over and decided that it was Chosul and that he was the trespasser.

When No came back and heard this he was very very angry, and decided at first to lay the case before the magistrate, but disliking the publicity it would bring, abandoned the attempt.

Chosul set going a story to the effect that he and Pak-ssi had been keeping company for a long time and that she had been with child already four months. It was talked about everywhere.

Hearing this, Pak-ssi decided to face the music and lay her indignant case before the magistrate. She put her coat over her head to hide her face and made her way to the public yamen, where she told what she had been subjected to by Chosul and what lies he had spread.

But Chosul had already given bribes to each and every one so that the official servants were Chosul's henchmen. The recording secretaries pointed her out, saying, "She is a woman of ill-repute, as the stories about her have been heard for a long time."

The magistrate, Yun Ihyŏn, believed the official servants and so said, "If you were a decent woman, even though others spoke against you, you could prove by the lapse of time that you were innocent. Why do you come here to make a fuss?"

Pak-ssi replied, "If Your Excellency does not see justice done me in this case, I shall strike my throat through here and now and die in your presence."

Her determined appearance was very terrible to behold.

Yun Ihyŏn replied in an angry voice, "Do you think you can frighten me by any such threat as this? If you want to die, go home and die. Why is this knife flourished before me here? Away with you. Have her out, you servants."

The woman servants knocked and pushed her till they had almost got her out. On reaching the gate, Pak-ssi gave a great cry, ran the knife through her throat and died then and there, so that all who saw it beheld how terrible and tragic it was.

Alarmed beyond measure, the magistrate had her body taken away. Later, No came into the compound and gave him the full measure of his mind. Incensed at this, the magistrate shouted, "How dare you speak to your magistrate so?"

He had him reported to the Governor so that finally he was imprisoned in Andong.

Mansŏk the slave went to Seoul and when the King was out on a progress he struck the great bell and got a hearing.

The King inquired as to it and gave orders that the Governor of Kyŏngsang take note and see. But Chosul bribed this one and that, and so insured himself against any condemnation. He spread another report saying that Pak-ssi did not die by the knife but by poison that she took to hide the fact that she was with child. He found one old woman who said she had bought and one man who said he had sold it – all bribed, every one of them.

The matter hung fire for four years, during which time Pak-ssi's body was kept in No's house in an uncovered coffin. "After I have had vengeance I'll see her buried," said he.

Even after four years the body remained wholly unchanged – her face was fresh and fair as when alive. No odour was noticeable in the room and flies and insects avoided it altogether.

At this time the magistrate of Ponghwa was a man named Pak Siwŏn, a 6th cousin of Pak-ssi. He decided to look the matter up, and so had the cover of the coffin put aside till he could see the victim's face.

Mansŏk, being married as he was, had fallen under Kim's jurisdiction. A son and daughter were born to him but in view of all the terrible experiences that his mistress had been through, he cast these off saying, "Your master killed my mistress – you are my enemies. Though the relation of husband and wife is important, the claims of No come first. Go to your master; I shall die with my mistress, and vengeance I shall have, or die."

So saying, he went again to Seoul.

At this time Kim Sanghyu was Governor of Kyŏngsang. Mansŏk again struck the bell and the King took note and ordered a second investigation.

Carrying the coffin on his back, No brought it into the presence of the Governor. Suddenly there was a sound heard from the inside of the coffin, as of silk being torn. When No's servant took off the lid to see what it was, the Governor sent his servant to look as well, when lo, the face was the face of a living person, the cheeks red still and under her chin the mark of the knife. Her body was slim and comely in shape. Her flesh was as hard as stone with no sign of death or falling to decay.

The man who sold the medicine and the old woman who gave evidence were arrested and cross-questioned, whereupon they told that Chosul had given them each two hundred *yang* as a bribe and told them what to say.

The Governor made his report to the King, whereupon Chosul was arrested and punished, while Pak-ssi was recorded by the state as one of Korea's faithful women.

榮川 1) 儒生盧某有一子　過婚未幾而身死　其孀婦

朴氏　執喪以禮　孝奉舅姑　隣里稱之　來時率童

僕一人　而名則萬石者　盧家素貧寒　朴氏躬自

紡績　使奴樵汲　朝夕之供　未嘗闕焉　隣居金

祖述 2) 者　亦有班名　家計亦累萬金富者也

從籬隙見朴氏之妍美　心欲之矣　一日盧生欲

出他　借着揮項 3) 於祖述之家　祖述乘其不在家

使人探知朴氏之寢房　帶月着驄冠 4) 而入其家

時朴氏　獨在其寢房　房與其姑之房　隔壁而間

유소호의　박씨수각　문창외리성　우견월하인영
有小戶矣　朴氏睡覺　聞窗外履聲　又見月下人影

심절괴의　기이입고지방　기고괴이문지　밀어
心切怪疑　起而入姑之房　其姑怪而問之　密語

기유　고부상대이좌　시만석자　위조술지비부 5)
其由　姑婦相對而坐　時萬石者　爲祖述之婢夫 5)

숙어기가　적무일인　이홀어호외　유인려성왈
宿於其家　寂無一人　而忽於戶外　有人厲聲曰:

박과부여오유사　역이구의　사속출송운운
朴寡婦與吾有私　亦已久矣　斯速出送云云

기고려성　호동인이위왈　유적인래운　린가지인
其姑厲聲　呼洞人而謂曰:有賊人來云　隣家之人

거화이래　조술잉환귀기가　박씨고부　지위
擧火而來　祖述仍還歸其家　朴氏姑婦　知爲

조술야　로생귀래　문기어　이분불자승　욕정우관
祖述也　盧生歸來　聞其語　而忿不自勝 6)　欲呈于官

이공치소문지지호　잉고인지　기후조술
而恐致所聞之之好　仍姑忍之　其後祖述

우양언　우동중왈　박씨여오상통　잉이사오삭운운
又揚言 7) 于洞中曰:朴氏與吾相通　孕已四五朔云云

전설자자　박씨문지왈　금즉가이정관이설치의
傳說藉藉　朴氏問之曰:今則可以呈官而雪恥矣

이상엄면이입관정　명언조술지죄악　우언자가수
以裳掩面而入官庭　明言祖述之罪惡　又言自家受

무지상　시조술행화어관속　차일관속　구시조
誣之狀 8)　時祖述行貨於官屬 9)　且一官屬　俱是祖

술지노속야　형리배개언　차녀자래행음　소문지출
述之奴屬也　刑吏輩皆言　此女自來行淫　所聞之出

亦已久矣云　本倅尹彝鉉 10)　信聽官屬之言　以爲

汝若有貞節　則雖被人誣　久則自脫　何乃親入官

庭而自明乎　朴氏曰：自官卞白 11)　而不嚴處金

哥之罪　則妾當自刎 12) 於此庭下矣　仍拔所佩

小刀　而辭氣 13) 慷慨　本倅怒而叱曰：汝欲以此

而恐動 14) 乎　汝若欲死　則以大刀　自刎於汝

家可也　何乃以小刀爲也　斯速出去　仍使官婢推背

逐出官門之外　朴氏出門　放聲大哭　以其小刀

刎其頸而死　見者無不錯愕 15)　本倅乃驚動　使運

屍而去　盧生不勝其忿　入庭而語多侵逼 16)

本倅以土民 17) 之肆惡 18) 官庭　侵逼土主 19)　報營

盧生移囚於安東府矣　其奴萬石者　上京鳴金 20)

于駕前　有下該道查啓之判付 21)　行查則祖述以累

千金　行賂於洞人及營邑之下屬　至朴氏之死　則非

自刎而羞愧孕胎之說　服藥致死云　而貿藥之嫗

賣藥之商　皆立證　此亦祖述給賂於老嫗及商人而

然也　獄久不決　拖至四年之久　盧家以朴氏之屍

不斂而入棺　不覆盖曰：復此讐後　可改斂而葬

置越房者四年　而身體少無傷敗　面如生時　入其門

少無穢惡之臭 22)　而蠅蚋 23) 不敢近　亦可異矣

奉化 24) 倅朴始 [時] 源 25) 卽其再從 26) 甥妹也　往哭

其靈筵 27) 云故　余於逢場 28) 問之　則以爲啓棺

而而 [而] 見之　與生時無異云矣　萬石爲金哥

之婢夫　生一男一女矣　當此時　逐其妻而訣曰：

汝主殺吾主　卽讐家也　夫婦之義雖重　奴主之

分不輕　汝自還歸汝主　吾則爲吾主而死也云

而奔走京鄉　必欲復讐乃已　及金判書相休 29)

之按節時　萬石上京鳴金　啓下本道　更定查官而

^{궁 핵} 窮覈 30)　　^{로 가 담 래 박 씨 지 구 어 사 정} 盧家擔來朴氏之柩於查庭　　^{즉 중 유 렬 백} 則中有裂帛

^{지 성} 之聲 31)　　^{로 가 인 거 관 개} 盧家人去棺盖　　^{이 욕 시 지} 而欲示之　　^{사 관 사 관 비 험 시} 查官使官婢驗視

^{즉 면 색 여 생} 則面色如生　　^{량 협 유 홍 훈} 兩頰有紅暈　　^{경 하 상 유 검 자 지 혈 흔} 頸下尙有劍刺之血痕

^{복 첩 우 배} 腹帖于背　　^{이 기 부} 而肌膚 32)　^{견 여 석} 堅如石　　^{소 무 부 상} 少無腐傷　　^{약 물 매 매} 藥物賣買

^{지 상 인 급 로 구} 之商人及老嫗　　^{엄 국 문 지} 嚴鞫問之　　^{즉 시 토 실 왈} 則始吐實曰：　^{조 술 각} 祖述各

^{급 이 백 량 전} 給二百兩錢　　^{이 여 시 위 언 운} 而如是爲言云　　^{자 영 문} 自營門　　^{이 차 상 문} 以此狀聞

^{조 술 시 복 법} 祖述始伏法 33)　　^{박 씨 정 려} 朴氏旌閭 34)　　^{만 석 급 복} 萬石給復 35)　^운 云

1　榮川: a town in North Kyŏngsang Province; present-day Yŏngju 榮州.
2　金祖述: unidentified.
3　揮項 = *hwiyang*: a winter hat, similar to the Russian *ushanka*.
4　驄冠: cap (K. *kat*) made of horsehair.
5　婢夫: husband of a slave girl.
6　忿不自勝: lit. "cannot overcome indignation."
7　揚言: spread stories.
8　受誣之狀: lit. "situation where one is accused falsely."
9　官屬: secretary or servant attached to a local magistrate.
10　尹彛鉉: unidentified.
11　卞白 = *pyŏnbaek* 辨白: refute point by point.
12　自刎 = *chagyŏl* 自決: commit suicide by slitting one's throat.
13　辭氣: manner of talking.
14　恐動: threaten, blackmail.
15　錯愕: be surprised.
16　侵逼: exceed one's authority and encroach upon another's.
17　土民: the locals.
18　肆惡: make a scene; rant and rave.
19　土主: local magistrate.
20　鳴金: sound the gong.

21 判付 = *p'anha* 判下: grant royal sanction to a petition or report.

22 穢惡之臭: lit. "foul and repulsive smell."

23 蠅蚋: flies and gnats.

24 奉化: a town in North Kyŏngsang.

25 朴時源 [1764–1842; styled Ch'isil 穉實; sobriquet Ilp'o 逸圃; ancestral seat Pannam 潘南]: scholar-official under King Hŏnjong 憲宗 [r. 1834–49; 1827–49] from Yŏngju 榮州. His father was Pak Sap'yo 朴師豹 [dates unknown]. The *Kimun ch'onghwa* records his given name as "始源"; we have corrected this to 時源 in light of the forty-second entry ("A slave bangs a gong to wash away a false accusation": *Ch'angdu myŏngjaeng sŏl muwŏn* 蒼頭鳴錚雪誣冤) of the Karam edition of the *Tongya hwijip* (Assortment of *Yadam* of the East) held at Seoul National University.

26 再從: second cousin.

27 靈筵 = *yŏngjwa* 靈坐 ~ *pinso* 殯所: mortuary.

28 逢場: impromptu.

29 金相休 [?–1827; styled Kyeyong 季容; sobriquet Ch'och'ŏn 蕉泉; ancestral seat Kwangju 廣州]: scholar-official under King Sunjo 純祖 [r. 1800–34; 1790–1834]. He served as the governor of Kyŏngsang Province in 1822. His father was Kim Mut'aek 金茂澤 [dates unknown].

30 窮覈: investigate and uncover in detail.

31 裂帛之聲: lit. "sound of tearing silk."

32 肌膚 = *p'ibu* 皮膚: skin; flesh.

33 伏法 = *pokchu* 伏誅: be executed according to the law.

34 旌閭: commemorate loyal subjects, filial children, and chaste wives by erecting a gate of honour.

35 給復: exemption from corvée labour for loyal subjects and filial children.

Note by Professor Donguk Kim

In the Karam edition of the *Tongya hwijip* 東野彙輯 [Assortment of *Yadam* of the East] held by Seoul National University and in the Kyujanggak Library edition of the *Ch'ŏnggu yadam* 青丘野談 [*Yadam* of the Green Hills] (Volume 11, Entry 11; "Petitioning in front of the royal palanquin on the road, a royal servant makes his resentment heard": *So yŏllo ch'ungbok myŏngwŏn* 訴輦路忠僕鳴寃), the scholar No appearing in the story above is referred to as Min Pongjo 閔鳳朝.

The *Sunjo sillok* 純祖實錄 (Veritable Records of King Sunjo) recounts the actual event as follows:

[The king ordered that] a gate of honor be erected for Chaste Wife Pak-ssi. Pak-ssi was a widow of a *yangban* family. Falsely slandered by Kim Chosul of the same town, she slit her throat and demonstrated her innocence. Wicked elements stirred up trouble. The litigation dragged on for three years without resolution. Struck with sadness, her slave Mansŏk repeatedly implored, and at last she was acquitted. [The King] ordered the Ministry of Rites to report to the throne to finalize the matter. Mansŏk was recognized as "a loyal slave": during his lifetime, he was exempted from corvée labour and after death, a gate of honor was erected in his memory.

— Sukchong 22 (1582), 11th month, *siyu* 辛酉

명 렬 녀 박 씨 정 려　　박 씨 이 사 족 상 부　　위 본 군 인 김 조 술
命烈女朴氏旌閭　朴氏以士族孀婦　爲本郡人金祖述

소 무 핍　　자 재 결 실　　이 흉 도 번 란　　옥 정 삼 년　　미 득 결
所誣逼　自裁潔身　而凶徒翻亂　獄情三年　未得決

기 노 만 석　　음 읍 루 약　　시 득 폭 백　　령 례 조 품 처
其奴萬石　飲泣屢籥　始得暴白　令禮曹稟處

만 석 이 충 노　　생 전 급 복　　사 후 정 려
萬石以忠奴　生前給復　死後旌閭

———— **65** ————

The Dancing Girl's Two Guests

Vol. II: 38; n.d.; Diary XII, pp. 190–3 (with the title "A Dancing Girl"); 236.

There was a dancing girl in P'yŏngyang who was very pretty of face and highly skilled in the song and dance. From her youngest days her name was far famed.

She said to herself, "I have known many men but only two whom I never forget. One was so handsome that I can never forget him, while the other was so hateful and dirty that I can never forget him, either."

Someone asked how this was so and she replied: "When I was young I waited on the governor. We had a great celebration at the Yŏn'gwang Pavilion. At evening time when I was leaning over the railing, looking out at the long stretch of willows, I saw a handsome young lad come riding on a donkey as though he flew along with wings by the river bank.

"He called for a boat and came swiftly across and came in by the East Gate. The closer he came the more beautiful he was, his face and form truly were of the fairies.

"On seeing him I was so drunk and I started out and said I was going to the water closet. I watched where he went and saw him enter the inn just inside the East Gate. I made careful note of this and waited till the feast was over and then I dressed as an ordinary woman of the town and at night went to the inn aforementioned. I peeked in through the window and there was that beautiful boy, looking like an angel sitting before the lamp reading a book.

"I thought to myself, 'If I don't capture this pretty boy and sleep with him, I shall carry regrets that will keep my eyes open even after death.'

"So I coughed outside the sliding window.

"The young man asked, 'Who are you?'

"I replied, 'I am the daughter-in-law of the inn-master.'

"He again asked, 'Why have you come here in the dark?'

"I replied, 'There are so many guests come that I have no place to sleep and am forced to ask if I may have the upper end of the room.'

"He replied, 'Why yes, come in.'

"I then came in and took my place in the shady part of the room; the young man did not pay any attention to me but sat in his most dignified way and read his book.

"When it grew late, he put out the light and turned in to sleep.

"I then pretended to be ill and moaned in pain.

"The young man asked, 'Why do you moan? Are you ill?'

"I replied, 'I am subject to attacks of this kind and have pain; the room is cold here where I am lying and that has caused it.'

"The young man said, 'If that is so come here behind me where it is warm, and sleep.'

"I went and lay down behind him, and though I was there for ever so long, he made no move to touch me.

"At last I said, 'I do not know Your Excellency, but I am wondering if you may not be a eunuch.'

"The young man replied, 'Eunuch? What do you mean by eunuch?'

"I made reply, 'I am not really the daughter-in-law of the inn-master but am an official dancing girl. Today I saw your handsome form as you came and loved you so that I came to have a sight of your face. I am not an ugly person myself in face, and you are not yet old in years, but young. So here we are – we are all alone by ourselves and yet you do not in the least turn toward me and so I ask: if you are not a eunuch, what are you?'

"The young man laughed and replied, 'You are a dancing girl, are you? Why did you not tell me from the first that you were so! I thought you were the master's daughter. Since that is so, undress and let us sleep together.'

"So we slept and I found he was a lad who knew all about dancing girls. We had our fill of love and, when morning came, arose. He put his baggage in order and as he made ready to go, he said to me, 'We met all unexpectedly and have for one night fulfilled our destiny together and now we have to part. We have no definite time set to meet again. What shall we say on such a parting as this? I have nothing else to give to show my love for you but just a verse that I shall write for you on your dress skirt. Spread it out for me.' And then he wrote:

> The moving stream comes like a guest goes,
>   The mountain like the maid must watch it go.
> The cold night watch beneath the curtain walls,
>   Hears rain that falls and leaves that patter near.

"He wrote this verse, dropped his pen and was gone.

"I took him by the sleeve and holding him, asked his name. But he laughed and said, 'I am a lover of the hill and stream who harries everywhere. My name has nothing to do with it.' and so he left.

"Again when I was attached to the governor, on a certain day, the soldier who kept the gate came in to tell the governor that a *tongji** who had charge of his farm near Seoul had arrived and desired to see him.

"'Show him in,' said the governor.

"When he came in I saw him, a great hulk of a fellow, from some wild country place. He wore rough clothes and string shoes and had a faded red girdle about his waist, with gold buttons behind his ears that looked like dirty brass. His eyes and eyebrows were fearful to behold, his face too ugly for words, and his head like some constable of hell.

"Before he had made his bows, the governor asked, 'How comes it that you have made this long journey?'

"He replied, 'I have not come for anything to eat or wear as I have enough of these things. But I have always longed to flavour one of the famous P'yŏngyang dancing girls. That's why I've come.'

"The governor laughed and said, 'If that is your wish, look them over and take your choice.'

"Hearing that response, he came straight in to where we were. The girls all ran as for their lives while he chased after us and, catching one, he looked at her and said, 'Ugly' and let her go. He caught another and said, 'You're too fat,' and let her go. Then he caught me and said, 'This one will do alright.' He took me off into a corner and then and there outraged me. I had not strength enough to resist him. I wanted to die but could not and so I just had to yield.

"A little later when I got rid of him, I went home and had a hot bath over and over but the disgust that overcame me lasted for days so that I could not eat. So horrible was he that I have never forgotten him to this day."

* See note 16 below.

平壤有一妓　姿質歌舞　少時擅名 1)　自言　閱人多矣

有未忘二人　一則妍美而不能忘　一則醜惡而

不能忘也　人或問其故　對曰：少年時　侍巡使道 2)

宴于練光亭 3)　夕陽時依欄而望長林　則有一少年

佳郎騎驢　飛也似馳　到江邊　呼船而渡　入大同門 4)

風儀動盪 5)　望之如神仙中人　心神如醉　托以如厠

下樓而審其處　則卽大同門內店舍也　詳知而

待宴罷　改粧村婦服飾　乘夕而往其家　從窓隙

窺見　則如玉美少年　看書于燭下　自念如此佳郎

如不得薦枕 6)　則死不瞑目 7)　仍咳嗽 8) 於窓外

其少年問爲誰　答曰：主家婦也　又問何爲昏夜到此

答曰：弊舍商賈 9) 多入　無寄宿處故　欲借上堗 10)

一席而寢矣　曰：然則入來可也　渠仍開門而入

坐於燭火之背　則少年目不斜視　端坐看書　更深後

乃滅燭而臥　渠作呻吟之聲　少年問何爲有痛聲

對曰：曾有胸腹痛矣　今因房堗冷　宿疾復發矣

其人曰：若然則來臥於我之背後溫處　渠仍臥

于背後　食頃而又不顧　渠仍言曰：行次 11) 不知

何許人　而無乃宦侍 12) 乎　其人曰：何謂也　渠曰：

妾非主人婦　而乃是官妓也　今日練光亭上

瞻此行次之風儀　心甚艷慕　作此樣來此

冀其一面矣　妾之姿質　不至醜惡　行次年紀

不至衰老　靜夜無人之時　男女混處　而一不顧眄

非宦而何　其人笑曰：汝是官物乎　然則何不早言

吾則認以主人之婦而然矣　汝可解衣同寢可也

仍與之狎　其風流興味卽一花柳場蕩男子也

兩情歡洽　及曉而起　促裝將發　對渠而言曰：

意外相逢　倖結一宵之緣 13)　遽爾相分　後會難期

別懷何言　行中別無他可情表之物　可留一詩

仍使渠擧裳幅而書之曰：

水如遠客流無住　山似佳人送有情

銀燭五更羅幌 14) 冷　滿林風雨作秋聲

書畢仍投筆而去　渠仍把袖而泣問居住姓名

則笑而不答曰：吾自放浪於山水樓臺之人也

居住姓名不必問　仍飄然而去　渠仍還家後

欲忘而不可忘　每抱裳詩而泣　此姸慕而難忘者也

嘗以巡使道守廳妓侍立矣　一日　門卒來告

모 처 사 음　　　모 동 지　　　래 알 차　　　재 문 외 의　　　순 사 사
某處舍音 15) 某同知 16) 來謁次　在門外矣　巡使使

지 입 래 즉　　　견 일 반 대 촌 한　　　포 의 초 혜　　　요 대 반 투
之入來卽　見一胖大村漢 17)　布衣草鞋　腰帶半渝 18)

지 홍 대　　　로　　　현 금 관　　　이 순 시 동 색　　　미 목 녕 한
之紅帶　顱 19)　懸金圈 20)　而純是銅色　眉目獰悍 21)

용 모 추 악　　　즉 일 천 봉 장 군　　　래 배 지 전　　　순 사 문
容貌醜惡　卽一天蓬將軍 22)　來拜之前　巡使問

여 하 위 이 원 래 야　　　대 왈　　　소 인 의 자　　　불 구　　　별 무
汝何爲而遠來也　對曰：小人衣資 23)　不苟 24)　別無

소 망 어 사 도 야　　　평 생 소 원　　　욕 득 일 개 가 기 이
所望於使道也　平生所願　欲得一箇佳妓而

창 정　　　위 시 이 불 원 천 리 이 래 야　　　순 사 소 왈　　　여 약
暢情 25)　爲是而不遠千里而來也　巡使笑曰：汝若

유 차 심　　　즉 가 어 차　　　택 일 흡 의 기 야　　　궐 한 문 명　　　직 입
有此心　則可於此　擇一洽意妓也　厥漢聞命　直入

수 청 방　　　제 기 개 미　　　궐 한 추 후 축 지　　　착 일 이 모 불 미
守廳房　諸妓皆靡 26)　厥漢追後逐之　捉一而貌不美

우 착 일 이 운　　　신 풍 불 합　　　급 도 거　　　착 이 견 지 즉 왈
又捉一而云　身豊不合　及到渠　捉而見之則曰：

족 가 용　　　잉 포 지 장 우 이 강 간 지　　　거 어 차 시　　　이 력
足可用　仍抱至墙隅而强奸之　渠於此時　以力

약 지 고　　　불 득 적 타 구 사　　　불 득 이 임 기 소 위　　　소 언
弱之故　不得適他求死　不得而任其所爲　少焉

탈 신 이 귀 가　　　이 온 수 욕 신　　　이 비 위 막 정　　　수 일 불 능 식
脫身而歸家　以溫水浴身　而脾胃莫定　數日不能食

차 시 추 악 이 난 망 자 운 이
此是醜惡而難忘者云爾

1 擅名: win a name for oneself.
2 巡使道 = *kamsa* 監司 ~ *kwanch'alsa* 觀察使: another name for a provincial governor.
3 練光亭: a famous pavilion by the Taedong River 大洞江 in P'yŏngyang.
4 大同門: a famous gate located on the eastern side of P'yŏngyang.
5 風儀動盪: possess a well-built physique and a beautifully plump face.
6 薦枕: lit. "recommend one's pillow" = render one's services to someone in bed.
7 死不瞑目: lit. "[already] dead, [yet] unable to shut ones' eyes" = unable to die in peace.
8 咳嗽: cough.
9 商賈 = *sangin* 商人: merchant, trader.
10 上埃: the end of a room closest to the heat source.
11 行次: (honorific) going and coming of a person, or the person himself.
12 宦侍 = *hwan'gwan* 宦官 ~ *naesi* 內侍: eunuch.
13 一宵之緣: karmic bond formed through a one-night stand.
14 羅幌: silk curtain, silk hanging screen.
15 舍音: (*idu* term) *marŭm*; native Korean word for a superintendent overseeing sharecroppers.
16 同知: originally a junior second-grade post attached to the Office of Ministers-without-Portfolio (Tongji chungch'u pusa 同知中樞府事). Later, a generic form of address for untitled and unranked elderly men.
17 一胖大村漢: a big fat country bumpkin.
18 半渝: half-faded.
19 顱: head; crown of the head.
20 金圈 = *kŭmgwanja* 金貫子: gold buttons on a headdress.
21 眉目獰悍: lit. "eyebrows and eyes are fierce and vicious" = a ferocious look.
22 天蓬將軍: ugly demon.
23 衣資: lit. "clothing materials or the cost thereof" = livelihood.
24 不苟: not wretched.
25 暢情 = *t'ongjŏng* 通情: share intimacy with.
26 靡: swarm around and fall over.

————— **66** —————

A Wonderful Dream

Vol. II: 40; n.d.: Diary XIV, pp. 52–3; 238.

As a boy, Kim Ŭngsun, who was vice president of a Board, had a dream in which he saw the South Gate of Heaven open and heard a voice call, "Kim Ŭngsun-*a*,* take this that I give you."

Kim stepped down into the court and there he saw a black lacquered box descend. He looked at it and saw written on the top *mu-ch'ŏm i-jo* (Honour Your Ancestors). He opened the box and inside he found a book wrapped in a silk wrapper. He unwrapped it and there was his life with all its happenings written out – all its joys as well as its sorrows and at the end his death was marked for such a year, such a month, such a day, and such an hour. His highest rank was given as Minister of Ceremony.

Kim awoke and wondered greatly. At once he lit his lamp and wrote out all that he remembered and later on he found all came perfectly true.

When the day appointed for his death had come, he dressed in his ceremonial robes, made his bow before his ancestral tablets and then called his children and friends and spoke his farewell words to each: "I am to die at such-and-such time today and yet I have never attained to the rank of Minister of Ceremony which gives me occasion to question."

He was then but Vice-Minister.

When the time came he lay down and breathed his last and the word came to King Yŏngjong (1725–76),[†] who said, "I intended to appoint Kim to the Ministry of Ceremony but neglected to do so. Have this title put on the label that marks his coffin."

A very strange happening.

When he was a secretary of a Board (*sŭngji*), Kim Yŏngjong wrote with his own hand, "You are a descendant of Sŏnwŏn – Honour Your Ancestors (*mu-ch'ŏm i-jo*)."

This was the message that was written on the box that came down from heaven.

---

* "-*a*": vocative particle used to summon or address close friends and intimates.

† Here and below Gale renders Yŏngjo as Yŏngjong. Gale's reign dates are off, and should be 1724–76.

金叅判應淳 1) 少時得一夢 夢中南天門開 而叩聲

呼名曰：金某受此 金台 2) 乃下堂 而立於庭

則自天下一漆函 受而見之 則上以金字 大書以

無添爾祖 開而見之 則中有錦袱之裏冊者 [子]

披而見之 則卽自家平生推數 3) 也 一生休咎 4)

皆書日時 末云 某(年)月日時死 而位至禮判云云

金台覺而異之 仍擧火而逐年錄之于冊子矣 無不

符合 至將死之日 整衣冠 辭家廟 會子姪知舊

面面告訣曰：今日某時 吾將棄世 而禮判尚不得爲

亦可異也云 盖此時 位尙叅判矣 迨 5) 其時 仍臥而

奄忽 6) 訃聞 英廟嗟歎曰：吾欲除禮判 而未果者也

銘旌可書以禮判爲敎 事亦異矣 嘗以承旨入侍

英廟以御筆 書以仙源 7) 之孫 無忝爾祖八字賜之

亦符于夢中之書

1 金應淳 [1728–74; styled Hoewŏn 會元; ancestral seat Andong 安東]: scholar-official under King Yŏngjo [r. 1724–76; 1694–1776]. He was posthumously honoured as senior second-grade Minister of Rites (Yejo *p'ansŏ* 禮曹判書). His ancestor was Kim Sangyong 金尚容 [1561–1637]. See note 7 below.

2 台: a generic term of address for officials holding junior second-grade posts and above.

3 推數: prognosticate.

4 休咎: good and ill omen.

5 迨: reach (a place/state).

6 奄忽: suddenly.

7 仙源: sobriquet of Kim Sangyong 金尚容 [1561–1637; styled Kyŏngt'aek 景擇; ancestral seat Andong 安東; posthumous epithet Munch'ung 文忠]: scholar-official under King Injo [r. 1623–49; 1595–1649]. Kim Sangyong committed suicide when Kanghwa Castle fell to the Manchus during the second Manchu invasion, in the *pyŏngja* year [1636; Pyŏngja horan 丙子胡亂].

—— **67** ——

Hong Sanghan

Vol. II: 40; n.d.; Diary XII, pp. 59–61; 239.

Minister Hong had reached eighty years of age, when his grandson Ŭimo in the winter of *kyemi** matriculated with great success. In his joy, Hong had music and dancing that lasted for days. The crowds that came to see were each given a bowl of soup and a stick of broiled fish. For a month and more, this kept up.

Hong's son, minister Naksŏng, was at that time a Vice-President of a Board. He was a most reserved and silent man, correct in all his ways. He disliked display of any sort and was disturbed by this feasting and yet there was no way by which he could suggest to his father its discontinuance. He thought of his relatives as to whether there was any who might use his influence on this behalf.

Now there was a man, greatly gifted, named Kim Isin – a cousin of his mother – whom he asked to urge on his father that this cease.

Having consented, Kim *kong*† called in minister Hong and congratulated him on his great and unexampled prosperity and then at the end added a warning against too great a display, lest misfortune follow.

Minister Hong looked at him, laughed and said, "When you came, did you have to do with my son on the way? I am a man of no ability and no virtue but the fortune of the sages has come my way. I have risen to the highest rank there is, and my age is eighty and over. I have seen my son's son graduate – and because I am so glad the people of the world point at me and say, 'Minister Hong of Kongdong has seen his grandson graduate and has gone clean crazy.' Take note of this. After I am dead this fine house of mine will gather thick with dust while our official son will sit fixed and dead as the Buddha. What kind of house do you call that? No dictating to me, please."

So he called the singing girls and had them sing.

Ashamed of his attempt, Kim *kong* sat in silence.

Minister Hong said again, "In today's hazing of the new graduate, the graduates have shown not the first sign of originality. It proves that the world is on the decline. I regret this very much."

Hearing this, Kim *kong* said farewell and took his departure and on the way met minister Kim Ŭngsun. He was at that time Keeper of the Seal‡ and also Chief of the Military Bureau so that great crowds attended him. Seeing Kim, he descended from his horse.

Kim *kong* asked, "Where are you going?"

Kim Ŭngsun replied, "I am on my way to see Minister Hong of Kongdong."

Kim *kong* (Isin) said, "I saw my uncle Hong just now and he said so-and-so about the world today. I wish you would wait here for a little and have the graduate called and the singing girls as well."

Kim Ŭngsun said, "Good. Let it be done." He had his horse wait at Kwangt'ong Bridge and sent a servant to call the new graduate.

Minister Hong asked, "Who calls him?"

The servant replied, "The Royal Preceptor, Kim Ŭngsun."

"Where is he now?" asked the old man.

"He is by the Kwangt'ong Bridge," was the reply.

The old man then said, "He's a fine lad, he."

Again a servant came to ask that singing girls be sent as well.

On hearing this, Minister Hong arose and announced, "Ah-ha, he's a wonderful boy, that lad."

With a staff in hand, he followed out after the procession and stood in the street.

Kim Isin rode out also with the graduate on the same horse, [the graduate's] face marked with ink.

Kim Ŭngsun, seeing the old man standing in the street, descended from his horse and inquired, "How is Your Excellency?"

274   Hong Sanghan

The old man patted him on the back, saying, "I thought all the people in the world were dead and putrid, but I find you live, a live man, living among all these dead."

* *kyemi*: the year 1769.
† *kong* is: a form of address for holders of high-ranking official posts.
‡ "Keeper of the Seal" is Gale's mistranslation of "玉堂" (*oktang*), another name for the Office of the Special Counselors (Hongmungwan 弘文館).

홍 판 서 상 한　　　　년 팔 십　　　기 손 의 모　　　　등 계 미
洪判書象漢 1)　　年八十　　其孫義謨 2)　　登癸未 3)

동 증 광 사 마　　　홍 판 서　　매 일 장 락　　이 만 정 관 광 자
冬增廣司馬 4)　　洪判書　　每日張樂　　而滿庭觀光者

매 인 궤 일 기 탕　　병 일 관 륙 적　　매 매 여 시　　태 근 일 삭
每人饋一器湯　　餠一串肉炙 5)　　每每如是　　殆近一朔

기 백 윤 상 공 락 성　　시 이 아 경　　재 가　　이 위 인 근 졸
其伯胤相公樂性 6)　　時以亞卿 7)　在家　　而爲人謹拙 8)

매 이 성 만 질 　질 　탕 　위 우　　이 무 계 간 지　　구 일 친
每以盛滿迭 [跌] 宕 9)　爲憂　　而無計諫止　　求一親

척 중 기 망 인　　욕 간 지　　김 도 정　　리 신　　다 재 선 변
戚中期望人 10)　欲諫之　金都正 11)　履信 12)　多才善辯

이 이 성 륙 촌 간 야　　홍 상 청 래　　이 도 기 사　　요 사 간 지
而異姓六寸間也　　洪相請來　　而道其事　　要使諫止

김 공 견 홍 판 서　　선 찬 기 복 력　　이 말 내 이 성 만 위 계
金公見洪判書　　先讚其福力　　而末乃以盛滿爲戒

홍 판 서　　문 이 미 소 왈　　여 래 시　　견 아 자 호　　오 이 무
洪判書　　聞而微笑曰 : 汝來時　　見兒子乎　　吾以無

재 무 덕 지 인　　조 우 성 세　　위 제 숭 품　　년 유 팔 순 의
才無德之人　　遭遇盛世　　位躋崇品 13)　　年踰八旬矣

우 견 손 아 지 등 과　　여 시 행 락　　세 인 개 목 지 왈　　공
又見孫兒之登科　　如是行樂　　世人皆目之曰 : 公

洞 14) 某位一品　年八十　見孫兒科慶　而發狂云爾

則庸何傷乎　汝第見之　吾死之後　清風堂 15) 上

塵埃堆積 16)　叅判塊坐 17)　於一處　其象如何　汝之言

不願聞也　仍妓而進歌曲　金公無聊而坐　洪判書

又言曰：近日少年輩　呼新來 18)　而無一人有風度

可謂衰世 19) 矣　豈不慨惜也云云　金公辭歸之路

逢金判書應淳 20) 於路　時以玉堂 21)　兼軍門從事

多率帶隸　而見金公　下馬于路左　金公問何往

金台答曰：欲往見金公洞洪進士矣　金公乃言曰：

洪叔之言　如此如此　君須立馬於此　而呼新恩 22)

又使出妓樂而前導也　金公曰：好矣　仍立馬

廣通橋 23)　送隸呼新恩　洪判書問誰也　曰：

壯洞 24) 金應敎 25) 也　問在何處　曰：方在某橋上矣

洪判書擊節 26) 曰：此兒甚奇矣　已而一隸又來

전 기 락 지 출 송　　홍 판 서 문 이 기 왈　　차 아 우 가 기 의
傳妓樂之出送　洪判書聞而起曰：此兒尤可奇矣

잉 부 장 이 수 출 동 구 외　　립 어 가 상　　김 태 사 신 은　　동 기
仍扶杖而隨出洞口外　立於街上　金台使新恩　同騎

일 마　　묵 말 기 면　　이 전 도 이 행　　견 홍 판 서 지 립 어 로 상
一馬　墨沫其面　而前導以行　見洪判書之立於路上

하 마 문 후　　즉 파 수 무 기 배 왈　　금 세 지 인　　개 사 시 의
下馬問候　則把手撫其背曰：今世之人　皆死屍矣

여 독 생 의　　문 자 절 도
汝獨生矣　聞者絕倒

1　洪象漢 [1701–69; styled Unjang 雲章; ancestral seat P'ungsan 豊山; post-humous epithet Chŏnghye 靖惠]: scholar-official under King Yŏngjo 英祖 [r. 1724–76; 1694–1776]. Posthumously honoured as Prime Minister (yŏngŭijŏng 領議政). His father was Hong Sŏkpo 洪錫輔 [1672–1729].

2　洪義謨 [1743–1811; styled Ijung 而中; sobriquet Haudang 何愚堂, Kŭmsihŏn 今是軒; ancestral seat P'ungsan 豊山; posthumous epithet Hyohŏn 孝獻]: scholar-official under King Sunjo 純祖 [r. 1800–34; 1790–1834]. His father was Hong Naksŏng 洪樂性 [1718–98].

3　癸未: the year 1763 (Yŏngjo 39).

4　增廣司馬: supplementary examination given infrequently on certain felici-tous occasions to select classical and literary licentiates (saengwŏn 生員 and chinsa 進士, respectively).

5　一串肉炙: pieces of meat on a skewer.

6　洪樂性 [1718–98; styled Chaan 子安; sobriquet Hangjae 恒齋; ancestral seat P'ungsan 豊山; posthumous epithet Hyoan 孝安]: scholar-official under King Chŏngjo 正祖 [r. 1776–1800; 1752–1800]. His father was Hong Sanghan (see note 1).

7　亞卿 = ch'amp'an 參判: second minister.

8　謹拙: punctilious yet maladroit.

9　盛滿趺宕: go on a spree, indulge oneself in merry-making; binge.

10　期望人: a promising person.

11　都正: senior third-grade posts belonging to the Office of Royal Genealogy (Chongch'inbu 宗親府), Office of the Royal Clan (Tonnyŏngbu 敦寧府), and the Bureau of Military Training (Hullyŏnwŏn 訓練院).

12　金履信: unidentified.

13 崇品: a generic term for a junior first-grade official (Chosŏn dynasty).

14 公洞 = So Sogongju-dong 小公主洞: lit. "little princess's neighbourhood" = present-day Sogong-dong in Seoul.

15 淸風堂: name of Hong Sanghan's guesthouse.

16 塵埃堆積: dust and dirt accumulate.

17 塊坐: kneel; crouch.

18 呼新來: lit. "call *sillae*"; *sillae* refers to new civil service examination passers or the occasion itself. "Call *sillae*" indicates a kind of hazing ritual conducted by seniors to congratulate new civil service examination passers. The ceremony involved seniors drawing designs on the *sillae*'s face in ink and ordering him around.

19 衰世 = *malse* 末世: end of the world.

20 金應淳 [1728–74; styled Hoewŏn 會元; ancestral seat Andong 安東]: scholar-official under King Yŏngjo [r. 1724–76; 1694–1776]. A descendant of Kim Sangyong 金尙容 [1561–1637], he was posthumously honored as a Minister of Rites. See Story 66 above.

21 玉堂 = Hongmungwan 弘文館: Office of the Special Counselors.

22 新恩 = *sillae* 新來: see note 18 above.

23 廣通橋: the name of the bridge in what is now Kwanggyo 廣橋 in Seoul.

24 壯洞: a neighbourhood located in present-day Hyoja-dong 孝子洞 and Ch'angsŏng-dong 昌成洞 in Chongno-gu 種路區, Seoul.

25 應敎: senior fourth-grade official belonging to the Office of the Special Counselors (Hongmungwan 弘文館).

26 擊節: slap one's knees in time to a musical beat.

--- **68** ---

Kwak the Magician

Vol. II: 41; n.d.; Diary XIV, pp. 53–6; 240.

Kwak Sahan was a native of Hyŏnp'ung, Kyŏngsang, a descendant of Mangudang (Kwak Chaeu). When he was young he studied for the examination and thus engaged, he met a magician and learned his arts, which included astrology, geomancy, and the law of the *yang* and *yin*. But his home was very poor.

His ancestral burial hills were near his home. Here people trespassed every day, feeding their cattle and cutting wood. He had had no chance to grow pines about the graves as they were destroyed as soon as planted.

One day he walked about his enclosure and planted stakes to indicate the boundary. He set up a notice saying, "There will be unheard of punishment meted out to trespassers here."

He gave warning to people of the village to keep away and not approach the stakes, but all laughed over it.

There was one bold, rough fellow who defiantly went straight to the hill and began to cut wood, when suddenly the heavens began to whirl around him and the earth to revolve like a top. The winds blew and thunder roared; swords and spears suddenly appeared pointing at him, closing every means of escape.

He was frightened out of his wits and fell in a swoon. Hearing of this, his mother came in fear and consternation to Kwak and prayed for his life.

In a great outburst of anger, Kwak said, "I gave explicit orders and this fellow has defiantly run counter to what I said; what occasion have you to come thus and bother me? I have no concern about this."

In tears and agony, the mother wept before him for the space of a meal till Kwak went and brought him out.

From that time on, no one dared venture near.

Kwak's uncle fell ill and the physician said, "If he could have some mountain ginseng he would recover, but not otherwise."

The son came and he sought Kwak, saying, "My father is most seriously ill and I have no means of getting mountain ginseng, but I know that you, cousin, have power to do what I cannot. Could you not get me a few roots that would assuredly save his life?"

Kwak knitted his brows, saying, "This is a very difficult thing to do but since the case looks so serious I shall do my best to help."

So he took his cousin with him and went up the ridge to the rear of his house till they came to a certain place and there was a little knoll under the pines. There was a patch of ginseng growing.

He chose three of the largest and dug them and prepared the requisite potion, saying definitely, "Say nothing about this and on no account think of going yourself to dig more."

The medicine was given and the uncle recovered.

The cousin had taken careful note of the road on his way back and later took occasion when his cousin was away to go secretly and get some more, but it turned out a different place altogether from what they had seen the other day. He was alarmed at this and sighed and later told his cousin all about it.

Sahan laughed saying, "The other day when you and I went together we went to the Chiri Hills (Turyu). How would you expect to find your way there?" said he.

Once when he was in his house he swept out his inner room and said to his wife, "I have some work to see to in this room for three or four days. Don't open the door or look in through the chink but wait till I come out by myself."

So he went in and closed the door behind him.

The people of the house left him as he desired, and a few days later, hearing no sound, his wife grew anxious lest he had died. She looked in through the window when suddenly she saw that the room had changed into a great river. Along the river was a pavilion and in it she saw her husband playing the harp with five or six of the genii sitting about him and fairies dressed in the mists of the morning and cloud-like robes, some blowing pipes, some strumming the strings of their instruments and some dancing.

The wife gave a great start and, filled with wonder, did not dare mention it.

On the appointed day, the husband opened the door and came out and gave his wife a scolding for looking in upon him. "If you do so again," said he, "I'll take myself off and leave you for good."

He had a special friend who came and made request that he might see just once the great generals of the past.

Kwak laughed, saying, "This is not a difficult matter to bring about but I have my doubts as to your strength to bear it."

The friend said, "If I could only see them once I'd really not care whether I died or not."

Kwak laughed again, saying, "Very well – since you put it so, let's do so."

Then Kwak had him put his arms about him from behind and, taking firm hold, said, "Keep your eyes closed now till I tell you to open them and then see what is before you."

He shut his eyes and heard only the sound of wind and thunder. In a little Kwak said, "Open your eyes."

He opened them and suddenly found they were sitting on a giddy mountain peak. Frightened to death and dizzy, the friend asked where they were.

"This is Kaya *san*," said he.

A little later Kwak arranged his dress in an orderly way, burned incense and began beckoning to ☐ persons. A great wind then arose and an army of great generals came down from midair. Generals of the ☐

States – Chin, Han, Tang, Song, all known by name – appeared: men of most commanding appearance and with faces of greatest power, some in armour, some with swords at their sides, all crowded about.

In a spasm of fear, the friend suddenly lost consciousness and fell by the side of Kwak.

Kwak then gave orders that they all go but the friend still remained unconscious for some time and then gradually came to.

Kwak said, "Didn't I tell you? With such strength as you possess to make such a foolish request! You'll be ill over this. I'm very, very sorry. Take hold of my waist again."

And just as they had come they returned home. A little later the man fell ill of nervous fears and died a little later.

Kwak could do all sorts of supernatural things. He lived till he was over eighty and was as strong as a youth of twenty. One day, without any illness, he was translated into the World to Come. He had many friends and it is only a score of years or so since he died.

郭思漢 1) 玄風 2) 人 而忘憂堂 3) 後孫也 少時業科工

嘗遇異人 傳秘術 通天文地理陰陽等書 家甚貧

其親山 4) 在於境內 樵牧日侵 無以禁養 5) 一日

周行山下 挿木而標之曰 : 人或有冒入此標之內

則必有不測之禍云 而戒飭洞人 使勿近一步地

人皆笑之 有一年少頑悍之漢 6) 故往其山下樵探

入其木標之內 則天旋地轉 風雷飛動 劒戟森嚴

無路可出 其人魂迷神昏 仆之于地 其母聞之而急

래　애걸우곽생　곽생로왈　오즉정령계지이불준
來　哀乞于郭生　郭生怒曰：吾卽丁寧戒之而不遵

하래뇌아　아즉불지　기모체읍이애걸　식경후
何來惱我　我則不知　其母涕泣而哀乞　食頃後

궁자왕이휴출　자기후　인막감근　기중부　병중
躬自往而携出　自其後　人莫敢近　其仲父 7) 病重

이의언약득용산삼　즉가료운운　기종제　래간왈
而醫言若得用山蔘　則可療云云　其從弟 8) 來懇曰：

친병극중　이산삼무가득지망　형지포재　제지자야
親病極重　而山蔘無可得之望　兄之抱才　弟知者也

합구수근이치료호　곽생빈미　왈　차시중난지사
盍求數根而致療乎　郭生顰眉 9) 曰：此是重難之事

이병환여차　불가불극력주선　잉여지　상후록
而病患如此　不可不極力周旋　仍與之　上後麓

지일처송음지하　유평원즉일삼전야　택기최대
至一處松陰之下　有平原卽一蔘田也　擇其最大

자삼근이채지　사작약이　이계지왈　차사물
者三根而採之　使作藥餌 10) 而戒之曰：此事勿

출구　차물생갱채지념　기종제급귀전용　이과득
出口　且勿生更採之念　其從弟急歸煎用　而果得

효　래시식기정도　급삼소재처　승기종형지불재
效　來時識其程道　及蔘所在處　乘其從兄之不在

잠왕견지　즉비부향일소견처야　경아차탄이귀
潛往見之　則非復向日所見處也　驚訝嗟歎而歸

대기형　도차상　곽생소왈　향일여여소왕처즉두
對其兄　道此狀　郭生笑曰：向日與汝所往處卽頭

류산　야　여기가갱섭기경야　여시운기　일일재가
流山 11) 也　汝豈可更躡其境耶　如是云其　一日在家

淨掃越房　戒其妻曰：吾在此　將有三四日所幹之

事 12)　切勿開戶　且勿窺見　待限日　吾自出來矣

仍闔戶 13) 而坐　家人依其言置之矣　過數日後

其妻甚訝之　從窓隙窺覵 14)　則房中變成一大江

江上有丹靑之一樓閣　而其夫在其樓上　援琴鼓之

五六鶴氅衣 15) 羽者 16) 對坐　而霞裳霧裙之仙女

或吹彈　或對舞　其妻驚異　不敢出聲　至期日

開戶而出　責其妻之窺見　日後復如是　則吾不可

久留此矣　有切己之窺知人　願一見萬古名將之神

生笑曰：此不難　而但恐君之氣魂 17) 不能抵當

而爲害也　其人曰：若一見之　雖死無恨　生笑曰：

君言既如是　第依我言爲之　其人曰：諾　郭生

使抱自家之腰　而戒之曰：但且闔眼　待吾聲

始開眼可也　其人依其言爲之　兩耳但聞風雷之聲矣

이 이 사 개 안 시 지　즉 좌 어 고 봉 절 정 지 상 의　기 인 창
已而使開眼視之　則坐於高峯絶頂之上矣　其人惝

황　지　즉 내 시 가 야 산　야　소 언　곽 생 정 의 관
怳 18) 之　則乃是伽倻山 19) 也　少焉　郭生整衣冠

분 향 이 좌　약 유 소 지 휘 호 소 자 연　미 기　광 풍 대 작
焚香而坐　若有所指揮呼召者然　未幾　狂風大作

무 수 신 장　종 공 이 하　구 렬 국 진 한 당 송 지 제 명 장 야
無數神將　從空而下　俱列國秦漢唐宋之諸名將也

위 풍 름 름　상 모 당 당　혹 대 갑　혹 장 검　좌 우 라 렬
威風凜凜　狀貌堂堂　或帶甲　或杖劍　左右羅列

기 인 혼 미 신 혼　부 복 어 곽 생 지 측　이 이 곽 생 사 각 퇴 출
其人魂迷神昏　俯伏於郭生之側　已而郭生使各退出

이 기 인 혼 질　의　곽 생 대 기 초 성 이 언 왈　오 기 불 운 호
而其人魂窒 20) 矣　郭生待其稍醒而言曰：吾豈不云乎

군 지 기 혼 여 차　이 망 자 간 아　필 경 득 병　량 가 탄 야
君之氣魂如此　而妄自懇我　畢竟得病　良可歎也

우 사 포 요 여 래 시 양　이 귀 가 의　기 인 득 경 계 증
又使抱腰如來時樣　而歸家矣　其人得驚悸症 21)

불 구 신 사 운　개 다 신 이 지 술 지 견 어 인 자　년 과 팔 십
不久身死云　蓋多神異之術之見於人者　年過八十

강 건 여 년 소 인　일 일 무 병 이 좌 화　운　령 남 지 인
康健如年少人　一日無病而坐化 22) 云　嶺南之人

다 유 친 지 자　이 기 사 불 과 수 십 년 운 의
多有親知者　而其死不過數十年云矣

1　郭思漢: unidentified.
2　玄風: a town in North Kyŏngsang Province.
3　忘憂堂: sobriquet of Kwak Chaeu 郭再祐 [1552–1617; styled Kyesu 季
綏; ancestral seat Hyŏnp'ung 玄風; posthumous epithet Ch'ungik 忠翼]:
general of a righteous army fighting during the Japanese Invasions, served

under King Sŏnjo宣祖 [r. 1567–1608; 1552–1608]. His father was Kwak Wŏl 郭越 [1518–86].

 4 親山: one's parents' graves.
 5 禁養: restricted forest area.
 6 頑悍之漢: ferocious man.
 7 仲父: father's younger brother.
 8 從弟: younger cousin.
 9 嚬眉: furrow one's brow.
10 藥餌: lit. "medicinal food."
11 頭流山: another name for Mount Chiri 智異山.
12 所幹之事: business needing one's attention.
13 闔戶: shut the door.
14 窺覰: peek through at; spy on.
15 鶴氅衣: lit. "crane-feathered clothes." A *ch'angŭi* is a wide-sleeved garment that was part of an official's casual attire.
16 羽者 = *ugaek* 羽客: winged Daoist immortal.
17 氣魂: chutzpah, intrepid spirit, self-confidence.
18 惝怳: hurried, flustered.
19 伽倻山: Mount Kaya, a mountain straddling Sŏngju County 星州郡 and Hapch'ŏn County 陜川郡 in North Kyŏngsang Province.
20 魂窒: lose consciousness, black out.
21 驚季症: lit. "heart-pounding symptom."
22 坐化: depart from this world while seated.

——— **69** ———

Kwŏn of Andong

Vol. II: 45; n.d.; Diary XII, pp. 92–6; 243.

There lived a certain Kwŏn in Andong, a man of great learning and of highly respected character such that he was recommended by the governor for office and made Keeper of the Tomb of Queen Cho of Injong, his age being sixty. He was well-to-do but he had lost his wife; neither had he any children or near relatives.

At this time Kim Uhang, who afterward became a Minister of State, was superintendent of the tomb and had come out to supervise a matter of work being done on it. So they found occasion to become acquainted and pass the time together. On a certain day a soldier who was on guard brought a trespasser who been cutting wood inside the tomb enclosure.

Kwŏn reprimanded him for what he had done and was about to order him beaten, when he saw that he was an unmarried man with the boy's queue still down his back. He was in tears and seemed to have no words with which to reply.

Looking him over carefully, Kwŏn recognized that he was not a low-class man but evidently a member of the aristocracy and so he asked, "Who are you, and how came you here?"

The man replied, "I am ashamed and rendered speechless. A son of an officer of state, I lost my father early in life and my old mother is now seventy-one years of age. I have a sister who is thirty-five, not yet married. I myself am thirty and have no wife. So my sister and I care for our mother, I gathering the wood while she sees to the water and the meals. Our home is near the tomb enclosure and now that we have this very terrible cold upon us, I was unable to go far to seek wood and so I have done this wrong. I know full well that I deserve punishment," and again he cried.

When Mr. Kwŏn saw his tears he felt sorry for him and so he turned to Superintendent Kim and said, "This is a worthy man and surely one to be pitied. Suppose we let him off free."

Kim laughed and said, "Let him go."

Kwŏn then said to the lad, "Learning your circumstances, I feel sorry for you and so I shall show you special leniency but don't commit this offence again."

He then gave him a measure of rice and a chicken and said, "Take this with you and see to the needs of your mother."

The boy expressed his profound thanks and left. But now many days later he was taken again for a light offence. Kwŏn scolded him soundly. When the lad broke into a loud wail and said, "I have been unmindful of all Your Excellency's kindness to me. I know that I am thus twice guilty but I could not bear to see my mother suffering from the cold, and with all this snow about, there was no way of going elsewhere. I have no face to look up or allow myself to be seen."

Again moved by the pitiful case of the man, Kwŏn wrinkled his brows and thought, and again concluded to let him off. Sitting at his side, Kim smiled and said, "You can't expect to move this fellow by a measure of rice and one chicken. I have thought of another plan that would doubtless move him. Will you do as I suggest?"

Kwŏn wanted to know what it was that he proposed. Kim said, "Your Excellency has no wife and no child. How about it if you should marry that lad's sister and make her your second wife?"

Kwŏn stroked his long white beard and said, "I am an old man, but still I am young yet as regards strength."

Catching at this word of his, Kim called the lad and said, "Keeper Kwŏn here is a most upright and kindly gentleman with means enough at his disposal, but he has no wife and no son. Your sister is already beyond the marriageable age and as to her general qualifications I cannot speak. If you have her marry here, you'll have a place of refuge. Would this not be a good plan?"

The boy said, "I have an old mother and so I cannot decide of my own will. I'll go and talk it over with her."

He went and soon returned, saying, "I went and told my mother and she said, 'Our home has belonged to the gentry for many generations, and now it has come to this plain of great need. We have known of no such cases as this before, but yet it is better than not marrying at all.' She shed tears as she gave her consent."

Kim was very happy at this and urged the matter with great zeal and so the matter was arranged and carried out in a few days. The bride was the daughter of an ancient, famous clan and a gifted and worthy woman.

One day Kwŏn came to call on Kim and said, "You used your kind efforts to secure me an honest wife and now I am sixty years of age. I have nothing to ask in the way of favour so I have decided to go back to my native district and have come to say good-bye."

Kim asked, "You will take your wife along but how about the other members of her family?"

Kwŏn replied, "I'll take them all."

Kim said, "That's right – the good and noble thing to do."

So he had wine brought and they gave their farewell greetings.

Twenty-five years later, Kim had become a great officer of state. He went as Governor of Andong and on the day after his arrival a caller came and sent in his card and asked to see him. On the card was written: 'Kwŏn, formerly keeper of a tomb.' Kim did not recognize the name at first but later remembered his old friend of the tomb and reckoning up his age he knew that he was eighty-five. He hurried out and greeted him in the kindest way. He had a child's face and snow-white hair; with no one to help him and no staff to aid his steps he quickly mounted the stairway like a fairy among men. Kim took him by the hand and greeted him with no end of questions. He gave him wine to drink and food of the most lavish preparation. He ate with hearty zest just as of yore.

Kwŏn said, "Your humble dweller in the country meeting you, a master of the capital today, counts it God's good blessing. You were the one who urged my marriage and had me in my old age win a good and honest woman and now I have two sons and we have grown old together. My two boys have had some grounding in the Classics and they have passed their exams in the capital, a pair of glad □s. Tomorrow is their triumphant return home and now Your Excellency has come here. You really must come out to my place. My coming to call today sooner than the required formality is on this account."

On hearing this, Kim was greatly delighted and offered his heartfelt congratulations, saying that he would go with pleasure.

Kwŏn then arose and took his departure.

The day following Kim took with him musicians and dancing girls with food and dainties, and left early and found Kwŏn's home among the hills and streams – a delightful retreat with flowers and bamboos about in great abundance. There was a pavilion and a summer hall, beautiful to behold – a most delightful home. The master came out to meet him. Word got abroad like the wind and clouds that the Governor Kim had come to call on Kwŏn.

In a little, the two new graduates came into view wearing their caps and scholars' coats. They won the hearts of everybody. Before each was a white certificate carried in a roll, with pipers leading the way. Sightseers lined the way like a wall and all heralded the praise of Kwŏn.

While this was going on Kim called the new graduates and made them do their stint. He asked their age and found the oldest twenty-four and the second twenty-three. Thus had Kwŏn renewed the broken threads of his married life and had two sons in succession. He talked with them and found them handsome as the phoenix bird and in letters, precious as jewels. He pronounced them both alike in age and appearance. Kim was unlimited in his praise while the old father looked on with delight.

While they were thus delighting themselves, Kwŏn pointed out an oldish person sitting at the side and asked, "Does Your Excellency know this person? He is the one who trespassed and got into trouble over the wood. He is now fifty-five years of age."

With music and singing they spent the happy occasion. Kim asked the governor to stay the night and go next day. "My joy today is all due to you. Your condescending to come today is a God and not man.

So he spent the night and talked the long night through. On the following morning Kwŏn had wine passed and then several times seemed desirous of speaking but failed.

Kim inquired, "Have you something you would like to say?"

Kwŏn then answered, "Our old wife has always desired to make some return for the kindness done her and now you have come to visit our humble house, my wife would like just once to come forth and make her bow. She thinks nothing of the proper forms necessary to observe but desires to make her glad acknowledgment. Pardon her wish in this matter, please, and step into the inner room of my house and have her pay her respects. Will you not kindly consent? You are to my old wife as the Heaven and Earth itself and your favour like that of one's parents. What reason to refuse?"

Kim could not refuse this appeal and stepped in and here he found a mat spread and there they met. The old wife came forth and bowed before him. She was moved so greatly that her tears flowed.

Kim noticed also two young women who were dressed neatly and well. They also bowed. These were the daughters-in-law. Thus the three sat and silently did him honour. By their faces you could see how much they loved and how highly they regarded him.

A moment later there came forth refreshments, the very finest.

Kwŏn then invited Kim into a little side room where there was a little child of some six or seven years whose head was covered with darkish hair and whose hands held the doorsill. Its eyes were bright as it watched Kim approach. It looked as though it saw and knew and then again as though its thoughts were elsewhere.

Kwŏn pointed to it and said, "Does Your Excellency know who this person is? This is the old mother of the man who filched the wood. She is now ninety-five. Hear what she is saying: 'Make Kim Uhang Minister of State, make Kim Uhang Minister of State.' For twenty-five years this has been her one and only prayer and today this is her petition still. Such persistent praying as this God will assuredly hear."

When Kim heard this he smiled.

Later Kim became Minister of State in the days of Sukchong and had charge of the royal physicians and saw to the health of Prince Yŏning (afterward Yŏngjong). He told Prince Yŏning about his experiences and told also the story of Kwŏn *ch'ambong* from beginning to end.

Hearing this, Yŏngjong was greatly interested – a wonderful story, he thought, so that after he became king an examination was held. Later among the various names of the candidates he saw the name Kwŏn so-and-so of Andong. This was a grandson of Kwŏn the Grave Keeper.

Yŏngjong gave special orders, saying, "The late minister Kim told me of Kwŏn and what a wonderful experience he had had. And now his grandson has passed the special examination. Is this not a wonderful story?"

He ordered him made a keeper of a tomb so that he might follow in the steps of his grandfather. All the people of Kyŏngsang counted this a special honour.

安東權某　以經學行義　登道薦 1)　仕徽陵 2)

叅奉 3)　時年六十　家富饒　新喪配　內無應門之童

外無朞功之親 4)　時金相宇杭 5)　爲本陵別檢 6)

適有陵役　與之合直 7)　一日　陵軍捉犯樵人以

納　權公據理責之　將答罰之　樵人卽老總角也

涕泣漣漣 8)　無辭可答　權公察氣色　決非常漢也

問汝何許人也　總角曰：言之慙也　小生簪纓後裔 9)

早孤而老母年今七十有一　有一妹　年至三十五尙

未嫁　小生年三十　未有室　娚妹樵汲以奉養　家近

火巢 10)　而今當極寒　不能遠樵故　有犯樵　知罪

지 죄　잉 우 체 읍　권 공 견 기 체 읍　홀 생 측 은 지 심
知罪　仍又涕泣　權公見其涕泣　忽生惻隱之心

고 위 김 공 왈　가 긍 재 기 정　특 사 지 하 여　김 공 소 왈
顧謂金公曰：可矜哉其情　特赦之何如　金公笑曰：

무 방　권 공 왈　문 여 정 리 가 긍 고　특 방 지　갱 물 범 죄
無妨　權公曰：聞汝情理可矜故　特放之　更勿犯罪

사 일 두 미 일 척 계 왈　이 차 귀 양 로 친　총 각 감 사 이 거
賜一斗米一隻鷄曰：以此歸養老親　總角感謝而去

수 일　우 견 착 어 범 초　권 공 대 책 지　총 각 실 성 곡 왈
數日　又見捉於犯樵　權公大責之　總角失聲哭曰：

고 부　성 의　고 지 량 죄 구 범　이 불 인 로 친 지 호 한
辜負 11) 盛意　固知兩罪俱犯　而不忍老親之呼寒

적 설 지 중　차 무 초 채 지 로　금 즉 거 두 무 지　권 공
積雪之中　且無樵採之路　今則擧頭無地 12)　權公

우 생 측 은 지 심　축 미　량 구　불 인 태 치　김 공 재
又生惻隱之心　縮眉 13) 良久　不忍答治　金公在

방 미 신　왈　척 계 두 미　불 능 감 화　제 유 호 양 도 리
傍微哂 14) 曰：隻鷄斗米　不能感化　第有好樣道理

의 아 언 부　권 공 원 문 기 설　김 공 왈　로 인 상 배
依我言否　權公願聞其說　金公曰：　老人喪配

이 무 자　총 각 지 매　취 위 계 실 하 여　권 공 랄
而無子　總角之妹　娶爲繼室何如　權公捋 15)

기 백 수 왈　오 수 년 로　근 력 족 가 위 야　김 공 췌 기 의
其白鬚曰：吾雖年老　筋力足可爲也　金公揣其意

수 초 총 각 근 전 왈　피 권 참 봉　충 후 군 자 야　가 계 요 족
遂招總角近前曰：彼權叅奉　忠厚君子也　家計饒足

상 배 이 무 자　여 지 매 과 년 미 가　역 미 지 범 절 지 하 여
喪配而無子　汝之妹過年未嫁　亦未知凡節之何如

이 여 지 작 배　즉 여 가 의 탁 유 소　기 불 호 재　총 각 왈
而與之作配　則汝家依托有所　豈不好哉　總角曰：

가 유 로 모　불 감 천 편　당 왕 의 언　거 이 부 반 왈
家有老母　不敢擅便 16)　當往議焉　去而復返曰：

왕 고 로 모　즉 로 모 왈　오 가 세 세 벌 열　금 지 쇠
往告老母　則老母曰：吾家世世閥閱 17)　今至衰

체 지 극　수 전 세 미 행 지 사　불 유 유 어 폐 륜　호
替之極 18)　雖前世未行之事　不猶愈於廢倫 19) 乎

읍 이 허 지　김 공 희 지　수 력 권 지　연 길　이 급 급 성 례
泣而許之　金公喜之　遂力勸之　涓吉 20)　而急急成禮

과 시 명 가 후 예　녀 중 현 부 야　일 일　권 공 래 견 김 공
果是名家後裔　女中賢婦也　一日　權公來見金公

왈　뢰 군 지 력 권　득 차 량 배　오 년 이 칠 [륙] 십
曰：賴君之力勸　得此良配　吾年已七 [六] 十

하 소 구 호　영 귀 향 리 고　래 별 의　문 부 인 솔 귀
何所求乎　永歸鄉里故　來別矣　問夫人率歸

즉 기 가 구 처 하 여 야　답 왈　병 솔 거 의　김 공 왈
則其家區處何如耶　答曰：並率去矣　金公曰：

대 선 재　잉 작 주 상 별　후 이 십 오 년　김 공 시 득 비 옥
大善哉　仍酌酒相別　後二十五年　金公始得緋玉 21)

출 재 안 동 도 관　익 일　유 일 민　납 자　청 알　전 참 봉
出宰安東到官　翌日　有一民　納刺 22)　請謁　前參奉

권 모 야　김 공 량 구 시 기 득 휘 릉 반 료 사　이 계 기 년 기
權某也　金公良久始記得徽陵伴僚事　而計其年紀

즉 팔 십 오 세 야　급 위 요 견　동 안 백 발　불 부 불 장
則八十五歲也　急爲邀見　童顏白髮　不扶不杖

표 이 입　약 신 선 중 인　악 수 서 회　설 주 찬 관 대
飄而入　若神仙中人　握手敍懷　設酒饌款待 23)

음담여상 권공왈 민지득배성주 어금일 천야
飮啖如常 權公曰：民之得拜城主 [24] 於今日 天也

민뢰성주권혼 만득량우 련생이자 지금해로
民賴城主權婚 晚得良耦 [25] 連生二子 至今偕老

이이자초학시문 전예 어경사 탁련벽 진사
而二子稍學詩文 戰藝 [26] 於京師 擢連璧 [27] 進士

명일즉도문일야 성주적리 차부 기가무하림
明日卽到門日也 城主適涖 [28] 此府 豈可無下臨

지거야 민급청알자 량유이야 김공경하불이
之擧耶 民急請謁者 良有以也 金公慶賀不已

쾌허지 권공사거 명일 김공휴기락 비주찬
快許之 權公謝去 明日 金公携妓樂 備酒饌

조왕지 견기거 계산수려 화죽예여 루사
早往之 見其居 溪山秀麗 花竹翳如 [29] 樓榭 [30]

온창 호가거야 주인하계영지 원근풍동
穩敞 [31] 好家居也 主人下堦迎之 遠近風動 [32]

빈객운집 아이량신은래도 복두 앵삼 풍채
賓客雲集 俄而兩新恩來到 幞頭 [33] 鶯衫 [34] 風彩

동인 마전량립백패 쌍적료량 관자여도
動人 馬前兩立白牌 [35] 雙笛寥亮 [36] 觀者如堵

함자차 공지복력 김공련호신은 문기년 즉백
咸容嗟 [37] 公之福力 金公連呼新恩 問其年 則伯

이십사 계이십삼 권공속현 지익년 우익년
二十四 季二十三 權公續絃 [38] 之翌年 又翌年

련득쌍옥 야 여지수작 용모즉란고 야 문장
連得雙玉 [39] 也 與之酬酢 容貌則鸞鵠 [40] 也 文章

즉완염 야 가위난형난제 김공흠탄불이 로주
則琬琰 [41] 也 可謂難兄難弟 金公歆嘆不已 老主

人喜色　可知座間　權公指在傍一老人曰：城主知

此人乎　此是昔年犯樵人也　計其年數　則五十五也

遂設樂以娛之　主人仍請留宿曰：民之今日之慶　皆

城主之賜也　城主之適臨蓬蓽 42)　天與之　非人力也

遂止宿穩話　翌朝　權公進酒饌侍坐　口欲言而囁嚅 43)

不敢發　金公曰：有所欲言乎　權公乃言曰：

老妻平日爲城主結草之願　而今幸臨陋地　一拜尊

顏　則至願遂矣　女子之不思體面　只有感恩之心

容或無怪 44)　願城主暫入內室受拜　恐未知何如

且城主之於老妻　德如天地　恩猶父母　何嫌之有

金公不得已入內　軒上設席迎坐　老夫人出拜於前

感極而悲　淚涕汍瀾 45)　又見兩少婦　凝妝盛飾 46)

隨後而出拜　其子婦也　三夫人黙然侍坐　其愛

戴之意 47)　溢於顏色　遂進滿盤珍羞　權公請

김공어협방전　　견년가위륙칠세치아　　　발칠흑
金公於夾房前　見年可爲六七歲穉兒 48)　髮漆黑

봉송　　수집창달　이립　방동형연　　암암　시인
鬔鬆 49)　手執窓闥 50) 而立　方瞳瑩然 51)　黯黯 52) 視人

정신약존약무　　권공지지왈　성주지차인호
精神若存若無 53)　權公指之曰：城主知此人乎

시범초인지자친　야　금년구십유오세　기구중
是犯樵人之慈親 54)　也　今年九十有五歲　其口中

유성　성주시세청지　비타성야　김우항배정승
有聲　城主試細聽之　非他聲也　金宇杭拜政丞

김우항배정승　이십오년　축원여일　상금구불절
金宇杭拜政丞　二十五年　祝願如一　尙今口不絶

성　지성안득불감천호　김공청지　리연　이소
聲　至誠安得不感天乎　金公聽之　犂然 55) 而笑

기후김공과배상우숙묘　조　이공이약방도제조
其後金公果拜相于肅廟 56) 朝　而公以藥房都提調 57)

왕시연잉군　환후　영묘　잠저　시봉호야
往視延礽君 58) 患候　英廟 59) 潛邸 60) 時封號也

설기평생환적　어급권참봉　서기전말　영묘문
說其平生宦蹟 61) 語及權叅奉　敍其顚末　英廟聞

심기지　등극후　식년　창방일　우견방목중
甚奇之　登極後　式年 62) 唱榜日 63)　偶見榜目中

안동진사권모　내시권공지손야　자상특교왈
安東進士權某　乃是權公之孫也　自上特敎曰：

고상신김우항설권모지사　심희사야　기손우첩
故相臣金宇杭說權某之事　甚稀事也　其孫又捷

사마　사불우연　특제재랑　사지승무기조
司馬 64)　事不偶然　特除齋郎 65)　使之繩武其祖 66)

령인　영지언
嶺人 67) 榮之焉

1 道薦: (provincial governor) recommend to the court a capable person within one's jurisdiction.

2 徽陵: tomb of Queen Changnyŏl 莊烈王后 [1624–88], wife of King Injo [r. 1623–49; 1595–1649].

3 參奉: junior ninth-grade posts in local yamen; they encompass *ch'ambong* 參奉 – caretakers of ancestral halls (*sadang* 祠堂), royal tombs, and gardens (*nŭngwŏn* 陵園) – and the Office of Royal Genealogy (Chongch'inbu 宗親府).

4 朞功之親: lit. "close relative who will don mourning apparel."

5 金宇杭 [1649–1723; styled Chejung 濟仲; sobriquet Kappong 甲峰; ancestral seat Kimhae 金海; posthumous epithet Ch'ungjŏng 忠靖]: scholar-official under King Sukchong 肅宗 [r. 1674–1720; 1661–1720]. His father was Kim Honggyŏng 金洪慶 [1621–91].

6 別檢: junior eighth-grade post belonging to the Bureau of Ceremonial Tents (Chŏnsŏlsa 典設司).

7 合直 = *happŏn* 合番: serve on night duty together.

8 漣漣: tears streaming down.

9 簪纓後裔: descendants of a *yangban* family.

10 火巢: the perimeter of a gravesite that has been cleared of trees and bushes as a precaution against forest fires.

11 辜負: let down, disappoint, go back on, contravene.

12 舉頭無地: lit. "no place to lift one's head" = ashamed.

13 縮眉: knit one's brow.

14 微哂: lit. "a wee smile."

15 捋: stroke.

16 擅便 = *ch'ŏndan* 擅斷: make an arbitrary decision.

17 世世閥閱: clan that has rendered meritorious service from generation to generation.

18 衰替之極: lit. "extreme decline."

19 廢倫: lit. "affront to morality"; here, for a man or woman to fail to marry.

20 涓吉: select an auspicious day for a wedding or similar happy occasions.

21 緋玉: silk robes and jade headband buttons; part of the formal attire of a *tangsanggwan* 堂上官 (lit. "officials of the upper end of the hall" = officials higher than senior third rank.)

22 納刺 = *t'uja* 投刺: send in one's credentials to request a first audience.

23 款待 = *hwandae* 歡待: warm reception.

24 城主: another name for a local magistrate.

25 良耦 = *yangbae* 良配: good spouse.

26 戰藝: talent-based competition between two individuals.

27 連璧: lit. "a pair of jade pieces": two brothers passing the civil service examination at the same time.

28 涖 = *ri* 莅 = *puim* 赴任: report for duty at one's new post.

29 翳如: thick and lush.

30 樓榭: tower or pavilion.

31 穩敞: comfortable and spacious.

32 風動: lit. "wind moves": the music begins.

33 幞頭: hat worn by a successful passer of the civil service examination.

34 鶯衫: light yellow-green clothing worn by a successful passer of the civil service examination.

35 白牌: a white piece of paper certifying classical licentiates (*saengwŏn* 生員) or literary licentiates (*chinsa* 進士) as passers of the preliminary civil service examination (*sokwa* 小科).

36 嘹亮: (for sound) clear-toned and high-pitched.

37 咨嗟: marvel, exclaim.

38 續絃: lit. "re-string one's instrument"; remarry (said of a widower).

39 雙玉: a pair of jade pieces in the shape of a boy.

40 鸞鵠: lit. "*luan* bird and swan" = brilliant personage. A *luan* is a mythical phoenix-like bird.

41 琬琰: beautiful jade.

42 蓬蓽: lit. "roof made of mugwort and beans" = "my humble abode."

43 囁嚅: mumble.

44 容或無怪: within the realm of possibility, and therefore not strange.

45 淚涕汍瀾: weep with tears streaming down one's face.

46 凝妝盛飾: heavily made up and decked out.

47 愛戴之意: lit. "desire to happily attend upon someone."

48 稺兒: child.

49 鬐鬆: full head of hair.

50 窓闌 = *ch'angmun* 窓門: window.

51 瑩然: brilliant.

52 黯黯: jet-black.

53 若存若無: sometimes there, sometimes not.

54 慈親: (humilific) one's own mother.

55 怦然: startled and afraid.

56 肅廟: temple name for King Sukchong 肅宗 [r. 1674–1720; 1661–1720].

57 藥房都提調: *yakpang* is another name for the Royal Clinic (Naeŭiwŏn 內醫院), the bureau in charge of medical and pharmaceutical supplies in the palace. *Tojejo* is a senior first-grade official belonging to the Naeŭiwŏn.

58 延礽君: the title of the future King Yŏngjo when he was still a prince.

59 英廟: temple name of King Yŏngjo [r. 1724–76; 1694–1776].

60 潛邸: the period preceding the ascendance to the throne of a king or dynastic founder; his residence during that time.

61 宦蹟: career trajectory.

62 式年: the regularly scheduled civil service examination year, or the examination taking place thereupon; refers to the years *cha* 子, *myo* 卯, *o* 午, and
yu 酉, i.e., every fourth year.

63 唱榜日: the day when the names of the civil service examination passers
were announced.

64 司馬 = *samasi* 司馬試 = *sokwa* 小科: another name for the preliminary
examination for classics and literary licentiates (see note 35).

65 齋郎: a junior ninth-grade post such as *ch'ambong* 參奉, caretakers of ancestral halls (*sadang* 祠堂) or royal tombs and gardens (*nŭngwŏn* 陵園).

66 繩武其祖: continue working in the hereditary professions of one's ancestors.

67 嶺人 = *yŏngnamin* 嶺南人: a person from Kyŏngsang Province.

—— 70 ——

Geomancy and Whatnot

Vol. II: 49; n.d.; Diary XIV, pp. 56–9; 246.

Kim *p'ansŏ* (Chief of a Board) was gifted with the power to read
men. One day in passing through the city, he saw an overgrown boy
with his hair down his back and dressed in ragged clothes, and a face
withered and dry. He brought him home with him and asked him who
he was. His reply was, "I lost my parents early in life and could find no
relatives and so I have gone from market to market begging. I do not
know my name but my age is fifteen."

The minister said, "If you will remain at my house, I'll clothe and
feed you."

He gave him the name Kim Tong.

The boy, most grateful, remained and asked that he might be taught
the character. Day by day and months by months he made marked
progress and could remember all he learned. He was like an invisible
spirit at the pen, a lad indeed gifted with the greatest skill.

The minister greatly loved him and never let him leave his side. He
was naturally a bad sleeper and in the mid hours even whenever he
called Kim Tong he would respond at once and come. Others remarked
on this as very exceptional.

Day after day at the home of the minister, Kim Tong lived in the
library where he read the books and took special interest in astrology.

The minister asked him about it and Kim Tong told him a little of what he had found and they talked about the influences of the stars. It was as though Kim Tong had read and mastered all. He did not talk of it, however, to anybody else but pretended ignorance.

The minister loved him as his very own and talked over everything with him. He urged him to get married but Kim Tong opposed. Then some ten years passed by when one night the minister called him, but there was no answer. He took a light and went to see but there was no trace of him whatever. It was as though he had lost his own hands in losing Kim Tong. He lost his appetite and cared nothing for sleep.

Four days later Kim returned, all unannounced, his face all smiles. The minister, in alarm but pleased, said, "How is this that you went off without telling me – where have you been? Have I failed in something that you have acted so? How is it you look so happy?"

Kim Tong replied, "Your Excellency has failed in nothing. When I have a quiet moment I'll tell you."

In the night he again asked, whereupon Kim said, "I am not a Korean but a Chinese son of a minister Kak-no.* My father fell under disfavour through an evil minister's opposition and was sent into exile to Sandy-Gate Island (Samundo). All our relatives were scattered and exiled likewise. My father is a great expert at astrology and when he left for exile, he said to me, 'In fifty years, I'll be released and come home. If you remain here in China you'll be in danger of the enemy; go east to Chosŏn and remain there till I come home.'

"So I begged all along the way till I came here, where I have become the recipient of your kindness, wide and great as the sea. You have brought me up and taught me. I shall never be able in this life to repay your kindness to me. My going the other night without a word was to the Hill of the Five Fairies in Kwach'ŏn. There I was watching the stars when I suddenly learned by them that my father had returned. I was then obliged to say to you that I must return home and yet without some return for all you have done, I could not think of it. I went to the hills to find a propitious site for burial. There beneath the Five Fairy Hill, I found a place. I would like you to come and see it tomorrow."

The minister gave a great start and so went as requested the next day. There Kim Tong pointed out one spur, saying, "This is a propitious site. Make haste and have your father's remains transferred here."

When the lucky day came they marked out the site and Kim Tong again said, "You will have a numerous and noted posterity and five ministers of state will come forth from among them."

So he wrote out the instructions. Then he returned home, bowed and spoke his farewell.

On his departure, the minister was digging the ground according to his directions. When he had gone down some seven feet, they came to a flat rock that was propped up on each side; as it was pressed slightly it moved up and down.

He had heard from Kim Tong that they would come on a rock and so he ceased digging and awaited the hour for the lowering of the coffin, lighting lamps at the corner of the site.

Now the minister had a steward, specially beloved, who went down into the grave and, being surprised at the shaking of the rock, desired to find if anything was underneath it. He found he could lift up the flat stone and underneath he found four jade images that served as props to the flat stone, and in the middle one as well. The one in the middle was slightly higher than the others and because of this the stone was unsteady.

The steward gave a great start of fear and let the flat stone fall back with a crash, whereupon he heard that the jade dolls had broken. He thought in his fear, "I have been greatly loved and favoured by His Excellency and yet I have now spoiled this special grave site for him. Disaster will follow this as sure as this world. I did not intend any such thing, an accident it was, but it means death for me nevertheless. I do not dare to go and tell it."

When the time came the coffin was lowered and following this, if there was the slightest illness or trouble in the home, the steward's heart was all on fire. There were several of these but they all recovered.

Kim Tong returned to China, his native country, where he found his father returned from exile and in charge of office, while his enemies had all died under the knife. Here the two who had passed through so great danger – together again. How happy they were!

Kim Tong graduated and became a Doctor of the Hallim. One day his father inquired, "You received so much kindness from the Korean, Kim. How do you expect to make return for it?"

The Hallim said, "I showed him a very special site for burial."

"What kind of site?" asked the father. The Hallim then told him about it. The father gave a start, saying, "You have brought disaster on your

best friend. The five jade dolls in the tomb accord with the five mountain peaks. The peak in the middle is an unlucky one. After a measure
of prosperity they will all perish. Why did you not look at it closely?"

The Hallim now saw his mistake but there was no help for it.

The father then said, "All your enemies are now dead. You have the
□□□ for the □. You must get a special commission and go to Korea
and get the friend to change the site at once for a propitious place."

The Hallim did as the father directed and went to Korea as Second
Envoy, where he met his friend the minister at the Bright Snow Hall
(Myŏngsŏlgung). They talked of the past and all they had known. He
called him "Kind Father." He then told of his own father's news. The
minister listened and in great distress, not knowing what to do, turned
to the steward who was nearby.

The steward then came forward and told how he had let the stone fall
and had □-ed the middle image.

When he said this the minister's face lighted up and he said,
"Misfortune has gone with it and good luck followed all □ to us.
The stone that at first teetered, when finally laid, rested square and
they wondered at it. When they put the coffin down a great thunder
storm arose and struck the middle peak, smashing it to pieces – a proof
that luck was with them. The Hallim was greatly □-ed and said the
minister's family will now become great. He returned home and told
his father.

* "Kak-no" 閣老, taken as a proper name, is Gale's mistranslation for "a minister."

김 상 서 모 유 지 인 지 감　　　　일 일　　　견 로 방 유 총 각
金尙書某有知人之鑑 1)　　一日　　見路傍有總角

의 복 람 루　　형 용 초 췌　　휴 귀 기 가　　문 여 시 하 허 인 야
衣服襤褸　形容憔悴　携歸其家　問汝是何許人也

대 왈　　조 실 부 모　　사 고 무 친　　행 걸 어 시　　성 명 역
對曰：早失父母　四顧無親　行乞於市　姓名亦

불 자 지　　년 즉 십 오 세 야　　상 서 왈　　여 류 주 오 가
不自知　年則十五歲也　尙書曰：汝留住吾家

의 식 불 핍 야　　잉 사 명 왈　　김 동　　총 각 감 사　　거 수 월
衣食不乏也　仍賜名曰：金童　總角感謝　居數月

원학서　일취월장　과일성송　운필여신　진기재야
願學書　日就月將　過日成誦　運筆如神　眞奇才也

상서애지중지　수유불리　상서소무수　수심야지중
尙書愛之重之　須臾不離　尙書素無睡　雖深夜之中

일호즉김동응대　제공　겸　개미　급　야　김동재
一呼則金童應對　諸公 [僚] 皆未 (及) 也　金童在

상서가　일입서루　번열　서적　우침간성력지서
尙書家　日入書樓　繙閱 2) 書籍　尤眈看星曆之書 3)

상서고지즉략언기오지　여지양흘　각　고금
尙書叩之則畧言其奧志　與之揚扢 [推] 4) 古今

즉여송숙문　여타인언　도회　불답　상서애지여자
則如誦熟文　與他人言　韜晦 5) 不答　尙書愛之如子

매사상의　권지취처　즉고사불원　여시과금십년
每事相議　勸之娶妻　則固辭不願　如是過今十年

일일야　호지즉김동불응　거촉시지　묘무형적
一日夜　呼之則金童不應　擧燭視之　杳無形跡

상서여실좌우수　침식불감　제사일　김동홀래현
尙書如失左右手　寢食不甘　第四日　金童忽來現

희색만면　상서경희왈　여하불고이거　거향하처
喜色滿面　尙書驚喜曰：汝何不告而去　去向何處

오기대여지심　유미진이연야　차여유희색하야
吾豈待汝之心　有未盡而然耶　且汝有喜色何也

김동소왈　비야　당종용고지　야간우문지　김동왈
金童笑曰：非也　當從容告之　夜間又問之　金童曰：

오비조선인야　중국각로　지자야　부친조간신지참
吾非朝鮮人也　中國閣老 6) 之子也　父親遭奸臣之讒

원배사문도　원근제족　개피산배　부친심지성력
遠配沙門島 7) 遠近諸族　皆被散配　父親深知星曆

之數　臨行敎小子曰：五十年當赦還　而汝在中國

則必死於奸臣之手　東出朝鮮　則後必生還云云

遂轉轉流乞 8)　至於此　幸蒙大監河海之澤　養育之

敎誨之　此生此恩　無以爲報　日前不告而去者

登果川 9)之五鳳山 10)　仰視星象 11)　父親已赦還

矣　小子當告歸　而報恩之心　切於中　遍求山

地於五鳳山下　得一明穴 12)　而明日請共往觀之

尙書驚且異之　翌日　共往五鳳山下　指一阜曰：

此是吉地　急行大監親山 13)緬禮 14)　擇日裁穴 15)

又曰：子孫昌盛　出五相國矣　立標而識之

還家拜謝而別　尙書如其言　將行緬禮　開壙七尺

出盤石　石之四面有罅 16)　而以手壓之　則微有搖

動　尙書旣聞盤石之說於金童故　將待時而下棺

懸燈於墓閣而坐　尙書之愛傔 17)一人　獨往壙中

異其石之搖動　欲知其中之有何物　暗自手　揭而

視之　見其石底　四隅有玉童子　捧石而立　中有一

玉童　又捧之　而稍長於四隅之玉童　此所以石搖也

傔人驚訝之　急下盤石之際　琤然 [18] 有折玉之聲

傔人大驚之心語曰：吾受恩於大監家而誤了此吉地

後必有灾禍 [19]　吾雖無心之致　生不如死　然不忍

實告　時至下棺　封墳而來　尙書家　或有些少憂患

則傔人心焉如燬 [20]　危而復安者屢矣　金童還入中國

閣老果赦還登庸　奸臣已被誅　父子相逢於萬死之

餘 [21]　其喜可知　金童登第　而爲翰林學士　一日

閣老問　汝酬恩於朝鮮金某　何以報之　翰林曰：

占一吉地　指示而來矣　閣老曰：何許吉地乎

翰林櫽言入之　閣老驚曰：遺慘禍 [22] 於恩人矣

地中五箇玉童　應山外不峯　而中峯凶煞 [23] 也

猝貴而亡　汝何不審詳也　翰林悟悔無及

閣老曰：凶黨已誅　今大赦天下　汝以頒赦 24)

往朝鮮　使之急急改葬　更占吉地而來　翰林如其敎

以副使 25) 出來　會金尙書於明雪宮 26)　敍舊愴新 27)

呼以恩爺　遂言其父親之意　尙書聞甚罔措之際

其愛傔隨來　竊聽之　出言其時折玉所以然也

尙書恱然 28) 曰：此來轉禍爲吉偶合也　開壙時

搖動之盤石　下棺時安接不搖　固已異之　及下棺後

忽晴雷 29) 乍起　霹靂 30) 壞了山外中峯之大巖石

此其驗也　翰林大喜曰：尙書家　子孫大昌矣

使還復其言於閣老

1　知人之鑑: discerning judgment of human nature or other people's talents.
2　繙閱: open up a book to peruse it.
3　星曆之書: books on astronomy and astrology.
4　揚推: discuss in a general fashion.
5　韜晦: hide one's talents or learning.
6　閣老: appellation for a minister in the Ming Dynasty.
7　沙門島: an island belonging to Shandong Province 山東省.
8　轉轉流乞: go around begging.

 9 果川: a town in Kyŏnggi Province.

10 五鳳山: a mountain located in Koch'ŏn Village in Ŭiwang, a market town in Kyŏnggi Province.

11 星象: a constellation's appearance.

12 明穴: lit. "bright hole" = auspicious burial site.

13 親山: a mound where one's parents are buried.

14 緬禮: exhume and bury elsewhere.

15 裁穴: decide on a burial site and dig a grave.

16 罅: gap.

17 愛傔: a steward (kyŏmjong 傔從) whom one dotes on.

18 琤然: sound of jade clacking or breaking.

19 灾禍 = chaeang 災殃 = anghwa 殃禍: calamity, disaster.

20 如燬: feel panicked as if burning up in a fire.

21 萬死之餘: as a consequence of a near-death experience.

22 慘禍: brutal calamity.

23 凶煞: harmful spirit.

24 頒赦: spread the news of a special amnesty.

25 副使: deputy commissioner who escorts the chief envoy (chŏngsa 正使).

26 明雪宮: likely the name of a palace.

27 敍舊愴新: lit. "in a discussion of past affairs, nostalgic sorrow is renewed."

28 怳然: be/get engrossed in something.

29 晴雷: a bolt from the blue.

30 霹靂: thunderclap.

—— 71 ——

Yi Tongak (Cousin of T'aektang)*

Vol. II: 50; n.d.; Diary XII, pp. 198–9; listed in Diary XVI, p. 178,
as "Yi Tong-ak, the Mistaken Wife"; 247.

Master Yi Tongak, befriended after marriage on the night of the fifteenth of the first moon, set out to hear the great bell in Chongno ring.†

Later, overcome somewhat by drink, he went along Shoe-shop Street and then sat down to rest unconscious by an entrance door.

A few minutes later women servants of the house looked out and seeing him, said chatting to one another, "Our young master, overcome by new year's drink, is lying here."

They took him in hand and led him into the inner room where the young wife was.

Yi was wholly unaware of what had taken place. Under the light he slept with the young bride, but when morning came he realized that he was in someone else's home, not the home of his wife.

He asked of the young woman, "Whose house is this, please?"

The young woman, also aroused as to suspicion, inquired, "Who are you, pray?"

They then knew that a great error had been committed and were both frightened.

The young people of this home had been married only three days and the bridegroom, hearing the sound of the bell, had gone off to see friends and not having returned, the servants had brought Yi Tongak by mistake into this room.

Yi asked of the young woman, "What shall we do about it?"

She replied, "I had a dream last night and you have come in answer to it. According to proper form, I have only death before me and I should die. I am the last surviving child of an old *yŏkkwan*[§] family. If I die my parents will have no place to lay their head. I see nothing for it but to become your secondary wife, if you will permit it, and to care for my aged parents."

Yi replied, "I had no thought of doing such a thing as this and you had no thought to entangle me in this illicit relation. I see no reason why you should not do as you say and yet I fear my old father, who is most exacting in his ways, and I am so young – not yet twenty – and have not passed my exams. For me who belongs to the literati, it will be very difficult to have a concubine."

She replied, "There is one way out of it. You could leave me with your aunt."

He replied, "Yes, I could do that."

She again said, "Then let's go at once – only let's not tell either your folks or mine. Give all your attention to your examination and let us not see each other until after you have graduated and then we could tell our parents."

Yi did as she suggested and placed her with his aunt, where she was put to sewing. They were like mother and daughter.

When the home of the bride had awakened, they could find no trace of either bride or groom and were terribly alarmed and fearful over it. Only when they had gone to the house of the bridegroom and made inquiry, did they realize that she had run off with some other man. To cover over the disgrace of it, they made out that the new bride had suddenly died and had a make-believe corpse prepared and buried.

Yi Tongak did not again see his young second wife but kept strictly at his studies and in a few years had passed high.

Then he told his parents and had his second wife acknowledged and when they attempted to make the matter known to her people, the young woman said, "There is no question in my mind. When you send word my people will not believe it. You must send some of the silk I had at my wedding as a proof that your words are true. The silk was given to my ancestor by the Emperor when he was in Peking. There is none other like it anywhere. This was used to border my quilt when I was married. This you must send to prove what you say."

Thus they did, and the old *yŏkkwan* and his wife came and seeing their daughter were glad and sorrowful both together. They met Master Yi and saw that he was indeed a gentleman. The whole story was told and the old *yŏkkwan* said, "God indeed has done it. We had no place of refuge in view but now we have. Therefore, I give all my land and goods, servants, etc., to Your Excellency."

On this account, Yi Tongak became possessor of great riches.

His second wife was good and wise in her management of the home. In all her affairs, she was a woman of order. Thus has Yi's home outlasted all these generations – "The drunken man's house," they call it. Her children's children were many in number and her posterity all prospered.

* The parenthetical iinformation was supplied by Gale. T'aektang 澤堂 is a sobriquet of Yi Sik 李植 [1584–1647; styled Yŏgo 汝固; ancestral seat Tŏksu 德水; posthumous epithet Munjŏng 文靖), a scholar-official during the reign of King Sŏnjo 宣祖 [r. 1567–1608; 1552–1608]. Yi Sik is known by other sobriquets such as Namgung *oesa* 南宮外史 and T'aekku *kŏsa* 澤癯居士.

† Gale's first sentence is difficult to read, and there are words in the translation that have no counterparts in the original *hanmun* text, perhaps an indication of confusion on his part.

§ *yŏkkwan*: hereditary non-literati officials who served as interpreters (Chinese, Japanese, Mongolian, and Manchu) in diplomacy and trade.

東岳 1) 李公　新娶後　上元 2) 夜　聽鍾於雲從街 3)

醉過履洞 4) 前路　倚一門而臥　俄而婢僕輩來誼曰：

新郎醉倒此 仍扶入其家新房 而公渾不省矣

洞房華燭 與新婦同寢 翌曉睡覺 則別人之室也

非聘家也 公問新婦 此是誰家 新婦疑之 反詰之

相與錯愕 盖其家新婦過婚禮之三日也 新郎亦

聽鍾夜遊 仍爲不來 東岳誤入此室也 公問新婦曰:

何以處事則好也 新婦曰：吾有夢兆之符合 此亦

緣分 以婦女之道言之 吾辦一死可也 然吾亦屢

世譯官家無男獨女也 吾死 父母老無依托之所

不忍於此 不獲已從權之計 5) 願爲小室 且奉養老親

以從 [終] 年何如 公曰：吾非故犯也 君非亂奔 6)

也 從權無妨 而但家有老親 庭訓 7) 甚嚴 吾年

未弱冠 且未登第 以書生畜小室 豈不難乎

新婦曰：無難也 君之姨姑之家 8) 或有置我之所乎

曰：有之 曰：然則今急起 與我偕行 置我於其家

使兩家莫知之　君必登第　而未第前　誓不相面

登第後　實告于兩家老親　以爲團聚之計如何

公如其言　區處於其寡居姨母家　助其針綿［線］

相依如母女以過　新婦家　朝起視之　則新郎新婦

不知去向　大驚怪　往探新郎家　始知（與）假郎偕

遁　遂秘其事　假稱以新婦暴疾不起　假斂虛葬之

東岳更不接面於小室　晝夜勤工　文章大達矣　不

幾年　登高科　始告老親　率來小室　又欲通小室家

則小室曰：不必信也　出給新婚時紅錦衾領 [9] 曰：

以此爲信　此錦在昔年　遠祖入燕時　皇帝所賜也

天下所無之異錦　獨吾家有之　以爲新婚時衾領而已

見此必信　遂如之　老驛見其女［其］　悲喜交至

且見李公　宰相人也　問其始終曰：天也　吾老夫妻

後事有托矣　無他子女　以其家貲 [10] 奴婢田宅　悉付

之（公爲）長安甲富也　其小室　賢而有智　治産業

奉巾櫛 11)　皆有閨範 12)　李公家　至今以世富稱　李

[履]洞第宅　皆[乃]醉人[入]之第也　小室子孫

且繁衍 13)　云爾

1 東岳: sobriquet of Yi Annul 李安訥 [1571–1637; styled Chamin 子敏; ancestral seat Tŏksu 德水; posthumous epithet Munhye 文惠]: scholar-official under King Injo 仁祖 [r. 1623–49; 1595–1649]. His father was Yi Hyŏng 李泂 [dates unknown].

2 上元: the year's first full moon; the fifteenth day of the first month of the lunar calendar.

3 雲從街: old name for Chongno 種路.

4 履洞: Sinjŏn-ko. A neighbourhood famous for shoe shops in what is now Chung-gu, Seoul, covering Ŭlchiro 3-ga, Chŏ-dong 2-ga, and Ch'o-dong.

5 從權之計: lit. "resolution resorting to expediency" = a solution that deviates from conventional, orthodox means but results in a moral outcome.

6 亂奔 = ŭmbun 淫奔: lascivious behaviour.

7 庭訓: the precepts of one's father.

8 姨姑之家: the house of one's maternal or paternal aunt.

9 紅錦衾領: breast-ties (coat strings) made of red silk.

10 家貲: household assets.

11 奉巾櫛: lit. (of a married woman) "hold up the towel and comb"; submit to one's husband.

12 閨範: the rules and etiquette of womenfolk.

13 繁衍: prosper.

——— 72 ———

The Reward of Virtue

Vol. II: 54; n.d.; Diary XIV: pp. 62–4; 251.

Good Story*

The Kims of Kangnŭng had among their posterity a certain scholar who had been reduced to great poverty and could hardly provide bean soup for his people to live on. His old mother said to her son, "Your house used to be rich and well-to-do and had slaves whose posterity have now gone to live on the islands of Chŏlla Province. Go you south, collect the dues □ from them and set them free."

She then gave him his deeds of slave ownership and sent him on his way.

With these in his possession he arrived at the island and here he found a village of a hundred houses and more, all sons of his slaves. He showed the deeds of ownership when they all came round him in a great company and made their bow. From them all he collected several thousands of *yang*. Having paid thus, they asked as to their freedom and in view of what they had so liberally paid, he burned his deeds and announced that they were free.

He then loaded his money on pack ponies and started on his way, his road leading by the Silk River (Kŭm-gang). It was then winter and very, very cold. As he approached he saw three people by the river bank – an old man, an old woman, and a young woman, all crying and holding on to each other as though to prevent each and every one plunging into the stream.

Amazed at this kind of action, Kim asked what it meant. The old man made reply, "I had an only son who was secretary to the governor of Ch'ungch'ŏng who has offended by embezzling public funds; the limit of time given him to pay up has passed so that tomorrow is his day of death. We have no possible means of raising the amount and I cannot bear to stand to see my son die and so I prefer to drown myself in this river, but my wife and daughter-in-law are determined to die by my side and yet they do not want to see me plunge in. Thus we are holding back each other and crying."

The scholar asked, "How much are you in debt and how much would it take to save him?"

The answer was, "If we had a few thousand *yang* we could save him."

The scholar then said, "I have here with me now several loads of ransom money from a town of slaves that I owned. I can let you have what you need. Take this and pay the amount."

He then gave it, whereupon the three said in tears and expressions of thanks, "You have saved us three – what can we do to return the kind favour? Please come to our house and rest before you proceed on your way."

The scholar said in reply, "The time is short and the way long, while my parents have waited for me many days. I cannot wait," and so he was off and did not ever look back.

The three paid off their debt and on that day the son was set free. All the house was rendered grateful and prayed for blessing on their stranger, though they did not know where he lived or what was his name.

When he had returned home his old mother was delighted to see him safe and sound. She also asked as to how he had fared with the slaves and was more delighted than ever to see the money he had brought.

The scholar also told of what had taken place at the Kŭmgang River, whereupon the old mother patted him on the back and said, "My son, indeed, my son!"

The old woman died at a great age and once again the house fell into the deepest poverty. All the forms and necessaries that go into a funeral he was unable to provide.

Going with the geomancer, he walked over the hills and after making a wide survey he came to a place that the geomancer greatly praised as a spot destined to riches and happiness. But there was a great house just below that forbade the use of it. They asked of the townsfolk whose house it was and found it belonged to their master, with fields all about it on the flat lands. There was a large town of the servants of this lord.

The scholar said to the geomancer, "How can we ever come into possession of such a site as this? However, let us go to this place, as the day is late, and sleep the night there."

So they entered the house where a young man received them in the guest room and had them given an evening meal.

Kim was sitting before the lamp with many anxious thoughts in mind about the site he would so like to have. He sighed to himself when suddenly from the inner room there came forth a young woman who threw open the door and bounded in. She took hold of Kim and burst into tears and seemed rendered speechless. The young man gave a great start and asked the young wife the meaning of such actions as this. She replied, saying, "This is the gentleman who saved our lives at the Silk River."

The young man also took hold of him and expressed his gratitude in tears. The old mother heard this and came hurrying in □ to join in their tearful thanks. They sat before the light and asked concerning all that had come to pass since last they met.

The young woman ever since that day had kept a lighted candle and had offered prayers to God that he would have them meet again the man who had □ -ed them and make some return for all his kindness. The young husband had given up his work as office secretary and had returned to the country and finally come here to live and became a great millionaire. The young woman had watched through the chink to see what guests visited the guest room. She was young and bright and once seen was never forgotten for her whole heart had been given to God in this matter.

They asked as to why he was a mourner, whereupon Kim told the whole story and how he had come looking for a propitious site.

The people of the house were greatly relieved and most anxious to forward his wishes. They said, "We shall take all charge of the necessaries for burial. Please bring the dead."

He sent his own servants as bearers and also had a chariot for the wife to ride and had all the members of the family come.

When the burial was over and a few days had passed, Kim gave over to the scholar the deeds of his house, his fields and servants, and said they would move away to another place.

But the mourner refused, saying, "Where will you go?"

The reply was, "We have another place quite the equal of this where we can live. All that we have here we got from you and so they are not really ours. Please accept of them."

Kim's children were numerous, princely and highly accomplished, known and heard □□ world.

* Gale's editorial note is located separately from his translation, in Diary XVI: p. 178.

강 릉 김 씨 일 사 인　　가 빈 친 로　　핍 숙 수 지 공　　기 로 자
江陵金氏一士人　家貧親老　乏菽水之供 1)　其老慈 2)

어 자 왈　　여 가 선 세　　본 이 부 칭　　노 비 지 산 재
語子曰：汝家先世　本以富稱　奴婢之散在

湖南島中者　不知其數　汝往推刷 3) 也　仍出示篋中

奴婢文記軸　士人持劵　往島中　百餘戶村落

自占居生　皆奴僕子孫也　見劵羅拜　遂收斂數

千金贖之　士人燒其劵　駄錢而還　路過錦江 4)

邊　時冬月甚寒　見江邊一翁一媼一少婦入水

而互相拯出 5)　扶持痛哭　士人怪問之　老翁曰：

吾有獨子　吏役於錦營 6)　以逋欠 7) 在囚　屢

違定限　明日卽死日　而分錢粒米　無可辦出

不忍見獨子之被刑　吾欲投水而死　老妻少婦

共欲死於此　而不忍見入水　互相拯出　仍與痛哭矣

士人曰：若有錢幾何　則可以償逋也　曰：數千金

可以勾當 8) 矣　士人曰：吾有推奴錢 9) 幾駄　洽

滿數千　以此償之　卽與之　其三人又大聲哭曰：

吾輩四人之命　因此得生　將何以報恩　願入吾家

留宿而去　士人曰：日暮道遠 10)　老親倚門 11) 久矣

不可留連　卽馳去不顧　三人仍以此物　盡償宿逋 12)

當日　其子放出獄門　渾室感祝士人　而居住姓名

亦莫知之　士人歸家　老慈喜其無恙而還　又問

[聞] 推奴如意　益喜之　問其贖良之財　何以輸還

士人對以錦江事　其老慈　拊其背曰：是吾子也

後老慈　以天年終於家　家益剝落 13)　初終拮据 14)　萬

不成樣　金哀 15) 與地師 16) 一人　步行尋山　遍踏諸山

到一處　地師大讚之　富貴福祿　不可形言之地也

山下有一大家舍　問於村人　則人 [金] 老家也

良田美畓　遍於一野　村落撲地 17)　皆其奴僕也　顧

地師而言曰：如許 18) 之地　何以占得乎　然而日已暮

留宿彼家而去可也　入其室　有一少年　迎接客室

待以夕飯　金哀對燈而坐　悲懷弸中 19)　山地關心

장우이이　급　홀　자내실일소부　개호돌입　부김
長吁而已　急 [忽]　自內室一少婦　開戶突入　扶金

애대곡지　기색불능언　기소년　경문기고　소부왈
哀大哭之　氣塞不能言　其少年　驚問其故　少婦曰：

차시금강소봉지은인야　소년우포이곡지　로옹
此是錦江所逢之恩人也　少年又抱而哭之　老翁

로온　문차언　우돌출포이곡지　곡지명등　상대
老媼　聞此言　又突出抱而哭之　哭止明燈　相對

각문년조　사실　과불상　의　개소부일자기후
各問年條 20) 事實　果不爽 21) 矣　盖少婦一自其後

야즉분향축천　원봉은인　이보기덕　기부역퇴리
夜則焚香祝天　願逢恩人　以報其德　其夫亦退吏

촌거이사우차　치산졸위거부　이소부매어외실
村居移徙于此　治産猝爲巨富　而少婦每於外室

규시객인지래　심찰기용모　년소안명지인야
窺視客人之來　審察其容貌　年少眼明之人也

견이기득　개기지성감천야　잉문조간지유
見而記得　盖其至誠感天也　仍問遭艱之由 22)

김애언급가후산지사　기가유공불급　답왈
金哀言及家後山地事　其家猶恐不及 23) 答曰：

폄장지절　오가자당지　제왕인행　이래야
窆葬之節 24) 吾家自當之　第往靷行 25) 而來也

발인제구급담군　개이노복치송　겸송교마
發靷諸具及擔軍 26) 皆以奴僕治送　兼送轎馬

솔기내권　이병래　폄례졸곡후　김가헌노복전
率其內眷 27) 而幷來　窆禮卒哭後　金家獻奴僕田

댁문권　청사거　김애왈　거장안지　답왈　우유
宅文劵　請辭去　金哀曰：去將安之　答曰：又有

별 업
別業 28)　足以資生矣　此物都是喪主之福力　非吾

가 지 소 유 야　원 물 사 언　기 후 김 애 지 자 손 혁 창
家之所有也　願勿辭焉　其後金哀之子孫赫昌 29)

관 면　어 세 야
冠冕 30) 於世也

1 菽水之供: lit. "service with beans and water" = serve someone with meagre food.
2 老慈 = *nomo* 老母: one's aged mother.
3 推刷: track down runaway slaves to bring back or extract payment for their manumission.
4 錦江: a river running between South Ch'ungch'ŏng Province and North Chŏlla Province.
5 互相拯出: save each other.
6 錦營: headquarters of the governor of Ch'ungch'ŏng Province.
7 逋欠 = *p'ojo* 逋租: inability to pay taxes.
8 勾當 = *kamdang* 堪當 ~ *tamdang* 擔當: undertake; take charge of.
9 推奴錢: money received through the manumission of a slave.
10 日暮道遠: lit. "the day is done and the road is far."
11 倚門: lit. "lean against the door": a metaphor for parents awaiting their children.
12 宿逋: taxes owed.
13 剝落 = *pakt'al* 剝脫: (household) be in financial straits.
14 初終拮据: painstakingly carry out a funeral.
15 金哀: refers to Kangnŭng Kim in the story (otherwise unknown).
16 地師 = *chigwan* 地官: geomancer.
17 撲地: cover the ground in abundance.
18 如許 = *yŏch'a* 如此: like this; like that.
19 弸中: filling one's heart/chest.
20 年條: chronicle of events by year.
21 不爽: has no discrepancy.
22 遭艱之由: lit. "reason to encounter a difficulty."
23 猶恐不及: lit. "worry [something] might not reach [the desired destination]" or (b) "not worth worrying about."
24 窆葬之節: procedure for interring the coffin.
25 靷行 = *parin* 發靷: move a corpse.

26 擔軍: pallbearer.
27 內眷 = *kwŏnsok* 眷屬: wife and the rest of the family members.
28 別業 = *pyŏlchang* 別莊: cottage; country house.
29 赫昌: brilliant prosperity.
30 冠冕: high-ranking post.

———— 73 ————

A Certain Kim *Sanggun**

Vol. II: 55; Diary XII, pp. 181–2, 185; listed in Diary XVI, p. 178,
as "A Dead Spirit Appears"; 252.

When he was young, a certain minister Kim along with two or three of his friends went to the Yŏngwŏl Temple that is situated beneath Paengnyŏn (White Lotus) Peak to study.

On a certain day all the friends with him had occasion to return home and he was left alone. Late into the night he was reading his book by a lighted lamp when he heard in the hills a strange crying as of a woman. It came closer and closer and finally ceased just in front of his window.

Hearing this and counting it a strange and eerie thing, Kim inquired, "Are you a spirit or are you a human being?"

A woman's voice replied with a long deep sigh, "I am a spirit."

Kim said in answer, "The dark world of spirits is one thing and this world of light another. How comes it that you make your presence known here?"

The spirit replied, "I have a matter of wrong that pertains to my past life that I want to put right and no one is available for this but yourself."

He opened the window and looked out but there was nothing. He then heard a whistling from the upper air and a voice said, "I was afraid if I showed my face you would get a fright and so I have refrained from doing so."

Kim said, "Never mind, show it anyway."

Then suddenly a young woman appeared with her hair down and her face streaming with blood.

Kim said, "What wrong have you suffered, tell me."

Her answer was, "I was the daughter of a *yŏkkwan* (official interpreter) and was married off to one of our own class. But when we had been married only a few days, my husband, led astray by another woman, scolded me and beat me. Finally, put up to it by the evil woman who was his tempter, he charged me with adultery and in the night he stabbed me with a sword and killed me and threw my body among the rocks where it has not been found. He has deceived my parents by saying that I have run away with another man.

"I was most unjustly murdered, but more than that my name is blackened by the evil report he gave. I shall never in all ages to come be able to wipe out this disgrace."

The scholar said in reply, "You are indeed to be pitied, but how on earth can I ever requite your wrongs?"

She replied, "In such a year on such a day you will pass a successful examination and such an office will come to you, and you will rise to be Minister of Justice. When you become that, it will be easy for you to requite my wrongs."

Thus saying, she was gone.

On the day following he went as indicated to the spot and there he found a bloody corpse. He came back and resumed his studies but said not a word of it to anyone.

As the spirit had foretold, he passed his examination and rose by swift promotion to be Minister of Justice. He remembered still what the spirit had said to him and he gave orders to have such-and-such a translator arrested.

He asked, "Do you know anything of anyone who died unjustly near Yŏngwŏl Temple?"

"I do not know," said he.

He then had him taken under arrest to Yŏngwŏl Temple and there the body was found. He was shamed ☐ and having no word of excuse to offer, said, "I did it."

The parents of the dead girl were called and ordered to see it buried, while the translator was condemned.

On that night, with a light burning before [him], [Kim] sat watching the night through at the temple. Again the spirit came before his window, cried ☐ thanked him for his kindness. He saw her again but her hair was done up in a ☐☐ and her dress well ordered.

He then asked the spirit of his prospects and what he should do.

She replied, "On such a day you will have such a rank, and on such a date on account of a special reason you will rise to the highest place of all. On such a day you will die in the service of the state and after your death your sons and sons' sons will live forever.

She was gone and as she had indicated so everything came to pass,
even his death for his country which she foretold.

* See note 1 below.

김 상 군　　모　　소 시 여 친 우 수 인　　독 서 어 백 련 봉
金相君 1) 某　少時與親友數人　讀書於白蓮峯 2)

하 영 월 암　　일 일　　친 우 개 유 고 환 가　　야 심 독 좌
下映月菴 3)　一日　親友皆有故還家　夜深獨坐

명 등 간 서　　홀 유 녀 인 곡 성　　여 원 여 소　　종　영　월 암
明燈看書　忽有女人哭聲　如怨如訴　從（映）月菴

자 원 이 근　　지 어 창 외 이 지　　공 괴 지　　단 좌 불 동
自遠而近　至於窓外而止　公怪之　端坐不動

문 왈　　귀 호 인 호　　녀 인 장 우 이 답 왈　　귀 야　　공 왈
問曰：鬼乎人乎　女人長吁而答曰：鬼也　公曰：

연 즉 유 명 유 수　　안 감 상 유　　녀 인 왈　　오 유 전 생 해
然則幽明有殊 4)　安敢相糅 5)　女人曰：吾有前生解

원 사　　이 비 공 즉 막 가 해　　욕 소 원 이 래　　공 개 호 시 지
冤事　而非公則莫可解　欲訴冤而來　公開戶視之

불 견 기 처　　유 소 어 공 중 왈　　현 형 즉 공 치 공 경　　공 왈
不見其處　有嘯於空中曰：現形則恐致公驚　公曰：

제 현 지　　언 파　　일 소 부 피 발 류 혈　　이 립 어 전　　공 왈
第現之　言罷　一少婦披髮流血　而立於前　公曰：

소 하 원 호　　녀 인 왈　　오 내 역 관　　지 녀 인 야　　가 우 모
訴何冤乎　女人曰：吾乃驛官 6) 之女人也　嫁于某

역 관　　신 혼 미 기　　가 부 혹 어 음 부　　매 아 구 아　　말 내
驛官　新婚未幾　家夫惑於淫婦　罵我毆我　末乃

신 기 음 부 지 참　　위 아 유 순 분 지 행　　야 반 이 검 자 아
信其淫婦之讒　謂我有鶉奔之行 7)　夜半以劒刺我

기 지 우 영 월 암 절 벽 지 간　인 무 지 자　태　오 부
棄之于映月庵絶壁之間　人無知者　紿 8) 吾父

모 왈　음 분　이 거　오 오 사 어 비 명　고 원 야　우 몽 불
母曰：淫奔 9) 而去　吾誤死於非命　固冤也　又蒙不

결 지 명 천 고 천 양　차 원 난 세　공 왈　원 귀 수 가 긍 측
潔之名千古泉壤 10)　此冤難洗　公曰：冤鬼雖可矜惻

오 하 이 해 지　녀 인 왈　공 모 년　필 등 과　모 년 력 모 직
吾何以解之　女人曰：公某年　必登科　某年歷某職

모 년 필 위 추 조 형 참 의　추 조 형 옥 지 관　야
某年必爲秋曹刑 [參] 議 11)　秋曹刑獄之官 12) 也

해 원 기 불 이 재　잉 사 거　익 조　잠 시 절 벽 지 간　유 일
解冤豈不易哉　仍辭去　翌朝　潛視絶壁之間　有一

녀 시　내 작 야 소 견 자 야　선 혈 림 리　유 약 신 사 자 연
女屍　乃昨夜所見者也　鮮血淋漓　有若新死者然

반 이 독 서　비 불 발 설　후 과 여 기 언　등 과 력 직 지
返而讀書　秘不發說　後果如其言　登科歷職至

추 의　공 기 득 원 녀 지 소 즉 부 아 설 좌 기　착 래 모 역
秋議 13)　公記得冤女之訴卽赴衙設坐起 14)　捉來某驛

신 문 왈　여 지 영 월 암 원 사 지 인 호　기 인 저 두　수 여
訊問曰：汝知映月菴冤死之人乎　其人抵頭 15)　遂與

지 공 왕 영 월 암　검 험　기 인 어 색 즉 복　수 초 원 녀
之共往映月菴　檢驗　其人語塞卽服　遂招冤女

지 부 모　사 지 매 장　모 역 즉 치 지 벽　당 야　공 우 입
之父母　使之埋葬　某驛則置之辟　當夜　公又入

영 월 암　병 촉 독 좌　기 인 읍 사 어 창 외　정 기 환 고
映月菴　秉燭獨坐　其人泣謝於窓外　整其鬟髻 16)

의 복 초 초　비 복 구 일 용 야　공 사 지 근 전　갱 문
衣服楚楚 17)　非復舊日容也　公使之近前　更問

前程　女人曰：公某年某職　某時某事　位至大官

而某年爲國辨死 18)　然後令名 19) 無窮　子孫大昌矣

仍辭去　公黙［點］檢平生　若符合契 20)　果於某年

終至死於國事　而永垂 21) 令名

1 相君 = *sanggong* 相公: minister.
2 白蓮峯: Paengnyŏn Peak, a summit between Pukkajwa-dong, Sŏdaemun-gu, and Ŭngam-dong, Ŭnp'yŏng-gu, in Seoul.
3 映月菴: a Buddhist hermitage near Paengnyŏn Peak.
4 幽明有殊: lit. "there is a difference between this world and the netherworld."
5 糅: mix, intermingle.
6 驛官 (error for 譯官): professional interpreter.
7 鶉奔之行: lascivious and promiscuous behaviour.
8 紿: deceive.
9 淫奔: lewd and promiscuous.
10 泉壤 = *kuch'ŏn* 九泉 = *hwangch'ŏn* 黃泉: the netherworld.
11 秋曹參議 = Hyŏngjo *ch'amŭi* 刑曹參議: Third Minister of Punishment (junior third grade).
12 刑獄之官: official in charge of incarceration and punishment.
13 秋議 = Hyŏngjo *ch'amŭi* 刑曹參議: See note 11 above.
14 坐起: lit. "sit and stand up": official at work in office.
15 抵頭: shake one's head.
16 鬟髻: tie one's hair into a bun.
17 楚楚: fresh and crisp.
18 爲國辨死: lit. "for the sake of one's country, make efforts and die" = die in the line of duty.
19 令名: beautiful name.
20 若符合契: dovetail with; match up exactly.
21 永垂: immortalize; preserve forever.

——— **74** ———

Yi Chiham

Vol. III: 1; Box 9:21, pp. 113–14; Diary XII:68–9 (crossed out).
Also listed in XVI: 178 as "Yi Chi-Ham's Providing Money"; 262.

Yi Chiham was exceedingly bright from his very earliest years. He understood the powers that govern the heavens and the laws that move the earth, the science of the physician, fortune-telling and all sorts of magic. There was nothing he did not know. He could foretell the future with exactness so that he was known by the people of his time as a god-man.

He used to tie a gourd to each foot and one to his walking-stick and then start over the water. He went all about the world to Dongting and to the Xiao and Xiang Rivers in China. Everywhere he would wander about the Four Seas. He used to remark that the sea had five colours according to its five compass points.

Notwithstanding his knowledge, however, he was very, very poor. His home was cold and he had but little food to eat and yet he did not seem to trouble about it in the least.

One day as he was seated in his inner room his wife suddenly broke out, "People call you a Superior Man on account of your spiritual gifts and powers; but we have nothing to eat and no wood for the fire. Why don't you try your magic hand for a little in making things easier for me?"

He laughed and said, "Since your ladyship requests it, I'll consent to do as you say for once."

He then called their woman servant and, giving her a brass dish, said, "Take this dish outside the West Gate to the Governor's Bridge and when you get there you will find an old woman going by who will offer you a hundred cash for it. Sell it and bring the money."

The servant went as directed and sure enough an old woman offered to buy it and so the maid took the price and returned.

Again he ordered her, saying, "Take this hundred cash and go outside the Little West Gate to the market where you will see a man with a straw hat on his head who has a pair of chopsticks and spoon for sale. You buy them for that amount."

The servant went and there was the man with the straw hat and a spoon and chopsticks, just as foretold. On buying them it was found that they were made of silver.

Again he commanded her, saying, "Take these things outside the West Gate to the street just before the Provincial Governor's Office where a servant will appear looking for a spoon and chopsticks. He will give you fifteen *yang* for them."

The servant went as directed and matters turned out just as the master foretold and she brought home the fifteen *yang*. He then gave one *yang* to the servant and said, "The old woman who bought the brass dish from you earlier in the day did so because she had lost her own. Now, however, she has found hers and wants to sell the one you let her have. Go and give her back the money."

The servant went and lo, there was the woman distressed over the dish she had bought and anxious to get rid of it, and so she gave back the *yang* she had received and brought back the dish. Yi then gave the dish and the money to his wife and said, "Now let us have some breakfast and dinner as well."

His wife exclaimed, "Wonderful! Do it again."

But Yi Chiham laughed and said, "That's enough, no need to do it more."

Thus was he a man of spiritual power.

리 토 정 지 함
李土亭之菡 1)　　生而穎悟 2)　　天文地理醫藥卜筮 3)

術數之學 4)　無不通曉 5)　　未來之事　豫先知之

世皆稱以爲神人　兩足係一圓瓢 6)　杖下又係一圓瓢

行于海水之上　如踏平地　無處不往　如瀟湘 7)

洞庭 8) 之勝　皆目見而來　周行四海　以爲海有五色

分四方中央　而隨其方位而同色云　家甚貧寒

朝夕無以供　而不以介于心一日　坐於內堂　夫人曰：

人皆稱君子有神異之術云　見今之粮　將絶火 9)

矣　何不試神術而救此急也　公笑曰：夫人之言

既如此　吾當少試之矣　命婢子　持一鍮器 10)

而諭之曰：汝持此器　往京營 11) 橋前　則有一老嫗

以百錢願買矣　汝可賣來　婢子承命而往

則果有願買之老嫗　一如所指教　仍捧價 12)

而來　又命曰：汝持此往小西門 13) 外市上　則有蒻

笠人 14)　以匙箸 15) 將欲急賣矣　汝以此錢買來

婢子又往　則果符其言　持匙箸來納　卽銀匙箸也

又命曰：持此而往畿營 16) 前　下隷方失其銀匙箸

而來求同色者　示此則可捧十五兩錢　汝可賣來　婢

子又往見　則又符其言　捧十五兩而來　更以一兩錢

給婢子而言曰：買器之老嫗　初失食器而欲代之矣

금 언 득 기 소 실 지 기　　　이 욕 환 퇴　　　　여 가 환 퇴 이 래
今焉得其所失之器　　而欲還退 17)　汝可還退而來

비 자 우 왕 견　　과 연　　잉 환 퇴 기 기 이 래　　이 기 전 여 기
婢子又往見　　果然　　仍還退其器而來　　以其錢與器

전 우 부 인　　사 작 조 석 지 비　　부 인 갱 청 가 수　　즉 소 왈
傳于夫人　　使作朝夕之費　　夫人更請加數　　則笑曰：

여 사 족 의　　불 필 첨 가　　기 신 이 지 사　　류 다 여 차
如斯足矣　　不必添加　　其神異之事　　類多如此

1　李之菡 [1517–78; styled Hyŏngjung 馨仲; sobriquet T'ojŏng 土亭; ancestral seat Hansan 韓山; posthumous epithet Mun'gang 文康]: scholar-official during the reign of King Sŏnjo 宣祖 [r. 1567–1608; 1552–1608]. His father was Yi Ch'i 李穉 [1477–1530].

2　穎悟: clever.

3　卜筮: divination.

4　術數之學: science of divination.

5　通曉: have penetrating mastery of.

6　圓瓢: round gourd.

7　瀟湘: the Xiao and Xiang Rivers, south of Lake Dongting, famous for their beauty.

8　洞庭 = 洞庭湖: Lake Dongting in northeastern Hunan Province, China.

9　絶火: lit. "stop the fire": too poor to even cook.

10　鍮器: brassware.

11　京營: cover term for the capital guard units, including the Military Training Office (Hullyŏn togam 訓鍊都監), the Royal Guards' Command (Ŏyŏngch'ŏng 御營廳), the Command of the Southern Approaches (Suŏch'ŏng 守御廳), the Capital Garrison (Kŭmwiyŏng 禁衛營), the Command of the Northern Approaches (Ch'ongyungch'ŏng 摠戎廳), and the King's Bodyguards (Yonghoyŏng 龍虎營).

12　捧價: commodity prices.

13　小西門 = 西小門 = Soŭimun 昭義門: another name for the Great West Gate (Sŏdaemun 西大門) in Seoul.

14　蒻笠人: person wearing a conical hat of woven reeds.

15　匙箸: spoon and chopsticks.

16　畿營: headquarters of Kyŏnggi Province.

17　還退: give back.

————— 75 —————

The Return of the Spirit of Yi Kyŏngnyu

Vol. III: 1; Diary XIV, pp. 66–7, 70;
listed in Diary XVI, p. 178, as "The Return of the Soul of Yi Kyŏngnyu"; 263.

Yi Kyŏngnyu was an officer of the War Department who took part in the Japanese War of 1592. His second older brother had cast aside his pen and given himself wholly to the bow. When General Pyŏn went out to meet the enemy the second brother was sent as special aide of the state but in their royal order Yi Kyŏngnyu's name found a place instead of that of his brother. The brother said, "My name was the one proposed to the state and even though they have written yours, I'll away."

Kyŏngnyu replied, "My name is written there, hence I should go," and so he made ready, bade his mother goodbye and joined the forces. They went first to the Yŏngu region where they were defeated and fled. The soldiers were without a general and all reduced to confusion. Kyŏngnyu then heard that the general of the local forces was in Sangju. Hurrying thither, he met Yun Sŏm and Pak Chi and made one with them.

Again they fought but again were defeated and all the army broken up, Yun and Pak both being killed. Kyŏngnyu, gathering the remaining forces together, had his servant wait with his horse ready. The servant wept, saying, "We have come to this pass; hasten back to Seoul, will you not?"

Kyŏngnyu laughed and said, "When the state comes to this pass, what purpose for me to live?"

He then called for a pen and wrote out a last message to his parents and his older brother and placed it in the collar of his coat, telling his servant to see it safely delivered. Then he turned to face the enemy. The servant, however, took him in his arms and would not let him go.

Kyŏngnyu said, "Your love and faithfulness pass all bounds – I shall have to do as you say. But I am very hungry just now. Go and get me a meal and hurry back."

The servant believed his word and departed and went to get a meal but when he returned his master was gone. The servant, seeing how strongly the enemy was entrenched, wept and went away.

After making this request and getting rid of his servant, Kyŏngnyu went straight for the enemy. He killed a number of the enemy with his own hand and in return was himself killed. At the time, he was twenty-four years old and it was the twenty-fourth day of the fourth moon, and the place was the plain outside the north gate of Sangju.

The servant took his horse and returned to Seoul, where all the house learned the terrible news. The letter was dated the twenty-fourth day and that day became the sacrificial day. The servant no sooner had come home and done his faithful part but he too fell ill and died; the horse also refused to eat and died too. His clothes and headdress were all placed in order in a coffin and buried in Kwangju in Tolma Township where his ancestors were. Also the servant and horse were buried too.

The literati of Sangju built an altar and there offered sacrifices while the state gave him the posthumous rank of Chief of Secretaries (*tosŭngji*).

In the year *ŭlmyo* (1795) King Chŏngjo wrote with his own hand the name "Altar of Loyal Hearts" and gave it to mark the place. A house was erected to the north of the altar and the command was given to offer sacrifices to these four faithful men in spring and autumn.

Kyŏngnyu died on the battlefield but nightly he visited his house in Seoul. His voice, his □, his face were just as when alive. He would talk to his wife Cho-ssi just as when he lived. She would have food prepared and offer it and he would eat just the same and yet the food was in no way consumed. When the day darkened he would come and when the cock crew he would retire.

His wife asked of him where his body was, saying that if she but knew she would see that it was buried.

He replied in a sad and mournful way, "In all the heaps of bones buried together how could one ever tell? Leave it where it is. The ground, too, is all right where they are buried."

He told her how to do in regard to household matters just as when alive.

After the first anniversary he came down only every other day and after the Great Sacrifice of the second year he bade farewell, saying, "I shall not come again."

At this time his son who became a district magistrate was four years old. He stroked his head and said as he sighed, "He will pass his examination, but alas, he will have his troubles. At that time I shall come again."

He then passed out of the door leaving no mark or trace behind.

Twenty years and more afterwards when Kwanghae was on the throne his son passed his examination and made his obeisance before the family shrine; a voice from midair was heard calling his *sillae** so that everyone wondered.

The grandmother was at that time ill, it being the sixth moon. She was thirsty and asked for an orange to slake it. She said that she was sure an orange would cure her but there was no way to get any such fruit. Several days afterward there was heard a voice from the air calling, "Hyŏng-*nim!*" (older brother).

The dead man's older brother hurried down into the court and looked up and from the clouds came three oranges.

"My mother is calling for oranges and so I got these from Dongting that I now offer."

Then he was gone.

The brother offered the oranges and her sickness was cured.

When Yi Chae (Toam Munjŏnggong) wrote the inscription for Yi's tablet he put on it *Kongni t'ugyul sin hwanghol hye* (from the sky he threw the oranges)[†] a dream indeed it seemed. This is a proof indeed of its reality.

When the day of sacrifices came and the doors were shut, there was a sound of chopsticks and spoon. A relative of his, son of a councilor, Yi Pyŏnghyŏn, made a record saying he had heard these sounds when he was young and shared in the sacrifice, but of late it is not heard again.

Whenever there was a sacrifice in that home there was found hair in the bread, but when the sacrifice was over the sound was heard of someone calling a servant. The sound seemed to come from the guest room.

The servant replied, "Yes."

The word that succeeded was, "Have the fellow that made the bread arrested. A spirit hates man's hair in the food that is offered – why did you not look more carefully? You must be beaten for this."

And so he was paddled on the legs. From this time the greatest care possible was taken in the sacrifice.

---

* *Sillae* refers to new civil service examination passers or the occasion itself. "Call *sillae*" indicates a kind of hazing ritual conducted by seniors to congratulate new civil service examination passers. The ceremony involved seniors drawing designs on the *sillae*'s face in ink and ordering him around.

† The *hanmun* for "*Kongni t'ugyul sin hwanghol hye*" is "空裡投橘　神恍惚兮." In Gale's original translation, he parses the phrase into four segments as "Kongni t'ugyul sinhwang holhye," giving a disyllabic rhythm to it.

리공경류
李公慶流 1)　以兵曹佐郎 2)　當壬辰倭亂　而其仲氏 3)

투필공무직　조방장　변기　출전시　이기중씨종
投筆供武職　助防將 4)　邊機 5)　出戰時　以其仲氏從

사관　계하　이명자오이공서지　중씨왈　이오계하
事官 6)　啓下　而名字誤以公書之　仲氏曰: 以吾啓下

이오서여명　오가왕의　공왈　기이오명계하즉
而誤書汝名　吾可往矣　公曰: 既以吾名啓下則

오당왕　잉속장　이사우자친　창황부진　변기
吾當往　仍束裝　而辭于慈親 7)　蒼黃赴陣　邊機

출진우령우　대패이도　군중무주장　잉대란　공문
出陣于嶺右 8)　大敗而逃　軍中無主將　仍大亂　公聞

순변사　리일　재상주　단기치부지　여윤공섬
巡邊使 9)　李鎰 10)　在尙州　單騎馳赴之　與尹公暹 11)

박공지　동처막하　우전불리　일진함몰　윤박
朴公篪 12)　同處幕下　又戰不利　一陣陷沒　尹朴

량공개피해　공출진외　즉노자견마이대지　견이읍
兩公皆被害　公出陣外　則奴子牽馬而待之　見而泣

고왈　사이도차　원속속환락　가야　공소왈　국사
告曰: 事已到此　願速速還洛 13)　可也　公笑曰: 國事

여차　오하인투생　잉색필　고결우로친급
如此　吾何忍偸生 14)　仍索筆　告訣于老親及

백씨　장우포거　중　사노전지　욕환향적진
伯氏 15)　藏于袍裾 16)中　使奴傳之　欲還向賊陣

즉노자포이읍불사　공왈　여성역가가　오당종여언
則奴子抱而泣不捨　公曰: 汝誠亦可佳　吾當從汝言

이오기심　여가득반이래　노자신지불의　심인가
而吾飢甚　汝可得飯而來　奴子信之不疑　尋人家

걸반이래　즉공이불재의　노자망적진　통곡이귀
乞飯而來　則公已不在矣　奴子望賊陣　痛哭而歸

공이득반위탁이송노　잉회신　갱부적진　수격
公以得飯爲托而送奴　仍回身　更赴敵陣　手格 17)

살수인　이잉우해　시년이십사　사월이십사일　이
殺數人　而仍遇害　是年二十四　四月二十四日　而

상주북문외평야　기노견마이래　거가시문흉보
尙州北門外坪也　其奴牽馬而來　擧家始聞凶報 18)

이발서일위기일이시거애　기노자도이병사
以發書日爲忌日而始擧哀 19)　其奴自到而病死

마역불식이폐　이소유의관　렴이입관　장우광
馬亦不食而斃　以所遺衣冠　斂而入棺　葬于廣

주돌마면선영지좌록　이기하우장노여마　상주
州突馬面先塋之左麓　而其下又葬奴與馬　尙州

사림설단이행조두례　자조가증직　도승지
士林設壇而行俎豆禮 20)　自朝家贈職 21)　都承旨 22)

을묘　정묘　조이친필서충신의사단　건각
乙卯 23)　正廟 24)　朝以親筆書忠臣義士壇　建閣

어북반　명사삼종사병향　이춘추행사　공졸후
於北畔　命使三從事並享　而春秋行祀　公卒後

매야래가중　성음소모　완여생시　대부인조씨수작
每夜來家中　聲音笑貌　宛如生時　對夫人趙氏酬酌

무이평석　매구찬이진　즉음담여생시　이후내견지
無異平昔　每具饌而進　則飲啖如生時　而後乃見之

음식여전　매어일혼후시래　림계명즉출문이거
飲食如前　每於日昏後始來　臨鷄鳴則出門而去

부인문공지유해재어하처　약지지즉장반장의　공초
夫人問公之遺骸在於何處　若知之則將返葬矣　公愀

然 25) 曰：許多白骨堆中 何由辨知乎 不如置之爲好

且吾之白骨所埋處 亦自無害矣 其家事區處 一如

平時 小祥 26) 後 間日 27) 降臨矣 及大祥 28) 時 乃

辭曰：從今以後 吾將不來矣 時公子府使公 29)

年四歲矣 公撫而嗟歎曰：此兒必登第而不幸

當不幸時然 而伊時吾當更來 仍出門 伊後更無

形影 其後二十餘年後 光海朝 公之子登第 謁廟

之時 自空中呼新恩進退 30) 人皆異之 公之母親

常有病患 時則六月間也 喉渴思橘 若得喫

則病可解矣 無由得橘 數日後 空中有呼兄聲

伯氏公下庭而仰視 則雲霧中 公以三橘投之曰：

老親念橘故 吾於洞庭 31) 得來矣 可以進之 仍

忽不見 以橘進之 病患卽差 此時 陶菴 32) 李

文正神道碑 33) 銘曰：空裡投橘 神恍惚兮云者

즉차야　매당기신　행사시　합문　지후　즉필유
卽此也　每當忌辰　行祀時　閤門 34) 之後　則必有

시저　성　기서족　병현　어인왈　오소시참사
匙箸 35) 聲　其庶族 36) 秉鉉 37) 語人曰：吾少時參祀

매문차성의　근일이래　미상문운의　기가행사시
每聞此聲矣　近日以來　未嘗聞云矣　其家行祀時

병유인모지입자　파사후문지　즉외사유호노지성
餠有人毛之入者　罷祀後聞之　則外舍有呼奴之聲

가인괴이청지　즉출자사랑　노자승명이입　즉사
家人怪而聽之　則出自舍廊　奴子承命而入　則使

착치증병비자분부왈　신도기인모발　여하불찰
捉致蒸餠婢子分付曰：神道忌人毛髮　汝何不察

여죄가달　잉명달초　자시매당기신　수년구지후
汝罪可撻　仍命撻楚 38) 自是每當忌辰　雖年久之後

가인불감소홀언
家人不敢少忽焉

1　李慶流 [1564–92; styled Changwŏn 長源; sobriquet Pan'gŭm 伴琴;
　　ancestral seat Hansan 韓山]: scholar-official under King Sŏnjo 宣祖
　　[r. 1567–1608; 1552–1608]. His father was Yi Chŭng 李增 [1525–1600].
　　He was killed on the battlefield during the Imjin (1592) War.
2　兵曹佐郎: senior sixth-grade post belonging to the Ministry of War.
3　仲氏: another's second-eldest brother; here it refers to Yi Kyŏngsim 李慶深
　　[dates unknown].
4　助防將: general who defends the borders during wartime.
5　邊璣: unidentified.
6　從事官: junior sixth-grade post belonging to the garrisons (Kunyŏng 軍營)
　　and the Capital Police (P'odoch'ŏng 捕盜廳).
7　慈親: polite way to refer to one's own mother in front of others.
8　嶺右: western side of Kyŏngsang Province.
9　巡邊使: military envoy inspecting the border regions.
10　李鎰 [1538–1601; styled Chunggyŏng 重卿; ancestral seat Yongin 龍仁;
　　posthumous epithet Changyang 壯襄]: military official under King Sŏnjo

[r. 1567–1608; 1552–1608]. He was a descendant of Yi Paekchi 李伯持 [?–1419].

11 尹暹 [1561–92; styled Yŏjin 汝進; sobriquet Kwajae 果齋; ancestral seat Namwŏn 南原; posthumous epithet Munyŏl 文烈]: scholar-official under King Sŏnjo [r. 1567–1608; 1552–1608]. His father was Yun Usin 尹又新 [dates unknown].

12 朴篪 [?–1592; styled Taegŏn 大建]: scholar-official under King Sŏnjo [r. 1567–1608; 1552–1608].

13 還洛: return to the capital.

14 偸生: eke out a living.

15 伯氏: another's eldest brother; here it refers to Yi Kyŏngham 李慶涵 [1553–1627; styled Yangwŏn 養源; sobriquet Mansa 晚沙; ancestral seat Hansan 韓山]. His father was Yi Chŭng 李增 [1525–1600].

16 袍裾: hem of one's outerwear.

17 手格: fight with one's bare fists.

18 凶報: lit. "bad news" = notice of death.

19 舉哀 = *palsang* 發喪: sending out an announcement of death and/or initiating funerary protocol.

20 俎豆禮 = *chesa* 祭祀: ancestral rite.

21 贈職: lit. "confer official posts or promote" = confer official posts upon or promote meritorious officials, loyal subjects, filial children, and other deserving individuals.

22 都承旨: chief royal secretary (senior third rank) belonging to the Royal Secretariat (Sŭngjŏngwŏn 承政院).

23 乙卯: the year 1795 (Chŏngjo 19).

24 正廟: the years from 1776 to 1800; the reign years of King Chŏngjo.

25 愀然: desolately.

26 小祥: ancestral rite commemorating the first death anniversary.

27 間日 = *kyŏgil* 隔日: every other day.

28 大祥: ancestral rite commemorating the second death anniversary.

29 府使公: Yi Che 李穧 [dates unknown], son of Yi Kyŏngnyu.

30 新恩進退: (new civil examination passer) pay one's respects.

31 洞庭 = 洞庭湖: Lake Dongting in Hunan Province, China.

32 陶菴: sobriquet of Yi Chae 李縡 [1680–1746; styled Hŭigyŏng 熙卿; ancestral seat Ubong 牛峰; posthumous epithet Munjŏng 文正]: scholar-official under King Yŏngjo 英祖 [r. 1724–76; 1694–1776]. Yi Chae's father was Yi Manch'ang 李晚昌 [1654–84].

33 神道碑: gravestone erected along the road beside the tomb of a high-ranking official (junior second grade or above).

34 闔門: lit. "shut the door" = sever communication with the outside; refers
   to putting up a screen or closing the door during an ancestral rite in order
   not to disturb the honoured ancestor enjoying the food prepared by his
   or her descendants.
35 匙箸: spoon and chopsticks.
36 庶族 = *chwajok* 左族: relatives of secondary sons and their descendants.
37 秉鉉: unidentified.
38 撻楚: whip someone's calves.

—— **76** ——

The Secret Commissioner

Vol. III: 6; n.d.; Diary XIV, pp. 74–6; listed in Diary XVI, p. 178,
as "The Secret Commission"; 270.

When young, Prince Yŏngsŏng Pak Munsu went along with his maternal uncle to Chinju and there he met a certain dancing girl and became
completely entangled in her looks. They made an oath to live together
and to die one and the same day.

On a certain day when he was in his study he saw a terribly ugly-
looking wench go by with water on her head. She was pointed out to
him in a laughing way, saying, "Yon woman is nearly thirty years of age
but because she is so horribly ugly she has never come to know the law
of the dual principle. It is said that if any one has the courage to come
into relation with her, he'll be blessed with great good luck and good
blessing will attend him."

Pak heard this and that night the same woman went by his place. He
called her and asked that they share the same pillow. She was delighted
at this good fortune and so took her departure.

When he returned to Seoul, he passed his examination and for ten
years went around the country as a Secret Commissioner and finally
reached Chinju. He went at once to the home of the dancing girl whom
he had formerly known, stood outside the gate and asked for something to eat.

An old woman came out, looked at him for a time and said, "Alas,
alas!"

Pak then asked, "What do you mean by 'alas'"?

The old wife's answer was, "Your face looks like a Master Pak who used to be here three or four officials past and gone, that's why I say 'alas!'"

Pak replied, "I am one and the same person."

The old woman gave a start of wonder and asked, "What does this mean? Going about thus like a beggar I never dreamed to see. Come in, however, and have something to eat before you go."

Pak went in and sat down and then asked, "Where is your daughter?"

Her reply was, "She is just now at the official quarters where her turn is," while she went on preparing the meal.

Suddenly there was the sound of a foot-fall and the daughter appeared. Her mother said to her, "Mister Pak, your friend has come."

The daughter asked, "When, and why has he come?"

The mother's reply was, "He is in a very pitiful condition, his hat broken and in ragged clothes – just a beggar. As to how it has come about, he was driven away from his uncle's for some reason or other. Now he is a wandering waif who has come as far as here where he used to live years ago. He has his friends too among the writers. I expect he hopes to get something from them."

When the daughter heard this she turned very angry and said, "Why do you tell me all this? What concern of mine is it, pray?"

The mother answered, "He has come hoping to see you and you have come. Go in and see him."

The daughter's answer was, "Why see him? What's the use? I have no wish to see any of his kind. Tomorrow is the birthday of the magistrate and all the magistrates of the district are coming with music and dancing, with the girls of the district dressed for the occasion. My clothes are in the press in the room and I must get them out. Please, mother, go in and get them for me."

The mother replied, "How do I know your clothes? Go in and get them yourself."

There being no help for it she opened the door and went in with a very angry countenance. She never turned once to look at him but opened a box and got out her clothes. Without once looking back she went out.

Pak then called the mother and said, "Such cold treatment as this means that I shall not stay here. I am off."

The mother took him by the sleeve and said, "She's only a child and has no sense. Don't be angry at her, please. The meal is all ready. Please wait a minute and dine before you go."

Pak replied, "I have no desire to eat," and at once went away and sought out the ugly woman slave's abode. Here she was carrying water just as she used to do and now returned. Giving a look at Pak for a little, she said, "Alas, alas!"

Pak inquired, "Why do you say 'alas', on seeing me?"

The slave's answer was, "You look just like a Pak who used to live here in the library. That's why I said 'alas!'"

His answer was, "I am that very person."

At once she threw down the bucket from her head, took hold of him with her two hands, and bursting into tears asked, "What does this mean and why such a condition? My house is nearby here – come please."

Pak followed her and found a little room. Here he entered and sat down. Here the slave in tears inquired as to how this had come about and Pak replied as he had done to the mother of the dancing girl.

She gave a start of alarm and said, "How ever could you have become so poor? I thought you were destined to great office. Did I ever dream of your coming to this? Please stay today at my home."

She took from an old case a plain suit of silk and asked him to put it on in place of the one he had.

Pak replied, "Where did you get such a suit as this?"

"This I bought by many years' carrying water. I saved up and so had it put aside. My thought was that if I ever met the master again, I'd make a present of it to him."

Pak refused it, however: "I have come here in these old clothes. If I suddenly put on this fine suit people would wonder what it means. I'll wear it by and by. Leave it as it is."

The woman went into the kitchen and made ready his evening meal. She then went into the rear court and there she went into a long talk with someone as though she was scolding him. There was a sound also of beating, smashing, fighting.

Wondering what this could mean, Pak Munsu asked the reason.

Her answer was, "We worship the spirits here in the south. Ever since I saw you before, I have placed a shrine here where I have prayed morning and evening that the master may advance in rank and office and become widely known. If this god has any spiritual power how comes it that you are seen in this plight? For this reason I have smashed it all to pieces."

Pak laughed and thought the matter over but was deeply moved.

Then she brought in the evening meal. Pak ate it all greedily and there he slept the night. He asked that his morning meal be prepared early: "I have a journey to make," said he and left.

First he went to the Ch'oksŏk Pavilion (*a Kunsan maid here in the Japanese War committed suicide for her country*) and hid behind the main hall. When the sun rose officials began to make ready, placing mats, and raising awnings, and a little later the magistrate and his officers came out. Then all the magistrates of the outlying districts came. Pak suddenly came out of his place of hiding and took a seat without □. He faced the military governor and said, "I am a mere passer, but I wanted to have a share in this fine celebration."

The military governor replied, "Sit there in a corner and look on. That's all right."

In a little, tables of food and drink were brought in, pipes played and the dance began. Pak's own particular dancing girl sat back to back with the host magistrate of Chinju, beautifully dressed and adorned to a fine finish – she was as pretty as a picture.

The military governor looked at her and said to the host, "I hear you have been carried captive by her yonder. You look rather thin and worn."

The host laughed and said, "How could you ever think such a thing? This is merely my concubine. I have nothing to do with her."

The military governor laughed and said, "Don't tell me any such thing."

He then called her and had her pour out the drink. She did as bid, giving a glass to each in their order of rank.

Pak then asked, "I too can drink. Give me a glass, too."

The military governor said, "Give it to him."

She poured it out but gave it to one of the men servants and asked him to pass it to the beggar. Pak laughed and said, "I too am a man and want the girl to bring it."

The host then twisted his face and said, "Take what's given. Never mind about the dancing girl's hand."

Pak then took it and drank.

Foods of various kinds were now brought out and placed before each on large tables but only a dish or two were placed before Pak. He asked, "Why do you make such a distinction between people of one and the same rank?"

The host grew angry at this and said, "Where gentlemen gather, how comes it you make such a row? Take what you want to eat and be gone. What do you mean by all this chatter?"

Pak then grew angry and said, "Am I not a gentleman, too? I have a wife and children. I have a beard as well. Why treat me as though I were a boy?"

The host grew very angry at this and said, "This tramp comes here with his impudence. Put him out."

He ordered his servants to get him out of the place. The servants stood beneath the dais and shouted to him to come down at once.

Pak said, "Not a foot shall I move. Let the boss get out himself."

Fearfully angry at this, the host said, "The creature is crazy. Why don't you servants have him out?" Thus he shouted.

The ☐ servants then seized him by the sleeves and pushed him from behind, whereupon Pak gave a great shout, saying, "All you move out of here."

Before he had finished the servants of the commissioner rushed in, saying, "The Secret Commissioner has come!"

Hearing this, from the military governor down all turned pale and were at a loss what to do. Pak then took his seat on the dais and said, "Please move down for a little."

Now, from the military governor down, all put head dress and hat in order and asked permission for an interview.

After the ceremony was over, Pak ordered that the dancing girl be arrested and her mother also be called. He said to the girl, "How did I treat you in days gone by? Though the hills fall and sea dry away, we swore that our love would never fail. Now when I come thus, you should have thought of our love and treated me kindly. But instead you have been angry and acted in an ugly way. There is a saying that if you can't give money to a beggar you have no right to break his dish. You assuredly have failed in this. You should be beaten to death. But what's the use of this?"

He had her slightly beaten.

Then he said to her mother, "You have acted much better; for your sake I'll not kill her."

He ordered rice and meat to be given. He said also, "Call the woman I met here," and had her sit at his side. He put his hand on her and said, "Here is a woman with heart indeed. Let her be raised to the rank of Chief Dancing Girl and let her take charge of the others."

The other girl he degraded to the rank of water carrier. He called the chief writer and said, "Give her two hundred *yang*, the woman who had treated me well."

령 성 군 박 문 수　　　소 년 수 왕 내 구　　진 주　　임 소
靈城君朴文秀 1)　少年隨往內舅 2) 晉州 3) 任所

면 일 기 이 대 혹　　상 서 이 피 차 동 일 사 생　　일 일
眄一妓而大惑　相誓以彼此同日死生　一日

재 서 실 유 일 추 악 지 비 자 급 수 이 과　　제 인 지 소 이 언 왈
在書室有一醜惡之婢子汲水而過　諸人指笑而言曰：

차 녀 년 근 삼 십　　이 이 추 악 지 고　　상 불 지 음 양 지 리
此女年近三十　而以醜惡之故　尚不知陰陽之理 4)

운　　여 유 근 지 자　　즉 가 위 적 선　　필 획 신 명 지 우　　의
云　如有近之者　則可謂積善　必獲神明之佑 5) 矣

문 수 문 기 언　　기 야　　궐 녀 우 과　　잉 호 입 이 천 침
文秀聞其言　其夜　厥女又過　仍呼入而薦枕 6)

궐 녀 대 락 이 출　　급 환 락 등 과　　십 년 지 간
厥女大樂而出　及還洛登科　十年之間

승 암 행 지 명　　도 진 주　　방 기 소 면 지 기　　가
承暗行之命 7)　到晉州　訪其所眄之妓 8) 家

립 어 문 외 이 걸 반　　즉 자 내 일 로 구 출 래 숙 시 왈
立於門外而乞飯　則自內一老嫗出來熟視曰：

괴 재 괴 재　　문 수 문 로 구 왈　　하 위 여 시 야　　로 구 왈
怪哉怪哉　文秀問老嫗曰：何爲如是也　老嫗曰：

군 지 안 면　　흡 사 전 전 등 내　　박 서 방 주 양 자 고　　괴
君之顏面　恰似前前等內 9) 朴書房主樣子故　怪

지 의　　문 수 왈　　오 과 연 의　　로 구 경 왈　　차 하 사 야
之矣　文秀曰：吾果然矣　老嫗驚曰：此何事也

불 의 서 방 주 작 차 걸 객 이 래 야　　제 가 입 오 방 내
不意書房主作此乞客而來也　第可入吾房內

소 류 끽 반 이 거　　문 수 입 방 좌 정　　문 군 지 녀 안 재
小留喫飯而去　文秀入房坐定　問君之女安在

答曰：方以本府 10) 廳妓 11) 長番而不得出來矣云

而方爇火 12) 炊飯　忽有曳履聲　而其女來至廚下

其母曰：某處朴書房來此矣　其女曰：何時來此

而緣何故而來云耶　其母曰：其狀可矜　破笠弊衣

卽一丐乞兒　問其委折　則見逐於其外家前前使道家

今方轉轉乞食而來　以此處曾是久留地　吏隷輩面熟

故　欲得錢兩(而)委來 13) 云矣　其女作色曰：此等說

何爲對我而言耶　其母曰：欲見汝而來云　旣來矣

一次入見可也　其女曰：見之何益　此等人不欲見之

明日兵使道 14) 生辰　守令多會　張樂矗石樓 15)

營本府以妓輩衣服事　申飭至嚴　吾之衣箱中有

新件衣裳矣　母氏出來也　其母曰：吾何以知之

汝可入而持去也　其女不得已開戶而入　面帶怒色

不轉眸而開箱出衣　不顧而出去　文秀乃呼其母

이 언 왈　주 인 기 여 시 랭 락　오 불 가 구 류　종 차 서 의
而言曰：主人旣如是冷落　吾不可久留　從此逝矣

기 모 만 지 왈　년 소 불 해 사 지 기　하 족 책 야　반 기 숙 의
其母挽止曰：年少不解事之妓　何足責也　飯幾熟矣

소 좌 끽 반 이 거 가 야　문 수 왈　불 원 끽 반　잉 출 문
少坐喫飯而去可也　文秀曰：不願喫飯　仍出門

우 심 기 비 자 지 가　즉 기 비 자 상 급 수 의　급 수 이 래
又尋其婢子之家　則其婢子尙汲水矣　汲水而來

견 기 상 모　량 구 숙 시 왈　괴 재 괴 재　문 수 문 왈
見其狀貌　良久熟視曰：怪哉怪哉　文秀問曰：

하 위 견 인 이 칭 괴　기 비 자 왈　객 지 모 양　흡 사 향 래 차
何爲見人而稱怪　其婢子曰：客之貌樣　恰似向來此

읍 책 방 박 서 방 고　심 절 괴 지 대 왈　오 과 연 의　기 비
邑冊房朴書房故　心竊怪之對曰：吾果然矣　其婢

자 거 수 분 우 지　파 수 대 곡 왈　차 하 사 야　차 하 양 야
子去水盆于地　把手大哭曰：此何事也　此何樣也

오 가 불 원　가 해 왕　문 수 수 이 왕　즉 유 수 간 두 옥 의
吾家不遠　可偕往　文秀隨而往　則有數間斗屋矣

입 기 방 좌 정　읍 문 기 개 걸 지 유　대 여 아 자 대 기 모 지 언
入其房坐定　泣問其丐乞之由　對如俄者對妓母之言

기 녀 경 왈　일 한　여 차 재　오 이 위 서 방 주 대 달 의
其女驚曰：一寒 16) 如此哉　吾以爲書房主大達矣

기 료 도 차　금 일 즉 원 류 오 가 운　이 출 일 추 상 즉 주
豈料到此　今日則願留吾家云　而出一麤箱卽紬

의　일 습　권 사 개 복　문 수 왈　차 의 종 하 출 호
衣 17)　一襲　勸使改服　文秀曰：此衣從何出乎

대 왈　차 시 오 지 적 년 급 수 고 세　야　취 전 무 차
對曰：此是吾之積年汲水雇貰 18) 也　聚錢貿此

세 인 봉 의 이 치　　차 생 약 우 서 방 주　　즉 욕 이 표 고 정 야
貰人縫衣以置　此生若遇書房主　則欲以表故情也

문 수 사 왈　　오 어 금 일　　이 폐 의 래 차　　금 홀 착 차 신 건
文秀辭曰：吾於今日　以弊衣來此　今忽着此新件

의 복　　즉 인 기 불 괴 아 호　　종 당 착 지　　고 치 지　　기 녀 입
衣腹　則人豈不怪訝乎　從當着之　姑置之　其女入

주 이 비 석 선　　입 후 면　　구 눌 눌　　약 유 질 언 자　　연
廚而備夕饍 19)　入後面　口吶吶 20)　若有叱焉者　然

우 유 렬 파 기 명 지 상　　문 수 괴 이 문 지　　즉 답 왈　　남 중
又有裂破器皿之狀　文秀怪而問之　則答曰：南中 21)

다 유　　경 귀 신　　자　　의　　오 자 송 서 방 주 후　　설 신 위
（多有）敬鬼神（者）矣　吾自送書房主後　設神位

이 조 석 기 도　　지 원 서 방 주 립 신 양 명 의　　귀 약 유 령
而朝夕祈禱　只願書房主立身揚名矣　鬼若有靈

즉 서 방 주 기 지 차 경 야　　이 시 지 고　　아 자 렬 파 이 소 화 의
則書房主豈至此境耶　以是之故　俄者裂破而燒火矣

문 수 인 소 이 감 기 의　　이 이 구 석 반 이 진　　문 수 둔 복
文秀忍笑而感其意　而已具夕飯以進　文秀頓服 22)

이 류 숙　　평 명 최 반 왈　　오 유 소 왕 처　　잉 출 문　　선 왕 촉
而留宿　平明催飯曰：吾有所往處　仍出門　先往矗

석 루　　잠 복 어 루 하　　일 출 후　　관 리 분 분 수 소　　사 연
石樓　潛伏於樓下　日出後　官吏紛紛修掃　肆筵

설 석　　소 언　　병 사 급 본 관 출 래　　린 읍 수 령 십 여 인
設席 23)　少焉　兵使及本官出來　隣邑守令十餘人

개 래 회　　문 수 돌 입 상 좌　　향 병 사 이 언 왈　　과 거 객 자
皆來會　文秀突入上座　向兵使而言曰：過去客子

욕 참 성 연 이 래 의　　병 사 왈　　제 좌 일 우　　관 광 무 방 의
欲參盛筵而來矣　兵使曰：第坐一隅　觀光無妨矣

이 이 배 반 랑 자　생 가 조 촉　굉　　　기 기 녀 립 어 본
而已盃盤狼藉　笙歌嘈囃[轟]24)　其妓女立於本

관 배 후　복 식 선 명　함 교 함 태　병 사 고 이 소 왈
官背後　服飾鮮明　含嬌含態　兵使顧而笑曰：

본 관 근 일 대 혹 어 궐 물 야　신 색 불 여 전 의　본 관 소 이
本官近日大惑於厥物耶　神色不如前矣　本官笑而

답 왈　녕 유 시 리　지 유 명 색　무 실 사 의　병 사 소 왈
答曰：寧有是理　只有名色　無實事矣　兵使笑曰：

필 무 시 리　잉 호 사 행 배　기 기 행 배　이 차 차 진 전
必無是理　仍呼使行盃　其妓行盃　而次次進前

문 수 청 왈　차 객 역 선 음　원 청 일 배　병 사 왈　가 진 주
文秀請曰：此客亦善飲　願請一盃　兵使曰：可進酒

기 내 작 주　급 지 인　왈　가 급 피 객　문 수 소 왈　차
妓乃酌酒　給知印 25) 曰：可給彼客　文秀笑曰：此

객 역 남 자 야　원 음 기 수 지 배 주　병 사 여 본 관 작 색 왈
客亦男子也　願飲妓手之盃酒　兵使與本官作色曰：

음 즉 호 의　하 원 기 수 호　문 수 잉 수 이 음 지　진 선 이
飲則好矣　何願妓手乎　文秀仍受而飲之　進饌而

각 인 지 전　구 시 대 탁　이 자 가 지 전　불 과 수 기 이 이
各人之前　俱是大卓　而自家之前　不過數器而已

문 수 우 언 왈　구 시 반 야　이 음 식 하 가 층 하　호
文秀又言曰：俱是班也　而飲食何可層下 26) 乎

본 관 로 왈　장 자 지 회　하 가 여 시 지 번　득 끽 음 식
本官怒曰：長者之會　何可如是至煩　得喫飲食

사 가 속 거　하 위 다 언 야　문 수 역 로 왈　오 역 비 장 자 호
斯可速去　何爲多言也　文秀亦怒曰：吾亦非長者乎

오 이 유 처 유 자　수 발 창 연　즉 오 기 해 소 호　본 관 로
吾已有妻有子　鬚髮蒼然 27) 則吾豈孩少乎　本官怒

曰：此乞客忘［妄］悖矣　可以逐出　仍分付官隷

使逐送　官隷立於樓下呵叱曰：斯速下來　文秀

曰：吾何以下去　本官可以下去矣　本官益怒曰：

此是狂客也　下隷輩焉敢不爲曳下乎　號令如霜

而知印輩擧袖推背　文秀高聲曰：汝輩可出去

言未已　門外驛卒大呼曰：暗行御史出道矣　自兵

使以下　面無人色　而蒼黃幷出　文秀高坐而笑曰：

固當如是出去矣　仍坐於兵使之座　而自兵使以

下各邑守令　皆具帽帶請謁　一一入現　禮罷後

文秀命　捉入其妓　又呼其母　而分付於妓曰：

年前吾與汝　情愛何如　山崩海渴　而情好不變

爲約矣　今焉吾作此樣而來　則汝可念舊日之情

好言慰問可也　何爲發怒也　俗云不給糧而破瓢者

正謂汝也　事當卽地打殺　而於汝何誅　仍略施笞

罰 28) 謂妓母曰：汝則稍解人事　以汝之故　姑不

殺之　命給米肉　又曰：吾有所眄之女　斯速呼來

仍使汲水之婢升軒而坐於傍　撫之曰：此眞有情女

子也　此女陞付妓案 29)　使行行首 30) 事　而某妓

降付汲水婢　仍招入本付吏房　毋論某樣錢二百兩

速持來以給其婢子而去矣

1 朴文秀 [1691–1756; styled Sŏngbo 成甫; sobriquet Kiŭn 耆隱; ancestral seat
  Koryŏng 高靈; posthumous epithet Ch'unghŏn 忠憲]: he was honoured
  as Prince Yŏngsŏng 靈城君 for his meritorious work during the Yi Injwa
  Rebellion of 1728. He served as a secret royal inspector (*amhaeng ŏsa*
  暗行御史). Numerous Chosŏn stories depict him on duty. His father was
  Pak Hanghan 朴恒漢 [1666–98]. Many anecdotes regarding his days as
  a secret inspector survive.
2 內舅: maternal uncle.
3 晉州: a town in South Kyŏngsang Province.
4 陰陽之理: the principle of *yin* and *yang* (as it relates to men and women).
5 神明之佑: help from the spirits of heaven and earth.
6 薦枕: (of a *kisaeng* or a secondary wife) wait on someone in bed.
7 暗行之命: a royal order to travel incognito to act as the eyes and ears of
  the king.
8 所眄之妓: a *kisaeng* with whom one has an especially intimate relationship.
9 等內: for the duration of an official's term of office.
10 本府: (for a local magistrate) "my yamen."
11 廳妓 = *such'ŏng kisaeng* 守廳妓生: a *kisaeng* who attends a local magistrate
  in bed.
12 爇火: make a fire.
13 萎來: lose courage; be dejected, dispirited.
14 兵使道 = *pyŏngma chŏltosa* 兵馬節度使: commander-in-chief of any army
  (junior second-grade military post).

15 矗石樓: a pavilion by the Nam River in South Kyŏngsang Province.
16 一寒: destitution.
17 紬衣: silken clothing.
18 雇貰 = *koga* 雇價: wages.
19 夕饍: supper.
20 吶之: mumble; stutter.
21 南中: in the southern region.
22 頓服: gulp down food or medicine.
23 肆筵設席: prepare banquet seats.
24 嘈轟: make boisterous sounds.
25 知印 = *t'ongin* 通引: a factotum belonging to a local administration.
26 層下: belittle, sneer at, make light of.
27 蒼然: faded with age, hoary.
28 答罰: (a form of punishment) flogging with a bamboo stick or a wooden cane.
29 妓案: roster of *kisaeng* officially registered to a local yamen.
30 行首: leader of the pack; here, a head *kisaeng* (*haengsu kisaeng* 妓生).

——— **77** ———

Pak's Help

Vol. III: 8; n.d.; Diary XIV, pp. 79–81; 271.

While Pak Munsu was a Secret Commissioner on his way about, he was overtaken by night and had no food to eat. He was very hungry and so hurried into the first house he came to. Here he found a boy of about fifteen alone. He asked something to eat from this lad, whereupon the boy replied, "I have only my mother with me and we are very, very poor. It is several days since we have had a warm meal. I am afraid we have nothing to offer."

The Commissioner sat tired out and hungry.

The boy looked up several times at a paper package on the shelf in the room with something of a shamed look on his face. He then took down the parcel and went into the inner room. There were three or four rooms in the house. The inner room was just across the court from the guest room.

Pak could hear the boy call his mother: "Mother, there is a guest who has just now called who has had nothing to eat and he asks that we provide him a meal. We must try to do something for him and yet we have nothing on hand. Shall I use what we have in this package?"

The mother replied, "Then how about your father's sacrifice, if you use that?"

The boy said, "That would never do and yet I cannot bear to see this gentleman left unsupplied when he is hungry."

The mother then took it and prepared a meal.

When Pak heard this conversation, he felt very sorry for them and as the boy returned, Pak asked what package this was and what conversation they had had.

His reply was, "I cannot tell you anything but the truth. Our father's sacrificial day is near at hand and fearing we might have nothing on hand for the meal, we had one measure put away that I had wrapped up. Even though we went hungry I did not intend to use it. Seeing Your Excellency so hungry and having nothing to eat before you, I could not do anything but use this. If you had not heard this, I would not be ashamed."

When morning came, a servant came before the house and called, "Pak *toryŏng,** come out!"

The boy begged the servant, saying, "I cannot go today."

Hearing this surname, Pak asked what clan he belonged to and found it was his very own. He also inquired as to who had come and was told it was the deputy magistrate's servant.

"Having come of age, I heard that the deputy had a daughter of marriageable age and so made request for marriage. The deputy took offence at this, seeing I was so poor, and so has sent this servant to arrest me. They have sent several times, taken me, and have made sport of me by his people; and now he sends again."

Pak Munsu said to the servant, "I am an uncle of this boy and I shall go in his place."

He had breakfast and went following the servant. The deputy sat in state and ordered him to be arrested and brought in, when suddenly Pak sprang with lively steps up to where the deputy sat and said, "My nephew is an aristocrat higher than you, deputy though you be. He is poor and that's why he asked marriage with your daughter. If you do not wish it, say so and let the matter end there. Why have you arrested him thus and insulted him in this way? You have presumed on your authority to do thus."

When he had heard this, the deputy flew into a rage and had his servant summoned at once, whereupon he soundly rated him, saying, "I ordered you to bring the boy Pak and you bring this mad creature to me instead. Is this the way you insult your master? You shall be put down and beaten on the buttocks!"

Munsu gradually let from his sleeve the point of his horse-mace and roared at the deputy, "How do you dare to act as you have done?"

When he saw this, the deputy turned ashy pale and hurried down from the dais and bowed with his face to the ground saying, "I have done wrong and am worthy of death, worthy of death."

The Commissioner said, "Will you join marriage with this man or not?"

His reply was, "How could I think of refusing?"

The Commissioner said, "Looking up the calendar I find four days hence is a lucky day. I shall come with the bridegroom. Get ready then everything for the marriage."

The deputy replied, "I'll do it just as you say, Sir."

When Munsu had gone out of the gate, he repaired to the town and held a session making his presence known. He said to the official, "I have a nephew who lives in such-and-such place, who is engaged to the daughter of the deputy. The marriage will take place on the appointed day. Will you please see that food and necessaries are sent from the yamen to the wedding."

The magistrate said, "This is a very happy occasion. Be sure I'll see that all the necessaries are on hand. I'll do as you command."

The Commissioner then summoned the surrounding magistrates, had his own attendants see the bridegroom on his way, and made his headgear and dress. The Commissioner then put on his ceremonial dress, and riding a chair, came in state. The house of the deputy had a great tent created like a canopy of heaven with food and supplies without number. On the highest seat sat the Commissioner while the various officials sat around □ in order. It was a great day of glory for the house of the deputy.

When the ceremony was over the bridegroom came forth and bowed to the Commissioner who then gave a command that they arrest the deputy.

The deputy bowed with his face to the ground, saying, "I have obeyed the commands of Your Excellency. What is my fault?"

The Commissioner responded, "How many fields and how much property have you?"

He replied, "So much."

The Commissioner then said, "Will you give half to your son-in-law?"

The deputy replied, "As Your Excellency says, I'll be glad to do so."

The Commissioner said, "How many servants and cattle have you, and what furniture?"

His reply told all.

The Commissioner said, "Give half of all you have to this son-in-law."

"I give it," was his reply.

"Bring paper," commanded the Commissioner: "Have it written out."

As witness he wrote first "The Secret Commissioner Pak Munsu" and the second was the magistrate of the place, the third another magistrate so-and-so and so on. He then stamped it with the Commissioner's seal and made his way to another county.

* *toryŏng*: a Korean expression for an unmarried *yangban* man.

기 은 박 문 수　　　이 수 의　　　행　　　전 향 타 읍　　　일 만 불 득 식
耆隱朴文秀 1) 以繡衣 2) 行　轉向他邑　日晚不得食

파 유 기 색　　　잉 향 일 인 지 가　　　즉 지 유 일 동 자　　　이 년 근 십
頗有飢色　仍向一人之家　則只有一童子　而年近十

오 륙 의　　　잉 향 전 걸 일 우 반　　　즉 대 왈　　　오 즉 편 친 시 하
五六矣　仍向前乞一盃飯　則對曰：吾則偏親侍下 3)

이 가 계 빈 궁　　　절 화 이 수 일　　　무 반 여 객　　　문 수 곤 비 소 좌
而家計貧窮　絶火已數日　無飯與客　文秀困憊少坐

동 자 루 첨 견 옥 루　　　지 지 낭　　　미 유 참 연 지 색　　　이 즉
童子屢瞻見屋漏 4) 之紙囊 5) 微有慚然之色 6) 而卽

해 낭 입 내　　　수 간 두 옥 호 외　　　즉 기 내 당 야　　　재 외 문 지
解囊入內　數間斗屋戶外　卽其內堂也　在外聞之

즉 동 자 호 모 왈　　　외 유 과 객　　　실 시 청 반　　　인 기 기 불 가 고
則童子呼母曰：外有過客　失時請飯　人飢豈不可顧

야　　　량 미 절 핍　　　무 이 공 반　　　이 차 취 반 가 야　　　기 모 왈
耶　糧米絶乏 7) 無以供飯　以此炊飯可也　其母曰：

如此而汝親之忌事 8) 將闕之乎 童子曰：情理雖

切迫 而目見人飢 何可不救乎 其母受而炊之

文秀聞其言 心甚惻然 童子出來 文秀問其由

則答曰：客子旣聞知 則不得欺矣 吾之親

忌不遠 無以過祀故 適有一升米 作紙囊懸之

雖闕食而不喫矣 今客子飢餓 而無供飯之資 不得

而已以此炊飯矣 不幸爲客子所聞知 不勝慚愧

云云 方與酬酌之際 有奴子來言曰：朴道令斯

速出來 其童子哀乞曰：今日則不得去矣 文秀問

其姓 則是乃同宗 9) 也 又問彼來者爲誰 曰：此邑

座首 10) 之奴也 吾之年紀已長 聞座首有女通婚

則座首以爲見辱云 而每送奴子 捉我而去 捽曳 11)

侮辱 無所不至 今又推捉 12) 矣 文秀乃對奴

而言曰：吾乃此童之叔也 吾可代往 飯後仍隨奴

자이왕　즉좌수자고좌　이사지착입운　문수직상
子而往　則座首者高坐　而使之捉入云　文秀直上

청좌이언왈　오질지반벌　유승어군　이특이가
廳坐而言曰：吾姪之班閥　猶勝於君　而特以家

빈지고　통혼어군의　군여무의　즉치지가야
貧之故　通婚於君矣　君如無意　則置之可也

하매매착래시욕　군이읍중수향 13)　이유권력이연야
何每每捉來示辱　君以邑中首鄉 13)　而有權力而然耶

좌수대로　착입기노이질지왈　오사여착래박동
座首大怒　捉入其奴而叱之曰：吾使汝捉來朴童

이여하위착차광객이래　사여상전견욕호　여죄당태
而汝何爲捉此狂客而來　使汝上典見辱乎　汝罪當笞

문수자수중　로시마패 14) 왈　여언감약시　좌수일견
文秀自袖中　露示馬牌 14) 曰：汝焉敢若是　座首一見

이면여토색　강우계하부복왈　사죄사죄　문수왈
而面如土色　降于階下俯伏曰：死罪死罪　文秀曰：

여가결혼호　대왈　언감불혼　문수우왈　오견력
汝可結婚乎　對曰：焉敢不婚　文秀又曰：吾見曆

삼명 15) 즉길일　이일오당여신랑해래의　여가비혼구
三明 15) 卽吉日　伊日吾當與新郎偕來矣　汝可備婚具

이대　좌수왈　경락　문수잉출문　직입읍내이출도
以待　座首曰：敬諾　文秀仍出門　直入邑內而出道

위기본관왈　오유족질이재어모동　여차읍수향통
謂其本官曰：吾有族姪而在於某洞　與此邑首鄉通

혼　이기재모일　이시혼구급연수　자관비급위호
婚　而期在某日　伊時婚具及宴需　自官備給爲好

본관왈　차시호사　하불우조　수당여명　우청린
本官曰：此是好事　何不優助　須當如命　又請隣

읍 수 령 　 당 일 문 수 청 신 랑 어 자 가 하 처 　 구 관 복
邑守令 當日文秀請新郎於自家下處 16) 具冠服

이 문 수 비 위 의 수 후 　 좌 수 지 가 　 운 막 련 천 　 배 반 랑 자
而文秀備威儀隨後 座首之家 雲幕連天 盃盤狼藉

좌 상 어 사 주 벽 　 제 수 령 개 렬 좌 　 좌 수 지 가 　 일 층
座上御史主壁 17) 諸守令皆列坐 座首之家 一層

생 광 휘 의 　 행 례 후 　 신 랑 출 래 　 어 사 명 나 입 좌 수
生光輝矣 行禮後 新郎出來 御史命拿入座首

좌 수 고 두 왈 　 소 인 의 분 부 　 행 혼 례 의 　 어 사 왈
座首叩頭曰：小人依分付 行婚禮矣 御史曰：

여 전 여 답 기 하 　 왈 　 기 석 수 의 　 왈 　 분 반 급 녀 서 호
汝田與畓幾何 曰：幾石數矣 曰：分半給女婿乎

좌 수 고 왈 　 언 감 불 연 　 어 사 왈 　 노 비 우 마 기 하
座首告曰：焉敢不然 御史曰：奴婢牛馬幾何

기 명 집 물 역 기 하 　 답 왈 　 기 구 기 필 기 건 기 개 의 　 왈
器皿什物亦幾何 答曰：幾口幾匹幾件幾個矣 曰：

우 위 분 반 급 녀 서 호 　 답 왈 　 언 감 불 연 호 　 어 사 즉 명 서
又爲分半給女婿乎 答曰：焉敢不然乎 御史卽命書

문 기 　 이 증 인 수 서 어 사 박 문 수 　 차 서 본 관 모 모 읍 쉬
文記 而證人首書御史朴文秀 次書本官某某邑倅

렬 서 이 답 마 패 　 잉 이 전 향 타 처
列書而踏馬牌 仍而轉向他處

---

1 朴文秀 [1691–1756; styled Sŏngbo 成甫; sobriquet Kiǔn 耆隱; ancestral seat Koryŏng 高靈; posthumous epithet Ch'unghŏn 忠憲]: a scholar-official under King Yŏngjo [r. 1724–76; 1694–1776].
2 繡衣: lit. "silken clothing" = *amhaeng ŏsa* 暗行御史: secret royal inspector.
3 偏親侍下: support a single parent.
4 屋漏: northwest corner of a room.
5 紙囊: sack made of paper.
6 慚然之色: look of mortification/humiliation/shame.

 7 絶乏: be/get exhausted; run out of.

 8 忌事 = *chesa* 祭祀: ancestral rite.

 9 同宗 = *chongssi* 宗氏: families who share the same surname and ancestral seat.

10 座首 = *agwan* 亞官 = *suhyang* 首鄉: head of a local yamen (*hyangch'ŏng* 鄉廳).

11 捽曳: yank by the tresses of one's hair.

12 推捉: hunt down and arrest.

13 首鄉 = *chwasu* 座首: see note 10.

14 馬牌: lit. "horse disc" = a metal disc used for identification purposes by officials when moving from one post-station to the text. One side was marked with the maximum number of horses allowed.

15 三明: on the third day; two days after tomorrow.

16 下處: lodging place of an honoured traveller.

17 主壁: seat of highest honour located in the centre of the room, or the person who occupies it.

--- **78** ---

Examples of Courage

Vol. III: 11; Diary XIV, pp. 84–5; 276.

General Sin Yŏch'ŏl when young went to the Hullyŏn Commons for archery practice and on his return he was insulted by a drunken soldier attached to the Guard of the Hullyŏn. Sin kicked him with such force that the man fell down and died. Yi Wan was then General of the Guard and to his house Sin made his way. Here he sent in his card and was invited in. After greetings, General Yi asked Sin why he had come.

Sin replied, "My name is so-and-so; a little ago as I returned from the archery □ I was insulted by one of Your Excellency's soldiers and I kicked him so that he died. What are the consequences in a case like this?"

General Yi laughed and replied, "Murder means death to the doer. Three Feet of Board* with the offence marked settles it. There is no escape from the law."

Sin replied, "Death is death, but to die for one common soldier is not the fate of a gentleman. How would it be if I kill a general and die with some show about it?"

General Yi asked, "Does this mean that you want to kill me?"

Sin said, "Your soldiers are of no use. Five paces and less and I have done the deed."

General Yi laughed and said, "Wait a little."

He then called the captain and said, "I hear there is a soldier dead drunk lying on the road as though he was dead, making a pretence. Have him carried here."

The servants went at once and had him brought, placed down and beaten and then taken out. Then he was said to be killed by the general and so nothing further was said about it.

General Yi asked Sin to stay a while and said, "You are a young man of great promise. Come see me often."

He loved him as his own son.

One day the General called him and said, "There is a house of a friend of mine near here where the people have died of typhoid – the whole household. And there is no one to see to the burial. I have prepared all the necessaries. Would you go this evening and see them taken away?"

Sin took the order, came at night, and lit a light, whereupon he found five corpses in the room. He had them wrapped in linen one, two, and just as he came to take charge of the third, suddenly it jumped up and gave Sin a stinging blow across the cheek and knocked out the light.

Undaunted by this, Sin seized fast hold of his wrist: "What mean you? What sort of action is this?"

He called for a light and saw the corpse laughing from ear to ear. It was none other than General Yi who had lain down among the corpses to try Sin's courage and see what mettle he was made of.

* "Three feet of board" (*samch'ŏk*): military law.

申大將汝哲 1)　少時習射于訓練院 2)　歸路都監

軍一人乘醉詬辱 3)　公乃蹴殺 4) 之　直入李貞翼公浣 5)

家通刺 6) 使之入來而寒暄罷 李公問何爲來見

申公對曰：某名某也 俄於射亭 而歸路都監

軍士如斯如斯 某果蹴殺之矣 此將奈何

李公笑曰：殺人者死 三尺至嚴 焉敢逭律 7)

申公曰：死則一也 殺一軍士而死 非丈夫之事也

欲殺其大將而死如何 李公曰：汝欲殺我乎 申公曰：

五步之內 公不得恃其衆也 李公笑曰：第姑俟之

仍分付於都監執事曰：聞軍卒一人 乘醉臥於街上

托以佯死須擔來 下隷承命而擔來 則拿入決棍

8) 而出之 仍以無事 李公使留之曰：汝大器也

可親近往來 愛之如親子姪 一日召而言曰：吾親

知人家在不遠 而以染疾 9) 擧家皆死 無人殮襲 10)

諸具吾已備置 今夜汝可往其家 躬自殮襲可也

申公承命 而至夜執燭而往 則一房之內有五尸

잉 이 포 목
仍以布木 11)　　次次斂之　　至第三尸　　將殮之時
차 차 렴 지　지 제 삼 시　장 렴 지 시

홀 연 시 기 이 타 협
忽然尸起而打頰 12)　　燭乃滅矣　　申公少不驚動
촉 내 멸 의　신 공 소 불 경 동

이 수 안
以手按 13) 之曰：焉敢如是　公呼人　爇燭 14) 而來
지 왈　언 감 여 시　공 호 인　설 촉　이 래

기 시 대 소 기 좌
其尸大笑起坐　乃是李公也　盖李公欲試其膽氣 15)
내 시 리 공 야　개 리 공 욕 시 기 담 기

이 선 와 시 측
而先臥尸側

1　申汝哲 [1634–1701; styled Kyemyǒng 季明; ancestral seat P'yǒngsan 平山; posthumous epithet Changmu 莊武]: military official under King Sukchong 肅宗 [r. 1674–1720; 1661–1720]. His father was Sin Chun 申竣 [dates unknown].
2　訓鍊院: (Chosǒn Dynasty) Office of Military Training.
3　詬辱: slander and dishonour.
4　蹴殺: kick someone to death.
5　李浣 [1602–74; styled Chingji 澄之; sobriquet Maejukhǒn 梅竹軒; ancestral seat Kyǒngju 慶州; posthumous epithet Chǒngik 貞翼]: military official under King Hyǒnjong 顯宗 [r. 1659–74; 1641–74]. His father was Yi Suil 李守一 [1554–1632].
6　通刺: send in one's calling card; seek an audience by presenting one's card.
7　逭律: evade the law.
8　決棍: flog.
9　染疾 = chǒnyǒmbyǒng 傳染病: contagious disease; epidemic.
10　殮襲: dressing a corpse for burial.
11　布木: linen and cotton.
12　打頰: slap someone on the cheek.
13　按: caress.
14　爇燭: light a candle.
15　膽氣 = 膽力: courage, mettle.

——— **79** ———

Prophets of the Shade

Vol. III: 16; n.d.; Diary XIV, pp. 89–90; 284.

While Vice-President of the College of Literature, Yi Chŏngbo (*p'ansŏ*)* became a mourner and so resigned office. He went on a journey to Ch'ungch'ŏng Province to the graves of his ancestors and after seeing them, suddenly a messenger met him saying that his only son was very ill. In great excitement, he started on his return journey and reached a place called Sŏngch'o-*chŏm*† as the evening fell.

There were a group of dried herring merchants stopping here who had arrived before him. Yi Chŏngbo went into a little room on the other side of the court. It was a bright moonlit night and he was quite sleepless so he sat up to pass the time. One of the group of herring peddlers came out of his room opposite and after urinating, he looked up at the sky and then called to a companion to come out.

A moment later another man came out and they sat down together. The one pointed out the stars saying, "Yonder star in Taurus runs counter to so-and-so just now; we shall have a great rain tomorrow that will not cease for days. Let's get up early and make sure of crossing that stream or we shall be blocked."

The one man said, "Let's do so."

Thus they talked together. The other inquired, "Do you know that magistrate whom we met on the road today?"

The reply was, "He is the magistrate of Yŏnggwang."

"What sort of man is he?" inquired he.

"He is a fine-looking man."

"But has he no untoward marks about him?"

"In ten years from now he will dance his part on the examinations cart – a terrible portent, surely."

Again he asked, "Do you know the guest who came here today to this inn?"

"Yes, he is a very fine gentleman. He shall rise to the place of minister."

He again asked, "Do you not see any special mark between his eyes?"

"His marks are clear and fine and yet he is destined to have no posterity. He has heard of his ☐ son's illness already, but his son really died yesterday. He is not likely to ever have another son."

When Yi heard this in his room he was greatly alarmed and opened the door, whereupon the two men made their escape into the room and a snoring like thunder was the only noise.

Yi called out, "Who was that who was talking here just now? I want to see him."

But there was no one to reply.

A little later the cock crew and all the guests arose, had breakfast and took their way.

Yi also had his horse fed and started out.

When the afternoon had come a great rain fell and the stream overflew its banks and many people failed to cross. When he arrived home the first news was that his son was dead, just as was foretold.

Later the magistrate of Yŏnggwang, Sin Ch'iun, died as a rebel against the state in the year *ŭrhae*.

* *p'ansŏ*: senior second-grade minister of the Six Ministries (Yukcho 六曹), comprising Personnel (Ijo 吏曹), Tax (Hojo 戶曹), Rites (Yejo 禮曹), War (Pyŏngjo 兵曹), Justice (Hyŏngjo 刑曹), and Public Works (Kongjo 工曹).

† *"chŏm"*: tavern.

李判書鼎輔 1) 以副學 2) 遭故 3) 一日 往省湖中 4) 先山

聞獨子病報 蒼黃復路 到省草店 5) 而日暮 貫目 6)

(貫目靑魚)商人十餘人 先入店矣 李公處于越小房

夜深月明 不寐坐 一商人開戶而出溺 仰見天象

忽呼同伴之字 7) 曰： 某也出來 而已一人又出

相對而坐 一人指示星辰曰： 畢星 8) 犯某星 明午

필대우　수일불지의　진조　기동　월모천가야　일인
必大雨　數日不止矣　趁早 9) 起動　越某川可也　一人

앙시왈　연의　잉여지수작　일인문왈　금일소봉
仰視曰：然矣　仍與之酬酌　一人問曰：今日所逢

수령행　차　여지지호　왈　문시령광　쉬야　왈
守令行（次）　汝知之乎　曰：聞是靈光 10) 倅也　曰：

기인하여　왈　풍의동탕　의　왈　기면목능무
其人何如　曰：風儀動盪 11) 矣　曰：其面目能無

흉기호　왈　십년지후　필무어차상의　지흉지상야
凶氣乎　曰：十年之後　必舞於車上矣　至凶之像也

왈　금일입차점상인지지호　왈　극귀인　견금사
曰：今日入此店喪人知之乎　曰：極貴人　見今似

귀지재상지반의　왈　기간간득무소현지기야
貴至宰相之班矣　曰：其眉間得無所現之氣耶

왈　기형극청수　자궁　심귀　필문독자병보이거
曰：其形極淸秀　子宮 12) 甚貴　必聞獨子病報而去

연이작일오후　이불구의　잉이무사가려의
然而昨日午後　已不救矣　仍以無嗣可慮矣

리공문이아이지　개호이시지　즉이인잉입방내　비
李公聞而訝異之　開戶而視之　則二人仍入房內　鼻

성여뢰　리공고성왈　아자수작지인수야　원일견지
聲如雷　李公高聲曰：俄者酬酌之人誰也　願一見之

련성이무응자　미기계명　행인개기이최반출문
連聲而無應者　未幾鷄鳴　行人皆起而催飯出門

리공역말마　이발　과오후　대우과주　천거창일
李公亦秣馬 13) 而發　過午後　大雨果注　川渠漲溢

<ruby>행</ruby><ruby>인</ruby><ruby>수</ruby><ruby>일</ruby><ruby>불</ruby><ruby>통</ruby>　<ruby>도</ruby><ruby>가</ruby><ruby>즉</ruby><ruby>기</ruby><ruby>자</ruby><ruby>이</ruby><ruby>사</ruby>　<ruby>과</ruby><ruby>부</ruby><ruby>기</ruby><ruby>언</ruby>　<ruby>이</ruby><ruby>령</ruby>
行人數日不通　到家則其子已死　果符其言　而靈

光倅卽申致雲 14) 也　乙亥謀逆 15) 伏誅

1 李鼎輔 [1693–1766; styled Sasu 士受; sobriquet Samju 三洲; ancestral seat Yŏnan 延安; posthumous epithet Mun'gan 文簡]: scholar-official under King Yŏngjo 英祖 [r. 1724–76; 1694–1776]. His father was Yi Usin 李雨臣 [1670–1744].

2 副學 = *pujehak* 副提學: senior third-grade post belonging to the Office of Special Counselors (Hongmungwan 弘文館).

3 遭故 = *chogan* 遭艱 = *tanggo* 當故: suffer the death of one's parents.

4 湖中: Ch'ungch'ŏng Province.

5 省草店: tavern in a place named Sŏngch'o. According to the *Survey of Geography of Korea* (*Tongguk yŏji sŭngnam* 東國輿地勝覽), Sŏngch'o is listed as a place name in Anak County 安岳郡 in Hwanghae Province, and Kŭmsan County 金山郡 and Kŏch'ang County 居昌郡 in Kyŏngsang Province.

6 貫目: dried herring. Cf. vernacular Korean *kwamegi* ← *kwa[n]mok-i* → *kwam-oyki* → North Kyŏngsang dialect *kwamegi* "id." In other words, the dialect term *kwamegi* "dried herring" is in origin a Sino-Korean word meaning "[fish] strung up through the eyes."

7 同伴之字: the name of one's companion.

8 畢星: the twelfth star in the twenty-eight mansions of Chinese astronomy.

9 趁早 = *chinjŭk* 趁卽 ~ *chinsi* 趁時: immediately, promptly, on the spot, from the get-go.

10 靈光: a town in South Chŏlla Province.

11 風儀動盪: possess a well-built physique and a beautifully plump face.

12 子宮: good fortune with one's posterity.

13 秣馬: feed one's horse.

14 申致雲: unidentified.

15 乙亥謀逆: incident involving a subversive message posted at an inn in Naju 羅州 in 1755 (Yŏngjo 31).

—— **80** ——

Yang Pongnae

No page numbers; n.d.; in Diary XII, pp. 182–4; 288

Yang Pongnae Saŏn's father, who had never passed his literary exami-nation, went to Yŏngam as magistrate. He received permission for a short furlough and on his way back from the capital one day before he reached his destination, he arose early in the morning and started on his way. But before he reached the inn, he was tired out and his horse as well. He therefore went into a house by the way. It was the time of special farm work and all hands were in the fields. There was only a girl in the house of some twelve or thirteen years of age. She said to the servants that accompanied him, "I'll prepare dinner for you, please rest here."

A servant said, "You are only a young girl; how can you prepare food for our whole company?"

"I can easily do so – please do not be anxious on that score."

She then swept out the [quarters] and put things in order and said, "I'll prepare food for the Master, but you servants can stand good for your own."

Yang looked with wonder at the girl, so pretty of face and so sweet of voice – not a bit like a girl of the country. A little later she brought him his noonday meal, clean and neat beyond words.

They all praised her and wondered at her skill.

Yang called the girl to him and asked her age. She said twelve.

"What does your father do?" inquired he.

She replied, "He is one of the military guard of this town and he has gone with my mother to the fields to weed."

Yang loved this honest straightforward girl and gave her two fans – a blue and red one – and said laughingly, "These are my wedding gifts to you, please take them."

She took them and went into her room, opened her box and wrapped them in a red *furoshiki** and said, "I am putting them away here."

Yang asked, "Why do you wrap them up and put them away thus?"

Her reply was, "These are my wedding gifts of necessity; I put them away with greatest care."

All the people of the party looked on her with wonder and praised her comely ways.

Shortly after, Yang left and went on his way to his town and soon forgot all about her.

Several years afterward, the gatekeeper of Yang's home came in to say, "Such-and-such Military Secretary of the outlying district has come and wants to see Your Excellency."

Yang asked him in, but found he was a stranger whom he had never seen before.

Yang asked, "Who are you? And why have you come to see me?"

His reply was, "I am the Military Secretary of such-and-such a village. Your Excellency: on your return from Seoul several years ago, did you not call at our home and have a young girl there prepare your dinner for you?"

Yang said, "Why yes, that is so."

"Did you give her anything in the way of a pledge?"

He replied, "It's not a pledge. She was such a nice girl and did her work so well that I gave her a present."

He said, "The girl is my daughter and she is now fifteen. And while I have tried to make arrangements for her marriage, she says she has a pledge from the magistrate and will go nowhere else.

"I said in reply, 'Nonsense – what he said was only a joke. What use to □ of that!' But she refuses absolutely to listen to any other proposal. I have coaxed and threatened but she says she will die first and refuses utterly."

Yang said in reply, "How can I refuse your daughter's wish in this matter. Choose a day and let her come."

The day came about and he took her by a marriage ceremony as his secondary wife. He was a widower at that time and she was made the woman of the household.

In all her work and oversight of his home, she was more than a delight to him.

He was succeeded in office by another and so returned home and his wife loved his sons and daughters and she managed all his servants with a perfect hand.

She made all his relatives glad as well and when her presence was there, gladness and joy resulted.

All praised her excellent virtues, those above and those below.

She had a son called Yang Pongnae. He was a beautiful lad, born of the gods; his eyes had the light of other worlds in them. The face of the fairy, the form of the genie was he.

Some years later the father died and when in sorrow, the household went into mourning, with all the relatives assembled.

Pongnae's mother wept and said to those gathered: "You have all come □ and all □ our mourners. I want to ask of you a favour."

The mourners said in reply, "Whatever your kind heart shall suggest we shall assuredly do."

All the relatives gave their assent likewise.

She then said, "I have a son who is bright and promising. Still, according to the law of our land he is the son of a concubine, always regarded as inferior. What hope is there for him? Though you all love him and make no difference in your kind treatment, if I die he becomes my mourner and he will be seen and known then specially as my poor son. What hope will there be for him, I pray? If I die today there will be no such mark to mar his way. Therefore, I ask that you do not mourn for one who passes off today into the yellow shades."

They all said in reply, "No, no, please do not do so. We shall see that nothing will remain to mar his life and will make all □□□□□ from such an act."

"I thank you all so much for your kind thoughts but it will not serve as well as my dying now for my boy."

When she had finished thus she took a knife and, going to the side of her husband's coffin, thrust it through her throat and died.

All those assembled were struck with astonishment in fear and said, "This marvellous woman has died this □ of hers. Let's see it carried through."

They □ had her son made a real son.

Thus Pongnae became an official of state and a man whose name resounded through the state.

---

* *furoshiki* is a Japanese word for "wrapping cloth" (written 風呂敷 in Japanese) that was current in the foreign missionary community in colonial Korea.

양 봉 래 사 언　　지 부　　이 음 관　　위 령 암　　군 수　　수 유
楊蓬萊士彦 1) 之父　以蔭官 2) 爲靈巖 3) 郡守　受由

상 경　　환 관 지 로　　미 급 본 군 일 일 정　　효 기 작 행　　미 급
上京　還官之路　未及本郡一日程　曉起作行　未及

점 사　　인 마 피 곤　　위 심 로 방 려 사　　위 중 화　　지 계
店舍　人馬疲困　爲尋路傍閭舍　爲中火 4) 之計

時當農節 人皆出野 村中一空 一箇村舍 只有

一女兒 年可十一二歲 對下隷而言曰：吾將炊飯

須暫接於吾家可也 下隷曰：汝以年幼之兒

何可炊飯而供饋行次 5) 乎 對曰：此則無慮 須卽

行次好矣 一行無奈何 入門則其女子淨掃房舍 鋪

席而迎之 謂下隷曰：行次進支 6) 米 自吾家辦出矣

只出下人各名之粮可也 楊倅細察其女兒 則容

貌端麗 語音淸朗 少無村女之態 心甚異之 而已

進午飯 則其精潔踈淡 絶異常品 上下之人 皆

嘖嘖 7) 稱奇 楊倅招使近前而問年幾許 對曰：十二

歲矣 又問汝父何爲 對曰：此邑將校 而朝與吾母

出野鋤草 8) 矣 楊倅奇愛之 乃出箱中靑紅扇各一

而給之戲曰： 此是吾之送綵 9) 於汝之需 謹受之

其女子聞其言 卽入房中 出箱中紅色袱 而鋪之

前曰：此扇置之此袱之上　楊倅問其故　對曰：

旣是禮幣 10)　則莫重禮物　何可以手授受乎　一行

上下　莫不稱奇　楊倅遂出門而作行　到郡後忘

之　過數年後　門卒入告曰：隣邑某處將校某

來謁次此通刺 11)　矣　使之入來　則素昧之人 12)　也

楊倅問曰：汝之姓名云何　而緣何來而見　其人拜伏

而言曰：小人卽某邑之校也　官司 13)　再昨年京行

回路有中火於小人之家　而時有一女兒炊飯接對

之事乎　楊倅曰：然矣　又曰：伊時或有信物 14)

之給者乎　曰：不是信物　吾奇愛其女兒之怜俐

以色扇賞之矣　其人曰：此兒卽小人之女也　今年

爲十五歲矣　方欲議婚 15)　矣　女兒以爲吾受靈岩官

司禮幣　矢死不之他 16)　云云故　以一時戲言　何可

信之　欲使强之　則以死爲限　萬端誘之　難回其心

불득이래고의　양쉬소왈　여녀지호의　오하인배지
不得已來告矣　楊倅笑曰：汝女之好意　吾何忍背之

여수택일이래　오당영래의　급길기 17)　이례영
汝須擇日以來　吾當迎來矣　及吉期 17) 以禮迎

래위소실　시양쉬적환거 18)　이기녀처내지정당
來爲小室　時楊倅適鰥居 18)　以其女處內之正堂

이주궤음식의복　무불칭의 19)　급체귀본제 20)
而主饋飮食衣服　無不稱意 19)　及遞歸本第 20)

기무애적자녀독지　어제비복　각진기도　지어일
其撫愛嫡子女篤至　馭諸婢僕　各盡其道　至於一

문종당 21)　무불득기환심　예성 22)　일어상하내외
門宗黨 21)　無不得其歡心　譽聲 22) 溢於上下內外

산일자즉봉래야　신채 23)　준일　간목 24)　청수　정시
産一子卽蓬萊也　神彩 23) 俊逸　眉目 24) 淸秀　正是

선풍도골 25)　기년지후　양쉬작고애훼 26)　여례성
仙風道骨 25)　幾年之後　楊倅作故哀毀 26)　如禮成

복 27)　지일　종족함집　봉래지모　호읍이출좌언왈
服 27) 之日　宗族咸集　蓬萊之母　號泣而出座言曰：

금일렬위제회　제상인재좌　첩유일봉탁지사 28)
今日列位齊會　諸喪人在座　妾有一奉托之事 28)

기능긍허부　상인왈　이서모지현숙소욕탁자
其能肯許否　喪人曰：以庶母之賢淑所欲托者

오배안유불종지리호　제종지답역연　내왈
吾輩安有不從之理乎　諸宗之答亦然　乃曰：

첩유일자　이작인 29)　불지우미　연이아국지속
妾有一子　而作人 29) 不至愚迷　然而我國之俗

자래천얼 30)　거수성인　장언용재　제위공자
自來賤孼 30)　渠雖成人　將焉用哉　諸位公子

雖恩愛無間 31) 而妾死之後　將服妾母之服矣

如是則嫡庶顯殊矣　此兒將何以行世　妾當於今

日自決　若於大喪中彌縫 32)　則庶無嫡庶之別矣

奉望列位　哀憐將死之人　勿使飮恨 33) 於泉下 34)

諸人皆曰：此事吾輩相議好樣道理 35)　俾無痕跡矣

何乃以死爲期乎　蓬萊母曰：列位之意　雖可感

却不如一死之爲愈　言罷自懷中　出小刀　自刎 36)

於楊倅之柩前　諸人皆大驚而嗟惜 37) 曰：此人也

以賢淑之性　以死自決　而如是勤托　逝者之托

不可孤 38) 也　遂相議而嫡兄輩　視若親兄弟　少無嫡

庶之別　蓬萊長成之後　位歷士大夫之職　名滿一國

人不知其爲庶流云爾

---

1 楊士彦 [1517–84; styled Ŭngbing 應聘; sobriquet Pongnae 蓬萊, Wan'gu 完邱, Ch'anghae 滄海, Haegaek 海客; ancestral seat Ch'ŏngju 清州]: scholar-official under King Myŏngjong 明宗 [r. 1545–67; 1534–67] and a calligrapher. His father was Yang Hŭisu 楊希洙 [dates unknown].

2 蔭官: protected officials who entered the official bureaucracy on account of their parents' or ancestors' merits.

3 靈巖: a town in South Chŏlla Province.

4 中火 = *chungsik* 中食: lunch.

5 行次: (honorific) a traveller or his or her journey.

6 進支 = *chinji* 進止 = native Korean word *chinji* rendered in Chinese characters: (honorific) meal.

7 嘖嘖: praise.

8 鋤草: weed.

9 送綵 = *napch'ae* 納采 ~ *napp'ye* 納幣: red and blue/green silk sent by the groom's family to his bride's family as a wedding gift.

10 禮幣 = *yemul* 禮物: wedding gifts exchanged between the bride and the bridegroom.

11 通刺: send in one's calling card; seek an audience by presenting one's card.

12 素昧之人: a person whom one has never met before.

13 官司 = *kwana* 官衙: originally, yamen; here it refers to the magistrate himself.

14 信物 = *sinp'yo* 信標: token of memory given to someone setting out on a journey.

15 議婚: discuss marriage.

16 矢死不之他: swear upon death not to marry another.

17 吉期 = *kiril* 吉日: lit. "auspicious day"; date selected for a wedding ceremony.

18 鰥居: live as a widower.

19 稱意: be to one's liking.

20 本第 = *pon'ga* 本家: the main family; the head house.

21 一門宗黨: one's family and kinfolk.

22 譽聲: sounds of praise.

23 神彩: spirit and countenance.

24 眉目: facial features.

25 仙風道骨: exceptional appearance of a Daoist immortal.

26 哀毀: lit. "grief damage" = damage to the body caused by mourning for one's deceased parents.

27 成服: lit. "wear mourning" = donning mourning attire for the first time, on the third or fifth day of the mourning period.

28 奉托之事: a very important favour to ask.

29 作人 = *wiin* 為人: one's disposition, temperament, character.

30 自來賤孼: ignoble son born of a union between a man and his secondary wife.

31 恩愛無間: lit. "grace and love without reserve."

32 彌縫: temporary remedy; makeshift.

33 飲恨: hold a grudge against someone.

34 泉下 = *kuch'ŏn chi ha* 九泉地下 ~ *hwangch'ŏn* 黃泉: netherworld.
35 好樣道理: good method/solution.
36 自刎 = *chagyŏl* 自決: slit one's throat; commit suicide.
37 嗟惜: lament and be heartbroken.
38 孤: turn one's back on, forsake.

——— **81** ———

The Truth of Dreams

Vol. III: 21; n.d.; Diary XIV, pp. 98–101; 289.

Prince Haep'ung, Chŏng Hyojun, was thirty-eight years of age, poor, and wholly destitute. He had lost his wife three times in succession and had only two daughters but no son. He was a great-grandson of the son-in-law of King Tanjong. He not only offered sacrifices to his own ancestors but also to Tanjong; his mother, Queen Hyŏndŏk, Kwŏn-ssi; and to his wife, Queen Chŏngsun, whose three tablets he kept in his home.

Having lost his wife there was no one left to make the necessary preparations. He remained in a state of great anxiety in his home or sometimes went to General Yi Chin'gyŏng's home where he spent the time in playing chess. This Yi Chin'gyŏng was grandson of Yi Chunmin. At that time he was a captain of the guard, so he played chess with Chŏng.

One day Chŏng said all of a sudden to Yi, "I have something on my heart to say to you. Will you hear it?"

Yi replied, "I am your best friend. Why should I not hear whatever you have to say? Say it."

Chŏng hesitated and seemed afraid to speak it, but finally said, "My home has not only the sacrifices of several generations to carry on but has other spirits of the very highest to serve and honour but I am a widower and have no son so I fear that my line may be broken off altogether. A pitiful case, mine! If I had not you to speak to, to whom could I ever mention it? In this need of mine how about making me your son-in-law?

Yi suddenly turned red and asked, "Are you joking or is it in earnest that you speak? My daughter is only fifteen – how could she ever become a companion to one nearly fifty? You are havering, surely. Do not mention it again. Or you will be considered a fool altogether."

With a face filled with shame, Chŏng cut off intercourse with this home and did not go again.

Ten days or so after this General Yi had a dream in which the outer gate quarters and the court were filled with commotion. It sounded as though the king was out on procession and going to call.

Suddenly a man dressed in official robes came in and said, "His Majesty is now going to call on you. Make haste and meet him."

In a state of great excitement, Yi hurried out and bowed low in the court. A moment later the king appeared, a young man, dressed beautifully in jewels and gems. He entered and took his place in the main hall and then called Yi to come to him. He said, "Chŏng Hyojun desires to marry with your house; how do you regard this?"

Yi arose and bowing afresh, said, "What can I say in view of this command of my king? My daughter, however, is only fifteen years of age while Chŏng is thirty years and more older. How could they marry?"

The King said in reply "Never mind about the difference in age but let them be married."

Having said this he took his departure.

In a state of distress, Yi awoke from his dream, got up and went into his wife's room. Here he found his wife sitting with the light burning. She asked of him, "How come you thus in the night? Are you not asleep?"

Yi then told of his dream and his wife replied, "I, too, dreamed the same. Surely this is a very strange, remarkable thing."

Yi replied, "This is a most extraordinary thing. What shall we do about it?"

The wife replied, "A dream is a vain, foolish thing. Why pay attention to it?"

Ten days or so later, Yi again dreamed a dream where the king came again. His face wore an anxious look as he said, "I gave you certain orders some time ago. How comes it that you have not carried them out?"

In a great state of fear, Yi said, "I have done very wrongly. I'll see to it at once and have it carried out."

On awaking he again told his wife, saying, "I've had that dream again and regard it as God's word to me. If we run counter to God, we'll assuredly meet with great misfortune. What had we better do?"

His wife replied, "I don't care if we do have this dream – this thing is impossible. How could I think of giving the daughter I love so dearly as a fourth wife to a beggar like that man Chŏng? I don't care whether it's God or man who decides it – I'll not consent even though I die."

Yi was greatly disturbed by this and deeply afraid and could neither eat nor sleep. Ten days or so later he had another dream in which the king came again and said, "I told you it a few days ago and assure you that this is not only God's will, this union, but the man Chŏng means great blessing to you; no evils will befall you in it, but blessings only. I have instructed you most explicitly. What does this refusal mean, I ask of you? A great disaster is impending over your head."

Alarmed beyond words, Yi arose, bowed, arose and bowed again. Said he, "I'll do at once as Your Majesty commands."

Again the king spoke to him, saying, "I know it is not you who refuses but your wife with her heart hardened against it. I must punish her. Have her arrested and brought here."

In a flash of the eye all the instruments of torture were placed in order and his wife was brought out. The king said, "Your husband wants to carry out what I command him, but your opposition has hindered him doing so. What do you mean by it?"

He then ordered her to be beaten. And the batons were laid on her shins four or five times.

In fear of her very life, Yi's wife cried out, saying, "I'll not do so again but shall assuredly follow what you command."

The king then returned to the palace and Yi awoke and went into his wife's room. There his wife began to tell him of a dream she had as she sat rubbing her knees. Here were marks of the batons that he had seen laid on. On this, the two in the greatest fear possible held a conference and decided to carry out the marriage. So the next day they called Chŏng and asked, "Why have you not been to see us these days?"

Hearing this, Chŏng came at once. Yi met him and said, "Were you offended at what I said the other day and have not come since? Since then, though, I have thought over it again and again and have come to the conclusion that if I do not help you no one else will. So even though it means an eternal regret to my daughter, I'll send her to you. Be my son-in-law, then. This is my definite decision, so there need be no other talk. There need be no occasion for you to go home to write out the 'Four Pillars' of it. Do it here and now."

He gave him a sheet of paper and had them written out. He then opened up his calendar and after reckoning up, decided on such-and-such a day as lucky, signed the contract and let Chŏng go.

On waking the day following, his daughter said to her mother, "I had the most wonderful dream last night. I saw father's friend with whom he plays chess turn into a dragon and he said to me, 'Take my sons.' I lifted up my skirt and received them and here were five little dragons that wormed about and wriggled here and there. While I was receiving them, one of them fell to the earth and broke its neck and died, a very unlucky happening."

When her parents heard this, they were greatly startled.

When the maid was married to Chŏng she had a child every year – five sons, all strong and well, who each passed his examination in the order of age. The first and the second sons became Presidents of Boards (*p'ansŏ*), the third was a Chief Justice (*taesahŏn*). The fourth and fifth were both literary graduates of great renown. The oldest grandson also passed his exam while Chŏng his grandfather still lived. A son-in-law also was a successful candidate. Chŏng, therefore, because of having five sons who were graduates, was advanced two degrees in rank and so became a *ch'amp'an*.*

He lived to be over ninety and saw his children and his children's children. Blessings were poured out upon him such as the world rarely sees. His fifth son went to Peking as secretary to the envoy; on his way back before he reached the Stockade Gate, he died, so he returned home in his coffin. Seeing this, Chŏng remembered the dream. His wife died three years before him.

When Chŏng was poor and in reduced circumstances he went to a friend's house and there met a fortune-teller who was asked by those present to tell their fortunes, but Chŏng did not ask him. The master, however, said to Chŏng, "This man is a great master of physiognomy – ask him and see."

Chŏng replied, "A man as poor as I, what use for him to have his face read?"

The fortune-teller then looked at him intently for a little and said, "Who is that gentleman over there? Though he is poor now he is destined to blessings beyond computation. After this season of poverty it will so come to pass that he will possess all the five blessings. There is no one else here who will begin to equal him."

Later it all came true as foretold. When Chŏng was first married, on the first night, in a dream he went to a friend's house and there he saw food laid out and all preparations made as for marriage but there was no bride.

He awoke and thought of how strange this dream was. Later his wife died. On the occasion of his second marriage, he again dreamed and again entered that house and had the same dream, though there was a bride but no swaddling clothes. Again his wife died. The third time he was married and on the first night he again went to the same house and saw the same display, while the little child had grown to be a girl.

Again his wife died and for the fourth time he was married and seeing his bride, recognized her as the maid he had seen in a dream.

It looks by this that all things were ordered. In Yi's dream the young king who came to him was Tanjong.

* *ch'amp'an*: second-rank minister (junior second grade) belonging to the Six Ministries.

海豊君鄭孝俊 1) 年三十八　貧窮無依　喪妻者三

而只有二女無一子　以寧陽尉 2) 之曾孫　本家奉先 3)

之外　又奉魯陵 4) 及顯德王后 5) 權氏魯陵王后 6)

宋氏三位神主　而無以備香火　在家愁亂 7)

每日從遊於隣居李兵使 8) 進卿 9) 家　以賭博 10)

爲消遣之資 11)　李卽判書俊民 12) 之孫也　時以堂下

武弁　日與海豊賭博矣　一日　海豊猝然而言曰：

吾有衷曲之言 13)　君其信聽 14) 否　李曰：吾與君

如是親熟　則何有難從之請乎　第言之　海豊攝嚅 15)

良久乃曰：吾家非但累世奉祀　且奉至尊 16) 之神位

而吾今鰥居 17) 無子絕嗣必矣　豈不肯悶 18) 乎　如非君

則吾何可開口　君其矜悶我情勢　能以我爲女婿乎

李乃勃然作色曰：君言眞乎假乎　吾女年今十五

何可與近五十之人作配乎　君言忘 [妄] 矣　絕勿

更發此沒知覺必不成之言可也　海豊滿面羞愧　無

聊而退　自此以後　更不往其家矣　其後十餘日之夜

李兵使就寢矣　昏夢中　門庭 19)　喧擾 20)　遠遠有警

蹕之聲 21)　一位官服者入來曰：大駕 22)　幸于君家

須卽出迎　李慌忙而下階　俯伏于庭　已而少年王

端冕珠旒 23)　來臨于大廳之上　命李近前而敎曰：

鄭某欲與汝結親 24)　汝意如何　起伏而對曰：　聖

敎之下　焉敢違咈 25)　而但臣之女　年未及笄 26)

鄭是三十年長　何可以作配乎　敎曰：年齒多少

不須較計　必須成婚可也　仍還宮　李乃悅惚而覺

卽起入內　則其妻亦明燭而坐問曰：夜未晚 [曉]

하위입래　리이몽사언지　기처왈　오몽역연
何爲入來　李以夢事言之　其妻曰：吾夢亦然

대시괴사　리왈　차비우연지사　장하이위지
大是怪事　李曰：此非偶然之事　將何以爲之

기처왈　몽시허경　하가신지운의　과십여일후
其妻曰：夢是虛境　何可信之云矣　過十餘日後

리우몽　대가우림　이옥색불예　왈　전유소
李又夢　大駕又臨　而玉色不豫 27) 曰：前有所

하교자　여하상금불봉행호　리황축　이사왈
下敎者　汝何尙今不奉行乎　李惶蹙 28) 而謝曰：

근당상량　위지의　각이언우기처왈　차몽우여시
謹當商量 29) 爲之矣　覺而言于其妻曰：此夢又如是

차필시천의야　약역천　즉공유대화의　장약지하
此必是天意也　若逆天　則恐有大禍矣　將若之何

기처왈　몽수여차　사즉불가성야　오하인이애녀
其妻曰：夢雖如此　事則不可成也　吾何忍以愛女

작한걸인사실호　차즉론론천정　여인정　사
作寒乞人四室乎　此則毋論天定 30) 與人定　死

불가종의　리자차지후　심심우공　침식불안의
不可從矣　李自此之後　心甚憂恐　寢食不安矣

과십여일후　대가우림우몽왈　향일하교어여자
過十餘日後　大駕又臨于夢曰：向日下敎於汝者

비단천정지연　차내다복지인야　어여무해이유익자
非但天定之緣　此乃多福之人也　於汝無害而有益者

야　루차하교　이종시거역　차하도리　장강대화의
也　屢次下敎　而終是拒逆　此何道理　將降大禍矣

리내황공　기복이대왈　근봉성교의　우교왈
李乃惶恐　起伏而對曰：謹奉聖敎矣　又敎曰：

此非汝之所爲　專由於汝妻之頑不奉命　當治其罪

仍下敎拿入　霎時 31) 大張刑具　拿入其妻而數之曰：

汝之家長欲從吾命矣　汝獨持難而不奉命　此何道理

仍命加刑　至四五杖而止　李妻惶恐而哀乞曰：何敢

違越　謹當奉敎矣　仍停刑而還宮　李乃驚覺而入內

則其妻以夢中事言之　捫膝 32) 而坐　膝有刑杖之痕

李之夫妻大驚恐　相與議定　而翌日請海豊曰：

近日何久不來云　則海豊卽來矣　李迎謂曰：君以

向日事　自外 33) 而不來乎　吾於近日　千思萬量 34)

非吾　則此世無濟君之困　雖誤却 35) 吾女之平生

斷當送歸于君家矣　君爲吾家之東床 36)　吾意已決

寧有他議　柱單 37) 不必　相請此席書之可也　仍以

一幅簡給而書之　仍於座上　披曆而涓吉 38) 丁寧

相約而送之　翌日之朝　其女起寢　言于其母曰：

夜夢甚奇　嚴君 [39] 之博友鄭生　忽化爲龍　向余

而言曰：汝受吾子　吾乃開裳幅而受　小龍五箇

蜿蜿蛇蛇 [40] 於裳幅之上　授受之際　一小龍落于

地　折項而死　豈不可怪乎　父母聞其言而異之

及入鄭門　逐年生産　生純男子　五人皆長成

次第登科　一男二男　位至判書　三男位至大司憲 [41]

四男五男　俱是玉堂 [42]　長孫又登第於海豊之生前

其婿又登第　海豊以五子登科　加二資 [43] 位至亞卿 [44]

享年九十餘　孫曾滿前　其福祿之盛　世所罕比 [45]

其第五男　以書狀 [46] 赴燕　回路未出柵 [47] 而作故

以其柩還　時海豊尙在　果符夢中之事　其夫人

先海豊三年而歿　海豊窮時　適於知舊之家　逢一

術士 [48]　諸人皆問前程　海豊獨不言　主人言曰：

此人相法神異　何不一問　海豊曰：貧窮之人　相

之何益　術士熟視曰：這位是誰　今雖如此困窮

其福祿無限　先窮後通　五福 49) 俱全之相　座上人

皆不及云矣　其後果符其言　海豊初娶時　醮禮 50)

之夕　夢入一人之家　則堂上排設　一如婚娶之儀

但無新婦　覺而訝之　喪妻而再娶之夜　夢又入其家

則又如前夢　而所謂新婦　未免襁褓 51)　又喪妻

三娶之夕　又夢入其家　則一如前夢　而稱以

新婦襁褓之兒　年僅十餘歲而稍長矣　又喪妻

及四娶　李氏門見新婦　則卽向來夢見之兒也

凡事皆有前定 52) 而然也　李兵使夢中下敎之君上

乃是端廟 53) 云爾

1 鄭孝俊 [1577–1665; styled Hyou 孝于; sobriquet Nangman 樂晚; ancestral seat Haeju 海州; posthumous epithet Chesun 齊順]: scholar-official under King Hyŏnjong 顯宗 [r. 1659–74; 1641–74]. He was honoured as Prince Haep'ung (Hae'punggun 海豊君) in 1656. His father was Chŏng Hŭm 鄭欽 [dates unknown].

2 寧陽尉: title (*pongho* 封號) conferred upon Chŏng Chong 鄭悰 [?–1461; ancestral seat Haeju 海州; posthumous epithet Hŏnmin 獻愍], the son-in-law of King Munjong 文宗 [r. 1450–52; 1414-1452]. Chŏng Chong's father was

Chŏng Ch'unggyŏng 鄭忠敬 [?–1443]. He married Princess Kyŏnghye 敬惠
公主 [1436–73], daughter of King Munjong.

3 奉先: perform a ritual ceremony for ancestors.

4 魯陵: King Tanjong 端宗 [r. 1452–5; 1441–57].

5 顯德王后 [1418–41]: the wife of King Munjong. She was the daughter
of Kwŏn Chŏn 權專 [?-1441], honoured as Prince Hwasan (Hwasan
Puwŏn'gun 花山府院君).

6 魯陵王后: Queen Chŏngsun, wife of King Tanjong 端宗 [r. 1452–5; 1441–57].

7 愁亂: distracted with worry.

8 兵使 = short for *pyŏngma chŏltosa* 兵馬節度使: Commander-in-Chief.

9 李進卿: unidentified.

10 賭博: gambling.

11 消遣之資: diversion, pastime.

12 李俊民 [1524–90; styled Chasu 子修; sobriquet Sinam 新菴; ancestral seat
Chŏnŭi 全義; posthumous epithet Hyoik 孝翼]: scholar-official under King
Sŏnjo [r. 1567–1608; 1552–1608]. His father was Yi Kongnyang 李公亮
[dates unknown] and his uncle was Cho Sik 曹植 [1502–72].

13 衷曲之言: lit. "earnest and heartfelt words."

14 信聽: trust, take seriously.

15 囁嚅: falter; hesitate to say.

16 至尊: (honorific reference to the king) most exalted and noble.

17 鰥居: live as a widower.

18 矜悶: pity; feel sorry for.

19 門庭: courtyard.

20 喧擾: noisy and boisterous.

21 警驆之聲: lit. "sounds made to clear the way for the royal procession."

22 大駕 = *ŏga* 御駕: royal palanquin.

23 端冕珠旒: wearing a diadem (headgear worn by the king).

24 結親: enter into matrimony with.

25 違咈: go against, disobey.

26 笄: lit. "ornamental hairpin" = rite-of-passage ceremony for a betrothed girl.

27 玉色不豫: uncomfortable expression on the royal visage.

28 惶蹙: be/get awe-stricken and cower or shrink.

29 商量: mull something over.

30 天定: lit. "heaven decides/dispenses."

31 霎時: in a moment, in a flash.

32 捫膝: caress one's knees.

33 自外: distance oneself from.

34 千思萬量: lit. "think one thousand times, calculate ten thousand times" =
give ample thought to.

35 誤却: spoil/ruin a plan.

36 東床: (honorific) someone else's new son-in-law.

37 柱單 = *saju tanja* 四柱單子: (for prognostication purposes) piece of paper bearing the year, month, day, and hour of one's birth.

38 涓吉 = *t'aegil* 擇日: pick an auspicious day for a wedding ceremony.

39 嚴君: (honorific) one's own father.

40 蜿蜿蛇蛇: wriggle like a snake.

41 大司憲: junior second-grade official belonging to the Office of the Inspector-General (Sahŏnbu 司憲府).

42 玉堂: informal name for the Office of the Special Counselors (Hongmungwan 弘文館) or official posts attached to it.

43 加二資: confer two additional ranks upon an official.

44 亞卿: any second minister (any *ch'amp'an* 參判), ranking just below *chŏnggyŏng* 正卿.

45 世所罕比: incomparable to anything else in the world.

46 書狀 = *sŏjanggwan* 書狀官: a temporary post given to an official escorting Chosŏn envoys to foreign countries.

47 柵 = *ch'aengmun* 柵門: gate in the border area at Fenghuang City 鳳凰城 in Manchuria 滿洲; used as the customs area between Chosŏn and Qing.

48 術士 = *sulga* 術家: prognosticator or face reader.

49 五福: Five Blessings = longevity (*su* 壽), wealth (*pu* 富), health (*kangnyŏng* 康寧), love of virtue (*yuhodŏk* 攸好德), and natural death (*kojongmyŏng* 考終命).

50 醮禮 = *hollye* 婚禮: wedding ceremony.

51 襁褓: swaddling clothes.

52 前定: predetermined.

53 端廟: King Tanjong 端宗 [r. 1452–5; 1441–57].

——— 82 ———

Ilt'ahong

Vol. III: 23; Diary XII, pp. 199–200, 50–2, 54–5 (all crossed out);
two-page typed fragment in 9:12 (pages numbered 3 and 4); three typed
pages in 9:13; see also "Ta-hong" in Korean Folk Tales: Imps, Ghosts, and
Fairies, translated from the Korean of Im Bang and Yi Ryuk by James S. Gale
(J.M. Dent & Son, 1931), pp. 219–33, for a translation of a different
version of the same story found in Im Pang's Records of the Invisible
Workings of Heaven (Ch'ŏnyerok 天倪錄); 290.

Sim Ilsong lost his father early in life and so neglected his education altogether. From his earliest boyhood he gave himself up wholly to dissolute ways. Day and night loose women were his sole delight. On occasions of public gathering, or when singing women or dancers met together, he was always to be found. With uncombed head, old shoes on and ragged clothes, he would thrust himself into everyman's company, devoid of shame, so that gradually he became known and pointed out by passers as the mad son of Sim.

One day in accord with his general habit he went to a feast at the home of one of the ministers named Kwŏn, where were singing girls dressed in red and green and blue. He paid no heed to those who smiled with contempt upon him, or spat as he went by. Though thrust aside or ordered off the place, he ignored it all and sat boldly through.

There was among the singing women a young girl of special note whose name was Ilt'ahong or Red Bud. She had recently come from Kŭmsan, Chŏlla Province. Her beauty of face and skill of song and dance made her the favourite of all the guests assembled. The boy, Sim, had heard of her too and so took occasion to find a place near her, while she seemed to feel no dislike for him or displeasure in the least. Rather, she took careful measure of the lad, made note of his actions and seemed deeply impressed. At last she arose as though to go, making a sign with the hand that he follow while she quietly withdrew.

When she passed him she whispered, "Where is your home?"

Sim told her where, and in just which house he lived.

Then Red Bud said, "You go first and I'll follow. Wait for me; remember, I shall not fail you."

Intoxicated with delight at this good fortune beyond all his hopes, he went home, swept his room, put his house in order, and waited.

Just as the sun was going down, Red Bud arrived according to her word.

Hardly knowing what he did, Sim sat beside her while they talked together. Just then a servant from the inner quarters, happening to look in upon them, saw this and then went at once and told the mother.

Ever anxious about this dissolute son of hers, the mother was on the point of calling him in order to administer a severe rebuke, when Red Bud asked that the servant make request for her to call. Sim then gave orders that she go and tell his mother that a stranger wished to speak to her.

Bowing low in the court before the step-way, she said, "I am a singing girl recently come from Kŭmsan. Today when I was at our official feast your son came in, and while all the people pointed at him with scorn, and said, 'Behold the fool,' in my inner soul I saw him rise to fame and fortune and become a noted minister in days that are to be. I realize that the craze for women that possessed him is like an evil demon in his soul, and that if it be not bridled, it will be his death and destruction; yet that can only be done by degrees and gently. From today on I propose to give up my profession as a singing girl and spend my life in his service. His pens, his books, and his paper shall be my constant care, and his future success my single purpose in life, and so I make a request that your ladyship give consent to this. If I had only selfish ambitions to fulfil, I should never come to live in the poverty of your home, or give my life for one known to everyone as a fool. His success shall be my care and even though I be by his side, I shall guard strictly against his giving himself over to wanton pleasure."

The mother said, "My poor lad in the loss of his father lost also his hopes of an education. Mad folly has been his one and only ambition; authority is brushed aside and his own will and way is all he ever knows. On this account my heart bleeds night and day. How comes it that you should be my unexpected hope, or that you should set my foolish boy in the way of honour? Could you but do it, my gratitude would know no bounds. It is not a question of doubt that would make me hesitate nor one of shame, for no greater dishonour can come to me than what I have already suffered; but my house is so poor that frequently morning and evening meals are lacking. You are a girl accustomed to everything a gay life can give – how could you face the hardships here?"

Red Bud replied, "Please don't let that be a matter of anxiety, for I shall be satisfied."

From that day on she bade a long farewell to the giddy life of the dancing girl, and hid herself from all those who knew her. With her own hand she combed the lad's hair and did his washing. When morning came she had him take his book and go straightway to the village teacher.

On his return his studies were continued and kept at through every waiting hour. She marked off each day's appointed task. On the slightest sign of indifference her displeasure was the goad, and her threat to leave the spear that pricked him on. While Sim loved her dearly he gradually came to fear her, and so kept hard at work till the time came for his appointed marriage.

However, in possession of Red Bud, Sim refused all other such ideas. Knowing this, she asked the reason and then reprimanded him, saying,

"You are the son of an ancient family and have before you the highest hopes of the nation. It would be madness for you to join your fortunes with a low-class singing girl. Whatever happens I shall never be the cause of the ruin of the house of Sim – never. If you insist on this and refuse marriage, I shall go and return no more."

In fear, Sim consented and was married to another.

In a way most humble and with sweet sincerity, Red Bud served the new mistress just as she served the mother. She saw, however, that Sim should not spend overmuch time in the company of his wife. Only on certain days could they meet and beyond these appointed times she stood stern guard at the door.

Thus the years passed. Sim's dislike of study increased as time went by. One day he threw his book at Red Bud's feet, rolled over and said, "Though you try ever so hard to make me a scholar it will not work; I hate it – so what do you propose to do?"

Knowing that it was no use to argue with him in regard to his indifference, Red Bud took advantage of the occasion when he was absent to see the mother: "The young master's dislike of study has increased more and more of late. All my efforts and every bit of will that I can bring to bear has failed to make it a success. There is nothing for me now but to go. My going will rouse him, if possible, to his need. Please do not think, however, that I will never come again. When I hear of the young master's passing his examination successfully I shall return at once."

So she arose, made her bow and turned to leave, when the mother took her by the hand and cried, saying, "Since you came, dearest, my mad boy has been restored to reason as by a master hand. It is all due to you. Why do you lose heart and go away over a little matter like this indifference of his?"

Red Bud said, "Were my heart wood or stone it might be less hurt, but as it is, this parting is exceedingly sad and hard to bear. Still, there is no other power that will rouse him to his need. If the young master learns that I have gone and will return only when he has passed a successful examination, I know he will work, even though in anger. At the farthest, six or seven years will suffice to give him success; perhaps even four or five. I shall guard myself for his sake from every unworthy touch, and await his graduation. Please tell him, will you."

Thus she left in tears, and going to a certain minister who was old and had no wife, said, "I am a person who has met with great misfortune and have no place of refuge; may I be one of your lowest servants and prove my faithfulness in seeing to your Excellency's needs?"

Seeing how comely she was and hearing her expression of sincerity, the old minister gave consent.

From that day on Red Bud went into the kitchen and did her bravest part to make the old man's meals a delight to him. She soon became his cheer and hope. Said he, "For an old man like me to have met with one who so kindly sees to dress and fare as you do, is surely wonderful. Let me make a contract that you be my daughter from now on, share all I have and be the mistress of my house."

When Sim returned and found Red Bud gone, he suddenly awoke from his dream and asked, "Where is she?"

His mother replied, "She left this reprimand concerning you as she departed: 'You refuse to go on with your studies. With what possible countenance can you hope to meet the world?' This is her agreement to return, when you pass the *kwagŏ*, and we know she is a woman of her word. If you do not pass, you have no likelihood of ever seeing her again. Do now as you please."

When Sim heard this he was overwhelmed with grief; the joy of his heart was gone. For several days he went here and there throughout the city making inquiry, but no trace of her could he find. At last he swore an indignant oath, saying, "I am the castaway of a woman; with what face can I behold the light of day? She has promised to come back when I graduate. I shall write this on my heart, enter anew on my studies and set my determination to meet her again. If I do not pass my examination and see her face I shall have no object left in life."

He closed the door against all guests and kept at his studies night and day. Thus the years moved slowly along till he passed through the "Dragon-Gate" as the prize-man of his class.

On the day on which he rode as winner through the streets he went to see some of the older officials and make his bow. Thus it was he entered Red Bud's home.

The old minister received him with great delight, and as they talked over things of the past and the honours of the day, food was brought in from the inner quarters. When Sim saw the table prepared so specially, his face suddenly changed colour.

The old minister inquired, "Why do you look with such startled fear on this food?"

He then told all about Red Bud and added, "My effort to win in the lists today was that I might meet her again. As I look at this table before me it reminds me of Red Bud whom I lost and so my heart is sad."

The old minister then inquired as to her age and looks and then added, "I have an adopted daughter whose origin I have never been able to definitely locate; I wonder if she could possibly be the one you refer to?"

Before the old man finished speaking the screen from the rear moved gently aside and a pretty girl stepped in. She dropped on her knees, threw her arms round the new graduate and burst into tears.

Sim arose and bowing to the old minister, said, "Kind father, you must give her back; she is my lost Red Bud who is found."

Startled at this, the old man said, "I am at the time of life ready every day to die, and by this young woman I have been sustained in health and happiness; if I give her up I shall be bereft of both my hands. This is the strangest thing surely that I have ever heard. I see, however, how you love each other and in view of it I cannot but yield my willing consent."

Sim arose, gave a deep bow and gave expression to his unbounded thanks.

It was then late at night. With Red Bud on the horse before, he rode beneath a torchlight procession to his home and on reaching the gate he shouted, "She is found, mother, she is found!"

Delighted beyond words, the mother met Red Bud at the middle gate, took her by the hand and led her in. Joy filled all the house and so this lost thread was once again restored.

Sim later became secretary of the Home Office, when one night Red Bud, gathering her skirts about her, said to him, "For ten years and more now I have had but one thought and that was to bring my young master to a place of honour such as you hold today. Even my own father and mother have been forgotten in this one consuming purpose of life. My only regret has been my parents. I had hopes that you might be appointed magistrate of Kŭmsan and that I might accompany you to see them. Thus indeed, all my wishes would be fulfilled."

Sim replied, "That is easy enough." He made request of the King and was sent to Kŭmsan so he took Red Bud with him on his way. Inquiring as to her parents, he found them both alive and well. Three days after his arrival Red Bud prepared food and drink and went to her home and there for three days made a great feast in honour of her parents and relatives. She gave them rich presents of clothing and other things and said, "Official quarters are different from a private home, and official visits are different from private visits. If I visit or see you too frequently there will be talk on the part of others that may mar my master's office. I shall not come again and we must have no goings or comings. Just think of me as in Seoul and observe a strict rule as regards this."

Thus she made her bow and departed.

One day some months later she suddenly sent a servant to ask the master to come to her room; but Sim, being busy with official business at the time, could not go. Again the servant came and urged him to come quickly.

Startled by this, he hurried to her room where he found that Red Bud had put on a new skirt and spread new mats on the bed where she was lying. Without any special reason for it but with a look of sadness, she said, "Today I am to leave you, my dear master, and go on my most distant journey. I wish for you long life and every blessing. Do not sorrow for me, please, but gently bid me go. My one wish is that I be buried by the site chosen for my master's grave."

With this word she passed away.

In deep distress and grief, Sim said, "I came here on account of Red Bed and now she is dead and gone. No concern further have I with this world's affairs."

He sent in his resignation at once and asked to be set free. Her coffin was borne to Kŭmgang and he wrote concerning her:

We bear her form upon the willow cart
A soul more dear than all the world beside;
The falling rain drops sorrow on her beir,
And say Dear Heart – farewell, farewell.

沈一松喜壽 1) 早孤 2) 失學 自編髮 3) 時 專事豪宕

日夜往來於狹斜靑樓 4) 公子王孫 5) 之宴

歌娥舞女 6) 之會 無處不往 蓬頭突鬢 7) 破屐弊衣 8)

少無羞澁 9) 人皆目之以狂童 10) 一日 又赴權宰宴席

雜於紅綠叢中 11) 唾罵 12) 而不顧 毆逐而不去

妓中有少年名妓一朶紅者 新自錦山 13) 上來

용모가무 독보일세 심동모기명 접석이좌 홍소
容貌歌舞 獨步一世 沈童慕其名 接席而坐 紅少

무염고지색 시이추파 미찰기동정 잉기여측
無厭苦之色 [14] 時以秋波 [15] 微察其動靜 仍起如厠

이수초심동 심동기이종지 홍부이어왈 군가하재
以手招沈童 沈童起而從之 紅附耳語曰：君家何在

심동상언모동제기가 홍왈 군수선왕 첩당수
沈童詳言某洞第幾家 紅曰：君須先往 妾當隨

후즉왕의 행사지 첩불실신의 심동대희과망
後卽往矣 幸俟之 妾不失信矣 沈童大喜過望 [16]

선귀가 소진이사지 일미모 홍과여약이래
先歸家 掃塵而俟之 日未暮 紅果如約而來

심동불승흔행 여지접슬이수작 일동비자내이출
沈童不勝欣幸 與之接膝而酬酌 一童婢自內而出

견기상 회고어기모부인 모부인이기자지광탕위우
見其狀 回告於其母夫人 母夫人以其子之狂宕爲憂

방욕초이책지 홍최호동비이래왈 오장입알어
方欲招而責之 紅催呼童婢而來曰：吾將入謁於

대부인의 심동여기언 호비사통 즉홍입래배어
大夫人矣 沈童如其言 呼婢使通 則紅入來拜於

계하왈 모시금산신래기모야 금일모재가연회
階下曰：某是錦山新來妓某也 今日某宰家宴會

적견귀댁도령 제인개이광동목지 이이천첩지
適見貴宅都令 諸人皆以狂童目之 而以賤妾之

우견 가지기대귀인기상 연이기기대추조
愚見 可知其大貴人氣像 然而其氣大麤粗 [17]

가위색중아귀 금약불억제 즉장지불성인지
可謂色中餓鬼 [18] 今若不抑制 則將至不成人之

境矣　不如因其勢而利導之　妾自今日　爲道令

斂跡於歌舞花柳之場 19)　與之周旋於筆硯書籍之間

冀其有成就之道矣　未知夫人意下如何　妾如或

以情欲而有此言　則何必取貧寒寡宅之狂童乎

妾雖侍側　決不使任情受傷 20)　矣　此則勿慮焉

夫人曰：吾兒早失家嚴 21)　不事學業　全事狂蕩

老身無以制之　方以是晝宵惱心 22)　矣　今焉何來

好風　吹送如汝佳人　使吾家之狂童　得至成就

則可謂莫大之恩也　吾何嫌何疑　然而吾家素貧

朝夕難繼　汝以豪奢之妓女　其能忍飢寒而留此乎

紅曰：此則少無嫌　萬望 23)　切勿慮　遂自其日

絕跡於娼樓 24)　隱身於沈家　其梳頭洗垢之節 25)

終始不怠　日出則使之挾冊　學於隣家　歸後坐於

案頭　晨夕勸課　嚴立課程　少有怠意　則勃然作色

以別去之意恐動 26) 沈童愛而憚之 課工不懈 及到

議親 27) 之時 沈童以紅之故 不欲娶妻 紅知其意

詰其故 乃嚴責曰：君以名家子弟 前程萬里 何

可因一賤娼 而欲廢大倫 28) 乎 妾決不欲因妾之故

而使之亡家矣 妾則從此去矣 沈童不得已娶妻

紅下氣 29) 怡聲 30) 洞洞屬屬 [燭燭] 31) 事之如老夫人

使沈童 定日限 四五日入內房 一日許入其房

如或違期 則必掩門不納 如是者數年矣 沈童

厭學之心 尤倍於前 一日 投書於紅而臥曰：

汝雖勤於勸學 其於吾之不欲何 紅度 32) 其怠慢之心

有不可以口舌爭也 乘沈生出外之時 告于老夫

人曰：阿郎 33) 厭讀之症 近日尤甚 妾雖以誠意

亦無奈何矣 妾從此告辭矣 妾之此擧 卽激勸之

策 34) 也 妾雖出門 何可永辭乎 如聞登科之報

則須當卽地還來矣　仍起而拜辭　夫人執手而泣曰：

自汝之來　吾家狂悖之兒　如得嚴師　幸免蒙學 35) 者

皆汝之力也　今何因一厭讀之微事　舍 36) 我母子

而去也　紅起拜曰：妾非木石　豈不知別離之苦乎

然勸激之道　惟在於此一條　阿郎歸　聞妾之告辭

而以決科後更逢爲約之言　則必也發憤勤學矣

遠則六七年　近則四五年間事　妾當潔身而處

以俟登科之期矣　幸以此意　傳布于阿郎　是所望也

仍慨然出門　遍訪老宰無內眷 37) 之家　得一處

見其主人老宰而言曰：禍家餘生 38)　苦無托身之

所　願得厠［側］婢僕之列　俾效微誠　針線酒食

謹當看檢矣　其老宰見其端麗聰慧　憐而愛之

許其住接　紅自其日　入廚備饌　極其甘旨　適其

食性　老宰尤奇愛之　仍曰：老人以奇窮之命 39)

행득여여자　의복음식　편어구체　금즉의뢰유지
幸得如汝者　衣服飲食　便於口體　今則依賴有地

오기허심　여역탄성　자금결부녀지정가야　잉사지
吾既許心　汝亦殫誠　自今結父女之情可也　仍使之

입처내사　이녀호지　심생귀가　즉홍이무거처
入處內舍　以女呼之　沈生歸家　則紅已無去處

괴이문지　즉기모부인전기림별시언이책지왈
怪而問之　則其母夫人傳其臨別時言而責之曰：

여이염학지고　지어차경　장이하면목립어세호
汝以厭學之故　至於此境　將以何面目立於世乎

거기이여지등과위기　위기인야　필무식언지리
渠既以汝之登科爲期　爲其人也　必無食言之理

여약불득결과　즉차생무갱봉지기　유여임의위지
汝若不得結科　則此生無更逢之期　惟汝任意爲之

심생문이망연　여유실의　수일편방어경성내외
沈生聞而憫然　如有失矣　數日遍訪於京城內外

종무종적　내시우심왈　오위일녀지견기　이하안
終無蹤跡　乃矢于心曰：吾爲一女之見棄　以何顏

면대인　피기유과후상봉위약　오당각의 工課40)
面對人　彼既有科後相逢爲約　吾當刻意 工課

이위고인상봉지지　이여불득과명　이불여약　즉
以爲故人相逢之地　而如不得科名　而不如約　則

생이하위　수두문사객41)　주소불철기주독　재42)
生而何爲　遂杜門謝客　晝宵不撤其做讀　才

과수년　외첩룡문43)　생이신은44)　유가45)지일
過數年　嵬捷龍門　生以新恩　遊街之日

편방선진46)　로재즉심지부집47)야　력로배알
遍訪先進　老宰即沈之父執也　歷路拜謁

則老宰欣然迎之　敍古話今 [48]　留與從容做話

而已　自內饋饌　新恩見盃盤饌品　愀然 [49] 變色

老宰怪而問之　則仍以紅之始末詳言之　且曰：

侍生之刻意做業　期於登科者　全爲故人相逢之地

也　今見饌品　則完是紅之所爲也　故自爾傷心矣

老宰問其年紀狀貌而言曰：吾有一箇養女　而不

知所從來矣　無乃此女乎　言未畢　忽有一佳人

推後窓突入　抱新恩而痛哭　新恩起拜於主人曰：

尊丈今則不可不許此女於侍生矣　主人曰：

吾於垂死之年 [50]　幸得此女　依以爲命　今若許送

則老夫如失左右手矣　事甚難處　而其事也甚奇

相愛也如此　吾豈忍不許　新恩起拜　而僕僕稱謝 [51]

時日已昏黑　與紅幷騎一馬　以炬火導前而行　及門

疾呼母夫人曰：紅娘來矣　其母夫人　不勝奇喜

구급　　어중문지내　　집홍지수이승계　　희일어당우
屨及 52) 於中門之內　執紅之手而升階　喜溢於堂宇

부속전호의　　심후위천관랑　　일석　　홍렴임
復續前好矣　沈後爲天官郎 53)　一夕　紅斂袵 54)

이언왈　　첩지일단심성　　전위진사　　지성취
而言曰：妾之一端心誠　專爲進賜 55) 之成就

십여년　념불급타　　오향부모지안부　　역불황문지의
十餘年　念不及他　吾鄕父母之安否　亦不遑問知矣

차시첩지일야부심　　자야　진사금당가위지지
此是妾之日夜拊心 56) 者也　進賜今當可爲之地

행위첩　구금산재　　사첩득견부모어생전　즉
幸爲妾　求錦山宰　使妾得見父母於生前　則

지한필의　심왈　차시지이지사　　내치소
至恨畢矣　沈曰：此是至易之事 57)　乃治疏 58)

걸군　　과위금산쉬　설홍해왕　부임지일　문홍지
乞郡 59) 果爲錦山倅　挈紅偕往　赴任之日　問紅之

부모안부　즉과개무양　과삼일후　홍자관부　성구
父母安否　則果皆無恙　過三日後　紅自官府　盛具

주찬이왕기본가　배견부모　회친당　　삼일대연
酒饌而往其本家　拜見父母　會親黨 60)　三日大宴

의복수용지자　극기풍후　이유기부모이언왈
衣服需用之資　極其豊厚　以遺其父母而言曰：

관부이어사실　　관가지내권　우유별어타인
官府異於私室 61)　官家之內眷　尤有別於他人

부모여형제　여혹인연　이빈삭　　출입　즉초인언
父母與兄弟　如或因緣　而頻數 62) 出入　則招人言 63)

루관정　아금입아지후　일입불득갱출　역불득빈빈
累官政　兒今入衙之後　一入不得更出　亦不得頻頻

상통　이재경양지지　물부왕래상통　이엄내외지분
相通 以在京樣知之 勿復往來相通 以嚴內外之分

잉배사이입　일미상통우외　기과반년　내비이소
仍拜辭而入 一未相通于外 幾過半年 內婢以少

실지언래청입　적유공사　미즉기　비자련속래청
室之言來請入 適有公事 未卽起 婢子連續來請

공괴지입내이문지　즉홍착신건　의상　포신건침석
公怪之入內而問之 則紅着新件 64) 衣裳 鋪新件寢席

별무질양　이안대처창지색　이언왈　첩어금일
別無疾恙 65) 而顔帶凄愴之色 66) 而言曰：妾於今日

영결진사　장서지기　야　원진사보중　장향영귀
永訣進賜 長逝之期 67) 也 願進賜保重 長享榮貴

이물이첩지고이구회　언　첩지유체　행반장어
而勿以妾之故而疚懷 68) 焉 妾之遺體 幸返葬於

진사선영지하시소원야　언파엄연이몰　공곡지통
進賜先塋之下是所願也 言罷奄然而歿 公哭之痛

잉왈　오지출외　지위홍랑지고야　금언거이신사
仍曰：吾之出外 69) 只爲紅娘之故也 今焉渠已身死

아하독류　잉정사단　이도체　이기구동행금강
我何獨留 仍呈辭單 70) 而圖遞 71) 以其柩同行錦江 72)

유금강추우명정　습의시가인읍별시지도망시
有錦江秋雨銘旌 73) 濕疑是佳人泣別時之悼亡詩 74)

1 沈喜壽 [1548–1622; styled Paekku 伯懼; sobriquet Ilsong 一松; ancestral seat Ch'ŏngsong 青松; posthumous epithet Munjŏng 文貞]: scholar-official under King Sŏnjo 宣祖 [r. 1567–1608; 1552–1608]. His father was Sim Kŏn 沈鍵 [1519–50].

2 早孤: lose one's father at a young age.

3 編髮 = *pyŏnbal* 辮髮: queue of an unmarried man.

4 狹斜青樓: brothel.

5 公子王孫: scion of a noble family.

6 歌娥舞女: lit. "singing ladies and dancing girls" = *kisaeng*.
7 蓬頭突鬢 = *pongdu nanbal* 蓬頭亂髮: lit. "mugwort head, disorderly hair" = dishevelled, unkempt hair.
8 破屐弊衣: lit. "broken wooden clogs and worn-out clothes."
9 羞澁: bashful, timid.
10 狂童: unruly, out-of-control child.
11 紅綠叢中: lit. "in the midst of *kisaeng* wearing multi-coloured clothes."
12 唾罵: spit and swear at something or someone despicable.
13 錦山: a town in the southern extremity of South Ch'ungch'ŏng Province.
14 厭苦之色: lit. "a look of contempt and disgust."
15 秋波: amorous glance.
16 過望: exceed one's expectations.
17 麤粗: rough and coarse.
18 色中餓鬼: lit. "sex-starved devil."
19 歌舞花柳之場 = *hwaryugye* 花柳界: lit. "place of singing, dancing, and flowers and willows" = the pleasure quarters, red-light district.
20 任情受傷: lit. "ruin one's health with lustful behaviour."
21 家嚴 = *kach'in* 家親: (honorific) one's father.
22 晝宵惱心: worry day and night.
23 萬望: hope earnestly.
24 娼樓: brothel.
25 梳頭洗垢之節: lit. "washing up and combing one's hair" = morning ablutions.
26 恐動 = *konggal* 恐喝: threaten, intimidate, blackmail.
27 議親 = *ŭihon* 議婚: discuss marriage.
28 大倫 = *honin* 婚姻: marriage, in the sense of being one of the important moral obligations in life.
29 下氣: compose oneself, soothe one's nerves.
30 怡聲: tender voice.
31 洞洞燭燭: ever so respectful and circumspect.
32 度: comprehend; fathom.
33 阿郞 = *sŏbang-nim*: respectful term of address for one's husband.
34 激勸之策: lit. "strategy of using shock to persuade."
35 蒙學: young child's studies.
36 舍 = 捨: discard.
37 內眷: one's wife; female members of a family.
38 禍家餘生: descendant of a calamity-ridden family.
39 奇窮之命: unfortunate destiny.
40 刻意: lit. "inscribe an intention" = keep something in mind.
41 杜門謝客: shut the door and decline to meet guests.

42 才 = 纔: barely, narrowly.

43 嵬捷龍門: win first place in the state examination.

44 新恩: new civil examination passer.

45 遊街: festive procession for someone who has just passed the civil service examination.

46 先進: someone who has preceded one in passing the civil service examination.

47 父執: father's friend; senior man who is one's father's age.

48 敍古話今: recount the past and discuss the present = catch up on things.

49 愀然: worriedly, anxiously.

50 垂死之年: an age approaching death.

51 僕僕稱謝: thank profusely.

52 履及: come out to greet someone without putting one's shoes on properly = greet someone ecstatically.

53 天官郎: appellation for officials of the Board of Personnel.

54 斂衽: adjust one's attire; tidy oneself.

55 進賜: *naŭri* = vernacular Korean for "master, sir" rendered in sinographs.

56 拊心: a grudge lodged in one's heart.

57 至易之事: an extremely easy affair.

58 治疏: write a memorial.

59 乞郡: (for a *munkwa* examination passer) request a government post near one's hometown in order to serve aged and/or ill parents.

60 親黨 = *ch'inch'ŏk* 親戚: one's family circle; kin.

61 私室 = *saga* 私家: one's own (private) home.

62 頻數: frequent, incessant.

63 招人言: lit. "invite people's words" = instigate rumours.

64 新件: brand-new object.

65 疾恙 = *chilbyŏng* 疾病: disease; illness.

66 凄愴之色: plaintive, sorrowful face.

67 長逝之期: lit. "day of eternal departure" = death.

68 疚懷: lament a death in the family.

69 出外: government post away from the capital; provincial government post.

70 呈辭單: submit a letter of resignation.

71 圖遞: angle for a different government post.

72 錦江: Kŭm River; a river that runs through North Chŏlla Province and South Ch'ungch'ŏng Province.

73 銘旌: red mourning banner bearing the name, government post, and rank of the deceased, written in white, that is buried with the coffin.

74 悼亡詩: eulogy.

—— **83** ——

A Man of Virtue

Vol. III: 26; n.d.; Diary XIV, pp. 101–3; 291.

When young, Hong Uwŏn (Namin) (graduated in 1645) was making a trip through the country and on his way stopped at a certain inn. There was no master but a young woman in charge, only of about twenty years of age or so. She was very pretty. But there was in her face the expression of one given up to illicit ways.

She saw how young and handsome Hong was and smiled as she received him. She assumed the most attractive air and was so attentive to him that one could not fail but be attracted. Hong, however, paid no attention but sat down in the room. She came into the room again and again, felt the floor and asked him if it was warm enough and quite comfortable. She looked with smiley face upon him, but Hong sat unmoved and scarcely deigned reply.

As the night grew late Hong lay down in the room farther from the fire while she slept in her room at the other inn just over the fire.

She softly called, "I fear your room is uncomfortable and cheerless – come in and share this room."

Hong said, "This room is all right. One night will do me no harm and so I'll stay here."

The woman again said, "Are you afraid you will transgress the law that divides the sexes? I am only a low woman so it will make no difference though you come in here and sleep. Come in, please."

Hong made no reply, but as he took note of her he saw that she was determined to overcome his scruples. He therefore took the rope of his load and tied the door fast so that it could not be opened and thus he slept.

The woman then said to herself, "I wonder if this guest is a eunuch. I have invited him two or three times to have him come to my bosom and take his fill of love, yet he pays no heed whatever but has made his door fast instead. He surely is the queerest creature that ever breathed God's air."

She sighed to herself.

Hong paid no heed whatever but went fast asleep. In the midst of his dreams he thought he heard muffled struggles in the adjoining room. A moment later he heard someone cough in the courtyard just outside of his room and a voice asked, "Is Your Excellency asleep?"

With a sudden start of fear and doubt, Hong answered, "Who are you and what have you to do with me, I pray?"

The reply was, "I am the master of this house; please unfasten the door and light the candle as I have something to say to you."

Hong unfastened the door whereupon the master came in with a light and sat down, poured out a glass of wine and said, "Please drink."

Hong inquired as to what this meant: "If you are the master of this house, where were you during the day and why should you come thus at midnight?"

The master said, "Your Excellency escaped the greatest danger last night that could ever come to a human being. My wife, though a pretty woman, was given up to adulterous ways. Whenever I went away she would take occasion to carry this practice on and though I have tried again and again to catch her in the act, I have failed.

"Today with this intent I said to her that I was going away, but instead I took a sharp knife and hid in the rear garden and so I heard all that was said between you and her. If you had fallen a victim to her, you would have died tonight under my knife, but you – with the true heart of a gentleman and a spirit of iron – resisted her from first to last and even made your door fast. I respect and honour you more than words can say.

"This drink I offer is from a grateful heart. She tried to seduce you but failing, worked her will on a boy Kim from across the way and as I caught them in the act I finished them both off under this knife. Since such a state of affairs has come about I urge Your Excellency to start at once. If you linger here you will assuredly find yourself in trouble. I, too, am going to make my escape."

In the greatest fear, Hong made fast his bundles and set out. The master then set fire to his house and accompanied Hong several *ri* on his way and then said his farewell and departed from him, saying, "Your Excellency will assuredly become a man of mark. We shall not likely ever meet again. Take good care of yourself, I pray you."

And so he left with an evident deep impression of Hong's worth.

After Hong had graduated he went as a Secret Commissioner □□ and reaching a mountain district he found one lonely house. As the day was late he put in there with the desire to sleep the night when, seeing the master, he recognized him as the young man whom he had met before. He called him and said, "Don't you know me?"

He replied, "I have not seen your honorable face before, how could I know you?"

Hong said, "Did you not come to such-and-such a place and on such-and-such a day meet a guest with whom you talked? You set fire to the house and went with me for several *ri*. Do you not recollect?"

He then gave a start and made a low bow in front of him. "I am sure Your Excellency has passed his examination and has come to a place of official service."

Without any reserve, Hong told him that he was a Secret Commissioner and then asked, "How do I find you here in this lonely place?"

His reply was, "I went to a neighbouring village and lived and was married again. She also is very pretty and I feared she might be tempted to evil with so many people about and that I should have a repetition of the experience I have gone through. I came here to this lonely place to live."

洪宇遠 1) 少時作鄕行 住一店幕 無男子主人 而只

有女主人 年可卅餘 2) 容貌頗美 其淫穢之態 3)

溢於面目 見洪之年少貌美 喜笑而迎之 冶容納媚 4)

殆不忍正視 洪視若不見 坐於房中 其女頗數 5)

入來 手撫房突 [堗] 6) 而問曰：得無寒乎 時以

秋波 7) 送情 洪端坐不答 至夜深 洪臥于上房

女則臥于下房 微以言誘之曰：行次 8) 所住之房

漏 [陋] 湫 9) 何不來臥于此房乎 洪曰：此房足

可容膝 10) 挨過 11) 一夜 何處不可 不必更移他房

女又曰：行次或以男女之別爲難乎 吾儕常賤有何

男女之可別 斯速下來爲好矣 洪不答 微察其氣色

則必有鑽穴 12) 來㤼之慮 13) 仍以行中麻索 14) 縛其隔

壁之戶 15) 而就寢矣 其女獨語曰：來客無乃宦官乎

吾以好意再三誘 [諭] 之 使入於佳人之懷中 而穩

度良夜 16) （則）不害爲風流好事 17) 而聽 [使] 我

漠漠 甚至於縛房戶 可謂天字 [宇] 怪物 18) 可恨

可恨 洪佯若不聞而就睡矣 昏夢之中 忽聞下房

有怪底聲 19) 而已窓外有咳嗽聲 20) 曰：行次就寢乎

洪驚訝而應曰：汝是何許人 而問我何爲 對曰：

小人卽此家之主人 今將欲開戶擧火有所可白之事 21)

耳 洪乃起坐而開戶 則主人持火而入 明燭而坐

進酒肴一案而勸之 洪問曰：此何爲也 汝是主人

則晝往何處　而夜深後始來　主人漢曰：行次今夜

經無限危境矣　小人之妻　貌雖美　而心甚淫亂

每乘小人之出他　行奸無常　小人每欲捉贓 22)

而終未如意　今日必欲捉奸　稱以出他　懷利刃

匿于後面矣　俄者行次酬酌　已悉聞之　行次如或

爲其所誘　則必也殞命於小人之劍頭矣　行次以士大

夫心事 23)　鐵石肝腸 24)　終始牢拒 25)　至於鎖門之境

小人暗暗欽歎之不暇　敢以酒肴　以表此歎服之心

厥女欲誘行次　事不諧意 26)　則淫心難制　與越邊金

總角同寢故　小人以一刀　斷其男女之命　事已到此

行次須即地出門可也　小留則恐有禍延之慮 27)

小人亦從此逝矣　洪大驚起　趣裝 28) 而出門

主人漢仍舉火燒其家　與洪同行數十里　仍分路

而作別曰：行次早晚必顯達　此別之後　後會難期

萬望 29) 保重 懇懃致意 30) 而去 洪登第後 以繡

衣 31) 暗行山谷間 只有一草舍 日勢已暮 仍留宿

見其主人 則卽是厥漢 呼問曰：汝知我乎 主人曰：

未嘗承顏 32) 何以知之 洪曰：汝於某年某邑某地

逢一過客 有所酬酌 夜間放火其家 而與我同

行數十里之事也 汝能記憶乎 主人怳然而覺

迎拜曰：行次其間必也做第 而就仕矣 洪不以諱之

以實言之 仍問曰：汝何爲獨處於四無隣里之地乎

對曰：主 [小] 人自其後 寓居于隣邑 又娶一女

而貌亦妍美 若在村閭熱鬧之中 33) 或恐更有向日

之事故 擇居于深山無人之地云矣

1 洪宇遠 [1605–87; styled Kunjing 君徵; sobriquet Namp'a 南坡; ancestral seat Namyang 南陽; posthumous epithet Mun'gan 文簡]: scholar-official under King Sukchong 肅宗 [r. 1674–1720; 1661–1720]. His father was Hong Yŏng 洪榮 [1567–1624].

2 什餘: twenty-some years old.

3 淫穢之態: lascivious and promiscuous behaviour.
4 冶容納媚: lit. "beautiful face, coquettish eyes."
5 數: be frequent.
6 房堗: Korean hypocaust (heated floor).
7 秋波: an amorous glance.
8 行次: (honorific) a traveller or his/her journey.
9 陋湫: dirty and desolate.
10 容膝: lit. "(barely) allow knees" = small, confined space.
11 挨過: get along with difficulty.
12 鑽穴: lit. "bore a hole" = an illicit union between a man and woman.
13 來悧之慮: be concerned that someone will come and threaten.
14 麻索: hemp rope.
15 隔壁之戶: door between two rooms.
16 穩度良夜: spend a pleasant night.
17 風流好事: a nice, romantic affair.
18 天宇怪物: a freak of nature.
19 怪底聲: strange, low voice.
20 咳嗽聲: sound of coughing.
21 可白之事: a matter to report.
22 捉贓: catch red-handed.
23 心事: one's heartfelt intentions versus the truth of the matter.
24 鐵石肝腸: unwavering fidelity.
25 牢拒: resolutely hold one's ground.
26 諧意: meet one's expecations.
27 禍延之慮: worry about possible repercussions.
28 趣裝: hurriedly pack for a journey (*yŏjang* 旅裝).
29 萬望: earnestly hope.
30 致意: convey one's thoughts.
31 繡衣: lit. "brocaded silken clothing" = *amhaeng ŏsa* 暗行御史: secret royal inspector.
32 承顏: lit. "receive the face" = meet someone honourable.
33 熱鬧之中: lit. "in the midst of all the commotion."

———— **84** ————

Yi Changgon

Vol. III: 27; see "The Troubles of 1498: Yi Chang-kon" in Diary XII: 55–9
(crossed out); "Yi Chang-kon" in *Old Corea*, pp. 92–4.
Published in *Korea Magazine*, Sept. 1918, pp. 396–400; 292.

Yi Changgon 李長坤
(THE TROUBLES OF 1498 AD)

In the reign of King Yŏnsan a great disturbance broke out in the capital
and among others who made their escape was a certain Yi who held the
rank of *kyori*, Keeper of the Records. He fled for his life to Posŏng
County in Chŏlla Province. Overcome by thirst as he hurried along, he
saw a girl dipping water from a stream and asked for a drink. She
dipped her gourd, but before passing it to him, she stripped some willow leaves from a branch that overhung the stream and threw them
into the water.

He thought this a peculiar thing to do and asked, "When I am so
thirsty and in so great a hurry, why do you scatter leaves over the water
that I have to drink?"

"Seeing Your Excellency so overheated, I was afraid you might take
harm from drinking too fast, and so I scattered these leaves," was her
answer.

Impressed by this, the man inquired where she lived, and she replied,
"I am the daughter of a basket-weaver and live in yonder little cabin."

Yi followed her to her home and said to the master, "I desire to become your son-in-law and live with you; please take me."

Consent was given and there he lodged.

But for a son of Seoul's ancient nobility to learn to become a basket-
maker was out of the question. Day succeeded day with nothing done
as he slept out the long hours. The father- and mother-in-law, both of
them indignant at this, scolded him soundly: "We took you in order
that you might help us in our basket-making, but instead of proving a
help you are an abominable loss – you simply eat your meals and sleep.
Nothing but a scrap-bag you are, to throw good food into."

From this day on they gave him only half the ordinary amount,
though night and morning his young wife, sorry for him, brought him
the scrapings of the pot, unknown to her parents.

Her kindness was rewarded, for their love for each other deepened day by day.

Thus three years passed till Chungjong ascended the throne (1506) and all the world was changed. Those who had been sentenced to death were pardoned and honoured and reappointed to office. Yi's name, too, was on the restored list, but he like others was lost to view and no one knew where he was. Advertisement was made as to this to all corners of the land and the rumour of it spread everywhere.

Yi was startled to hear the news, and as it happened to be the first day of the month and the time for the basket-maker to make his offering of baskets to the magistrate, he said to his father-in-law, "On this occasion I'll take the baskets and see them safely to their destination."

The father-in-law replied in a high key, "You, you lazy dog, you don't know east from west; how could you take these baskets to the magistrate? I never go myself without having a terrible time of dispute with the unreasonable creature, for he constantly refuses this and that and orders them back, telling me to bring better. How do you think he would treat *you*? No, no, no, you can't take the baskets."

But the daughter said, "Please let him try, father, it will do no harm."

The basket-maker was persuaded by his gentle daughter, and so Yi took the load on his back and went to the official yamen, where he boldly walked straight into the compound and shouted out in a loud voice, "The basket-maker has come with his baskets – ahoy!"

The magistrate happened to be an old soldier friend of Yi's. Startled by this bold announcement, and suddenly realizing who he was, he hurried down the step-way, took him by the hand and led him up to the special place of honour. "Friend of friends, wherever have you been, and how do you come to me in such a guise as this? The Government is out in search for you everywhere, and a notice from the Governor's office is here on your behalf. Go to Seoul at once; make no delay."

He had food and drink prepared, and fitted him out with a new suit of clothes.

Yi said, "I was under sentence of death and so stole into a basket-maker's home and hid away, and thus I have survived these years. Never did I expect again to see such a day as this."

The magistrate sent word to the Governor saying that Yi *kyori* was in the county of Posŏng, and made ready post-horses to send him swiftly and safely to Seoul.

Yi replied, "But I cannot forget the kindness shown me these past three years by my wife whom I greatly love. I must go now and say my word of greeting to her and to my master. You will please come for me tomorrow morning."

The magistrate yielded and gave his consent to the plan.

Yi again changed his dress to the old basket-maker's garb and went forth to his home. He greeted his father-in-law thus: "This time he took the baskets, and all without a word."

The old man replied, "He did, did he? Well, well! They say that even a thousand-year-old hawk can be taught the work of a falcon. This must be true for even my son-in-law has done his part once as a man. Wonderful! Wonderful! Give him an extra spoonful or two of rice," he shouted to his wife.

The next morning Yi got up early and swept the court, whereupon the old father-in-law, seeing him, shouted out, "Yesterday my son-in-law made a success of those baskets, and today he sweeps the court clean as a whistle. I shouldn't wonder to see the sun rise in the west today. Ha! Ha!"

When Yi then took a mat out and spread it out on the ground, the old man asked, "Look here, what are you at, putting a good mat like that out on the dirty ground?"

Yi replied, "The magistrate is coming today, so I am making ready."

The old basket-maker laughed an ironical laugh and said, "What wild talk is this? The Magistrate come to such a place as we have? Addle-headed idiot! Seeing what the fool is about now, I begin to mistrust yesterday; I shouldn't wonder if he threw those baskets away and came home to make an empty boast about it."

Before he had finished speaking, however, the magistrate's secretary came bounding in all out of breath with a beautifully coloured mat that he spread out in the court, saying, "His Excellency is on his way."

Hearing this, the man and his wife were greatly alarmed, and ran to hide. A moment later they heard the official criers shouting to clear the way, when suddenly the magistrate arrived, alighted from his horse, and went into the room to greet the son-in-law most politely and ask him how he had spent the night. A moment later he inquired, "Where is our sister, I pray? Have her come in."

Yi called, "Come and make your bow to the magistrate."

With a plain wooden pin through her hair and in simplest linen dress, she appeared and made her bow. Though evidently poor in circumstances, her face and form marked her as a young woman of good intelligence.

The magistrate treated her with marked deference and said, "Dr. Yi, in the days of his desperate need, found you to be his friend and your service has proven more to him than any other person's could possibly have been; are you not to be honoured?"

The woman drew her dress modestly around her and replied, "I am a woman, the lowest of the low, and though it fell to my lot to care for this my master, I had no idea who he was, and so I fear that in my treatment of him there have been many defects and no end of lack to do him honour. My failures and faults rise up before me and render me wholly unworthy of the kind words you have spoken. Your coming today to our poor home means honour beyond every dream, but I fear, it being so great, it may presage misfortune."

Hearing this, the magistrate sent a servant to call the basket-maker and his wife, had them treated to refreshments and spoke kindly to them. A little later other magistrates began to come in. The Governor sent his secretary to present his word of greeting. The court of the basket-maker's house was crowded with the horses and servants of state.

Yi *kyori* said to his friend concerning his wife, "She belongs to the lowest class, undoubtedly, and yet she and I are one, and we cannot be separated. For these years she has served and aided me with all her strength, and now that I have come to a place of honour I cannot forget her faithfulness. Please provide a chair so that I can take her along."

The magistrate at once acceded to this request, had a chair made ready and saw her start with him.

When Yi went to the palace to bow his thanks before King Chungjong (1506), His Majesty gave command that he be admitted at once. The king then inquired all about where he had been, and what had befallen him, and Yi told him the story.

On hearing it, the king nodded his head and said, "This woman must never be treated as one of low station again. I make her your wife to take the place of your kindred who have been killed, with all the honour that goes with it."

Long years they lived together, Yi and his beloved wife. There was no honour of the state that did not come his way, and many sons and daughters were born unto them. This Yi *kyori* was Yi *p'ansŏ*, Changgon 李長坤, a great and noted minister.

燕山朝 1) 士禍大起　有一李姓人　以校理 2)

亡命　行到寶城 3) 地渴甚　見一童女汲於川邊

趨而求飲　其女以瓢盛水　而摘川邊柳葉

浮之中而給之　心竊怪之　問曰：過客渴甚

急欲求飲　何乃以柳葉　浮水而給之也　其女對

曰：吾視客子甚渴　若或急飲冷水　則必也生病故

故以柳葉浮之　使之緩緩飲之之故也　其人大驚

異之　問是誰家女　則對曰：越邊柳器家女 4) 云

其人隨其後而往柳器匠家　求爲其婿而托身焉

自以京華 5) 之貴家 [客]　安知柳器織造乎

日無所事　以午睡爲常　柳匠之夫妻怒罵曰：

吾之迎婚 [婿]　期欲助柳器之役矣　今焉新婚

只喫朝夕飯　晝夜昏睡　卽一飯囊 6) 也云　而自

伊日　朝夕之飯　減半而饋之　其妻憐而悶之

每以鍋底黃飯 7)　加數而饋之　夫婦之恩情甚篤

如是度了數年之後　中廟改玉 8)　朝著一新 9)

昏朝 10) 沈廢之流 11) 一幷赦而付職 12) 李生還付官職

行會 13) 八路 14) 使之尋訪 傳說藉藉 李生聞於風便

而時適朔日 15) 主家將納柳器於官府矣 李生乃謂

其婦翁 16) 曰：今番則官家朔納柳器 吾當輸納矣

其婦翁責曰：如君渴睡漢 17) 不知東西 何可納

器於官門乎 吾雖親自納之 每每見退 18) 如君者

其何以無事納之乎 不肯許之 其妻曰：試可乃已

盍使往諸 19) 柳匠始乃許之 李乃背負而到官門

直入庭中 近前高聲曰：某處柳匠 納器次來待矣

本官乃是李之平日切親之武弁也 察其貌 聽其言

乃大驚起而下堂 執手而延之上座曰：公乎公乎

晦跡於何處 而乃以此樣來此乎 朝廷之搜訪已久

營關 20) 遍行 斯速上京可也 仍命進酒饌 又出

衣冠改服 李曰：負罪之人 偸生 21) 於柳器匠家

至于今延命而度　豈意天日之復見也　本官仍

以李校理之在邑　成報于巡營 22)　催發馹騎 23)

使之上京　李曰：三年主客之誼　不可不顧　且有糟

糠之情 24)　吾當告別主翁　今將出去　君須於明朝

來訪吾之所住處　本官曰：諾　李乃換着來時衣

出門而向柳匠家言曰：今番柳器　無事上納矣

主翁曰：異哉　古語云　鵰老千年能搏一雉云

信非虛矣　吾婿亦有隨人爲之事乎　奇哉奇哉

今夕當加給數匙飯矣　翌日平明　李早起灑掃門庭

主翁曰：吾婿昨日善納柳器　今則又能掃庭　今日日

可出於西矣　李乃鋪藁席 25)　于庭　主翁曰：鋪席何爲

李曰：本府官司　今朝當行次故　如是耳　主翁冷笑

曰：君何作夢中語 26)　也　官司主何可行次於吾家乎

此千不近萬不近之荒說 27)　也　到今思之　昨日柳器

지선납운자　필시위기　로상이귀　작과장지허어야
之善納云者　必是委棄[28]　路上而歸　作誇張之虛語也

언미이　본관공리　지채석이천천　이래　포지
言未已　本官工吏[29]　持彩席而喘喘[30]　而來　鋪之

정중이언왈　관사주행차　금방래도의　류장부처
庭中而言曰：官司主行次　今方來到矣　柳匠夫妻

창황실색　포두이닉우리간　소언　전도성　급
蒼黃失色　抱頭而匿于籬間　少焉　前導聲[31]　及

문　본관기마이래　하마입방　여서별래한훤
門　本官騎馬而來　下馬入房　與敍別來寒暄[32]

잉문왈　수씨　하재　사지출래　리내사기처래배
仍問曰：嫂氏[33]　何在　使之出來　李乃使其妻來拜

기녀이형채포군　래배어전　의상수폐　용의한아
其女以荊釵布裙[34]　來拜於前　衣裳雖弊　容儀閑雅

유비상천녀자　본관치경왈　리학사신재궁도
有非常賤女子　本官致敬曰：李學士身在窮途

행뢰수씨지력　득지우금일　수의기남자　무이과차
幸賴嫂氏之力　得至于今日　雖意氣男子　無以過此

하불흠탄호　기녀렴임이대왈　고이지천지촌부
何不欽歎乎　其女斂衽而對曰：顧以至賤之村婦

득시군자지건즐　전매　여시지귀인　기어접대
得侍君子之巾櫛[35]　全昧[36]　如是之貴人　其於接對

주선지절　무례극의　획죄대의　하감당존객지치사
周旋之節　無禮極矣　獲罪大矣　何敢當尊客之致謝

관사금일강림어상천루추　지지　영요　극의
官司今日降臨於常賤陋湫[37]　之地　榮耀[38]　極矣

절위천첩지가　공유손어복력야　본관청파　명하예
窈爲賤妾之家　恐有損於福力也　本官聽罷　命下隸

초 입 류 장 부 처　궤 주 사 안　의　이 이 린 읍 수 재
招入柳匠夫妻　饋酒賜顔 39) 矣　已而隣邑守宰

락 속　래 견　순 사　우 송 막 객　이 전 갈　류 장 지
絡續 40) 來見　巡使 41) 又送幕客 42) 而傳喝　柳匠之

문 외　인 마 열 뇨　관 광 자　여 도　리 위 본 관 왈
門外　人馬熱鬧 43) 觀光者 44) 如堵　李謂本官曰：

피 수 상 천　오 기 여 지 적 체　필 작 배 의　다 년 복 로
彼雖常賤　吾旣與之敵體 45) 必作配矣　多年服勞 46)

성 의 비 지　오 금 불 가 이 귀 이 이　원 차 일 교 해 행
誠意備至　吾今不可以貴而易　願借一轎偕行

본 관 즉 지 득 일 교　치 행 구 이 송　리 어 입 궐 사 은 지 시
本官卽地得一轎　治行具以送　李於入闕謝恩之時

중 묘 명 입 시　이 부 문 류 리　지 전 말　리 내 주 기
中廟命入侍　而俯問流離 47) 之顚末　李乃奏其

사 심 실　상 재 삼 차 탄 왈　차 녀 자 불 가 이 천 첩 대 지
事甚悉　上再三嗟歎曰：此女子不可以賤妾待之

특 승 위 후 부 인　가 야　리 여 차 녀 해 로　이 영 귀 무 비
特升爲後夫人 48) 可也　李與此女偕老　而榮貴無比

다 유 자 녀　차 시 리 판 서 장 곤　지 사 운 이
多有子女　此是李判書長坤 49) 之事云耳

1 燕山朝: the years 1494–1506; the reign of Yǒnsangun 燕山君.
2 校理: senior fifth-grade post belonging to the Office of the Special Counselors (Hongmungwan 弘文館).
3 寶城: a town in South Chŏlla Province.
4 柳器家女: lit. "daughter of a wicker weaver."
5 京華 = *kyǒngsa* 京師: thriving Seoul.
6 飯囊: lit. "rice pouch" = good-for-nothing.
7 鍋底黃飯: lit. "browned rice on the bottom of the cauldron" = crust of scorched rice (*nurungji*).
8 中廟改玉: lit. "Restoration of Righteousness by King Chungjong" = enthronement of King Chungjong 中宗 [r. 1506–44; 1488–1544] in 1506.

9 朝著一新: new court officials take up new posts under a new reign.

10 昏朝: lit. "chaotic court"; refers to the reign of Yŏnsangun [r. 1494–1506; 1476–1506].

11 沈廢之流: people who have taken refuge or been driven out.

12 付職: serve in a government post.

13 行會: policy-related briefing led by a senior official for his subordinate.

14 八路: the eight provinces of Chosŏn.

15 朔日: the first day of the lunar month.

16 婦翁 = *changin* 丈人: father-in-law.

17 渴睡漢: sleepyhead; late-riser.

18 見退: be turned down, rejected.

19 盍使往諸: Why not send [him there]? 盍 is a fusion character composed of 何 (how) and 不 (not) – lit. "why not." 諸 is likewise a fusion character, composed of 之 (object pronoun) and 於 (locative marker).

20 營關: official documents released by the provincial headquarters.

21 偸生: connive for undeserved longevity.

22 巡營 = *kamyŏng* 監營: provincial administrative headquarters.

23 駔騎 = *yŏngma* 驛馬: post-horse for official use.

24 糟糠之情: lit. "love [during the time] of plain food": affection for one's wife based on earlier times spent together in poverty.

25 藁席: straw mat.

26 夢中語: sleep talking.

27 荒說: preposterous talk, nonsense.

28 委棄: abandon and disregard.

29 工吏: (during the Chosŏn period) the Office of Works belonging to a local yamen.

30 喘喘: ahem; dry cough.

31 前導聲: lit. "sounds made to clear the way for officials en route."

32 寒暄: salutation and greeting; inquiry after a person's health.

33 嫂氏: older or younger brother's wife.

34 荊釵布裙: lit. "a hairpin made of thorns and a coarse skirt made of hemp."

35 巾櫛: lit. "towel and comb" = serve one's husband well.

36 全昧: not know at all.

37 陋湫: dirty and desolate.

38 榮耀: glorious and brilliant.

39 賜顏: treat someone socially inferior with kindness.

40 絡續: go on forever.

41 巡使 = *kamsa* 監司 ~ *kwanch'alsa* 觀察使: provincial governor.

42 幕客 = *pijang* 裨將: unranked military attendant or envoy attached to a regional government office who escorted provincial governors (*kamsa* 監司),

magistrates of strategic regions (*yusu* 留守), military commanders (*pyŏngsa* 兵使), naval commanders (*susa* 水使), and foreign envoys (*kyŏnoe sasin* 遣外使臣).

43 熱鬧: in the midst of a boisterous throng.

44 觀光者: onlookers.

45 敵軆: treat with the propriety due to an equal.

46 服勞: undertake an onerous task.

47 流離: drift without a fixed abode.

48 後夫人: honorific term for someone's second wife (*husil* 後室).

49 李長坤 [1474–?; styled Hŭigang 希剛; sobriquet Hakko 鶴皐, Kŭmhŏn 琴軒; ancestral seat Pyŏkchin 碧珍; posthumous epithet Chŏngdo 貞度]: scholar-official under King Chungjong [r. 1506–44; 1488–1544]. He was exiled to Kŏje Island in 1504 during the Literary Purge of the Kapcha Year, but fled to Hamhŭng and lived among the low-born who were hereditary butchers and wicker craftsmen (*paekchŏng* 白丁). After the "Rectification of King Chungjong," he was reemployed at the court. His father was Yi Sŭngŏn 李承彦 [dates unknown].

85

The Faithful Bride

Vol. III: 29; n.d.; Diary XIV, pp. 103–4 and 106–7; 293.

There was a scholar who lived in Ch'ungch'ŏng Province who was married to a girl whose home was distant some twenty miles. On the first night of their wedding, the groom went into the bride's room and there sat talking to her late into the night, when suddenly there was a sound as of thunder with which the front door smashed in and a great tiger bounded in upon them.

He caught up the groom and was off in a trice. In a flash of light the bride was after him and then seizing the beast by the hind leg did not let him go. Away he went up the rear mountain like a dragon on the wing.

Indifferent to every danger, the bride held on over rocks, pits, thorns, and thickets till her dress was torn to tatters, her hair dishevelled, and all her body covered with blood. Thus the beast ran on for miles and miles. At last exhausted, the beast flung the bridegroom aside and made off. The bride hurried at once to restore her husband. She felt him over and found that life still was present. She then looked here and there to see if there was any means of succour and at last spied a house just below the hill with a small, lighted window at the back.

Knowing that the tiger had gone far enough by this time, she found her way down to the house and entered by the back gate and here she found five or six people drinking together with heaps of refreshments before them. Seeing a bride come stepping in with her face still bearing marks of the rouge and cosmetics and blood on her face and body as well and all her clothes torn, they were astounded and fell on their faces before her.

The bride said, "I am a human being – please do not be startled at my appearance. There is a man on the hill just at the back here, but whether dead or alive I cannot tell. Won't you come at once and lend help?"

They all returned to a reasonable consciousness, and with torches started up the hill. Here they found a young man lying on the ground all but dead. They looked him carefully over and what was their astonishment to find he was the son of their master.

In his fears, the master had him carried and placed in the room and there they gave him restoratives and medicine. After a watch of the night or two he came to. Then the whole house awaked to what had really happened. The master had called a few friends to make glad over his wedding and lo it was behind this house that this had happened. Then it was that they understood that the young woman was the bride. They had her come into the room and had her given some soup.

The day following they sent news to the bride's home. The parents on both sides were wonder-struck and delighted and greatly moved by her faithfulness. The scholars in that district memorialized the governor and had a gate of honour erected to her and her name was recorded among Korea's faithful women.

湖中 1) 一士人　行子婚於隣邑五六十里　新郎醮禮 2)

夜　入新房　與新婦對坐　夜將深　一聲霹靂　後門

破碎　忽有一大虎　突入房中　嚙 3) 新郎而去

신부창황급기　내포호후각불사　호직상후산
新婦蒼黃急起　乃抱虎後脚不舍 [4]　虎直上後山

기행여비　이신부한사수거　불계암학지고하
其行如飛　而新婦限死隨去　不計岩壑之高下

형극　지총월　의상파렬　두발산란　편신류혈
荊棘 [5]　之叢樾 [6]　衣裳破裂　頭髮散亂　遍身流血

이유불지　행기리　호역기진　잉포기신랑어초암
而猶不止　行幾里　虎亦氣盡　仍抛棄新郎於草岸

지상이거　신부시내수습정신　이수무신체
之上而去　新婦始乃收拾精神　以手撫身體

즉명문　하　미유온기　사고찰시　즉암하유일인가
則命門 [7]　下　微有溫氣　四顧察視　則岸下有一人家

후창미유화광　탁　기호행지기원　내심경　이하
後窓微有火光　度 [8]　其虎行之既遠　乃尋逕 [9]　而下

개후호이입　즉적유오륙인회음　효핵　랑자
開後戶而入　則適有五六人會飲　肴核 [10]　狼藉

홀견신부지입　만면지분화혈이응　편신의상수
忽見新婦之入　滿面脂粉和血而凝　遍身衣裳隨

처이렬　망지즉일녀아　제인개경부어지　신부내왈
處而裂　望之卽一女兒　諸人皆驚仆於地　新婦乃曰:

아시인야　렬위　행물경동　후암유인　이방재사
我是人也　列位 [11]　幸勿驚動　後岸有人　而方在死

생미분지중　걸급구　제인시수습경혼　일제거화
生未分之中　乞急救　諸人始收拾驚魂　一齊舉火

이상후암　유소년남자　강부　암상　기식장진
而上後岸　有少年男子　僵仆 [12] 岸上　氣息將盡

제인시심시　즉내주인지자야　주인대경　거이와지
諸人始審視　則乃主人之子也　主人大驚　舉而臥之

방내　관이약수등물　과수경후내소　거가시야경황
房內　灌以藥水等物　過數頃後乃甦　擧家始也驚惶

종언경행　개신랑지부　치송혼행　이적회린우
終焉慶幸 13)　盖新郎之父　治送婚行　而適會隣友

음주지제　이즉기가후야　시지기녀자지위신부
飲酒之際　而卽其家後也　始知其女子之爲新婦

연치우방　궤이죽음　익일통우부가　량가부모
延置于房　饋以粥飮　翌日通于婦家　兩家父母

막불경희　탄기지성고절　향리다사　이기사
莫不驚喜 14)　歎其至誠高節　鄕里多士　以其事

정관　정영　지승정표지전　운이
呈官 15) 呈營 16) 至承旌表之典 17) 云爾

1　湖中: Ch'ungch'ŏng Province.
2　醮禮 = *hollye* 婚禮: wedding ceremony.
3　嚼: made-in-Korea sinograph meaning "(tiger) attacks/mauls/carries off (a person) in its mouth."
4　不舍: not let go of.
5　荊棘: thorns and brambles.
6　叢樾: dense forest.
7　命門: solar plexus, pit of the stomach.
8　度: comprehend, reckon.
9　尋逕: find a path, find one's way.
10　肴核: snacks of drinks and fruit.
11　列位: all of you, everyone (similar to "ladies and gentlemen").
12　僵仆: fall facedown.
13　慶幸: serendipitous auspicious occasion.
14　驚喜: be pleasantly surprised.
15　呈官: report to the local magistrate.
16　呈營: report to the provincial magistrate.
17　承旌表之典: receive the honour of public recognition of one's filial piety and chastity (*chŏngp'yo* 旌表).

——— **86** ———

Kim *Kamsa*

Vol. III: 29; n.d.; Diary XII, pp. 90–2; 294.

Governor Kim Ch'i, whose special name was Namgok, was father of Kim Paekkok (Tŭksin). From his earliest years he was an adept at the casting of fortunes. No end of events were fulfilled just as he had foretold. In the days of our darkest history he attained to the office of *kyori* but later on he repented of his part with a government so misdirected and on excuse of ill-health he resigned office. He built a house in Yongsan and lived there. He closed his doors and hid away from the world. When callers came, he had them turned away on the claim that he was ill.

On a certain day the servant came in to say that a Sim from South Mountain had called. Kim's reply was, "The honoured guest did not know that his humble servant was ill so has come by mistake. I have already cut myself off from the affairs of the world and am so sorry that I cannot see you."

Thus he turned him away.

Kim had frequently read his own fortune and he had learned that a person having in his surname the radical for "water" would save him from the greatest danger. Just now he thought, "If this name Sim has 'water' for radical, I wonder if he is the man who is destined to save me?"

He at once sent his servant and had the guest recalled. Now this man was Sim Kiwŏn.

Sim came back as the servant had indicated and Kim got up, saying, "I am an old man and have already long cut myself off from affairs of the world. Your Excellency has come to call on me but I turned you away on account of sickness. I am very much ashamed."

Sim replied, "I have never yet met Your Excellency, but I have long heard that you can divine as no other and I have come in a very bold way to propound a question or two. I am now a poor scholar of forty years of age, and my fortune is wholly ill-favoured and so I wish you to look upon my affairs and with your marvellous eyesight tell me what my future is to be."

From his sleeve he drew forth a paper on which was written his four birth dates (*saju*).* He went on to say, "On my way here I met a friend who, learning that I was coming to have my fortune told, asked me to have his told, too, and gave me his dates. I could not refuse and so brought it, too."

Looking over the dates given, Kim said, "You have great riches and good fortune so strong – nothing greater could be hoped for."

A moment later he drew out still another person's dates: "This man does not desire riches or good fortune. His one wish is to be free from disease and live long. How long will he live, pray?"

Kim looked it over and called a servant to bring a table and spread a mat. He put on his official robes, knelt down before it and opening the paper with the birth dates on the table, offered incense and said,

"These dates are precious beyond word to say – very wonderful, indeed – such as one would never hope to see."

Sim then arose and said, "I must go now."

Kim said, "I am an old man, ill and full of anxiety and worry. Stay and comfort me and pass the night."

He remained there and spent the night and when it was late and no one else was by, he said to Sim, "I was born unlucky into this world and my name has been soiled with the evil government we have lived under before I realized it. Thus I have made excuse of sickness and came here to shut my door. Ere long this government will fall and a great change will come. I know why you came to enquire of me and the thought back of it. Do not look upon me as an outsider but as a closest friend. Let me hear all, I pray you, every word."

With a sudden start, Sim said, "No, no, nothing of the kind – no such thoughts are mine."

But in the end he told him all.

Kim replied, "Your wishes will all come about, no doubt or fear need be yours. What time have you decided to make your start?"

His reply was, "On such-and-such a day."

Kim then sang over to himself a formula pertaining to the day and said, "The day you suggest is good but for a great work such as you have in mind, you should have these three characters *sal-p'a-rang* (Death, Break, Wolf) in the day you begin. For a little affair the day you suggest is all right but for a great work, this other day is needed – I'll choose you a day instead."

And so he opened his calendar and said, "The 16th of the 3rd moon is the day of greatest fortune. This day has in it *pŏm-sal + p'a-rang* (Death and destruction to the wolf). On that day someone will go to give information against you but it will not succeed and all will turn out well in the end."

Greatly wondering at this, Sim said, "If that is so, will Your Excellency also lend your name for our list?"

Kim's reply was, "I have no desire for my name to be there; one thing only I ask, and that is that you succour me on the day that I am destined to misfortune."

Sim replied, "I'll certainly do so," and was gone.

When the reform of the state came about and the day for a settlement came, Kim's name also was included in the list of the guilty, but Sim opposed it and he saved his friend and finally made him Governor of Kyŏngsang.[†]

* "Four birth dates" indicates the four elements: the year, month, day, and hour of one's birth. *Saju* "four pillars" refers to these four dates.

† Gale's translation stopped here. The rest of the story deals with Kim Ch'i as a ghost.

金監司緻 1) 號南谷 栢谷金得臣 2) 之父也 自少精於

推數 3) 多奇中 4) 神異之事 仕昏朝 5) 爲弘文校理 6)

晚始悔之 托病解官 7) 卜居 8) 于龍山 9) 之上 杜門

晦跡 10) 謝絶人客 一日 侍者來告曰：南山洞 11)

居沈生請謁云矣 金公謝曰：尊客 12) 不知此漢

之病廢 13) 而枉顧 14) 乎 人事之廢絶已久 今無延迎

甚可恨歎云而送之 金公平日 每以自家四柱 推數

平生 則當得水邊人之力 可免大禍 忽爾思來客

旣水邊姓　則斯人也　無乃有力於我　急使侍者

追還於中路　此是沈器遠 15) 也　沈生隨其奴還來

則金公連忙起迎曰：老夫廢絶人事者久矣　尊客

枉屈　適有採薪之憂 16)　有失迎拜之禮　慚愧無地

客曰：曾未承顔 17)　而竊聞長者 18)　精通推數云故

不避猥越 19)　敢以來質　某以四十窮儒　命途奇窮 20)

今此之來　欲一質定 21) 於神眼之下矣　仍自袖中

出四柱而示之　且曰：某之來時　有一親切之友

又以四柱托之　難以揮却 22)　不得已持來矣　金

公一見之　極口稱讚曰：富貴當前　不須更問矣

最後客又出示一四柱曰：此人不願富貴　只願平生

無疾恙 23)　且欲知壽限 24)之如何而已　公瞥眼 25) 一覽

卽令侍者　鋪席置案　起整冠服　斂膝危坐 26)　以其

四柱　置之書案上　焚香而言曰：此四柱貴不可言

有非常人之命數　可不欽 27) 哉　沈生欲告退　公曰：

老夫病中愁亂　難遣尊客　幸且暫留以慰病懷可也

仍使之留宿　至夜深無人之時　公乃促膝而近前曰：

某實托病　老夫不幸出身於此時　曾染跡 28) 於朝廷者

晚而悔悟　杜門病蟄　而朝廷之翻覆 29) 不久矣

君之來質　吾已領畧 30)　幸勿相外而欺我　以

實言之可也　沈生大驚　初欲諱之　末乃告其故

公曰：此事可成　少無疑慮　將以何日擧事乎

曰：定于某日矣　公沈吟良久曰：此日吉則吉矣

此等大事　擇日有殺破狼之日 31) 然後可矣　某日

若於小事則吉矣　擧大事則不可也　某當爲君

更擇吉日矣　仍披曆熟視曰：三月十六日果吉矣

此日犯殺破狼　擧事之際　必也先有告變 32) 之人

而少無所害　畢竟無事順成矣　必以此日擧事可也

심대이지　　내왈　　약연　　즉공지명자　　근당록입어
沈大異之　乃曰：若然　則公之名字　謹當錄入於

오배록명책자의　　공왈　　차즉비소원　　단명공
吾輩錄名冊子矣　公曰：此則非所願　但明公 33)

성사지후　　행구수사지명　　비불급화　　시소망야
成事之後　幸救垂死之命 34)　俾不及禍　是所望也

심쾌락이거　　급지갱화　　지일　　다이김공지죄
沈快諾而去　及至更化 35)　之日　多以金公之罪

불가원언　자　심내극력구지　　초배　　령남백
不可原言 36)　者　沈乃極力救之　超拜 37)　嶺南伯

이졸　　공상이자가사주　　문우중원　　술사
38) 而卒 ‡　公嘗以自家四柱　問于中原 39)　術士 40)

즉서이일구시　　시왈　　화산　　기우객　　두재일지
則書以一句詩　詩曰：花山 41)　騎牛客　頭戴一枝

화운운　막효기의　　급위령백　　순도안동　　졸환점
花云云　莫曉其意　及爲嶺伯　巡到安東 42)　猝患痁

질　편문견각지방　　즉혹이위당일도기흑우
疾 43)　遍問譴却之方 44)　則或以爲當日倒騎黑牛

즉즉추　운운고　　의기언　　기우이주행정중　　재하
則卽瘳 45)　云云故　依其言　騎牛而周行庭中　纔下

우이와방중　　두통극심　　사일기　　이안지　　문기명
牛而臥房中　頭痛劇甚　使一妓　以按之　問其名

즉일지화야　　홀억중원인시구　　탄왈　　사생유명
則一枝花也　忽憶中原人詩句　歎曰：死生有命

내명포신석　　환착신의　　성복정침이서　　시일삼척
乃命鋪新席　換着新衣　盛服正枕而逝　是日三陟 46)

쉬　모재아　　홀견공성추종　　입문　　경이기영왈
（倅）某在衙　忽見公盛騶從 47)　入門　驚而起迎曰：

公何爲而越他道　來訪下官也　金公笑曰：吾非生人

俄者已作故　方以閻羅大王 48) 赴任之路歷見君

而且有所托者　某方赴任　而恨無新件章服 49)

君念平日之誼　幸爲辦備否　三陟倅　心知其虛誕 50)

而因其强請　出篋中緞一疋而給之　則金公欣然

受之　告辭而去　三陟（倅）大驚訝　送人探之

則果於是日　沒于安東府巡到所矣　以是之故

金公爲閻羅大王之說　遍行于世　朴久堂長遠 51)

與金公之子栢谷　切親之友也　曾於北京推數而來

則書以某年某月當死云云矣　當其月［年］正

初　委送人馬　邀栢谷以來　授以一張簡而書之

栢谷曰：書以何處　久堂曰：欲得君之一書

（呈）于老［先］尊長 52) 前矣　栢谷悅惚而不書

久堂曰：君以吾爲誕乎　勿論誕與不誕　第爲我書之

재삼간청　백곡부득이거필　구당구호이사지서왈
再三懇請　栢谷不得已擧筆　久堂口呼而使之書曰：

모지절우박모　수장지어금년야　행복망특수긍련
某之切友朴某　壽將止於今年也　幸伏望特垂矜憐

비연기수운운　이외봉서부주전　내봉서이모자
俾延其壽云云　而外封書父主前　內封書以某子

[자모]　백시운운　서필　구당정소일실　여백곡분향
[子某]白是云云　書畢　久堂淨掃一室　與栢谷焚香

분기서왈　금이후　오지면의　과온도　기년
焚其書曰：今而後　吾知免矣　果穩度 53) 其年

과수십년후시몰　사근탄망 [망]　이김공지정백
過數十年後始歿　事近誕忘 [妄]　而金公之精魄 54)

대이어인의　기후　매야성추솔　렬등촉　왕래어
大異於人矣　其後　每夜盛騶率　列燈燭　往來於

장동　락동　지간　혹봉지구　즉하마이서회
長洞 55) 駱洞 56) 之間　或逢知舊　則下馬而敍懷

일일지야　일소년효과락동　봉김공어로상　문왈
一日之夜　一少年曉過駱洞　逢金公於路上　問曰：

령감종하이래호　김공왈　금효즉오지기일야
令監從何而來乎　金公曰：今曉即吾之忌日也

위향음식이거　제물불결　미득흠향　창결　이귀
爲饗飲食而去　祭物不潔　未得歆饗 57) 悵缺 58) 而歸

잉홀불견　기인즉왕기가　가재창동　주인파제
仍忽不見　其人即往其家　家在倉洞 59) 主人罷祭

이출의　이기수작전지　백곡대경　직입내청
而出矣　以其酬酌傳之　栢谷大驚　直入內廳 60)

편심제물　무일불결지물　이병이　지중　유일인모
遍尋祭物　無一不潔之物　而餅餌 61) 之中　有一人毛

거 가 경 송　기 후　우 유 일 인 봉 어 로　즉 김 공 왈
擧家驚悚　其後　又有一人逢於路　則金公曰：

오 증 차 견 타 인 지 강 목　이 미 급 환　제 기 권 기 장
吾曾借見他人之綱目 62)　而未及還　第幾卷幾張

유 금 백 지 협 치　자　일 후 환 송 지 시　여 혹 불 심
有金箔紙挾置 63)　者　日後還送之時　如或不審

즉 금 백 유 유 실 지 려　수 이 차 언 전 오 가　수 상 심 송 이
則金箔有遺失之慮　須以此言傳吾家　須詳審送而

가 야　기 인 귀 전 기 어　백 곡 수 견 강 목　즉 김 백 과 유 지
可也　其人歸傳其語　栢谷搜見綱目　則金箔果有之

인 개 이 지　기 외 다 유 신 이 지 사　이 불 능 진 기 언
人皆異之　其外多有神異之事　而不能盡記焉

‡ Gale's translation ends here.

1　金緻 [1577–1625; styled Sajŏng 士精; sobriquet Nambong 南峰, Simgok
　　深谷; ancestral seat Andong 安東]: scholar-official under King Injo 仁祖
　　[r. 1623–49; 1595–1649]. His father was Kim Sihoe 金時晦 [1542–81].
2　金得臣 [1604–84; styled Chagong 子公; sobriquet Paekkok 栢谷; ancestral
　　seat Andong 安東]: scholar-official under King Sukchong 肅宗 [r. 1674–
　　1720; 1661–1720]. He was posthumously honoured as Prince Anp'ung
　　安豐君. His father was Kim Ch'i.
3　推數: tell a person's fortune; prognosticate.
4　奇中: make an extraordinarily accurate guess.
5　昏朝: lit. "dark court": refers to the reign of Kwanghaegun 光海君 (r.
　　1608–23; 1575–1641).
6　校理: fifth counsellor of the Office of the Special Counselors (Hongmungwan
　　弘文館)
7　托病解官: resign from an official post using illness as a pretext.
8　卜居: select a place to live via prognostication.
9　龍山: a neighbourhood in Seoul.
10　杜門晦跡: lit. "shut the door and cover one's tracks."
11　南山洞: a neighbourhood at the foot of Nam Mountain.
12　尊客: honorable guest.

13 病廢: lit. "ill and disabled."

14 枉顧 = *wanggul* 枉屈 = *wangnim* 枉臨: (deferential) be visited by someone.

15 沈器遠 [?–1644; styled Suji 邃之; ancestral seat Ch'ŏngsong 靑松]: scholar-official under King Injo 仁祖 [r. 1623–49; 1595–1649]. For his meritorious contribution to the enthronement of King Injo, he was honoured as Ch'ŏngwŏn puwŏn'gun 淸原府院君, royal father-in-law. His father was Sim Kan 沈諫 [dates unknown].

16 採薪之憂 = *pusin chi u* 負薪之憂: (humilific) my illness.

17 承顔: (deferential) meet someone for the first time.

18 長者: your esteemed/honoured father.

19 猥越: presumptuous; impertinent; insolent.

20 命途奇窮: lit. "life path is hapless": be born under an unlucky star.

21 質定: assess the situation and decide accordingly.

22 揮却: reject dismissively; spurn; cast aside.

23 疾恙 = *chilbyŏng* 疾病: chronic sickness.

24 壽限 = *sumyŏng* 壽命: life span.

25 瞥眼 = *pyŏlgyŏn* 瞥見: catch a glimpse of; glance at.

26 斂膝危坐: kneel in such a way that one's body rises straight up.

27 欽: delightfully dutiful.

28 染跡: traces of uncleanliness.

29 翻覆: overturn.

30 領畧: hear the gist of and get a rough idea about.

31 殺破狼之日: the *shao po lang* day; i.e., the day on which bad luck disappears. *Shao po lang* refers to three stars in Chinese astrology.

32 告變: lit. "inform the authorities of a coup d'état."

33 明公: (honorific) form of address for a top-ranking official.

34 垂死之命: life that is hanging in the balance; i.e., about to expire.

35 更化 = *panjŏng* 反正: lit. "return to the correct path."

36 原言: words of forgiveness.

37 超拜: promote an official by allowing him to skip a rank.

38 嶺南伯 = *yŏngbaek* 嶺伯: governor of Kyŏngsang Province.

39 中原: Central Plain of China, i.e., centre of Chinese civilization.

40 術士: diviner.

41 花山: old name for Andong, North Kyŏngsang Province.

42 安東: village in North Kyŏngsang Province.

43 痁疾 = *hakchil* 瘧疾: malaria.

44 譴却之方: lit. "plan to rebuke and decline."

45 卽瘳: immediately recover from an illness.

46 三陟: a coastal village in Kangwŏn Province.

47 騶從 = *ch'ubok* 騶僕: servant escorting a master.

48 閻羅大王: Yama, King of Hell.

49 章服 = *kwanbok* 冠服 = *kwandae* 冠帶: official attire.

50 虛誕: preposterousness.

51 朴長遠 [1612–71; styled Chunggu 仲久; sobriquet Kudang 久堂, Sŭpch'ŏn 隰川; ancestral seat Koryŏng 高靈; posthumous epithet Munhyo 文孝]: scholar-official under King Hyŏngjong 顯宗 [r. 1659–74; 1641–74]. His father was Pak Hwŏn 朴烜 (dates unknown).

52 先尊長: (honorific) someone's deceased father.

53 穩度: live an untroubled life.

54 精魄 = *chŏngnyŏng* 精靈 = *hollyŏng* 魂靈: spirit of the dead.

55 長洞: a neighbourhood that used to straddle present-day Ch'ungmu-ro, Namdaemun-ro, and Hoehyŏn-dong in Seoul; also known as Changhŭnggot-kol, because Changhŭnggo 長興庫 (the royal warehouse for paper supplies and tents) used to be located there.

56 駱洞: T'arak-kol 酡酪洞, located in the same vicinity as Chang-dong (see note 55) so called because it housed an establishment that sold milk. Kol, meaning "neighbourhood," is the vernacular Korean gloss for the sinograph tong 洞.

57 歆饗: (for a spirit) accept offerings.

58 悵缺: feel enormously disappointed.

59 倉洞: Ch'ang-gol, in the same vicinity as Chang-dong and Nak-tong (see notes 55 and 56); so called because Sŏnhyech'ŏng 宣惠廳 (Agency to Bestow Blessings) used to be located there.

60 內廳: place for preparing and/or storing food.

61 餅餌: rice cake.

62 綱目 = *Zizhi tongjian gangmu* 資治通鑑綱目 (*Outlines and Details of the Comprehensive Mirror*): Zhu Xi's 朱熹 [1130–1200] critical restructuring according to "outer guidelines" (*gang* 綱) and "details" (*mu* 目) of *The Comprehensive Mirror to Aid in Government* (*Zizhi tongjian* 資治通鑑) by Sima Guang 司馬光 [1019–86].

63 挾置: insert.

——— **87** ———

Tonggye's Maid

Vol. III: 32; n.d.; Diary XIV, pp. 107–9; 295.

When a young lad, Chŏng On (1569–1641 AD) was already noted among the literati as a coming man. He had matriculated and was on his way to graduating exercises when he met a mourner's chair in white. This chair sometimes went ahead of him and sometimes behind. A maid-servant followed behind. Her plaited hair came down to her heels while her face was very pretty. Her gait also was one of perfect grace as she tripped along and all her ways seemed most refined. All those on horseback with him watched her with the deepest interest. Said they, "How pretty this dainty maid!"

From time to time she looked back, and always toward Chŏng On.

Thus it went on for some time and they all joked together and said, "Knowledge and skill in the character are with Chŏng, but as for looks we can any of us beat him. How comes it her looks are all directed toward him? One can never tell the ways of the world."

And thus they laughed. A little later the white chair entered a village.

Still sitting on his horse, Chŏng said, "Twenty *ri* beyond this place is an inn. If you will go on there and await me, I'll sleep here and pick you up early tomorrow morning."

The friends said in reply, "We have all had our hopes fixed on you, and now we are out on a thousand-*ri* journey and we cannot think of separating even for a little. You have met this seductive wench and have foolishly fallen in love with her and are filled with □ thoughts, ready to forsake us and go after her. There is no accounting for people or what they will do."

Chŏng On laughed but made no reply, laid on the whip and followed the chair and the little maid.

Reaching the gate that she had entered, he found a large and stately mansion with the outer guestroom quite vacated and bare. Here Chŏng On alighted and sat down on the vacant verandah. The maid following the chair went into the inner quarters and in a little came out again. Her face lighted up with smiles so that he felt quite in love with her. She then said, "Please do not remain seated on this cold verandah but come into my room and rest for a little."

Chŏng On followed her into her room and found it clean and neat in the most perfectly ordered manner. In a little his evening meal came forth and though the food was simple it was most tasty. The servant said, "I'll go in and straighten up the kitchen and will then return."

So she went and by the first watch of the night returned, sent her relatives to another room, and came in and knelt down before Chŏng.

Smiling, Chŏng inquired, "How did you know I was coming here that you had food prepared and lodging ready?"

She answered, "Though I have escaped the mark of being ugly and my age is seventeen, I have never yet lifted my eyes to any man. Today, however, on my way here I looked up at Your Excellency not once but many times. Now, though you are a high □ valiant lord you do not treat anyone with contempt. My venturing to address you thus is because I have an exceedingly sad story to tell, and one of deadly resentment. I wish to seek your power to redress the wrong and set matters right. I wonder how you will regard what I have to say."

She then began to cry and her manner was one that deeply moved him. Chŏng asked what this could mean and the cause.

She replied, "My master was the only son of a line of only sons and he unfortunately became married to an adulterous woman, and in his early years he died at the hands of this woman's adulterer. He had no near relatives or friends who could right his wrong and take vengeance for what he had suffered. I alone know of this and have seen it all. This resentful heart has filled my soul till today and yet being only a woman I can do nothing. My only hope was to offer myself to some heroic heart in return for his hand of vengeance. Today this wicked woman returned to her own home for a night and now we are on our way back. I saw Your Excellency and at once recognized that you stood far above your fellows and that your courage excelled them all. This explains my desire to see you. I looked my love and my regard for you and so brought you here. The one who ruined our home is here to carry on their nefarious intercourse. Here is a rare opportunity to rid the earth of him. I would that Your Excellency would take this opportunity to mete out vengeance."

Chŏng replied, "Your thought is a very worthy one. I am only a scholar and quite alone with nothing in my hand. How could I carry out such a proposal as this?"

The servant replied, "I had that thought in mind and have long had in hiding a bow and arrows. And though Your Excellency is not a practised archer you can still draw a bow. One shot of this bow and he is finished – however defiant his spirit may be."

She then brought him the bow and they went together into the inner quarters. Looking in through the chink of the window, the light was burning and all the room aglow. Here was a great fat fellow with his outer garments rolled back and his broad chest showing while he dallied with this unhappy woman. The fellow sat next to the door of the room.

Chŏng drew the bow back to his ear and let fly through the chink, straight at the chest of the offender through which it drove to the wall. He fell over at once. He drew again intending to make an end of the woman as well, when the maid stayed his hand and had him desist and urged him to depart at once, saying, "Though the woman deserves to die I have long been her servant and cannot forget this relationship; my hand must not be lifted against her. Leave her alone."

Thus they hurriedly returned to their own room and on her urgent request they made ready and left the inn, she following him.

Chŏng had an extra horse that carried his load and here he had her ride.

They went on for several *ri* till they came to the inn where his companions were lodged. Still it was dark and after a time he found where they were. His companions were all awakened in startled wonder to see him bringing a maid-servant with him. One man among them drew an expression of deep seriousness and said, "I used to think that you, Chŏng, were a scholar and a gentleman till today I saw you taken captive by this woman. We would never have dreamed you would have been so captivated. Does a gentleman ever act so?"

He gave him a severe and stern reprimand.

Chŏng laughingly replied, "I have not done this from a licentious motive and I knew full well how a gentleman should order his ways. There is a reason for this that you will know by and by."

Then he made his way to Seoul, taking her along and putting her in a room by herself. Chŏng passed his exams and when all ceremony was over and he was returning to his country home he took the maid along. Later he made her his secondary wife. She was good and virtuous as well as very beautiful. There was nothing she was not equal to and all she did was □ a perfect □. Everyone in the house who knew her praised and loved her.

鄭桐溪蘊 1) 少時與洞中名下士 2) 數人 作會試 3)
之行 中路逢一素轎 4) 或先或後 5) 而後有一
童婢隨去 而編髮 6) 垂後及趾 7) 容貌佳麗 冉冉 8)
作行 擧止端麗 9) 諸人在馬上皆目之曰：美艷
而童婢頻頻顧後 10) 而獨注目於桐溪
如是而行半餉 11) 諸人相與戲言 文章學識
固可讓於輝彥[遠] 而至如外貌 何渠 12)
不若輝彥[遠] 而厥女奚獨屬情 13) 於輝彥[
遠]乎 世事之未可知如此矣 相與一笑 未幾
其轎子向一村閭而去 桐溪立馬而言曰：
過此卅餘里地 14) 有店舍 15) 君輩且歇宿 16) 而待我
我則向此村而寄宿 明曉當追到矣 諸人皆曰：
吾輩之期望 17) 輝彥[遠]者何如 而今當千里科行
聯轡 18) 同行 不可中路相離 今於路次逢妖女

空然爲情欲所牽　妄生非意之心　至欲舍同行而

作此妄行　人固未易知　知人亦難　桐溪笑而不答

促鞭向其女之所去村　及其門則一大家舍　外廊 19)

則廢已久矣　桐溪下馬而坐於外廊之軒上矣

其童婢隨轎入內　少焉出來　笑容可掬　仍言曰：

行次 20)不必坐此冷軒　暫住小婢之房　桐溪隨入其房

則極其精潔　已而進夕飯　亦疎淡而旨　其婢曰：

小婢入內灑掃廚下而出矣　仍入去　至初更 21)出來

揮送其親屬而避之　促膝而坐 22)於燭下　桐溪笑而

問曰：汝何由知吾之來此　而有所排設也　婢曰：

小人面貌免醜 23)而行年十七　未嘗擧眼而對人

今午路上屬目 24)於行次者非止一再 25)則行次

雖是剛腸男兒　豈或恝然 26)耶　小人之如是者

竊有悲寃之懷 27)欲借行次而伸雪 28)未知行次倘

能肯從否　仍揮淚而顔色凄然 29)　桐溪怪而詰其故

則對曰：小婢之上典　以屢代獨子　娶一淫婦　靑年

死於奸夫之手　而旣無强近親屬 30)　無以雪寃復讐

而只有小婢一人知其事　而寃憤之心　結于胸膈

而自顧以一女子之身無所施　只願許身於天下英雄

假手而雪憤矣　今日　上典之淫妻　自本家還來

故小婢不得已隨後往來矣　路上見行次諸人之

中　行次之容貌頗不埋沒　而膽氣有倍於他人

眞吾所願者也　以是之故　以目送情誘之而致此

奸夫今又相會　淫虐狼藉　此誠千載一時　行次幸

乘機而圖之　桐溪曰：汝之志槩 31)　非不奇狀［壯］

而吾以一介書生　赤手空拳 32)　遽行此大事乎

童婢曰：吾有意而藏置弓矢者久矣　行次雖不知射法

豈不知彎弓而放矢 33) 乎　若放矢而中　則渠雖

凶獰之漢 34)　豈有不死之理哉　仍出弓矢而與之

偕入內舍　從窓隙窺見　燭火明亮 35)　一胖大漢 36)

脫衣而露胸　與淫婦相抱戲謔 37)　無所不至

而其坐稍近於房門　桐溪乃滿酌 [彎張] 38) 而

從窓穴射去　一矢正中厥漢之背　洞胸而仆 39)

又欲以一矢　射其淫婦　童婢揮手止之　促使出

外曰：彼雖可殺　吾事之久矣　奴主之分既嚴

吾何忍自吾手殺之　不如棄之而去　促行至渠房

收拾行李 40)　隨桐溪而出　桐溪適有餘馬載卜之者

不得已載後而同行　行幾里　訪同行之科客所住處

則時天色未明　艱辛搜覓而入門　則同行驚起而見

桐溪與一女子同行矣　一人正色言曰：吾於平日以

揮彦 [輝遠] 謂學問中人矣　今忽於路次携女而行

君之有此行　吾儕意慮所不到也　士君子行事固

여시호　정색책지　동계소왈　오기위탐색지도
如是乎　正色責之　桐溪笑曰：吾豈爲貪色之徒

불지사군자지행작차거야　개중자유위절
不知士君子之行作此擧也　箇中自有委折 41)

종당　지지의　잉여지상경　치지점막　동계과
從當 42) 知之矣　仍與之上京　置之店幕 43)　桐溪果

중회시　방방후환향지일　우여지솔래　잉작부실
中會試　放榜後還鄉之日　又與之率來　仍作副室

기인온공연미　백사무불가의　가향칭기현숙의
其人溫恭姸美　百事無不可意　家鄉稱其賢淑矣

1 鄭蘊 [1569–1641; styled Hwiwŏn 輝遠; sobriquet Tonggye 桐溪; ancestral seat Ch'ogye 草溪; posthumous epithet Mun'gan 文簡]: scholar-official under King Injo 仁祖 [r. 1623–49; 1595-1649]. His father was Chŏng Yumyŏng 鄭惟明 [1539–96].

2 名下士: renowned scholar/literary figure.

3 會試: second-stage examination in the capital taken by passers of the first-stage examination (*ch'osi* 初試).

4 素轎: lit. "plain palanquin" = unadorned palanquin that marks a funeral procession.

5 或先或後: now in front, now behind.

6 編髮: braided hair, queue.

7 垂後及趾: hanging down the back as far as the heels.

8 冉冉: move with a lilt.

9 擧止端麗: prim and proper comportment.

10 頻頻顧後: lit. "look back frequently."

11 半晌: half the morning; a quarter of a day.

12 何渠: "Who on earth … ?" (rhetorical question)

13 屬情: grow fond of, grow attached to.

14 廿餘里地: lit. "a place at a distance of twenty-something *ri*."

15 店舍 = *chŏmmak* 店幕 ~ *chumak* 酒幕: tavern; a place where travellers purchase a meal or stay the night.

16 歇宿: rest and stay.

17 期望: anticipate and hope.

18 聯轡: lit. "connected reins" = travel side-by-side.

19 外廊 = *sarang* 舍廊: reception room for male guests.

20 行次: (honorific) traveller or his journey.
21 初更 = *kabya* 甲夜: 7–9 PM.
22 促膝而坐: lit. "press one's knees and sit" = sit side-by-side/intimately.
23 免醜: escape ugliness.
24 屬目 = *chumok* 注目: pay attention to.
25 非止一再: lit. "not stop at once or twice" = repeatedly.
26 恕然: look down upon, treat with contempt.
27 悲寃之懷: sorrowful and resentful sentiment.
28 伸雪 = *sinwŏn sŏlch'i* 伸寃雪恥: lit. "recount one's resentment and cleanse
   oneself of shame" = redress an injustice.
29 凄然: bleakly and sorrowfully.
30 强近親屬: immediate relatives.
31 志槩: integrity and constancy.
32 赤手空拳: lit. "bare hands and bare fists" = unarmed.
33 彎弓而放矢: nock an arrow and shoot.
34 凶獰之漢: ferocious-looking man.
35 明亮: light and bright.
36 一胖大漢: a big-boned, fat man.
37 戲謔: jest, rib, poke fun at, fool around.
38 彎張: draw a bow to full draw.
39 洞胸而仆: lit. "(something) penetrates a person's chest and [makes the
   person] collapse."
40 行李: travel baggage.
41 委折 = *kokchŏl* 曲折: ins and outs; twists and turns.
42 從當: as a matter of course.
43 店幕 = *chŏmsa* 店舍: inn.

—————— 88 ——————

A Gifted Woman

Vol. III: 33; n.d.; Diary XIV, pp. 109–13; 296.

No good as a story.

U Hahyŏng was a man of P'yŏngsan, poor in this world's goods, though
he had graduated as an archer and was sent to the River (Yalu) districts
of northwest Korea on guard. There he saw a woman servant who

carried the water at the official quarters. She was fairly good-looking. Hahyŏng took her and lived with her.

One day this woman said to Hahyŏng, "You, a graduate, have made me your concubine. What do you propose to give me in the way of return?"

He replied, "My house is poor and here I am one thousand *ri* away from its meagre supply without a thing in hand. I have taken you simply to have you see to my clothes and my stockings and keep them in order. What salary do you expect to come your way?"

The woman answered, "I know it well, but I have given myself to you and I'll see to your clothes. Don't be anxious."

Hahyŏng said further, "I don't expect you to clothe me."

The woman from this time on worked busily to mend and weave and had him well clothed and fed.

When the time of his office had expired and Hahyŏng was making his plans to return, the girl asked, "When you return, will you seek office in Seoul?"

Hahyŏng replied, "I have nothing and know no special friends and know no way to remain in Seoul. No such hopes are mine. I shall go back to my ancestral home and live there."

The woman said, "As I study your face and manner I realize that you are no common man. I see ahead of you high office and official preferment. You are gifted sufficiently for any such office. Why should you stay where there is no means of living? That would be a sad case, indeed. I have some money laid up – six-hundred *yang* of cash. I'll give you this. Get yourself a saddle, horse and other necessaries with this. Do not go back to the country, but to Seoul and seek office. In less than ten years, you will find you have won out. I am a low-class woman and have no power to preserve my chastity. I'll betake myself to a place I know and when you have attained to office that very day I'll come."

This they agreed and she urged on him to take good care.

Having thus come into possession of means, Hahyŏng was greatly moved by this kindness. He shed tears as he said his good-byes.

When she had let him go she went to the home of a widower captain and made application to him. The captain noticed her as a woman above the ordinary and made her his wife.

His home was sufficient in means and well-to-do and she said to him, "How much have you in the way of means left over from your former wife? Let me know definitely: how much in the way of grain, money, silks, grasscloth, cotton, dishes, and odds and ends? Will you please write them all out and give me the list?"

The captain said, "A husband and wife simply use what there is and when it's gone they get more. What doubts have you that you desire to do so?"

The woman replied, "Not so. I pray you do as I request."

The captain then made it out as she requested. She read it and hid it among her clothes in the press. She busied herself and saw abundantly to her husband's needs. She said to the captain, "I am slightly educated and like to read the Official Gazette when I live in the country. Will you not please get it for me so I can see it?"

The captain did as she requested and had her see the paper.

In following this for several years, she finally found that U Hahyŏng had passed all his tests and was now high up in military rank and was about to be appointed magistrate of some rich county. Later she saw that he had bade Seoul good-bye and was on his way to his post. The woman then said to the captain, "My coming here was not with the intent to stay for good but only for a little and now I am obliged to speak a long farewell."

The captain gave a great start and asked the reason.

She replied, "There is no reason to ask the cause. I have a definitely appointed place to go to. Don't think of me anymore, I pray you."

She then showed the list of things as he had written them out. "For these seven years I have been your wife and have had charge of this house. If there's one thing lacking I shall be greatly disturbed. There are none less than there were. But in many cases there are three and four times as many as there were. I am so glad of this."

She then said her farewell and with a servant that carried her effects she dressed as a man and with a straw hat on her head set out toward the county where Hahyŏng was.

Hahyŏng had only just arrived in his place that very day and the woman appeared and said that she was a person who had a lawsuit to be □-ed so she entered the court.

She said, "I have a word to say and would prefer to come close and speak it by my own mouth."

The magistrate thought this peculiar that a woman should suggest that she come up on the terrace to speak and he did not give consent at first but finally yielded. She was no sooner up on the terrace than she asked to come close to the window.

Moved by this peculiar desire, the magistrate gave consent.

She said, "Do you not know me?"

He replied, "I have just arrived – how do you suppose I could know people here?"

She answered, "When you were in such-and-such a place as border guard do you not recollect one who lived with you?"

The magistrate then looked sharply at her, jumped up, quickly took her by the hand and led her into his room.

He asked, "Why have you come in such a guise as this? I only arrived yesterday and now you are here. This is a strange coincidence."

They were mutually most glad and talked over all that they had gone through in the meanwhile. At this time Hahyŏng's wife had died and so he made this woman his wife and put her in charge of all his house. She cared most kindly for his son born of the first wife and took such wise charge of all the servants and had everything so well ordered. She was kind and yet severe.

All the people of the district praised her. She used to say to her husband, "Give something to the *ajŏn* secretary and have the Gazette brought me every month."

She read it faithfully and so was posted on the things of the world. She waited to see who was likely to become Minister of Home Affairs and lost no opportunity to pay her respects there. When the particular person came to power, naturally he praised U and his house and so had him appointed to this and that rich county and so her house grew and prospered and more than ever she rewarded her friends. Little by little he rose to the rank of General and now he was nearing eighty years of age. Finally he resigned and went to his home in the country.

The woman followed the required custom in mourning and wore sack cloth, saying to her stepson, "Your father was quite a high military officer in the country and he rose to ranking General and lived till eighty, a long and happy life. There was nothing left for him to wish. I too have only done my duty – no praise is due me. Still I did what I could to have him rise in rank till we arrived here and so I have also finished my course.

"I was a low-class woman of the border districts who became the second wife of a military officer and have gone here and there on official duty and have lived well. My glory has had its fill. What regrets could I possibly have? When my master lived, he made me mistress of all his house. Naturally I could be such. Now you have attained to high office* and your wife, my daughter, understands all. I hand it all over to you."

On hearing this, the son and daughter-in-law wept, saying, "Not so. Our house's prosperity today is entirely due to our mother. We would have your help and direction for the future. Why do you propose to resign it all?"

She replied, "No, not so. If I do not step aside the affairs of the family will be rendered confused."

So then she wrote out a list of all the articles of furniture and utensils, and gave it to her daughter-in-law who went to the large room and there lived while the mother moved to the smaller room by herself.

She said, "I shall not come out again," and so shut the door, cut off all supply and died.

The son and daughter wept and cried, saying, "Our mother was a rare woman indeed. We cannot treat her other than our real mother."

So they buried her with all honour. After three months the funeral □ and then they built a shrine for her where sacrifices could be offered.

When they had finished the father's sacrifices as well, they started off to bury their father but they could not lift the father's coffin. Even a hundred could not lift it. They all said, "I expect it is because his thoughts are with his wife."

So they made her a coffin too and when they started off together his was possible to lift easily. All wondered at this. They buried them, [him on the side of the main road to P'yŏngsan facing west, and her a dozen or so paces to his right facing east].†

* This is Gale's mistranslation. The original reads: "You are now a grown-up."
† The translation in the square brackets is ours. The last two lines of Gale's manuscript are impossible to read.

禹兵使夏亨 1) 平山 2) 人也　家貧初登科　赴防 3)

于關西 4) 江邊之邑　見一汲水婢 5) 之免役者

貌頗免醜　夏亨嬖之　與之同處　一日　厥女謂夏

亨曰：先達 6) 既以我爲妾　將以何物爲衣食之資乎

對 [答] 曰：吾本家貧 況此千里客中 手無 [有] 所

持者乎 吾旣與汝同室 則所望不過澣濯垢衣 7) 補

綻弊襪 8) 而已 其何物之波及 9) 於汝乎 其女曰：

妾亦知之熟矣 吾旣許身而爲妾 則先達之衣資

吾自當之 須勿慮也 夏亨曰：此則非所望也

厥女自其後 勤於針線紡績 10) 衣服飮食 未

嘗闕焉 及赴防限滿 夏亨將還歸 厥女問曰：

先達從此還歸之後 其將留洛 11) 而求仕乎 夏亨曰：

吾以赤手之勢 12) 京中無親知之人 以何糧資留京乎

此則無可望矣 欲從此還鄉 老死於先山之下爲計

耳 女曰：吾見先達容儀氣像 非草草之人 13) 也

前程優可至閫帥 14) 男子旣有可爲之機 何可坐於無

財而埋沒於草野乎 甚可歎惜 吾有積年所聚銀貨

皆可至六百兩 以此贐 15) 之矣 可備鞍馬及行資

幸勿歸鄉　直向洛下而求仕焉　十年爲限　則可以有

爲也　吾賤人也　爲先達何可守節　當托身於某處

先達作宰本道然後　卽日當進謁矣　以是爲其期

願先達保重保重　夏亨意外得重財　心窈感幸

遂與其女揮淚作別而行　其女送夏亨之後　轉

托於邑底鰥居 16) 之一校家 17)　其校見其人物之

伶俐　與之作配而處　家頗不貧　其女謂校曰：

前人用餘之物爲幾許　凡事不可不明白爲之

穀數爲幾許　錢帛布木爲幾許　器皿雜物爲幾許

皆列書名色及數爻　而作長件記 18)　校曰：夫婦之間

有則用之　無則措備可也　何嫌何疑而有此擧也

女曰：不然　懇請不已　校乃依其言而書給之

其女受而藏之衣笥 19)　勤於治産　日漸富饒　女謂

其校曰：吾粗解文字 20)　好看洛中之朝報政事 21)

盍爲我每每借示於衙中乎　校如其言　借而示之

數年之間政事　宣傳官 22) 禹夏亨　由經歷 23) 而陞副

正 24)　乃除關西腴邑 25) 也　其女自其後　只見朝報

某月日某邑倅禹夏亨辭朝 26) 矣　其女乃謂校曰：

吾之來此非是久留計也　從此可以永別矣　其

校愕然而問其故　其女曰：不必問事之本末

吾自有去處　君勿留戀 27) 乃出向日物種長件記

以示之曰：吾於七年之間　爲人之妻　理家産萬

一有一箇之減於前者　則去人之心　豈能安乎

以今較前　幸而無減　或有一二三四倍之加數者

吾心可以快活矣　仍與校作別　使一雇奴負卜 28)

而作男子粧　着平陽子 29)　徒步而行夏亨之郡

夏亨莅任 30) 纔一日矣　托以訟民 31) 而入庭曰：

乃有所白之事 32) 願升階而白活 33)　太守怪之

初則不許　末乃許之　又請近窓前　太守尤怪而許之

其人曰：官司[34] 倘[35] 識小人乎　太守曰：吾新到之初

此邑之民　何以知之　其人曰：獨不念某年某地

赴防時同處之人乎　太守熟視　急起把手而入于

房而問曰：汝何作此樣而來也　吾之赴任之翌日

汝又來此　誠一奇會[36] 彼此不勝其喜　共敍中間阻

懷[37] 時夏亨喪配[38] 矣　因以其女入處內衙正堂[39]

而總家政　其女撫育其嫡子　指使其婢僕　俱有法度

恩威幷行　衙內洽然稱之　每勸夏亨　托于備局[40] 吏

給錢兩而得見每朔朝報　女見之而揣度[41] 世事

時宰之未及爲詮官[42] 而未久可爲者　必使厚饋

如是之故　其宰相秉軸[43] 則極意吹噓[44] 歷三四

腴邑　家計漸饒　而饋問 [餉] 尤厚　次次陞遷

位至節度使[45] 而年近八十以壽　終于鄉第　其女治

喪如禮 過成服 46) 謂其嫡子喪人曰：令監以鄕曲武弁

位至亞將 47) 位已極矣 年過稀年 48) 壽已極矣

有何餘憾 且以我言之爲婦事夫 自是當然道理 何

必自矜 而積年費盡誠力 贊助求仕之方 得至于今

吾之責已盡矣 吾以退方賤人 49) 得備小室於武宰 50)

享厚祿於列邑 吾之榮亦極矣 有何痛寃之懷

令監在世時 使我主家政 此則不得不然 而今

喪主如是長成 可幹家事 51) 嫡子婦當主家政

自今日請還家政 嫡子與婦泣而辭曰：吾家之

得至于今 皆庶母之功也 吾輩只可依賴而仰

成今何爲而遽出此言也 女曰：不可 不如是

家道亂也 乃以小大物件器皿錢穀等屬 成件記

一并付之 嫡子婦使處正堂 而自家退處越邊 52) 一

間之房曰：自此一入而不可出 仍闔門 53) 而絶粒 54)

수 일 이 사　　적 자 배 개 애 통 왈　　오 지 서 모　　비 심 상 인
數日而死　嫡子輩皆哀痛曰：吾之庶母　非尋常人

하 가 이 서 모 대 지　　초 종　　후 장 사　　대 삼 월 장 행
何可以庶母待之　初終 55) 後葬事　待三月將行

별 립 묘 이 사 지　　급 병 사 지 장 기 이 박　　장 천 구 이 인 행
別立廟而祀之　及兵使之葬期已迫　將遷柩而靷行 56)

담 군 배 불 득 거　　수 십 백 인 무 이 동　　제 인 개 왈
擔軍輩不得舉　雖十百人無以動　諸人皆曰：

무 혹 계 의 어 소 실 이 연 야　　내 치 기 소 실 지 인　　장 행 동 발
無或係意於小室而然耶　乃治其小室之靷　將行同發

즉 병 사 지 구 경 거 이 행　　인 개 이 지　　장 우 평 산 지 대
則兵使之柩輕舉而行　人皆異之　葬于平山地大

로 변　　서 향 이 장 자　　병 사 지 분 야　　기 우 십 여 보 지
路邊　西向而葬者　兵使之墳也　其右十餘步地

동 향 이 장 자　　기 소 실 지 분 운 이
東向而葬者　其小室之墳云爾

1 禹夏亨 [dates unknown; sobriquet Hoesuk 會叔, ancestral seat Tanyang 丹陽]: a military official under King Yǒngjo 英祖 [r. 1724–76; 1694–1776]. He passed the military service examination in 1710 (Sukchong 36). He served as Commander-in-Chief in the army (*pyǒngma chǒltosa* 兵馬節度使) in Hwanghae Province and Kyǒngsang Province. He died at the age of sixty-four. His father was U Sunp'il 禹舜弼 [dates unknown].

2 平山: a town in Hwanghae Province.

3 赴防: take up a new post in the border region.

4 關西: P'yǒngan Province.

5 汲水婢: a slave girl in charge of fetching water.

6 先達: scholar who has passed the civil service examination but has yet to be appointed to an official post.

7 瀚濯垢衣: launder dirty clothes.

8 補綻弊襪: darn socks.

9 波及: spread, have repercussions.

10 針線紡績: needlework and weaving.

11 留洛: stay in the capital.

12 赤手之勢: have nothing but one's bare hands.

13 非草草之人: lit. "not an ordinary person."

14 閫帥: lit. "leader of the doorsill, commander of the threshold"; polite term for a Commander-in-Chief in the army or navy (*pyŏngma chŏltosa* 兵馬節度使 or *sugun chŏltosa* 水軍節度使).

15 贐: give a memento to someone setting out on a journey.

16 鰥居: live as a widower.

17 校家: officer's house.

18 件記: vernacular Korean *idu* term for an inventory of people or things.

19 衣笥: clothes chest made of bamboo.

20 粗解文字: lit. "comprehend (Chinese) characters a little bit."

21 朝報政事: lit. "morning gazette and official business." Also known as "notices" (*kibyŏl* 奇別, 寄別) or "morning paper" (*choji* 朝紙), *chobo* refers to the official daily gazette issued by the Royal Secretariat (Sŭngjŏngwŏn 承政院) of the Chosŏn Dynasty. *Chŏngsa* refers to official business regarding appointments and dismissals of officials (*immyŏn ch'ulch'ŏk* 任免黜陟).

22 宣傳官: royal messengers (junior ninth grade to senior third grade).

23 經歷: junior fourth-grade official handling administrative duties belonging to the Office of Records of Meritorious Subjects (Ch'unghunbu 忠勳府), the State Tribunal (Ŭigŭmbu 義禁府), the Military Command Headquarters (Toch'ongbu 都摠府), etc.

24 副正: junior third-grade official belonging to the Office of Royal Genealogy (Chongch'inbu 宗親府), the Office of Royal Kinsmen (Tonnyŏngbu 敦寧府), the Royal Stables and Transportation Office (Saboksi 司僕寺), and the Government Arsenal (Kun'gisi 軍器寺).

25 腴邑: a well-off town.

26 辭朝: (for a newly appointed official) bid farewell to the king before departing to take up one's post.

27 留戀: anticipate and long for.

28 負卜: carry baggage. "卜" *pok* is an *idu* expression for baggage.

29 平陽子 = *p'yŏngnyangja* 平凉子 (made-in-Chosŏn Chinese-character expression designed to represent the native Korean word *p'aeraengi*): "conical hat made of bamboo strips, typically worn by mourners or people of low status."

30 莅任: be/get newly appointed or take up a new position.

31 訟民: lit. "a person filing a lawsuit or lodging a petition to have one's case heard."

32 所白之事: a matter to be reported.

33 白活: *idu* expression read as *palgwal* "(for commoners) submit a written or oral report to a government office."

34 官司 = *kwana* 官衙: lit. "government office." Here, the magistrate himself.

35 倘: perhaps, perchance.

36 奇會: strange and unexpected encounter.

37 中間阻懷: the emotions built up over a long separation.

38 喪配: lose one's spouse.

39 正堂: inner quarters.

40 備局: Border Defence Council (Pibyŏnsa 備邊司).

41 揣度: comprehend, fathom.

42 詮官: a cover term for Minister of Personnel (Ijo p'ansŏ 吏曹判書) and Minister of War (Pyŏngjo p'ansŏ 兵曹判書), the ministers who managed the selection of civil and military officials.

43 秉軸: assume a position of power.

44 吹噓: exaggerate someone's achievements as a way of nominating him for a government position.

45 節度使 = Pyŏngma chŏltosa 兵馬節度使: Commander-in-Chief.

46 成服: lit. "don mourning attire" = donning mourning attire for the first time on the third or fifth day after the deceased person's death.

47 亞將: cover term for junior second-grade military posts such as Chief Commander of the Police Bureau (P'odo taejang 捕盜大將), Commander of the Royal Bodyguards (Yongho pyŏlchang 龍虎別將), Lieutenant Commander of the General Directorate for Military Training (Togam chunggun 都監中軍), and Second Minister of the Ministry of War (Pyŏngjo ch'amp'an 兵曹參判).

48 稀年 = *kohŭi* 古稀: seventy years old.

49 遐方賤人: a country bumpkin from a faraway place.

50 武宰: lit. "military prime minister" = a military official at the rank of Prime Minister.

51 可幹家事: able to manage household affairs.

52 越邊: the opposite side; the other side.

53 闔門: close the door.

54 絶粒: stop eating grain; stop eating.

55 初終: lit. "beginning and end" = period from the burial of the deceased (*ch'osang* 初喪) until the "ceasing of the wailing" ceremony (*cholgok* 卒哭), a memorial service held in the third month after burial.

56 靷行 = *parin* 發靷: commence a funeral procession.

—————— **89** ——————

The Results of Faithful Sacrifice

Vol. III: 35; n.d.; Diary XIV, pp. 113–14; 297.

The family of the Kims of Ch'ŏngp'ung fell low in the scale and lost all their standing. The father of Kim Hwasun lived at Sagŭn in Kwangju but was very poor with no friends whom he could call his own.

Cho Sŏgyun came and lived as his near neighbour. Though he had come here to live he had not brought his books from Seoul. He heard that there was a copy of the *Kangmok** in Kim's house.

Hearing of this, Cho asked the loan of it and Kim gave consent. But though he had given this some time ago, he failed to send the book. Cho wondered what this could mean and if it was because he disliked to lend it.

It was the time of the Tano festival. Cho's maidservant had just returned from Kim's house and said, "I have just seen the sacrificial ceremony at Kim's and assuredly it is a ceremony worth the name. The sacrifices in the master's house, while there is an abundance of things, are not so perfectly performed as at the Kims'. The spirits in our home will, I fear, refuse the offering that we make. The spirits in Kim's home are evidently present and partake before your very eyes."

Mrs. Cho asked the servant how she made this out, whereupon she replied, "I have just been to the Kims' and they were preparing for the Tano festival. The main hall and the court were as clean as possible – not an atom of dust or disorder. Mr. Kim and his wife had their old clothes washed till they were as white as snow and with bodies bathed they dressed thus. They spread mats and, for want of something better, had placed books to serve as a table and on there were placed the sacrificial offerings. These included rice, soup, vegetables, and fruit. This was all they had. There were not many dishes but the food was most clean. Here they placed the table and the husband and wife passed the glass, bowed, and sat kneeling, all most strictly according to the rule. With all their heart and to the observance of every detail they carried through the ceremony. I stood by the side and watched till my hairs stood one by one on end, and I seemed to see the very spirits. The sacrifice in our master's house, if one were to make a comparison, is not worthy of the name of sacrifice at all. Today I saw a real sacrifice, indeed."

Mrs. Cho told this to her husband and Cho now realized that Kim's not sending the *Kangmok* was because he had need of it in his sacrifices instead of a table or stand. Hearing this, Cho wondered greatly at once and went and called on Kim. He congratulated him and said, "I have heard that your acts have by their faithfulness caused people to wonder. You will be blessed assuredly! I am so glad for this. I would like to take the responsibility of teaching your son. Will you consent to it?"

Kim consented most gladly and Kim Hwasun went to Cho's for study, and later he studied with Pak Chamya and became recommended as a great scholar for office. His son became a prominent governor and from that time forth the family became widely known. Later five ministers were born from three generations of the family – a great and noble house.

* *Kangmok = Zizhi tongjian gangmu* 資治通鑑綱目 (*Outlines and Details of the Comprehensive Mirror*). See note 6 below.

청 풍 김 씨 조 선 　　중 엽 심 미 　　김 화 순 　　지 부 모
淸風金氏祖先 1) 　中葉甚微　金和順 2) 之父某

거 재 광 주 사 근 평 　　이 심 빈 천 　　인 무 지 자
居在廣州肆覲坪 3) 　而甚貧賤　人無知者

조 락 정 석 윤 　　적 비 린 　　이 거 　　자 경 중 신 래 책 자
趙樂靜錫胤 4) 　適比隣 5) 而居　自京中新來冊子

다 미 수 래 　　김 지 가 　　적 유 강 목 　　조 공 문 이 원 차
多未輸來　金之家　適有綱目 6) 　趙公聞而願借

즉 락 지 이 구 이 종 불 송 지 　　락 정 심 절 아 지
則諾之已久而終不送之　樂靜心窃訝之

의 기 인 석 　　이 불 차 의 　　시 당 중 오 일 　　조 씨 비 자
意其吝惜 7) 而不借矣　時當重五日 8) 　趙氏婢子

자 김 가 이 래 언 왈 　　아 자 견 김 씨 댁 행 사 지 의
自金家而來言曰：俄者見金氏宅行祀之儀

진 개 행 제 사 　　여 오 상 전 댁 제 사 　　제 수 수 풍 결
眞箇行祭祀　如吾上典宅祭祀　祭需雖豊潔

불급어김씨댁　신도　필불향지　김씨댁　즉신기
不及於金氏宅　神道 9)　必不享之　金氏宅　則神其

양양　여강흠　의　락정부인　문기유즉기비왈
洋洋 10)　如降歆 11)　矣　樂靜夫人　問其由則其婢曰：

아왕김씨댁　방욕행절사　청상계하　개이쇄소
俄往金氏宅　方欲行節祀 12)　廳上階下　皆已灑掃

무반점진구　김반내외　정세폐의여설색
無半點塵垢 13)　金班內外　淨洗弊衣如雪色

이일신목욕이착지　포신석건　건석　우상
而一身沐浴而着之　鋪新席件 [件席]14)　于上

상치책자　기책자상　진설제물　불과반갱　소
上置冊子　其冊子上　陳設祭物　不過飯羹 15)　蔬

채　과품　이이　기수수소　이품극정　출주
菜 16)　果品 17)　而已　器數雖小　而品極精　出主 18)

후　기부처헌작배궤　개유법도　성경비지
（後）　其夫妻獻酌拜跪　皆有法度　誠敬備至

소인립기방　불각모발송연　황견신령지래격
小人立其傍　不覺毛髮悚然 19)　怳見神靈之來格 20)

오지주인댁제사　비지어차　가위유여불제지탄
吾之主人宅祭祀　比之於此　可謂有如不祭之歎 21)

진개제사　금일시견지운의　부인이기언　전우락정
眞箇祭祀　今日始見之云矣　夫人以其言　傳于樂靜

시지강목지불즉차　개이행사지고야　김가무상탁
始知綱目之不卽借　盖以行祀之故也　金家無床卓

이기책대용고야　락정문이이지　즉왕견김씨이
以其冊代用故也　樂靜聞而異之　卽往見金氏而

하왈　문군유지행　필유여경　가불흠탄
賀曰：聞君有至行　必有餘慶 22)　可不欽歎 23)

오 욕 성 취 령 윤
吾 欲 成 就 令 胤 24)　　미 가 허 지 부
未 可 許 之 否　　김 대 락 이 허 지
金 大 樂 而 許 之

김 화 순 수 학 우 락 정 지 문
金 和 順 受 學 于 樂 靜 之 門　　후 우 위 박 잠 야
後 又 爲 朴 潛 冶 25)　　문 인
門 人

이 학 행
以 學 行　　천 등 음 사
薦 登 蔭 仕 26)　　자 기 자 감 사 공
自 其 子 監 司 公 27)　　시 현 달
始 顯 達

후 유 삼 세 오 공
後 有 三 世 五 公 28)　　위 대 가 언
爲 大 家 焉

1　祖先 = *chosang* 祖上: ancestor.

2　金和順: lit. "Kim, [the magistrate of] Hwasun" = Kim Kŭkhyŏng 金克亨 [1605–63; styled T'aesuk 泰叔; sobriquet Sach'ŏn 沙川, Unch'on 雲村; ancestral seat Ch'ŏngp'ung 淸風] when he was serving as magistrate of Hwasun County in Chŏlla Province. Kim Kŭkhyŏng was a scholar-official under King Hyojong 孝宗 [r. 1649–59; 1619–59]. His father was Kim Inbaek 金仁伯 [1561–1617].

3　肆覲坪 = Sagŭnp'yŏng 沙斤坪 ~ Sagŭnbŏl: plain near present-day Sagŭn-dong, Sŏngdong-gu, Seoul. Judging by the alternate characters 沙斤, which are typically used as phonograms in Korean sources, we speculate that "Sagŭn-" is vernacular Korean for a native place name or native verb form.

4　趙錫胤 [1605–54; styled Yunji 胤之; sobriquet Nakchŏng 樂靜; ancestral seat Paekch'ŏn 白川; posthumous epithet Munhyo 文孝: scholar-official under King Injo 仁祖 [r. 1623–49; 1595–1649].

5　比隣 = *küllin* 近隣: close neighbour.

6　綱目 = *Zizhi tongjian gangmu* 資治通鑑綱目 (*Outlines and Details of the Comprehensive Mirror*): Zhu Xi's 朱熹 [1130–1200] critical restructuring according to "outer guidelines" (*gang* 綱) and "details" (*mu* 目) of *The Comprehensive Mirror to Aid in Government* (*Zizhi tongjian* 資治通鑑) by Sima Guang 司馬光 [1019–86].

7　吝惜: cherish, prize, be reluctant to part with; begrudge, stint.

8　重五日 = Tano 端午: the fifth day of the fifth month, known as the Double Fifth Day (Festival) in China.

9　神道 = 神靈: divine spirit, supernatural being.

10　洋洋: unreserved and unconstrained manner.

11　降歆: lit. "[spirits] descend and enjoy the offerings."

12　節祀: seasonally observed sacrificial rites.

13　塵垢: lit. "dust and dirt."

14 新件席: newly woven straw mat.

15 飯羹: rice and soup offered up at a sacrificial table.

16 蔬菜: vegetables and edible wild plants.

17 果品: fruits.

18 出主: (at an ancestral worship rite) take out the spirit tablet of the deceased ancestor (*sinju* 神主).

19 毛髮悚然: hair stands on end.

20 來格: reach, arrive at.

21 不祭之歎: lamentation over an improperly prepared ancestral worship rite.

22 餘慶: auspicious events happening to someone due to his or her ancestor's good deeds.

23 欽歎: admire a beautiful deed.

24 令胤: (honorific) "your esteemed son(s)."

25 朴潛冶: sobriquet of Pak Chigye 朴知誡 [1573–1635; styled Inji 仁之; ancestral seat Hamyang 咸陽; posthumous epithet Munmok 文穆]: scholar-official under King Injo 仁祖 [r. 1623–49; 1595–1649]. His father was Pak Ŭngnip 朴應立 [dates unknown].

26 蔭仕 = *ŭmgwan* 蔭官 = *ŭmjik* 蔭職: lit. "official position [gained through] stealthy [benefaction]": entering into the state bureaucracy via "protected appointment" (*ŭmsŏ* 蔭敍), i.e., appointment due to one's ancestors' merits or illustrious political career; also known as "white bones going south" (*paekkol namhaeng* 白骨南行).

27 監司公: Master *kamsa*; here it refers to Kim Ching 金澄 [1623–76] and Kim So 金沼 [dates unknown], two sons of Kim Kŭkhyŏng 金克亨 [1605–63].

28 三世五公: lit. "three generations, five high-ranking officials" = a family / clan producing five high-ranking officials (*konggyŏng* 公卿) over three generations.

———— **90** ————

The Andong Wizard

Vol. III: 36; n.d.; Diary XIV, pp. 114–16; 298.

Yu Sŏngnyong (Sŏae) (1542–1607), while he lived in Andong, had his brother* with him, **Yu Unnyong** 柳雲龍 (**Kyŏmam** 謙庵). He was most simple and wholly ignorant of everything. People said he did not know the difference between wheat and barley, while his own family gave him the nickname *Ch'isuk* the "Blockhead"[†] and Sŏngnyong regarded him as nothing.

This brother once said, "I have really something to say to you but your place is always in such confusion and uproar that I can't do it. Call me sometime when you have no guests and all is quiet. I have something of the greatest importance to tell you."

Once when there were no callers and all was quiet he sent a man to call Blockhead. With an old head cap and tattered clothes, he came and with great delight said, "Let's have a game of *paduk*."

Sŏngnyong said, "But you have never played *paduk*. If you think to play it without practice, you'll only lose."

He said this because he, Sŏngnyong, was a most noted player. Blockhead replied, "Good player or poor player, never mind that. Let's try a hand."

There being no help for it, Sŏngnyong yielded though he wondered what thought could possibly be back of it. The older brother clapped down one piece on the sounding board and before half the board had been used Sŏngnyong was defeated hopelessly and could not find a turn. From this time on Sŏngnyong recognized that his brother's stupidity was all put on, not real. He bowed down before him, saying, "Brother, we have lived half our lives together and you have deceived me thus. I feel you have done me a wrong that I can never have requited. From today on I want you to tell me how to do and what to say."

"What deception have I ever practised, pray? This game is purely a matter of chance. You, a man of the world rising in office – what could a poor rustic like me teach? Still I may tell you that tomorrow a certain priest will come this way and ask you for a night's lodging. Don't receive him, I pray you. Though he asks a hundred times, refuse him. Tell him to go to the rear village and find a lodgment in the little huts there. Write this in your head and make no mistake about it."

Sŏngnyong said, "I'll do as you tell me."

On the day following, a priest did come and sent in his name card at which Sŏngnyong invited him in. His face was shining and full of determined vigour – about forty years of age. When asked where he lived, he replied that he lived in Odaesan, of Kangnŭng, and that he had come on a visit of sight-seeing to Kyŏngsang. He had seen all the places of note and was now on his way home. But he had heard of Sŏngnyong's great wisdom and excellence and he wished just once to see him. As now the day was late, he asked for a place to sleep the night and take his departure in the morning.

Sŏngnyong replied, "My rooms are engaged and I am sorry I cannot put up a stranger. There is a small temple just back of the village where you will find a lodging place. Sleep there and come and see me in the morning."

So the priest urged his request, but he refused and so there being no help for it, he followed a servant that Sŏngnyong sent to the little temple at the rear.

At this time the older brother disguised himself as a hermit and took a maidservant who was dressed as a priestess (*sadang*) and himself, as though he were owner of the little temple. He had on a special cap and coat as worn by hermits and went outside the gate to meet the priest with a low bow, saying, "Whence comes his High Excellency, Your Reverence, to my humble dwelling?"

The priest bowed his recognition and came in and sat down. The hermit prepared the evening meal but first treated him to a glass of wine. The priest tasted of it and, smacked his lips, saying, "This wine is fragrant and highly flavoured – not ordinary drink at all. Where did you get it?"

The hermit replied, "This old dame used to be a dancing girl who sold drinks and here she puts up now. It is her skills that prepared it. Do not refuse it, I pray you, but drink as much as your heart desires."

The evening meal now came forth, greens and vegetables from the hills and plain, very clean and fresh. The priest ate his fill and, dead drunk, fell over quite unconscious. Only late at night did he awake to consciousness when he felt an uncomfortable pressure on his chest. Opening his eyes, he saw the hermit sitting on his breast and stomach.

He had a knife in hand and with flashing eyes he called, "You low-down priest – how dare you play any tricks like this? The day you came across the sea, I knew of it. How can you think to deceive me? If you speak the truth and the whole truth you may find a way to live but if not your days are numbered, speak now."

The priest prayed for his life: "Here I am up against death, how could I dare to speak one word that was not true. I am a Japanese, not Korean, and the Shogun Hideyoshi just now is planning the destruction of your country. His only fear is Yu Sŏngnyong and so he has sent me ahead to assassinate him. I am spied out by your wonderful vision. If you now spare me I promise that never again will I do such as this."

The Blockhead replied, "War on us is something that is in the hands of God and cannot be blocked by man's weak hands. I shall never at- tempt to fight against God. I shall see, however, even though there is war here, that Andong is □. If the Japanese soldiers come here, not one of them will ever return home again. What object would I have in taking your poor wasted life? I set you free. Go and tell Hideyoshi and let him know that I am here."

So he let him go. The priest bowed a hundred times and said, "I'll never do it again – ever again."

He covered his head and ran for his life.

He returned and told Hideyoshi. Hideyoshi gave a great start and sent word to his soldiers, saying, "Not one foot on Andong territory – remember."

Thus was all Andong made safe and secure.

* The original reads 叔 (*suk*; uncle). Gale translates it as "older brother Suk." At first blush, this appears to be a simple mistranslation of the character 叔 (uncle) as a given name Suk. However, note that Gale also goes on to identify the protagonist's name as Yu Unnyong. Like many other *yadam*, this story survives in many different versions, one of which indeed introduces the protagonist as Yu's older brother, not his uncle. Given this fact, Gale's translation indicates that he and his pundits had foreknowledge of this other version and mixed up their *Kimun ch'onghwa* entry and what they had read or heard about this other version, with the result that two different identities become conflated into "older brother Suk."

† The original consists of 痴 (*ch'i*; blockhead, idiot) and 叔 (*suk*; uncle) to mean "blockhead uncle."

柳西崖成龍 1) 居安東 2) 家　有一叔　爲人蠢蠢

無識 3) 可謂菽麥不辨 4) 家間呼曰：痴叔　心甚易之

叔每曰：吾有從容可道言　而君之家每患喧撓 5)

如有無客靜寂之時　可請我　我有千萬繁說話

云云矣　一日　適無人而從容矣　使人請痴叔

則叔以弊冠破衣　欣然而來曰：吾欲與君　賭一局棋

未知如何　西崖曰：叔父平日未嘗着棋　今忽對局

恐非侄之敵手也　蓋西崖之棋法　高於一世者也

叔曰：高下何論　姑且對局可也　西崖强而對局

心窃訝之　其叔先着一子　未至半局　而西崖之

局全輸[輪]6)　不敢下手　始知其叔之韜晦7)

俯伏而言曰：猶父8)猶子9)之間　半生同處　如是

相欺　下懷10)不勝抑鬱　從今願安承敎　叔曰：

豈有欺君之理也哉　適偶然耳　君既出身於世路

則如我草野之人　有何可敎之事乎　然而明日必有一

僧來訪而請宿矣　切勿許之　雖千萬懇乞　而終始

牢拒11)　使指後村草菴而寄宿可也　須銘心勿誤

西崖曰：謹奉敎矣　及到其日　忽有一僧通刺12)

使之入來　狀貌堂堂　年可三四十許人也　問其居

則居在江陵13)五坮山14)矣　爲覽嶺南山川而來

편간명승　금방복로　이절복문대감청덕아망
遍看名勝　今方復路　而窃伏聞大監淸德雅望 15)

위당금제일운고　이식형지원　잠래배알
爲當今第一云故　以識荊之願 16)　暫來拜謁

금즉일이만의　원차일석이기숙　이위명조발
今則日已晚矣　願借一席而寄宿　以爲明朝發

행지지야　서애왈　가간적유사고　금불가이
行之地也　西崖曰：家間適有事故　今不可以

생면인　류숙　차촌후유불암　가이차중숙의
生面人 17)　留宿　此村後有佛菴　可以此中宿矣

대조하래가야　기승만단간걸　이일향뢰각
待朝下來可也　其僧萬端懇乞　而一向牢却 18)

승불득이수동향촌후지암　차시　치숙이비자
僧不得已隨童向村後之菴　此時　痴叔以婢子

장출사당　양　자가작거사양　이승건포갈
粧出舍堂 19)　樣　自家作居士樣　以繩巾布褐 20)

출문합장　배이영왈　하래존사　강림우박루지지
出門合掌　拜而迎曰：何來尊師　降臨于薄陋之地 21)

승답례이입좌정　거사정비석반　이선이일호지
僧答禮而入坐定　居士精備夕飯　而先以一壺旨

주　대지　승음이감지왈　차주지청렬　비상
酒 22)　待之　僧飮而甘之曰：此酒之淸冽 23)　非常

하처득래　대왈　차로구즉차읍지주모기로퇴
何處得來　對曰：此老嫗卽此邑之酒母妓老退

자야　상유구일지수법이연야　원존사물혐랭담
者也　尙有舊日之手法而然也　願尊師勿嫌冷淡

이진량즉행의　잉진석반　산채야속　극기정결
而盡量則幸矣　仍進夕飯　山菜野蔌 24)　極其精潔

其僧飽喫　而泥醉昏倒矣　夜深後　始覺而胸膈

悶鬱 25)　擧眼而視之　則其居士騎坐胸腹之上

手執利刀 26)　張目叱之曰：賤僧焉敢　汝之渡海之日

吾已知矣　汝其瞞我乎　汝若吐實　則或有饒貸之

道 27)　而不然　則汝命盡於卽刻矣　從實直告可也

其僧哀乞曰：今則小僧之死期已迫矣　何可一毫

相欺乎　小僧果是日本人也　關伯 28)　平秀吉 29)

方欲發兵　謀陷本國　而所忌者　獨尊家大監故

使小僧　先期來此　以爲先圖之地 30)　矣　今者現露

於先生神鑑 31)　之下　幸伏望寄我一縷之殘命　則勢

[誓]不敢復作此等事　痴叔曰：我國兵禍　乃是天

數所定　難容人力　吾不欲逆天　吾鄉則雖兵革

之禍 32)　吾在矣　優可救濟　倭兵如躡 33)　此境　則俱

不旋踵 34)　矣　如汝螻蟻之命 35)　斷之何益　寬汝禿頭 36)

<ruby>而</ruby> 이 <ruby>送</ruby> 송 <ruby>之</ruby> 지　<ruby>傳</ruby> 전 <ruby>于</ruby> 우 <ruby>平</ruby> 평 <ruby>秀</ruby> 수 <ruby>吉</ruby> 길　<ruby>使</ruby> 사 <ruby>知</ruby> 지 <ruby>我</ruby> 아 <ruby>國</ruby> 국 <ruby>之</ruby> 지 <ruby>吾</ruby> 오 <ruby>在</ruby> 재 <ruby>也</ruby> 야　<ruby>仍</ruby> 잉 <ruby>釋</ruby> 석 <ruby>之</ruby> 지

而送之　傳于平秀吉　使知我國之吾在也　仍釋之

其 기 僧 승 百 백 拜 배 稱 칭 謝 사 曰 왈　不 불 敢 감 不 불 敢 감　抱 포 頭 두 鼠 서 竄 찬　而 이 去 거

其僧百拜稱謝曰：不敢不敢　抱頭鼠竄 37) 而去

歸 귀 見 견 平 평 秀 수 吉 길　備 비 傳 전 其 기 事 사　秀 수 吉 길 大 대 驚 경 異 이　勅 칙 [勅 칙] 軍 군 中 중

歸見平秀吉　備傳其事　秀吉大驚異　勅 [勅] 軍中

以 이 渡 도 海 해 之 지 日 일　無 무 敢 감 近 근 安 안 東 동 一 일 步 보 地 지　一 일 境 경 賴 뢰 以 이 安 안 過 과 矣 의

以渡海之日　無敢近安東一步地　一境賴以安過矣

1 柳成龍 [1542–1607; styled Igyŏn 而見; sobriquet Sŏae 西厓; ancestral seat P'ungsan 豊山; posthumous epithet Munch'ung 文忠]: scholar-official under King Sŏnjo 宣祖 [r. 1567–1608; 1552–1608]. His father was Yu Chungyŏng 柳仲郢 [1515–73].

2 安東: a town in North Kyŏngsang Province famous for its tenacious conservatism and Confucian scholarship.

3 蠢蠢無識: slow-witted, foolish; "not very swift."

4 菽麥不辨: lit. "cannot tell beans from barley" = ignorant of practical matters = a fool.

5 喧撓: disturbance, commotion.

6 全輪: lit. "completely encircled" = (in a game of *paduk*) all of one's stones are encircled by the opponent's stones.

7 韜晦: conceal one's talents.

8 猶父: uncle (on the father's side).

9 猶子: nephew.

10 下懷 = *hajŏng* 下情: (humilific) my feelings.

11 牢拒: decline resolutely.

12 通刺: send in one's calling card; seek an audience by presenting one's card.

13 江陵: a coastal town in Kangwŏn Province.

14 五坮山: Mount Odae 五臺山 in P'yŏngch'ang County 平昌郡 in Kangwŏn Province.

15 淸德雅望: lit. "pure virtue, elegant renown."

16 識荊之願: desire to meet a person whom one admires.

17 生面人: utter stranger.

18 牢却: refuse resolutely.

19 舍堂 = *sadang* 寺黨 ~ 社堂: itinerant troupe of singing and dancing girls and prostitutes.

20 繩巾布褐: headdress made of hempen cords and clothes made of roughly
   woven ramie cloth.
21 薄陋之地: squalid, shabby place.
22 旨酒: tasty booze.
23 清冽: clean and chilled.
24 山菜野蔌: edible plants growing in the mountains and wild fields.
25 胸膈悶鬱: lit. "lower chest contracts and feels constricted."
26 利刀: sharp knife.
27 饒貸之道: magnanimity.
28 關伯 *kanpaku*: (in Japan) title given to the regent = the highest bureaucrat
   assisting the emperor.
29 平秀吉 = Toyotomi Hideyoshi 豊臣秀吉 [1536–98]: general during the
   Sengoku period 戦国時代 [1467–1573] who instigated the Imjin Wars
   [1592–3 and 1597–8].
30 先圖之地: preemptive attack; a plan to kill Yu Sŏngnyong.
31 神鑑: prescience; amazingly discerning eye.
32 兵革之禍: calamities of war.
33 躪: tread, step on.
34 旋踵: turn on one's heel; return whence one came.
35 螻蟻之命: lit. "the life of mole crickets and ants" = insignificant individuals.
36 禿頭: tonsured/bald monk.
37 鼠竄: lit. "scurry away like a mouse."

———— **91** ————

A Warning to General Li Rusong

Vol. III: 40; n.d.; Diary XIV, pp. 116–18; 300.

In the days of Sŏnjo when the Great Japanese War came to pass, General
Li Rusong of the Mings received commands to come East and aid us.
After he had driven out the Japanese from P'yŏngyang, he entered the
city and seeing how fair the city was with its surroundings, thoughts of
possessing it for himself overtook him. His impulse was to get rid of
Sŏnjo who was now in Ŭiju and reign instead.

One day he ordered a great feast for his officers and aides in the
Yŏn'gwang Pavilion, when he saw someone – an old man – pass on a
black bullock.

The soldiers shouted at him: "Who are you that you dare pass there?"

But he paid no attention, held to his bridle rein, and went slowly on. On this, Rusong grew very angry and ordered him arrested and brought. Now while the cow seemed to be going very leisurely, the soldiers who followed to make his arrest could not catch up. The General was so angry that he jumped on his fast horse himself, drew his sword and followed. The cow was just a little distance ahead and yet the thousand-mile-a-day mule that Rusong rode could not catch up. It crossed the hill, passed over the stream, and then entered a mountain village and there the rider tied his cow to a willow tree on the bank of the stream before which was a grass-thatched house. The bamboo gate was flung open. Thinking this stranger must be in the house, Rusong left his mule and with his sword drawn entered the house. The old man arose and met him on the open verandah.

Bursting with anger, Rusong said, "Who are you? I'd like to know. Who does not know God or man, but goes by in this bold and ill-mannered way? I represent the Emperor, with a million troops under my command and have saved your country from destruction. You must know me and yet you go riding by with no manners whatever. You shall die for it!"

The old man laughed as he replied, "I am a man of the hills, true enough, and I know right well the great General of the Mings. I did what I did today to you to inveigle you to my house which I could do in no other way. My name is so-and-so, and I have a very urgent message to lay before Your Excellency and yet it is most difficult to express it in words. Though I would rather have avoided any such interview, I could not help it and so brought you here."

The General asked, "What urgent message have you for me? Let's hear it."

The old man replied, "I have two sons, very worthless fellows, who neither study nor do they engage in agriculture but make their living by robbery and brigandage. They pay no heed to what their parents tell them and care nothing for age or experience but are makers of mischief only. I am helpless to repress them. I have heard that your spiritual powers are more than a master for the whole world. I beg your spiritual help against these sons of mine."

Rusong asked, "Where are they?"

His reply was, "They are just back of this hill in the little thatched hall."

With sword drawn, the general went in search and there he found two young men busy at the study of the character. He shouted, "You are a disgrace to your home. Your father asks that I destroy you both. Now take this stroke that I mean to deal out to you."

So he raised his knife yet the young men made no sign of fear and never moved, but quietly closed their book and took their bamboo marker and warded off Rusong's strike. All his efforts to strike them were of no avail. One young man then turned on the General and gave a smashing blow with his bamboo that broke the General's sword into pieces. Rusong was all out of breath with the perspiration breaking out on him.

A moment later the old man entered, and in his fierce anger to his sons said, "How dare you act in this outrageous way – go and sit back there."

Li Rusong then turned to the old man and said, "These sons of yours are not ordinary men at all. I have no power over them. I cannot carry out your wishes."

The old man laughed and said, "What I said to you was all a joke. These lads have something in the way of strength and yet I alone am more than a match for any ten of them. With commands from the Emperor, Your Excellency has come and saved our army and has rid us of this horde of midnight owls* (Japanese) and have made our nation ☐. With songs of victory you will return to your country and your name will live forever in history. Yours has been the work of a great General, indeed.

"But now Your Excellency fails to see this and has other thoughts in mind that never should be harboured by a true general. I have done this today to prove to Your Excellency that we have men also in our country. If you do not put away these thoughts but enter on your darkened scheme, though I am old, I shall see that your life pays the price for this evil. So be careful, I pray you – be careful. I recall, however, the fact that I have spoken too plainly to you. Forgive me, I pray you."

The General remained quiet for a half hour or so with lowered head and then raised his head and said, "I'll do as you say."

And so he left.

* Gale has followed the manuscript, which has the incorrect 梟 (owls) for 島 (island).

宣廟 1) 壬辰之亂 2)　天將 3) 李提督如松 4)　奉旨東援

平壤之捷後　入據城中　見山川之佳麗　懷異心

有欲動搖宣廟　而仍居之意　一日　大率僚佐 5)

設宴于練光亭 6) 上　江邊沙場　有一老翁

騎黑牛而過者　軍校高聲辟除 7)　而聽若不聞

按轡 8) 徐行　提督大怒　使之拿來　則牛行不疾

而軍校輩無以追到　提督不勝忿怒　自騎千里名騾 9)

按劍而追之　牛行在前不遠　而騾行如飛　終不可及

踰山度水 10)　行幾里　入一山村　則黑牛係於

溪邊垂楊樹　前有茅屋　竹扉 11) 不掩　提督意其老

人之在此　下騾杖劍而入　則老人起迎於軒上

提督怒叱曰：汝是何許野老　不識天高　唐突至此

吾受皇上之命　率百萬之衆　來救汝邦　則汝必無

不知之理　而乃敢犯馬 12) 於我軍之前乎　汝罪當死

로인 소 이 답 왈　오 수 산 야 지 인　기 불 지 천 장 지 존 귀 호
老人笑而答曰：吾雖山野之人　豈不知天將之尊貴乎

금 일 지 행　전 위 요 장 군　이 욕 왕 비 소　지 계 야
今日之行　全爲邀將軍　而欲枉鄙所 13)　之計也

모 절 유 일 사 지 봉 탁　난 이 언 어 도 달　고　불 득
某窃有一事之奉托　難以言語導達 14)　故　不得

이 행 차 계 야　제 독 문 왈　소 탁 심 사　제 언 지
已行此計也　提督問曰：所托甚事 15)　第言之

로 인 대 왈　비　유 불 초 아　이 인　불 사 사 농 지 업
老人對曰：鄙 16)　有不肖兒 17)　二人　不事士農之業 18)

자 행 강 도 지 사　불 솔 부 모 지 교 훈　불 지 장 유 지 별
恣行强盗之事　不率父母之教訓　不知長幼之別

즉 일 화 근　이 오 지 기 력　무 이 제 지　절 복 문 장 군 신 용
即一禍根　以吾之氣力　無以制之　窃伏聞將軍神勇

개 세　욕 차 신 위 이 제 차 패 자　야　제 독 왈　재 어 하 처
盖世　欲借神威而除此悖子 19)　也　提督曰：在於何處

답 왈　재 어 후 원 초 당 상 의　제 독 안 검 이 입　유 량 소 년
答曰：在於後園草堂上矣　提督按劍而入　有兩少年

공 독 서 의　제 독 대 성 질 왈　여 시 차 가 지 패 자 호
共讀書矣　提督大聲叱曰：汝是此家之悖子乎

여 옹 욕 사 제 거　근 수 아 일 검　잉 휘 검 거　격　지
汝翁欲使除去　謹受我一劍　仍揮劍擧 [擊] 之

즉 기 소 년 불 동 성 색　서 이 수 중 서 증 죽　한　지
則其少年不動聲色 20)　徐以手中書證竹 21)　捍 22)　之

종 불 득 격 이 이　기 소 년　이 기 죽　영 격 검 인　검 인
終不得擊而已　其少年　以其竹　迎擊劍刃　劍刃

쟁 연　일 성　절 위 량 단 락 지 의　이 제 독 기 천 한 류
錚然 23)　一聲　折爲兩端落地矣　而提督氣喘汗流 24)

소언　로인입래질왈　소자언감무례호　사지퇴좌
少焉　老人入來叱曰：小子焉敢無禮乎　使之退坐

제독향로인이언왈　피패자용력비범　무이조
提督向老人而言曰：彼悖子勇力非凡　無以阻

저당　기부미부　로인지탁재　야
[抵]當 25)　豈負[未副]老人之托哉[也]

로인소왈　아언희이　차아수유려력　이거십
老人笑曰：俄言戲耳　此兒雖有膂力 26)　以渠十

배　불감당로신일인　장군영황지　동원이래
輩　不敢當老身一人　將軍迎皇旨 27)　東援而來

소제　효도구　사아동재전　전　기업
掃除 28)　梟[島]寇 29)　使我東再奠[全]基業 30)

장군창개환귀　명수죽백　즉기비장부지사업호
將軍唱凱還歸 31)　名垂竹帛 32)　則豈非丈夫之事業乎

장군불차지사　반회이심　차기소망어장군자재
將軍不此之思　反懷異心　此豈所望於將軍者哉

금일지거　욕사장군　지아동역유인재지계야
今日之擧　欲使將軍　知我東亦有人材之計也

장군약불개도　이집미　즉오수로의　족가
將軍若不改圖 33)　而執迷 34)　則吾雖老矣　足可

제장군지명　면지면지　산야지인　어심당돌
制將軍之命　勉之勉之　山野之人　語甚唐突

유장군수찰　이서지　제독반향무어　저두상기
惟將軍垂察 35)　而恕之　提督半餉無語　低頭喪氣 36)

잉락락이출문운이
仍諾諾而出門云爾

1 宣廟: temple name of King Sŏnjo 宣祖 [r. 1567–1608; 1552–1608].
2 壬辰之亂: the Japanese invasion of 1592 (Sŏnjo 52).

3 天將: lit. "Heavenly General" = term used by Koreans to refer to Chinese generals, reflecting Chosŏn's Sinocentric foreign relations.

4 李如松 Li Rusong [?–1598; styled Zimao 子茂; posthumous epithet Zhonglie 忠烈]: a Ming general. His father was Li Chengliang 李成梁 [1526–1615].

5 僚佐: assistant, retainer, attaché.

6 練光亭: a pavilion by the Taedong River in P'yŏngyang.

7 辟除: lit. "avoid and exclude" = blocking traffic on the occasion of a high-ranking official's procession.

8 按轡: lit. "take the reins" = assume control.

9 千里名驥: lit. "a fabled mule that travels one thousand *ri* a day."

10 踰山度水: lit. "go over mountains and cross rivers."

11 竹扉: gate made of bamboo twigs.

12 犯馬: dare to pass someone of superior social standing on a horse.

13 鄙所: squalid, shabby place.

14 導達 = *chŏndal* 傳達: convey a message.

15 甚事: what matter.

16 鄙: (humilific) I, myself.

17 不肖兒: lit. "a child who fails to resemble its parents" = unfilial, unworthy child.

18 士農之業: till the field by day and study by night.

19 悖子 = *p'aeryuna* 悖倫兒: immoral, depraved person (child).

20 不動聲色: (of the voice or facial expressions) not waver, not skip a beat.

21 書證竹: bamboo strip used as a reading aid.

22 捍 = *pangŏ* 防禦: defend.

23 錚然: sound of metal clanging; metallic sound.

24 氣喘汗流: lit. "breathe with gasps and drip sweat."

25 抵當: difficult to match, defend against.

26 膂力 = *yongnyŏk* 勇力: physical prowess.

27 皇旨: the Emperor's order, bidding.

28 掃除: sweep away, wipe out.

29 島寇: lit. "island marauder" = Japanese pirates.

30 基業: groundwork; foundation of the state.

31 唱凱還歸: lit. "return home singing a triumphant song."

32 竹帛: lit. "bamboo and silk" = history.

33 改圖: lit. "change plans/intentions."

34 執迷: be obdurate, obstinate.

35 垂察: approach/undertake with due consideration.

36 低頭喪氣: lit. "lower one's head and lose spirit."

—— **92** ——

The Wife of Kim Ch'ŏnil

Vol. III: 41; n.d.; Diary XIV, pp. 118–21; 301.

The wife of Kim Ch'ŏnil, whose origin is uncertain, did no work whatever from the day she was married. She used to sleep all day.

Her father-in-law scolded her, saying, "Though you are a good daughter-in-law, you don't know the duties of a daughter-in-law. This is indeed a great defect. A woman has her duties to perform and here you have married and should take charge of the house and its affairs, but instead of this you only sleep – all day long, too."

She replied, "Though I desire to do my part in the home, what can I do with nothing in hand to do it with?"

The father-in-law felt anxious and sorry for her and so gave her a few score bags of rice □, four or five maidservants, and two or three cattle, saying, "With these do you think you can manage the home?"

She replied, "This is quite enough."

She then called her servants to appear before her and said, "Your master has given you to me. Do now what I tell you. Put this grain on these cattle and go to such-and-such a deep mountain gorge in Muju. Cut timber and build a house. Use this grain for food supply, fire the hills and get them ready for cultivation; when autumn comes, come and let me know what the result of the harvest is. Take the millet, hull it and use it for seed grain next year. Do this each year."

Thus ordered, the servants went off to the mountain district in Muju.

After a few days, the wife said to her husband, "If a man has no money and no grain, he is hindered from any work to do. How is it that you do not think of this?"

The husband replied, "I am under the orders of my parents and get all I need from them. How can I be expected to have money or grain?"

She replied, "I hear that in this town a certain Yi has no end of wealth heaped up, but that he thinks only of playing chess. Why don't you go and work a thousand bags' bet with him?"

Kim replied, "Yi is a first-class hand at chess and has no equal, while I am quite unpractised. I could never think of such a thing."

His wife answered, "That is easy enough – no difficulty whatever. Bring the chess board and come here."

So they sat face to face and she taught him all sorts of moves and combinations. Kim Ch'ŏnil was himself a man of great parts and clear intelligence and half a day's teaching was sufficient to give him special skill.

His wife said, "Now you are quite sufficiently equipped. Go and make proposition of three games, the one winning two being counted the winner. In the first game give the victory to him and in the second and third beat him by only a mere shade and after you have got all the grain necessary, suggest one game more. This time, show your very best and don't give him a chance to set his finger to the board."

Consenting to this view, Kim Ch'ŏnil went next day to the house and asked that they have a game of chess for a wager.

Yi laughed and said, "You and I have lived in the same town for many years and yet I have never heard that you can play chess. What can induce you to come now and suggest a game? I am at a loss to know. You are not equal to me as a player and so would only lose – let's not have it."

Kim replied, "After we have played, we can talk about who is best and who poorest. Why say we should not play?" Thus he urged him.

Yi said, "If we play we shall play for a wager. I never play otherwise. Let's lay a wager."

Kim said, "You have three or four heaps of one thousand bags each of unhulled rice grain – let that be your wager."

Yi said in reply, "I can wager my thousand bags, but what will you wager in response?"

Kim's reply was, "I, too, will make it one thousand bags."

Yi said, "You are under the orders of your parents. Wherever could you get one thousand bags to venture this?"

Kim answered, "Wait till we settle the game and then I'll tell you. If I lose, I shall be ready to ☐ not one thousand only."

Yi then, compelled thus, made ready the game and they decided on three games.

At first Kim allowed himself to be beaten and Yi laughed: "I told you so. You cannot play against me. Why do it?"

Kim Ch'ŏnil said, "We have two games left yet. Wait and see before we say anything."

Yi wondered over what this boldness could mean and so again played and was beaten both times.

Yi was startled by this and said, "Very strange, this, surely – what law governs the likes of this? I'll give you your thousand bags as I promised, but let's try one more game."

Kim consented and this time Yi played his very best but he never had the slightest chance. Kim laughed and said, "Let's end with this," and so he returned home.

He told his wife and she replied, "I already knew."

Kim said, "Now that we have come into possession of this rice, what shall we do with it?"

His wife said, "You have friends, some who are too poor to marry, some too poor to arrange burials for their parents, some too poor to live. □ them up and help them and among them, whoever they may be, if you find any especially gifted, make special friends of them and as you bring them here I'll see to their refreshments."

Kim did as his wife suggested.

One day his wife invited her father-in-law, saying, "I would like to do something in the way of farming. Will you let me have five days' ploughing [allotment] near the town?"

The father-in-law consented and she had the fields ploughed and then she planted gourd seeds. The larger gourds she had gathered and lacquered black and then put away. In a few years she had five *kan* filled with these. She had the blacksmith called and had him make two imitation gourds out of iron. These she placed with the others in the store room. People seeing it had no idea what it meant.

When the Imjin War came and the Japanese army made its great invasion Kim's wife said to him, "My suggesting that you aid and help and specially ally yourself with men of gifts was in preparation for this great need today! Arouse the loyal soldiers; I have settled on a place in Muju where your parents may find refuge – the place where I sent the servants to carry on farming. They have a house there ready, and grain. So you will have no need to feel anxious on our account. I shall stay here and see to supplies for the troops that they may have a constant replenishment."

Delighted at his wife's wisdom, Kim consented fully and called together his loyal soldiers. All who had been favoured by Kim came in crowds to aid. In less then ten days, he had an army of four or five thousand. Each carried a huge gourd at his belt and when they retreated, they cast aside the metal gourd.

Seeing this great weight, the Japanese gave a start of wonder and said, "Each of their soldiers carries a huge thing like this and yet they run under the weight of it like a mountain deer. They are strength and agility personified."

So they never ventured to attack Kim's troops but were ordered to return before them without striking a blow. As a result, whenever they saw Kim's forces, the Japanese troops lay down their arms without a fight.

Kim's extraordinary merit was all due to his wife's strong support.*

* Gale omits this last line from his translation. Instead he added, "Kim was finally killed in a fight at Chinju."

金倡義使 1) 千鎰 2) 之妻　不知誰家女子　而自于歸 3)

之日　一無所事　日事晝寢　其舅 4) 戒之曰：汝誠

佳婦　而但不知爲婦道　是可欠也　大凡　婦人皆有

婦人之任　汝旣出家　則治家營産 5) 可也　而不

此之爲　日以午睡爲事乎　其婦對曰：雖欲治産

赤手空拳 6)　何所藉 7) 而營産乎　其舅悶而憐之

卽以租數三十包奴婢四五口牛數隻給之曰：如此

足可爲營産之資乎　對曰：足矣　仍呼奴婢近

前曰：今則汝輩旣屬之於我　當從吾之指揮

汝可馱 8) 穀於此牛　入茂朱 9) 某處深峽中　伐木作家

이 차 조 작 농 량　　　이 근 경 화 전　　매 추 이 소 출 도 수
以此租作農粮 10)　　而勤耕火田　　每秋以所出都數 11)

래 고 어 아　　속 즉 작 미　　저 치　　매 년 여 시 가 야
來告於我　　粟則作米 12)　　儲置 13)　　每年如是可也

노 비 배 승 명　　이 향 무 주 이 거　　거 수 일　　대 김 공 이 언 왈
奴婢輩承命　　而向茂朱而去　　居數日　　對金公而言曰：

남 아 수 중 무 전 곡　　즉 백 사 불 성　　하 불 념 급 어 차　　공 왈
男兒手中無錢穀　　則百事不成　　何不念及於此　　公曰：

오 시 시 하 인 사　　의 식 개 뢰 어 부 모　　즉 전 곡 종 하 이 판
吾是侍下人事 14)　　衣食皆賴於父母　　則錢穀從何以辦

출 호　　부 왈　　절 문 동 중 리 생 모 가　　적 루 만 재 화　　이
出乎　　婦曰：窃聞洞中李生某家　　積累萬財貨 15)　　而

성 기 도 박 운　　랑 군 하 불 일 왕　　이 천 석 지 로 적　　일 괴
性嗜賭博云　　郎君何不一往　　以千石之露積 16)　　一塊 17)

위 도 호　　공 왈　　차 인 이 도 국 일 수　　유 명 어 세　　오 즉
爲賭乎　　公曰：此人以賭局一手 18)　　有名於世　　吾則

수 법 심 졸　　차 등 사　　하 가 생 심 도 박　　부 왈　　차 이 여 이
手法甚拙　　此等事　　何可生心賭博　　婦曰：此易與爾

제 이 박 국 지 래　　잉 대 좌 이 훈 지　　제 반 묘 수　　수 수 지 휘
第以博局持來　　仍對坐而訓之　　諸般妙手　　隨手指揮

김 공 역 기 걸 지 인　　야　　반 일　　대 국　　진 법 효 연
金公亦奇傑之人 19)　　也　　半日 20)　　對局　　陣法曉然 21)

기 부 왈　　금 즉 우 가 도 박　　군 자 이 삼 국 량 승　　위 도
其婦曰：今則優可賭博　　君子以三局兩勝 22)　　爲賭

초 국 즉 양 수　　이 이 삼 국　　즉 근 근　　결 승　　기 득 로
初局則佯輸 23)　　而二三局　　則堇堇 24)　　決勝　　旣得露

적 후　　피 필 욕 갱 결 자 웅　　차 시 즉 출 신 묘 지 수　　사 피 불
積後　　彼必欲更決雌雄　　此時則出神妙之手　　使彼不

得下手 25) 可也　金公然其言　明日躬往其家　請賭

博局　則其人笑曰：君與我同閈 26) 未聞君之賭博矣

今忽來請者　未知其故也　且君非吾之敵手　不必

對局　金公曰：對局行馬 27) 然後　可定其高下　何必

預先斥罷 28) 仍强請至再三　其人曰：若然則吾於平

生對局　則必賭　以何物爲賭債 29) 乎　公曰：君家

有千石露積三四塊　以此爲賭可乎　其人曰：吾則以

此爲賭　君則以何物爲賭乎　公曰：吾亦以千石

爲賭　其人曰：君以侍下之人事　不少之穀　從何判

[辦] 出乎　金公曰：此則勝負判決然後　可言之事

吾若不勝　則千石何足道哉　其人勉强 30) 而對局

以兩勝爲限　初則金公佯輸一局　其人笑曰：然矣

君非吾之敵手　吾不云乎　金公曰：猶有二局矣　第

又對局　李生心異之　又復對局　連輸二局　李生驚

아 왈　이 재 이 재　령 유 시 리 호　기 허 지　천 석 불 가
訝曰：異哉異哉　寧有是理乎　既許之　千石不可

불 급　즉 당 수 지　제 우 갱 도 일 국 의　김 공 허 지　부 대
不給　卽當輸之　第又更賭一局矣　金公許之　復對

박 국　시 출 신 묘 지 수　리 생 세 궁 력 진　불 득 하 수 의
博局　始出神妙之手　李生勢窮力盡 31)　不得下手矣

김 공 소 이 파　귀 대 기 처 이 언　즉 처 왈　오 이 료 지　의
金公笑而罷　歸對其妻而言　則妻曰：吾已料知 32) 矣

공 왈　기 득 차 재　장 언 용 지 호　처 왈　군 자 지 소
公曰：既得此財　將焉用之乎　妻曰：君子之所

친 인 중　궁 혼 궁 상　급 빈 불 능 자 생 자　량 의 분 급
親人中　窮婚窮喪 33)　及貧不能資生者　量宜分給

무 론 원 근 귀 천　여 유 기 걸 지 인　즉 여 지 허 교
毋論遠近貴賤　如有奇傑之人　則與之許交 34)

이 축 일 요 래　즉 주 식 지 비　오 자 판 비　김 공 여 기 언 이
而逐日邀來　則酒食之費　吾自辦備　金公如其言而

행 지　일 일　기 부 인 우 청 우 기 구 왈　식　욕 사 농 업
行之　一日　其婦人又請于其舅曰：媳 35) 欲事農業

리 외 오 일 경 전　가 사 허 경 호　기 구 허 지　어 시 경
籬外五日耕田 36)　可使許畊乎　其舅許之　於是畊

전　이 편 종 호 종　대 숙 이 작 두 용 호　사 지 착 칠
田　而遍種瓠種 37)　待熟而作斗容瓠 38)　使之着漆

매 년 여 시　충 오 간 고　우 사 야 장　련 출 이 개 여 두 용
每年如是　充五間庫　又使冶匠　鍊出二箇如斗容

호 양　병 치 우 고 중　인 막 효 기 고　급 임 진 왜 구 대 지
瓠樣　竝置于庫中　人莫曉其故　及壬辰倭寇大至

부 인 위 김 왈　오 지 평 일 권 군 자　이 휼 궁 제 빈　교 결
夫人謂金曰：吾之平日勸君子　以恤窮濟貧 39)　交結

영남　　욕어차등시　　득기력고야　　군자창기의병
英男 40)　欲於此等時　得其力故也　君子倡起義兵

즉구고피란지지　　오이경기　　어무주지　　유옥유곡
則舅姑避亂之地　吾已經紀 41)　於茂朱地　有屋有穀

서불이군자지우　　오즉재차　　판비군량　　사불핍절
庶不貽君子之憂　吾則在此　辦備軍粮　使不乏絶 42)

야　김공흔연종지　　수기의병　　원근지평일수은자
也　金公欣然從之　遂起義兵　遠近之平日受恩者

개래부　　순일지간　　득정병사오천　　사군졸　각
皆來附　旬日之間 43)　得精兵四五千　使軍卒　各

패칠호이전　　급회진　　지시　　유기철주지호어로
佩漆瓠而戰　及回陣 44)　之時　遺棄鐵鑄之瓠於路

이거　　왜병대경왈　　차군인　인개패차호　　기행여비
而去　倭兵大驚曰：此軍人　人皆佩此瓠　其行如飛

기용력가지기무량　　수상여계칙　　무감영기봉
其勇力可知其無量　遂相與戒飭 45)　無敢迎其鋒 46)

이시지고　　왜병견김공지군　　즉불전이피미
以是之故　倭兵見金公之軍　則不戰而披靡 47)

김공다건기훈　　개부인찬조지력
金公多建奇勳 48)　盖夫人贊助之力

1 倡義使: a temporary government post conferred upon a person who has raised a righteous army.

2 金千鎰 [1537–93; styled Sajung 士重; sobriquet Kŏnjae 健齋; ancestral seat Ŏnyang 彦陽; posthumous epithet Munyŏl 文烈]: general of a righteous army during the reign of King Sŏnjo 宣祖 [r. 1567–1608; 1552–1608]. During the Imjin Wars, when Chinju Castle fell to the Japanese, he drowned himself in the River Nam 南江.

3 于歸: (of a new bride) move into one's husband's home; (of a woman) get married.

4 舅 = *sibu* 媤父: (for a woman) father-in-law.

5 營産: make a living, manage the household economy.

 6 赤手空拳: bare-fisted.
 7 所藉: capital, funds.
 8 駄: bale; load baggage onto.
 9 茂朱: a town in North Chŏlla Province.
10 農粮: food supplies to be consumed during the farming season.
11 都數 = *ch'ongsu* 總數 ~ *ch'ongaek* 總額: total amount.
12 作米: hull.
13 儲置: gather up and accumulate; store away.
14 侍下人事: a person living with his or her parents.
15 累萬財貨: wealth worth tens of thousands of gold pieces.
16 露積: stacks of grain remaining in the fields after the harvest.
17 一塊: a lump, bundle.
18 賭局一手: (in *paduk*) player with superior skills.
19 奇傑之人: heroic, gallant man.
20 半日: half a day.
21 曉然: have an insight into; have penetrating knowledge of.
22 三局兩勝: two out of three.
23 輸: be defeated in a competition.
24 堇堇 = *kŭn'gŭn* 僅僅: narrowly, with difficulty.
25 下手: make a move; (in gambling) low-level player.
26 同閈: from the same neigbourhood.
27 行馬: (in a game of *paduk*) move a piece.
28 斥罷: defeat, vanquish.
29 賭債: one's bet, wager; the stakes.
30 勉强: do under duress.
31 勢窮力盡: lit. "morale is dampened and strength is exhausted."
32 料知: figure out.
33 窮婚窮喪: unable to conduct weddings or funeral ceremonies due to
   poverty; a person in such a situation.
34 許交: allow someone to become one's friend.
35 媳 = *sikpu* 息婦: daughter-in-law.
36 五日耕田: a piece of land that can be cultivated in five days.
37 遍種瓠種: plant gourd seeds all around.
38 斗容瓠: *twiungbak* – vernacular Korean word for "calabash scoop" (a scoop
   made from a dried gourd), rendered in sinographs.
39 恤窮濟貧: relieve the poor.
40 英男: hero, gallant.
41 經紀 = *kyŏngyŏng* 經營: operate/manage with sound fundamentals.
42 乏絶: run out, run short.
43 旬日之間: for ten days.

44 回陣 = *t'oejin* 退陣: retreat, fall back.

45 戒飭: admonish, warn.

46 鋒 = *yebong* 銳鋒: lit. "knife blade": fierce, overwhelming force; brunt.

47 披靡: lit. "fall pell-mell"; submit to superior forces like reeds bending before the wind.

48 奇勳: exceptional merit.

—— **93** ——

High-born Prince and Worthy Girls

Vol. III: 43; published under this title in *Korea Magazine*, November 1918, pp. 502–7; Diary XIV: 121–4 with the titles "Five Daughters Married" (crossed out), "The Right Kind of Girl" (crossed out), and finally "Providence Aids the Right Kind of Girl"; the manuscript translation is crossed out with the note "Oct. 7, 1918"; Gale's draft Table of Contents (Diary XVI: p. 179) lists the title as just "Providence Aids"; also, 9:21, pp. 102–5 (typed-up); 303.

On account of his faithful service during the trying days of the Hideyoshi Invasion, Yi Kwangjŏng was made Prince Yŏnwŏn, or Duke Yŏnwŏn as would be said in England. He went as envoy to the Mings in 1602 AD and by his upright character and high attainments won great respect of the Chinaman — Editors.

Yi Kwangjŏng,* while magistrate of Yangju County, had a falcon and a keeper who used to hunt with him. One day this hunter went out in search of game, but did not return till the next morning. He had hurt his foot, it seems, and came limping home. Seeing this, the master asked what had befallen him. He laughed as he replied, "Yesterday when I let the falcon loose after a pheasant, he missed it and let it go. After searching right and left in vain, he finally alighted on a tree in front of the [former] Deputy Magistrate Yi's house. With much difficulty I finally induced him to come back to me and perch on my arm and then turned to make my way home. Suddenly I heard voices from within the garden enclosure talking in a very lively manner and I glanced through the paling to see what it was about. There I beheld five strong, husky girls swinging along the hill-side, hand in hand. I was filled with fear as I looked upon them, afraid lest they might pounce out upon me, and so I ran for my life and in doing so fell and hurt my foot.

"It was then late in the day and growing dark. On second thought, I wondered who they were, and what they were about, and resolved to hide behind the fence in the long weeds and hear what they had to say. They were talking together and one said, 'We are quite alone here; let's play at county magistrate.'

"'Delighted!' answered the others.

"The tallest among them, about thirty years of age, I should think, then took her seat on a rock with her sisters just before her. One she named the Deputy Magistrate, one the Secretary of Justice, one the Public Crier and one the Constable-Runner.

"She, the Magistrate, then issued the following order: 'Arrest the Deputy and bring her here.'

"The Secretary of Justice called to the Crier and gave the order that the Deputy be arrested. The Crier shouted to the Runner to carry out this command at once. The Runner made off at full speed and in a trice had the Deputy arrested and brought. She knelt humbly before the Judge, when the Magistrate, in a loud voice gave forth the charge thus: 'Marriage is one of the first laws of society, and yet your youngest daughter, we take note, is past the marriageable age and not married. What shall we say as to her older sisters? How comes it that you have disregarded this law of nature in such a shameful way and left your children unmarried? Surely you deserve to die.'

"The Deputy bowed low with her face to the ground and said, 'How is it possible that your humble servant could be ignorant of this fault? I know it full well, but I'm as poor as carking poverty can make one, and so have no means by which to arrange a marriage.'

"The Magistrate replied, 'Marriage should be carried out according to one's means. All it needs is a pair of quilts and a bowl of water across which to plight one's troth. How dare you say, "No means." Such talk is nonsense.'

"The Deputy said, 'Your humble servant's problem is not that of one daughter only, nor even two. How could I ever be expected to find husbands for all these?'

"The Magistrate stopped her at once, saying, 'Let me not hear a word of it. If you had any zeal in the matter you'd find them soon enough. I have heard that Deputy Song of such-and-such a place has a son, and Vice-Deputy An of another place, also Deputy Chŏng, and Vice Kim, and Ch'oe. They all have sons. You could apply for any of these. They are all of your own social class; what reason, pray, for not taking the necessary steps?'

"The Deputy said, 'I'll do as Your Excellency commands, but I am so poor that they are not likely to respond to any such invitation.'

"The Magistrate went on: 'You ought to be soundly paddled for this sin of yours, but for the present, I'll let you off. Get the matter seen to at once. If you don't, you'll be severely dealt with, rest assured.'

"She called the Runner to have the Deputy put out and dismissed.

"The five of them laughed over this scene and with many words and much hilarity, dispersed. It was a most amusing performance. Leaving the place, I found an inn where I passed the night and so returned."

Hearing this story, Prince Yŏnwŏn laughed likewise and, calling the present deputy, asked about Yi as to his antecedents, how he was circumstanced, his children, etc.

The deputy replied, "He is the senior deputy of this county, but is as poor as poverty. He has no sons, but five daughters. Because of his being poor, his five daughters have all passed the marriageable age without a chance to wed."

On learning this, Prince Yŏnwŏn sent through his secretary and signed by him a letter asking deputy Yi as to his health, etc. Shortly after Yi appeared at the official headquarters, Prince Yŏnwŏn remarked, "You are a deputy, I understand, of this county, and know all the points of law. I have wanted to consult with you for some time on important matters, but have had no chance to meet you."

He then inquired as to how many sons he had.

The deputy replied, "My luck is surely the worst you have ever heard of, for I have not a single son but only five useless daughters."

"Have you married them off?" inquired Prince Yŏnwŏn.

The reply was, "Not a single one of them."

The magistrate again asked, "How old are they?"

He replied, "The youngest of them is past the marriageable age."

Prince Yŏnwŏn then asked the same questions that the daughter who played at magistrate had asked, and the old deputy answered just as the deputy daughter had done.

He then went on, "In such-and-such a deputy's house there are sons, and in such-and-such another house …" just as the daughter had said at the mock trial.

The deputy's reply was, "I'm so poor that I am sure none of these would consent."

Prince Yŏnwŏn said, "I'll be the go-between and see that your daughters are properly married."

And with that he dismissed him. He then dispatched his secretary to the five officials referred to and had them summoned.

"Have you any unmarried sons?" he inquired.

The reply was, "Yes, we have."

"Have you not yet decided on their marriage?"

"Not yet," was the answer.

Prince Yŏnwŏn then went on, "I have heard that in such-and-such a deputy's home there are five daughters; why should you not marry there?"

The five hesitated over this and gave no answer.

The Prince than assumed a severe attitude: "He is a county official; so are you. Your station in life is the exact counterpart of his. Your not wanting to marry is solely on account of his being poor. Shall the poor man's daughters then have no chance to marry at all? I am socially a step higher than you and yet even my good office in this matter seems hardly acceptable to you."

He then took out five sheets of paper and had one given to each. "Write, each of you," said he, "the Four Points that constitute a marriage application."

His words were stern and full of command.

Fearing trouble, the five knelt humbly before him and said, "We'll do as Your Excellency commands," and so they wrote each his application.

The Prince took them in the order of their sons' ages and appointed them to the daughters accordingly.

He then called for drink and refreshments and entertained them bountifully, giving to each as he left a large roll of grass-cloth: "Have an outer robe made of this," said he. He added, "I'll see to all the expenses involved in these weddings so you need have no anxiety on that account."

He had the day chosen at once and in due time the marriages were celebrated. He sent supplies of cloth, cotton goods, silk, money, and grain in abundance to deputy Yi's house, and on the day of the wedding he himself went and took a most interested part. The screens used, the mats, and the awning were all sent from his official headquarters. Five tables were placed side by side in the wide court where five bridegrooms and five brides bowed toward each other and plighted their troth.

The sightseers were packed like walls on the four sides, and all were most appreciative of the goodness of the Prince. Later many children were born to these five homes who passed their examinations and attained to high rank and responsible office. How much this unexpected favour of Prince Yŏnwŏn had to do with happy homes and joyful faces!

* Subsequently honoured as Prince Yŏnwŏn; see note 1.

延原府院君李光庭 1) 爲楊牧 2) 時　養一鷹

使獵夫 3) 每作山行　一日　獵夫出去　經宿而還

傷足而行蹇 4)　公怪而問之　笑而對曰：

昨日放鷹獵雉 5)　雉逸而鷹逃　四面搜訪

則鷹坐某處李座首門外大樹上故　艱辛呼鷹

而臂之 6)　將欲復　路之際　忽聞籬內　有喧撓之聲 7)

故　自籬間窺見　則有五介處女　豪健如壯男樣

相率而來　氣勢甚猛故　意其或被打　急急避身

足滑而傷　時日勢幾昏 8)　心甚訝之　隱身於籬

下叢樾 9) 之中而聞之　則其五處女相謂曰：

今日適從容　又當作太守戲 10) 乎　僉曰：諾

其中大處女　年可三十　高坐石上　其下諸處女

各稱座首 11) 刑房 12) 吸［及］唱 13) 使令 14) 名色

侍立於前 而已太守處女出令曰：座首拿入

刑房處女呼吸［及］唱處女而傳分付 吸［

及］唱處女呼使令處女而傳分付 使令承令

而捉下座首處女 拿而跪于庭下 太守處女

高聲數 15) 其罪曰：婚姻人之大倫也 汝之末女

年已過時 則其上之兄 從此可知矣 汝何爲

而使汝之五女 空然幷將廢倫 16) 乎 汝罪當死

座首處女 俯伏而奏曰：民 17) 豈不知倫紀之重乎

然而民之家計赤立 18) 婚具實無可判［辦］之望

19) 矣 太守曰：婚姻稱家之有無 20) 只具單衾 21)

勺水成禮 22) 有何不可之理乎 汝言太迂濶 23) 矣

座首曰：民之女 非一二人 郎材 24) 亦無可求之處矣

太守口叱曰：汝若誠心廣求 豈有不得之理乎

以鄕中所聞言之　某村之宋座首吳別監 25)　某村之鄭

座首金別監崔鄕所 26)　家　皆有郎材　如是則可定汝

五女之匹矣　此人輩與汝地醜德齊 27)　有何不可之理

座首曰：謹當依下敎通婚　而彼必以民之家貧

不肯矣　太守曰：汝罪當笞　而今姑十分參酌

斯速定婚而成禮可也　否者後當嚴處矣　仍命拿出

五介處女　仍相與大笑一鬨 28) 而散　其狀絕倒 29)

仍而作行　寄宿於旅舍　今始還來矣　延原聞而

大笑　召鄕所　問李座首來歷　與家勢子女之數

則以爲此邑曾經首鄕 30) 之人　而家勢赤立無子

而有五女家貧之故　五女已過時　而尙未成婚矣

延原卽使禮吏 31) 告目 32) 請李座首以來　未幾來謁

公曰：君是曾經鄕所而解事 33) 云　吾欲與之議事

而未果矣　仍問子女之數　則對曰：民命途奇窮 34)

未育一子　只有無用之五女矣　問俱已婚嫁否

對曰：一未成婚矣　又曰：年各幾何　對曰：

第末女　已過時矣　公乃以俄所聞太守處女之分付

一一問之　則其答果如座首處女之答　公乃歷數 35)

某座首某別監某鄉所之家　而依太守處女之言而

言曰：何不通婚也　對曰：渠必以民之家貧不願矣

公曰：此事吾當居間 36) 矣　使之出去　又使禮吏

請五鄉所而問曰：君家俱各有郎材云　然否　對曰：

果有之　問已成娶否　對曰：姑無定婚處矣　公曰：

吾聞某村某座首之家有五女云　何不通而結親 37)

乎　五人躊躇 38) 不卽應　公正色曰：彼鄉族 39) 此鄉

族　門戶相適　君輩之不欲　只較貧富而然也

若然則貧家之女　其將編髮而老死乎　吾之年位

比君輩　何如不少之地　既發說　則君輩焉敢

불 종 호　내 출 오 폭 간　사 치 우 오 인 지 전 왈
不從乎　乃出五幅簡　使置于五人之前曰：

각 서 기 자 사 주 가 야　성 색 구 려　오 인 황 공 부 복 왈
各書其子四柱可也　聲色俱厲　五人惶恐俯伏曰：

근 봉 교 의　잉 각 서 사 주 이 납　공 이 기 년 기 지 다 소
謹奉敎矣　仍各書四柱以納　公以其年紀之多少

정 기 처 녀 지 차 제　잉 궤 주 효　우 각 사 저 포　일 필 왈
定其處女之次第　仍饋酒肴　又各賜苧布 40) 一疋曰：

이 차 위 도 포 지 자　우 분 부 왈　리 가 오 녀 지 혼 구
以此爲道袍之資　又分付曰：李家五女之婚具

자 관 비 급　본 가 물 려 야　즉 사 지 택 일　기 재 수 일 지 간
自官備給　本家勿慮也　卽使之擇日　期在數日之間

잉 송 포 백 전 곡　사 비 혼 수　이 일　공 출 왕 리 가　병 장
仍送布帛錢穀　使備婚需　伊日　公出往李家　屏幛

포 진 지 속　자 관 차 설　렬 오 탁 어 정 중　오 녀 오 랑
41) 布陳之屬 42) 自官借設　列五卓於庭中　五女五郞

일 시 행 례　관 자 여 도　무 불 흠 탄 연 원 지 적 선　기 후
一時行禮　觀者如堵 43) 無不欽嘆延原之積善　其後

승　번 연　이 현 달 자　개 유 적 선 지 여 경 운 이
承 44) 繁衍 45) 而顯達者　皆由積善之餘慶云爾

1　李光庭 [1552–1627; styled Tŏkhwi 德輝; sobriquet Haego 海臯, Nurong
　　訥翁; ancestral seat Yŏnan 延安]: he was honoured as Prince Yŏnwŏn
　　延原府院君. His father was Yi Chu 李澍 [1534–84].
2　楊牧: magistrate of Yangju 楊州, Kyŏnggi Province.
3　獵夫: hunter.
4　行蹇: walk with a limp.
5　放鷹獵雉: lit. "release a falcon to hunt pheasants."
6　臂之: have one's falcon perch on one's arm.
7　喧撓之聲: boisterous and disorderly voices.
8　幾昏: almost dark.
9　叢樾: a stand of trees forming a dense thicket.

10 太守戲: lit. "the game of *t'aesu* [head of the local yamen]."

11 座首 = *agwan* 亞官 = *suhyang* 首鄉: head of a local yamen (*hyangch'ŏng* 鄉廳).

12 刑房: a petty clerk (*ajŏn* 衙前) in charge of penal administration at the local yamen.

13 及唱: a crier servant boy at the local yamen.

14 使令: a page boy at the local yamen.

15 數: enumerate.

16 廢倫: lit. "contravene morality": remain unmarried or fail to marry.

17 民: (humilific) "we" used by a commoner to local government officials.

18 赤立 = *chŏkpin* 赤貧: destitute.

19 可辦之望: prospect of procuring.

20 稱家之有無: manage according to one's family circumstances.

21 單衾: a single set of bedding.

22 勺水成禮: lit. "complete the [wedding] ceremony (over) a bowl of water."

23 迂闊: clueless, ignorant of the ways of the world.

24 郎材: husband material.

25 別監: deputy *chwasu* at the local administrative organ.

26 鄉所 = *yuhyangso* 留鄉所 ~ *hyangch'ŏng* 鄉廳: local yamen or the head thereof.

27 地醜德齊: lit. "(two families') land, reputation, and virtue are on a par."

28 大笑一闋: have a big laugh.

29 絶倒 = *p'obok chŏlto* 抱腹絶倒: hold one's sides with laughter; have a laughing fit.

30 首鄉 = *chwasu* 座首: see note 11.

31 禮吏 = *yebang* 禮房: a petty clerk (*ajŏn* 衙前) in charge of the Office of Rites at the local yamen.

32 告目 *komok*: vernacular Korean *idu* 吏讀 expression referring to a letter written by a commoner to a *yangban* recipient.

33 解事: savvy.

34 命途奇窮: lit. "life's journey exceptionally needy" = born under an unlucky star.

35 歷數: count things one by one, enumerate.

36 居間: broker, middleman.

37 結親: become related by marriage; enter into matrimonial relations with.

38 蹰躇 = *chujŏ* 躊躇: hesitate, falter.

39 鄉族: lit. "local lineage": family/lineage that can undertake various clerical posts such as overseer (*chwasu* 座首) and assistant (*pyŏlgam* 別監) at the local yamen.

40 苧布: ramie fabric.

41 屏幛: *pyŏngjang* 屏帳 ~ *pyŏngp'ung* 屏風: folding screen.

42 布陳之屬: random assorted items laid out for display.

43 觀者如堵: lit. "spectators (standing) like a wall."

44 後承 = *husa* 後嗣 ~ *huson* 後孫: descendants.

45 繁衍 = *pŏnyŏn* 蕃衍 ~ *pŏnsŏng* 繁盛 ~ *pŏnch'ang* 繁昌: prosperity.

—— 94 ——

A Second Wife under Difficulties

Vol. III: 47; Diary XIV: 124–30; published in *Korea Magazine*,
January 1919, pp. 22–9;
also 9:21, pp. 109–12 (typed-up); 304.

A gentleman by the name of Kwŏn, well-to-do and prosperous in all his affairs, lived in Andong. He was a very severe and exacting man, however, and ruled his house with a rod of iron. One son only did he have whom he had married off early in life. His daughter-in-law turned out a jealous and evil-minded wench, most difficult to get along with. No one could manage her but her father-in-law. He held her in by main force with bit and bridle.

When anything specially roused Kwŏn's ire, he would spread his mat in the main hall and sit like an ogre, master of the supreme court. Sometimes he would have disobedient or disorderly servants beaten to death. In case of a fault that did not call for so severe a handling and yet merited punishment, he would beat them till blood marks impressed their lesson upon their naked body. Such was the fear of him that when he spread his mat on the open hall the whole house trembled and waited with bated breath to see whose turn next it was to die.

Now the daughter-in-law was away once while the son had gone to pay his respects to his wife's parents. On his way back he was overtaken by rain and took shelter in an inn where he found a young man sitting in the open verandah, a palanquin in the court, and five or six fine horses tethered in the open stall. There seemed to be a great number of men and women servants about, as though some woman of the gentry were making a journey under their special care.

The young man arose to greet Kwŏn and then had wine and refreshments ordered. The wine was very good and the refreshments likewise.

They inquired as to each other's name and where they lived and while Kwŏn gave frank and full answers, the first comer gave his surname only and nothing more. He refused to tell. Said he, "Here I am on a journey, overtaken by rain, and find refuge in a country inn and now meet this very agreeable friend – how delightful."

So they drank together. "Let's drink till we are drunk," said the friend, and Kwŏn agreed and was the first to be overcome. He rolled over and lay unconscious till midnight when he awoke and opened his eyes in wonder. There was no evidence of the young man anywhere, but instead, he seemed to be in the inner quarters of the household. At his side was a young woman dressed in white, very comely, about eighteen years of age.

Her face and general appearance bespoke of a refinement such as one finds in the homes of the gentry of the capital.

Kwŏn gave a great start and asked, "How came I here and who are you that you find yourself in this room with me?"

The young woman, apparently overcome by shame, made no reply. He asked again and again but still no answer was forthcoming. When he further insisted, however, she spoke in a low voice: "I am from Seoul, where our family holds high rank and office. At fourteen I was married and at fifteen lost my husband. My father also died and so my older brother became master of the house. A most exacting and difficult person he is and his special dislike seemed the idea of having to live a life with his widowed sister. Contrary to ancient custom he sought to marry me off again till the matter became a scandal in our clan that threatened no end of disgrace. Finally my brother gave up his plan. Instead, he made ready a palanquin and took me off with servants and supplies not specifying where we were bound for. Hence it comes that I am here. His idea was to rid himself of the whole unhappy matter by putting me off on the first likely person we met. Yesterday when you were overcome by wine he had you brought in here and immediately took his departure."

She pointed to a box and said, "There are five or six hundred *yang* there that will serve as clothing and food for my life to come."

Greatly surprised at this strange occurrence, Kwŏn went out and looked about and lo, all had gone. There was no sign of anyone about except two stupid-looking maid-servants.

He then returned to the inner room and so passed the night. But as he thought over the affair, the fear and terror of his father arose before him.

For him to take a concubine thus was out of the question and would assuredly end in an awful scene. His wife's jealous and venomous disposition would add doubly to his difficulties. What could he do? However much he thought and pondered it over, there seemed no way out of the difficulty. His strange meeting with this refined young woman was the cause of a head-splitting ache to him.

He waited till breakfast was over and then ordered the two maids to stay fast by their mistress and guard her. To her he said, "I have a very unreasonable father to deal with, so I must go first and see him before I bring you. Wait here for a day or so."

He then called for the master of the inn and gave him special instructions.

Instead of returning home he went direct to the house of a friend who was a specially wise and far-seeing man and told him fully of the dilemma that he found himself in and asked help.

The friend thought for a time and then said, "You are in a difficulty, I admit. I am afraid I know of no special plan and yet there is one thing I would like to try. You go home and in a day or two I'll order a feast and invite my friends. On the day following you do the same and invite your friends and I'll see what can be done."

Kwŏn then returned home and in a few days a servant of this friend came with an invitation. It read: "Wine and refreshments in abundance and many good friends gathered together. We need you to complete our joy – come at once."

Kwŏn told his parents and then went. On the day following he said to his father, "So-and-so entertained me yesterday; I must order a return feast today and have him here."

His father gave a willing consent and so the board was spread and many guests invited. As they came they went first of all to speak to Kwŏn's father and make their bow.

Kwŏn Senior said, "You youngsters are here for a good time and yet you have not invited me; what kind of treatment is that?"

The reply was, "If Your Excellency were to take the place of the host, we youngsters would be under such constraint that we would not dare to move. Your exalted nature is dignified and severe beyond our little world so that even this coming and bowing takes all the courage we have. How could we possibly venture on an entertainment together. If you, Sir, were present it would kill all the joy and freedom of the occasion."

Kwŏn laughed and said, "When people meet to drink and have a good time, what account do they take of age and rank? I am going to be master of ceremonies today, so you must just put aside all your fears and have a good time. Never mind how often you fail to keep the law of exact deportment, I shall have no desire to reprimand or correct you. Have a good time and so let me have a day of relief from all my grinding cares."

On hearing this, the young people were delighted and thus they mixed together, old and young.

They raised their glasses and when they had partaken freely the wise young man came forward to elder Kwŏn and said, "I have a story to tell, a very wonderful story of what happened long ago. It will make Your Excellency laugh – that's why I tell it."

Kwŏn said, "Good. Let's hear."

The young man then went on with the story of Kwŏn's son and how he had met with the young woman, but he told it all in terms of an old-fashioned tale.

The elder Kwŏn expressed his appreciation every little while, saying, "Very wonderful, indeed. Such things as this used to happen in days gone by, but one never hears of anything of the kind now."

The wise young man inquired, "If Your Excellency should come on such a surprise as this, how would you act? Suppose you should meet such a person in the night – would you accept of her or not? Then afterwards would you bring her home or would you cast her away?"

The elder Kwŏn replied, "Being a man, if I were to meet such a one I could not do otherwise than accept of her, and bring her home, of course. To cast her aside would be to give her over to a life of evil."

The young man said, "Your Excellency is of a specially stern nature and I know you would not fall a victim as easily as the ordinary man. I doubt if you would deign to look upon her."

Kwŏn shook his head and said, "Not a bit of it – I should do quite otherwise. Under such circumstances I should forget all else. This man's going into the inner-room was not his affair; he was so placed by others, so it was not an offence as though he had designed it. A young man meeting a beautiful girl thus could not do otherwise – the girl, too, being of good family and in circumstances most pitiful. If he had taken her but for the moment and then cast her aside she would have died of shame and mortification, and a most grevious sin it would have been on his part. No gentleman would ever do that."

The young man again asked, "Then Your Excellency thinks that under such circumstances there would be nothing else for a man to do?"

Elder Kwŏn said, "Certainly he would have to do so. To do otherwise would prove him a man of very poor spirit, indeed."

The young man then said, "This is not an old story at all, but something that has happened to your own son even this very day. Your Excellency has said two or three times that to do otherwise than take her would be a great wrong. I am so happy to think that your son will not die for this offence of his but live."

Hearing this, Kwŏn was silent for a moment and then with a countenance suddenly changed to wrath, he exclaimed, "Away with you all – I'll settle this matter."

The guests scurried off in a state of wild alarm, while the old man called in a loud voice, "Spread the mat in the main hall."

All the people of the house were struck with fear and wondered now who had come in for punishment.

The old man sat on the mat and roared out in a stentorian voice, "Bring me the straw chopper at once."

In wild alarm, the servants brought it and the plank as well that goes below. Again he called, "Bring my son at once and have his head off."

He was brought at once and his neck placed where the sheaf of straw should go.

The old man shouted out at him, "You ill-begotten boy! With the smell of milk still on your lips and without asking your parents anything about it you have dared to take to yourself a concubine. A disgrace to your home you are. You have done this before my very eyes while I live – what evil deeds will you be up to, pray, when I die? There is no hope in such a creature as you living. Better off with your head and done with all these abominable worries."

When he had said this he shouted to the servant, "Down with the knife and off with his head."

All the household were paralyzed with fear and stood with faces pale as death. The young man's wife and his mother hurried into the court where they pleaded with tears for his life. Said they, "His offence merits death, and yet we ask: how can you think of beheading your only son?"

They cried and begged him to desist.

Old Kwŏn shouted his disapproval and ordered them ejected from the court. The old woman went, but not the young man's wife. She beat her head upon the ground till blood covered her face, saying, "I am guilty of disobedience, I know, and yet I would remind you that this is your only son. How can you do such a thing as this and cut off forever the family sacrifice? Take me instead, I pray, and let me die in his place."

Kwŏn roared out, "A rascal like this brings disgrace not only upon his house but upon his ancestors as well. Better kill him here and now and put an adopted son in his place. Still, whether he live or whether I take an adopted son in his place, the honour of the home is gone all the same. Since we are ruined anyhow let it be a clear-cut ruin with no rag-ends to it. Off with his head!"

The servants answered, "Yes, Sir," and yet refused to press down the knife.

The young wife took on at such a terrible rate that old Kwŏn shouted, "You and your jealous ugly disposition could not tolerate another woman in the house for a minute. What a combination it would be and what a dreadful time we would have of it. 'Tis better that I do away with this wretched creature and make an end of it."

The daughter-in-law said, "I have a face to save and a heart, too. Seeing such a pass as this how could I ever think of being jealous again? If you will but forgive this offence, I'll be most careful that we live in peace hereafter for all time. Be not anxious on my account, but only grant forgiveness and spare his life."

The old man said, "It's all very well for you to say these fair words in the face of today's uproar, but I know right well that your heart's not in it."

The daughter-in-law replied, "How could you say so? I mean it all. If I show the slightest failure in this direction, let God deal death to me, and let the devils take off my head."

The elder Kwŏn then replied, "This may be true while I live, but after I'm dead I'll not be here to take account of your tricks, and this contemptible creature will have no power over you. That also would bring ruin to the house. Better have off his head and so insure ourselves against disgrace in the future."

The daughter-in-law went on, "Please do not say so. Even though Your Excellency depart this life, I shall forever guard against such a mind. If I fail, may I be a dog or a pig. I swear it and give my pledge."

The old man said, "Then if you really mean to swear, write it out on a paper and sign it."

She wrote it out: *If I break this oath in the slightest degree, let me be counted as one who eats his father's and mother's flesh.* She added: *If after this oath of mine Your Excellency will not grant my request I shall commit suicide with this knife here and now.*

The old man Kwŏn said, "Let him go, let him go."

He then called the head servants and gave orders: "Take a four-man chair with servants and horses and go to such-and-such an inn and bring my son's secondary wife with you."

Thus ordered, the servant brought her and at once she paid her respects to her father-in-law and mother-in-law and also bowed to the first wife and so they lived together. The daughter-in-law did not dare ever again to lift her voice and to old age they were a happy family living in joy and sweet accord.

安東權進士某者　家計饒富　性嚴峻　治家有法

有獨子而娶婦　婦性行悍妬難制　而以其舅之嚴

不敢下 [使] 氣 1)　權如有怒氣　則必鋪席於大廳而坐

或打殺婢僕　若不至傷命　則必見血而止　以此

鋪席於大廳　則家人喘喘 2)　知其有必死之人也

其子之妻家在於隣邑　其子爲見其妻父母而行

歸路遭雨　避入於店舍　先見一少年坐於廳上

而廐有五六匹駿馬　婢僕又多　若率內眷之行 3)

與權少年　仍爲寒暄 4)　而以酒肴饌盒勸之

酒甚淸冽 5)　肴又豐旨 6)　相問其姓氏與居住

權生則以實之　先來少年則只道姓氏　而不肯言所

在處曰：偶爾 7) 過此　避雨而入此店　幸逢年輩佳朋

豈不樂乎　仍與之酬酌　而醉爲期　權少年先醉倒

夜深後始覺　擧眼審視　則同盃之少年已無形影 8)

而自家則臥於內室　而傍有素服佳娥　年可十八九

容儀端麗　知其非常賤　而的是洛下 9) 卿相家婦女也

權生大驚訝　問曰：吾何以臥於此處　而君是誰

家何許婦女　在於此處乎　其女愁 [羞] 澁 10)

而不答　叩之再三　終不開口　最後過數食頃

始低聲而言曰：吾是洛下門地 11) 繁盛之仕宦家女子

十四出嫁　十五喪夫　而嚴親又早世　娚兄 12) 主家矣

兄之性熱 [執] 滯 13)　不欲從俗而執禮使幼妹寡

居也　欲求改適 14) 之處　則宗黨 15) 之是非大起

皆以汚辱門戶　峻辭嚴斥 16)　兄不得已罷議　因

其轎馬駄我而出門　無去向處而作行　轉而至此

其意若遇合意之男子　則欲委而托之　自家因以避之

以遮諸宗之耳目者也　昨夜乘君之醉　而使奴子

負而入臥內　而家兄則必也遠走　仍指在傍之一箱

曰：此中有五六百銀子　以此使作妾衣食之資云爾

權生異之　出外而視之　則其少年及許多人馬　幷

不知去處　只有蒙騃 17) 之童婢二人在傍　生還入內

與其處女同寢而已　思量則嚴父之下　私自卜妾 18)

必有大擧措　且其妻悍妬之性　必不相容　此將奈何

千思萬量　實無好箇計策　反以奇遇之佳人爲頭痛

待朝　使婢子　謹守門戶　而言于其女曰：家有嚴

親　歸當奉稟而率去　姑少俟之　申飭店主而出門

直向親朋中有智慮者之家　以實告之　願爲之劃策

其友沉吟良久曰：大難大難　實無好策　而第有

一計　君於歸家之數日　吾當設酒席而請之矣

君於翌日　又設酒席而請我　我當自有方便之

計矣　權生依其言　歸家之數日　其友人送伻 [19]

懇請以適有酒肴　諸益 [20] 畢會　此席不可無兄

兄須賁臨 [21] 云　權生稟其父而赴席　翌日　權生稟

于其父　某友昨日擧酒有邀　而酬答之禮　不可闕也

今日略具酒饌　而請邀諸友　則似好矣　其父許之

爲設酒席而邀其人又邀洞中諸少年　諸人皆來

先拜見於權生之老父　權曰：少年輩迭相 [22] 酒會

而一不請老我　此何道理　其少年對曰：尊丈若

主席　則年少侍生　坐臥起居 [23]　不得任意爲之

且尊丈性度嚴峻 [24]　侍生輩暫時來謁　十分操心

或恐其見過　何可終日侍坐於酒席　尊丈若降臨

則可謂殺風景 [25] 矣　老權笑曰：酒會豈有長幼之

序 26) 乎　今日之酒　我爲主矣　擺脫 27) 其拘束之儀

終日湛樂 28)　君輩須百番失儀於我　我不汝責　盡歡

而罷　以慰老夫一日孤寂之懷也　諸少年一時敬諾

長幼雜坐而擧觴　酒至半　其多智之少年近前曰：

侍生有一古談之奇事　請一言之以供一粲 29)

老權曰：古說極好　君試爲我言之　其人乃以權少

年之客店奇遇　作古談而言之　老權節節稱奇曰：

異哉異哉　古則或有此等奇緣　而今則未得聞也

其人曰：若使尊丈當之　則何以處之　中夜無人之際

絶代佳人在傍　則其將近之乎　否乎　旣近之　則

其將率畜乎　抑棄之乎　老權曰：旣非宮刑之人 30)

則逢佳人於黃昏　豈有虛度 31) 之理乎　旣同寢席

則不可不率畜　何可等棄 32) 而積惡乎　其人曰：

尊丈性本方嚴　雖當如是之時　而必不毀節 33) 矣

老權掉頭 34) 曰：不然不然 使吾當之 則不得不

毀節矣 彼之入內 非故爲也 爲人所欺 此則非

吾之故犯也 年少之人 見美色而心動 自是常事

彼女旣以士族行（此）事 則其情戚 35) 矣 其地窮 36)

矣 如或一見而棄之 則彼必含羞含寃 37) 而死

豈非積惡乎 士大夫之處事 不可如是齷齪 38) 也

其人又問曰：人情事理 果如是乎 老權曰：豈有

他意 斷當不作薄幸［行］人可也 其人笑曰：此非

古談 卽胤友 39) 日前事也 尊丈旣以事理當然

再三質言 40) 而有敎 則胤友庶免 41) 罪責矣 老權

聽罷 半餉無語 仍正色厲聲曰：君輩皆罷去 吾有

處置之事矣 諸人皆驚怯而散 老權仍高聲曰：斯速

設席於大廳 家中人皆悚然 42) 不知將治罪何許

人矣 老權坐於席上 又高聲曰：急持斫刀 43)

以來　奴子慌忙承命　置斫刀及木板於庭下　老權又

高聲曰：捉下書房主 44)　伏之斫刀板　奴子捉下

權少年　以其項　置之刀板　老權大叱曰：悖子 45)

以口尙乳臭 46) 之兒　不告父母而私蓄小妾者　此是

亡家之行 47) 也　吾之在世　猶尙如此　況吾之

身後 48) 乎　此等悖子　留之無益　不如吾在世之時

斷頭以杜後弊可也　言罷　號令奴子　使之擧趾 49)

而斫之　此是上下惶惶 50)　面無人色 51)　其妻與子婦

皆下堂而哀乞曰：彼罪雖云可殺　何忍於目前

斷獨子之頭乎　泣諫不已　老權高聲而叱　使退去

其妻驚怯而避　其子婦以頭叩地　血流被面而告曰：

年少之人　設有放恣自擅之罪 52)　尊舅血屬　只此

而已　尊舅何忍行殘酷之事　使累世奉祀　一時

絶嗣 53) 乎　請以子婦之身代其死　老權曰：家有悖子

이 망 가 지 시　　욕 급 조 선 의　　오 령 살 지 어 목 전　　갱 구
而亡家之時　辱及祖先矣　吾寧殺之於目前　更求

명 사　　가 야　　이 차 이 피　　망 즉 일 야　　불 여 망 지　　건 정
螟嗣54) 可也　以此以彼　亡則一也　不如亡之　乾淨55)

지 위 유 야　　잉 호 령 이 사 작 지　　노 자 구 수 응 락
之爲愈也　仍號令而使斫之　奴子口雖應諾

이 불 인 가 족　　기 자 부 읍 간 익 고　　로 권 왈　　차 자 망
而不忍加足　其子婦泣諫益苦　老權曰：此子亡

가 지 사 비 일 의　　이 시 하 지 인　　이 천 자 축 ［ 축 ］ 첩
家之事非一矣　以侍下之人　而擅自畜［蓄］妾

기 망 조 56) 일 야　　이 여 지 한 투　　필 불 상 용　　여 차 즉 가
其亡兆56) 一也　以汝之悍妬　必不相容　如此則家

정 일 란　　기 망 조 이 야　　유 차 망 조　　불 여 조 위 제 거
政日亂　其亡兆二也　有此亡兆　不如早爲除去

지 위 호 야　　자 부 왈　　첩 역 시 구 인 면 인 심 의　　목 견 차
之爲好也　子婦曰：妾亦是具人面人心矣　目見此

등 광 경　　하 가 념 급 어 투 지 일 자 호　　약 몽 존 구 일 번 용 서
等光景　何可念及於妬之一字乎　若蒙尊舅一番容恕

즉 자 부 근 당 여 지 동 처　　소 불 실 화 의　　원 존 구　　물 이
則子婦謹當與之同處　少不失和矣　願尊舅　勿以

차 위 려　　특 하 광 ［ 광 ］ 탕 지 은 57)　　로 권 왈　　여 수 박
此爲慮　特下廣［曠］蕩之恩57)　老權曰：汝雖迫

어 금 일 거 조　　이 유 차 언　　필 야 면 락 이 심 불 연 의　　부 왈
於今日擧措　而有此言　必也面諾而心不然矣　婦曰：

령 유 시 리　　여 혹 유 근 사 차 등 지 언　　즉 천 필 극 지　　귀 필
寧有是理　如或有近似此等之言　則天必殛之　鬼必

주 지 의　　로 권 왈　　여 어 오 지 생 전　　무 혹 연 의　　이 오
誅之矣　老權曰：汝於吾之生前　無或然矣　而吾

死之後 汝必復肆其惡 58) 此時吾已不在 悖子不

敢制 則此非亡家之事乎 不如斷頭以絶禍根 婦曰:

焉敢如是乎 尊舅下世 59) 之後 如或有一分非心

則犬豚不若 60) 當矢言而納侉 61) 矣 老權曰:

若然則汝以矢言 書紙以納 其子婦書禽獸之盟 62)

且曰: 一有違背之事 子婦父母之肉 可以生啗 63)

矣 矢言至此 而尊舅終不信聽 有死而已 老權

乃赦而出之 仍命呼首奴 64) 分付曰: 汝可率轎馬

人夫 往某店 迎書房主小室而來 奴子承命而率來

行見舅姑之禮 又禮拜於正配 65) 而使之同處

其子婦不敢出一聲 到老和同 66) 人無間言 67) 云爾

1 使氣: throw a tantrum.
2 喘喘: be/get nervous or anxious.
3 內眷之行: a journey made by the womenfolk of a household.
4 寒暄 = *munan* 問安: exchange greetings and engage in small talk.
5 清冽: clear and ice-cold.
6 豊旨: abundant and tasty.
7 偶爾 = *uyŏn* 偶然: coincidentally.
8 形影: form and shadow.

9 洛下: the capital.

10 羞澁: feel ashamed/embarrassed.

11 門地: lit. "gate and basis" = lineage and social standing.

12 甥兄: (girl's) older brother.

13 執滯: inflexible, obstinate.

14 改適 = *kaega* 改嫁: remarry.

15 宗黨: all the relatives in the family.

16 峻辭嚴斥: lit. "stern refusal and resolute rejection."

17 蒙騃: lit. "immature; young and foolish" = have yet to pass the civil service examination.

18 卜妾: take a secondary wife.

19 伻: servant, messenger.

20 諸益 = *cheu* 諸友: one's friends.

21 賁臨 = *pirae* 賁來: (honorific) someone's visit.

22 迭相 = *kyodae* 交代: rotate, take turns.

23 起居 = *tongjŏng* 動靜: stand up to greet an honoured guest.

24 性度嚴峻: strict personality and demeanour.

25 殺風景: kill-joy.

26 長幼之序: lit. "the order of the old and the young" = respect for seniority.

27 擺脫: relax one's attention to rules and propriety.

28 湛樂: enjoy for a long time.

29 粲: have a good laugh.

30 宮刑之人: a person who has been castrated.

31 虛度: spend days in vain; let an opportunity go to waste.

32 等棄: make light of and discard.

33 毀節: compromise one's fidelity.

34 掉頭: shake one's head in disagreement.

35 情戚 = *chŏngch'ŏk* 情慽: pitiable circumstances.

36 地窮: wretched situation, hard plight.

37 含羞含寃: harbor shame and resentment.

38 齷齪: fussy over details, pernickety.

39 胤友 = *yunu* 允友: (deferential) your son.

40 質言: make a straightforward comment, speak plainly.

41 庶免: narrowly avoid.

42 悚然: trembling in fear.

43 斫刀: a fodder chopper (operated with the foot).

44 書房主: one's husband (read *sŏbang-nim* with the vernacular Korean honorific suffix -*nim*).

45 悖子 = *p'aeryuna* 悖倫兒: prodigal son.

46 口尙乳臭: lit. "mouth still smells of breast milk" = be born yesterday; be still in swaddling clothes.

47 亡家之行: lit. "a deed that will ruin one's family."

48 身後: after death.

49 擧趾: lift one's heel.

50 惶惶: trembling with fear.

51 面無人色: lit. "face not looking human" = *sasaek* 死色 = a deathly pall.

52 自擅之罪: lit. "crime of insolence."

53 絶嗣: cessation of the family line.

54 螟嗣: adopt a son to continue the family line.

55 乾淨: tie up loose ends, arrange a tidy conclusion.

56 亡兆: sign of impending ruin.

57 曠蕩之恩: grace of special amnesty.

58 肆其惡: lit. "let loose with one's evil ways."

59 下世 = *pyŏlse* 別世: depart this world.

60 犬豚不若: worse than dogs and pigs.

61 納侤: respond to the local government's summons.

62 禽獸之盟: lit. "pledge of wild beasts" = a pledge that the breacher of the contract can be treated as a wild beast.

63 生啗: chew something raw.

64 首奴: head slave(s); the most senior slave.

65 正配 = *chŏngsil* 正室: legal, primary wife.

66 到老和同: lit. "live together until old age."

67 間言 = *igan* 離間: lit. "alienating, estranging words."

———— 95 ————

The Man That Might Have Been

Vol. III: 52; n.d.; Diary XIV, pp. 130–3; 306.

Yi Wan was a special friend of King Hyojong and was sent by him to strike a blow at the Manchus. He sought for suitable help in this undertaking and even when he was out on a journey he took note of passers and whenever he saw a suitable person he would take him home and make a contract with him. According to his special ability, he would recommend him to the government.

Once when he was Commander-in-Chief he asked leave to pay a visit to his ancestral tombs. On his way when passing Yongin County, he stopped at an inn where there was a man unmarried, with his hair down his back, about thirty years of age. He was about ten feet high with a face one foot long. He was very, very thin with only his bones showing through his skin. His hair was short* and curly and the clothes he wore were of linen and quite insufficient to cover his body. He lolled back on the mud platform of the inn and there drank from a great bowl of spirit as a whale might drink in the sea.

Yi Wan took him in at a glance and marked him as a wonder. He alighted from his horse and went and sat on the bank nearby. He then sent a servant to call this odd stranger.

He came, but not the first sign of manners was there. He came and sat down in a free and easy way on a stone.

Yi Wan asked him his name and he replied, "My name is Pak T'ak."

"What is your family?" asked Yi.

"I am of a family of the gentry but my father died early in life and my old mother alone remained. We were poor and so nothing remained for me but to gather wood and sell it on her behalf."

Yi went on, "I saw you drinking *sul*† just now; will you have some wine?"

His reply was, "I never refuse an extra glass."

Yi then sent a servant with a *yang* of money to buy drink and for this amount got two big jars of Korean beer.

Yi Wan took one glass and drank and handed the glass over to the stranger, who took it without a word of refusal and drank the whole thing.

Yi Wan said, "You are buried out here in the country in the hunger and cold and yet your make assures me that you are no common man but one to be greatly used. Have you heard of me? I am the Commander-in-Chief, Yi Wan. Just now the state has some great matters on hand and is calling for capable men. If you come with me, you will have no need to raise the question of wealth and influence."

The young man said, "I have an old mother and I cannot make any promises."

Yi Wan said, "If that be the case, I wish to go and see your mother and make my bow to her. Show me the way, will you?"

He followed some ten *ri* or so and finally arrived at the house. It was a most dilapidated place of two or three *kan*‡ unfit to keep out either wind or weather.

The young man went first of all into the room and a little later, came out with an old worn mat which he spread out before the front gate and the old lady came out to receive the guest.

Her head was all in a tangle and she wore a linen skirt. About sixty years of age she must have been. They bowed to each other to be seated and when they had taken their places, Yi Wan said, "I am the Commander-in-Chief, Yi Wan. I am out on a journey to see to our family graves and have met your son on the way. One glimpse proved to me that he was destined for great things. Your Ladyship has this wonderful son – I congratulate you again and again."

The old mother arranged her dress in an orderly manner and replied, "Here in this wild country, my boy has grown up without his father, and has failed to make use of his early years for study, and has grown up wild as a mountain bird or a beast of the wilderness. Your Excellency has praised him beyond measure. I am ashamed to hear it."

Yi Wan replied, "Your Ladyship, even though you live in the uncultured country, you probably know of the world's doings. We are just now planning for great affairs in the government and are looking for the right man. I see your boy and cannot think of saying goodbye to him. We must go together and share in the affairs of state. This lad says he will not go without the consent of his mother. I could not ask him to do otherwise and so I have come to petition you to let him go with me. Will you not grant it?"

The old mother said, "An ignorant boy from this most uncultivated region – what use can he possibly be in this great undertaking you speak of? Besides, he is my only child. We depend on each other for our very life. It is difficult for him to go far away. I cannot let him go."

Yi Wan urged most insistently two or three times whereupon the old mother said, "A man is born to a wide world of thought and effort. If I give him once to the state, he will have no chance to think again of this poor old life of mine. Since Your Excellency has such urgent thoughts on behalf of your country, I cannot but consent."

Greatly delighted, Yi Wan made his farewell and left. He took the lad with him and they went together to Seoul and entered the palace and went straight to audience.

The King spoke saying, "You went to the country to see your family tombs. How is it that you have returned so soon?"

Yi Wan replied, "On my way to the country, I met a very rare and gifted man whom I have brought back with me."

The King called for him and he came in with tangled head and protruding temples on each side of his head, looking like a beggar lad of some sort or other. He came straight in without a single sign of ceremony of any kind and sat down cross-legged such as no one ever does before the King.

The King laughed and said, "How come you to be so poor and thin?"

He replied, "If a great man fails to win the favour of the world, this condition is inevitable."

The King made reply, "Your words are worthy of the great."

He then turned to Yi Wan and said, "What office shall we appoint this lad to?"

Yi replied, "He is like a wild beast from the hills as yet. I shall take him for a time and shall polish him off and after he has learned something, he will then be ready for some office."

The King gave his consent to this.

Yi Wan kept the lad near him and had him well-dressed and fed. He taught him the laws of war and other things and he learned with great rapidity.

He advanced with the advancing days till all his ignorant ways were dropped off.

Whenever he saw Yi Wan, the King asked persistently for Pak T'ak as to how he was getting on.

Yi Wan made reply that he was getting on all right and thus some two years or so passed.

Whenever he talked to Pak T'ak about an attack on the northern enemy, Yi Wan found his ideas and plans superior to his own. Yi Wan was delighted at this and told the King of it. It was only a little later, however, that King Hyojong went as a guest to heaven.

Pak T'ak followed the mourners and wept louder than any other. His eyes were swollen and he shed tears of blood.

Day after day, morning and evening he shared in the group of mourners till the seven moons of burial[§] were over and then he came to Yi Wan and desired to say his last and long farewell.

Yi Wan said, "What do you mean by this? I love you as my own child – how can you think of casting me aside in this easy way?"

His reply was, "Do you think I do not know how Your Excellency has loved me? I did not come for food and clothes. We had a great and good King whose rule inspired me to attempt my all for the state; and now that God's mercy is withdrawn and he has left us, I have no further thoughts of any work to do. This is indeed a case for the great man to weep over. Though I am under orders of Your Excellency, there is no longer any place where I can be used. To remain simply because we know and love each other is a useless expense only and one that no man should consent to; better that I go."

He wept and said his farewell and went back to the country and took his mother and hid himself away in the hills. No one knew what became of him. Song Siyŏl used to tell this story and sigh over him.

* "With his hair down his back" indicates that the young man did not wear his hair braided, which was the custom for unmarried men, and does not necessarily mean that his hair was long.
† *sul* is a generic term for alcoholic beverages.
‡ *kan* = the size of a room (usually 7 to 8 feet square).
§ "Seven moons of burial" refers to the duration of a state funeral.

리 정 익 공 완　　　하 효 묘　　권 주　　　　장 모 북 벌　　　광 구 인 재
李貞翼公浣 1)　荷孝廟 2)　眷注 3)　將謀北伐 4)　廣求人材

수 어 행 로 상　　　여 견 인 지 모 지 괴 위　　　즉 필 연 치 지 문
雖於行路上　如見人之貌之魁偉 5)　則必延致之門

수 기 재 이 천 우 조　　증 이 훈 장　　　득 가 소 분　　　행 도 요
隨其才而薦于朝　曾以訓將 6)　得暇掃墳 7)　行到龍

인　　점 막　　유 일 총 각　　년 근 삼 십 허 지 인　　신 장 기 십 척
仁 8)　店幕　有一總角　年近三十許之人　身長幾十尺

면 장 일 척 수 골 릉 층　　　단 발 봉 송　　　포 갈 불 능 엄 신
面長一尺瘦骨稜層 9)　短髮鬅鬆 10)　布褐不能掩身

거 좌 토 청　　　지 상　　이 일 와 분 탁 료　　　음 여 장 경
踞坐土廳 11)　之上　以一瓦盆濁醪 12)　飲如長鯨 13)

공 어 마 상　　별 견 이 이 지　　　잉 하 마　　　좌 우 안　　상
公於馬上　瞥見而異之　仍下馬　坐于岸上

사 인 초 기 동 이 래　　　궐 동 불 위 례　　우 거 좌 우 석　　상
使人招其童以來　厥童不爲禮　又踞坐于石上

公問其姓名　答曰：姓朴名鐸 14) 也　又問　汝之

地閥何如　答曰：自是班族　而早孤家有偏母

而家貧負薪而養之　又問　汝飲酒　能復飲乎　對曰：

卮酒 15) 安足辭　公命下隷　以百文錢 16)　沽酒而來

而沽濁醪二大盆以來　公自飲一椀　以其器　擧以

給之　厥童少無辭讓羞澁之意　連倒二盆　公曰：

汝雖埋沒草野　困於飢寒　骨相非凡　大用之人也

汝或聞我名乎　我是訓將李某也　朝廷方營大事

遍求將帥之才　汝若隨我而去　則富貴何足道哉

厥童曰：老母在堂　此身未敢以許人也　公曰：若然

則吾當升堂拜君母　而家安在　汝須導前　行十餘里

抵其門前　不蔽風雨　數間斗屋也　厥童先入門

而已出一弊席　鋪之柴門外　（有一老嫗）出而迎

之　蓬頭布裙　年可六十餘　相與讓席坐席 [定]

公曰：某是訓將李某也　掃墳之行　路逢此兒

一面可知其人傑　尊嫂 17) 有此奇男　大賀大賀

老婦斂袵而對曰：草野之間　無父之兒　早失學業

無異山禽野獸 18)　大監過加詡獎 19)　不勝慚愧公曰：

尊嫂雖在草野　時事必有及聞者矣　見今朝廷方營

大事　招延人材　某見此兒　不忍遽別　欲與之同行

以圖功名　則此兒以無親命爲辭故　不得已躬來敢請

幸尊嫂許之否　老婦曰：鄕曲愚蠢之兒 20)　有何知識

而敢當大事乎　且此是老身之獨子　母子相依爲命

有難遠離　不敢奉命矣　公懇請再三　老婦曰：

男子生而志在四方　旣許身於國家　則區區私情有不

敢顧矣　且大監之誠意如是　則何敢不許乎　公大喜

卽辭其老婦　與其兒偕行　還歸洛下　詣闕請對 21)

上下敎曰：卿旣作掃墳之行　何爲徑還 22) 也

公奏曰：小臣下鄕之路　逢一奇男子　與之偕來矣

上使之入侍　則蓬頭突鬢 23)　旣一寒乞之兒 24)

直入榻前　不爲禮而踞坐　上笑而敎曰：汝何瘦瘠

之甚也　對曰：大丈夫不得（志）於世　安得不然乎

上曰：此一言　奇且壯矣　顧李公曰：當除何職乎

公曰：此兒姑未免山野禽獸之態　臣謹當率畜家中

磨以歲月　訓戒人事然後　可以責一職事矣　上許之

常置之左右　豊其衣食　而敎以兵法及行世之要

聞一知十　日就月將　非復舊日痴蠢樣子　上每

對李公　必問朴鐸之成就　公每以將進奏達　如

是度數年矣　公每與朴鐸　論北伐之事　則其出謀發

慮　反有勝於自家　公乃大奇之　將奏達而大用之

未幾孝廟賓天 25)　朴鐸隨人參哭班 26)　痛哭不已　至

於目腫 27) 而淚血　每日朝夕　必參哭班　及因山禮 28)

畢　告公以永訣　公曰：此何言也　吾與汝　情同父子

汝何忍舍我而去耶　對曰：豈不知大監眷愛之恩哉

某之來此　非爲哺啜之計 [29] 也　吾英雄之聖主在上

可以有爲於世矣　皇天不弔 [30]　奄遭大喪 [31]　今則天下

事無可爲者　此誠千古不禁英雄 [英雄不禁] 淚者也

吾雖留在大監門下　無可用之機　且拘於顔私 [32]

浪費衣食　而逗留 [33] 不去　亦甚無義　不如從此逝矣

仍揮淚拜謝　而歸鄉　與其母　離家而入深峽　不知

所終　尤齋 [34] 先生　常對人　道此事而嘆 [嗟] 嘆

1　李浣 [1602–74; styled Chingji 澄之; sobriquet Maejukhŏn 梅竹軒; ancestral seat Kyŏngju 慶州; posthumous epithet Chŏngik 貞翼]: military official under King Hyŏnjong [r. 1659–74; 1641–74]. His father was Yi Suil 李守一 [1554–1632].

2　孝廟: temple name of King Hyojong 孝宗 [r. 1649–59; 1619–59].

3　眷注: win the favour and confidence of someone.

4　北伐: "Northern Expedition," i.e., the anti-Manchu military campaign of later Chosŏn.

5　魁偉: well-built and robust.

6　訓將 = *hullyŏn taejang* 訓鍊大將: Commander-in-Chief of the General Directorate of Military Training (Hullyŏn togam 訓鍊都監), a junior second-rank military post.

7　掃墳: lit. "tomb sweeping": ancestral worship rite performed at the ancestral burial site to mark a special occasion.

 8 龍仁: a town in Kyŏnggi Province.
 9 瘦骨稜層: skinny yet with a large frame and tough appearance.
10 鬅鬆: unkempt hair.
11 土廳: dirt floor.
12 濁醪: *makkŏlli* = milky rice brew.
13 飮如長鯨: lit. "drink like a large whale."
14 朴鐸: unknown.
15 巵酒: alcoholic beverage contained in a cup = small amount of alcohol.
16 百文錢 = *paekp'un mun* 百分文 = one *yang* 兩. *Yang* is a unit of traditional Korean coinage.
17 尊嫂: (deferential) married woman; here, "you."
18 山禽野獸: lit. "mountain birds, wild beasts."
19 詡奬: boast about and recommend.
20 鄉曲愚蠢之兒: lit. "stupid and slow country bumpkin."
21 請對: (for a subject) request an audience with the king to discuss an urgent matter.
22 徑還: return via a shortcut.
23 蓬頭突鬢 = *pongdu nanbal* 蓬頭亂髮: unkempt hair.
24 寒乞之兒: lit. "wretched beggar child."
25 賓天 = *pungŏ* 崩御: passing away of the king.
26 哭班: the ranks of the mourning officials at a state funeral.
27 目腫: swollen eyes.
28 因山禮: proprieties for a state funeral.
29 哺啜之計: plan to make ends meet.
30 皇天不弔: lit. "High heaven is indifferent."
31 大喪 = *kuksang* 國喪: state funeral.
32 顔私 = *chŏngni* 情理: personal feelings.
33 逗留: linger on.
34 尤齋: sobriquet of Song Siyŏl 宋時烈 [1607–89; styled Yŏngbo 英甫; ancestral seat Ŭnjin 恩津; posthumous epithet Munjŏng 文正]. Song Siyŏl was a scholar-official under King Hyojong. His father was Song Kapcho 宋甲祚 [1574–1628].

—————— **96** ——————

Yi Wan and the Robber Chief

Vol. III: 53; n.d.; Diary XIV, pp. 134–6; 307.

When Yi Wan (1602–74) was a young man he went to the hills on a hunting expedition. Following the chase, he got deep into the hills. The day was late and though he looked here and there, there was no sign of a house anywhere. He was disturbed by this and hastened his horse along a little path that he found in the long grass. He crossed a number of hills and reached a place where was a deep defile. Here he found a large tiled house. He alighted and rapped at the door but no answer came. He waited for the space of a meal or so, when a girl came forth, saying, "You must not stay here. There is danger. Go at once."

Seeing the girl, Yi Wan thought that she was about twenty years of age. Her face and form were neat and attractive. He said to her, "This is a secluded region and the day is late with tigers and leopards all about. I have found this place with the greatest of difficulty. Why do you forbid my entrance?"

The girl answered, "I am afraid that if you stay here, you will suffer death."

Yi Wan said, "If I stay outside, I shall die by the tiger; death itself is better inside than out."

He pushed the door open and went in.

Seeing that there was no way of preventing his entrance, the girl showed him the way into a room.

He sat down and asked why she had indicated that he could not stay here.

The girl said, "A chief of a group of bandits lives here and I am the daughter of the bourgeoisie, but was carried away by the robber chief. I have been here for a number of years, and yet I have never found a chance of escape. The chief has gone off on a hunting expedition and has not yet returned. Later in the night he will come and if he sees a guest here he will have both our heads off with one strike. I do not know who you are but yet I do not wish to see you die to no purpose at the hands of a robber. Should I not be anxious?"

Yi Wan laughed and made reply: "There is danger, I admit, and yet I must have my supper. Make haste and prepare it."

The girl gave him of the rice already prepared for the robber chief, and after he had dined well, he asked the girl to share his room.

The girl resisted him and said, "If we do as you say what will be the end of it?"

Yi Wan said, "Here we are in this fix. Though we sleep together, we shall die; though we refrain, we die. Here we are in the quiet with no one near, and even though we have nought to do with each other, who will believe it? Life and death are at the disposal of God. What's the use of fears over this?"

And thus they slept together.

In the passing of a watch of the night, there was the sound of steps approaching and then the loosening of saddles and the tossing down of heavy bundles.

The girl's form trembled and her face turned pale and she said, "The chief has come. What shall we do?"

Yi Wan paid no attention to this whatever, when suddenly a great giant of a fellow, ten feet high with wild eyes and a "sea mouth" wide slit, a great defiant face, and a manner most fearful to behold appeared. He stood with a sword in his hand and half under the influence of drink entered the room. Seeing a stranger lying in his room, he shouted out, "Who are you? Who dares come here to commit adultery with another man's wife?"

With no end of leisure in his manner, Yi Wan said, "I came to the hills on the chase for game when the day overtook me and so I came here to spend the night."

The robber chief shouted, "You are a bold-livered scoundrel. If you wish to stay the night, why don't you sleep in the outer quarter instead of here in the inner room to take possession of another man's wife? This means death to you. You are an ill-mannered weasel, as well, who does not even know how to greet the master of the house but lies stretched out in his presence. What manner of behaviour is this? Have you no fear of death whatever?"

Yi Wan laughed and said, "I have come here and found your wife. Even though I had confined myself to the outer room, would you have believed that we had kept part? We mortals have to die sometime or other; death offers no fears to me. Do as you please."

The robber chief then bound Yi Wan with a great rope and tied him up to the ridge log of the roof after which he said to his wife, "There is some game out on the verandah. Cook and bring some of it."

In a state of inexpressible fear, the woman went out trembling. Here were wild pigs and deer that she cut up and made ready, cooked and brought in on a huge platter.

The chief then called for drink and drank two or three glasses. He then took his sword and cut up the steak and ate it in great pieces. He then stuck the point of his sword into another piece and said, "How can one eat alone when he has a guest? You are doomed to death. But still try this steak and see what you think of it."

And so he passed it on to Yi.

Yi opened his mouth and munched away at it, without the slightest sign of fear, anxiety, or alarm. The robber chief then looked at him and said, "You are made of great stuff – a mighty chief, you surely are."

Yi replied, "If you intend to kill me, have it done and over with. What's the sense of this delay? What's the sense of talking of mighty chiefs or great stuff?"

The chief then threw down his knife, arose, and untied Yi's hands with one of his hands and had him sit down beside him. Then he said, "You are indeed a wonder. Your like I have never seen. You have a great future before you and will be a wall and shield to the state. How could I ever kill such a one as you? From now on you are my special friend for whom I would die. Even though that girl is my wife, since you have had knowledge of her, she is yours to do as you please. She is mine no longer. The goods and plunder I have here in my storehouse are all at your service. Do not refrain, I pray you. If a great man undertakes to do great things on earth, he must have materials and supplies. I shall follow you and I ask you to save me from a great piece of misfortune that lies ahead."

He so said, arose and disappeared.

Yi Wan then took the young woman on the horse he rode and loaded the goods and supplies on the horse that remained and took his way out of the hills.

Later when Yi Wan became an officer of state he was put at the supreme head of the troops and also made Superintendent of Police. When a certain robber chief was brought up for examination, he saw his face and recognized him as the chief he had met and went and told the king of it, and so got the man off. He was made a non-commissioned officer in the army. Finally, by good behaviour, he was made an officer of the state and later a general.

貞翼公 1) 少時　射獵于山間　逐獸而轉入深山

日暮且四顧無人家　心甚慌忙 2)　按彎而尋草路

歷盡數岡　到一處　則山凹之處 3)　有一大瓦家

仍下馬叩門　則無一應者　居食頃　一女子自內而出

曰：此處非客子暫留之處　斯速出去　公見其女子

則年可十餘　而容貌頗端麗　公對曰：山谷深矣

日勢暮矣　虎豹橫行之地　艱辛尋覓人家而來

則如是拒絕何也　女曰：在此則有必死之慮故也

公曰：出門而死於猛虎　寧死於此處　仍排門而入

女子料其無奈何　遂延之入室坐定　公問其不可

留之故　女曰：此是賊魁之居也　妾以良家女

年前爲此賊魁所標畧 [剽掠] 4)　在此幾年　尚不

得脫虎口 5)　賊魁適作獵行　姑未還　夜久必來

若見客子之留此　則妾與客　當授首於一劍之刃

客子不知何許人　而空然浪死 6) 於賊魁之手　豈不

悶哉　公笑曰：死期雖迫　不可闕食　夕飯斯速備來

女子以其賊魁之飯進之　公飽喫後　仍抱女而臥

其女牢拒曰：如此而將於後患何　公曰：到此地頭 7)

削 8) 之亦反 9) 不削亦反　靜夜無人之際　男女同處

一室　雖欲別嫌 10) 人孰信之　死生有命　恐懼何益

仍與之交　偃臥自若 11) 居數食頃　忽聞剝啄之聲 12)

又有卸擔之聲 13) 其女戰慄　而面無人色曰：

賊魁至矣　此將奈何　公聽若不聞而已　一大漢

身長十尺　河目海口 14) 狀貌雄偉　風儀獰猂 15)

手執長劍　半醉而入門　見公之臥　高聲大叱曰：汝

是何許人　敢來此處　奸人之妻　公徐曰：入山逐獸

日勢已昏　寄宿於此　賊魁又大叱曰：汝是大膽

既來此處　則處于外廊可也　何敢入內室　犯他人

之妻　已是死罪　汝以客子　而見主人　不爲禮　偃
臥而見之　此何道理　如是而能不畏死乎　公笑曰：
到此地頭　吾雖貞白一心　男女分席而坐　汝豈
信之乎　人之生斯世也　必有一死　死何足懼也
汝任爲之　賊魁乃以大索　縛公懸之樑上　顧謂其
妻曰：廳上有山獸之獵來者　汝須洗而炙來　其
女戰戰 16) 出戶　宰割 17) 山猪獐鹿 18) 等內［肉］　爛熟
而盛于一大盤以進之　賊魁又使進酒　以一大盆　連
倒數盃　拔劒切肉而啗之　更以一塊肉　挿于劒鋩 19)
曰：何可置人於旁而獨喫乎　渠雖當死之漢　可使
知味　仍以劒頭肉與之　公開口　受而啗之　小無疑
慮恐怯之色　賊魁孰視曰：是可謂大丈夫矣
公曰：汝欲殺我　則殺之可也　何爲而如是遲延
又何大丈夫小丈夫之可言乎　賊魁擲劒而起　解其縛

把手就坐曰：如君之天下奇男　吾初見之矣　將大

用於世　爲國杆 [干] 城 20)　矣　吾何以殺之　從今

以後　吾以知己許之　彼女子雖是吾之妻眷　君已

近之　則卽君之內眷也　吾何可更近也　且庫中

所積之財帛　一一付之君　君其勿辭　丈夫有爲

於世　而手無錢財　何以營爲　吾則從此逝矣　日後

必有大厄　君必捄 [救] 我　語罷飄然而起　仍不

知去向　公以其馬　駄載其女　且以廐上所係馬四

盡載財帛而出山　其後公顯達　以訓將 21)　兼捕將 22)

時自外邑　捉上一大賊魁　將按治之際 23)　細察其

狀貌　則卽其人也　乃以往事　奏達于榻前　仍

白放 24)　而置之校列 25)　次次推遷 26)　至於武科　位至

閫任 27)　云耳

1　貞翼公 ＝ Yi Wan 李浣 [1602–74; styled Chingji 澄之; sobriquet Maejukhŏn 梅竹軒; ancestral seat Kyŏngju 慶州; posthumous epithet Chŏngik 貞翼]:

military official under King Hyŏnjong 顯宗 [r. 1659–74; 1641–74]. His father was Yi Suil 李守一 [1554–1632].

2 慌忙: helter-skelter; flustered.

3 山凹之處: concavity in a hill or a mountain.

4 剽掠: threaten and snatch = abduct; plunder.

5 虎口: lit. "tiger's mouth" = tiger's den; a dangerous predicament.

6 浪死: die in vain; die a dog's death.

7 到此地頭: [since] things have reached this state/plight.

8 削: snatch away.

9 反 = *panyŏk* 反逆: committ treason; rebel.

10 別嫌: take pains to alleviate suspicion.

11 偃臥自若: lit. "recline in a relaxed manner as if nothing is the matter."

12 剝啄之聲: lit. "sound of knocking at the door."

13 卸擔之聲: lit. "sound of putting down luggage."

14 河目海口: lit. "eyes as big as a river and mouth as big as the ocean" = have striking facial features.

15 獰猂: merciless and fierce.

16 戰戰: trembling in fear.

17 宰割: slaughter a beast and butcher it.

18 山猪獐鹿: wild boar and deer.

19 劍鋩: the blade of a sword.

20 干城: lit. "shield and castle" = soldier who protects the state.

21 訓將 = Hullyŏn taejang 訓鍊大將: Commander-in-Chief of the General Directorate of Military Training (Hullyŏn Togam 訓鍊都監), a junior second-rank military post.

22 捕將 = P'odo taejang 捕盜大將: one of the two commanders-in-chief of the Police Department (P'odoch'ŏng 捕盜廳), a junior second-rank military post.

23 按治之際: lit. "when it was time to punish the crime."

24 白放: be declared innocent and released.

25 校列: the ranks of military officials.

26 推遷: be promoted and move to a different place.

27 閫任: lit. "doorsill duty/threshold duty" = Pyŏngsusa 兵水使 = both army Commander-in-Chief (Pyŏngma chŏltosa 兵馬節度使) and naval Commander-in-Chief (Sugun chŏltosa 水軍節度使).

——— **97** ———

A Man of the Mings

Vol. III: 55; n.d.; Diary XIV, pp. 136–8; 308.

After the year *kapsin* of Chongzhen, when the Mings had fallen, many of them came to Korea. Among these was one who had been an officer of the state, who cut his hair, put on a black coat, became a priest, and came to Seoul. Here he remained for a half year or so when he said to his disciple, "I have heard that the master Song Siyŏl just now is in consultation with the king in regard to some great matters of the state and that a certain Sin Man also is called in. I desire greatly to meet these two and see what order of man they are."

With his disciple, he went to Hoedŏk on the way near the halfway station, where they met Uam on his way up to the capital. The priest made his way and bowed low before the master Song.

Song Siyŏl dismounted at once and, with a glad countenance, said, "I meet the most excellent teacher here in the street, where I have no means to entertain you as in my home and this I regret. Will you not come to Seoul with me? When we get there I would like you to come to my place, for I have something to talk over quietly with you."

He agreed and so they separated and each went on his way.

The priest then turned and said to his disciple, "The master Song had no sooner cast his eye on me than he recognized that I was a man with ideas in my soul. I, too, have seen him and a great man I truly know him to be, who has work before him. He answers the questions of my soul. I would like now to go see Sin Man."

So they started for Chinjam, and while seeking Sin's house, they came before the door.

At this time Sin was eating his noonday meal when he looked up with a glad countenance and said, "Whence comes this teacher? Come in, come in."

The priest excused himself two or three times, whereupon Sin spat out the food he was eating and, taking him by the sleeve, had him come in and gave him a seat. He said, "You have come a long way and will be famished and yet my house is so poor that I have nothing special to offer you. Come and share my bowl with me."

The priest declined, saying, "I just dined at yonder inn. Please do not suggest such a thing."

Sin said, "I am here eating – how can I let you sit by unrefreshed?"

And so he forced him to eat. He was delighted far beyond that of an ordinary friend.

The priest then arose and said he would go. Just outside the door, he said to his disciple, "This man also is born to great deeds. When one finds such men in the government as Song and such in the country as this man Sin, one need have no fears as to success attending one's way; but only after a great king takes his place on the throne could such fine men be put to good use. I want now to see the king and find what he is like."

Again he returned to Seoul and made a stay. Just at this time, King Hyojong was out at Nodol, inspecting a review of his troops, and the priest joined the crowd of sightseers and got his view of the heavenly face. He then went in a hurry to a quiet spot by himself where he lifted up his voice and wept.

In wonder over this, his disciple asked the reason, whereupon the priest wiped his eyes and said, "I had a heart to strike a blow for king and state but it's gone for good. I saw the king's face and, while you might say he was great and highly enlightened and ready for the greatest undertaking, there is the expression of the dead in his face, and he will not live beyond this year (1660). This is God's appointment. Oh God, oh God! Why did you give us one who could do so much and now take him away?"

And so he wept and cried. In ten days or so the king died.

Later the priest was never seen again.

崇禎甲申 1) 以後 皇朝 2) 遺民之東來者 甚多 有一

仕宦人 削髮衣緇而來歸京師者 過半年 忽謂其

上佐僧曰：吾聞懷德宋相 3) 某 方贊助國家大議

鎮岑申生 4) 亦預 5) 其事云 此是吾日夜所冀望者也

吾將見此兩人之何如樣 仍與上佐 向懷德

未及半程　路逢尤齋 6) 之上京　仍合掌而拜于馬前

先生仍下馬　欣然而言曰：吾與禪師　草草 7) 相逢

於路次 8) 甚可恨也　禪師今當向洛乎　入洛之日

必來訪我於所住處　以爲從容酬酌之地可也　僧曰：

諾　與之相別而行　其僧顧謂上佐曰：宋相一擧目

以知我之爲有心人　且吾察其狀貌　可謂英雄　百

事可做　庶副 9) 吾願矣　第向鎭岑　見申生之何如人

仍向鎭岑路　訪申生之家　及門則舟村 10) 方對

午饌　欣然而笑曰：禪師從何而來也　斯速升堂

其僧再三告辭　舟村吐哺 11) 而手自携裾 12) 而上

之坐定　舟村曰：禪師遠來　必有飢思　吾家貧

無以別供一案　可與我共喫一盂飯　僧辭曰：小僧

俄於客店已療飢　不必俯念　舟村曰：主人旣對飯

而何可使客闕飯乎　強與之共喫　其欣款之心 13)

無異於平生知舊 僧告辭而退 出門謂其上佐曰：

此人亦可當大事之人也 朝野俱有此等人 何患大

事之不成 然而必有大有爲 14) 之君 然後

可用此等人物 吾第觀主上之何如也 更留京數月

孝廟 15) 適親行閱武於露浦 16) 之上 僧從觀光人叢中

一瞻天顔 急向靜僻處 放聲大哭 上佐驚怪而問之

則掩涙而言曰：吾之一片苦心 今焉已矣 吾觀主

上 天日之表 17) 可謂英雄聖明之主 18) 可以有爲

而但屍氣 19) 滿面 壽限盡於今年之內 天乎天乎

既出其人 又何奪之速也 哀痛不已 其後一旬之間

孝廟賓天 20) 而其僧不知去處云矣

1 崇禎甲申: the year 1633 (Injo 22) = the fall of the Ming and the establishment of the Qing.

2 皇朝 = imperial court = *myŏngjo* 明朝: the Ming dynasty.

3 懷德宋相: Minister Song of Hoedŏk = Song Siyŏl 宋時烈 [1607–89; styled Yŏngbo 英甫; sobriquet Uam 尤庵, Ujae 尤齋; ancestral seat Ŭnjin 恩津; posthumous epithet Munjŏng 文正]: scholar-official under King Hyojong 孝宗 [r. 1649–59; 1619–59]. His father was Song Kapcho 宋甲祚 [1574–1629]. Hoedŏk is a town near Taejŏn 大田.

4 鎭岑申生 Master Shin of Chinjam = Sin Man 申曼 [1620–69; styled
　 Manch'ŏn 曼倩; sobriquet Chuch'on 舟村; ancestral seat P'yŏngsan 平山;
　 posthumous epithet Hyoŭi 孝義]: studied under Song Siyŏl and was the
　 eldest grandson of Sin Hŭm 申欽 [1566–1628] and son of Sin Ingnyung
　 申翊隆 [?–1657]. Chinjam is a town near Hoedŏk.

5 預 = ch'amyŏ 參與 ~ ch'amye 參預: partake in.

6 尤齋: Song Siyŏl. See note 3 above.

7 草草: busily, hurriedly.

8 路次 = tojung 途中: on the way; halfway.

9 副 = puŭng 副應: comply with; fit the bill.

10 舟村: sobriquet of Sin Man. See note 4 above.

11 吐哺: spit out the food in one's mouth.

12 携裾: grab the hem of someone's clothes.

13 欣款之心: wholehearted welcome.

14 有爲 = yunŭng 有能: able, competent.

15 孝廟: temple name for King Hyojong 孝宗 [r. 1649–59; 1619–59].

16 露浦: Nodolgae, an estuary in Noryangjin 鷺梁津, a ferry-crossing in
　 Seoul.

17 天日之表: appearance like that of the sun in the sky.

18 聖明之主: lit. "king of sagacity and light."

19 屍氣: lit. "the air of a corpse" = the pall of death.

20 賓天 = sŭngha 昇遐: (deferential) the death of a ruler.

———— 98 ————

A Visit to Hell by Kwŏn Chŏk

[No source cited]; Diary XIV, pp. 138–40; listed in Diary XVI, p. 178,
as "A Visit to Hell"; 311.

Kwŏn Chŏk was a descendant of Kwŏn P'il and lived at Yŏnsan,
Ch'ungch'ŏng Province, in the village of Pan'gok. He had won a name
for filial piety but died at forty years of age.

The whole house was plunged into mourning but as time passed
they noticed that a measure of warmth was noticeable in his breast and
so they refrained from binding up his form for burial.

One day passed and at the close of it he suddenly came to life, saying,
"I died and what I saw proves that the world's talk about a myŏngbu*

is not foolish talk after all. I lost my consciousness in my sickness and suddenly I heard my name called by the spirit soldiers. I was startled awake and went outside the gate to see what it meant and there I saw the spirit soldiers and followed them. I lost all knowledge of the points of the compass. There was a great and wide road that led to a certain place that had an official yamen in it. I stood outside the gate while the soldiers went in and announced, 'We have arrested and brought Kwŏn so-and-so.'

"They were told to have him in and in I went and prostrated myself in the courtyard. I saw before me a great judge with royal robes on, who asked of the spirit soldiers, 'Where did you arrest him?'

"They replied, 'We took him in Yŏnsan.'

"The one wearing the royal robes shouted out, 'I ordered you to arrest an unfilial Kwŏn of Suwŏn; why have you arrested the faithful Kwŏn of Yŏnsan? This man is booked to live till eighty and he is now only forty. Send him back at once.'

"The spirit soldiers were startled out of their wits and pushed me out.

"I was inside of Hades and yet I did not have a single moment in which to bow to my parents. I regret this very much. I came away under force for I wanted to see them so much. On the way out, I saw two children playing by the roadside. When they saw me, they smiled, took hold of my robes and tried to follow me. Looking at them more closely, I found they were my own little children who had died.

"I was so startled and rendered sad by this that I went back through the main gate of Hades and begged the great judge saying, 'I am a man of the outer world and have come here to Hades and now am to go back. Such an opportunity as this is surely very rare. I am here and have not yet seen my parents. This is not the part of a filial son. Will you not please give me this pleasure even though but for a moment?'

"The judge shook his head, saying, 'This is not permitted – now return at once.'

"I cried and begged again and again but he refused to the last. I then asked if he would let me take the two children, but he refused again, saying, 'Your appointed destiny is to be deprived of these children. If you are determined to take them, one is to be born to a certain Kim's house in Sangju. You must go to Kim's after the child is born and take it there.'

"I then came away, unable to do anything. The children wept and cried as they followed me. The soldiers, however, pushed them back and drove them off. I felt so sorry and upset that I asked the soldiers if I could see my parents just once and said, 'I have not seen them. Tell me, however, where they live.'

"The soldiers pointed out a little pavilion and said, 'There. Though it looks quite near, it is very far away and you cannot go. Hurry away,' they said.

"I did not see my parents and could not take my two children. My mind was terribly upset and sore and finally the soldiers pushed me so that I fell face forward, with my wits all gone. Finally I awoke."

Everybody hearing this thought it most strange. He lived till eighty and had no son, though he was honoured by the state for his filial piety. He used to say year after year, "I want to see a lad in the house of a certain Kim of Sangju but I don't know which Kim. It is too uncertain and weird that I do not dare to send anyone on the errand."[†]

* *myŏngbu*: Offices of the Netherworld.

† "I do not dare to send anyone on the errand" shows that Gale's translation is in error. The correct translation reads, "This affair is extremely preposterous and remains inconclusive. So the story goes."

權判書禰 1) 石洲鞸［鞸］2) 奉祀孫 3) 也　居在連山 4)

盤谷 5)　以孝聞於世　年四十而死　擧家發喪

而以胸膈 6) 間有一線溫氣故　姑未襲斂矣

過一日　忽爾回甦而言曰：吾死而見所見

則世人所謂冥府之說　果不虛矣　吾於病中

精神昏昏　忽聞鬼卒高聲而呼我姓名　驚訝而

出門　隨鬼卒而　不知東西 7)　但見大路濶而長

行幾里 到一處 則有一如官府樣 吾則立於門外

鬼卒先入而告曰：權某捉來矣 使之拿入

吾俯伏於庭下 則有一大殿坐王者服色者

問鬼卒曰：捉來於何處 對曰：捉來於連山地矣

如王者者厲聲曰：吾使汝捉來水原 8) 居不孝

子權姓人矣 何爲誤捉連山孝子權姓人也

此人壽限 9) 已定於八十 尙有四十年 斯速還送

鬼卒惶蹙 10) 而聽命 推我出門故 吾以既入冥府

不得一拜父母而歸 心甚痛缺 11) 勉强而出道見

兩介童遊戲於道傍 見我而欣然牽衣 而欲隨行

熟視之 乃是前日夭折之兩兒 心甚慘愕 12) 更入門

而懇乞於殿上人曰：陽界 13) 之人入冥府而還歸

則此是不易得之機 14) 也 既入而不得見父母而歸

則此豈人情也哉 伏望暫許使之一面 殿上人

掉頭曰: 此則不可不可　斯速出去　吾乃再三

涕泣而哀乞　終不許　吾乃又懇請兩兒之率去

則又不許曰: 汝之命數　自來無子　不可以許

如欲率去　則一童當使托生於尙州 15) 金姓人

家矣　汝可於後日率去於陽界上　吾無奈何

出門　則兩兒號哭而欲隨　爲鬼卒所逐　心甚慘痛 16)

且以一見父母之意　懇請於鬼卒曰: 雖不得一拜

可指示我所住處　鬼卒指一處小亭曰: 此雖相望之地

程道甚遠　不可以往　仍促行　吾以父母之不得一拜

兩兒之不得率來　心甚痛寃之際　鬼卒自後推而

仆于地　精神怳惚　仍以驚覺矣云云　人皆異之

其後年果八十而無嗣　以孝旌閭 17) 常對人言曰:

尙州金吏家兒　欲率來見之　而不知名字之爲誰

且 [此] 事甚妖誕 18) 而不 [未] 果 19) 云矣

1 權禰 [1675–1755; styled Kyŏngha 景賀; sobriquet Ch'angbaekhŏn 蒼白軒; ancestral seat Andong 安東; posthumous epithet Hyojŏng 孝靖]: scholar-official under King Yŏngjo 英祖 [r. 1724–76; 1694–1776]. He served as Minister of Rites (Yejo *p'ansŏ* 禮曹判書). He was honoured with a commemorative arch (*chŏngmun* 旌門) for his filial piety.

2 權韠 [1569–1612; styled Yŏjang 汝章; sobriquet Sŏkchu 石洲; ancestral seat Andong 安東]: scholar-official under Kwanghaegun 光海君 [r. 1608–23; 1575–1641]. His father was Kwŏn Pyŏk 權擘 [1520–93].

3 奉祀孫: descendant responsible for carrying on the ancestral rites.

4 連山: a town in Nonsan County 論山郡 in South Ch'ungch'ŏng Province.

5 盤谷: a town in Yŏnsan 連山.

6 胸膈: lower chest; one's mind/heart.

7 不知東西: lit. "not know East from West" = be disoriented.

8 水原: a town in Kyŏnggi Province.

9 壽限 = *sumyŏng* 壽命: (preordained) life span.

10 惶懾: shrink in fear.

11 痛缺: searing pain.

12 慘愕: be appalled by a shocking scene.

13 陽界: this world; the world of mortals.

14 易得之機: lit. "easily obtainable opportunity."

15 尙州: a town in North Kyŏngsang Province.

16 慘痛: miserable, wretched, pitiable.

17 旌閭: erect a gate at the entrance to a village to recognize its filial children, loyal subjects, or faithful wives.

18 妖誕: preposterous.

19 未果: lit. "remain inconclusive."

———— **99** ————

A Question of Conscience

Vol. III; 60; Diary XIV, pp. 10–11;
typed up in *Miscellaneous Writings* 30, pp. 161–2, and in *Old Corea*,
pp. 95–6; 312.
Gale's two renditions differ enough to warrant reproduction
in full below.

A Question of Conscience

The question is often raised as to how far conscience
rules in East Asia. To be found out in a wrong we know is
a dreadful fate; or to be exhibited to the public with
loss of "face" is often more feared than death itself,
but the inner heart which no eye sees, how far is its
condemnation to be reckoned with? Can it really influence
the understanding and the soul? Again the question is
asked, How far will the Oriental sacrifice his personal
interests to do an act of pure justice? Many casual
observers would say that he will never do it.
The accompanying story throws light on these great
questions, and like a parable impresses its message
perhaps better than a sermon.

Hwang In'gŏn, who graduated from the Confucian College in 1714 AD,
spent much of his time as a young man in a Buddhist monastery where
he studied the Chinese classics. Here he met a young priest who became his sworn friend, ran his errands, furnished him with supplies,
and took every occasion to meet all his needs. They had everything in
common, he and this priest, and Hwang found him more and more
faithful and true as the days went by. He made him part and parcel of
his permanent service till finally he rose to a place of political influence,
when suddenly his priest disappeared and could not be found anywhere. Hwang thought of him day and night and longed to see his face.

Some years later he was appointed Governor of Kyŏngsang Province,
and one day, while making his round of the different districts, he suddenly caught a glimpse, past his chair flap, of someone standing at the
side of the way. Noticing that he looked like his former friend, he sent a
servant to inquire, and lo it was the man.

Overjoyed, Hwang had a horse provided for him and wherever he
went he had the priest go as well, had him sleep in the same room and
be his most intimate companion. On returning to his headquarters at
Taegu, he gave him a room next to his library, and saw to his needs with
the greatest of care.

One day he called the priest and said, "There is an old saying that
runs, 'A single spoon of rice merits its return of favour.' How many

spoons have I received from you, might I ask? I have silks and stores in great abundance and yet if I gave you half of all I possess it would still be too little to express my heart. Unfortunately, you are a priest who dresses in coarse cloth and eats the poorest vegetarian fare. What is gold or silk to such as you? If you could only cut yourself off from the Buddhist connection I would see that you had a beautiful home with lands and abundant goods to spare. How does this strike you?"

The priest replied, "I thank you very much for your kind thought for me, but I have made a vow with my soul and can never go back on it."

Thinking this strange, Hwang inquired, "What vow, I pray, and for what reason?"

But the priest only laughed and made no reply.

Hwang was determined, however, to know what it meant and asked again and again.

The priest's answer was, "What reason for Your Excellency to know?"

Hwang then followed this with other questions but the priest gave no answer.

Then Hwang ordered his attendants and other listeners out and went on to say: "You have some secret on your soul, and you know we keep nothing back from each other – let me know."

Unable to withhold the truth further, the priest replied, "Before I knew you I was an irreligious young man and one day as I passed along the road I saw a very pretty girl quite by herself digging greens among the grave mounds. Seeing no one near, I went up to her and made evil proposals, but she withdrew, resented what I said and apparently was determined to resist me with all her strength of body and soul. Unable to persuade her, I used force, tied her hands and feet, and having done her every dishonour, I unfastened her and hurried away to an inn where I slept the night.

"In the morning I overheard people talking together and learned that a young woman of known integrity had committed suicide. A word was added, 'Some rascal or other must have done her dishonour to cause her to take her own life.'

"I was terribly frightened on hearing this; pity also for the poor girl took possession of me. Not being sure that the rumour was true I stealthily made my way back to the neighbourhood to find that it was really so. I went in to view her body and there on her hands and feet were the marks of where I had bound her.

"The people said, 'Someone must evidently have violated her when she was thus made fast. We shall let the magistrate know, and have the scoundrel sought out and punished.'

"On hearing this, my hair stood on end and in the altar of my soul I said, *'Why did I ever do such a thing? My not resisting this guilty passion has brought an innocent woman to so dreadful an end. There is no pardon for such as I in heaven above or on earth beneath. God will assuredly smite me.'* I thought of this and thought of it till I was almost mad and wondered if there was any atonement for such a sin as mine.

"I finally decided that only hardships of the world could make amends, that they must be my portion hereafter, and not an atom of joy was ever again to enter my life. In this decision I became a priest of the Buddha. I donned the black coat as a mark of the oath I had sworn. It is therefore impossible for me to accept of your kindness and break with my soul's decision. Never again can I go back to earth. This happened long ago and only because you insisted on knowing do I tell it today."

Hwang had seen before in the list of crimes of his province that there was one not yet requited from long years ago. The time agreed, the day, the month, the year just as he had been told.

On seeing this, the Governor said, "Though you and I are the best of friends, and love each other dearly, the law must take its course," and so he handed him over to the judges. The priest was condemned and died, and after his death the Governor gave him a great and honourable funeral.

*　*　*　*　*

From *Old Corea*

A Question of Conscience

The question is sometimes raised as to how far conscience rules in East Asia. To be found out in a wrong, we know, is a dreadful misfortune; or to be exhibited to the public with loss of "face" is often more feared than death itself; but the inner heart, which no eye sees, how far is its condemnation to be reckoned with? Can it readily influence the understanding and the soul?

Two hundred years ago there lived in Corea a well-known man by the name of Hwang In'gŏm. He graduated from the Confucian College IN THE YEAR THAT GEORGE THE FIRST CAME TO THE THRONE OF ENGLAND — 1714 — and rose to be an officer of the first rank. While preparing for the rigid examination of that day, he spent much of his time in a Buddhist monastery. The quiet of the surroundings, pine trees and rippling streams were conducive to study, and the priesthood were always more than ready to run his errands and do his service.

Among those he met was a young man of more than ordinary ability, a sincere disciple of the Buddha who took great delight in waiting on him and attending his every wish. Hwang made him part and parcel of his service, and kept him as his special help till he rose to a place of great influence, when suddenly the priest disappeared.

Some years later he was appointed Governor of Kyǒngsang Province, and one day, while making his round of the different districts, he suddenly caught a glimpse past his chair-flap of someone standing by the side of the way who reminded him of his former friend. He sent a servant to inquire and lo, it was the man.

Overjoyed, Hwang took him back into his employ, had a horse provided for him and had him accompany him wherever he went. On return to his official quarters in Taegu, he had a room set apart for him next to the library and saw to his needs with the greatest care.

One day he called the priest and said, "There is an old saying that runs, 'Every spoon of rice merits its return of favour.' How many spoons have I received from you? I have silks and stores in great abundance, and yet if I gave you half of all I possess, I would still fail to express my heart. Unfortunately, you are a priest who dresses in coarse cloth and eats poor vegetarian fare. What is silk or gold to such as you? If you could only cut yourself off from the Buddhist connection I would see that you had a beautiful home with lands and abundant goods to spare. How does this strike you?"

The priest replied, "I thank you very much for your kind thought, but I have made a vow with my soul and can never go back on it."

Thinking this strange, Hwang inquired, "What vow, I pray, and for what reason?" But the priest only laughed and made no reply.

Hwang was determined, however, to know and asked again and again.

The priest's answer was, "What reason for Your Excellency to know?"

Hwang then followed this with other questions but the priest gave no answer. Then Hwang ordered his attendants and other listeners out and went on to say, "You have some secret hidden from me, and you know we keep nothing back from each other – let me know."

Unable to refuse further, the priest replied, "Before I knew you, I was an irreligious young man who had no thought of the Buddha, or the Law, and sought my own will only. One day as I passed along the road

I saw a very pretty girl quite by herself digging greens among the grave mounds. No one being near, I went up to her and made evil proposals, but she drew back, resented what I said, and seemed determined to resist me at all costs. Unable to persuade her, I used force, tied her hands and feet, and having done her every dishonour, I unfastened her and hurried away to the inn where I slept the night.

"In the morning I overheard people talking together and learned that a young woman of known integrity had committed suicide. A word was added, 'Some rascal must have wrought her ruin to cause her to take her life.'

"I was terribly frightened on hearing this. Pity also for the poor girl took possession of my soul. Wishing to know whether the awful rumour was based on fact or not I made my way to the neighbourhood to find that it was really so. I went in to view her body and there on her hands and feet were the marks of where I had bound her. The people said, 'Someone must evidently have violated her when she was thus made fast. We shall let the magistrate know and have the scoundrel sought out and punished.'

"On hearing this, my hair stood on end and in the altar of my soul I said, 'Why did I ever do such a thing?' My guilty passion has brought this innocent girl to a dreadful death. There is surely no pardon for such a sinner as I in heaven above or earth beneath. God will assuredly smite me. I thought of it, and thought of it till I was almost mad, and wondered if there was any atonement for such a sin as mine. I finally decided that only the hardships of the world could make amends, and that they must be my portion hereafter, with not an atom of joy entering my life. In this decision I became a priest of the Buddha and donned the coarse black coat as a mark of the oath I had sworn. It is, therefore, impossible for me to accept of your kindness and break with my soul's decision. Never again can I go back to earth. This happened long ago and only because you insisted on knowing do I tell it today."

Hwang had seen before in the list of crimes of his province that there was one not yet requited from long years ago. The time agreed, the day, the month, the year, just as he had been told.

On seeing this, the Governor said, "Though you and I are the best of friends, and love each other dearly, the law must take its course," and so he handed him over to the judges. The priest was condemned and died, and after his death the Governor gave him a great and honourable funeral.

황판서인검　　소시독서산사　유일승진성사역
黃判書仁儉 1)　少時讀書山寺　有一僧盡誠使役

량자여결　즉거매간간자당　유무상자　종시불
糧資如缺　則渠每間間自當　有無相資　終始不

태　황파감기성이애기인　급현달　기승절적
怠　黃頗感其誠而愛其人　及顯達　其僧絶迹

황매념지　이불득견　심상한탄　기위령백
黃每念之　而不得見　心常恨嘆　其爲嶺伯 2)

출순지로　유일승피좌로방　황자교중　별안견지
出巡之路　有一僧避坐路傍　黃自轎中　瞥眼見之

사시궐승　내명예초사근전　즉과시차승　불승흔
似是厥僧　乃命隷招使近前　則果是此僧　不勝欣

행　잉명일기　재이수후　야매동침　무애여자질
幸　仍命一騎　載而隨後　夜每同寢　撫愛如子侄

급환영　치지책실　공궤심풍결　일일　초이위왈
及還營　置之冊室　供饋甚豊潔　一日　招而謂曰：

고인유일반지덕필보　오어여　해단일반이이재　오
古人有一飯之德必報　吾於汝　奚但一飯而已哉　吾

즉전백유족　수할반이여지　무소불가　이여이산승
則錢帛裕足　雖割半而與之　無所不可　而汝以山僧

의갈식초　전백수다　장안용재　여약장발이퇴속
衣葛食草　錢帛雖多　將安用哉　汝若長髮而退俗 3)

즉비단가산지요족　오당위여도발신지계　의
則非但家産之饒足　吾當爲汝圖拔身之計 4) 矣

여의여하　승왈　사도위소승지의　비불감사
汝意如何　僧曰：使道爲小僧之意　非不感謝

이소승유구구미집　욕이차종　무의어출세야
而小僧有區區迷執 5)　欲以此終　無意於出世也

黃怪而問之 則僧笑而不答 黃再三强問 終始牢諱 6)

黃又詰之 則僧終不言 黃辟左右 促膝而問曰:

汝之所執 必有所以 而吾於汝之間 有何諱

秘之事 7) 從實言之可也 僧始乃勉强而言曰:

小僧不知使道之前卽俗人也 某年偶經山谷中

有一新塚 前有一素服女子採蔬 8) 而貌頗姸美

四顧無人故 逼 9) 而欲犯 則抵死不從故 乃以衣

帶 縛其四肢而强奸之 仍解其縛 而行數十里

宿於店幕 翌朝 聞傳說 則以爲某處守墓之節婦

昨夜自決 不知何許過人 必也强淫而致死云云故

心甚驚動 10) 而哀憐 猶慮傳聞之未詳 委往 11) 其

近處而探之 則果是的報 12) 而其手足縛痕宛然

人皆曰: 必也縛其手足而强淫 至於此境云云

卽報于地方官 使之跟捕兇身 13) 云矣 一聞此說

毛髮悚然　悔之哀之　仍以自量　則吾不忍　一時之

欲　致使節婦至於此　卽天地間難容之罪也　神明

必降之以殃矣　左右思量　欲得贖罪之方而不可得

又自念以爲吾旣負此大罪　當喫盡天下之風霜　小

無生世之樂然後　庶可贖罪　仍削髮爲僧　以不脫緇

衣 14)　矢于心矣　今何以使道之厚恩　變幻 15)　初意乎

以是之故　不欲還俗矣　事已久遠　下問又切故

不得已吐實 16)　矣　日前巡使適見道內殺獄文案 17)

則有此獄事　而殆近數十年　兇身尙未得捕者也

年月日無一差爽 18)　乃嘆曰：吾與汝　雖親切之間

公法不可廢也　仍命隷拿下抵之法 19)　厚給葬需云矣

1 黃仁儉 [1711–65; styled Kyŏngdŏk 景德; ancestral seat Ch'angwŏn 昌原; posthumous epithet Chŏnghyo 貞孝]: scholar-official under King Yŏngjo [r. 1724–76; 1694–1776]. In 1760, he was appointed Governor of Kyŏngsang Province. His father was Hwang Chae 黃梓 [1689–?].

2 嶺伯: Governor of Kyŏngsang Province.

3 退俗 = *hwansok* 還俗: (for a monk) resume secular life.

4 拔身之計: a strategy for passing the civil service examination in order to enter government service.

 5 迷執: be a stickler about something.
 6 牢諱: hide facts or be evasive.
 7 諱秘之事: a clandestine affair = "a dirty little secret."
 8 採蔬: gather edible wild plants.
 9 逼 = *p'ippak* 逼迫: browbeat, pester.
10 驚動: be startled and shaken.
11 委往: sneak over to.
12 的報: accurate report.
13 兇身 = *sinbyŏng* 身柄: culprit, guilty party.
14 緇衣 = *sŭngbok* 僧服: a monk's robe.
15 變幻: fluctuate; change unpredictably.
16 吐實: "fess up."
17 殺獄文案: an interrogation report concerning a murder case.
18 差爽: discrepancy.
19 抵之[以]法: administer according to the applicable laws.

——— **100** ———

The Impudent Priest

Vol. III: 63; n.d.; Diary XIV, pp. 140–2; 314.

There was a man of Sangju called Ko Yu. He was a strong, honest, straightforward, and clean-hearted man who had passed his literary examination. He had been magistrate of several different circuits. Wherever he went, he put an end to all sorts of wrongdoings in the past of the secretaries. He was like a spirit in his looking into the deeds and actions of another – like Zhao Guanghan of the Kingdom of Han. Wherever he went he made his term of office resound with praise, so true and faithful he was. While he was appointed to Ch'angnyŏng, Kyŏngsang Province, he cleared away many doubtful cases that had been left undecided.

At this time there was a famous priest named Nam P'ung who was somewhat educated and really very bright. He had many friends among the high officials of Seoul. He was head of the Memorial House of the Faithful, and so presumed on his lawful power to unlawful things. Wherever he went, he imposed upon the magistrate and his underlings. Even the provincial governors had to treat him as an equal. If this was not wholly granted, the official would soon find himself out of favour and dismissed. Hence it came that appointments and dismissals in the province were made at the bidding of this priest. In each county he carried on his nefarious work, as well as in each temple. Everyone hated him, priest and lay alike, and yet they were powerless in his hands.

Now Nam P'ung had an occasion to pass by Ch'angnyŏng County. On the occasion of going in to see the magistrate, he ordered the servants to open the central gate. He went straight in and made no obeisance. Ko Yu had already planned with his runners that if he came in he would arrest the offender, and now as he entered he had him under arrest at once. He hurled insults at the magistrate and roared his protestations in a great volume, so the magistrate Ko had him killed then and there. Some days later there came letters from Seoul, a host of them, all asking that special treatment be given to Nam P'ung.

At that time, Cho Ŏm happened to be governor of the province and had issued an order that no drink of any kind be allowed. Ko Yu of Ch'angnyŏng did not transmit the order and it came to a question of punishment of Ko's deputies. Ko went in to see the governor, but before presenting himself he bought drink, and got very drunk, and then went in to see the governor, and said, "I have drink in my own county, but it is such poor stuff. Now coming in here to the governor's centre, I find drink in every house – number one drink. I have not the capacity to drink all I should."

Knowing this, the governor gave a grin but gave no further reply.

Ko Yu was made magistrate of many other counties, but he did not catch the smallest fraction of squeeze, coming back just as poor as he went.

There was a secretary in Sangju whom he took about with him as his steward. Whatever was left over of official supplies he gave to his steward, and by this means the steward lived.

After Ko Yu's death, his children were so poor that they could not live, while the steward now was eighty years and over. He called his sons and grandsons one day to him and said, "The reason we are so rich and well provided for is due to the kindness of Ko Yu. While I was in Magistrate Ko's employ, I often wished to make him gifts, but in view of his strict honour and with the fear that he might not accept it, I refrained. So it has passed until today. I learned that his family now is in great poverty. Shall we simply hold to our own peace and let it go? If a man forgets to be grateful for past favours, God will punish him with troubles. From the time that I accompanied His Excellency, I bought certain rice fields and certain monies I have in the top storey. I want to give return. Go tomorrow and bring Ko's grandson to me."

The sons and grandsons bowed and said that they would do so.

They went and returned to say that there was some reason that prevented his coming. It happened that Ko's grandson had come that day to the official centre and so called on the old steward for a moment. The steward's sons and grandsons, seeing him coming, however, had him sent off so that he could not get in.

Ko's grandson was very angry at this, when suddenly he met a friend and told him of the treatment he'd received. The friend came and told the old man. On learning this, the old man gave a great start, called his sons and grandsons, had them paddled, and at once rented a chair and started for Ko's place, where he bowed in front of Ko's gate.

In great alarm, Ko came out to see the old man whereupon the old man said, "I want you to come with me at once."

He went and here the old man treated him with wine and snacks, saying, "All I have and all I am is due to the kindness of your grandfather. I have thought of you often and have something special set aside for your benefit. Please accept of it, I pray you – do not refuse."

He gave him the deeds for the rice field, two hundred bags a year and one thousand *yang* of money. Then he sent him to his house and Ko became a rich man.

A man of Sangju told me this and so I wrote it.

高裕 1) 尙州 2) 人也　爲人剛直廉潔　以文科　累典 3)

州郡　而官人不敢干囑 4)　其發奸擿伏 5) 之

神如漢之趙廣漢 6)　到處以得治著名

其爲昌寧 7) 也　前後疑獄 8) 之裁決事　多神異

有僧南朋 9)　薄有文華才藝者　交結洛下權貴 10)

以表忠祠 11) 院長　怙勢行惡 12)　所到之處　守宰奔

趨 13) 下風 [風下]14)　雖以道伯之體重　亦與之

抗禮 15)　小有違咈 16)　則守宰每每罪罷　道內黜陟 17)

皆出於此僧之手　貽弊各邑　行惡寺刹　無僧俗

舉皆側目 18)　而莫敢誰何　南朋適有事　過昌寧

使開正門而入　見本倅而不爲禮　高裕豫使官隸約定

使之捉下　則其凌辱之說　恐喝之言　不一 19) 而足 20)

遂卽地打殺　居數日　京中書札之來　不可勝記 21)

皆以南朋爲托矣　趙尙書曮 22) 之爲嶺伯 23) 也

道內設酒禁　以昌寧之不禁　至有首吏鄉 [鄉

吏]24) 推治 25) 之境　高裕一日至營下　使下隸

買酒以來　大醉而入見巡使曰：昌寧一境　雖有酒

而薄不敢飲矣　今來營下　則無家不釀　可謂大酒

下官無量而飲云云　巡使知其意　微笑而不答云矣

歷州縣　一毫不取歸　則食貧如初　尙州吏屬一人

每以傔從相隨　廩俸 26) 或有餘　則必擧而給之

其人以此饒居　高裕之沒後　其孫貧不能聊生

其時其傔人　年已八十餘　一日　謂其子與孫曰：

吾家之致此富饒者　皆高官司 27) 之德也　吾非不知

官司在世時　以錢穀納之　而恐累淸德　設或納之

必無許受之理故　忍而至今矣　聞其宅形勢　莫不

成說　於吾輩之心安乎　人而背恩忘德　天必殃之

吾自初留意　而買處 [置] 某處畓　又樓上所儲錢矣

將以此納　汝於明日　須往邀其宅孫子書房以來

其子與孫拜應曰：諾　及其日　來言曰：有故不得來

云矣　此時高之孫　適入城內　歷路暫訪其家　則其

人之子與孫　自外揮逐　使不得接迹　高生大怒而去

適逢邑底親知人　言其痛駭之狀 28) 其人來問于老者

老者大驚　招子與孫　以杖敺之　使貰乘轎　騎而卽

往其家　待罪門外　高生驚訝而出見　老者强請同行

至其家　接以酒肴　乃言曰：小人之衣食　無非先令

監之德也　小人爲貴宅　而留意經紀 29) 者　兹以奉獻

幸勿辭焉　仍出畓券之每年收二百石 30) 者　及錢千

兩手標而送之　高生之家　仍以致富云　尙州之人

來傳此事始末故　兹錄之

1 高裕 [1722–79; styled Sunji 順之; sobriquet Ch'udam 秋潭; ancestral seat Kaesŏng 開城]: scholar-official under King Chŏngjo [r. 1776–1800; 1752–1800]. He served as magistrate of Ch'angnyŏng 昌寧, and was a fifth-generation descendant of Ko In'gye 高仁繼 [1564–1647] and son of Ko Kyusŏ 高奎瑞 [dates unknown].

2 尙州: a town in North Kyŏngsang Province.

3 典: be in charge of, govern.

4 干囑 = *ch'ŏngch'ok* 請囑 ~ *ch'ŏngt'ak* 請託: ask a favour of; beseech; solicit.

5 發奸摘伏 = *palgan chŏkpok* 發奸摘伏: lit. "reveal the cunning, point out the hidden" = bring to light hidden affairs and uncover unjust deeds.

6 趙廣漢: courtier (styled Zidu 子都) under Emperor Xuandi of the Former Han Dynasty 前漢 (202 BC–AD 8). When he served as chief magistrate of the Capital (京兆尹 Jing Zhao Yin), he was renowned for his uncanny ability to "reveal the cunning, point out the hidden."

7 昌寧: a town in South Kyŏngsang Province.

8 疑獄: lit. "suspicious criminal case" = large-scale criminal case, usually involving bribery.

9 南朋: unidentifiable. In the Koryŏ University edition of *Kyesŏ Yi Hŭip'yŏng's Miscellany* (*Kyesŏ chamnok* 溪西雜錄; prefaced in 1828), the same story has as its protagonist a Nam Myŏng 南明.

10 權貴 = *kwŏnsega* 權勢家: powerful, influential family.
11 表忠祠: shrine commemorating the loyalty of Buddhist Masters Sŏsan 西山
   大師 [1520–1604] and Songun 松雲大師 [1544–1610], located in Miryang
   密陽 in South Kyŏngsang Province.
12 怙勢行惡: lit. "relying on the strength of others do evil deeds."
13 奔趨: flee, speed away.
14 風下: customs become corrupted.
15 抗禮: impartial treatment.
16 違咈: run counter to, deviate from.
17 黜陟: lit. "[of government employment] cast away (the evil) and promote
   (the good)."
18 側目: lit. "side eye" = look askance at out of fear.
19 不一: lit. "not one" = many.
20 足: suffice.
21 不可勝記: lit. "unable to manage to record all" = too much to record.
22 趙曔 [1719–77; styled Myŏngsŏ 明瑞; sobriquet Yŏngho 永湖; ancestral seat
   P'ungyang 豊壤; posthumous epithet Munik 文翼]: scholar-official under
   King Yŏngjo 英祖 [r. 1724–76; 1694–1776]. He was appointed governor of
   Kyŏngsang Province in 1758 (Yŏngjo 34). His father was Cho Sanggyŏng
   趙尚絅 [1681–1746].
23 嶺伯: governor of Kyŏngsang Province.
24 首鄉吏 = *chwasu* 座首: overseer (*hyangni*) at the local yamen.
25 推治: arrest and punish.
26 廩俸: = *nŭmnyo* 廩料 ~ *kwanhwang* 官況: stipend of an official in a local
   government office.
27 官司 = *kwana* 官衙: local yamen or its head.
28 痛駭之狀: lit. "deplorable and scandalous situation."
29 經紀 = *kyŏngyŏng* 經營: manage and administer.

———— 101 ————

The Magistrate of Andong,
Whose Friend Wanted to Be Inspector

Vol. III: 64; n.d.; Diary XIV, pp. 142–3, then Diary XV, p. 7 (crossed out); 315.

There was a minister once upon a time who had a friend that had studied with him. He was a specially good student, gifted with great ability.

Not withstanding this, he had failed at his examinations so that his family was reduced to great poverty. So poor was he that he could not care even for his own kith and kin. Later his friend the ex-minister was to be sent as magistrate to Andong, a sort of exile for an offender.*

This scholar friend came to him quietly and said, "Your Excellency is going as magistrate to Andong; I would like to ask your kind favour to requite myself in □ goods. If you will kindly do this, I see a way by which I can live comfortably all the rest of my life."

The minister answered, "If I go to Andong I can see you fitted out with a new suit of clothes and something to eat – what has that to do with all your future life? Foolish thought!"

The friend said, "I am not asking from Your Excellency money and goods, but merely that you make me *tosŏwŏn* – inspector of the literati schools."†

The minister replied, "Andong is the centre of the *ajŏn* class and they have already appropriated all such offices. The Inspector's office is the fattest field they have – how could I ever give this to a Seoul *yangban*? This could never be done."

The friend made answer: "I am not asking Your Excellency to get it for me by force. I shall go ahead and shall enroll myself among the *ajŏn* of the county. After my name is once enrolled in the book of the *ajŏn*, what difference will there be?"

The minister said, "Even though you go first, how could you get your name recorded in the *ajŏn*'s book?"

The man answered, "After Your Excellency has entered office, when the people come in with lawsuits, I would like you to call out your decisions in learned language which the others cannot write out. On proof of this, let them be dismissed from office. Not only so, but the head *ajŏn* must also be called and reprimanded. Do that every time a lawsuit comes before you. By this way I can attain to the office of Inspector of the Schools.†

"Also: all communications that come in and pass my hand, I want you to praise my writing specially. Let this method be carried on for a time and then announce that you will examine candidates for chief *ajŏn* and that it be open to all applicants – let such an order go forth. I can then be appointed to the office of Inspector. If you do so, I will take notes on outside matters as well and let you know what I hear. I shall have your name and fame sounded abroad and your wisdom will be made most manifest."

The minister said, "Very well, try it and see how it works."

So he went first to Andong and said he was an *ajŏn* who had got into difficulties in another county and had made his escape here. He went to an inn and ate there and then went to the *ajŏn*'s offices. He worked for them, did their accounts, and they all saw how bright and efficient he was, as well in the character as in reckoning. The *ajŏn* all treated him with marked distinction. They had him eat with the *ajŏn* who had charge of supplies.

He was appointed to office. Seeing how skilfull and well equipped he was in writing, reckoning, and the like, all the *ajŏn* treated him with special favour and had him sleep at the *ajŏn*'s office. There they discussed various documents.

When the new magistrate came and took up office, he found the court full of petitions and lawsuits awaiting him. He had his decisions called out and ordered to be written, but the *ajŏn* failed to keep up with him. Then in anger he had them arrested and had them furiously beaten. In a single day, a host were punished in this fashion. Orders to the military quarters and directions to the people, he ordered back for rewriting and had the writers beaten along with the chief *ajŏn*. It was as though the *ajŏn* had fallen on a state of war. They did not dare approach this fearsome magistrate.

However, whenever the writing of the new *ajŏn* came before the magistrate, he accepted of it quietly. The group of *ajŏn* gathered around him as the one source of safety.

On a certain day, the magistrate said to the chief *ajŏn*, "I heard when I was in Seoul that in Andong there were many famous scholars but now that I have come and seen with my own eyes, I can only say that I am most disappointed. Not a single one do I find who will in any way pass muster. Will you from your office call together the best scholars and writers and have a trial of skill till we see?"

The chief *ajŏn* on this order came forth and a subject was given for them to write on.

The magistrate looked over the results and the stranger came forth first of all. He then asked, "Who is this *ajŏn*?"

The chief replied, "He is not an *ajŏn* of this county but one who has lost his place in another county and came here and came to stay with me."

The magistrate said, "He is best of all, both in his □ and also his wording. I hear he is an *ajŏn* from another county and therefore there is no reason why he should not be here. Appoint him here and let him be the chief *ajŏn* of questions of law."

The chief *ajŏn* did as he was ordered and so from this day on, this *ajŏn* did the work of laying questions before the magistrate.

From the time that he was directly appointed to office there were no more reprimands and no more punishments. From the chief down all drew a long breath and said how all goes well. All went well. The magistrate made this man also the chief collector of taxes and this he carried out; all went well with no complaints.

The *ajŏn* took a dancing girl and made her his concubine, bought a house and there lived. Whenever he went in to the magistrate with documents in hand, he also brought notes of all he heard outside and left this underneath the mats. The magistrate read these by himself. Because of this, the secrets of the people and the tricks of the *ajŏn* were all made known as by the spirits. All looked upon him in fear.

The next year he was again made chief of the tax collections. He grew rich by reason of the share he fell heir to. This he sent by exchange notes to Seoul. While the magistrate remained in Andong he suddenly disappeared and was gone. All in the *ajŏn*'s office were filled with fear and consternation.

The chief came in and told how this special *ajŏn* was gone.

The magistrate said, "Did he take his concubine or not?"

"No – he left his house and his concubine, and is gone."

The magistrate said, "Has he any debts to pay?"

The answer was, "No."

Then said the magistrate: "It is a strange affair. I expect he is a wandering spirit – let him go."

He came back home, bought house and fields, and lived in affluence. Later he passed his exams and was magistrate of several counties.

---

* Gale has mistaken "適出" (*chŏkch'ul*) to mean "be exiled off [to Andong]." The correct meaning is "happen to go off [to Andong]."

† Gale errs in translating 都書員 (*tosŏwŏn*) as "inspector of the literati schools." The correct meaning is "petty clerk (*hyangni*) in charge of tax and accounting at the local yamen." See note 5 below.

古有一宰相　有同硯之人 1)　文華贍敏 2)　而屢屈

科場 3)　家計貧寒　窮不能自存　宰相適出補安東倅

其友來見　乘閑而言曰：令監今爲安東倅　今則吾

可以得聊賴之資 4)　非但聊賴　可以足過平生矣

宰相曰：吾之作宰　助君衣食之資可也　何以足過平

生乎　此則妄想也　其人曰：非爲令監之多助給

錢財也　安東都書員 5)　所食夥多　以此給我則好矣

宰相曰：安東鄉吏之邑也　都書員　吏役之優窠 6)

豈有許給於京中儒生耶　此則雖官威　恐無以得

成矣　其人曰：非爲令監之奪而給之也　吾先

下去　當付吏案 7)　既付吏案之後　有何不可之理耶

宰相曰：吾[君]雖下去　吏案其可容易付之耶

其人曰：令監到任後　民訴題辭 8)　順口呼 9) 之

刑吏 10)　如不得書之　則罪之汰 11) 之　又以此等刑吏

之隨廳 12)　治首吏 13)　每每如是　則自有可爲之道

凡干文字上　如出於吾手　則必稱善　如是過幾日

出令以刑吏試取 14)　無論時任及閑散 15)　文筆可

堪者　幷許赴而試之　則吾可自然居首 16)　而得爲

刑吏矣　爲刑吏之後　都書員一窠　分付則好矣

若然則外間事　吾當隨聞隨錄以進矣　令監可

得神異之名矣　宰相曰：若然則第爲之也　其人

先期 17)　下去　稱隣邑之逋吏 18)　寄食旅舍　往來

吏廳 19)　或代書役　或代看檢文書　人旣詳明 20)

文筭又優如　諸吏皆待之　使之寄食於吏廳庫直 21)

而宿於吏廳　諸般文字　與之相議　新官到任後

盈庭民訴　口呼題辭　刑吏未及受書　則必捉下猛棍

一日之間受罪者　不知其數　至如報狀 22) 及傳令

必執頉 23) 而嚴治　又拿入首吏　以刑吏之不擇

每日治之　以是之故　吏廳如逢亂離　刑吏無敢

近前　文狀去來　此人之筆迹　如入則必也無事

以是之故　一廳諸吏　唯恐此人之去也　一日

分付首吏曰：吾於在洛時　聞本邑素稱文鄉 24)

以今所見　可謂寒心　刑吏無一人可合者

自汝廳　會時任吏　及邑底人之有文筆者　試才以入

首吏承命而出　題試之　以諸吏文筆入覽　則此

人居然 25) 爲魁矣　仍問曰：此是何許吏　對曰：

此非本邑之吏　卽隣邑退吏　來寓於小人之廳者也

乃曰：此人之文筆最勝　聞是隣邑吏役之人也

則無妨於吏役　其付吏案而差刑吏也　首吏依其

言爲之　自是日此吏獨自擧行　自其吏之爲刑房

一未有致責治罪之擧　自首吏以下　始乃放心

廳中無事　及到差任之時 26)　特兼都書員而擧行

無一人敢有是非者　其人畜一妓而爲妾　買家而居

每於文牒擧行之際　必錄外間所聞　置之方席而出

본쉬암지견지　이시지고　민은　리간　촉지여신
本倅暗持見之　以是之故　民隱27)　吏奸28)　燭之如神29)

민리개습복　명년우사겸대도서원　량년소득
民吏皆慴伏30)　明年又使兼帶都書員　兩年所得

태지만여금　암암환송경제　본쉬과체　지전
殆至萬餘金　暗暗換送京第　本倅瓜遞31)之前

일일야　잉기가도주　리청거개황황　수리입고
一日夜　仍棄家逃走　吏廳擧皆惶惶　首吏入告

즉왈　여기첩해도호　대왈　기가기첩　단신도주의
則曰：與其妾偕逃乎　對曰：棄家棄妾　單身逃走矣

왈　혹유소포　호　왈　무의　왈　연즉역시괴사
曰：或有所逋32)乎　曰：無矣　曰：然則亦是怪事

자시부운종적　임지가야운의　기인환가　매택매토
自是浮雲蹤跡　任之可也云矣　其人還家　買宅買土

가요　기후등과　루전주군운의
家饒　其後登科　累典州郡云矣

1 同硯之人: lit. "person [with whom one shares] the same inkstone" = a fellow student.

2 文華贍敏: lit. "literary efflorescence flourishes and is clever."

3 屢屈科場: lit. "fail numerous times at the civil service examinations."

4 聊賴之資: a means upon which to rely.

5 都書員: top position in the yamen, responsible for collecting local taxes.

6 優窠: premier position.

7 吏案: roster of petty officials and clerks (*ajŏn* 衙前).

8 題辭: local magistrate's verdicts in civil cases.

9 順口號: call out in order.

10 刑吏: petty officials (*ajŏn* 衙前) belonging to the Chamber of Punishments (*hyŏngbang* 刑房) in a local administration.

11 汰 = 淘汰: dismiss, lay off.

12 隨廳: select an underling to serve in the yamen.

13 首吏: head *ajŏn*.

14 試取: choose someone by competitive examination.

15 閑散: lit. "idle and slack" = retired officials or such an official's carefree life.

16 居首: occupy first place.

17 先期: go ahead of, go in advance of.

18 逋吏: clerks and petty officials who have embezzled public property or evaded taxes.

19 吏廳 = *ich'ŏng*: office where local clerks and petty officials go about their business.

20 詳明: attentive and smart.

21 庫直 = *kojigi* (vernacular Korean word inscribed in Chinese characters): keeper of the storehouses attached to the yamen.

22 報狀: official report submitted to one's superior.

23 頉: problem, hitch.

24 文鄕: village famous for having produced numerous literary figures.

25 居然: calmly, still, unperturbedly.

26 差任之時: at the time of one's official appointment.

27 民隱: secrets harboured by the commoners.

28 吏奸: wickedness of local clerks and petty officials (*ri* 吏 = *ajŏn* 衙前).

29 燭之如神: see through, have penetrating knowledge like that of a spirit.

30 慴伏: be cowed.

31 瓜遞: rotation to another post upon completing a term of office.

32 所逋: damage or loss to government property.

──────── **102** ────────

The Fortune-Teller's True Prophecy

Vol. IV: 1; translated 13 June 1921; Diary XVI, pp. 179–80; 321.

Pak Isŏ (Pich'ŏn; `graduated 1558`) was the son of Pak P'yo.* He was liberal, kind and good, and specially beloved by his friends and an intimate of my own (Yi Tŏkhyŏng, graduated 1590).

In the winter of 1619 I returned home from the office of the governor of Hwanghae Province. The next day Pak came to see me and we had a long talk. A blind fortune-teller, Chi Ŏkch'ŏn, came at the same time and Pak said, "This blind fortune-teller is greatly skilled at his work and I have long wished to meet him."

Pak then wrote out his *saju* (birth year, month, day, and hour) and gave it to me, so that the blind man might not know. He asked me to inquire of the fortune-teller. I asked and Chi the blind man answered, "The year *sinyu* (1621) will be a fated year."

556 The Fortune-Teller's True Prophecy

I was greatly disturbed by this.

Seeing this, Pak himself asked, "This is my *saju*. Am I to die in the year *sinyu*?"

Chi, who was old and looked like an ancient devil of some kind, answered quietly: "I look again and find that in the year *sinyu* a propitious star will arise and save you. I fear, however, that among your children one will die."

Pak asked no more but got up and went away. After he had gone I asked further myself.

His reply was: "In the year *sinyu* he will meet with an accident and die. No escape from it, I fear."

In the autumn of the year *kyŏngsin* (1620), he went as envoy to Peking and because of a war with the northern barbarians, the road by Liaodong was blocked. Nothing remained for him but to come by sea. In the fifth moon of the year 1621, he was wrecked and drowned. Chi's words came true.

In the year *kapcha* (1624), I went as envoy to Peking by sea. I offered a sacrifice on the seashore for Pak Isŏ. In the fourth moon of the year 1625, I finished my work and came by way of Dengzhou† to take ship.

When I came on board that night, Pak Isŏ came with a bag of wine to wish me well on the way. We talked for a long time most intimately together, just as though he had been alive. I awoke and felt so grateful and yet so sad. We went on our way some six or seven days but saw not a sign of rough weather and reached home.

Was this not due to the good wishes and prayers of Pak? Our love for each other when we lived still remained with me – alas!

---

* Gale writes Pak Yul instead of Pak P'yo. We speculate that he and his pundits misread 票 (*p'yo*) as 栗 (*yul*)

† Dengzhou: 登州, present-day Penglai 蓬萊 in Shandong Province 山東省.

泌川朴參判彛舒 [敍]1) 字錫吾　遯溪栗 2) 之子也

忠厚善良　篤於朋友　與爾 [余] 最親　己未 3) 冬

余以海伯 4) 遞來　翌日早朝　錫吾來見　坐語良久

盲人池億千 5) 又來　錫吾曰：此盲善卜　欲見久之

以小紙書給四柱曰：令須問之　余取問之　池盲曰：

來辛酉 6) 年大不吉　余甚無聊　錫吾察余辭色　親問

曰：此吾命也　辛酉當有死亡之患耶　池盲素老神

旋答曰：更思之　辛酉有吉星來救　故當有膝下之痛

錫吾更不問而起　余又問之　則辛酉必有橫死之厄

似難免矣　錫吾果於庚申 7) 秋赴京　以奴故 [胡]8)

陷遼路　經由水路出來　辛酉五月　溮海而沒

池盲之言驗矣　後甲子 9) 余以奏請使 10) 由水路赴京

祭錫吾於海邊　乙丑 11) 四月竣事　回到登州

登船之夜夢　錫吾以囊酒來餞　慇懃敍話　宛如平日

覺來不勝感愴　船行六日　少無風波之險　來泊我

國地方　豈非錫吾之靈黙佑而然耶　平日相厚之誼

無間幽明　嗚呼悲哉　「竹窓閑話 12)」 李德泂 13) 撰

1 朴彝敍 [1561–1621; styled Sŏgo 錫吾; sobriquet Pich'ŏn 泌川; ancestral seat
   Miryang 密陽; posthumous epithet Ch'unggan 忠簡]: scholar-official under
   Kwanghaegun 光海君 [r. 1608–23; 1575–1641]. His father was Pak Yul 朴栗
   [1520–69]. His original name was Munsŏ 文敍.
2 朴栗 [1520–69; styled Kwanjung 寬仲; sobriquet Tun'gye 遯溪; ancestral
   seat Miryang 密陽]. His father was Pak Tŏngno 朴德老 [dates unknown].
3 己未: the year 1619 (Kwanghae 11).
4 海伯 = Hwanghae *kamsa* 黃海監司 = Hwanghae-do *kwanch'alsa* 黃海道 觀
   察使: governor of Hwanghae Province.
5 池億千: unidentified.
6 辛酉: the year 1621 (Kwanghae 13).
7 庚申: the year 1620 (Kwanghae 12).
8 奴胡: barbarians, referring to the Later Jin Dynasty 後金 (founded in 1616).
9 甲子: the year 1624 (Injo 2).
10 奏請使: lit. "messenger of formal requests" = [Korean court] envoys on a mis-
    sion to China to convey requests or suggestions concerning grave matters.
11 乙丑: the year 1625 (Injo 3).
12 「竹窓閑話」: miscellany by Yi Tŏkhyŏng 李德泂 [1561–1613].
13 李德泂 [1566–1645; styled Wŏnbaek 遠伯; sobriquet Chukch'ŏn 竹泉;
    ancestral seat Hansan 韓山; posthumous epithet Ch'ungsuk 忠肅]: scholar-
    official under King Injo 仁祖 [r. 1623–49; 1595–1649]. His father was Yi O 李
    澳 [dates unknown].

———— 103 ————

A True Fortune-Teller

Vol. IV: 2; translated 13 June 1921; Diary XVI, p. 180; 324.

Yu Sŏngjŭng (graduated 1610), Governor of P'yŏngan Province,* died
and his dead spirit took possession of one of the Sukch'ŏn yamen slaves
so that he could tell fortunes. People showed him great respect and
trusted him.

In 1627, Governor Chŏng Munik, whose style was Wido, was appointed to go as envoy to Mukden and reached Sungnyŏnggwan. Here
he asked how his journey would fare – lucky or unlucky?

A chair was placed on an open verandah with a red cloth over it. The
yamen slave sat just before it. A little later the slave wrote on a piece of

paper a prayer calling for the spirit. The yamen slave sat just before it. From midair came a sound of accompanying voices. There was no appearance, but the red cloth danced up and down and settled as though sat upon.

A voice then spoke, asking, "Is your Excellency well?"

His speech and manner was just as when alive.

Chŏng said, "I am on my way now as an envoy among the savages. Tell me my luck on the way."

The reply was, "When you get about halfway there, you will be disturbed by a slight affair, but no danger will result. You will go and come without misfortune."

Chŏng again asked, "How are my parents, please? I have not seen them for many days."

The reply was, "I will send and find out."

After an interval long enough to eat half a meal, he said, "Your house is quite well – don't be anxious. However, in front of your guest room is a black bamboo that has broken off in the middle."

Chŏng again asked, "Will you remain long here?"

He replied, "I will go next year to a Chinaman's house in Zhejiang and transmigrate. I doubt if we shall meet again. May you go and come in peace."

The *ara – pik'yŏ sŏra*† sounds awoke again and then the slave took on the colour of a living man again.

When Chŏng reached Nangja Mountain, he got a fright on account of a Chinaman's affair with a Manchu, but he came back home safely. There he saw a large stalk of the black bamboo broken off, just as had been said.

---

* In the original, the protagonist is identified as a "governor." However, Gale's translation erroneously identifies him as "Governor of P'yŏngan Province" when in fact he was Governor of Kangwŏn Province in real life.

† Gale's transcription of a Korean expression for "Hey, there – stand aside!"

유 감 사　 성　 증　 사 후　 기 신 강 빙 어 숙 천　 관 노　 첩 유
兪監司（省）曾 ₁) 死後　其神降憑於肅川 ₂) 官奴　輒有

응　 인 개 경 이 신 지　 정 감 사 문 익　 자 위 도　 정 묘 강
應　人皆敬而信之　鄭監司文翼 ₃) 字衛道　丁卯講

화　　후　　이통신사　　장부심양　　도숙령관
和 4) 後　以通信使 5)　將赴瀋陽 6)　到肅寧館 7)

욕문행리　길흉　설의자어청상　이홍복부지　초관
欲問行李 8) 吉凶　設椅子於廳上　以紅袱覆之　招官

노립계하　아이관노행묵　색흑　공중유가벽지
奴立階下　俄而官奴行墨 [色黑]　空中有呵辟之

성　지관문이지　수불견기형　이의자홍보표
聲 9) 至官門而止）　雖不見其形　而椅子紅袱飄

기　현　유래거지상　잉왈　위도근래무양부
起　顯 10) 有來據之狀 11)　仍曰：衛道近來無恙否

서구　완여　생시　정왈　오봉사초입로중
敍舊 12) 宛如 13) 生時　鄭曰：吾奉使初入虜中 14)

미지길흉하여　답왈　행도중로　잠유경동지사
未知吉凶何如　答曰：行到中路　暫有驚動之事 15)

연불족려　당무사왕래의　정우문　오리친　가
然不足慮　當無事往來矣　鄭又問　吾離親 [家]

정일구　안부하여　답왈　오　즉　당팽탐　반향
庭日久　安否何如　答曰：吾（卽）當伻探 16)　半餉

내왈　대댁　평안　물이위려　군초당전오죽　최대
乃曰：大宅 17) 平安　勿以爲慮　君草堂前烏竹　最大

자중절　이승목보철운　정우문왈　군구재차호
者中折　（以繩木補綴云）　鄭又問曰：君久在此乎

답왈　오어명년당환생어중국절강　인가
答曰：吾於明年當還生於中國浙江 18) 人家

차후갱난상견　위도호거호거　우유가벽지성　관노
此後更難相見　衛道好去好去　又有呵辟之聲　官奴

시유인색　정지랑자산　인한인사경동　급준
始有人色　鄭至狼子山 19)　因漢人事驚動　及竣

^{사 환 가}　^{과 견 오 죽 대 자 중 절}　^{일 여 기 언}　^{이 재}　^국
事還家　果見烏竹大者中折　一如其言　異哉　「菊

^{당 배}　^배　^어
堂俳 [排] 語 20)」

1　兪省曾 [1576–1649; styled Chasu 子修; sobriquet Ugok 愚谷; ancestral seat
　　Kigye 杞溪]: scholar-official under King Injo 仁朝 [r. 1623–49; 1595–1649]
　　and Governor of Kangwŏn Province. His father was Yu Taeŭi 兪大儀 [dates
　　unknown].
2　肅川: a town in P'yŏngwŏn Prefecture in South P'yŏngan Province.
3　鄭文翼 [1571–1639; styled Wido 衛道; sobriquet Songjuktang 松竹堂; an-
　　cestral seat Ch'ogye 草溪]: scholar-official under King Injo 仁祖 [r. 1623–49;
　　1595–1649]. He was an official envoy to Shenyang 瀋陽 in 1631 (Injo 9).
　　After his return, he served as Governor of Ch'ungch'ŏng Province. His
　　father was Chŏng Ŭngt'ak 鄭應鐸 [dates unknown].
4　丁卯講和: peace treaty made between Qing and Chosŏn in 1627 (Injo 5;
　　the chŏngmyo year) after the first Manchu invasion (Chŏngmyo horan
　　丁卯胡亂).
5　通信使: goodwill missions to neighbouring states like Japan.
6　瀋陽 Shenyang: capital of Liaoning Province 遼寧省.
7　肅寧館: a guesthouse located in Sukch'ŏn 肅川 in present-day P'yŏngan
　　Province.
8　行李 = saja 使者 = sasin 使臣: envoy, but here used to mean "travel gear."
9　呵辟之聲 = kado chi sŏng 呵導之聲 ~ kalto chi sŏng 喝道之聲: sound
　　of slaves clearing the way for high-ranking officials of the Office of
　　the Censor-General (Saganwŏn 司諫院) and the Office of the Special
　　Counselors (Hongmungwan 弘文館) on their way to and from work.
10　顯: (deferential) ancestral tablet.
11　來據之狀: the appearance of taking one's place.
12　敍舊: catch up on past events.
13　宛如 = wanyŏn 宛然: vividly, distinctly.
14　虜中: in the land of barbarians.
15　驚動之事: alarming matter.
16　伻探: have a servant inquire into.
17　大宅: (honorific) your house.
18　浙江: Zhejiang Province.
19　狼子山: name of a mountain.
20　「菊堂排語」: a literary miscellany by Chŏng T'aeje 鄭泰齊 [1612–?]:
　　scholar-official under King Hyojong 孝宗 [r. 1649–59; 1619–59].

——— **104** ———

Trick Played on a Dancing Girl

Vol. IV: 4; translated 14 June 1921; Diary XVI, pp. 180–1; 330.

Kwŏn Kyŏngyu (styled Kunyo) and Yu Sunjŏng (styled Chiong) were both gifted in study when young. They went to the hills to study. There they found a young lad studying with a Buddhist priest.

The two asked him who he was: "You are a pretty boy; have you a sister?"

The lad replied, "I have a sister who was a dancing girl at Naju. Her name is Okpuhyang (Perfumed Jade Flesh). Her name was Tŏgo (Virtue Raven). She was greatly gifted, as well as beautiful – the most noted in all the county. She was chosen from among the county dancing girls to come to Seoul and is now at Kyobang, the music centre. Here, too, she is specially noted as a singer."

The two were greatly desirous of seeing this beauty and could not stifle their longings. They made a bargain: "Whichever of us two first graduates will have first privilege of calling Okpuhyang."

They asked also after the Naju home where she lived, the houses, the streams, the streets, the trees, the flowers, and made a careful mental note of it. Two or three years later they both graduated with honours. Yu became the lawmaker or judge of Hamgyŏng while Kwŏn became a Hallim scholar.* When the Hallim met to feast and make glad he saw at last Okpuhyang singing among the others. She was a matchless beauty.

Kwŏn had her called and asked her, "Do you know me?"

Hyang-i† said, "I don't."

Deceiving her, Kwŏn then said, "When you were a dancing girl in Naju, I was a young scholar and went by. The magistrate of Naju had you share the pillow with me. I went to your house and spent a day or two. Your mother was so-and-so; your older sister such-and-such, and your younger thus-and-such. There were such-and-such trees before your house, flowers, stones, etc."

All these descriptions were correct.

"When we parted, you said to me, 'If your humble servant ever goes to Seoul as a dancer and Your Excellency should gain the exam, let us meet there for a second acquaintance.' Have you forgotten?"

Hyang-*i* was mystified by this and after thinking for a moment said, "Your words are all true, every one of them. Your face, however, is not one that I have ever seen before, and yet this must have happened as you say. I have gone so many times to the east side to sleep and to the west side with Mr. Chang and Mr. Yi and who not, that I doubtless have forgotten."

She sighed to think of this lapse of memory. That night they shared together.

* Hallim 翰林 scholar: diarists (such as *ponggyo* 奉敎, *taegyo* 待敎, *kŏmyŏl* 檢閱) belonging to the Office of Royal Decrees (Yemungwan 藝文館).
† Hyang-*i* = short for Okpuhyang + -*i* (Korean diminutive suffix).

權景裕 1) 君饒　柳順汀 2) 智翁　少有才名　嘗隷習業

課於山寺　有少年亦學字於山僧　權與柳問之曰：

汝何人　觀汝貌妙 3)　亦有汝妹乎　對曰：有一妹

本羅州 4) 籍妓 5)　名玉膚香　少名德烏　才色甲於鄉

曩歲 6) 擢入京中教坊 7)　亦有聲藝　二人情不自抑

約曰：吾二人中　先及第者必取香　且問羅州鄉

家所在里巷　花木川石之類　心記之　二三年

二人俱捷科 8)　柳爲永平道 9) 評事 10)　權爲翰林 11)

翰林宴見香妓於歌妓中　果絕艷也

權曰：汝識我耶　香曰：未諳 12) 也　權卽誆之曰：

여 예 라 주 시　여 이 포 의　과 지　통 판　모 사 여 천 아 침
汝隸羅州時　余以布衣 13)　過之　通判 14)　某使汝薦我枕

여 귀 여 가　류 숙 수 일 내 거　여 모 모　여 형 제 모
余歸汝家　留宿數日乃去　汝母某　汝兄弟某

문 전 수 기　화 기 천 기 석 기　총 불 망 망
門前樹幾　花幾川幾石幾　摠不妄 [忘]

차 여 결 아 지 언 왈　첩 행 예 경 기　랑 역 부 첩 과
且汝訣我之言曰:　妾幸隸京妓　郎亦復捷科

즉 차 일 생 재 합 지 기 야　여 망 지 호　향 이 지 랑 구 왈
則此一生再合之期也　汝忘之乎　香異之良久曰:

한 림 소 교 성 여 시　이 면 목 여 낭 시 소 견 수 불 류　필
翰林所教誠如是　而面目與曩時所見雖不類　必

유 차 사 명 의　단 첩 동 가 서 가　장 랑 리 랑　간
有此事明矣　但妾東家西家 15)　張郎李郎 16)　間

서　망 지 의　인 허 희　불 지　시 야 소 성 약　약 성
胥 17)　忘之矣　因嘘唏 18)　不止　是夜素成約 [約成]

송　추　강 랭 화
「松 [秋] 江冷話」 19)

1 權景裕 [?–1498; styled Kunyo 君饒; sobriquet Ch'ihŏn 癡軒; ancestral seat Andong 安東]: scholar-official under Yŏnsan'gun 燕山君 [r. 1494–1506; 1476–1506]. His father was Kwŏn Chil 權輊 [dates unknown].
2 柳順汀 [1459–1512; styled Chiong 智翁; ancestral seat Chinju 晉州; posthumous epithet Munsŏng 文成]: scholar-official under King Chungjong 中宗 [r. 1506–44; 1488–1544]. His father was Yu Yang 柳壤 [dates unknown].
3 貌妙: beautiful appearance.
4 羅州: a town in South Chŏlla Province.
5 籍妓: a *kisaeng* registered in the government roster.
6 曩歲: last year.
7 教坊: the Bureau of Music, where *kisaeng* were trained in singing and dancing.
8 捷科: success in the civil service examinations.

 9 永平道: Hamgyŏng Province 咸鏡道.

10 評事: senior sixth-grade military post at the provincial level.

11 翰林: senior ninth-grade chronicler (*kŏmyŏl* 檢閱) attached to the Office of Royal Decrees (Yemungwan 藝文館).

12 未諳: cannot remember.

13 布衣: a scholar not yet appointed to a government office.

14 通判 = *p'angwan* 判官: junior fifth-grade position in a local magistracy.

15 東家西家: lit. "house in the east, house in the west" = this house and that.

16 張郎李郎: lit. "Mister Chang and Mister Yi" = this person and that.

17 胥: all.

18 噓唏: sob, become choked with tears.

19 「秋江冷話」: miscellany compiled by Nam Hyoon 南孝溫 [1454–92].

––––––– **105** –––––––

The Famous Dancing Girl, Hwang Chin

Vol. IV: 4; translated 14 June 1921; Diary XVI, pp. 181–2; 331.

Yanggok So Seyang, when young, was strong in his purposes and resolutions. He used to say, "To fall before a pretty girl is proof that one is no man."

He had heard that there was a very beautiful dancing girl in Songdo called Chin, more remarkable than any other in the world. He made a bargain with his friend, saying, "Though I should spend a month with this girl, I could leave her without any emotion and have never another thought of her. At the end of that period of time, if I should spend one day more, you may mark me as no man."

He then went to Songdo where he met Chin-*i*. She was indeed a marvellous beauty. He at once made acquaintance with her for a month. So he passed the time. The day following was to mark their departure. He went with her into the South Pavilion, where they drank and had a feast. Chin-*i* did not seem to be disturbed at their parting in the least, but said, "I have to leave you, Sir – how can we part without one word? I'll write you one of my poor verses as a parting message."

So Seyang said, "Good."

Chin wrote the verse and presented it:

The odong leaves spread deep the autumn court,
    Amid the frosts the golden flower blooms.
… *
Tomorrow morn we part and go our way,
    Long reaches of blue sea immeasurable lie.

She sang it over and said, "Do these words not point to me?"
Hearing this, So decided to stay a few days more.†

* Gale's translation skips two lines.

† Gale's manuscript translation here continues after an empty line with two other
   stories about Hwang Chini that are in fact independent entries in the *Kimun ch'ŏnghwa*
   (nos. 334 and 335). However, Gale does not identify the *Kimun ch'ŏnghwa* sources.
   Two other snippets about Hwang Chini follow, but because they are from the
   Kyŏnch'ŏmnok 見睫錄 (Looking Up at One's Eyelashes) and *Chunggyŏngji* 中京誌
   (Gazetteer of Kaesŏng), we do not include them here.

소 양 곡 세 양   소 시 이 강 장   자 허   매 왈
蘇 陽 谷 世 讓 1)   少 時 以 剛 腸 2) 自 許   每 曰：

위 색 소 감 혹   비 남 자 야   문 송 도   창 진 이
爲 色 所 感 [惑]   非 男 子 也   聞 松 都 3) 娼 眞 伊 4)

재 색 절 세   여 제 우 약 왈   오 여 차 희 동 숙 삼 십 일
才 色 絶 世   與 儕 友 約 曰： 吾 與 此 姬 同 宿 三 十 日

즉 당 리 절   불 부 일 호 계 념   과 차 한   약 갱 류 일 일
卽 當 離 絶   不 復 一 毫 係 念   過 此 限   若 更 留 一 日

즉 여 배 이 오 위 비 인 야   행 도 송 도   견 진 이   과 명 기 야
則 汝 輩 以 吾 爲 非 人 也   行 到 松 都   見 眞 伊   果 名 妓 也

잉 여 교 환   한 일 월 류 주   명 당 리 거   여 진 등 남 루 음 연
仍 與 交 懽   限 一 月 留 住   明 當 離 去   與 眞 登 南 樓 飮 宴

진 소 무 한   창   별 지 색   지 청 왈   여 공 상 별   하   가
眞 少 無 恨 [悵] 別 之 色   只 請 曰： 與 公 相 別   何 (可)

무 일 어   원 정 졸 구 가 호   공 허 지   진 즉 서 진 일 률 왈
無 一 語   願 呈 拙 句 可 乎   公 許 之   眞 卽 書 進 一 律 曰：

월 하 정 오 진　　상 중 야 국 황
月下庭梧盡　霜中野菊黃

루 고 천 일 척　　인 취 주 천 상
樓高天一尺 5)　人醉酒千觴 6)

류 수 화 금 랭　　매 화 입 적 향
流水和琴冷　梅花入笛香

명 조 상 별 후　　중 억 　 정 의 　 벽 파 장
明朝相別後　重憶 [情意] 碧波長

음 영 탄 왈　　오 비 기 인 재　　갱 류 기 일　　　수 촌 만 록
吟咏歎曰 : 吾非其人哉　更留幾日　「水村漫錄 7)」

1 蘇世讓 [1486–1562; styled Ŏngyŏm 彦謙; sobriquet Yanggok 陽谷; ancestral
  seat Chinju 晉州; posthumous epithet Munjŏng 文靖]: scholar-official under
  King Chungjong 中宗 [r. 1506–44; 1488–1544]. His father was So Chap'a 蘇
  自坡 [dates unknown].
2 剛腸: be valorous; have pluck/chutzpah.
3 松都: old name of Kaesŏng 開城, Kyŏnggi Province.
4 眞伊: Hwang Chini 黃眞伊 [real name Chin 眞; styled Myŏngwŏl 明月; appellation Chinnang 眞娘]; originally from Songdo (Kaesŏng). Some sources
  claim that she was a secondary daughter by a certain Hwang *chinsa* while
  others claim that she was the daughter of a blind woman. "Secondary" here
  refers to a social status during Chosŏn ascribed to children born of a man of
  elite status (i.e., *yangban*) and a non-*yangban* concubine, and to descendants
  of such children.
5 天一尺: one *cha* away from heaven = very high. One *cha* equals ten *chi* (*ch'on*
  寸), approximately the width of a person's thumb at the knuckle.
6 千觴: one thousand cups of wine.
7 「水村漫錄」: collection of *sihwa* ("remarks on poetry") by Im Pang 任埅
  [1640–1724], scholar-official under King Sukchong 肅宗 [r. 1674–1720;
  1661–1720].

—— **106** ——

The Famous Dancing Girl, Hwang Chin, Continued I

No source given; Diary XVI, p. 182; 334.

Chin, the famous dancing-girl, was the daughter of a blind dancing-girl of Songdo. She was the most famous dancer of her times. She was in her manner and bearing like a man, and a good musician and sweet singer. She loved to frequent the hills and streams from the Diamond Mountains. She went to the Ever White Mountain of China.* She finally reached Kŭmsŏng.

The magistrate of Kŭmsŏng made a feast and outing for the governor of Chŏlla and crowds of dancing-girls were present. Chin, in a poor dress and undecorated manner, made her appearance as though she were a beggar and lousy. Undaunted she stood. She sang and played. The other girls were rendered speechless by this.

She was a friend and companion of Sŏ Hwadam (1489–1546), played the harp and poured out drink for him and made his way full of delight. She said, "Even the priest, Chijok, who had given thirty years to facing the wall, fell before me. Hwadam and I also were the closest friends for years and yet we never overstepped the limits of good form. He was indeed a Holy Man."

When Chin was dying, she commanded the people of her house, saying, "Don't cry. Let music and dancing accompany my funeral."

They sing her songs even till today, a very wonderful person.

She once said to Hwadam, "There are three supreme things in Songdo!"

"What are they, may I ask?" said Hwadam.

She said, "The falls of Pagyŏn; the master Hwadam, and I, the dancing-girl."

Hearing this, Hwadam laughed.

---

* Gale's translation is in error here. The Diamond Mountains are part of the T'aebaek mountain range. See note 5.

眞伊 1) 開城 2) 盲女之女　一代名妓也　倜儻 3) 有男子

氣像　工琴善謳　嘗遨遊山水　自楓巖 4)　歷太白 5)

智異 6)　至錦城 7) 州　官方宴節使　聲妓滿座　眞娘以

弊衣膩面 8)　直坐其上　捫虱自若 9)　謳彈無少怍 10)

諸妓氣慴 11)　平生慕徐花潭 12) 爲人　必携琴釃酒 13)

詣花潭　盡歡而去　每言　知足老禪　三十年面壁 14)

亦爲我所壞　惟花潭先生　昵處 15) 累年　終不

及亂　是眞聖人　將死　命家人曰：愼勿哭出葬

以鼓樂導之　至今歌者　能謳其所作　亦異人也

眞娘常白于花潭曰：松都有三絕　先生曰：云何

曰：朴淵瀑布及先生曁 16) 少［小］的 17) 也　先生聞之

乃爲笑之　「巴人識小錄」 18)

1　眞伊: Hwang Chini 黃眞伊 [real name Chin 眞; styled Myŏngwŏl 明月;
　　appellation Chinnang 眞娘]: originally from Songdo (Kaesŏng). Some
　　sources claim that she was a secondary daughter by a certain Hwang
　　chinsa while others claim that she was the daughter of a blind woman.
2　開城: Songdo 松都 in Kyŏnggi Province.
3　倜儻: be spirited and harbour grand ambitions.

4 楓巖 = P'ungak 楓嶽: the autumn colours in the Diamond Mountains (Kǔmgangsan 金剛山).

5 太白: the mountain range between Ponghwa County 奉化郡 in North Kyŏngsang Province and Samch'ŏk County 三陟郡 in Kangwŏn Province.

6 智異 = Mount Chiri: the mountain at the nexus of Hamyang County 咸陽郡 and Sanch'ŏng County 山青郡 in South Kyŏngsang Province, Namwŏn County 南原郡 in North Chŏlla Province, and Kurye County 求禮郡 in South Chŏlla Province.

7 錦城: another name for Naju 羅州 in South Chŏlla Province.

8 膩面: dirty face.

9 捫虱自若: nonchalantly pick lice from one's person.

10 怍: feel ashamed or embarrassed.

11 氣懾: feel intimidated.

12 花潭: sobriquet of Sŏ Kyŏngdŏk 徐敬德 [1489–1546; styled Kagu 可久; ancestral seat Tangsŏng 唐城; posthumous epithet Mun'gang 文康]: scholar-official under King Chungjong [r. 1506–44; 1488–1544] and son of Sŏ Hobŏn 徐好蕃 [dates unknown].

13 醨酒: lit. "filtered alcoholic beverage" = newly brewed alcohol, delicious alcohol.

14 面壁: lit. "face the wall" = a Buddhist meditation method whereby monks sit staring at a wall.

15 昵處: get along intimately.

16 暨 = 及: and; along with.

17 小的: *soenne* = (humilific) I (used by servants and slaves to their master).

18 「巴人識小錄」: *Sŏngong chisorok* 惺翁識小錄, a miscellany compiled by Hŏ Kyun 許筠 [1569–1618], scholar-official under Kwanghaegun 光海君 [r. 1608–23; 1575–1641] in 1611.

——— **107** ———

The Famous Dancing Girl, Hwang Chin, Continued II

No source given; Diary XVI, p. 182; 335.

Chin-*i* heard that Sŏ Hwadam was unlike ordinary people of the world. He cared not for rank or office, though a great scholar and deeply learned. She made a trial of him by putting on a boy's dress and appeared as a student of the character, bowed low, and said, "I have heard that the *Book of Ceremony* says that men wear a leather belt and women a silken girdle. I, too, long to learn the character and so I have put on the girdle and come like a student."

Hwadam laughed and went on to teach her. Chin-*i* took advantage of the night to sleep close to him to wake his passions. This she did many days but she never shook his firm resolve.*

* The original text alludes to a Buddhist tale. Gale has left out all the Buddhist allusions in his translation.

眞娘 1) 聞花潭 2) 高踏不仕 3) 學問精深 欲試之

束條 [條] 帶 4) 挾大學 5) 往拜曰： 妾聞禮記 6) 曰：

男鞶革 7) 女鞶絲 8) 亦志學 帶絲而來 花潭笑而

晦之 眞乘夜相昵 如魔登 9) 之附摩 10) 阿難 11) 者累日

終不少撓 12) 「於于野談 13)

1 眞伊: Hwang Chini 黃眞伊 [real name Chin 眞; styled Myŏngwŏl 明月; appellation Chinnang 眞娘]: originally from Songdo (Kaesŏng). Some sources claim that she was a secondary daughter by a certain Hwang *chinsa* while others claim that she was the daughter of a blind woman.

2 花潭: sobriquet of Sŏ Kyŏngdŏk 徐敬德 [1489–1546; styled Kagu 可久; ancestral seat Tangsŏng 唐城; posthumous epithet Mun'gang 文康]: scholar-official under King Chungjong [r. 1506–44; 1488–1544] and son of Sŏ Hobŏn 徐好蕃 [dates unknown].

3 高踏不仕: lit. "lofty step, not serve" = remove oneself from worldly affairs and decline to serve in a government post.

4 條帶: braided sash.

5 大學 = *Daxue*: one of the *Four Books* (四書) in the Confucian tradition. Some sources say it was compiled by Zengzi 曾子 [505–436 BC], a disciple of

Confucius [551–479 BC]. It comprises the Three Principles (三綱領) and the Eight Articles (八條目). The Three Principles are "manifest virtue" (明德), "love of the people" (親民), and "ultimate goodness" (至善). The Eight Articles are "get rid of material desires" (格物), "acquire knowledge" (致知), "be sincere" (誠意), "rectify one's thoughts" (正心), "cultivate oneself" (修身), "put one's family in order" (齊家), "govern the country" (治國), and "bring peace to all under heaven" (平天下).

6 禮記 = *Liji*: one of the *Five Classics* (五經) in the Confucian tradition; a compilation of discourses on "propriety" (禮) drawn from sources from the Zhou 周 [1046–256 BC] through the Qin-Han periods 秦漢 [221 BC–AD 220].

7 鞶革: wear a leather belt.

8 鞶絲: wear a silken/cotton sash.

9 摩登 = Madŭngga 摩登伽 = Matangi: a member of the untouchable caste (chandala) in India. Here, "Madŭngga" specifically refers to Prakriti, a girl of the chandala class who falls in love with Ananda, a disciple of the Buddha.

10 附摩: caress, stroke.

11 阿難 = Ananda 阿難陀: cousin of the Buddha. Famous for his vast knowledge and keen memory, he was one of the ten disciples of the Buddha.

12 撓 = *kulbok* 屈服 = *tongyo* 動搖: waver, succumb, vacillate.

13 「於于野談」: collection of stories compiled by Yu Mongin 柳夢寅 [1559–1623], scholar-official under Kwanghaegun 光海君 [r. 1608–23; 1575–1641].

———— **108** ————

A Strange Psychic Phenomenon

Vol. IV: 6; translated 15 June 1921; Diary XVI, p. 183; 337.

Song Ŭnggae once said to me that his father's cousin, Song Kyuam, when he died (he died from state poison) died without the knowledge of his family – they knew it not.

At that time, however, the tablet in the room rapped loudly. Thinking this very strange, they opened the doors to see and they found the tablet of Kyuam's father had come down from the shelf and stood on the table. It beat upon the wall with its top – a very disturbed state, evidently.

Later they learned the government poison was administered that day and that he had died.

송 응 개 상 위 여 언 기 당 숙 규 암 공 장 사 일
宋應漑 1) 嘗謂余言　其堂叔圭菴 2) 公將死日

가 인 실 미 지 유 조 령 기 가 신 주 방 내 각 유
家人實未知有朝令 3)　其家神主房內　覺有

각 각 성 괴 이 시 지 즉 규 암 부 공 지 주
閣閣聲 4) 怪而視之　則圭菴父（公）之主

자 하 령 상 지 창 외 이 두 고 벽 사 작 민 백 박 지 상
自下靈床至窓外　以頭叩壁　似作悶怕［迫］之狀 5)

이 이 문 금 오 랑 압 약 부 적 소 거 운 후 청 쇄
已而聞金吾郞 6) 押藥赴謫所去［云］　「鰈鯖瑣

록 어
錄［語］」 7)

1 宋應漑 [1536–88; styled Kongbu 公溥; ancestral seat Ŭnjin 恩津]: prominent leader of the Easterner Faction (Tongin 東人) and scholar-official under King Sŏnjo 宣祖 [r. 1567–1608; 1552–1608]. His father was Song Kisu 宋麒壽 [1507–81].
2 圭菴: sobriquet of Song Insu 宋麟壽 [1487–1547; styled Misu 眉叟; ancestral seat Ŭnjin 恩津; posthumous epithet Munch'ung 文忠]: scholar-official under King Myŏngjong 明宗 [r. 1545–67; 1534–67]. During the purge of the *ŭlsa* year (1545; Injong 1), he was serving as Left Assistant Magistrate (*chwayun* 左尹; junior second grade) at the Magistracy of the Capital (Hansŏngbu 漢城府) but was discharged and sentenced to drink a bowl of poison. His father was Song Seryang 宋世良 [1473–1539].
3 朝令: order of the court.
4 閣閣聲: sound of knocking.
5 悶迫之狀: the appearance of being wracked with worry.
6 金吾郞 = 都事 = *Kŭmbu tosa* 禁府都事: junior eighth-grade or junior sixth-grade post in the State Tribunal (Ŭigŭmbu 義禁府).
7 「鰈鯖瑣語」: miscellany compiled by Yi Chesin 李濟臣 [1536–83].

—— **109** ——

A Hundred Years

Vol. IV: 6; translated 15 June 1921; Diary XVI, p. 184; 341.

Min Taesaeng was over ninety years of age. All his friends came to see him and offer congratulations on the first day of the year.

One of their number said, "I hope Your Honour may live to be a hundred."

On hearing this, Min flew into a rage, saying, "I am now over ninety. If I live only to be one hundred, I have but a year or two left. How comes it that you wish me dead in a year or two?"

He had him kicked out.

Another relative came forward and said, "The wish was that you, Our Good Uncle, should live one hundred years more."

Min was made glad by this, saying, "This is indeed a propitious wish."

He had him well fed and treated.

閔同知 1) 大生 2)　年九十餘　元日 3) 諸侄 [姪]（來）謁

一人進曰：願叔享壽百年　閔怒曰：我年九十餘

若享百年　只有數年　何口之無福如是　遂出 [黜] 之

一人進曰：願叔享壽百年　又享百年　閔喜曰：

此眞領 [頌] 禱之休 [休]4) 也　於是　乃厚饋而送之

「慵齋叢話」 5)

1 同知 = *tongji chungch'u pusa* 同知中樞府事: junior second-grade post in the Office of Ministers-without-Portfolio (Chungch'ubu 中樞府).
2 閔大生 [dates unknown]: scholar-official under King Sŏngjong 成宗 [r. 1469–94; 1457–94]. His son-in-law was Han Myŏnghoe 韓明澮 [1415–87].
3 元日: New Year's Day.
4 頌禱之体: lit. "form of eulogizing and supplicating" = congratulatory comportment.
5 「慵齋叢話」 : miscellany compiled by Sŏng Hyŏn 成俔 [1439–1504; styled Kyŏngsuk 磬叔; sobriquet Yongjae 慵齋; ancestral seat Ch'angnyŏng 昌寧; posthumous epithet Munjae 文載].

——— 110 ———

Yun Pyŏn (Graduated 1522 AD) (Chijogam)

Vol. IV: 23; n.d.; Diary XV, pp. 56, 59, 62; 411.

In the days of Chungjong* lived Yun Pyŏn who held the office in charge of the soldiers' supplies. In the year *chŏnghae* (1527) he was transferred to the Office of Justice, while in that day Kim Allo was in full power. He had power of life and death and power of office as well, and he made slaves of any whom he pleased.

There was a man with a great posterity who were all arrested by this man and were to be enslaved. At that time, the Minister of Law was Hŏ Hang, who worked in accord with Kim Allo, a perfect terror in the matter of punishing, and so punished those men. These raised their voices in protest and because they were helpless they pretended to be guilty.

Yun Pyŏn was filled with questions as to the justice of this. He got hold of the evidence of these people and looked it over till he was thoroughly convinced that they had been badly dealt with. He then wrote out a statement to use in their defence. The time happened to be the end of the year, a time when petitions are made to the king. Yun took his statement and went boldly in to the king. The king glanced it over and at once decided that it was a case of injustice, so the whole family were released. All the tangled matters pertaining to the family were unravelled in a day and they were set free. Yun Pyŏn was up in years at the time and he had no children. He was anxious about this.

In the following year he went as magistrate to Sukch'ŏn. He went to see the ministers to say goodbye and on his way home was crossing the Kwangt'ong Bridge. There he met an old man who came and bowed before his horse. He looked but did not know the man. He, however, said, "I am only a common man, but I was arrested and suffered at the hands of such-and-such an official and was made a slave and had no place where to speak my wrongs till Your Kindness interposed and we all lived – me and my posterity. This grateful act is written on my heart and I have longed for some way to express my thanks but have failed. In the year *kyesa* (1553), you will have a son. He will not last long and his power and influence will be of short duration, but one thing he will do well."

He then drew from his sleeve a paper roll and passed it with his two hands.

Yun Pyŏn examined it and found written: "In the year *kyesa*, a son will be born." On the other side was written: the character *su* for "life," then the character *pu* for "riches," then *kwi* for "office," and then the three characters *ta-nam-ja*, "many sons." The bottom of the paper was "wishes for blessing." No name was attached.

Yun asked, "Who wrote this?"

The old man said, "When your child is born, take this paper and go to Yujŏm Temple in the Diamond Mountains. Then, if you take five hundred pairs of wax candles and make your prayer before the Buddha, you will indeed know just what joy and great blessing means. Then, indeed, will my grateful heart find its satisfaction."

He urged him many many times.

Yun desired to ask his reason for this and whence he came. But he made a hasty bow and was gone. Greatly astonished over this, Yun came home and hid the paper until the year *kyesa*, when true to the prophesy, a son was born – a beautiful child.

Yun went out over to Yujŏm Temple and there made a liberal offering to the Buddha. He took the paper that had been given him and filled in the blank with his own name and placed it before the Buddha.

When he had ended his prayers he went to take the paper away when he noticed beneath the character for life (*su*), he found two characters *ka-chil* ("true-old generation"). Beneath the character for *pu* was *cha-jok* ("enough in itself"). Beneath *kwi* was written *mubi* ("no one like him"). Beneath *ta-nam-ja* was written *kae-kwi* ("all renowned"). All these eight characters were written in delicate blue of the delicate touch of a hair, all perfectly formed.

Yun could not make it out, and was greatly startled by it. He returned home. He made a wooden case and put this document safely away as though it were a gem of priceless value.

His son grew up and was known as Oŭm (Odong Shade). He lived to the age of seventy-eight and became prime minister, a man of abundant means. He had five sons, all men of distinction. His oldest one Pang, was prime minister. Hŭn, Hwi, and Hwŏn were all chiefs of Departments; U was a royal secretary.

Tusu became greatly renowned and is known by name to future generations. His sons and grandsons are many in number, holding the highest offices. One finds a short mention of this in the writings of Kim Sanghŏn in his "Life of Yun Pyŏn," but he does not tell of this spiritual part in the matter.

* Gale is in error. The original says 仁廟, temple name of King Injo.

尹公忭 1)　仁廟朝文科　官至軍資正 2)　歲丁亥 3)

爲刑曹正郎 4)　時金安老 5) 當國　恣行威福

認良民爲其奴僕　一人子孫數十口　皆被刑曹拘囚

判書許沆 6)　受安老旨　刑訊狼藉　寃苦切酷

勢將誣服　尹公獨疑之　將來彼民文案

反覈 [覆] 參考知其寃枉 7)　作一査卞 [辨] 之文 8)

將欲卞 [辨] 白　而適當歲末　啓覈 [覆]9) 之時

公持此入達　上一覽卽卞 [斥] 金家　盡釋其

囚數十（口）　蟠結之寃 10)　　一朝快申 11) 矣

時公年已衰　後娶久無子甚憂歎　翌年　拜肅川 12)

府使　歷辭朝紳　夕過廣通橋 13)　時日暮微雨

忽有一老翁　拜於馬前　公不能記　其人曰：

小人良人也　嘗爲一勢家迫脅　將壓爲賤

無所告訴　賴公之德　子孫數十人　皆獲保全　此恩

刻在心肺　常思報效　而不可得　然此後癸巳年 14)

當生男子　但年命福祿　不甚延長　有一事可救

得者　仍袖出一張紙　雙手奉呈　公看之　紙上書

癸巳年酉時生子　其左則書壽富貴多男子六字

每行書一字　而獨多男子爲三字　其右有祝願之文

而虛其姓名之位　公曰：此何爲　翁曰：兒生後

公以此紙　卽往江原道金剛山楡站［岾］寺 15)

備黃燭五百雙　供佛祝願　則必有慶祥陶［隆］厚

此足爲小人之報也　申囑重複 16)　公方欲問所從來

翁遽拜辭　仍忽不見　公大驚異　歸家藏深　及至癸

巳　果生男奇峻　公卽躬往楡站 [岾] 寺　依翁之言

厚設供佛　而塡書姓名於祝文所虛之處　薦于佛前

祝願畢　取看其（文）　則壽字下有可耋 17) 二字

富字下有自足二字　貴字下有無比二字　多男子下

有皆貴二字　凡八字皆深靑　細如毛髮而皆楷正 18)

莫知其所以然　公尤驚異之　歸而造櫃珍藏　其後兒

長　是爲梧陰 19)　壽至七十八　官至領相　富自裕足

五子皆貴顯　昉 20)　領相　昕 21) 暉 22) 暄 23)　皆宰列

旰 24)　知事　勳業赫然　耀當世而垂後世　孫曾繁昌

貂犀相襲 25)　事在淸陰集 26) 尹正墓誌中　而微著其事

不及於神怪

1 尹忭 [1495–1549; styled Kubu 懼夫; sobriquet Chijogam 知足庵; ancestral
　seat Haep'yŏng 海平]: scholar-official under King Chungjong 中宗 [r. 1506–
　44; 1488–1544]. His father was Yun Hŭirim 尹希琳 [dates unknown].

2 軍資正 = *Kunja kamjŏng* 軍資監正: Head of the Bureau of Military Supplies (senior third grade).

3 丁亥: the year 1527 (Chungjong 22).

4 刑曹正郎: senior fifth-grade Assistant Section Chief in the Ministry of Punishments.

5 金安老 [1481–1537; styled Isuk 頤叔; sobriquet Hŭiraktang 希樂堂, Yongch'ŏn 龍泉, T'oejae 退齋; ancestral seat Yŏnan 延安]: scholar-official under King Chungjong 中宗 [r. 1506–44; 1488–1544]. His father was Kim Hŭn 金訢 [1448–92]. Together with Hŏ Hang 許沆 [?-1537] and Ch'ae Mut'aek 蔡無擇 [?–1537], he is considered one of the "Three Evil Men [executed] in the *chŏngyu* year."

6 許沆 [?–1537; styled Ch'ŏngjung 清仲; ancestral seat Yangch'ŏn 陽川]: scholar-official under King Chungjong. His father was Hŏ Hwak 許確 [dates unknown]. Together with Kim Allo 金安老 [1481–1537] and Ch'ae Mut'aek 蔡無擇 [?–1537], he is considered one of the "Three Evil Men [executed] in the *chŏngyu* year."

7 冤枉 = *wŏnt'ong* 冤痛: feel mortified, resentful, galled.

8 查辨之文: written investigation report.

9 啓覆: appeal to the king on behalf of a criminal sentenced to death.

10 蟠結之冤: pent-up resentment.

11 一朝快申: settle a problem once and for all.

12 肅川: a town in P'yŏngwŏn prefecture 平原郡 in South P'yŏngan Province.

13 廣通橋 = Kwanggyo 廣橋: a bridge on Namdaemun-no in present-day Chung-gu, Seoul.

14 癸巳年: the year 1533 (Chungjong 28).

15 楡岾寺: a temple in Kansŏng County 杆城郡 in Kangwŏn Province.

16 申囑重複 = *sinsin tangbu* 申申當付: request/implore repeatedly.

17 可畫: can live until sixty to eighty years of age.

18 楷正: clear, printed-style calligraphy.

19 梧陰: sobriquet of Yun Tusu 尹斗壽 [1533–1601; styled Chaang 子仰; ancestral seat Haep'yŏng 海平; posthumous epithet Munjŏng 文靖]: scholar-official under King Sŏnjo 宣祖 [r. 1567–1608; 1552–1608]. He was honoured as Prince Haewŏn 海原府院君.

20 尹昉 [1563–1640; styled Kahoe 可晦; sobriquet Chichŏn 稚川; ancestral seat Haep'yŏng 海平; posthumous epithet Munik 文翼]: scholar-official under King Injo 仁祖 [r. 1623–49; 1595–1649]. His father was Yun Tusu 尹斗壽 [1533–1601]. He was honoured as Prince Haep'yŏng 海平府院君.

21 尹昕 [1564–1638; styled Sihoe 時晦; sobriquet Tojae 陶齋, Ch'ŏnggang 晴江; ancestral seat; Haep'yŏng 海平; posthumous epithet Chŏngmin 靖敏]:

scholar-official under King Injo 仁祖 [r. 1623–49; 1595–1649] and son of Yun
Tusu [1533–1601]. His original name was Yun Yang 尹暘.

22 尹暉 [1571–1644; styled Chŏngch'un 靜春; sobriquet Changju 長洲,
Ch'ŏnsang 川上; ancestral seat Haep'yŏng 海平; posthumous epithet
Changik 章翼]: scholar-official under King Injo 仁祖 [r. 1623–49; 1595–1649]
and son of Yun Tusu [1533–1601].

23 尹暄 [1573–1627; styled Ch'aya 次野; sobriquet Paeksa 白沙; ancestral seat
Haep'yŏng 海平]: scholar-official under King Injo 仁祖 [r. 1623–49; 1595–
1649] and son of Yun Tusu [1533–1601].

24 尹旰 [dates unknown; ancestral seat Haep'yŏng 海平]: son of Yun Tusu
尹斗壽 [1533–1601]

25 貂犀相襲: lit. "sable and rhinoceros take over each other" = continue to
occupy high-ranking posts.

26 「淸陰集」: *Collected Works of Kim Sanghŏn*. Ch'ŏngŭm is the sobriquet of
Kim Sanghŏn 金尙憲 [1570–1652; styled Sukto 叔度; ancestral seat Andong
安東; posthumous epithet Munjŏng 文正], scholar-official under King
Injo 仁祖 [r. 1623–49; 1595–1649]. His father was Kim Kŭkhyo 金克孝
[1542–1618].

—— 111 ——

Wŏlsa

Vol. IV: 24; n.d.; Diary XV, pp. 62–3; 413.

Yi Chŏnggwi* (Wŏlsa) was born in the same year as Min Hyŏngnam,
the year *kapcha* (1564 AD). They were great friends from their earliest
years, and studied together in the same room. Wŏlsa rose very early in
rank to the chief office of a department, while Min remained simply a
poor scholar.

Friends of Min who would meet to study the character, when they
saw Wŏlsa go by, would point at his state chair and say, "Your contemporary goes by."

Wŏlsa would stop his chair, alight and interfere with the students.
Min did not like this interference. He found at last a quiet nook where
no interference was likely and then had his students come, but Wŏlsa
sought him out even here.

Once they saw a blind fortune-teller passing by, whereupon Wŏlsa sent a man to call him. In an endeavour to upset the fortune-teller, Wŏlsa said, "We are all candidates for examination. Tell us how it will go and start with me."

He then gave his birth year, month, day and hour and inquired as to whether he would succeed or not. The fortune-teller made his reckoning and after a little, bowed and said, "Why do you deceive a poor creature like me? You have passed your examination long ago and, if I mistake not, are already head of a board."

Wŏlsa then inquired as to Min Hyŏngnam. The blind man said, "He is not yet graduated but will this year, and though late, will come to first rank and surpass you in honour and live to eighty and more – long past you. There is one thing more worthy of note that he will experience. He will be raised to the first rank twice."

All laughed at this and asked, "How can a plain scholar pass beyond the head of a board, and as for being twice-raised to the first degree – it's nonsense."

All laughed over it, paid the money, and let the fortune-teller go.

Min graduated that year and so fulfilled the fortune-teller's word. In the days of Kwanghae he was rewarded for service and suddenly raised to the first degree and was sent to meet the envoy from China as far as Ŭiju. At this time, Wŏlsa went to Peking as envoy and was on his way back and they met in Ŭiju in the T'onggunjŏng. The people prepared the seats for the festival and waited and placed two seats to the north as special place of honour. A follower of Min Hyŏngnam pushed Wŏlsa's seat lower down and said, "Our Chief is a man of one degree higher in rank. Why have you placed them side by side?"

So the seat was placed lower down to the east side.

In a little Wŏlsa came and when they met, he laughed and said, "I realize today that the fortune-teller was right."

Min rose higher still and was made a prince (Puwŏn'gun).

On the coup d'état of Injo, Min was degraded and was left only vice-president of a board. He lived, however, till he was ninety and won favour in that for his old age, he was made once more a minister of the first degree. The fortune-teller's words all came true.

---

* 龜, the character for the second element of the protagonist's given name, can be read either *ku* or *kwi*. In Gale's translation, the name Yi Chŏnggu is always Romanized as Yi Chŏnggwi.

月沙 1) 與閔貳相 2) 馨男 3)　俱是甲子同庚 4)

又少與親密同硯 5) 月沙早貴　位至正卿 6)

閔猶在布衣 7)　諸友做文會於路傍　月沙或過

則坐中輒指軒車而戲曰：君之同庚過矣

月沙亦必枉車騎　沮戲程工［上］　閔不勝其苦

嘗與親友會於矮［委］巷 8)　月沙又尋造坐　適有盲人

呼賣卜 9) 而過　使人呼之　月沙紿 10) 曰：此是科

儒之會　汝先推我命　仍自言其生年月日時曰：

可得今科否　盲人推而　良久拜曰：曷爲誑 11) 我病人

此命貴已久矣　似躋正卿之班矣　月沙又言閔命

盲曰：此命姑未第　而可捷今年之科　雖然其登一品

當先於相公　年又耆耊 12)　過於相公　且有一事可異

此命必再躋一品　諸人鬨然 13) 曰：以今白徒 14)

先躋正卿之上　必無是理　再躋一品　又不成說

一笑而罷　閔是年登第　光海朝　屢叅僞勳 15)

驟升 16)　一品　以遠使 17)　到龍灣 18)　是時　月沙奉使

于燕京而歸　相遇於統軍亭 19)　從人先設座以待之

誤連兩席於主壁 20)　閔公府隷斥退月沙席曰：我爺

爺品高　正使相公　安得幷坐　竟設席東壁　俄而月

沙至　相視而笑曰：今日始知其盲人推步之精 21) 也

其後　閔進秩爲府院君 22)　仁廟改玉 23)　幷削僞勳

閔降秩爲亞卿 24)　年過九旬　漸次升秩　又以壽職 25)

官判府使 [事]26) 卒　一如盲人之言

1 月沙: sobriquet of Yi Chŏnggu / Yi Chŏnggwi 李廷龜 [1564–1635; styled
  Sŏngjing 聖徵; ancestral seat Yŏnan 延安; posthumous epithet Munch'ung
  文忠]: scholar-official under King Injo 仁祖 [r. 1623–49; 1595–1649]; his
  great-great-grandfather was Yi Sŏkhyŏng 李石亨 [1415–77]. Yi Chŏnggu
  is one of the Four Literary Masters of the mid-Chosŏn period (四大文章家~
  漢文四大家).
2 貳相: lit. "second minister" = junior first-grade government post just below
  the three ministers (*sam chŏngsŭng*) at the State Tribunal (Ŭijŏngbu 議政府).
3 閔馨男 [1564–1659; styled Yunbu 潤夫; sobriquet Chiae 芝崖; ancestral seat
  Yŏhŭng 驪興; posthumous epithet Changjŏng 莊貞]: scholar-official under
  King Hyojong. During the reign of Prince Kwanghae 光海君 [r. 1608–23;
  1575–1641], he was a first-grade official. However, after the Restoration
  of King Injo (1623), he was stripped of all of his ranks and privileges.
  His position was restored to the first grade in 1653. His father was
  Min Pok 閔福 [dates unknown].

4 同庚 = *tonggap* 同甲: a person of the same age.

5 同硯 = *tongjŏp* 同接 ~ *tonghak* 同學: a fellow student.

6 正卿: a cover term for chief ministers of senior second-grade rank and above vis-à-vis vice-ministerial positions (*agyŏng* 亞卿); includes second ministers (*ch'amch'an* 參贊) of the State Tribunal (Ŭijŏngbu 議政府), ministers (*p'ansŏ* 判書) of the Six Boards (Yukcho 六曹), mayors (*p'anyun* 判尹) of the Bureau of the Capital (Hansŏngbu 漢城府), and directors (*taejehak* 大提學) of the Office of the Special Counselors (Hongmungwan 弘文館).

7 布衣 = *paegŭi* 白衣: literatus without an official posting.

8 委巷: winding back alleys.

9 賣卜: make a living from divination.

10 紿: deceive, trick.

11 誑: deceive, trick.

12 耆耋: seventy or eighty years of age.

13 閱然: noisily.

14 白徒: lit. "white feet": enter the bureaucracy without passing the civil service examination; any official with such a background.

15 偽勳: merit claimed under fraudulent pretences.

16 驟升 = *ch'wisŭng* 驟陞 ~ *ch'wijin* 驟進: unexpected promotion to a higher official rank.

17 遠使: lit. "faraway envoy" = *wŏnjŏpsa* 遠接使: an ad hoc government office assigned to officials who welcomed Chinese envoys.

18 龍灣 = village in Ŭiju 義州 in North P'yŏngan Province on the border with China. Called Yongman because of the presence there of the Yongman-gwan 龍灣館, where Chinese delegations were greeted by Chosŏn officials.

19 統軍亭: a pavilion in Ŭiju 義州 in North P'yŏngan Province by the Yalu River.

20 主壁 = lit. "main wall": the wall facing the main entrance of a room; the seat of honour, or the person who sits there.

21 推步之精: exquisite knowledge in astrological prognostication.

22 府院君: rank of nobility conferred upon royal fathers-in-law or senior first-grade merit subjects (*kongsin* 功臣).

23 仁廟改玉: the Restoration of King Injo in 1623.

24 亞卿: a cover term for vice-ministerial positions, as opposed to chief ministers (*chŏnggyŏng* 正卿). See note 6 above.

25 壽職: special official rank conferred upon officials over eighty years of age or commoners over ninety years of age.

26 判府事 = *p'an chungch'u pusa* 判中樞府事: first minister-without-portfolio (junior first grade).

——— **112** ———

Kim Yuk (1580–1658 AD)

Vol. IV: 28; "Kim Yuk." Diary XV, pp. 64–6; Preface, p. 66; 425.

Preface

Such fables as these are interwoven with the life
of the people. Names and dates are given in the most
extraordinary way. No one seems to question them.
The real and the unreal, the □ of reality and the □
of dreamland are not definitely defined as with us,
but mingle and mix in ways most surprising.

Kim Yuk (Chamgok), when he was a member of the Confucian College, sent a petition to the king against Yi Ich'ŏm, and asked that he be punished and thereby so offended his majesty that he was not allowed to try examination.

On this, he left the capital and went to live in the village of Chamgok in Kap'yŏng. There was in front of his house a pond where he kept fish. He used to throw them things to eat when he went to see them. There was among his fish a long, thin one whose name he did not know. He wondered over this fish. Whenever he would throw food to them, this fish came first to eat. This went on for several years till the fish was some four feet long. Then he showed himself less frequently, and remained much in hiding.

Once in a dream, Kim met a strange person with a very peculiar face who said, "I am the fish that lives in the pool. Tomorrow I'll change and take my departure for heaven. Don't be anxious but just keep out of the way."

In a little he awoke and wondered over this strange thing. Shortly afterwards, he moved away from that house and on the afternoon of the day of moving a sudden fall of rain came on with thunder and lightning. Then a great dragon arose from the lake wrapped about in dark clouds and took flight to heaven.

Later in the year 1623, when Kwanghae was expelled, Kim Yuk went to Naep'o on some business and went afoot. When he had almost reached his destination he saw before him a hill to cross with a white cloud on the top of it. Though he climbed the hill he did not yet know what the cloud meant.

Up he went, step by step, when suddenly a man came running after him, who called him, saying, "Will the gentleman wait a little?"

He turned on this and waited. The man seemed a mountain hermit by his appearance. He came with great speed and taking Kim Yuk by the hand, hurried with him up the hill. He scattered the cloud as they rushed on. Looking again, the white cloud turned out to be sea spray whipped up from a great tidal wave that had swept over the land. The hill his feet rested on a moment ago was now all under water. If it had not been for this stranger, Kim would certainly have been engulfed. Looking at the man more clearly, he recognized him as the stranger who had appeared to him in his dream. Kim Yuk asked who he was and whence he came, but the man made a hurried farewell and was gone without any answer. He crossed the hill and was already a speck in the distance.

Kim Yuk reached his destination and was still there living in an inn where he met a scholar. The scholar said, "Why do you not go up to the examination, instead of wasting time here?"

Kim said, "I have some matters that take me here and cannot do as you suggest."

He replied, "There is a great occasion for rejoicing just now, in fact, and a great exam will be held. If you miss the next four days, you will not be able to have a part. If you leave at once, I believe you can make it."

Kim replied, "I have a special matter, in fact, that I cannot leave, as it is one chance in a thousand – I cannot return so easily as you suggest."

The scholar said, "If you do not go, there will be no winner and the exam will prove a failure."

Kim wondered at this and at once started for Seoul. When he reached the gates, he learned that it was an exam in honour of the inquisition of Kwanghae. Kim entered and became the winner – a very strange thing.

潛谷 1) 金公　爲太學齋任 2) 時　上疏討李爾瞻 3)

請正法　被罪廢科 4)　遂避世居加平 5) 之潛谷村

宅前有小池養魚　常臨賞輒投食　有一魚細而長

막 지 기 명　　공 이 지 매 투 반　　차 어 필 선 지　　양 지 다 년
莫知其名　公異之每投飯　此魚必先至　養之多年

장 지 사 오 척　　기 대 한 출 희 현　　일 일 공 몽　　일 인 상 모
長至四五尺　旣大罕出稀見　一日公夢　一人狀貌

이 상　　래 고 공 왈　　오 내 지 중 어　　명 일 당 변 화 승 천
異常　來告公曰：吾乃池中魚　明日當變化升天

원 공 물 경 필 피 지　　기 각 이 지　　사 가 대 지　　기 일 오 후
願公勿驚必避之　旣覺異之　徙家待之　其日午後

백 주 폭　폭　　우 뢰 굉　　유 일 룡 기 어 지 중　　현 운 옹 지
白晝瀑 [暴] 雨雷轟 6)　有一龍起於池中　玄雲擁之

비 등 이 거　　기 후　　계 해 반 정　후　　공 유 사 어 내 포
飛騰而去　其後　癸亥反正 7) 後　公有事於內浦 8)

도 보 등 정　　수 지 소 왕 지 처　　망 일 소 현　　백 기 등 비
徒步登程　垂至所往之處　望一小峴　白氣騰飛

유 현 이 거 지　　막 지 위 하 물　　단 신 보 서 행　　홀 유 일
踰峴而去之　莫知爲何物　但信步徐行 9)　忽有一

　인　　종 후 질 호 왈　　거 인 소 주 소 주 운　　고 시 주 족
（人）　從後疾呼曰：去人小住小住云　顧視住足

기 인 일 거 사 야　　도 도 면 전　　설 공 지 수　　질 주 상 산
其人一居士也　走到面前　挈公之手　疾走上山

피 기 백 기　　내 해 일 수 창　　회 양 지 세　　출 몰 소 현
披其白氣　乃海溢水漲　懷襄之勢 10)　出沒小峴

비 차 인　　공 기 위 엄 몰　　시 기 모　　황 약 석 몽 소 견 자
非此人　公幾爲淹沒　視其貌　怳若昔夢所見者

공 욕 문 기 래 력　　기 인 거 고 사　　월 산 이 거　　아 경 지 간
公欲問其來歷　其人遽告辭　越山而去　俄頃之間

이 묘 연 의　　공 시 행 유 전 왕 처　　미 정 귀 기　　어 역 려
已杳然矣　公是行有轉往處　未定歸期　於逆旅 11)

中　遇一士子謂公曰：君何不赴擧而作此行也

公曰：吾有不得已之事　君言何可信而遽爾回程乎

其人曰：國有大慶　今方設科　若過四日　恐未及

君須自此卽回　庶可及矣　公曰：此行有萬不得已

之事　不可輕以回程　其人曰：君若不去　是無壯元

科事不成　公異其言　遂卽回程甫入城　其翌日卽

反正庭試 12) 也　公就試　果占壯元　甚可異也

1 潛谷: sobriquet of Kim Yuk 金堉 [1580–1658; styled Paekhu 伯厚; ancestral seat Ch'ŏngp'ung 清風; posthumous epithet Munjŏng 文貞]: scholar-official under King Hyojong 孝宗 [r. 1649–59; 1619–59]. His father was Kim Hŭngu 金興宇 [1564–94].

2 太學齋任: leader of boarding students at the Confucian Academy (Sŏnggyun'gwan 成均館).

3 李爾瞻 [1560–1623; styled Tŭgyŏ 得輿; sobriquet Kwansong 觀松, Ssangni 雙里; ancestral seat Kwangju 廣州]: influential official under Kwanghaegun [r. 1608–23; 1575–1641] and a leader of the Big Northerners (Taebuk 大北). His ancestor was Yi Kŭkton 李克墩 [1435–1503] and his father was Yi Usŏn 李友善 [dates unknown].

4 廢科: give up on the civil service examination.

5 加平: a town in Kyŏnggi Province.

6 暴雨雷轟: heavy rain and the sound of thunder.

7 癸亥反正: the Restoration of King Injo in 1623 (Kwanghae 15).

8 內浦: a bay.

9 信步徐行: walk slowly following where one's feet lead.

10 懷襄之勢: force that threatens to sweep away everything in its path.

11 逆旅 = *yŏgwan* 旅館: inn.

12 庭試: examination taking place inside the royal palace complex; examinations carried out in celebration of special occasions. For example, the rarely given *chŭnggwangsi* marked large-scale celebrations such as the enthronement of a new king or the thirtieth reign year of a king, or several smaller special occasions occurring within a short span of time. *Pyŏlsi* 別試 occurred more often and marked small-scale special occasions.

———— 113 ————

Yŏm Sido

Vol. IV: 35; n.d.; Diary XII, pp. 61–8 (crossed out);
Miscellaneous Writings II, no. 30, pp. 97–100; Box 9:21, pp. 105–8; 436.

A steward of Hŏ Chŏk's named Yŏm Sido lived in Sujinbang-gol, Seoul. He was a good and worthy man, and so received the appointment of Steward and was greatly loved and trusted.

One day Hŏ said to Sido, "Come tomorrow morning early as I have an errand on which to send you."

That night Sido played chess with his friends and drank rather freely so that next morning he overslept himself and knew not that day had dawned. He awoke with a start and hurried off along the way that took him over Kite Hill past Cheyonggam.* Near the top on the side of the road was a vacant lot and an old tree. Underneath the tree on the grass he saw a blue wrap with something tied within it. He went to see what it was and on lifting it up found it exceedingly heavy. Then he placed it in his sleeve and hurried along to Hŏ's house in Sajik-kol, where he immediately presented himself to his master and made confession of his late hour.

Hŏ said, "I have sent another man on the errand – never mind."

Sido then returned to his own room and opened the parcel and in it was two hundred and twenty *yang* of silver.

He thought to himself, "This is a great treasure. What anxiety and distress it must mean for him who has lost it. If I say nothing and just keep it, no fault will be ascribed to me; and yet getting wealth thus, by no effort of my own, means loss and not gain. I dare not have it in my own home so I shall take it and give it to my master."

Thus he took the silver and went to his master Hŏ and laid it at his feet, telling him how he came by it.

But Hŏ said, "What have I to do with what you have found? This is not mine."

Ashamed, Sido took it and went away.

A little later, however, Hŏ called him and said, "I heard a few days ago that the Head of the War Department had sold a horse for two hundred *yang* and that the purchaser was Kwangsŏng. I wonder if this money has anything to do with it? Go to Kwangsŏng's and make inquiry."

Now the Head of the War Department was Kim Ch'ŏngsŏng.

On the next morning early, Yŏm Sido went to the home of Ch'ŏngsŏng and the Head of the War Department asked him why he had come. His reply was, "I have not seen Your Excellency for so long a time that I have come to pay my respects. Is there anything that you have lost from your home?"

Kim replied, "Nothing that I know of."

Then he called a servant and said, "Where is the man that took that horse away? He has been gone now for two days and has not returned."

The servant made answer: "He has returned but he has been guilty of a great offence and so is afraid to appear before Your Excellency."

Kim replied in an angry voice, "What do you mean? Have that fellow arrested and brought here at once."

The servant was immediately brought in under force. Here he bowed low and said, "I am guilty of a great wrong and deserve a thousand deaths."

"What do you mean by 'wrong'? What have you done?"

His reply was: "I went to Master Kwangsŏng's in Chae-dong and there received the price of the horse, but on my way home I lost the money."

Very angry at this, Kim shouted, "You have made away with it by some fraud or other and now come to tell me that you have lost it."

A huge paddle was brought in with the intent to beat him to death, when Sido said, "Your Excellency, I have something to say. Please wait a moment about punishing him and ask him first how it came about."

Kim saw the justice of this and asked him.

The servant replied, "When I took the horse to Minister Kwangsŏng's, he made me ride him round a turn or two to see how he looked, and then he said, 'A splendid horse, indeed!' He praised his sleek coat and inquired, 'Did you feed this horse?'

"I replied that I had, and he said, 'You are certainly a faithful fellow to have done your part so well.'

"He then called me to him and inquired, 'Can you drink?'

"I replied that I sometimes drank a little. He then gave me three bowls of the finest liquor I ever tasted, and then counted out two hundred *yang* of silver. Besides this he added twenty *yang*, saying, 'I give you this for your faithfulness in feeding the horse.'

"I then said good-bye and came away, for it was dark. But I was so drunk that I could not walk, and after I had gone a little distance I fell over on the side of the road, but I have no idea where it was. In the night I came to and heard the Great Bell ringing. I managed to get back home but what became of the money, I cannot tell. I realized what I had done and realizing that my life would have to pay for it, I did not dare to let Your Excellency know."

Sido spoke here and said, "It is because I have found this money that I came here this morning. Here it is. The amount contained proves that it is one and the same."

Kim was greatly surprised by this and looking at him, said, "You are a wonder – certainly not an ordinary human being. But look – this is a lost article that you have found; half of it shall be yours. You shall have it."

Sido replied, "If I had had any desire for it I could have kept it all and nobody would have been the wiser. It is not mine and what I have done in no way merits any reward."

Hearing this, and realizing that he was speaking with a man of honour, Kim said nothing more about reward but simply repeated, "An honest man, an honest man."

He forgave the servant for his offence and then called for drink.

When Sido said his farewell and departed a young woman came after him and called, "Please, Sir – wait a moment, will you?"

Sido looked back and inquired as to what she wanted.

She replied, "The man who lost the money is my brother and he is my one support and stay. I live today by your kindness. How can I ever make return for the good favour you have done us? Just now the lady of the house, when she heard of this, in grateful wonder said she wished you to have something to eat before you go."

He then went into the hall and was treated to the finest of fare and the best of drink.

Sido ate appreciatively and then returned home.

In the year *kyŏngsin* (1680), his master Hŏ had to die by order of the King. Sido rushed in and made request that he be allowed to take half the poison dose and die as well, but the prison keeper pushed him aside and said, "Who are you?"

Thus Hŏ died and Sido raised a great cry and rushed forth like a madman, his thoughts of the world gone forever. He left his home and went away to the hills of Kangnŭng where he had a relative, but when he got there he found that he had become a priest and was gone. He then made his way to P'yohun Temple in the Diamond Mountains where he inquired, saying, "I wish to become a priest and am looking for a special master under whom I may study. Is there such a one here?"

They answered that back of Myogilsang[†] there is a little temple in the border of the wood where there was a great master – in fact, a living Buddha.

Sido went there to see and there indeed sat the sage, before whom he bowed, saying, "With all my heart I desire to serve Your Lordship."

He made request with all earnestness that his hair be cut and that he be permitted to take the vow; but the priest paid no attention to him whatever.

Sido then bowed low and remained in a sitting position until night came and it grew dark. The living Buddha then said, "There is rice on the shelf; why don't you set to and prepare it?"

He looked and true enough there was rice, which he took and made ready. Then again he knelt as before and continued so till morning.

When morning came the priest again said, "Why don't you prepare breakfast?"

This went on for five or six days without the priest showing the slightest sign of yielding to his wish.

Little by little Sido's mind changed in regard to the Buddha, and so he left the temple and went to a little thatched hut of two or three *kan* that stood some distance behind. As he entered, he suddenly saw a young woman of about sixteen years of age who was very beautiful of face.

Sido looked at her, was enamoured at once and laid his hand upon her arm, at which she drew a knife and made a threat to take her own life if he attempted to wrong her.

Sido desisted at once in great fear and asked kindly, "Where are you from?"

She replied, "I am from a village just outside the hills; my brother has become a priest and is now a student here under the master. Thinking this priest a prophet, my mother came to inquire as to the future. His reply is that I shall fall heir to a great evil in four or five years. He added, however, that if I came here to live I would not only escape the evil destined me but would meet one who in the end would be my husband.

"Believing this, my mother built this little house where she expects to live for a number of years. She has gone just now to our village and here I am alone, threatened by your coming. There being the destined evil spoken of by the priest and also the good, I dare not as yet become yours, even though I die. As I said, there is just the possibility of your being the one destined for me, but who knows? We have come to meet each other in this strange and unexpected way, so that I begin to feel that destiny may be in it. Let us wait till my mother comes and ask her."

Wondering over this mystery, Sido gave his consent. He then returned to the temple but again the priest was speechless. That night Sido felt that his whole heart was with the woman and not with religion and so the consent of the mother was what he awaited.

Early in the morning the master priest arose and suddenly threatened him, saying, "How dare such an evil creature as you come here and disturb me? Die! Die!"

With his six-ring staff he struck him.

In a state of inexpressible confusion, Sido made his escape and stood outside the temple. A little later the priest called him kindly and said, "When I saw your face, I felt that you were not one to ever become a priest, but that the woman in the little hut to the rear was destined for you. No doubt she is, but in any case, I don't want you here. Go away at once. There is an occasion of fear awaiting you and yet in the fear itself you will find your special joy."

He wrote him out eight characters:

i sŏng tŭk kŭm chak kyo ka yŏn.‡
"Her name is Kim, a happy mate from the Magpie Bridge."

In tears, Sido thanked him, took his departure, and went to P'yohun Temple, where suddenly, before he was seated, runners appeared and he was arrested, bound, blindfolded and taken in great haste back to Seoul. Here a great cangue was fastened round his neck. This was the time when all those attached to Hŏ were being arrested and among them his steward was taken too.

He was dragged by the constables to the place of interrogation and questioned with all the ministers sitting by. Among them was his old friend Ch'ŏngsŏng, though he did not recognize Sido. After being questioned a little, he was ordered back to prison.

Just then a serving woman bearing a luncheon table on her head for Ch'ŏngsŏng met him – the sister of the man who had lost the money. She went and told her mistress that she had seen Sido looking like a warlock with a cangue on his neck.

The mistress, also, anxious for him, sent a letter to Ch'ŏngsŏng in his behalf.

On learning this, Ch'ŏngsŏng ordered that Sido be brought before him at once and cross-questioned him without finding the slightest sign of suspicion. Then he said, "This fellow is an honest man – I know him from of old; how could he ever be among those counted 'rebels'?"

And so he ordered him set free at once.

Sido came forth from the prison where Kim, the man who had lost the money, was waiting to receive him with a new suit of clothes in hand. He took him to his house and treated him like a king. Here he was given money, a horse, and a fresh start in life.

Some little time later, a nephew of Hŏ Chŏk on the mother's side became magistrate of Sangju. It was then the Seventh day of the Seventh Moon, the time when the Weaving Damsel and the Herdman meet across the Magpie Bridge.§

Sido started south and reached Sangju late at night. The horse he rode had gone ahead of him and turned into a side road, making straight for an unknown house, while Sido followed along behind, trying to keep in touch with it.

He at last came to the place and found the horse tied in a stall. As he went in, a young woman who was arranging a bolt of linen out in the court made her escape into the house.

Sido was untying the horse when a woman came out and said to him, "Why are you loosing the horse that is tied? The horse knew where to come – why unfasten it?"

Not knowing what this meant, Sido bowed to her and said, "I have never seen you before; what do you mean by saying the horse knew where to come?"

The old woman asked him to sit down, said, "I'll tell you in a minute."

Just then there was heard the sound of sobbing and she turned and said, "Why do you cry? Are you happy at what has come to pass?"

More mystified than ever, Sido said, "Tell me at once what you mean?"

She replied, "Did you not meet a young woman once on a time in a little hut back of a temple in the Diamond Mountains?"

He said, "I did."

She then went on, "It was my daughter, and it is she who is now crying. Do you know definitely of the priest who occupied the little temple just in front? He was your relation from Kangnŭng. He is a prophet, indeed, who knows all the things – even the deepest and most hidden. The future lies open before him in every detail. He said of my daughter: 'She will find her mate in my cousin, Yŏm Sido, yet from now on for a time she will be followed by misfortune. But if she comes here for a time she will escape and her marriage will be made sure, though it will not be fully accomplished till such-and-such a day in Sangju County, Kyŏngsang, where they will indeed be united.' Thus it was that I took my daughter to be near the priest and escape the evil foretold. You came at the appointed time but I did not see you. Later the priest disappeared and was not seen again and thus I came here. This is the very day that I knew of a surety you would come."

Then she called her daughter. After some time she came and indeed she was the same as Sido had met in the Autumn Tint Hills, though prettier than ever.

Thinking over what had taken place, Sido was deeply moved, while she too was in tears.

In a little they had their evening meal – rare dishes prepared and made ready in advance. That night they were married and the eight characters written by the priest were all fulfilled.

Sido waited a few days and then went to Sangju to see the magistrate, to whom he told the story. Deeply interested in this, the magistrate gave him rich presents.

Sido's first wife had long been dead and his home he had left to be cared for by a relative, but he now returned with his wife and mother-in-law and took up life once more. His name was known in all the homes of the upper classes, and by the aid of Ch'ŏngsŏng he became a very rich man. He was called by all Yŏm *ŭisa* – Righteous Yŏm.

He lived long and happily with his wife and died at more than eighty years of age while his children live today in Anguk-tong, Seoul.

* The Bureau of Drapery Supplies in the palace.

† name of a hermitage.

‡ The Yonsei edition used by Gale reads "以姓得**金**鵲橋佳緣" (editors' emphasis). According to Professor Donguk Kim, this is the copyist's misreading and mistranscription of "以姓得**全**鵲橋佳緣" (editors' emphasis), meaning "Because of your surname you will attain safety and at the Magpie Bridge [is made whole] a beautiful reunion." Gale's translation of the phrase – "Her name is Kim, a happy mate from the Magpie Bridge" – suggests that he and his pundits, not realizing that 全 is a mistranscription, tried to make the best of what they had by understanding that sinograph to be the surname of the girl.

§ According to legend, the Herdman, a boy of humble origin, and the Weaving Damsel, a daughter of the Jade Emperor, were separated because they neglected their duties due to their intense love for each other. They were able to meet once a year on the seventh day of the seventh moon on a bridge formed by compassionate magpies. Their meeting alludes to a long-awaited reunion of a husband and wife.

허 적　　지 겸 인 렴 시 도　　　거 생 한 사　　수 진 궁 방
許積 1) 之傔人廉時道 2)　居生漢師 3) 壽進宮坊 4)

성 소 신 실 렴 개　　위 허 지 겸 종　　심 견 총 신　　일 일
性素信實廉介　爲許之傔從　甚見寵信　一日

허 위 시 도 왈　　명 효 유 사 환 처　　필 조 래　　기 야 시 도
許謂時道曰：明曉有使喚處　必早來　其夜時道

여 기 도　　음 박 취 수 심 농　　불 각 일 이 명 의　　급 기 분 왕
與其徒　飲博就睡甚濃　不覺日已明矣　急起奔往

로 과 제 용 감　　치 현　　견 로 방 공 대 유 일 고 목　　목 하
路過濟用監 5) 鴟峴 6)　見路傍空垈有一古木　木下

무 초 간　　유 청 복 로 현　　취 견 즉　　봉 과 심 밀　　거 지
茂草間　有靑袱露見　就見則　封裹甚密　擧之

심 중　　납 지 수 중　　주 도 사 동　　허 가　　이 만 래 청 죄
甚重　納之袖中　走到社洞 7) 許家　以晚來請罪

허 왈　　이 선 사 타 인　　여 하 죄 야　　시 도 퇴 우 청 하　　개 봉
許曰：已先使他人　汝何罪也　時道退于廳下　開封

즉 유 은 이 백 삼 십 량　　시 도 자 어 왈　　차 중 화 야　　기 주
則有銀二百三十兩　時道自語曰：此重貨也　其主

실 지　　기 심 우 황　　황　　불 언 가 지　　이 아 가 엄 이 유
失之　其心憂惶［遑］　不言可知　而我可掩而有

지 행 의　　차　　차　　무 단 횡 재　　재 소 민 비 길 상 야
之幸矣　此［且］無端橫財　在小民非吉祥也

기 불 가 휴 귀 어 가　　불 여 납 지 상 공　　수 장 은 취 허
既不可攜歸於家　不如納之相公　遂將銀就許

고 지 고 이 청 납　　허 왈　　여 지 소 득　　하 유 어 아　　차 이 지
告之故而請納　許曰：汝之所得　何有於我　且爾之

불 취　　아 하 취 지　　시 도 참 이 퇴　　아 이 허 소 위 왈
不取　我何取之　時道慙而退　俄而許召謂曰：

數日前聞　兵曹判書家馬　其價二百銀　而光城 8)

家將買之云　豈非此銀耶　汝試往問之

兵判卽淸城金公 9)也　時道如其言　翌日往謁焉

淸城問來現之意　時道曰：久未謁　爲問候而來耳

仍曰：貴宅寧［或］有所失耶　金公曰：無有　遽呼廳

下蒼頭曰：某奴持馬去已兩日　而尙無回報何也　蒼

頭曰：某奴稱有罪　不敢進現云　公嗔曰：是何言也

卽捉入某奴　一蒼頭押一奴跪於庭　且拜且言曰：

小人有罪萬死難釋　公問其故　對曰：小人往齋洞 10)

光城宅　受馬價而忽失之矣　金公大怒曰：奴訴

［詐］至此　汝乃弄奸沈沒而來誑我耶　將呼

大杖　欲撲殺之（際）時道仍請暫停刑　而備［俾］

陳失銀之由　金公悟而問之　奴曰：始持馬到相

公宅　光城命奴盤馬馳聚［驟］11)曰：果奇駿也

且嘉其肥澤曰：此馬爾之所喂 12) 耶　對曰：然

相公曰：人家奴僕方如此忠篤　誠可嘉也　仍呼

之前曰：爾能飲酒乎　對曰：然　相公命一大椀　酌紅

露旨烈 13) 者　連賜者三　卽計給銀二百兩　且加以

三十兩銀曰：此賞爾善喂馬之功也　小人辭出　日

（已）夕矣　醉甚不能步行　未幾倒臥路傍　不知

爲何處　而向夜微醒　忽聞鍾聲　雖（遂）强起而歸

不知銀封所落　罪犯如此　自知當死　趑趄不敢來現

時道始陳得銀來謁之由　卽以銀進　封識及數　果所

失者也　公大歎異之曰：汝非世人也　然（此）亦

已失之物也　今以其半賞汝　汝其勿辭焉　對曰：使

小人有貪財之心　當自取不言　其誰知之　旣非其有

惟恐或況 [溲]14)　何賞之有　公不覺悚然　改容不

復言賞銀事　咨嗟重複　呼酒勞之　奴罪得而快釋

時道辭出　有一年少女　從後疾呼曰：願丞 15) 少
留　時道顧問其由　女曰：俄者亡金［銀］者
乃吾兄也　吾倚以爲生　今賴丞得生　此恩當何報
吾入言于內　夫人極歎之　命賜酒饌　所以請留耳
卽設席廳下　旋入擎出一大盤　羅以珎羞美醞 16)
時道醉飽而歸　及庚申 17)　許以罪賜死　時道突入
持藥欲分飮之　都事曳出之　許旣死　時道狂奔亂呼
無復世念　仍棄家　遨遊 18) 山水　有族兄在江陵地
往訪則已爲僧　不知去處　遂往表訓寺 19)　問居僧
曰：吾欲依歸空門 20)　必得高僧爲師　誰爲可者
（居僧曰：）妙吉祥 21) 後　孤庵守座 22)　卽生佛也
時道往見　果有一僧趺［跌］坐入定 23)　時道前
伏　具陳誠心　服事之意　且請剃髮　辭旨懇切
僧若不聞　時道堅伏不起　日已昏黑　僧忽曰：

架上有米何不炊　起視果有米　炊食如命　夜後前伏

至朝僧又命之食　如是者五六日　僧終不言　而時

道意稱［稍］弛　出菴逍遙　見菴後　有茅廬數間

入其中　只見一幼女　年可二八　甚有姿色　時道不

勝婉戀之情 24)　遽前抱持欲犯之　女於懷袖之間 25)

拔出小刀欲自裁　時道驚怕遂止　問其所從來

女曰：吾本洞口外村女也　男兄出家於此山　師此

菴僧　母以菴僧神人　問女之命　以女有四五年大厄

若絶棄人間　來寓於此菴之房　可以導［度］厄 26)

且有佳緣　母信其言　縛茅於此　獨與女留住

爲數年計　母今暫還洞居　而遽爲人所迫　在此死境

是豈所謂大厄耶　旣無父母之命　雖死何可受汚

雖然此事非偶　神僧佳緣之言　亦必爲此　男女旣

一相接　更何他歸　當矢心 27)相從　但俟母之歸

明白成親 28) 不亦善乎 時道異其言從之 辭歸

菴中 僧又無言 其夜時道一心憧憧只在此女

無復問道之意 專俟翌朝母言之許 及朝睡起

僧忽起立大詬曰：何物怪漢 撓我至此 必死[殺]

乃已 取六環杖將奮擊 時道良貝[狼狽]而走

佇立 29) 菴外久之 僧招之前 溫言諭之曰：觀汝狀貌

非出家之人 後菴之女 終必爲汝之歸 從此直去

勿小蜘躕 30) 雖有小驚 福祿自此始矣 書給八字

以姓得金[全] 鵲橋佳緣 時道涕泣辭出 至表訓寺

席未煖 忽有譏捕軍 31) 突入 緊縛囊頭 32) 駄載驅疾

不數日抵京 具三木 33) 下杖[獄] 盖是時 許獄

34) 多株連 35) 追捉親近傔從 而時道緊入招辭 36) 故也

及金吾 37) 鞠[鞫]坐 38) 淸城與按獄 39) 諸宰列坐

羅卒捉時道入焉 時就訊者多 淸城不省其爲時道也

一次平問後復下獄　適淸城傳餐婢 40) 卽亡金[銀

]奴妹也　見時道鬼形着枷　大驚歸告夫人　夫人矜

惻　抵簡於淸城以警告　淸城始覺　卽命押入時道

盤[畧]詰無驗　乃曰：此本義士　其心事吾所深

悉　豈與於謀逆耶　卽命解釋　時道才[纔]出門

亡金[銀]奴　將新鮮衣服　已候之矣　遂同歸其家

接待極其意　給資本及馬　使之行商　而已[已而

]聞許之甥侄[姪]申厚載 41) 爲尙州牧使　往謁焉

時適七月七日　所謂牽牛織女相逢烏鵲橋成之日也

旣入州境　適日暮　馬疾馳驅而從僻路入一村家

時道落後入　則馬已係在廐中　而見一女　理織事[

絲]於庭中　避入屋中　時道欲解馬緤 42) 則有媼在

內而出曰：何必解馬緤　馬則知所歸矣　時道茫然

莫曉其意　拜且請曰：未曾拜現　莫省主母所諭

謂以馬知所歸者何也　嫗邀之坐曰：吾將言之

忽聞窓裡有哽咽聲 43)　嫗曰：何泣也　豈喜極而然耶

時道益疑之　亟請厥由　嫗曰：君於某歲　客遇一

女於金剛山小菴之後耶　曰：然　嫗曰：此吾女也

今泣者是也　亦知菴僧之所自來耶　此則君之江陵

族兄也　素以神僧　徹視無際 44)　知將來毫釐無差

45)也　嘗指吾女謂曰：此女與吾族弟廉某有因緣

第從今以後　有數年大厄　若來依於我　可以度厄

而自致成姻　然亦未同室　（其同室則）在於嶺南

尙州地　某年某月某日也　吾故將女就僧　欲度厄

而君果來過　吾適出未及見　厥後僧移庵而去

不知所向　君［吾］之子亦來寓此地寺宇　吾故隨

來在此　及至此日　因知君之必來也　因呼女出見

久之女出來　果是楓山所睹者也　顔狀益豊美　時道

不覺感愴 而女悲喜交并 但揮淚而已 俄進夕飯

珎饌盛列 皆預備者也 是夕遂成親 僧所言八字之

符 皆驗矣 時道留數日 往見尙州 [牧] 言其事

顚末 尙牧大異之 厚贈遺之 時時道之前妻 死

(已) 久矣 而家則托族人守之 時道遂與其女其母

歸京復居于舊宅 時道之名 播之縉紳 而淸城之所

以顧護者甚至 家頗饒富 皆稱廉義士 與其妻俱

享福壽 時道年八十餘死 今其諸孫 尙在安國洞 46)

1 許積 [1610–80; styled Yŏch'a 汝車; sobriquet Mukchae 黙齋; ancestral seat Yangch'ŏn 陽川]: scholar-official under King Sukchong 肅宗 [r. 1674–1720; 1661–1720] and a leader of the Murky Southerners (濁南). His father was Hŏ Han 許偘 [1574–1642].

2 廉時道 [dates unknown]: The story of Yŏm was first recorded in Kim Kyŏngch'ŏn's [1675–1765] "Tale of Yŏm Sit'ak" 廉時度傳.

3 漢師 = *kyŏngsa* 京師: the capital.

4 壽進宮坊: a magistracy in Susong-dong, Chongno-gu, Seoul. See note 5 below.

5 濟用監: the Bureau of Drapery Supplies in the palace. Located in present-day Susong-dong 壽松洞, Chongno-gu, Seoul.

6 鴟峴 = Songhyŏn 松峴 ~ (vernacular Korean) Solchae: a pass on the way to Anguk-tong from Kyŏngbok Palace.

7 社洞: a neighbourhood in present-day Sajik-tong, Chongno-gu, Seoul.

8 光城: refers to Kwangsŏng puwŏn'gun Kim Man'gi 光城府院君 金萬基 [1633–87; styled Yŏngsuk 永淑; sobriquet Sŏsŏk 瑞石; ancestral seat

Kwangsan 光山; posthumous epithet Munch'ung 文忠]. He was father-in-law of King Sukchong [r. 1674–1720; 1661–1720] and his father was Kim Ikkyŏm 金益兼 [1614–36].

9 清城金公 = Kim Sŏkchu 金錫胄 [1634–84; styled Sabaek 斯百; sobriquet Sigam 息庵; ancestral seat Ch'ŏngp'ung 清風; posthumous epithet Munch'ung 文忠]: scholar-official under King Sukchong [r. 1674–1720; 1661–1720]. His father was Kim Chwamyŏng 金佐明 (1616–71) and his grandfather Kim Yuk 金堉 (1580–1658).

10 齋洞: a neighbourhood in present-day Chongno-gu, Seoul.

11 盤馬馳驟: lit. "turn one's horse and gallop around."

12 喂: take care of a horse.

13 紅露旨烈: strong and delicious *honglujiu* 紅露酒 (an alcoholic beverage).

14 惟恐或涗: fear only that it might get dirty.

15 丞: "Sir" (honorific title used in reference to a commoner male).

16 珍羞美醞: dainty dishes and delicious alcohol.

17 庚申: the year *kyŏngsin* (Sukchong 6; 1680).

18 遨遊: go on a leisurely excursion; roam, travel.

19 表訓寺: a temple in the Diamond Mountains (Kŭmgangsan) supposedly built by the Silla Dynasty 新羅 [57 BC–AD 935] monk P'yohun 表訓 [dates unknown], one of the Ten Disciples of Ŭisang 義湘 [625–702].

20 空門 = *pulmun* 佛門: Buddhist monastic community.

21 妙吉祥: a hermitage in Pyŏksan 碧山, T'ongch'ŏn County 通川郡, in Kangwŏn Province.

22 孤庵守座: lit. "[at a] lonely temple, keep one's seat."

23 趺坐入定: sit straight up and meditate in the lotus position.

24 婉戀之情: lit. "sentiment of missing and longing for."

25 懷袛之間: lit. "inside one's clothing" = inside one's breast/heart.

26 度厄: lit. "avert calamity."

27 矢心: swear to oneself.

28 成親 = *honin* 婚姻: conduct a marriage ceremony.

29 佇立: stand vacantly/without expression.

30 蜘躕 = *chujŏ* 躊躇 = *chajŏ* 趑趄: hesitate, falter.

31 譏捕軍: members of the Capital Police (P'odoch'ŏng 捕盜廳) and the Five Military Garrisons (Ogunyŏng 五軍營), in charge of public security.

32 緊縛囊頭: bind a criminal's arms tight and put a sack over his head.

33 三木: lit. "three [kinds of] wood" = the three main instruments of corporal punishment = cangue (*hangswae* 項鎖), handcuffs (sugap 手匣), and shackles (*chokswae* 足鎖).

34 許獄 = lit. "Hŏ's incarceration": refers to the imprisonment of Hŏ Kyŏn 許堅 in 1680 (Sukchong 6). Hŏ Kyŏn was the secondary son of Hŏ Chŏk, the leader of the Southerner (Namin) Faction, and was accused by the Westerner (Sŏin) Faction of being the ringleader of a plot against King Sukchong to enthrone Prince Poksŏn 福善君 [?–1680], a son of Prince Inp'yŏng 麟坪大君 [1622–58]. As a result, the Southerner Faction lost footing at court.

35 株連: guilt by association; implicate another as accomplice to one's own crime.

36 招辭: document detailing a criminal's deposition.

37 金吾: *Kŭmo* = the State Tribunal (Ŭigŭmbu 義禁府).

38 鞫坐: place for interrogating criminals.

39 按獄: oversee court cases.

40 傳餐婢: slave girl who prepares and delivers meals.

41 申厚載 [1636–99; styled Tŏkpu 德夫; sobriquet Kyujŏng 葵亭, Sŏam 恕庵; ancestral seat P'yŏngsan 平山]: scholar-official under King Sukchong 肅宗 [r. 1674–1720; 1661–1720]. His father was Sin Hanggu 申恒耉 [dates unknown].

42 馬繼: lit. "horse rein."

43 哽咽聲: sound of wailing.

44 徹視無際: lit. "penetrating inspection without end" = have an exhaustive understanding of.

45 毫釐無差: not differ in the slightest.

46 安國洞: a neighbourhood in Chongno-gu, Seoul.

Professor Donguk Kim's Note

Another version of the same story is found in Entry 310 of the Yonsei University edition of *Kimun ch'onghwa*. There are several discrepancies between the two Yŏm stories. For example, in this other version, the protagonist's name reads Yŏm Hŭido 廉喜道. The "living Buddha" is not his cousin, but a brother of Yŏm's great-grandfather, and his dwelling place is identified as Wŏrhae Temple. Versions of the Yŏm story also appear in *Stories from the Green Hills* (*Ch'ŏnggu yadam* 青丘野談; Entry 108) and *Repeatedly Recited Stories of the East* (*Tongp'ae naksong* 東稗洛誦; Entry 16 of the Ewha University edition). The story translated by Gale above corresponds with Entry 436 of the Yonsei edition.

—— 114 ——

Yi Hangbok (A Very Dirty Story)*

Vol. IV: 38; n.d.: Diary XII, p. 78; 437.

In the days of King Sŏnjo, a law was passed forbidding any unlawful intercourse with the palace ladies-in-waiting. This was at a time when Yi Hangbok was in connection with the Office of Law and yet his steward fell under the offence marked here so that his life stood forfeited. Yi Hangbok took his case with consideration, but could think of no possible way to save him from the wrath of the king.

On a certain day a call came from the king to come and come at once. Yi Hangbok delayed his going and purposely lingered on his way.

When he arrived, the king asked him how it came that he was so late.

He replied, "I received the command of Your Majesty and was on my way. When I passed Chongno, I saw a great crowd of merchant-men laughing together over something. Thinking this strange, I stopped and asked them what it was all about.

"One of the onlookers said in reply, 'Listen – there was once a mosquito and a tick that met together. When the tick said to the mosquito, 'My stomach is distended to the breaking point and yet I have no way of getting rid of its contents; with your sharp bradawl I wish you'd poke a hole in me so that I can get relief.'

"The mosquito replied, 'Now what do you mean? Have you not heard that the steward of Yi Hangbok poked a hole already made and is to die for it? If I should attempt to poke where no hole has ever been, I'd be guilty of a still greater sin. What would the consequences be?'

"When I heard this I was impressed by it and giving it thought, I have thus come late. I am a great offender."

On hearing this, the king laughed and thought of Dongfang Shuo and his jokes in ancient days and forgave Yi's steward.

(Yi Ch'angjik† sees nothing vulgar in this.)

---

* "A Very Dirty Story" is Gale's comment.
† Yi Ch'angjik was one of Gale's trusted *hanmun* pundits.

선묘　조유방출궁녀　교간지률　오성　위지신사
宣廟 1) 朝有放出宮女 2) 交奸之律　鰲城 3) 爲知申事 4)

시기겸종범차률　장함중벽　오성민지　무계가해
時其傔從犯此律　將陷重辟 5) 鰲城悶之　無計可解

적자상패초　소　리공고어이각　후입시　상문
適自上牌招 6) 召　李公故於移刻 7) 後入侍　上問

이래하지　대왈　신승명입래　견종루가상시인
爾來何遲　對曰：臣承命入來　見鍾樓街上市人

족립　훤소　신이괴지　주마문지　관자답왈
簇立 8) 喧笑　臣以怪之　駐馬問之　觀者答曰：

유문여마랑충　상우　충위문왈　여복팽형
有蚊與馬閬蟲 9) 相遇　蟲謂蚊曰：余腹膨脝 10)

이무하공가설　이여리취　취천일혈여하　문왈
而無下孔可泄　以汝利嘴 11) 嘴穿一穴如何　蚊曰：

오시하언야　근문　리승지겸종　천기본유지혈
惡是何言也　近聞　李承旨傔從　穿其本有之穴

이장불면중률　오약강천불소유지혈　즉기죄장갱중
而將不免重律　吾若强穿不素有之穴　則其罪將更重

여하감여하감운운고　신청차언　아혹량구　이치
余何敢余何敢云云故　臣聽此言　訝惑良久　以致

계체　황공대죄　상미소지　이기위방삭　골계
稽滯 12) 惶恐待罪　上微笑之　以其爲方朔 13) 滑稽

수세　기겸종지죄
遂貰 14) 其傔從之罪

1 宣廟: the years from 1567 to 1608 = the reign years of King Sŏnjo 宣祖.
2 放出宮女: lit. "a former palace lady-in-waiting who has been discharged from her duties."
3 鰲城 = Yi Hangbok 李恒福 [1556–1618; styled Chasang 子常; sobriquet Paeksa 白沙, P'irun 弼雲; ancestral seat Kyŏngju 慶州; posthumous epithet

Munch'ung 文忠]: he was called Osŏnggun because he was conferred the
status of "prince" (*kun* 君).

4　知申 = *chisinsa* 知申事: early Chosŏn post (senior third grade) belonging
to the Royal Secretariat (Sŭngjŏngwŏn 承政院); later Chief Royal Secretary
(*tosŭngji* 都承旨).

5　重辟 = *hyŏngnyul* 刑律 = *chungjoe* 重罪: punishment meted out for serious
crimes.

6　牌招: (of a king) summon a subject through his secretary (*sŭngji* 承旨).

7　移刻 = *isi* 移時: after a long while, after a long delay.

8　簇立: densely packed.

9　馬閫蟲: a type of insect.

10　膨脝: swollen to bursting.

11　利嘴: (an insect's) sharp proboscis.

12　稽滯 = *chich'e* 遲滯: delay.

13　方朔 = Dongfang Shuo 東方朔 [ca. 160–93 BC]: known in Korea as Tong-
bank Sak, he served as a courtier under Emperor Wu of the Han Dynasty
漢武帝 [r. 141–87 BC; 156–87 BC] and was famous for his sense of humour.

14　貰: pardon a crime.

—— **115** ——

The Prince's Ghost

Vol. IV: 67; n.d.; 9:21 "A Trip to Japan," pp. 118–20; Diary XII, pp. 82–3
(crossed out); 581.

Prince Poksŏng, Yi Mi, a son of King Chungjong, was done to death by
Kim Allo.

Some years later when Yi Hangbok was a young man, he went to a
friend's house to study and there he saw a young woman come daily
and watch him by the paling.

One day when a great rain fell and he was sitting quite alone, the
woman came again and remained gazing at him for a very long time.

Thinking this very strange, Yi asked, "Why do you come here and
gaze at me?"

The woman said in reply, "I am a sorceress and the spirit that takes
possession of me desires an interview with Your Excellency."

Yi said, "Good – any time you wish to come."

That night the rain had ceased and there was light from the moon. Yi opened the window to look out, when suddenly he found a young man before him whose face was white as marble and his eyes and eyebrows like a pencilled picture. He wore a green coat and a red belt and moved leisurely as he stepped before him.

Yi put on his hat and robe and going out, bowed low and then led him into the room. Said he, "The ways of this mortal world and the land of the shadows are different – how comes it that we meet thus?"

The spirit drew a long breath and said, "I am the son of the King, Prince Poksŏng, and I was ruthlessly destroyed so that I still bear unrequited vengeance in my soul. I have wished to know what people of the world thought of my case, but most men are so weak in soul that they dare not face a dead spirit. You, however, though young, have a soul undaunted and are destined to special greatness, and so I have come to hear from you."

Yi answered, "We all have known of your innocence. Are you not aware of this?"

The spirit replied, "I saw it in the prayers that were written when sacrifice was made for me, but I thought it might have only been done for friendship's sake. I want to know what the people really think in their hearts."

Yi Hangbok replied, "The people all know that you are innocent, that you had died unjustly, and they extend to you their sincerest sympathy."

The spirit shed tears as he said, "Hearing this, my soul is satisfied. Though I die nine times, if I can have but such a just judgment accorded me I have no griefs to harbour."

He then called to the sorceress to bring fruits that she placed before Yi while he himself took his departure.

Yi accompanied him off but after a step or two he disappeared and was gone. Yi thought to himself, "What a strange experience!"

But he said nothing to anyone about it.

Later on in life when he went as an exile to the north country, he told it to Yi Tongak, an uncle of T'aektang (1584—1647 AD).

福城君 1) 嵋　中廟 2) 王子也　爲安老 3) 輩誣殺矣

其後　白沙 4) 李公少時　就友人家居業　隣居有少女

日日來仰視公　一日大雨　公獨坐　女復來仰視

公怪問之　女曰：我本巫人　有所憑神欲謁郎君

公曰：與之俱來　至夜雨止月微明　女曰：神至矣

開戶視之　少年男子也　貌如玉雪　眉目如畫　藍袍

紅帶　冉冉 5) 而來　公冠服出迎　揖讓而入　問曰：

幽明路殊　何爲相見　神噓唏曰：我王子福城君也

遭禍抱寃　欲聞世間公議如何　而凡人神魄類弱

無能接者　公雖年少　他日大貴　氣魄能相接

且言足徵神 [信]6) 故　願承一言之教　公曰：

伸寃久矣　神不聞乎　神曰　因祭告之知 [知之]

然此特出於親親之義7)　所欲聞者公議也　公俱 [具]

道世人所以哀愍其至寃者　神泣數行下曰：信然

雖更九死　無餘憾矣　仍令巫進果數品　遂辭去

공 출 송 지　수 보 이 멸　공 이 근 탄
公出送之　數步而滅　公以近誕 8)　終身不言　晩年北

찬 시　시 위 동 악　리 공 언　　동 평 문 견 록
竄時　始爲東岳 9)　李公言　「東平聞見錄」 10)

1 福城君 [?–1533; name Mi 嵋; posthumous epithet Chŏngmin 貞愍]:
  son of King Chungjong 中宗 [r. 1506–44; 1488–1544]. He and his mother,
  Kyŏngbin Pak-ssi 敬嬪朴氏 [?–1533], were executed for allegedly practic-
  ing black magic against the crown prince who became King Injo 仁祖
  [r. 1623–49; 1595–1649]. They were posthumously exonerated after the
  "crime" was revealed to have been hatched by Kim Hŭi 金禧 [?–1531],
  Kim Allo's 金安老 [1481–1537] son.
2 中廟: the years from 1506 to 1544 = the reign years of King Chungjong 中
  宗.
3 安老 = Kim Allo 金安老 [1481–1537; styled Isuk 頤叔; sobriquet Hŭiraktang
  希樂堂, Yongch'ŏn 龍泉, T'oejae 退齋; ancestral seat Yŏnan 延安]: scholar-
  official under King Chungjong 中宗 [r. 1506–44; 1488–1544]. His father was
  Kim Hŭn 金訢 [1448–92]. Together with Hŏ Hang 許沆 [?–1537] and Ch'ae
  Mut'aek 蔡無擇 [?–1537], he is considered one of the "Three Evil Men
  [Executed] in the *chŏngyu* year."
4 白沙: sobriquet of Yi Hanvgbok 李恒福 [1556–1618; styled Chasang 子常;
  ancestral seat Kyŏngju 慶州; posthumous epithet Munch'ung 文忠]. His
  father was Yi Mongnyang 李夢亮 [1499–1564].
5 冉冉: manner of walking slowly.
6 徵信: trustworthy.
7 親親之義: loyalty and obligations between relatives.
8 近誕: lit. "close to preposterousness."
9 東岳: sobriquet of Yi Annul 李安訥 [1571–1637; styled Chamin 子敏; ancestral seat Tŏksu 德水; posthumous epithet Munhye 文惠]: scholar-official
  under King Injo 仁祖 [r. 1623–49; 1595–1649]. His father was Yi Hyŏng 李泂
  [dates unknown].
10 東平聞見錄 = *Kongsa mun'gyŏnnok* 公私聞見錄: miscellaneous writings
  based on personal experience and hearsay, compiled by Chŏng Chaeryun
  鄭載崙 [1648–1723]. Chŏng Chaeryun was known as Tongp'yŏngwi
  東平尉, as he was King Sŏnjo's son-in-law. *Wi* 尉 was a title conferred upon
  royal sons-in-law beginning in 1451 (Munjong 1).

——— 116 ———

Kim Suon

Vol. IV: 68; n.d.; Diary XII, pp. 70–1; 584.

In the year 1486, Kim Suon was appointed public examiner and Kang Kwison (later a minister) was one of the candidates. The younger brother of Kang's father-in-law, Hŏbaek Sŏng Hyŏn, was at court and Kang's father, Hŭian, was also one of the Directors of Examinations. He said to Sŏng Hyŏn, "We have a great luck in graduates in our house – how about your going in and writing along with our Kwison?"

They did so and the first half was written by Kang and the latter half Sŏng wrote. At that time one of the examiners was Saga Sŏ Kŏjŏng, and his associates selected this paper as first and best of all. Kim Suon, however, being Chief Examiner, glanced it over without any special care. Just as the examiner in charge was going to mark it first, Suon told him to look it over again. Again and again it was reconsidered and gone over all night, till finally the examiner said "Let it be second."

Sŏ Kŏjŏng's associates asked, "But why not mark this first of all?"

Laughing, Kim Suon replied, "This is a patch-work done by two, not one – Kang and Sŏng."

They opened the envelope to find it Kang Kwison's writing. Suon said, "I know them for this reason: Kang studied with me and I taught Sŏng Hyŏn and so I know. Kang wrote to this point and Sŏng from here. How could □□□ to such a trick put into disorder our examination matter?"

All agreed with this as just.

金乖崖 1) 成宗丙午 2) 爲重試試官　時姜相黽

[龜]孫 3) 赴試　其婦翁之弟　成虛白倪 4)

以知申 5) 在省內　姜父晉山希顔 [孟] 6)

이 총 관　　입 직　　위 허 백　　왈　　오 가 련 과　　역 성 사 야
以摠管 7) 入直　謂虛白（曰：）吾家連科　亦盛事也

개 여 군 대 작 민　　귀　　손 지 책 호　　자 허 두 지 축
盍與君代作黽 [龜] 孫之策乎　自虛頭至軸 8)

강 제　　자 당 금 설 폐 지 종 성 제　　령 서 정 고 관
姜製　自當今設弊至終成製　令書呈考官

서 사 가　　등 개 탄 복　　당 위 제 일 괴 애 이 상 시
徐四佳 9) 等皆嘆服　當爲第一乖崖以上試

양 수 불 세 참 고　　시 관 서 등　　즉 왈　　갱 재 문 역 여 시
佯睡不細參考　試官書等　則曰：更再問亦如是

이 위 야 곤　　지 효 우 독 이 품 즉 왈　　차 상 가 야
以爲夜困　至曉又讀而稟則曰：次上可也

괴 문 지 왈　　차 문 하 이 미 참 등 야　　괴 애 소 왈
怪問之曰：此文何以未參等也　乖崖笑曰：

차 비 성 강 이 자 제　　당 위 장 원 의　　속 취 봉 미　　규 지
此非成姜二子弟　當爲壯元矣　速取封彌 10) 窺之

과 강 상 야　　괴 애 왈　　오 여 강 동 탑　　이 성 현 학 어 아
果姜相也　乖崖曰：吾與姜同榻　而成俔學於我

오 변 기 문　　자 차 지 피 강 작 야　　자 피 지 차 성 작 야　　거
吾辨其文　自此至彼姜作也　自彼至此成作也　詎 11)

가 위 기 소 만　　이 요 국 시 호　　중 개 복　　수 출 이 신 삼
可爲其所瞞　而撓國試乎　衆皆服　遂黜而申三

괴 종 호　　호　　부 위 괴　　파 인 지 소 록　　허 균
魁從護 [濩]12) 復爲魁 「巴人識小錄」13) 許筠 14)

---

1 乖崖: sobriquet of Kim Suon 金守溫 [1409–81; styled Mullyang 文良; sobriquet Sigu 拭疣; ancestral seat Yŏngdong 永同; posthumous epithet Munp'yŏng 文平]: scholar-official under King Sŏngjong 成宗 [r. 1469–94; 1457–94]. His father was Kim Hun 金訓 [dates unknown].

2 成宗丙午: lit. "the year *pyŏngo* during the reign of King Sŏngjong" = Sŏngjong 17 = 1486. In this year was held a re-test (*chungsi* 重試) for selecting *tangsanggwan* 堂上官 (lit. "officials of the upper end of the hall" = high-ranking officials whose rank reached higher than senior third).

3 姜龜孫 [1450–1505; styled Yonghyu 用休; ancestral seat Chinju 晉州; posthumous epithet Sukhŏn 肅憲; honoured as Prince Chinwŏn 晉原君]: scholar-official under Yŏnsangun 燕山君 [r. 1494–1506; 1476–1506]. His father was Kang Hŭimaeng 姜希孟 [1424–83].

4 成俔 [1439–1504; styled Kyŏngsuk 磬叔; sobriquet Yongjae 慵齋, Hŏbaektang 虛白堂; ancestral seat Ch'angnyŏng 昌寧; posthumous epithet Munjae 文戴]: scholar-official under King Sŏngjong 成宗 [r. 1469–94; 1457–94] and the brother of Sŏng Kan 成侃 [1427–56].

5 知申 = *chisinsa* 知申事: early Chosŏn post (senior third grade) belonging to the Royal Secretariat (Sŭngjŏngwŏn 承政院); later Chief Royal Secretary (*tosŭngji* 都承旨).

6 姜希孟 [1424–83; styled Kyŏngsun 景醇; sobriquet Sasukchae 私淑齋, Kugo 菊塢; ancestral seat Chinju 晉州]: scholar-official under King Sŏngjong 成宗 [r. 1469–94; 1457–94]. He was the son of Kang Sŏktŏk 姜碩德 [1395–1459] and brother of Kang Hŭian 姜希顔 [1418–65].

7 摠管: cover term for Commander (*toch'onggwan* 都摠管) and Deputy Commander (*puch'onggwan* 副摠管) of the Five Military Commands Headquarters (Owi toch'ongbu 五衛都摠府).

8 軸 = *ch'uk* 軸: the core of a piece of writing.

9 四佳: sobriquet of Sŏ Kŏjŏng 徐居正 [1420–88; styled Kangjung 剛中; ancestral seat Talsŏng 達城; posthumous epithet Munch'ung 文忠]: scholar-official under King Sŏngjong 成宗 [r. 1469–94; 1457–94].

10 封彌: write and seal off at the top of an examination paper the candidate's name, ancestral seat, and the names of his grandfather, great-grandfather, and great-great-grandfather.

11 詎: how; for what reason.

12 申從濩 [1456–97; styled Ch'aso 次韶; sobriquet Samgoedang 三魁堂; ancestral seat Koryŏng 高靈]: scholar-official under Yŏnsangun 燕山君 [r. 1494–1506; 1476–1506]. His grandfather was Sin Sukchu 申叔舟 [1417–75], and his father Sin Chu 申澍 [dates unknown].

13 「惺人識小錄」: *Sŏngong chisorok* 惺翁識小錄, a miscellany compiled by Hŏ Kyun 許筠 [1569–1618].

14 許筠 [1569–1618; styled Tanbo 端甫; sobriquet Kyosan 蛟山; ancestral seat Yangch'ŏn 陽川]: scholar-official under Kwanghaegun 光海君 [r. 1608–23; 1575–1641]. His father was Hŏ Yŏp 許曄 [1517–80].

——— 117 ———

Hwang Susin Cuts Off His Horse's Head

Vol. IV: 76; n.d.; Diary XVI, p. 141: 615.

Hwang Susin was son of Hwang Hŭi the great minister. He became enamoured of a dancing girl so that his father had to reprimand him. Susin gave a seemingly submissive answer but did not correct his evil ways. One day Susin, returning home, was met by his father who was dressed in ceremonial robes, hat and headgear, and met him at the gateway as he would meet a most distinguished guest.

Alarmed at this, Hwang bowed down to the earth and inquired the reason. Said Hwang Hŭi, "I treated you as a son, but you have not listened to what I said. This means that you do not regard me as your father. I want to try how it will work when I treat you as a guest."

Susin bowed down to the earth in deepest humiliation and asked that he might die for his sins. He never again had anything to do with the girl.

One day when he was drunk he rode his horse and the horse went into the dancing girl's house where he unconsciously slept. In the night he awoke and realized what he had done. In his anger, he struck the horse with his sword and killed it.

黃議政守身 1) 相國喜 2) 之子也 有所聘 [眄] 妓

鍾情 3) 特甚 喜嘗責之 守身唯唯而退 猶不悛

一日 守身自外至 其父正冠服出迎於門如大賓

守身懼而伏地 問其故曰： 吾以子待汝

而爾不聽 是不父我 以賓禮按之耳 守身叩頭請死

<ruby>궐</ruby>厥 <ruby>후</ruby>後 <ruby>갱</ruby>更 <ruby>불</ruby>不 <ruby>여</ruby>與 <ruby>기</ruby>妓 <ruby>상</ruby>相 <ruby>문</ruby>問　<ruby>후</ruby>後 <ruby>상</ruby>嘗 <ruby>부</ruby>扶 <ruby>취</ruby>醉 <ruby>횡</ruby>橫 <ruby>재</ruby>載　<ruby>마</ruby>馬 <ruby>입</ruby>入 <ruby>기</ruby>妓 <ruby>가</ruby>家 <ruby>인</ruby>因

<ruby>숙</ruby>宿 <ruby>언</ruby>焉　<ruby>야</ruby>夜 <ruby>반</ruby>半 <ruby>주</ruby>酒 <ruby>성</ruby>醒　<ruby>시</ruby>始 <ruby>각</ruby>覺 <ruby>기</ruby>其 <ruby>오</ruby>誤 <ruby>입</ruby>入　<ruby>대</ruby>大 <ruby>로</ruby>怒 <ruby>취</ruby>取 <ruby>검</ruby>劍 <ruby>참</ruby>斬 <ruby>기</ruby>其 <ruby>마</ruby>馬

「<ruby>어</ruby>於 <ruby>우</ruby>于 <ruby>야</ruby>野 <ruby>담</ruby>談」4)

1 Hwang Susin 黃守身 [1407–67; styled Kyehyo 季孝; sobriquet Ch'webu
 惴夫; ancestral seat Changsu 長水; posthumous epithet Yŏlsŏng 烈成]:
 scholar-official under King Sejo 世祖 [r. 1455–68; 1417–68]. His father was
 Hwang Hŭi 黃喜. See note 2 below.
2 黃喜 [1363–1452; original name Suro 壽老; styled Kubu 懼夫; sobriquet
 Pangch'on 厖村; ancestral seat Changsu 長水; posthumous epithet Iksŏng
 翼成]: scholar-official under King Sejong 世宗 [r. 1418–50; 1397–1450]. His
 father was Hwang Kunsŏ 黃君瑞 [1328–1402].
3 鍾情: dote on someone.
4 「於于野談」: miscellany compiled by Yu Mongin 柳夢寅 [1559–1623],
 scholar-official under Kwanghaegun 光海君 [r. 1608–23; 1575–1641].

Index

adultery, 319, 516

ajŏn (petty clerks), 168n5, 198n29, 441, 448n12, 488n31, 548–50, 554n10, 555n28

alcohol: beer, 506; drinking, 305, 517, 542; drunkenness, 174, 176, 457, 490, 591–2, 617; wine, 286–8, 457, 489, 491, 556

Andong, 255, 455, 458, 489, 548–9

animals: bamboo horse, 177; cows, 463–4; dogs, 6, 126n23, 127n27, 494, 505n60; dragons, 372, 373, 586; fish, 586; horses, 8, 138, 148, 199–200, 595, 617; *injak* (human-magpies), 70; leopards, 515; magpies, 69, 240–1, 596; robber chiefs, 149–50, 515–17; tailless dogs, 6; tigers, 56, 83–4, 89–90, 138, 172, 415–16, 515; and tiger skins, 131, 133

astrology, 277, 298

Board of Personnel (Ijo 吏曹), 82n11, 100n11

Board of Works (Kongjo 工曹), 165n2

Book of Ceremony (Liji 禮記), 571

Book of Changes (Yijing 易經), 65

Border Defence Council (Pibyŏnsa 備邊司), 82n10

bravery, 40, 355, 431

Buddha, 572nn9, 11, 576, 593

Buddhism, 42n8, 44, 83, 84, 533–4, 535–7, 562, 570n14; rituals, 47n19

Bureau of Drapery Supplies (Cheyonggam 濟用監), 605n5

Bureau of Military Training (Hullyŏnwŏn 訓練院), 276n11

Bureau of Music (Kyobang 敎坊), 134n3, 564n7

Bureau of the Palace Court (Aekchŏngsŏ 掖庭署), 76n5

Bureau of Royal Transportation (Saboksi 司僕寺), 61n19

Bureau of Translators (Sayŏgwŏn 司譯院), 209n26

burials, 55–6, 139, 148, 241, 245, 299–300, 442, 527, 535; ceasing of the wailing ceremony, 450n55; sacrifice, 56; seven moons, 508; tomb sweeping, 513n7

Capital Guard (Ŏyŏngch'ŏng 御營廳), 100n11, 326n11

Ch'a Ch'ŏllo 車天輅, 4n8

Comprehensive Mirror to Aid in Government, The (Zizhi tongjian 資治通鑑) (Sima Guang), 198n21, 429n62, 454n6
concubines, 306, 364, 439, 491, 493, 550, 567n4
Confucian Academy (Sŏnggyun'gwan 成均館), 34n2, 57, 76n7, 533, 535, 586; Confucius shrine at, 33
corruption: bribes, 254–6
crime: assassinations, 457; bandits, 515; murder, 181, 319, 354, 532–7; robber chiefs, 149–50, 515–17; thieves, 39; treason, 220n4; trespassing, 278, 287
Crown Prince Tutorial Office (Seja sigangwŏn 世子侍講院), 51n2
customs: basket-making, 405–7; *furoshiki* (wrapping cloth), 362, 364; honouring of ancestors, 270; *kyerye* (hairpin ceremony), 104n4; sword dances, 199

dancing girls, 15–21, 113, 132, 222–4, 237–8, 242–5, 262–5, 287, 335, 338–9, 383, 550, 562, 565–6, 568, 570–1, 617
Daoism, xliv, 68n4, 249n8, 284n16, 369n25
deception, 47, 457
destiny, 213, 235, 528, 594; *ch'ŏnsu* (fate), xlvi; fate, 66
Diamond Mountains, 229, 568, 570n4, 576, 593, 595, 606n19
Dongfang Shuo 東方朔, 608, 610n13
dreams, 137–8, 139, 151, 179, 201, 270, 306, 371–4, 398, 586–7

Easterner Faction (Tongin 東人), 573n1
education, xviii, xxii, 382–3

envoys, 7, 112, 149, 300, 373, 479, 556, 558–9, 582, 585n17
eunuchs, 263, 398
examinations, 6–7, 28, 33n4, 39, 41n4, 42, 54, 66, 69n11, 70, 76nn7, 9, 16, 189–90, 199, 217, 277, 289, 295n27, 296nn33, 34, 35, 297nn62, 63, 64, 306, 319, 328–9, 335, 358, 362, 373, 384–5, 397nn43, 45, 46, 59, 400, 437n3, 483, 517, 535, 540n4, 541, 548, 554n3, 582, 586–7, 587n12, 589n4, 614, 616n10; ad hoc civil service examination, 34n2; *alsŏng* examination, 33, 72–3; *changwŏn*, 76n16; *chŭnggwang-si*, 590n12; *kwagŏ* (examination), xxn20, 139, 385; *pyŏlsi* (special state examination), 69n14, 590n12; *saengwŏn chinsa si*, 208nn1, 3, 221n9; second stage, 437n3, 448n6; *siji* (examination answer sheet), 69n18, 76n9; *sillae-wi* (civil service examination), 217–18; special civil service examination, 76n7; "white feet," 585n14
exile, 298–9

fate. *See* destiny
Five Blessings, 373, 381n49
food, 8–9, 112, 148, 150, 250, 253, 272, 285, 287, 328, 338–9, 348, 431, 451; fasting, 26, 250; feasts, 6, 386, 463, 491, 568, 592; ginseng, 234, 278; meals, 200, 362, 385, 596; *miŭm* (rice gruel), 62; rice, 593; royal feasts, 82n8; wild pigs and deer, 517
fortune-tellers, 88, 323, 358–9, 373, 419–20, 555–6, 558–9, 581–2

Four Statesmen, 213. *See also* Cho
   T'aech'ae; Kim Ch'angjip; Yi
   Imyŏng; Yi Kŏnmyŏng
funerals. *See* burials

Gale, George, xxv, xxxviii
Gale, Harriet E. Gibson, xvin2
Gale, James Scarth, xvi, xviii, xx,
   xxviii, xliiin59, 32, 566, 596, 607;
   background of, xv–xviii; as
   bibliophile, xxiv; and "the
   character," xlvii–xlix; editorial
   freedom of, xxx–xxxiv; Gale-isms
   of, xliv–xlvii; Korean culture, as
   loyal to, xli; Literary Sinitic,
   admiration for, xix, xxi–xxiv,
   xxxiv–xxxvi; as misrepresented,
   xxxvii; old Korean literature,
   fascination with, xx–xxi; old school
   Korean Christians, influence on,
   xxiv; Romanization, system of,
   li–lii; resurgence of interest in,
   xxxix–xl; and sinographs, xlvii;
   source text of, xxvi–xxvii; style of,
   xlii–xliv; translation, philosophy
   of, l–li; translation process of,
   xxv–xxvi; as under-researched,
   xxxvii, xxxix; vernacular fiction,
   translations from, xlii; Western-
   Korean coevalness, xxxi, xxxin45
Gale, Hattie, xliiin59
Government Arsenal (Kun'gisi
   軍器寺), 41n5, 449n24
Great Japanese War, 463, 468n2. *See
   also* Hideyoshi Invasions; Imjin
   War
grief, 26, 385, 387. *See also* mourning

Hades. See *myŏngbu* (netherworld)
Haein Monastery, 187, 190–1, 198n30

Haep'ung, Prince 海豊君, 370–4.
   See also Chŏng Hyojun
Hamgyŏng, 115, 562
Hamhŭng, 119, 415n49
hanmun, xvii, xxxviii, xl, xlv, xlviii,
   l–liii, 329. *See also* Literary Sinitic
Ha Ŭngnim 河應臨, 28–9, 30n2
hazing, 273; call *sillae* (hazing ritual),
   277n18, 329
heaven, 270; *ch'ŏnŭi* (heaven's will),
   xlvii
Herdsman, 595–6
hermits, 35, 587
Hideyoshi Invasions (1592–8), xxxi,
   25n7, 49, 221n20, 327, 338, 479. *See
   also* Great Japanese War; Imjin
   War
Hŏ Chŏk 許積, 590–2, 594–5, 605n1,
   607n34
Hŏ Chong 許琮, 39–40, 41nn1, 2
Hoeŭn chapchi 晦隱雜誌, 6n1
Hŏ Hang 許沆, 575, 580nn5, 6,
   613n3
Ho Kyŏn 許堅, incarceration of,
   607n34
Hŏ Kyun 許筠, 18n8, 570n18, 616n13
holidays: bean porridge, eating of,
   44; beating of the gongs
   (*myŏngbal*), 43; beholding the
   moon, 44; Birthday of Sŏkkamoni,
   44; Day of One Hundred Seeds,
   44; drivers of devils (*pang maegwi*),
   43; fireworks (*p'okchuk*), 43;
   Flower Bread (*hwajŏn*), 44; Flower
   Morning (*hwajo*), 44; going to high
   places, 44; Great Night (*wŏnsŏk*),
   44; *kyŏngsin* day, 44; lanterns,
   hanging of, 44; New Year
   Greetings (*sebae*), 43–4; old year
   (*kwase*), 43; Pig Day, 44; Rat Day,